BOLD ASCENSION

BOOK TWO OF THE SUNDERED NATION TRILOGY

VAUGHN ROYCROFT

PRAISE FOR VAUGHN ROYCROFT

"With a fast pace and sweeping battle sequences, not to mention one of the best duels in fiction, The Severing Son will appeal to action-hungry readers of authors such as John Gwynne, George R.R. Martin, and Evan Winter."—*Philip Chase, BookTube's Dr. Fantasy*

"As the prophecies unfold and we learn more about our characters, I am not sure whether some of my favorites will end up being the saviors or the villains, and I find that incredibly exciting... I have a feeling that we are going to come out of this trilogy feeling like we were in the battles ourselves and there's no better feeling."—*Cassidee Lanstra, FanFiAddict*

"The author has almost the exact same writing style as my favorite epic fantasy author John Gwynne and I do not use those words lightly... The sequel can't get here fast enough..."—*Under the Radar SFF Books*

"I was engaged the whole way and found myself eager to continue on with the story once I reached the end. The storytelling is tight and feels like it easily could have been traditionally published."—*Books With Benghis Kahn*

"Indulge your tastes for dark prophecies, outcasts, heroes and knaves, peoples enslaved, and peoples in rebellion. And plenty of treachery. Besides all that, this is a love story, with swords—many are the moments of great feeling, among the flash of blades."—*Tom Bentley, author of Sticky Fingers*

CONTENTS

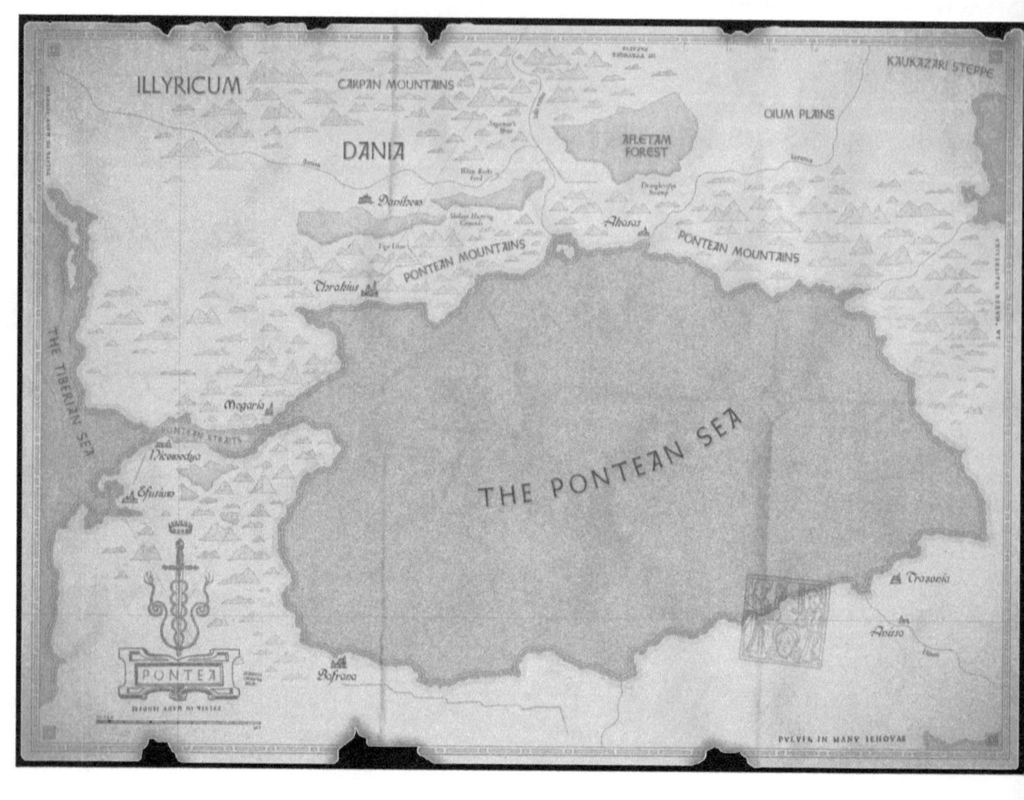

ILLYRICUM
CARPAN MOUNTAINS
DANIA
AFLETAM FOREST
OIUM PLAINS
KAUKAZARI STEPPE
Davihew
PONTEAN MOUNTAINS
Thrakius
Albanos
PONTEAN MOUNTAINS
THE TIBERIAN SEA
Mogaris
PONTEAN STRAITS
Vicoccolya
Efusino
THE PONTEAN SEA
PONTEA
Bofrana
Drosonia
Avisso
PVLVIS IN MANV IEHOVAE

CHARACTER LIST

<u>**The Gottari**</u>

The Amalus Clan (the lions):
Vahldan (eldest son of Angavar the Outcast)
Vahldan's Family:
Angavar (father, former Lion Lord, deceased)
Frisanna (mother, wife of Angavar, deceased)
Eldavar (younger brother)
Mara (sister)
Kemella (sister)

Desdrusan (Lion Lord of Dania, cousin to Angavar)
Teavar (Rekkr, royal guardsman)
Jhannas (Rekkr, royal guardsman)
Ermanaric (Rekkr, royal guardsman)
Arnegern (Rekkr, right hand to Vahldan, son of Vildigern)
Belgar (Rekkr and captain for Vahldan)
Herodes (Rekkr and captain for Vahldan)
Attasar (scribe and scholar to Vahldan)

Harma (an Amalus woman, daughter to Herodes)

The Wulthus Clan (the wolves):
Thadmeir (Wolf Lord of Dania)
Thadmeir's Family:
Urias (adopted brother and captain of the longhouse)
Aomeir (elder brother, deceased)
Theudaric (father and former Wolf Lord, deceased)
Amaseila (wife and priestess to Freya)
Amaga (daughter of Amaseila and Thadmeir, priestess to Freya)
Hloed (merchant, prominent member of the wool guild)
Gizar (prominent member of the Elli-Frodei, an order of shamanistic scholars)
Ulfhamr (captain of the Wulthus host based in Danihem, cousin to Thadmeir)

The Ponteans

Malvius (sea captain from Thrakius, son of Decebius, sister to Ligaia, disinherited)
Ligaia (daughter of Decebius, wife of Kluctus)
Decebius (anax of Thrakius and shipping magnate, father to Malvius and Ligaia)
Kluctus (husband of Ligaia, named heir to the Thrakian anaxship by Decebius)
Agoraki (kitchen boy in the Thrakian palace, adopted son of Apontia, known as Ago)
Apontia (maidservant in the Thrakian palace, enslaved during the war in Sassanada)
Neveka (a Bafranii woman, former slave turned prostitute in Akasas)
Dexicos (first mate of Malvius, known as Dex)
Sabas (former mate turned overseer of the docks and warehouses in Thrakius for Malvius)

Isidros (anax of Nicomedya, trading rival to Malvius)

Encho (Illyrican right hand to Isidros)

Zafan (Bafranii pirate captain, former slave, brother to Neveka)

Dah Arstra (high lord to the Haleez region of the Sassanadi Empire)

The Skolani

Elan (banished to become Vahldan's guardian, former Blade-Wielder, daughter of Ellasan)

    Keisella (queen of the Skolani)

    Icannes (princess, daughter of Keisella, near-sister to Elan)

    Sael (Wise One, a Dreamer/seeress, grandmother to Elan)

    Annakha (Wise One, a healer, near-sister to the queen)

    Ursellya (apprentice healer, daughter of Annakha)

    Anallya (Blade-Wielder and royal guardian)

    Kukida (Blade-Wielder and royal guardian)

    Alela (wet nurse)

    Hildeanna (Blade-Wielder, captain of the scouts of the eastern borders)

The Tiberians

Vernius (lord general of the Tiberian mobile reserve legions)

    Facerius (master commander of all Tiberian militum branches, including armies and navies)

    Mycanius (His Eminence, the Emperor of Tiberia)

    Avitus (imperial diplomat, or legatus, based in Megaria)

    Horius (provincial governor of Megaria)

PLACE NAMES &
GLOSSARY OF TERMS

Places:

Akasas—An ancient, walled city on the northern coast of the Pontean Sea. Located at the mouth of the Berezan River, Akasas was once a prominent port for Hellain traders.

Anaissa—A Sassanadi city on the River Haleez, high seat of Dah Arstra. An important trade center near the termination of the Peshtari trade routes. Because the mouth of the river is controlled by the Tiberian navy, goods are normally shipped from nearby Trazonia.

Bafrana—A port city on the southern shore of the Pontean Sea. Largest city and seat of power for the Bafranii people, a seagoing nation under the rule of their religious leader, the Sadhu.

Cispadaena—A large port city on the eastern side of the Tiberian Peninsula, Cispadaena is the home port of the Tiberian navy.

Dania—A river valley formed by the Pontean mountain range to the south and the Carpan mountain range to the north. Home of the Gottari, Skolani, and Carpan tribes.

Danihem—A stockade-fortified village in central Dania on the

Danian River. The longhouse of Danihem holds the seats of the lords of the ruling clans of the Gottari tribe.

Efusium—The Tiberian Empire's third largest city, a port on the Tiberian Sea, and home to the empire's largest library. A multiethnic city, Efusium is known for its vibrant cultural scene, the center of imperial fashion, art, and music.

Illyrica—the mountainous realm of the Illyrican tribes, located to the west of Dania and north of the Pontean Straits.

Megaria—A walled city founded by the Hellains at the opposite end of the Pontean Straits from Nicomedya, nearest to the Pontean Sea. Megaria is the seat of Pontea's provincial rector. The catapults of Megaria loom over the vital trade route for eastern goods to the Tiberian Empire.

Nicomedya—A walled city, largely populated by Hellains, at the opposite end of the Pontean Straits from Megaria, nearest to the Tiberian Sea. A vital trading city, Nicomedya is the center of the Tiberian slave trade.

Oium—A sprawling grassland, relatively featureless beyond its gently rolling hills.

Pontea—A province of the Tiberian Empire, Pontea encompasses the lands adjacent to the northern shoreline of the Pontean Sea, from the Pontean Straits in the west to Akasas in the east.

Thrakius—An ancient, walled city on the northern coast of the Pontean Sea. Due to its enclosed harbor and the marvel of its ancient seagates, Thrakius was long the Pontean stronghold of the Hellain navy. It remains a prominent trading port of the Tiberian Empire. Though Thrakius is but a shadow of its glorious past, it remains the largest imperial city in Pontea.

Trazonia—A port city controlled by Tiberia, once a part of the Sassanadi Empire, on the southeastern shore of the Pontean Sea at the edge of the mouth of the Bay of Haleez. Trazonia serves as the link from the overland Peshtari trade routes, vital to the spice trade throughout the Tiberian Empire. Dispute over control of the port led to the War of Two Empires between the Tiberians and the Sassanadi.

Because Trazonia is entirely surrounded by Sassanadi territory, accessible for Tiberians only via the water, tariffs are collected by both empires for the passage of goods.

Vigs-Utan—An aging stronghold at the head of the trail that leads through the Pontean Pass, consisting of a stone tower and ramparts surrounding the gateway to Dania. The tower remains the home of the Elli-Frodei—the order of the Wise Ones of the Gottari.

Glossary:

The Ananth-jahn—A trial in the form of a sword duel, granted to a petitioner to the dais chair and the Rekkr's council, to settle a perceived wronging or a slight of one's honor. The challenged has the right to select a champion to fight in his stead.

Hiatus—An annual period when shipping in the Tiberian Empire's territorial waters is shut down in order to avoid winter storm damage and loss. Sailing during hiatus is punishable by fine and is all the more dangerous due to the free reign of pirates.

The Fulhsna-Utanni—A part of the Mithusstandan (see below), in which the Skolani agree to supply Blade-Wielder guardians to the scions of the Gottari's ruling clans. Considered archaic and obsolete.

Futhark—Technically, any runic missive intended to convey a shared oath or law. To the Gottari, the futhark is the shared oath between the two ruling clans of the Wulthus and Amalus. The runes of the oath are inscribed on rings fastened to the hilts of the two futhark swords borne by the Lion Lord and the Wolf Lord.

The Jabitka—The mobile village of the Skolani. During the time of Vahldan and Elan's tale, the Jabitka is located in eastern Dania, south of the Danian River near the ford at Red Rocks.

Mithusstandan—The ancient oath between the Gottari and the Skolani in which the Skolani agree to safeguard the borders of their shared realm in exchange for Gottari weaponry (primarily the vaunted Gottari blades prized by the Skolani Blade-Wielders).

Qeins—A woman bonded to a Rekkr or chieftain of the Gottari, often of noble or landed birth. A qeins is a wife with rights and an inheritance outside of her marriage. Indeed, some qeins are more wealthy or prominent than their husbands. Esteemed priestesses are also granted the status of qeins.

Rekkr—A Gottari warrior who has claimed his name, pledged himself to one of the two ruling clans, and who owns his own weaponry and at least one warhorse.

The Urrinan—The prophesied calamitous end of the era in which the Tutona peoples shall rise to prominence from the ruins of the so-called civilized world of the imperials. To be wrought by the Bringer of Urrinan, who is foretold to arise from among the Gottari tribe.

DETAILED RECAP OF THE SEVERING SON

The Severing Son is the first volume of The Sundered Nation Trilogy—the tale of Vahldan of the Amalus and Elan of the Skolani. Bold Ascension is the second volume of their tale.

The Setup:

As our story opened, the security of Dania, home of the Gottari and Skolani tribes, was at risk. The Blade-Wielders (elite warriors of the Skolani tasked with guarding Dania's borders) pursued numerous Spali warbands raiding across Dania's eastern marches. The number of raids and the savagery of the raiders far exceeded the typical springtime incidences of Spali youths stealing sheep. The herdsmen most affected were the far-flung, among Dania's poorest, and mostly pledged to the Amalus clan of the Gottari. Their circumstances were a result of the exorbitant grazing prices of the wool guild, controlled by Wulthus clan landowners. As ever, the Wulthus were focused on the spring shearing and sowing of grains—activities that fed their coffers. Relatively unaffected by the raiding, the Wulthus opposed a mustering of warriors to quell the increased attacks.

In desperation, the Amalus herdsmen brought a seeress to appeal to the council of the longhouse in Danihem. AMASEILA, the daughter of a poor herdsman, claimed to speak with the voice of the goddess Freya. In the session, the Wulthus Lord THADMEIR found the claim of the seeress—a warning of a massive invasion of Dania by the Spali—shocking and alarming. He also secretly found Amaseila alluring. But when she implied that the son of the outcast Amalus chieftain ANGAVAR was the prophesied Bringer of Urrinan, the guildsmen named her a heretic. The charge provided a distraction that effectively postponed taking action to address the Spali incursions.

Angavar the Outcast lived and worked in a hidden mining compound high in the Carpan Mountains that bordered Dania and overlooked the eastern marches. His son VAHLDAN was fonder of carving than he was of training to stand as his father's second in the trial Angavar hoped to seek. The trial would've been to challenge Angavar's cousin DESDRUSAN's chieftainship of the Amalus clan. Desdrusan usurped the role through an elaborate setup which resulted in convicting Angavar for the slaying of his Wulthus rival, who was Thadmeir's older brother.

It was Vahldan who first spotted an approaching Spali warband heading for the compound. Angavar bid Vahldan to hide and protect their family in the mine while he stayed to defend the walled compound. Vahldan's concern for his father lured him out to discover that the Spali were led by the murderous elite warrior AUCHOTE. Seeking to run to his father's aid, Vahldan was set upon by Auchote himself. In response, Angavar exposed himself to divert the attack and save his son. Angavar was badly wounded, and once Vahldan helped him to safety inside the compound's walls, the attack mysteriously ceased. Still, the poison on the Spali weapon's tip ensured Angavar's wound was mortal. Father was forced to ask son to end his life honorably. Before he passed, Angavar implored Vahldan to seek the trail that would restore the family's honor and to bring those responsible for his downfall—and his murder—to justice.

Enter Elan:

The following morning, a Skolani Blade-Wielder named ELAN appeared to warn Vahldan and his family that the Spali were coming back. It had been Elan's Skolani host that had broken up the attack on the compound and put the Spali to flight. Together, they fled, with Elan leading the family to her tribal home village. Along the way, Elan and Vahldan were forced to fight together. The duo found respect and trust for one another. Upon arrival among the Skolani, Vahldan's pregnant mother was taken away to give birth. The baby arrived breech, which resulted in the tragic loss of Vahldan's mother.

Vahldan and his siblings were orphaned. The Skolani Queen KEISELLA tasked Elan with the guardianship of Vahldan and his younger siblings. She commanded Elan to take them to the long-house of Danihem to plea to Thadmeir to place the family in protective custody. Sending them to the Wulthus chieftain revealed the queen's mistrust of the Amalus leadership. The queen's daughter ICANNES, a highly skilled Blade-Wielder and near-sister to Elan, asked to accompany the group to act as a trainer to Vahldan to ready him for the possibility of a trial.

Along the way, after they were once again set upon by Spali, Vahldan became convinced that the Carpan priest TÚKASH, who originally led Angavar to the mine, was in league with Auchote. He also grew more certain that Desdrusan was in command of the murderous duo.

Reaching Danihem for Trial:

During an audience before Thadmeir, who was reluctant to help or to believe Vahldan's accusations, Icannes suggested that the solution could be found in granting Vahldan a trial against Desdrusan. Thadmeir reluctantly acceded. By law, those challenged were allowed to use a champion. Desdrusan selected his giant guardian TEAVAR. As the trial began, Amaseila—by then betrothed to Thadmeir and pregnant—touched Vahldan's hand and had a vision. She proclaimed him the Bringer and foretold of the glory he would win through Urrinan as well as the doom his role portended.

During the trial, through the communion he'd gained with his friend Elan, Vahldan was able to turn the rage he referred to as his ugliness into a clean and enhancing form of battle rage known as Thunar's Blessing. In the ensuing fight, Vahldan and Teavar found mutual respect, and ultimately they jointly chose to seek an honorable result in a draw, which outraged Desdrusan.

In the next longhouse council session, while determining Vahldan's post-trial fate, Icannes reappeared to report the onset of the Spali invasion. In response, Thadmeir granted Vahldan a temporary reprieve and ordered a total mustering for war. Thadmeir implored Vahldan to prove himself worthy of rejoining Gottari society. During the march to war, Vahldan was led to the hidden compound of his father's captain, BADAGIS. There he discovered how his father had spent years arranging for him to lead a host of well-equipped followers. Queen Keisella gathered a mustering of the Danian allies, and a strike plan was set in place. Vahldan volunteered to lead the secret mission that initiated the battle to repel the Spali from their position entrenched along the border.

Queen Keisella's War:

As the battle first began, Vahldan and Elan pursued Spali stragglers into the heart of a Spali encampment. After a fierce skirmish, they found themselves wounded, exhausted, and behind the lines of the ensuing battle. Out of harm's way and through shared concern and gratitude, the pair succumbed to enflamed passions. They were caught just as they surrendered to coupling. Any such contact violated Elan's oath as a Blade-Wielder. As a result of the transgression, Vahldan was turned over to Desdrusan's custody and Elan to Icannes's. In the aftermath of their initial victory, the allies pursued the retreating Spali through an ancient forest. At Desdrusan's behest, Icannes secretly made a deal with Túkash. The Carpan priest agreed to double-cross Auchote by setting him up in an ambush. Auchote sent Túkash out with his son in his place. Icannes also set up Vahldan, luring him to spring the trap. Vahldan took the bait, and in the process, he slayed both Auchote's son and their so-called ally Túkash.

Because of Desdrusan's offer of immunity to Túkash, the usurper was able to name Vahldan a murderer and place him on the penance line—an almost certain death sentence that would occur at the start of the coming battle. Vahldan found himself chained to, among others, his father's loyal scout, KEFFRIC. Resigned to fate, Vahldan secretly planned his vengeance on Desdrusan. While plotting and waiting for the inevitable, he also carved a kestrel charm, which he sent to Elan on the eve of battle.

As the battle lines formed, moments before Vahldan would have launched an attempt on Desdrusan's life, Keffric convinced him to seek to honor his father's memory instead by focusing on the Spali and Auchote. When Vahldan realized that Keffric was right, he looked to find Elan, and together they spotted the kestrel mates that had come to symbolize their connection soaring overhead. Still, each of them knew they would face their duty alone, though with renewed hope found in one another.

During the battle, the penance line fought their way to freedom, and Elan followed Icannes's small band in pursuit of Auchote's host fleeing behind the Spali lines. Elan was shocked and terrified to discover the immensity of the hidden Spali army. A massive attack was launched on the Gottari floundering in a swale. Vahldan was reunited with his host, and they remained at the fore of the Gottari counterattack. From above, Elan gleaned that Auchote had spotted Vahldan in the fighting and left her group to pursue Auchote. Just moments after Keffric sacrificed himself to keep Vahldan safe, Elan arrived to slay Auchote's henchman. Vahldan then faced Auchote, man to man. Auchote was surprised by Vahldan's boldness and skill and fled. After Vahldan's host fought their way to temporary respite, Vahldan retrieved his family sword, which had been cravenly abandoned by Desdrusan, who had fled the battle completely.

Bearing the heirloom sword, Vahldan and his host then rode against the crumbling Spali defenses. Their action inspired and roused the allies to victory. Vahldan won a great deal of acclaim, especially among the Amalus clan. In a ceremony of surrender, the Spali wished to submit to the Severing Son. Imbued by the ugliness after saying a prayer over Keffric, Vahldan spotted Auchote lurking at a safe distance and angrily vowed to hunt him down. The other leaders were aghast at Vahldan's display, but the rank-and-file warriors reveled in his swagger.

War's Aftermath:

After their victory, while Vahldan basked in the glory flowing from his admirers, Elan was called back to the Skolani camp to face charges that she had abandoned a fighting mate, which resulted in the woman being slain. Elan became convinced she would be stripped of her status as a Blade-Wielder. Icannes was called to a meeting in the queen's pavilion with Thadmeir's brother URIAS present. The two were old friends. Urias was sent by Thadmeir to ensure that Elan would be taken from Vahldan if he chose to follow through with a pursuit of Auchote's warband. Thadmeir feared that leading the Amalus warriors away might instigate the sundering of the Gottari nation, dividing those loyal to each ruling clan. Thadmeir hoped the prospect of losing Elan would keep Vahldan from leaving.

At the queen's meeting, Icannes and Urias were told that Urias was Elan's brother. The siblings were the grandchildren of the seeress SAEL, who had long foretold of the vital roles of Vahldan and Elan in the prophecy. Sael said that Urias and Icannes were bound by a similar shared destiny, also tied to Urrinan, which they both sensed to be true.

Later that same night, Vahldan sought the aid of Urias in allowing the Amalus clan to decide Desdrusan's fate without Wulthus or guild interference. With Urias's covert aid, Vahldan was able to challenge Desdrusan, and the usurper refused to fight back. Rather than execute him, Vahldan bid him to flee. After Desdrusan's flight, the clan elevated Vahldan by acclaim. They named him the rightful Lion Lord. He then vowed to lead them to pursue and finish off Auchote—the very move that Thadmeir had feared.

The following dawn, Keisella and Sael confronted Elan, forcing her to choose her own path forward. Elan had already all but decided to stay with Icannes and serve her near-sister during her likely assent to queenship. Elan was told that if she were to choose to follow Vahldan instead, she would be banished, as would any daughter that might be born to her.

Also at dawn, Vahldan was confronted by Thadmeir, who invited him to rejoin Gottari society as the presumed lord of the Amalus, to work to end corruption from within the system. Vahldan declined the offer, convinced that he could only gain the power he needed to overcome the guild by winning glory, which would deliver the acclaim of the common herdsmen.

Elan went to meet Icannes as the Skolani departed for home, and the two said a heartbreaking goodbye, for Elan had chosen Vahldan and banishment. Vahldan had left the meeting with Thadmeir in despair, believing that he had lost Elan forever. He was hugely relieved when Elan appeared to tell him that she was willing to commit to him for life, as kestrel mates would.

Into the Wider World:

Together and riding with their Amalus host, Vahldan and Elan pursued Auchote's warband across the plains. During a scouting mission, Elan realized she was no longer Skolani. She cut off her braids and rushed back to surrender to the communion with Vahldan that had been forbidden by her old oath.

The Amalus chased Auchote's warband all the way to the Pontean seacoast. There, before the walls of the Hellain city of Akasas, the Amalus defeated the Spali, with Vahldan vanquishing Auchote in the process.

Afterward, Elan saw Vahldan in the light of his victory. She recognized that he'd retained his true self—the young carver she had met in the compound. It made her fully realize her love for him. Before the battle, Vahldan had gleaned the worth of the ships in the Akasas harbor. Because he had Elan at his side, he recognized the potential of tapping into the wealth of Pontea, sensing that it may be what would break the wool guild's stranglehold in Dania.

Having been spurned by Vahldan, Thadmeir hurried back to Danihem to meet his new daughter, Amaga. The babe's mother recited the Song of the Bringer in the voice of Freya, reminding them of their daughter's foreseen connection to the Bringer of Urrinan.

Bold Ascension picks up right where The Severing Son left off—on the Pontean coast, in the Hellain city of Akasas.

"Tho' Lion's Son reclaims the blade
So too is spurned the futhark's glade
'Yond rock and vale his fame is sought
Kingdoms quail as empire's wrought..."
—from The Song of the Severing Son

PART ONE
SAILING TOWARDS DESTINY

CHAPTER I
A WORLD OF OPPORTUNITY

"Although my father was surprised by much that he encountered and learned as he stepped into the wider world of Imperial Pontea, he quickly adapted. Indeed, Vahldan swiftly began to thrive there.

In contrast, although Pontea was unsurprised by the arrival of yet another ambitious young chieftain of the Teutonics, the imperials were soon and repeatedly left astonished by the bold ascension of Vahldan of the Amalus Clan of the Gottari."—Brin Bright Eyes, Saga of Dania

MALVIUS WAS BORED. And hungover. The wine here was awful. Plus, he could hardly breathe. It was so stuffy in this forsaken tiny bedchamber. His supposed top-end lodging reeked of spilled wine, stale perfume, and night breath. He'd asked for the best, and this was what he'd received. Such a shitty little city.

He'd had such high hopes for this expedition. This was all his father's fault.

Not the siege. Or the shitty lodging. But his being stranded in this stinking backwater port when the siege had started—yes, for that

3

Malvius blamed Papa. As far as Malvius was concerned, his wretched circumstances sprang from the old man's ludicrous decree.

He had planned to stay in bed all day, and both of his employees seemed to be sticking to that plan. But now he was wide awake, and the light leaking in around the shutters told him it was still daytime. He closed his eyes and sighed. How long had he been stranded here? Was it two days or three? How does one keep track in a city like Akasas, where each day feels as bleak as the last? He wasn't a religious man, but he wondered if he should come up with a prayer to the gods, pleading for a change in circumstances. It was worth a try, and he had no other plans.

As he gathered his thoughts to compose his prayer, a low rumbling sound came to him. Perhaps he'd summoned the gods just by the rare thought of them. The rumbling increased, at first causing the glass lamp cover on the sideboard to rattle. A moment later, he felt the bed vibrating, then shaking. Beneath the rumbling came a low humming sound, as if a giant hive had been built in the surrounding walls of the chamber and had come alive.

One of his two employees quietly rose from the bed and went to the lone window. It was the one with the dark skin—likely Bafranii, he'd decided once he'd heard her accent. She lifted the louvered shutters. Jarring sunlight streaked into the room, searing Malvius's brain. Distant shouts and high-pitched cries drifted in on a gust of chilly air. The humming morphed into a mournful tone. Was it the distant chorus of some sort of horn?

Malvius sat up. "What's going on?" The Bafranii didn't bother looking at him or replying beyond a shrug. She seemed standoffish for someone being paid so well. The second employee woke with a start and sat up beside him, smearing her face paint by wiping the drool from the corner of her mouth. Daylight was not kind to this one. Beneath the smudged and smeared paint her cheeks were large-pored and creased by the wrinkles in the bed linens. Her eyebrows and faint mustache were as dark as his own hair, making it all the more obvious that the hair on her head had been dyed to its garish shade of yellow. He couldn't recall why he'd picked either of them. But, as with the wine, the pickings were sparse in this shitty corner of the Pontean.

Malvius rose from the bed, causing his temples to throb. He grabbed the flagon of shitty wine from the sideboard and shooed the standoffish one from the chair by the shutters. He dropped to a knee on the chair, took a slug of wine straight from the flagon, and peered through the louvers.

The visible end of the siege line of tattooed warriors was gone. From here he couldn't see their main camp directly outside the north gate, so he couldn't be sure of anything. The rumbling, mournful hum, and high-pitched cries swiftly faded. The only sound remaining was the drone and clatter of the bustling city directly below. Had his non-prayer been answered before he delivered it? Had the besieging raiders given up and moved on? Maybe the city fathers would finally open the gates, and he could sail his fleet away from this forsaken place. He looked at the sky, wondering if it was too late in the day to set sail. It seemed to be late afternoon—probably not wise, even if the shitty weather and rough seas that had driven them here had improved.

A knock at the door caused the girls to start. "Cap? It's me."

The muffled voice outside the door belonged to his first mate, Dexicos. Dex would only bother him for something big. "What's happening out there?"

"Not sure, Cap. Something odd."

"Just odd? Is it a good sort of odd?"

"Seems like it could go either way. I'm thinking you should come down to the wall." He'd assigned Dex to monitoring the situation outside the city walls. The man didn't venture such advice without good cause.

"I'll be right out." Malvius set aside the wine and started dressing. The blonde leaned back on the bed, blinking and pouting. The Bafranii girl rushed to dress, same as him. She seemed to have sensed the fret he'd heard in Dex's tone. He threw his cloak over his shoulders and reached into his belt pouch. All he had were gold vuliras—one was worth more than twice the nightly price for the both of them. He tossed it to the blonde, whose pout turned to delight. "You two will have to figure out how to split this."

The blonde nodded, still staring at the coin in her hand. "Of course," she rasped. They were her first two words of the day. The Bafranii girl scowled but said nothing and followed Malvius to the door. Neither had been much for conversation, but that wasn't what he'd paid for.

Dex came into view, already at the top of the stairwell. "Tell me," he said as he strode over.

"It's a lot to tell. Easier to have you see for yourself."

"Very well. Lead on." His man nodded and rushed down the narrow staircase. Malvius followed, barely able to keep up, with the Bafranii thumping along behind. Dexicos led him from the inn out onto the crowded lane. They started toward the north gate. Malvius looked back to find that the Bafranii girl had disappeared. The vendors lining the lane were closing early in spite of the fact that the streets were crowded. There was an ominous fret on the townsfolk's faces and in the drone of their voices. Clearly these folks were not celebrating the end of a siege.

The wall over the city's north gate loomed ahead. Dex led him to the base of the wall to one side of the closed gate and started up the stairs to the wall-walk, taking two steps at a time. Malvius followed at an increasing distance. The parapet of the wall was lined with sea captains and city fathers. The locals gawped with swiveling heads, holding their bows like unpracticed boys hoping to hit their first partridge but afraid to take the shot.

Malvius parted and pushed aside two graybeards, ignoring their indignation. He was astonished by the view. The tattooed steppe savages were indeed gone. But they'd been replaced.

Malvius gawped, struggling to make sense of the panorama. He swiftly realized that the large piles of corpses were those of the city's previous besiegers. Just as the makeshift corrals were filled with the steppe heathens' ponies. The ground was picketed with arrows and spears. A battle! That's what he'd heard. The fact that it was over was astonishing. How could so much have happened so quickly? And with such devastation to one side?

Even more astonishing was the sight of those responsible for this swift turn of events. He'd wondered earlier if he was hearing the coming of the gods. These were clearly men. But they were warriors unlike any he'd ever seen—clearly not the soldiers of either of the two empires. Most were mounted. Their horses were huge, as were their colorfully painted shields. Crimson banners snapped over their heads. To the man, they all wore chain armor and leather, most with dun or greenish woolen cloaks thrown behind their shoulders. Almost every one of them wore a sword at the hip or across their back, which was very unusual for warriors from the hinterlands. Swords were expensive, after all. As were horses! These warriors were not only well-equipped, they also held their backs straight and their chins high.

This was no rabble. Unlike the Kaukazari, there was no outrageous swagger to them. It wasn't the most uniform host Malvius had seen. Instead, each seemed a capable individual. Capable and lethal.

"Who are they?" Malvius wondered aloud.

"Teutonics!" a man down the line replied. "From the northlands."

"Gods help us," the old man beside Malvius added. "They're even worse than the Kaukazari heathens they slayed."

"Teutonics," Malvius repeated musingly, watching them trot back from chasing down the last of their tattooed foes, many dragging their victims from ropes tied to their saddles. Malvius couldn't be sure, but he saw no evidence that a single one of the city's original besiegers had survived. Moreover, it seemed few of the Teutonics had fallen. Their wounded were already being attended to, their dead laid out in neat rows.

A cheer went up from the field to his left. A group of the Teutonics was riding onto the plain, coming from the forest road to join their fellows gathering before the north gate. A roan horse bearing two riders led the arrivals. The setting sun shone upon the pair. From across the field, the victorious warriors lauded them, whooping and raising their fists in salute. As the pair came nearer, Malvius leaned over the parapet for a better look.

From among this impressive host, these two were the most astonishing by far.

The one riding pillion had flaxen hair that fell on broad shoulders. Even from afar, Malvius noted his angular features and his easy confidence.

But the rider in the saddle! It wasn't the cropped auburn hair that startled Malvius. His surprise was due to the fact that this fierce short-haired warrior was a woman. As far as he could tell, she was the only one. But what a woman she was. She had broad shoulders and bare, muscled arms. A sword hilt rose over her shoulder. Her cheeks were ruddy and her smile radiated.

Malvius couldn't pry his gaze away from the pair as they casually walked their mount to meet their companions on a rise in the meadow before the gate. Even from forty spans away, Malvius thought them one of the most magnetic and handsome couples he'd ever beheld. It seemed they'd emerged from the mists of legend.

"This is my captain here, Magister." Malvius forced himself to turn to Dex, who was leading a chinless man his way.

"Captain, I am Timaios, magister of Akasas," the chinless man said. Several grim graybeards stood at the magister's sloped shoulders.

"I am Malvius, son of Decebius." He bowed his head.

"Decebius of Thrakius is well-known here." Timaios squinted. "The four merchant ships in the harbor—all of them are yours?"

"The ships belong to my father, Magister. But they're currently at my command. Why do you ask?"

"We'd like to ensure that we have your support, Captain. You and your men could be a boon to our collective safety in what's likely to come next."

Malvius cocked his head. "I'm sorry, but what *is* likely to come next?"

The chinless man frowned. "An attack, of course. We've just gone from a stranding to a storm. We're likely to find ourselves fighting for survival, and I would like to know you and your men will stand with us. The gods willing, we can hold until an imperial garrison arrives."

"What makes you so sure things will worsen, Magister? You were already under siege. Perhaps these men merely came to help."

"Help? Can you not see? These are no steppe heathens. They're skilled killers."

"Evidently true. But they've removed a threat." Malvius's irritation slipped into his tone.

"Yes, but to what end?" the chinless magister demanded.

"Why don't you ask them?"

The magister's eyes went wide. "Ask them? Gods above, man. They're Teutonics! Have you not heard? Men like these have perpetrated some of the deadliest raids in imperial history."

Malvius sighed. He wished he could just sail away from this place —now more than ever. A moment before, this turn of events had provided a spark of hope within him. But the chinless magister's attitude was stamping it out. "Whatever their race, it seems pointless to guess at their intentions before seeking to learn them."

One of the graybeards pointed over the parapet. "Timaios—the Teutonics. They come."

Those clustered around Malvius all moved to the wall. A foursome of northmen came forth afoot, led by the magnetic couple. Flanking them were a slim young man and one of the largest warriors Malvius had ever seen. As they neared, Malvius's first impression was confirmed: The pair was strikingly charismatic— even more attractive than he'd thought. They were splattered with gore, as was their giant companion. The pair were clearly the host's leaders. The only new surprise was that they were younger than he'd surmised. That and, unlike most warlords Malvius had encountered, these two had fought and killed alongside those they led.

The male leader stood at the fore, but the thin young one spoke. "Brothers of the city! Our lord wishes to speak to whoever reigns here." His Hellainic was accented but otherwise perfect.

All eyes turned to the magister. Timaios swallowed and said, "What is it you want?"

The Teutonic leader spoke calmly in his own tongue, and the youth relayed. "As you can see, we have vanquished those who intended you harm. We have pursued these savages for many leagues, as they were guilty of grave atrocities in the north. They are much despised in our homeland. Our justice is yours this day."

Malvius couldn't wipe away his smile. "See there?"

The spokesman went on. "This journey, in pursuit of our mutual foe, cost us dearly. And we are far from hearth and kin. Our swift chase forced us to forego grazing and hunting along the way, leaving our stocks low and our horses thin. The only favor my lord Vahldan would ask in return for the liberation of your city is food and drink for his warriors and a bit of grain for our mounts. Perhaps a night or two of shelter and warmth for our wounded."

Malvius turned back to the graybeards. "Didn't I say? Your fears were obviously—"

"You see, Timaios?" the graybeard at the magister's shoulder interjected. "They want inside. They seek plunder and rape, just as we suspected."

Another said, "They're in range, Timaios. We could let loose a volley."

The first one nodded. "Yes, if we take down the chieftain, the rest may drift away."

Malvius couldn't believe what he was hearing. "I beg of you, Magister. Do not provoke them. You need not open your gates. Merely send out a few goats and geese, a dozen sacks of grain, and a barrel of ale for their efforts. This is all they ask."

"He's wrong!" the first graybeard exclaimed. "If you appease them, they'll never leave."

Malvius waved the fearmonger off. "Bah. Even if they decide to camp here for a few days, believe me, your drab little corner of the world will soon bore them into leaving. Then we can all get on with our lives."

Timaios's brows were knitting. "Lydas is right—feeding them will surely cause them to linger. And giving them ale would be inviting disaster. Having barbarians at the gates is one thing, but having well-fed, bored, and drunken barbarians is quite another. We'll do better to leave them hungry. Have Aristion call out the militia. We need every able body on the ramparts quickly." One of the graybeards scurried off.

Malvius opened his mouth to argue, but Timaios turned and called, "The citizens of Akasas thank you for defeating those who wrongfully sought to imprison free folk. Due to the hardship we have endured, there is no excess to spare here. Tell your lord to show himself more honorable than those he vanquished by moving on and leaving us in peace."

Malvius watched as the young man translated. The warrior woman bristled and spat, and the giant glared, hand on hilt. The young man's eyes were hard, but he spoke just as calmly as before. As they conferred, Malvius's eye was drawn to a black mass at the woman's belt. There was one on the belt of the leader as well. He focused and studied them. Hair... and blood. Gods, were those human scalps? He decided he'd best not point them out.

The translator turned back, shading his eyes against the setting sun. "Lord Vahldan is disappointed by your lack of gratitude. He wonders if you will reconsider and look to your stores again. He is interested only in gaining enough to sustain man and beast until we can see to our own needs. My lord considers this a fair request and knows that his men will not settle for less. He hopes to avoid the discontent your first answer is likely to bring."

"Ah, now come the threats," the graybeard Lydas said.

Malvius was beside himself. "Please, I will gladly pay for what they ask. At this point we must consider—"

"Enough." Timaios held up a silencing hand. His face reddening, the magister shouted down, "Fair? How is it that armed men at the gates dare to make demands and also speak of fairness? We say begone with insulting beggars! We shall never let the likes of you and your rabble inside to piss in our streets and defile our women. Never!"

Further back, more of the Teutonics were gathering to watch. As they received the translation, angry shouts erupted. The leader's female companion barked some sort of curse, made a crude hand gesture, and turned to storm off. For his part, the leader remained calm. But his glare smoldered. His reply was firm but still he did not raise his voice.

The sober translation arrived: "My lord Vahldan would have but one thing now and that is your name, you who casts such unprovoked venom." The youth pointed up at Timaios.

Timaios blanched. He took a step back from the parapet, his wet lower lip quavering. Lydas had not lost his bluster, though, and cried, "This is our magister, and he speaks for us all! His name is Timaios, son of Sosigenios!"

The Teutonics conferred a moment. The youth replied in Hellainic even as the leader and the big man strode off, openly showing their backs to the city's archers. "My lord Vahldan, chieftain of the Amalus clan of the Gottari nation, regretfully wishes to inform Timaios, magister of Akasas, that his city may now consider itself at war. He also adds, again with regret, that however your defeat comes about, he will personally see to your death."

Malvius sighed. The likelihood of the threat coming to fruition was too great to scoff. Timaios stared as if seeing his promised demise in a waking dream.

The young translator lingered. "Magister, if I might now speak for myself, Attasar, son of Halasar, I would beg of you: Seek to undo this. You must believe me when I say this is a fight you do not want. It's still not too late. Lord Vahldan is angry now, but he is also reasonable and just. My lord truly holds no designs on your city. Beg his forgiveness and his leave to make an offering. Seek an honorable end to this, for your city and for us."

Malvius looked hopefully to Timaios. No one spoke, so Malvius did. "If he does as you say, your lord will revoke his threats?"

Attasar paused. "Of this, I fear, I cannot be certain. But I am certain that if you do nothing, unnecessary woe is sure to follow." Attasar turned, as had the others, and strode off toward the already forming besieging lines of the Gottari host.

Still looking stunned, Timaios slunk away, his graybeards muttering and handwringing after him. Malvius scanned the scene, feeling even more trapped than before. In desperation he wondered if he could find a way to flee, even if he had to bribe someone. Or with this distraction, could he attempt to sail off in the dark? Surely a gatehouse guard could be enticed to let him and his crews out to the harbor.

Malvius looked back over the city to the sea glowing in the day's last light. The wind blew through his hair, and he saw that the waves were growing larger again. The masts of his ships docked in the harbor tipped and rocked. Storm clouds loomed to the south, just as the storm of war loomed outside the city's northern gates. It was dangerous enough to sail by night. By night and in a storm was too foolhardy even for him.

It seemed the ill fate of this ill-luck city was his to bear.

CHAPTER 2
BARBAROUS BEHAVIOR

"Though the Gottari routinely traded with the Hellains of Imperial Pontea, the contacts maintained by the Gottari wool guild were with merchants in Thrakius. As near as can now be told, the lesser port of Akasas had little contact with the Gottari. One would presume, based upon their reaction to the Amalus host, that any contact the Akasans had previously had with the tribes of the Teutonics had been disagreeable.

Vahldan's reception may have been unnecessary and foolish on the part of the Akasan city fathers, but who is to say whether or not their reaction was fortuitous? Certainly much that came of it would not have happened had my father not been spurned upon his arrival in Pontea."—Brin Bright Eyes, Saga of Dania

"Lie back and be at ease." Elan pushed Vahldan back onto the bed pallet she'd set up.

He resisted, propping himself on his elbows. "I'm trying to keep you from getting that stuff on our bedding."

"Stop your fretting," she said. "Trust me, *that stuff*, as you call it, will wash off."

Vahldan collapsed back, staring up at the pavilion ceiling, looking anything but restful. Elan stirred the pot of warm cleansing paste, scooped some out, and started low, smearing it on his calves. Vahldan raised his head to look. "It doesn't smell the same."

"This batch smells different because it is." Cedar bark she had in ample quantity. But she hadn't brought along any frankincense, and she hadn't found any cypress leaves. Elan had substituted ground pine needles and clove, mixed into lanolin along with the resin from some rosemary she'd found along the riverbank. It smelled reasonably close. "Now lie back," she commanded, working on his thighs. He did. "And close your eyes." He did that, too.

His muscles were like knots. His breathing came as a series of impatient sighs, and his eyebrows were furiously sparring. It was strange seeing him like this. Outside of sleeping, it was rare for the two of them to be nude together. Rarer still did Elan see him nude and not aroused. At least not *before* they'd made love. And she was rubbing his thighs! It made her certain that something was bothering him. "The point of a Skolani cleansing ritual, my love, is to rid the warrior of the tension of battle." Vahldan sighed again, louder. "If you're willing, the ritual can ease you back from the throes of Thunar's Blessing to the realm of the self."

He laughed. "I don't think it's working."

"Well…" She scooped out a glob of the paste with both hands and pounced, smearing it on his abdomen. He lurched and wriggled under her tickling. "You have to try."

"I *am* trying," he said, laughing.

"Are you?" Elan gently pressed him back. "Eyes closed," she said. He obeyed. She worked the slick, warm paste over his chest and up onto his shoulders, massaging as she spread it. "Now," she said, and she leaned over and softly kissed his lips. "Tell me."

A corner of his mouth quirked up. "What?"

"You know what. The thing that you're clinging to."

"How do you know I'm clinging to something?"

"You're obviously not surrendering to the process." Elan worked on the rigid bands of muscle at the base of his neck, then let her fingers slither down over his pectorals. "Do you really still think you can hide from me?"

Vahldan opened his eyes. His features softened. "No."

"Is it something that happened in the battle? Auchote?"

"He thought he had me," Vahldan mused, smiling. "So did I." His gaze grew distant and the smile faded. "Auchote said I'd never live up to my father. It's part of why I refused to give up. I just couldn't accept it. After all my father did for me, after all that I've caused to happen—"

"Vahldan," she scolded.

"What I mean is, after all we all went through, I just couldn't let Auchote be right. I couldn't let him win. I can't let any of them win. I need to..." He shook his head.

Elan put her face near his, filling his field of vision. "You do realize we've already won."

"I know." Vahldan looked and sounded less than convinced.

"Do you? Because you should. Think about it." Elan sat back and made a show of counting on her smeary fingers. "You beat Death's Grin. Your host eliminated the Paralatoe. You avenged your father's murder. You reclaimed the futhark sword and your rightful status. You brought glory to your clan and made your homeland safe. Through it all, you made sure your brother and sisters stayed safe. Have I missed anything?"

"I got the girl." He waggled his eyebrows.

"First, I'd hardly say you *got* me. Second, I'm not exactly *the girl*. Still, I suppose you have a point. And your point supports my point that it's no small list."

He laughed, but then turned his head, staring at nothing again. "I suppose," he said.

"But...?" Elan feigned tickling him again.

He clenched and grabbed her hands. "No fair."

Elan ceased her tickling effort. "I'll stop if you let it out."

Vahldan sighed a loud and long breath, a purposeful release. Still holding her hands, he said, "Did you see the way they looked at us?"

"Who? The city mouse?" Elan grinned. "I saw his face after Attasar told him you would find him and face him man to man. I think it pushed his next two shits into his trousers. Well, I hope he had trousers on."

Vahldan smiled but shook his head. "Not just him. All of them. The city folk. How could I have imagined they'd be grateful? Or at least intimidated. They just stared down at us. It's like... they're just so sure they're better than us. All I wanted was to talk, figure out our next steps. But no. There wasn't a chance. They looked at us like we were the stray hounds that scared off a pack of wolves outside their door. Worse—they wouldn't even toss us a scrap of food for the effort. They think we're savages, just like the Spali. Or maybe worse."

She raised her eyebrows. "Worse? Worse how?"

"Attasar says many imperials consider Tutona tribesmen to be barbarians—folk who should know better but who remain uncivilized."

"I almost hate to ask, but why should we care what they think of us?"

Vahldan's expression hardened again. "I've already told you. If I'm going to change things at home, I need to make something big happen. I wanted to find out about those ships. But now we're out here, besieging them just like the bedamned Spali were when we arrived. It's so stupid. I mean, those ships can just sail away. The ones I want to talk to aren't even trapped. It's like we're only proving them right—that we're contemptible barbarians. Irrelevant. They probably respect the pirates more. At least pirates are a real threat to them."

"Maybe they *are* right," she said. He frowned. Elan reached down to the pot and scooped up a handful of the paste. She straddled him as she smeared his chest, sliding her hands downward onto his stomach. "Since they're going to treat us like barbarians, maybe we should act like barbarians. But clever ones." She pressed her pelvis against him with a wicked grin.

She felt the stirring of Vahldan's arousal beneath her. Finally! He smiled but wore a puzzled expression. "Exactly what do you have in mind?"

Elan slid backward, working her hands over his hips, avoiding smearing any paste on his manhood. "Well, if a clever barbarian wants something, what should they do?" She poised her chin over his newfound arousal.

"They should"—his breath caught—"take it?"

"Aha," she purred and gave him a long, luxurious lick. He quivered and sighed. She poised herself again. "I say, if we're interested in a nice, long ship, we just..." She opened her mouth, moving oh-so-near to his now arcing cock.

"Oh, you barbarous wench. Tell me," he said. Gods, how she loved teasing him.

"We take it." She popped him in her mouth.

After only a couple of strokes, he hooked her under the arms and pulled her up to face him, gazing intently into her eyes. "I've never loved you more," Vahldan said as he entered her.

It occurred to her, even as they lost themselves to the rapture of fucking, that it was the first time Vahldan had actually told her he loved her. Elan knew he was still struggling to find himself, and that he still clung to the need to prove himself, to live up to the ridiculous expectations he shouldered in his father's name—to assuage the guilt he felt for Angavar's death.

In spite of it all, she found the expression oddly fitting in the moment. It confirmed her choice. She'd given up everything for this. She belonged to him. And they loved each other.

Whether this was a part of the prophecy or not, the whole of the wider world they'd discovered together was laid bare at their feet. Elan considered it theirs to take.

~

Malvius struggled to open his eyes. Once he managed it, he was sorry to have made the effort. His head throbbed. Gods, the wine was horrendous in this forsaken deathtrap of a city.

He rolled to find that the Bafranii whore was gone from his bed. And, as he dimly recalled, he'd forgone on her blonde companion. Had he even paid the Baffy? Had she robbed him? He flopped his legs over the side of the bed, tried to stand, and practically fell to his clothes. No, his purse was still on his belt and seemed untouched.

Had she figured out a way to escape the siege without taking him along? "Better not have, bitch," he murmured. Malvius instantly knew it was unfair speculation. She was clever—he'd gleaned that in spite of drinking what seemed to have been buckets of bad wine. Malvius suspected that her sort of cleverness made it all the more likely that he'd see her again.

He lifted a shutter louver to peek out. Sunlight all but stabbed his brain. Gods, how late was it? The city seemed quiet. He could see some of the Teutonics' tents in the distance but none of the warriors. Had their besiegers slept late as well? He slapped the shutters closed. Malvius recalled that their leader—one Lord Vahldan, as he had named himself—had claimed that a state of war would begin at dawn. Was this the Gottari's idea of war? Or had the magister come through with their demanded supplies? That seemed doubtful, as even paying them might still cost the chinless one his miserable life.

Someone knocked as he dressed. "Dexicos?"

"Yeah, it's me, Cap."

He opened the door. His first mate handed him a goblet of watered wine and a thick slab of warm bread, slathered in butter and partially wrapped in a cloth, so that he could keep his hands clean. Dex was as thorough as they came. "What's happening out there?" he asked as he took a bite.

"Storm blew over," Dex said as he went to reopen the shutters with a snap. "Smooth waters and light winds. Looks like we could get out this morning."

Malvius blinked in the blinding light. "Only if the bastards open the harborside gate."

"It'll happen," Dex said with a shrug.

"How do you figure?"

"I don't figure, you do." Dex grinned. "You'll think of something, Cap. You always do. I already sent Sabas to tell the other captains to be ready. It's nice and quiet out there. To me it feels like a good sign."

Ah, ever the optimist. Too bad Malvius couldn't think at all, let alone well enough to make a plan. He took another bite and chased it with a slug of the wine. The sharp pain in his temples miraculously started to dull. Maybe he would be able to think again. At some point. He wiped the butter from his mouth and handed back the cloth and goblet. He fastened his cloak and headed for the door. "What about the Teutonics?"

Dex followed him to the stairs. "No one seems to know, so I went to the wall to see for myself. Their horses are still grazing in a makeshift corral, but there's not even a sentinel in sight. It's a puzzle, but I'm hoping it means they no longer have their blood up. Or that they managed to drink away their grudge. Either way, seems possible that they'll move on."

"I suppose it's possible." He doubted it. It felt too much like wishful thinking. But of the pair of them, Malvius was the pessimist. It was one of the main reasons he needed Dex around.

They emerged onto the deserted lane. "Go and see how Sabas is faring. Keep your eyes and ears open. If the opportunity arises, we'll need to move fast." Dex nodded and took off at a trot toward the town square. Malvius set out for the harbor gate. Before he arrived at the closed gate, a bell clanged above him. Several militiamen called to one another on the wall. "Teutonics ahoy!" one called, pointing to the northeast.

Malvius took the steps two at a time. He arrived on the wall-walk and hurried to the parapet to scan the meadows beyond the harbor keep's wall. The Teutonics came in a cluster, all holding their shields edge to edge, both alongside their column and overhead. They looked like a cross between a turtle and a centipede. They disappeared from view behind the lower keep's outside gate even as a dozen archers lobbed useless potshots their way. Within a moment, echoing thuds revealed that the Gottari had brought a ram with them.

Rather than hitting the city's main gate, they sought to enter the harbor keep. Malvius glanced down at his fleet lined up in the dock slips below. Panic rose within him. Apparently, this Gottari lordling realized that the ships in this harbor were worth more than the whole of the city. Malvius's luck just kept getting worse.

He turned and spotted the hotheaded graybeard Lydas among the archers. Malvius grabbed the hothead's arm. "You've got to do something before they break the gate."

Lydas's eyes widened. "Just what would you have us do?"

"Go down there! Fight them!"

Lydas scowled. "Us? Why don't you and your men go down and fight them?"

"My men are sailors, not..." Malvius realized the folly of the conversation, turned, and hurried down the wall top to look back toward the market square. Where was Dex? He had to gather his men. Perhaps they could get to the boats and cast off before the gate broke. Neither Sabas nor Dexicos was in sight.

The next resounding boom of the ram was accompanied by the sound of cracking wood. Malvius slumped inwardly. Even if his crews were already gathered at the gate, ready to go, it would take too long to cast off. Besides, he could never send barely-armed sailors out there to face the kind of slaughter he'd witnessed the prior day.

The final thud resounded, morphing into a louder splintering sound. It was followed by a throaty cheer. Malvius hurried back to the parapet. He stood watching the shield-centipede skitter across the green of the outer keep to the docks. The intruders passed several fishing boats before they arrived at the dock to his current flagship, The Pontean Princess. The ship was his father's greatest pride—

certainly dearer to the old man than his children. The centipede stopped and a lone warrior appeared, sprinting out from the protection of the shields and down the protruding dock, slashing the moorings as he went.

"Shoot him!" Malvius cried to the gaping militiamen. But to no avail. Once they finally responded, their shooting was woeful. The young man was back to the safety of the shields in mere moments. The men of the shield-centipede gave his ship's hull a shove, sending her bumping out of the dock slip and setting her adrift in the harbor. The Gottari repeated the feat for each of his other three ships, plus the only other merchant ship in the port. Not a single bowshot came remotely close to impeding the predictable routine.

Malvius watched in horror as, one by one, the ships of his fleet all drifted far enough to be caught in the current of the river, to be inexorably pulled from the harbor to the sea. The Princess was the first to flounder into the quickening current. She even righted herself, moving toward the broad mouth of the river prow-first. Before she moved into the river's mouth, and the dangerous crashing waves of the rocky seacoast, a dripping rope rose from the dark river water downstream, ahead of his ships' progress and just beyond a bowshot from the outer keep walls. Apparently it was a series of entwined ropes. Gangs of barbarians scurried to tie off the ends of the woven ropes to a series of large trees on either bank.

His father's prize ship hit the taut rope braid and turned, the rope holding it broadside as the other ships bumped and banged together, collecting like chunks of ice on a dam.

The Teutonics of the shield-centipede hurried from the docks to the downstream gate. They pushed the crossbar free and were out of the keep in moments, running to join their companions downstream. Not a single assailant had been hit by the shitty archers of Akasas.

The Gottari archers on the banks, however, were much more accurate. They shot arrows fitted with lines and in no time the thieves were hauling Malvius's fleet to the riverbanks, where they tied and staked their prizes, tilting on their keels in the shallows.

Years prior, Malvius had returned to find one of his father's warehouses full of grain infested with rats. In his shock and rage, he'd screamed and thrown rocks at the rats, but the rodents had been utterly unconcerned. They had stood in the open, as if daring him to try to take back the grain. The same hopeless resignation came over him as he watched these nimble Teutonics scurrying onto and across his decks and leaping into his holds. All while Malvius's countrymen —the same bigoted dimwits who'd brought this about—stood gaping with useless bows in their hands.

The Gottari swiftly broke into the hold of the Princess. Mere moments later, the giant who'd stood at their leader's side appeared at the prow with one of the mini barrels of the rare Tiberian wine Malvius had procured before setting sail hoisted on his shoulder. The man easily held it while one of his fellows tapped the barrel. After they'd filled a dozen cups, the giant held the barrel aloft, letting the precious liquid gush from the tap into his mouth, over his face, and down his front side, inciting his mates to cheer.

Malvius turned from the sickening scene and almost bumped right into Lydas the Useless. "Told you they were trouble," the graybeard said, raising his chin.

"How prophetic of you," Malvius snarked.

Useless actually grinned. "But they didn't dare try for the inner gate, did they?"

Malvius managed to keep his fists at his sides. Gods, how he wanted to punch the dimwit. "Such a daring victory for you and your worthless archers!" he exclaimed. "And what have you saved? A few sacks of grain and a keg of your skunky ale? That and the skin of your spineless magister."

The man jutted his chin. "Untrue. Our actions kept the killers out. Many lives have been saved, including yours and those of your men."

Malvius's hands flew up to grab fistfuls of Lydas's tunic. "Why, you preening sprat! I may as well be dead. It should never have come to this. You could've at least tried to appease them. Or, at the very least, not insulted them. You worm-witted coin whores have ruined everything. My expedition is ruined. My entire family is ruined. And I have you idiots to thank."

He pushed the city's second biggest idiot aside as he released him and stalked to the stairs. "You'll be sorry for this," Lydas called after him.

Malvius paused. "I already am." He glanced back at the parapet, only briefly considering throwing himself down. No, he wouldn't give the idiots the satisfaction. Besides, there had to be less potentially painful ways to end his misery than falling to a grassy green.

He tromped down the stairs to seek one of them. He realized he could start by ending the pain in his temples and headed for tavern row. "There has to be something worth drowning myself in. Even in this forsaken deathtrap of a city."

"You know, Captain, you still owe me for last night." Malvius emptied his cup and tried to focus on the face of the interloper. The face was blurry so he refocused on pouring the last of his flagon. It mostly went into his cup.

The voice gave her away. It was the Bafranii girl. "The first of many debts to come, my dear," he said, smirking over his own slurring. "Alas, as of this very morn, I am hopelessly mired in arrears."

She leaned on his table wearing a flirty smile and a frock cut to show a generous portion of her shapely breasts. "Seeing you like this, I'm not sure I have the heart to collect."

"Ah. A whore with a heart. Who'd have imagined?" He took a drink and waved to the barman for another flagon. Ironically, or perhaps fittingly, he'd finally found some halfway decent wine. As a bonus, the pub in which he'd found it was in one of the darkest, quietest corners of Akasas. Malvius kicked the opposite chair out from under the table. "May I at least fill your cup?" She sat and held it out. "Where've you been hiding, lass?" It took effort to quash the slurring, so he gave up trying.

"Oh, I know the very best hiding places. Including this one." She indicated their surroundings. "I commend you for finding it."

"Good instincts, same as yours. Knowing from whence mine sprang makes me wonder why a whore with a heart would need them."

"Trust me, they're necessary." She sipped and cocked her head in approval of the wine before she went on. "Good heart or no, when bad things happen around here, folks who look like me tend to absorb misplaced blame."

"I would suppose. But in this case, since the bad thing that's happened is Teutonics rather than pirates from the homeland, I suppose your towheaded friend is the one in hiding, eh?"

She shrugged. "Could be. Her instincts aren't as good as mine."

"That I believe, too." Malvius liked her. She continued to surprise. "I wish it had been pirates. At least your kinsmen are gracious enough to take the cargo and leave the ships."

"Stolen ships are hard to sell. Plus, there's no honor in taking a man's ship."

"Well, you're not even a thief. You proved it this morning. A whore with a heart and with honor. The tale keeps getting better." Malvius pulled his coin purse from his belt and sat it on the table. "You could've taken it all. Now it's all I have left. What say we spend it together?"

She smiled archly. "Looks like there's enough left to release some pent-up frustration. Perhaps you'd enjoy taking it out on a dirty little pirate's daughter?"

Malvius couldn't think of a reason why not. There was a twinkle in her eye that suggested she was enjoying him as much as he was her. Or maybe she was just really good at her job. Either way, he admired her all the more for it. He scooted back and stood onto wobbly legs. Dexicos appeared at his elbow, holding him steady.

"The city elders are asking for you, Cap." Damn, the man had a knack for sneaking up on him. And for ruining any impending fun, too.

Malvius plopped back down. "Gods, spare me. What do those waddle-sweats want?"

"The Teutonics are demanding a meeting. They're holding our ships and cargo hostage. They want a parley to negotiate a settlement. Could be a chance to recover them."

Malvius massaged his temples to keep the tavern from spinning. "What, they're not sending out that chinless magister? I'd guess that letting the Teutonics slit his blubbery throat would be a solid step toward resolution."

"No one seems to know where he is," Dex said.

Malvius raised a brow to the Bafranii girl. "In one of your hiding spots perhaps?"

She shrugged. "I doubt it. But who knows? Desperation can be inspiring."

Malvius grinned and looked up at Dex. "If anyone could find that..." Looking up had been a mistake. He dropped his spinning gaze to the table. He belched and blew out his cheeks. It had nearly turned to a heave.

"Maybe I should get you something to eat," Dex suggested.

Malvius closed his eyes, swallowed, and shook his head. "Won't help. Not soon enough, anyway." He belched again. "Water."

Dexicos hustled to the rain barrel just outside the garden door and brought back a full ladle. Malvius drank, spilling a third of it down his tunic. "This is a good sign, Cap. Might be our last chance. I think you ought to go out there. If anyone can make this deal, it's you."

Damned optimists. "Considerate of you to offer me up," he said.

"I'd go with you, but they're insisting on one man. Seems like it's the only way to keep these city badgers from muddling it again."

Malvius couldn't argue the point. "One man, eh?" He turned to the Bafranii girl. There were two of her, so he closed an eye. "What did you say your name was, my dear?"

"I didn't. Not the real one, anyway. Why?"

"I've found that, when setting about bargaining, it's best for the parties to know one another's names." He straightened in the chair. "I am Malvius, son of Decebius. And you are...?" He extended a hand.

She frowned at his hand. "I already knew yours." She narrowed her gaze. "You're serious? Bargaining for what?"

"You'll only find out once I have your name. And yes, I'm serious. I never take bargaining lightly." He released a breathy belch. "No matter how drunk I get. Your name?"

She raised her chin and took his hand. "Neveka."

"Well, Neveka, I am prepared to offer you, say, one in twenty of the vulira from any profit I am able to salvage from my expedition."

Neveka squinted and stuck her chin out. "In exchange for what?" She tried to withdraw her hand, but he held it. Not to be a letch—she was helping him stay upright.

"For seeing to it that I get through the parley without falling on my face, of course."

Dex said, "I'm not so sure they'll accept more than one, even if the second is a woman."

"One in five," Neveka said. "And you take me along when you leave this cursed city."

Dex frowned but stayed quiet. Malvius grinned. "One in twelve."

"One in ten. *And* get me out of here." Neveka narrowed her gaze again.

"My dear, if you can help me get my ships back, yes. A tenth, *and* I'll happily take you wherever you like." They shook, and he released her. "You have something in mind, clever Neveka?"

"As he said..." She nodded to Dex. "They may not allow me to accompany you. But I have an idea that should work. I have a companion who can keep you upright. One whom the Teutons are unlikely to object to."

～

THE CALL RANG from the gatehouse, echoing from the walls of Akasas as the sun sank toward the mountains. The city gates creaked into motion. Vahldan signed to his captains to hold in place. The next step of his plan was officially underway. The last thing he'd wanted was for these fools to get spooked now. He had no desire to attack a walled city.

Vahldan sought for Thunar's Blessing by remembering the scornful faces of the city dwellers. He wanted to summon the resentment he'd felt the prior night. All that came was a low smoldering of the ugliness. For what was coming next he needed to be made of iron. Seeking the will to be hard and sharp only made him feel dull and floppy. The fear at the root of the ugliness wasn't for his personal safety. He needed this to go well. In spite of how they'd gotten to this juncture, Vahldan hoped he wouldn't need to kill the magister. It would be like killing a misbehaving mutt in front of its owners merely to prove a point.

Although he did hope that seeing that mouse of a magister would rekindle his rage. It was hard to stay angry after they'd so easily taken the ships. The successful theft was a victory, but he wasn't sure over whom, or what might be gained from it. He hoped there was someone other than the magister with whom to negotiate. It made Vahldan feel foolish that he couldn't figure out how to make the best of what they'd stolen. He only knew he had the dominant position. He could not relinquish the slightest bit of his advantage.

Leaving his host arrayed halfway back to the ships from the gate, Vahldan led his retinue to a spot just out of bow range from the walls. A figure was moving through the shadows of the city lane toward the gateway. Vahldan gripped his hilt and affixed what he hoped was an intimidating expression on his face. The figure emerged into the evening light. Vahldan didn't know whether to be relieved or infuriated. It wasn't the chinless magister but a man with curly black hair and a prominent nose, slumped on the back of a small donkey with his feet nearly dragging in the gravel on either side. The rider's head lolled with the gait of his little mount.

Elan harrumphed. "Where is the mouse? This is their idea of sending someone fit to bargain? He looks like he just woke up."

The rider squinted from one eye as he rocked toward them. He made it look like a feat that he managed to stay mounted. The rider reined in before them and smirked, his head still lolling.

"He's drunk," Elan spat. "They mock you. Send him away."

Vahldan smiled. "He does seem drunk. Maybe we should see what he has to say first."

"If he can still speak," Teavar said.

The man awkwardly drew his leg over and slid from the donkey, surprisingly landing on his feet. He kept one arm draped over the beast to steady himself. He was at least half a head shorter than every Gottari. His skin had a golden hue, and his unfocused eyes were as dark as his locks. Rather than a beard, the man wore the whiskers of a few days' growth. He was younger than Vahldan first thought, likely still in his twenties.

The drunk grinned and spoke in his own tongue, then hiccupped. Which made him laugh. Vahldan turned to Attasar, who relayed, "He asks that should we intend to kill him, that we do so quickly, as he feels his terror is beginning to sober him."

Vahldan couldn't help but laugh. He realized that this ridiculous ambassador had banished the ugliness from his belly. He couldn't help but feel grateful. He took a few steps forward and the man's smile withered. Vahldan followed the drunk's wary gaze to Elan who was standing at Vahldan's shoulder and holding a naked blade.

Vahldan chuckled and said to Attasar, "Ask him if it's Elan that terrifies him so."

Attasar spoke. With his eyes fixed on Elan, the drunk nodded. Vahldan said, "Tell him I consider him wise. Even a sober man should be afraid when confronting an angry Blade-Wielder." His followers laughed, and once Attasar translated, even the drunk laughed.

Elan feigned lunging at the man, and he flinched.

Vahldan said, "Be kind, darling. It wouldn't be seemly to have our bargaining opponent piss himself before the parley begins." The Gottari laughed again, and Elan sheathed Biter and crossed her arms over her chest.

"Ask him who he is and why he is here instead of the mouse," Vahldan said. "As if I can't guess."

Attasar questioned the man and he replied at length. "He says he is Malvius, captain of all but one of our captured vessels. He hails from Thrakius. He says he came out because if he loses his ships and his cargo, he might as well be dead. He wishes he had never made port here. He claims he tried to convince the city's elders to negotiate in good faith yesterday and was appalled by their lack of gratitude and respect. He says he came out because he realized he was the only man in the city with a sliver of sense. He says this still holds true even after his partaking in quite a lot of wine, consumed in the wake of witnessing us relieving him of his property." The Rekkrs laughed.

"That's all believable enough," Vahldan said sternly, veiling his excitement. "At least he has the sense to claim he supported us. Ask him what his cargo and ships are worth to him."

Attasar asked, and the man glanced back at the city, its wall-walk lined with watching figures. He spoke and Attasar relayed, "He says the value of the cargo is greater than the worth of this entire forsaken city. He said that although he realizes telling you so is fool-hardy, he is certain you would be better served in sailing away with the ships than in bargaining for anything they might have inside. He says that if you do sail off, he would only ask that you take him along, so that he can at least be done with this awful place and its idiot leaders."

Vahldan's head was completely clear of the haze of the ugliness. "Again, seems honest. Maybe almost too honest, so maybe he is deceiving us. But at least he's funny. Ask him how he's come to have such a fleet and such valuable cargos, and where he goes with them."

"He says he was taking it all to the realm of Trazonia, at the southeastern shore of the Pontean Sea. He set out during hiatus at great risk. He mentions the risk not just of being fined, but also from pirates and rogue bands of Sassanada thugs in all the ports he intends to visit. All of these risks he takes in order to leverage the maximum profit. If his venture were to somehow succeed, he would then be able to sail to the imperial markets in the spring with an even greater cargo of spices, silks, and winter fruits at a time when prices are at their peak and with little competition. If all had gone according to plan, Captain Malvius here would've returned home to Thrakius a very wealthy man. He claims it might have been the greatest trading expedition of our era. He risked everything to make the attempt and was driven to drink so much today because all seemed lost."

"Interesting," Vahldan said, studying the little man. Malvius was swaying less, and his eyes looked less unfocused. "Ask him why he would take such a gamble. Why reach so high?"

Attasar asked and relayed, "Malvius sought to eliminate all of his debts and to get himself out from under his domineering family's control. It's his father and his sister's husband who own these ships. He was to be his father's heir, but a dispute arose between them. He blames his sister, who has his father's ear. His father's disfavor has put his prospects in doubt." The image of Vahldan's father's disappointed face came to him. Attasar went on. "Malvius went to great lengths to secure the ships and crews in secret. He mentions that his men, too, have sacrificed and risked much. He says that because of this failure, his life is forfeit. Which led to his willingness to face the danger of meeting with you, my lord. The captain thought even a quick death by your hand to be preferrable to facing his men, his family, and his creditors."

Elan scowled. "Why would this fool admit to so much? Surely he seeks to trick us."

Vahldan studied the Hellain. He had the look of someone well-accustomed to deception and vice. But at the moment he also looked like someone who had nothing left to lose. The seeds of the idea Vahldan had had when he first saw the ships kept growing. It seemed more and more likely that it would bear fruit. "Whether it's a trick or not, it feels like providence. I know you consider the gods fickle. But maybe our boldness is being rewarded. Maybe we can benefit one another, this little sea captain and us."

"How so?" Teavar asked. "He's already told us there's little to be gained in the city."

"What could this drunk have to offer?" Arnegern added. "We already have his ships."

Vahldan looked out over the ships along the riverbank. Until the prior day, he'd never even seen a seagoing ship. Now he possessed five. Little good they did him. And yet... Perhaps even this little Hellain was a part of their providence. Perhaps he had only to figure out how.

"Well," Vahldan began, "he has admitted that his cargo is worth a fortune. We came here to eliminate a threat and to win glory. But we also came to stand up to Wulthus greed—to show them that our clan is to be reckoned with. Think about it. What do those who control the means to wealth fear more than anything?"

"An invading army?" Teavar ventured.

"Armies to repulse invaders can be recruited or even bought. Absent that, invading armies can almost always be bought off. Or the invaders get bored and move on. Armies need to be fed and kept invested in the need for an occupation. Those with means rarely suffer as much as the common man. And once an invader leaves, they often recover faster and grow stronger."

Elan wore a wry smile. "What the wealthy fear is wealth in the hands of another. Rivals."

"Exactly." Vahldan loved her clever mind. She was always right with him, if not ahead.

Belgar gestured toward the ships. "A fortune is now ours, is it not?"

"Ours for the moment," Vahldan said. "And at the moment, it's in the water."

Arnegern nodded. "Aye. And even if we unload the ships, we have no real way to haul what they hold. Nor a way to convert it to anything that *can* be easily carried from here."

"Right again. At least not its full worth." Vahldan was pleased. They were all staying right with him. "None of us even knows how to sail, let alone find these lucrative markets our little drunken friend mentions. We know he commands the crews. And I'll venture he's the best candidate to convert our plunder into the maximum reward. A reward we can really use. And, if anything he says is even close to true, it would be a reward that could save his life. And not just from us. This is a man who could be easily motivated to work with us. He could become a guide, of sorts. Lead us to the solution to all of our problems."

All of them fell silent, staring at the Hellain. The man started fidgeting, self-conscious.

Vahldan turned to Attasar. "You told me that some of the traders on the sea hire warriors as guards for the ships and as protection during their transactions."

Attasar nodded. "That's right, my lord."

"Ask Malvius here if he has ever done so."

Malvius's eyes narrowed, and he rubbed his chin as he replied. Attasar translated his words. "He agrees that it is common and that his father sometimes employs mercenaries. But that he has yet to find the right warriors. Ones that can be trusted."

Vahldan smiled. "Ask him if having good warriors for this trip might have helped him to avoid his current dilemma."

Upon receiving the translation, Malvius laughed. "Nai, nai!" he exclaimed, nodding.

"Ask him if having those same trusted warriors might turn his situation around—make the successful completion of his expedition more likely." Vahldan waved a hand, indicating his host, arrayed and waiting behind him.

As Attasar translated, Malvius's eyes began to gleam. "Captain Malvius agrees in principle. But he wonders how he might be sure that we are trustworthy," Attasar said.

Vahldan took a step closer, looming over the shorter man, wiping the smile from his face. "Ask him how well he has considered the alternatives to trusting us."

Malvius's eyes went wide. He spoke softly. Attasar relayed, "He takes your point, my lord. He hastens to add that he simply does not have the capacity to take on a host so large as ours." Malvius's gaze scanned the Amalus host. The Hellain's expression grew wistful, and he emitted a low whistle. "If I may, my lord," Attasar went on. "I'd guess that he is swiftly growing fond of the idea."

Teavar was outraged. "He ought to be! He's lucky to still be breathing."

Vahldan gestured for Teavar to calm down. His eyes met Malvius's, and the man gave him the slightest of nods. There was a strange communion between them. Like the nine realms were somehow falling into a rare alignment. This felt as if it were meant to be. "Ask him how large a host would be ideal," Vahldan said, holding the Hellain's gaze.

"He says that forty is a number that could both travel well, stave off piracy, and make an impression in the eastern markets. Though he adds that, as much as he admires our use of them, he would not have the means to transport our horses."

Vahldan nodded. "Ask him if the transactions he had hoped to make in the east could yet be made if he had command of his ships and such a host became available immediately."

The captain's grin grew as he received the translation. "He is sure it's so, my lord."

The Hellain urgently added something. "Captain Malvius says that he's reconsidered."

"Pah—I should've known," Elan said.

Malvius grinned as he bowed to Elan and went on, and Attasar relayed, "The captain has decided that the ideal number is a host of forty warrior men plus one impressive warrior woman. He thinks that such a number would all but assure the mission's success."

Vahldan laughed. "He's not wrong."

Malvius smiled and nodded. The Hellain's expression grew more sober as he pointed to the purse on his belt and began speaking again. Attasar relayed, "Such a host would be so valuable to him, Captain Malvius would be willing to offer one of every five gold pieces he earns from the expedition as compensation for their presence."

"One in five?" Elan spat. "Why should we barter with the fool? Has he already forgotten we have his ships and can just as easily take his life?"

Vahldan put his hand on her arm. "It's called a good bargaining position."

"This is beneath you," she said. "He's not worth the trouble. He dares wonder aloud if he can trust us? How can we trust him?"

"Oh, I think we can trust our little trader friend to always act in his own best interest. And we have a chance to insert ourselves into the course of his best interests. Just as he would keep himself in ours. And along the way, he can keep himself alive and prospering, and we can gain what we need to stand up to the wolves."

He stepped closer yet, chin to forehead with the cringing drunk. "Tell him one of two."

After Attasar translated, the shorter man blinked moisture from his eyes. Malvius's voice quavered as he replied. "He says that you may as well take the ships and kill him, for he must pay his crew and his creditors, or all is lost. Same as before he came out. He respectfully offers you one in four."

Vahldan saw that the man was holding his breath. To his credit, Malvius didn't look away. "One in three." He held up three fingers.

Malvius sighed out the breath he'd been holding, pursed his lips as if greatly pained, then held out his hand. Vahldan grasped his forearm, which seemed to surprise him, but he finally did likewise and smiled.

Their deal was struck. Vahldan sensed the scope of it. He felt the gods' smiles radiating down upon him. He'd sensed it right after the battle. This place and these ships could be the *really big thing* that he'd needed. And he had found it on the shore of the sea—the place that he'd always dreamed might carry him from the life of exile and the burden of expectation. The place he'd dreamed would lead to the life he was meant to live.

Indeed, the gods favored the bold.

Vahldan and his new partner were both grinning, but he noticed no one else was. Not even Elan. "I feel like the gods led us to this," he said to her.

"Of course," she said. "But we both know the gods are fickle. Remember that." She turned and walked through the parting host. The rest of them remained sullen, several of them glancing nervously out to sea. Vahldan remembered how cats felt about water. In order for his plan to have a chance, he had to ask forty of his lions to take to the sea and to travel to the unknown realms beyond it.

He hoped he could get forty to join him. And that no one would regret it. Including him.

CHAPTER 3
SEA LIONS

"*My father rarely spoke of his years at sea. Even when asked. I have often found myself wondering how strange it must have been for Vahldan, being so young and having never seen the sea, to find himself living aboard ships, ever traveling from port to port.*

My mother, on the other hand, often spoke of those days. Her bitterness over them was apparent. When I asked Elan if it was difficult, becoming accustomed to living on ships, she shrugged it off. Something she once said, I think, reveals much about her beyond how she felt about life at sea. I feel it sums up all of her years in Pontea. She said, 'Living on a boat was not so tough. It was living so close to so many people. That I never got used to.'"
—*Brin Bright Eyes, Saga of Dania*

"You've got to flow with the motion," Vahldan shouted to his squad of trainees. "Absorb it in the legs and keep fighting."

They looked like a group of confused children, stumbling and holding their arms out in awkward positions, fighting for balance rather than against their opponent. They hardly looked like the fearsome host of guardsmen he'd sold them as. The foredeck of the Pontea Princess—the fleet's flagship—suddenly plunged, causing Vahldan's innards to lurch. The bow crashed into the next massive swell, showering them all with frigid seawater. Half of his men staggered or fell, all of them heedless of their sparring partners.

Vahldan had barely kept his feet on that one. The leathers under his hauberk were heavy and soaked through. His mouth kept filling with spit and his head spun. Only Elan seemed unfazed by the increasingly rough seas, although she did look a bit pale. "Come on, lions," he roared. "Back on your feet! Keep your focus on your opponent. Those who keep their feet and stay focused will win the fight."

Ermanaric abruptly turned from his partner, staggered to lean over the rail, and spewed his breakfast into the Pontean. The sound of his retching triggered Vahldan's gag reflex. He swallowed to keep his own gorge in check. With her partner gone missing, Elan continued practicing her blade movements, looking graceful as ever. No surprise. She looked like she was fighting while crouched over her feet on the saddle as Hrithvarra maneuvered through a battle.

"The captain wants me to ask you again if you're sure about wearing armor?" Attasar had appeared at his side, and Malvius was with him. He hadn't even noticed their approach. Some combat trainer he was. He was no more accustomed to the sea than an actual lion, same as his men. "He says all he can do is fret that one of you will go overboard."

"Tell him I still feel it's worth the risk. If we're going to fight on ships, we need to be better than those we face. And the Amalus fight in armor. It's part of who we are."

His scribe relayed his words, but it hadn't been necessary. His little Hellain partner was already shaking his head, clearly dissatisfied. The longer they spent aboard the fleet, the better the lions and the Hellain sailors understood one another, even without a shared language. Although they were working on that, too. Malvius and his inner circle were teaching Vahldan, Elan, and several of his senior Rekkrs the Hellainic tongue. Meanwhile, both groups made a game of learning key words in the other's tongue, if only to toss jibes. Mostly good-natured jibes. Mostly.

The ship dropped into another trough and hit another cresting wave, this time sending nearly every sparring pair to the deck—all pretenses to sparring completely abandoned in the effort to stay aboard. Vahldan grabbed and held Attasar, who had already developed his sea legs in the travels of his youth. He glanced at Malvius as he regained his footing. Their ship's captain stood casually by, wearing an expression that revealed his dismay over what he was seeing. Vahldan could only imagine how pathetic the Amalus looked to their new partner. He felt dismayed, too. After all, he'd met Malvius with an army of hundreds behind him. Now he was fumbling through a completely new experience as the leader of just forty warriors. Warriors who were completely out of their element. On top of that, the Gottari were wildly outnumbered by foreigners who were experts in their new world. He kept expecting Malvius to revisit their bargain. To the Hellain's credit, there had been no sign of it.

"We will be better," he ventured in Hellainic.

The captain forced a smile and voiced what sounded to be one of his quips. "If you don't all drown in your armor first," Attasar said, translating.

"Tell him I better understand now why sailing is forbidden this time of year."

After his words had been relayed, Malvius's smile became genuine. "The captain says this is nothing. He suggests we pray to our gods that the seas remain as mild as this."

A shout echoed down from the aftcastle, and other sailors took up the call. Vahldan saw one pointing and tried to make out the object of their attention. "They've sighted another fleet of ships," Attasar told him.

Malvius called to his man at the tiller as they moved to the rail. The man called back. "Bafranii" was among the words in the reply.

"Likely pirates," Attasar said.

Vahldan shielded his eyes against the winter sun's glare, finally spotting them. At least three ships, definitely heading their way. Malvius cursed under his breath. "Can we outrun them?" Vahldan asked and gestured to indicate sailing away in the other direction.

Without awaiting translation, Malvius shook his head. He issued a string of commands, including one to Attasar. "The captain would like us to signal to the other crews to have every Gottari fully armed and on deck."

Malvius started toward the aftcastle ladder. "We are yet no good to fight," Vahldan called after the man in Hellainic.

"No need," Malvius called over his shoulder. He turned back with a grin. "I hope."

MALVIUS ORDERED the sails reefed and signaled the rest of the fleet to fan out on his portside aft. The Gottari scribe had managed to signal his fellows, and the warriors assigned to each ship lined up along the rails, in full view as he'd requested of them.

"Let them draw alongside," he told Dex as the Bafranii flagship came about. He hurried to the Gottari, calling to Attasar, "Line them up along the starboard rail, starting at the prow."

He came to appraise his guardsmen, soaked and looking miserable, most of them clinging to the rail like dock cats to a fishing boat's tether. "Tell them to loosen up," he told Attasar. Once relayed, the effort was apparent but far from convincing. "Tell them we need to look ready to fight," he told the scribe. The group turned their sour stares to him. He grinned and then pretended he was holding a sword, and he screwed his face into a fierce snarl and made a mocking growl. "You are confident!" he called, and Attasar relayed it.

Vahldan laughed, which finally loosened the others up.

The Gottari chieftain composed himself, raised his chin, and spoke in a tone that was full of command. The change in his men was dramatic. They were suddenly the fiercest looking batch of barbarians he could've hoped to have on his side.

The change came just in time. The Bafranii drew alongside and hailed him. "What is it you want?" Malvius called.

The pirates spoke among themselves. Even from two ships' lengths, Malvius saw their consternation. It was working. At last, a spokesman replied, "Since it is hiatus, we feared you were lost or in need of aid."

"We are grateful for your concern, but fear not. We are fine, regardless of the season." He lowered his voice and said to Attasar, "Have them look their meanest." The Gottari gripped their sword hilts and several even showed their teeth. A few slowly drew their blades. Malvius gave the Bafranii a grin. "I feel I must ask the same of you. Do you need our aid or guidance? My men would be happy to come aboard."

The Bafranii laughed among themselves, and the man who was most certainly their captain shouted directives to the tiller. The flagship shook out its reef, and the pirate fleet steered clear to head back the way they'd come. The final reply came. "Thank you, but no. We fear their weight would exceed our capacity." It incited more laughter from the pirate crew, which caused his own crew to start laughing. Lastly, the Gottari joined in. The two fleets parted ways to uproarious laughter.

With the danger behind them, Malvius gave his new partner a formal naval salute. Vahldan returned it with a courtly bow, full of charming self-deprecation. Whether or not they became better sea fighters, at the very least he'd acquired the fiercest looking guardians on the Pontean.

Gazing out from the ship's deck over the bustling docks and up the jammed lanes of Trazonia made Elan feel as ill as the worst weather at sea had. The land was relatively flat here, but the tiled roofs of the city seemed to sprawl to every horizon. The place was a riot of color and strange smells. She and Vahldan stood at the rail, trying to stay clear of the crew of the Princess as they secured the ship to the quay and began the unloading process. Only the flagship had been granted a slot on the quay, with the rest of the fleet at anchor in the brown waters of the harbor.

"Get us tied off and have the gangway lowered, but no one goes ashore before me," Malvius shouted as he strode by, heading for the ladder to the hold.

"I really think you should consider—"

"You have my orders, Dexicos," Malvius snapped over his shoulder.

"Aye, Cap," Dex called in response, though he still seemed unhappy.

Elan had gotten to the point where she understood most of what was said in their tongue, although she was often unsure in speaking it. It was humbling but necessary. The only path to competence was practice, which necessarily included failure. "Malvius is angry?" she ventured asking Dex.

Dex held up a finger, then directed two sailors to secure the gangway. The first mate came back to Elan and Vahldan. "Yes, Cap is angry," he confirmed. Elan gestured to indicate her confusion, hoping to coax more from him. Dex sighed. "He is angry that Isidros is here before us." Elan smiled and shook her head. Dex realized she still needed more information, and said, "Isidros is the anax of another city, and he is our biggest rival in trading. Either he got his men here before us, or he left them here since hiatus began. It means that he has already bribed the harbormaster and the city watch. We'll have to go through them to get our goods to the spice exchange. It's a huge market near the city center."

A sailor working nearby added, "Encho is already here. See?" The sailor pointed to a group of ruffians under an awning at the edge of the docks, watching them.

"Go through them?" Vahldan asked. His Hellainic wasn't even as good as hers, but evidently he was keeping up with the conversation.

Dex nodded. "Cap wants to go down alone to make a deal with them. They'll take a percentage of our goods before they allow the local wagon drivers to accept bids to haul for us."

"Who are those over there?" Elan pointed to another cluster of men, all wearing the same bright blue tunics and carrying spears topped with blades the length of their forearms.

"That's the city watch," Dex said with a frown. "As I said, Isidros will have already paid them off."

"Can we be he who pays city watch?" Vahldan asked. "Can they not be gone with rivals?" He pointed at this Isidros's men and signaled like he was shooing gulls off the deck.

Dex shook his head. "Not now. Not easily. The city watch will take anyone's coin, and Cap had planned on paying. But now we couldn't even get to them to ask how much more it would take. Not without a fight. If there's trouble, it might bring in the imperial garrison. Cap doesn't want to risk mucking up the whole deal. He has decided he will settle with Isidros."

"We lose part of treasure we come to get?" Vahldan stared at the other trader's ragtag ruffians. "To them?" His resentment was clear. It was a condition that could lead to the ugliness.

Dex gave a wry nod. "That's about it."

"They are no having weapons," Vahldan spat.

"No—here in Trazonia, no weapons are allowed on the docks or in the market. Not since the war with the Sassanada. Everyone knows that openly carrying weapons would bring the garrison out. Which would lead to fines, or worse."

"Worse?" Elan asked.

Dex squinted at her. "If the garrison hauls you away, you can never know what's next. Many of those taken end up on the slave blocks." The first mate headed off, calling orders to those tying off the lines and opening the hatches.

"I have an idea," Vahldan said, but he was already in motion. He called and beckoned, gathering the rest of the Gottari to their position next to the gangway. "Everyone disarm," he told them, unbuckling his sword belt. "Not even a belt knife."

"You can't be serious," Elan said as Teavar and the others followed suit, unbuckling their gear and piling it against the gunwale.

Vahldan gave her a grin that didn't meet his slightly crazed eyes. "The gods favor the bold, remember?" For weeks he'd been talking about finding a way to prove their worth as fighters to Malvius and the rest of the Hellains, but she didn't think this was it.

"Don't you think we should wait? We can't be sure what we're getting ourselves into." She argued with him even as she stripped off her own sword harness and slipped off her belt knife's sheath. She wasn't about to be left behind, but she hoped to delay him long enough to have Malvius or even Dexicos notice what he was up to.

It wasn't to be. She'd only just gotten herself disarmed when she found herself hurrying to follow him and the other eight Gottari, boots thumping down the gangway. Once on the docks, Elan hurried to walk at Vahldan's right shoulder with Teavar at his left. As she'd known he would, Vahldan headed straight for the rival traders under the awning. There were at least a dozen of them. And such a varied group they were. Some were as brown as Neveka, others had the golden hair of the Tutona. One man stepped to the fore. He had oily brown curls, a beak of a nose, and pock-marked cheeks. The man wore a cocky sneer and raised his chin, looking ready to issue a challenge.

"Greetings," Vahldan called cheerily in Hellainic. He sped his step, covering the last span in a heartbeat. "Greetings from Dania," he added and swung.

Elan didn't know Vahldan to be well-trained with his fists, but she suspected his father had seen to it. Either that or he landed a lucky punch. The shot audibly cracked into the man's jaw, dropping him to the docks like a tossed sack of grain.

Chaos erupted as all of the rival trader's men rushed in. The man nearest to Elan was about her height but he outweighed her by half with a neck as thick as the crown of his head. She cocked her arms back and threw her chin out as she rushed ahead, baiting him. He took the bait as she came within reach, swinging a chubby fist. Luckily he was as slow as an ox on the way to the plow.

Elan dropped backward and onto a hip as his arm swished over her, swinging her upper leg. Her boot connected with his knee just before she hit the dock boards. The man fell hard, crying out in pain. She got to her butt with her hands on either side, and the moment he hit the deck, she sprang into another kick, the bottoms of both boots solidly thumping in his chest. It put him flat on his back, wheezing and out of the fight.

She hopped to her feet to find the brawl abruptly ending. Those Dex had referred to as the city watch surrounded the entire fray, brandishing their blade-ended spears and barking orders. She quickly surmised that the Gottari had gotten the best of the larger group; at least half of their opponents were down, several of them bleeding and groaning. Teavar still held one man by the front of his tunic, forcing him to stand on his tiptoes. The giant still had his fist clenched and elbow cocked, ready to throw a final punch.

Malvius and Dex appeared to break the tense standoff with a flurry of apologetic-sounding phrases, spoken so fast Elan wasn't even sure which language was being used. Malvius went to a man who seemed to be the leader of the city watch and held out a sack of coins as he babbled.

The leader's eyes locked onto the coin sack. The man seemed agreeable and beckoned Malvius to step aside. Malvius turned to Dex and said, "Get them back, nice and slow."

Dexicos grabbed Vahldan by the arm and tilted his head. "Let's walk," the first mate said.

Vahldan nodded to the other Gottari and started back toward the gangway. Teavar released his unpunched opponent with a shove and followed, as did the others. Elan fell in beside Vahldan. She glanced back, relieved to find they were not being pursued or impeded.

"That was risky," she said. Vahldan only nodded but his smile was one of smug satisfaction. "Did I detect a bit of the ugliness back there?"

Any trace of a smile vanished. "Maybe. Just a bit."

"Best be careful of that," she suggested.

They started up the gangway, following Dex. He nodded but said, "It had to happen fast. I considered it worth the risk."

She was about to retort when Dex reached the ship's deck and turned back to the scene. "Looks like Cap got it done," Dex said. Elan looked to find Malvius already following behind them. The captain wore a sly smile and the city watch was herding the rival trader's sullen fighters away, some of them limping. Dex beamed. "Looks like we'll be able hire our own wagons. Better still, there's no sign that the garrison will be the wiser."

Vahldan didn't even try to hide his smug smile. "Looks like the risk paid off," he said.

"This time," she conceded, not entirely sure she was pleased by the outcome.

IN HIS YOUTH, Vahldan had idealized sea travel. He hadn't considered the isolation, depravation, and boredom. He hadn't imagined the repetitious meals, constant dampness, and bouts of seasickness. He hadn't spared a thought for the possibility of drowning, or for the fret that others may drown. He'd been naïve enough to focus on the exotic ports. He hadn't been wrong—the ports were indeed often wondrous and fascinating. Particularly Trazonia, which had dazzled them all. What he'd failed to conceive was how bewildering and ultimately tiresome it could become, moving from one exotic location to another. At least he and Elan and a few of the others were finally starting to make themselves understood in Hellainic, the primary language in all of Pontea. Although he could still understand it better than he could speak it, the ability made life abroad less bewildering.

Beyond the novelty and adventure of their new lives, in recent weeks, he'd begun to doubt he would ever get used to the danger—of constantly being on guard, of never knowing when a rival might attack or when a transaction might suddenly become violent. In every facet of their lives they remained the strangers. Most everyone who wasn't Gottari treated them with suspicion or even open hostility. They could never be sure who could be trusted or whether or not they were causing offense. In some ports they couldn't even rely on the weapons they'd trained with all their lives. They had only their mettle and their trust in one another's skill and vigilance. Hence they spent much of their time drilling and sparring. Although he'd finally conceded to Malvius in regard to wearing armor aboard ships. They now only donned armor when trouble seemed certain.

Slowly, out of necessity, the Gottari and the fleet's crews grew to tolerate one another. Over the months, once the Gottari had proved their worth a dozen times, and once the Gottari witnessed the adeptness of the crews in outmaneuvering competitors and potential waterborne threats, no small amount of appreciation—and even trust—grew between the two groups.

The worst of his worries was over the imperials, who posed a threat that would not abate.

There was no way around it—Vahldan and every member of his Amalus host were easily recognized as foreigners. Folk who looked and dressed like them were presumed to be barbarians—volatile, coarse, often drunk, and dimwitted. The Gottari were not citizens, paid no taxes, had no rights under the law. Indeed, much of what they had come to Pontea to do required them to operate outside of the law.

Making matters worse, their duty took them to the very places in which encountering officials of the Tibairyan government was most likely. They were routinely exposed to harbormasters and their minions, the vigiles of city law enforcement, Praetorian guardsmen at imperial palaces, and legionaries at garrison barracks and armories, which seemed always to be nearby or inside of every port district. Even while at sea, they risked encountering the imperial navy. The Amalus never knew when or where they might be questioned, harassed, or even beaten. Even Malvius operated at substantial risk. As a trading company who often skirted the laws of commerce, they could be boarded, fined, barred from markets, or suffer the seizure of cargo or even the impoundment of one or more ships.

For the Gottari, the worst outcome of any imperial confrontation was the threat of arrest. On any given day, for any reason—even those contrived on the spot—any member of the Amalus host might be detained or hauled away. Once in imperial custody, the threat of being sold as a slave grew serious. Slaves were too valuable for such opportunities to be passed up, even by low-ranking officers or minor bureaucrats. Any excuse for arrest would suffice.

Vahldan hated their status and resented being prejudged. But he was wise enough to keep those feelings to himself. Instead, he used the unfairness of it as motivation. One day he would achieve something that would change how the Tutona were viewed by the world forever.

Because of the wariness required in imperial cities, Vahldan found himself dreading their time in port. Their current journey would see them at sea for more than a week, running a load of grain from the Pontean Straits all the way to Trazonia. Malvius had taken the load simply to get them back to the eastern markets. Their cargo was perfectly legal, and they likely wouldn't face much imperial scrutiny even once their destination was reached. Even Isidros's crews rarely bothered trying to cut in on grain sales. The reward was minimal, hence the risk was low.

The summer weather was offering up calm seas and sunny warmth. Thus far they had earned more treasure than any of them had dared dream. Vahldan hadn't lost a man, or even had one suffer a serious injury, in months. Days like these should be savored.

Still, he found himself feeling disheartened. During the morning training session, he'd pushed the Gottari aboard the Princess to exhaustion, and still he was restless. In spite of the breezy warm weather, once they were dismissed, he'd been left alone on the fore-deck. He suspected they were all keeping their distance, even Elan. Beyond being demanding, he'd been brusque.

He continued working through his restlessness by practicing his sword movements with Bairtah-Urrin. While executing a reversal into a backhanded spin, as he'd intended, he chopped the blade into the mast behind him. What he hadn't intended was almost hitting the ship's captain, who'd approached in silence and was forced to stop short.

"I surrender," Malvius cried, and held up both open palms.

"Forgive me," Vahldan said in Hellainic.

"Damn, that was close." Malvius smiled and ran an index finger along the blade's edge, which was within easy reach, before Vahldan could pull it out and lower it. "I doubt it would've made me any prettier."

"Perhaps one should take care when another is to practice with a blade," he snapped. He instantly recognized how peevish he sounded.

"Whoa," Malvius said. "The lesson is noted."

Vahldan sighed. "Forgive me, too, for swinging hard words as well as a bare blade." He sheathed the sword and bowed his head.

"Tell me, my friend. Is all well with you?" Malvius reached up and gripped his shoulder. The fact that the Hellain was so much shorter than him made it feel awkward. Malvius quickly withdrew his hand.

"I am feeling a little off. It will pass."

Malvius nodded, as if it was foregone. "Tell me how I can help."

Vahldan squinted out over the endless blue of the Pontean. "I am not sure. The words are difficult to seek."

"Give it a try." Malvius wasn't going to give up.

He shrugged. "It is only that, well, there is no place that allows us..." He tried to think of the Hellainic words that would convey it. "No place that we can feel to be home."

The Hellain rubbed his chin. "Would you like to visit your home? It could be arranged."

Vahldan shook his head. "Not that. I did not have one. Not as most would name it. For me, no such place exists. What I am meaning is not a place but a feeling. When around the fire. With loved ones. Safe. Do you see my meaning?"

Malvius's grin seemed genuine. "I do. And I think I have just the remedy." He turned and called to the first mate on the aftcastle. "Dex! Signal the fleet. We're changing course."

"Aye, Cap. What's the new bearing?"

The captain glanced at Vahldan. "Northeast. We make for the Kynnya."

"Kynnya?" Dexicos frowned. "There's nothing there, Cap. No port, no nearby cities."

"That's exactly why we're going. We'll anchor in the cove and spend the night ashore." Malvius cocked his head at Vahldan. "Maybe two or three nights." He winked.

"Aye, Cap. Kynnya it is."

Vahldan had to admit it—the shore of Kynnya Cove felt more like home than any place he'd slept since he had left Dania. The area to the north and east consisted of forested slopes on rising foothills, and even the land to the west—a rocky labyrinth known as Orithya—had a similar feel to the rugged mountains near the mining compound where Vahldan had spent much of his youth. The Gottari had made a lovely camp in a bowl-like meadow surrounded by lush pines. The weather during the two days since their arrival had been mild and the cove was blissfully quiet other than the birdsong and gently lapping waves. The nights were chilly enough to keep them gathered near the fires and wrapped in their cloaks and blankets. During the first night, he and Elan had relished the shared bodily warmth while sleeping under a dark sky full of stars at the uphill edge of the camp. Elan seemed to delight in the smell of the pine needles beneath their bedding.

On the second morning, Vahldan had joined a hunting party. Before the high sun, Jhannas had taken down a doe, and the hunters had made swift work of butchering it in the field to carry it back to camp. Nearly all of the camp's fires were roasting a portion of the relatively fatty venison—on spits or in pots with freshly dug onions in a broth of ale—and the savory aroma filled the entire cove. The meal made for a delightful reprieve from their typical onboard fare of dried fish with cold rice or pickled turnips.

The stars reappeared as they finished eating, and only the occasional shared song could be heard, lulling the camp to slumber. Elan had built a small fire in their spot at the edge of the camp, where they could hear the whisper of the pine boughs in the night breeze. Vahldan sat by the fire, staring without focus into the flames, his carving knife and latest piece in his hands, giving the bird a final smoothing.

Elan returned from relieving herself and bent to kiss him. "Coming to bed?"

"In a bit," he said. "Trying to clear my head."

She smiled and caressed his cheek. "Carving always works wonders. It's nice to see you like this."

"Like what?"

She shrugged. "I can see the real you," she said. She stooped and gazed deeply into his eyes. "Even in the dark, I can see you in there. It's the version of you I met outside the mine."

He snorted a soft laugh. "That version of me had a lot to learn."

Elan cocked her head. "Oh, I think there's plenty that this version of you can learn by revisiting that one."

"May I come and bid you a good night?" A dark figure approached from the direction of the camp. "And perhaps offer you one last cup?" Malvius came into the firelight, holding a bottle in one hand and a cup in the other. Although most of his crew had chosen to sleep on the anchored fleet, Malvius and Neveka and around a score of the Hellains occupied the shoreline side of the camp. Malvius kept their Bafranii partner close, and her stoic presence seemed to be a steadying influence on him. Vahldan had grown to like and admire her, as had Elan.

"You may," Elan told him. "Although I fear I'm too exhausted to accept your wine, there is another wakeful spirit here who may be interested." As Malvius came the rest of the way, Elan bent and gave him a final peck. "Don't be too long," she said and stepped to the spot they'd lain to sleep the night before. She wrapped herself in their blankets and rolled to face away.

"Are you sure?" Malvius whispered and raised the bottle.

Vahldan reached for his cup and held it out to be filled. "There is no need to whisper." He nodded toward Elan. "That one can sleep through anything." Malvius poured for him and he took a sip. As usual, it burned on the way down. "Oh, this is much stronger than we have had." He had to wipe the tears from his eyes with the back of his hand.

Malvius loved to show off his special wines. His smile shone in the firelight. "Saurian. Distilled and aged. I've been saving it."

"It is very good," he offered, vowing to himself to not drink too much of it. He'd been feeling too good here to risk ruining his morning with the aftereffects he suspected this stuff would leave. He set aside the cup and took up his carving piece again.

"May I?" Malvius nodded to indicate he wanted to sit.

"Of course." Vahldan cut a few fine slivers. He glanced up to find Malvius leaning in, watching him. The man looked less than settled. Vahldan searched for the Hellainic words and came up with, "Something troubles the mind?"

"I only wish to make sure that your mind is untroubled, friend. Are you feeling better? Shall we stay here another night? A week?"

Vahldan shook his head but stayed focused on his work. "There is no need."

"I need to be sure," Malvius said. "These past months have been very good—for both of us, I know. But for me, what's happened is vast. We are able to make trades that were never possible for us before you and your host came along. I've made arrangements to settle up with my father, and I think we can even consider adding our own ships, rather than leasing his. Since you and the Gottari came aboard, we've been able to beat Isidros and others at their own game. Damn near every time." Vahldan gave him a look and a single nod. "What I mean is—I'm very happy. I'm in the best place I've been in long years. And I want to make sure you are, too."

"I joined with you to earn treasure, and we are earning it. So yes, we are happy."

Malvius leaned in again. "So, what's the endgame, if you don't mind my asking?"

Vahldan kept his eyes on his carving. "We have things we wish to do. In our homeland. I believe the treasure will help us to do them." He glanced up. "We, too, seek to set things right."

Malvius was unsettled again. "So how much do you think you need? To set things right."

Vahldan looked up. "I do not know. Not precisely. I believe I will feel it inside." He drew the fist holding the knife up to thump his chest. "In here," he said. "When I feel it, I will then know that the time has come to go back and to begin again."

Malvius leaned back and took a drink. "I suppose I'll just have to hope that the time is a long way off. For my new beginning has just begun." He laughed at his own quip.

Vahldan laughed too. Still, he felt the need to explain. He held up the carving and the knife. "I have always loved to carve. Since I was a boy." He held up the wood. "You see?"

Malvius squinted and smiled. "Say, that's pretty good. A seagull?" Vahldan nodded. "In flight, yet. Impressive."

Vahldan ran a finger along one of the spread wings. The perfect piece had come to him shortly after arriving ashore. He'd instantly seen that the bird had required his effort to release it. It seemed that the gods were insisting that he carve again. "It is not easy. This is but the third bird I have carved in flight. Elan wears the second—a kestrel—around her neck. You have seen it?"

Malvius hummed and nodded. "I have."

"The first was a hawk. The day I came near to having it done, like this." He indicated with the seagull. "That was the day my father was killed, and my childhood home was burned." Malvius's eyes went wide. "Foes of our people attacked our home."

"And the hawk burned in the fire?"

Vahldan frowned. "Yes and no. Before the attack, my father came to me. He was angry that I cared only for finishing the hawk. He wished me to be training to fight. We argued, and the bird broke. The hawk's wing flew into the hearth fire and burned." Malvius looked intrigued and yet puzzled. "I tell you this because that was the day my life forever changed. Because the bird broke, I am made to understand. It is not the wooden piece that matters." He held up the seagull. "It is the work that makes me who I am." He held up the knife. "And there is always more work to be done. We must work so that we remember who we are. We must then trust when our hearts tell us that our lives have changed and listen to hear what is next for us. I will continue to work and listen. It is all that I can promise."

He held out the seagull. "Do you see my meaning?" He gestured and Malvius took it. "For you," he added. "Now I must find more work." He smiled.

Malvius studied the bird. "I believe I do see," he said. His eyes met Vahldan's over the fire. "This is really mine, like a gift?" Vahldan nodded and Malvius struggled to stand. He held up the bird before him. "Then please don't take offense when I do this." He snapped off one of the wings and tossed it in the fire.

Vahldan momentarily relived the panic he felt that day and resisted the urge to reach for the wing as it burst into flame. He craned to meet the Hellain's eyes, trying not to scowl. "This is what you wished for my gift?"

"What I wish is for our lives to now be forever changed. Before we met, my father tried to break me. He, too, thought my focus was not on the right things. Since you came along, I find I am far from broken. My heart is telling me that what is next for my life includes having you in it." Malvius stowed the remainder of the bird in his belt pouch. "I shall keep the rest to always remind me of the need to work and to listen. Do you see *my* meaning?"

"I believe I do see," he repeated.

The Hellain bent to retrieve his cup and the bottle. He offered to pour a parting shot, and Vahldan shook his head. "To our new lives," Malvius said and raised his cup.

Vahldan raised his and they both drank.

"May you sleep as deeply as one who has found his home again, my friend," Malvius said, and he turned and strode into the darkness.

CHAPTER 4
NEGOTIATING A NEW WORLD

"I ONLY WISH you could see them in action," Malvius was saying. "They truly are a marvel of the ancient world. No memory or record of how they were made survives." Vahldan knew he was talking about the massive seagates of his home city, which stood open and through which they were finally sailing. But Vahldan couldn't be bothered about gates. He was too busy gawping beyond them into the enclosed harbor and at the city he'd heard so much about but had never before seen.

The Gottari had been at sea with Malvius for nearly two years, and during that time their new partner had stalwartly avoided taking them to his home city. Malvius had routinely sent lone ships and kept himself, the Gottari, and the fleet away. Although Vahldan's partner had continued to have dealings in Thrakius, including making payments on the ships they leased, he consistently said he would only go home to face his family when he could do so on his own terms. It was a sentiment Vahldan perfectly understood. It seemed the day had finally come.

The sight had been worth the wait. Vahldan was impressed by the gibbous moon-shaped harbor, completely enclosed within the city's stout walls, filled with over a dozen ships at anchor. He was awed by the bustle and breadth of the docks lined by a string of a half-dozen ships, which were tethered broadside along the quays. There were loading winches of various sizes and a long line of wagons being loaded or unloaded. The city immediately beyond the docks seemed to be lined with warehouses fronted by scores of vendors' carts.

Even more stunning was the view of the city beyond, sprawling across the mountainside. Row upon row of red-tiled roofs leaned over cobbled lanes, striating the slope. The city was crowned by a gray stone fortress sitting at the top. It was the conjuring of a fireside tale rendered in reality. The fortress had both turrets and tiered platforms, and Vahldan could only imagine the view that the top tier commanded—of the city and the sea and all Pontea. He'd seen dozens of cities since he'd set sail with Malvius, but none had captured his imagination like Thrakius did. The sight was almost as astonishing as his first view of the sea itself had been.

"What's all of that commotion in that broad center lane?" he asked, pointing to the bustling stretch of the hillside roadway, fringed with colored cloth.

"That's our market lane," Malvius said. "It's not so grand as the Spice Exchange of Trazonia, but it has its own sort of charm. One of the better arrays of goods in all of Pontea, if I do say so myself."

His choice of words and tone struck Vahldan as odd. For all of the complaining he did about his unfair treatment here in his home city, he was obviously still proud of the place.

"There's the signal. Looks like we have a quay," Malvius said, pointing to the newly vacated space along the dock. He started off toward the aftcastle. "Just wait until you see the surprise I've got in store for you, friends," he called back over his shoulder.

"For us?" Elan asked Vahldan. "What's that all about?"

"No clue," he said. "First I've heard of it."

Once the Pontea Princess was secured to the quay and the unloading process began, Malvius led the way down the gangway and onto the docks, moving through the bustle. Dexicos hurried at his heels. Vahldan kept them in sight. He had Elan and Teavar at his either shoulder and Jhannas trailing them. It wasn't difficult to follow as folks gave Malvius a wide berth. Vahldan noticed that no few of the dockworkers bowed their heads as he passed. Others called his name. It seemed everyone knew him and most seemed cheered to see him. Vahldan was surprised. Malvius had led them to believe that he was a wayward son, returning to a home in which he was no longer welcome. The folks on the docks seemed welcoming enough.

Malvius approached a grizzled fellow with graying whiskers, a full mop of wavy hair, and one arm in a sling. He wore a dockworker's togs. The man bowed at the waist as they approached. Surprisingly, Malvius opened his arms and embraced the man.

Keeping an arm slung around him, Malvius turned the man to face them. "My friends, meet Sabas. This man has forgotten more about ships and sailing than any of us will ever learn. Sabas runs things for me here in Thrakius." After introductions were made, Malvius said, "Are we ready?"

"Near enough, Cap," Sabas said. "You'll be able to see where things are headed, at least."

"Lead on, then."

Sabas led them up an alley between two massive warehouses. He made a quick turn into an even smaller alley, lined by warehouse walls. He stopped and slid a door open. They followed their guide into the shadows of the cavernous space. "We've finally cleared out all of the former owner's goods. Sold what we could, but most was worthless rot. Back here is where we're doing some of the complex carpentry. He led them toward a window's light near the back. There was a bench with tools and wood shavings on the floor. Vahldan saw that the adjacent area had a bed and table behind a low brick wall, next to a heating stove. Looked as though Sabas lived here. Vahldan couldn't imagine living in such a grim place.

Malvius was all smiles as he scanned the building. "The roof is sound?"

"Aye, Cap. Been through some downpours, and nary a drop."

"You've done well, Sabas. It'll be a real boon."

"Quite the bargain, too. Former owner keeled, and the family needed to cut loose quick."

Malvius went to the workbench. "Is the item I requested here?"

Sabas shook his head. "Took it over to the shipyards yesterday. Thought they should see it in its proper place." The grizzled sailor gave Vahldan a wink and a grin.

"No reason to dawdle, then," Malvius said and started back to the door.

On the way out, Vahldan fell in beside Dex. "Please explain. Why do we need a warehouse?" Dex gave him an arch look. "I mean, I understand that it is to store goods. But we normally sell the lots straight from the hold."

"Ah." Dex nodded his understanding. "It allows us to buy when prices are very low and then wait to sell if we believe they will rise later. For example, grain is cheap in late autumn but worth much more in the spring. Cap has a knack for sensing when to buy and whether to wait to sell. It will also allow us to parse a load or sort it. We'll be able to sell off a partial load and hold the remainder. You can trust Cap's instincts on this. The building will pay for itself in no time."

Vahldan found that he had indeed come to trust Malvius. At least when it came to earning profits. Besides, it wasn't as if the man had asked him to invest in the building. How could he complain? He glanced at Elan, who'd been listening. She gave him a single nod. Seemed she felt the same.

Once outside, Sabas led them on through a maze of alleys and then back toward the docks. When they emerged, they were at the far western edge of the docks, not far from the city walls. Before them, in an open yard, was a ship. A ship on land. It was clearly new —seemingly not quite complete—and held up on elaborate stilts and posts, with scaffolding along its sides. At least a half-dozen men were working on it. Vahldan had never seen anything like it. He'd never seen how far below the waterline the keel actually was or the look of an exposed rudder.

Malvius gave a whistle, obviously pleased. "She's a beauty, men," he called to the workers, walking toward the prow. His partner stopped short and held out both hands in delighted appraisal. "Vahldan, come see!"

He went to Malvius's side who pointed at the placard. Vahldan felt his cheeks flushing. His Hellainic was better than ever, and he rarely misunderstood what was being said. But he had no idea how to read the language.

Malvius glanced and realization struck. "Oh, sorry. It's the name of our new flagship. It says *Gullwing*. To honor the change you brought to my life and lead us to the next phase. She'll be the fastest freighter on the Pontean." Malvius beamed. "Well, what do you think?"

Vahldan felt so many things at once, it was impossible to sort them out. Surprise and gratitude, yes. The flush in his cheeks grew hot with shame, swiftly followed by resentment rising to form a knot in his chest. It felt like an exploitation of a private memory that he'd shared. How dare he flaunt it like this. It instantly burdened Vahldan with a dark secret. He hadn't told Malvius how the fight he'd had with Angavar had resulted in his death. Would he be reminded of that awful day every time he boarded this ship?

He also hated what seemed an attempt to drag him deeper into a life that he considered temporary. A ship's name was so permanent. For him, this partnership was far from permanent—a mere step on a ladder he was climbing. He and his men were guardsmen for hire, not shipping merchants. They aspired to so much more, and he'd been chosen to lead them to it.

Malvius was grinning, waiting. "It is good," he managed. His voice had cracked.

"Just good? That's all you've got?"

"I am happy," he added. "Happy for you to have such a fine ship. May she serve you well and long."

Malvius looked woefully dissatisfied, so Vahldan simply strolled toward the vessel, pretending to inspect the hull. Thankfully one of the workers came to offer Malvius a detailed progress report, and the awkwardness passed.

On the evening of their first overnight in Thrakius, Vahldan, Teavar, and Jhannas rode in a borrowed wagon with Malvius up to the palace on the hilltop. Malvius was meeting a merchant who sold exotic goods and fine wine selected specifically for the palace. The giants were enlisted not just as guardians but as muscle to help unload. All three Gottari gawped at the city life that surrounded them. The colors and smells and music and laughter were every bit as exotic as Trazonia, and yet the atmosphere seemed somehow more familiar. Hellainic nightlife seemed so jubilant and infectious —not so different from celebrations in Dania, if apparently more frequent.

"Once we arrive, I'd like to make the exchange quickly," Malvius said as the pair of draft horses clopped slowly up the hill. "In and out. I don't want to see anyone who lives there. Not tonight, anyway. I've made arrangements to leave everything in the keep's stables."

As they crested the hill, the wagon rolled onto a broad courtyard.

At the center was massive, decrepit tree. Beneath that was a statue of a Hellainic scholar, his pedestal rising from the center of a round pool with fountains trickling water from all four of the compass points. The water was stagnant with the leaves of the old tree. The far side of the courtyard was defined by the palace keep wall, but the other three sides were lined with what appeared to be stately homes, many with colonnaded terraces. Beyond the keep wall, the palace rose, looking ever grander as they drew nearer.

The wagon rolled through the archway of a gatehouse, and Malvius gave a wave to two guards standing beside the open gates. Rather than returning the wave, both men bowed their chins to their chests. Vahldan and Jhannas exchanged a curious look. Teavar scowled.

Rather than rolling onto the circular road leading to the stairway to the massive wooden doors of the palace, Malvius steered the team down a road that skirted the wall and led directly into a building with another arched entryway. In spite of its grand exterior, the building was indeed lined with horse stalls. The main tunnel led all the way through to an open exit.

The merchant was there waiting, along with several young groomsmen. The merchant ordered the grooms to help the giants unload. The merchant and Malvius strode off to the side, presumably to discuss business. There were more workers than there was space, so Vahldan stepped aside and wandered to the entrance. He stood gazing up at the magnificence of the palace. The elegant stonework, creeping with vines, spoke of antiquity, and yet the structure seemed modern and new. Nothing at all like the gloomy ramparts and tower at Vigs-Utan, the fortress at the Danian end of the Pontean Pass—the roadway from this city to his homeland.

Lights shone in the twilight from many of the palace windows. Staring up at the balconies made Vahldan wonder what it would be like to live here.

"Watching the bats?" Malvius appeared beside him.

"What? Bats? No, I hadn't noticed."

"The place is lousy with them. Which is an ironic way to put it, since they actually take care of a lot of the insects around here." Sure enough, Vahldan made out the dark shapes of them, swooping and swirling, chasing nightfall's flying insects.

Vahldan was formulating his first question for his partner when a voice called, "Master Malvius? I thought that was you."

"Ah shit," Malvius muttered. "So much for slipping in and out unseen."

An aging and slightly rotund Hellain strode toward them on a stone pathway, coming from a terraced garden. He was well-dressed, with a cropped beard and short hair. Malvius stepped forward to meet him. "Hello, Hesiod."

The man bowed formally and rose with a smile. "Welcome home, my lord," he said.

"Now, now, none of that lord stuff, remember?" Malvius fondly gripped the man's arm. "You're looking well."

"As are you." Hesiod had a gleam in his eye. The man looked past Malvius at Vahldan.

Malvius glanced, but then moved to block the man's view. "I brought a few of my men up to help with a load. Just some wine and exotic foods. You understand. Could never make this deal directly."

The man seemed to ignore the strange explanation. Vahldan felt like an imposition and started back inside. "Your sister was asking after you," Hesiod said. "Shall I run and fetch her?"

Vahldan stopped short. Malvius's sister was here?

"Gods no," Malvius said. "I'll come and see them both tomorrow. Please don't tell them I was here." Malvius turned to Vahldan and said, "Tell the others I'll be right in. We'll leave in a moment." His tone was curt.

He was being dismissed. *'I brought a few of my men up,'* Malvius had said.

Once they were all back in the empty wagon, and Malvius steered them out and around toward the gate, Vahldan could stay quiet no longer. "All right, partner. You're going to have to tell us what is going on. Your sister is here? Who was that man, and what is this place to you?"

Malvius gave him a side glance. "The man was my childhood manservant. Well, one of them. Hesiod works for my father, although they often don't get along. Which is something I have always found endearing about him. And yes, my sister and her dolt of a husband still live here with my father. This place was my childhood home."

"You lived here," Vahldan deadpanned. "In a palace."

Malvius looked over with a shy smile. "Sorry, I thought you knew."

"I knew your father was wealthy, but I..." He looked back as they exited the keep. "How long has your family lived here?"

"Oh, about ten generations, give or take." It made Vahldan wonder how many generations he would have to count back to get to the Amalus kings. He suspected it was a similar number. Malvius was grinning when he looked back. "My father is the city's magister as well as its largest employer. But beyond that, he is a descendant of the anaxship."

"What's that?" Vahldan asked.

"An anax is sort of a leftover from the old regional royal families. For my ancestors, this was our city to rule as a part of the Hellainic Empire, back before the Tiberians came. There was no central governance then, so each city and its surrounding region had their own anax, or ruler. My father still bears the title, same as Isidros does in Nicomedya. It's little more than a label now. Anaxes have almost no real power. Depending on the issue, my father is beholden to the city's garrison commanders or the rectors who are seated in Megaria, who both ultimately answer to the emperor. The Tiberian bureaucracy left the titles in place for two reasons. First, because they love pomp and ceremony as much as most of the anaxes. Second, because it creates the illusion of providing a voice to the regional ethnic traditions. Which helps them maintain control over the Hellains who live in Pontea. My people love their noble family lineages, regardless of how meaningless they've become to governance."

Things were starting to make more sense. Malvius often spoke of how unfairly he'd been treated by his family. The man had nothing kind to say of his father. He'd used the term *disinherited*. Vahldan saw that the term alluded to much more than losing his claim on a fortune made from shipping. "You have been trying to get back," he said.

"Get back?" Malvius frowned. "To live there?" He threw a thumb over his shoulder to indicate the palace. "Nah. The place is drafty, and most of the people who live up there are unpleasant." He laughed. Vahldan was trying to read him as night fell and they moved through shadows and snatches of light. Malvius felt his stare. "Seriously. My father loves that damn palace because it props up his ego. He loves the idea of looming over *his domain*. To do so requires a level of self-delusion. I've always hated that. My ideal home is aboard my own ship, on the open seas. These are my people." He smiled at the pedestrians, coming and going from eateries and pubs. "Here and down there." Malvius nodded downhill. "All the more so when they join my crews."

His partner wore a fond smile. "Down there on the docks—that's the real Thrakius. Sea trade is the lifeblood of this city. My father never truly understood that. Not like I've come to. To him, the shipping trade is a necessary evil, but it's so much more. The Tiberians may be the law, but the real traders truly run things here. The anax is a mere figurehead. And the current one never wanted to dirty his hands with a shrewd trade, let alone hold a tiller—feel his way to the best tack. The old man actually hates sailing, if you can believe it. To me, those are the things that make life worth living."

Vahldan twisted to look back at the palace, silhouetted in the night sky, windows twinkling over the city, almost like the stars that were starting to appear above it. "Every man has his own ideals, I suppose," he said.

VAHLDAN SUPPOSED they'd been lucky thus far. It had been made clear to him, again and again, that the greatest danger they faced in their lives here in Pontea came from the Tibairya. Not the citizens, or even the merchants, buyers, and bureaucrats, who were of every race and ethnicity within the imperial bounds and beyond. No, the real threat lurked in the form of the harbormasters and their guards, the city watchmen, or vigiles, and the members of the militum—the imperial warriors and the muscle.

They'd visited over a dozen imperial cities, including several along the coasts of the Tibairyan Sea, and had no serious encounters. But today the threat would be the greatest yet as they were docking at their first port on the Tibairyan mainland. Malvius ordered the oars to be drawn in as their fleet's new flagship coasted across the dark waters of the harbor toward the quay. He scanned the docks and sought to act natural as the crew of Gullwing scrambled to throw and secure the lines. Everyone went about their duties, but Vahldan sensed the tension felt by one and all.

Malvius appeared beside him. "Are you sure this is wise?" Vahldan asked, nodding to indicate his men, arrayed mostly along the dockside rail. In spite of the risk, the Gottari were well-armed and positioned to be apparent to those on the docks.

Malvius appraised his Amalus guardsman with a look of satisfaction and a nod. "We must make clear the downside of discourtesy," he said. "They're perfect."

Malvius had taught him early on: The strong impression of being capable of violence was its best prevention. Mutual respect made for smooth transactions.

It wasn't long before he spotted the caravan of tarp-covered wagons approaching, parting the crowds in the adjacent market-place. As the caravan arrived, large men jumped down from each wagon, spreading out to form a perimeter on the docks. If the guardsmen were armed, it wasn't apparent, but their purpose was clear. They were also there to make an impression, same as the Amalus.

"You were right," Vahldan said. "He has Tutona also."

"Oedias is thrifty, but he's no fool. Everyone knows Teutons are the best. By having them he's setting boundaries. Not just for us. Look." Malvius pointed. The dockworkers and passersby were all moving away, giving the Tutona mercenaries a wide berth. Malvius grinned and slapped Vahldan's back. "But don't worry. Soon all shall know that my Teutons are the best of the best. Besides, we have them outnumbered."

"You were right about the numbers, too." Vahldan had wanted to leave an equal number of guards on each of the other three ships in their current fleet, anchored beyond the harbor's mouth. Malvius had insisted on having the bulk of his lions aboard Gullwing.

Malvius tilted his head in acknowledgment. "It's like I always say. If you're sure you have what your counterpart wants, never hesitate to press your full advantage upon them. Sets the proper tone for the negotiation to come. Saves everyone from the trouble of bluster."

Since their first fight in Trazonia with Isidros's men, Vahldan had watched their reputation grow, and he saw its value. Even Malvius had grown to appreciate it. The Gottari wasted no time with tough talk or threats. When trouble struck, they did not hesitate. The violence they meted was silent, swift, and decisive. Even if it meant retreating without completing a deal. Pontea was coming to learn that Malvius of Thrakius and his Gottari would not be intimidated and would brook no trickery. It was making the trades they chose purer. Most of their counterparts knew what to expect and behaved accordingly.

Today's exchange, however, was an unknown. Malvius smelled a profit, but the risk remained uncertain.

The port's gangway was hoisted and secured. Several Tutona moved to the base, escorting Malvius's counterpart. The Tibairyan merchant was dressed in shimmering deep-blue robes. Malvius came to the top of the gangway to greet the man, with Vahldan and Elan at his shoulders.

"May I come aboard?" the merchant called in Hellainic.

Malvius summoned one of his charming grins. "But of course!"

The man started up the gangway with two of his Tutona close behind.

The trading partners bowed heads in unison. Without a word, Malvius beckoned the man toward the open hatch. Vahldan stiffened as the Tibairyan merchant strode past him. Despite standing a head shorter than Vahldan, the merchant appraised them as a herdsman would a breeding pair of prized sheep at auction. In contrast, the pair of Tutona following the merchant bowed their heads with open palms extended at either side—a warrior's deference. The guardians were larger and more muscled than most Hellains and Tibairya, but not extraordinary by Gottari standards. Without being too obvious, Vahldan scanned them for weapons. They likely had knives, but he detected no swords or cudgels.

Malvius led the trio of visitors to the six barrels already on the hoist platform, drawn and secured over the open hatch. Although most of Vahldan's men and Malvius's sailors were on the lookout for imperial intrusion, both the merchant and Malvius scanned the docks below before prying opening a barrel. Malvius held the lid, proffering the contents. The merchant dug through the contents a moment before taking a whole nutmeg. He drew a small knife and cut into it, first smelling and then tasting.

The merchant's smile was wry. "Top quality. Perfectly cured. And I am simply to trust that you've brought it out undetected?" Vahldan was glad the trader spoke in Hellainic rather than the Tibairyan tongue. He only knew a smattering of Tibairyan, though Malvius kept suggesting that he should learn it. Gaining fluency in Hellainic was difficult enough. Malvius continued to encourage every Gottari to learn the area's primary tongue, and he and his officers still offered language sessions, mostly in the form of word games and often filled with laughter. His men had complied until they could get by, but few remained as committed as he and Elan and his senior Rekkrs.

"Rest assured," Malvius said. "My source operates under the auspices of the Dah of Anaissa. Both he and the Dah are glad for the chance to spite our friends in the bureaucracy."

"What of the harbormaster in Trazonia?" the merchant inquired. "I am told he has many eyes and ears on the docks."

"Oedias, surely you know me better by now. I loaded this shipment up the River Haleez. We completely bypassed Trazonia. Instead, we took on water and supplies in Bafrana."

"What of the Straits?" Oedias was either very thorough or very suspicious. Perhaps both.

"We came through by night. I am quite sure none were the wiser for our passage."

Oedias raised a brow. "First you expect me to believe that you risked sailing deep into enemy territory to procure your load. That you then sailed right into the home port of pirates. And now you want me to believe that you slipped by both ends of the Pontean Straits by night? All while avoiding detection by every agent of our diligent imperial government?"

Malvius put his winsome grin back on. "As I say, my source has his reasons for dealing with me. And when it comes to illegal cargo, the Bafranii ask only for their fair share, which we gave. As for the Straits, it's not often you get such a favorable night wind this time of year. So yes, we're damn good. And a bit lucky. But we're practical, too. It's neither our first risky run nor our first shadow trade."

The merchant squinted. "A *bit* lucky." Oedias barked a laugh. "All right, Malvius. I suppose we'll have to trust that you're as good as you think you are and then pray we're as lucky as you've been."

"Of course. Sixty a barrel, then?"

"Sixty? That's larceny."

Malvius lowered his voice and raised an eyebrow. "Maybe so, but don't forget—it's the larceny that makes it tariff-free."

"Which also makes it riskier to resell. I'll give you forty-five, and I'll take it all."

Malvius rubbed his chin and hummed. "I suppose if you're willing to take all twenty-four barrels, I may be able to come down to fifty."

The merchant looked to his Tutona guards. One of them gave a barely discernible nod. To Malvius, Oedias said, "Done." He turned back to the Tutona. "Get the wagons in close. All hands in motion. I want this done quickly. Let us be gone before the harbormaster has even heard we've arrived."

Malvius clapped his hands and shouted down to the hold, ordering the rest of the barrels to be raised to the deck. A half-dozen Tutona hurried up the gangway to start rolling away barrels. The first wagon was loaded in mere moments. It moved clear and a second wagon replaced it. Tarps were dragged to cover each row as the barrels were set on the beds. Vahldan appreciated their efficiency.

He and Elan followed along as Malvius led Oedias to his quarters and then set themselves on either side of the closed door. The two were only inside briefly. When they emerged, Malvius was grinning and Oedias looked as though he'd been offered sour milk inside.

Another winch-load of barrels rose to deck level, and the Tutona instantly began rolling them off. There were too few men to clear the hoist, which caused a momentary delay. As they waited, Oedias frowned and gave Vahldan another once-over. "You know, Malvius, this would go faster if you had your Teutonic slaves pitch in."

Malvius was still buoyant. "I have two issues with your suggestion. First, my Teutonic friends are not slaves, for I keep none. Secondly, their job is to keep this transaction safe. That includes you and your men. Trust me, they are precisely where we both want them. They're quite good at what they do."

The merchant's lip curled as he stared at Vahldan. "Am I supposed to be stricken?"

Malvius laughed. "You ought to be. But I'd avoid seeking proof."

His partner came and put a fond hand on his shoulder. "You see, my good man, this is none other than Vahldan the Bold." Vahldan cringed. He hated the moniker. Elan considered it funny and teased him with it, which was how Malvius came to use it. Vahldan feared it would stick if they kept it up. "This man is the chieftain of the fierce Amalus clan of the mighty Gottari nation."

Oedias actually seemed impressed. "Gottari, eh? I have heard they are vaunted."

After the hoist was cleared, the merchant ambled off the deck without so much as a farewell. The crew lowered the winch for the last load. A few of Oedias's Tutona stayed behind. One of them kept glancing furtively at Vahldan and then over at Elan. Oedias climbed onto the bench of the lead wagon, and the Tutona workers hurried back up the gangway for what would be the last of the barrels. As they stood on deck, waiting for the last load to be hoisted into place, the man who'd been looking their way spoke in low tones to his companions. Which made all of them look at Vahldan.

As the winch began to creak with the load rising from the hold, the man came to Vahldan, bowing his head over hands pressed together before him. "If you forgive, I may ask?" the man said in broken Hellainic.

Vahldan almost walked away, but the man looked sincere. "What is it you wish?"

"Only knowledge." Another bow. "I wish to know if it can be true? That you are lord of lions, of the Gottari? He who rise from exile? He who defeat Para-lah-toe-ah? And she is gift of the Skolana queen?" He nodded toward Elan.

Vahldan frowned. He was surprised they'd heard of him. But he also wasn't sure why anyone from another tribe would care. He certainly had nothing to hide. "I am he," he admitted.

The man beckoned his fellows, speaking rapidly in his own tongue, which sounded similar to Gottari. They all rushed over and fell onto their knees in a semicircle around him, bowing their faces to the deck. The guard said, "We are honored, Great One. You are he who is to deliver us all in Hoo-Ree-Nahn—the rising of the Tutona. Our prayers go with you."

Vahldan looked around. The display had everyone staring, including Malvius. Several of the crew hooted and whistled. "Come, come," Vahldan scolded. "Enough of this. Rise now."

All of the Tutona reluctantly did as bidden. "We of the Rhugi leave you with much thanks. For your sacrifice, we cannot repay," the lead man said. They all backed away, bowing repeatedly as they returned to take the arriving barrels. "Much thanks," many of them echoed, tilting their heads as they rolled off the last of the lot.

Malvius appeared beside him, watching them descend the gangway. The Rhugian guard offered a final salute from the dock. "What in the broad blue was that all about?" Malvius asked.

Vahldan shook his head. "It is nothing. They mistake me."

Malvius arched an eyebrow and turned to Elan. She suppressed a smile. "Sorry," Malvius said, "but I'm not buying your load. I think there's a better story hidden in your hold."

Vahldan paused, searching for the right words. "It is not one I wish to offer. It is mine."

Malvius slapped his shoulder. "Well, my friend, know that I'm not going to quit haggling until you sell."

Vahldan sighed. "I would rather you let it go."

Malvius pulled a cloth sack from his purse and proffered it, waiting for Vahldan to put out his hand. "We can't have everything we seek." When he set the bag in his hand, it clinked softly, its weight significant. "Although there's much we can have, if we strive." Malvius laughed.

Vahldan knew it was the largest single payment for one stop that he and his men had yet received. This had been a risky run, and they weren't quite clear yet. Indeed, with every passing moment the risk of being hauled off to the nearest slaver's block only grew. It was a risk that none of the Hellains aboard faced. But it was a calculated risk—one that Vahldan, Elan, and all of his men had willingly accepted. This was why they had left Dania. Every risky deal put them another step closer to gaining the sort of wealth that would make a difference upon their return.

He offered Malvius a tilt of the head. "I suppose so," he conceded.

"Don't worry," Malvius said, grinning. "I'm willing to strive, too." As he started back to the aftcastle, Malvius spoke loudly, "Really? Vahldan the Bold, too shy to peddle a tale? About himself? That I will not buy."

AFTER THE CREW had eaten dinner, the wind had remained a bit gusty, so Malvius ordered the sails reefed as they headed into the evening. Dexicos had the till. Now that they had nothing to hide, it was prudent to ease back in order to approach the mouth of the Straits in the light of day. Vahldan, Elan, Teavar, and a few other Gottari were enjoying the cool breeze on the foredeck of Gullwing.

Malvius sensed an opportunity. He hadn't been able to get what he'd heard from Oedias's Teutonics out of his head. Vahldan's refusal to speak of it made him all the more curious.

He stopped at his cabin and grabbed two actual glass bottles from the case of fine brandy he'd acquired in Efusium. He put the bottles and as many cups as he could find on a tray and headed to the foredeck. The sun was setting behind them, but the low clouds that hung over the Tiberian hills off the port bow reflected its glory in hues from orange to purple.

When Vahldan saw Malvius coming, he tilted his head back and groaned. "Ah, no."

"What? I just thought you all deserved a nice libation after a successful venture." Malvius handed round the cups, pried out the first stopper, and started to pour. When they all had some, he lifted his cup. "Here's to—what was it?—he who shall deliver us all to..." He crinkled his nose. "Hoo-ree-doo, was it?"

Teavar's low laugh always brought to mind a jovial bear. Or an ornery one, depending.

"To the Bringer of Urrinan," Belgar said, evidently correcting his attempt.

"All right," Malvius said. "Time to draw back the hatches. What's all this about?"

"The Urrinan," Belgar began, "is a prophecy. One in which many believe."

"What does it prophesize?"

"The rising up of our people."

Malvius took a drink and wiped his mouth. "Your people? But Oedias's men were Rhugian, weren't they?"

Belgar nodded. "The prophecy is shared among many of the Tutona tribes."

Malvius raised his cup to Vahldan. "And our fine friend here figures into it somehow?"

"Somehow?" Elan grinned. "He's the key to the whole damn thing—destiny's lucky victim. Many who claim to know say he fits in perfectly."

"How so?"

"Is it not apparent?" Elan ran her fingers down the side of his face. "Could there be a more handsome choice?" Vahldan grew even more annoyed and playfully pushed her hand aside. Elan just laughed. "Actually, those who believe say it has to do with his blood-line and the happenstance of his birth."

This was getting better and better. Malvius poured another round. "Happenstance?"

"His family's exile, mostly," she said. "And a king shall arise from among the kingless, born of exile," Elan recited. In nearly flawless Hellainic, no less. Malvius was impressed.

Despite Vahldan's apparent irritation, Malvius was still intrigued. Plus, it was fun chatting with the Gottari about their world for a change. "So what's all this about our boy's sacrifice? Those Rhugians said some weird stuff—how they're praying for him, can never repay him. Are they talking about how you all hunted down the Kaukazari back in Akasas?"

Teavar shook his head. "The Rhugi make no war on Spali. They speak on a new war." The big man's Hellainic still lagged behind the others, but his grave tone conveyed plenty.

It seemed all of them were uncomfortable now. Malvius sensed he should drop it. But, damn, he couldn't recall being this curious. "Which new war is this?"

The silence stretched. Elan leaned to stare into her cup. "It's said the Urrinan will be ushered in by much..." She searched for the word. "Strife," she finally said. "The Urrinan is to be a—how do you say it? A cata..."

"A catastrophe?"

Elan gave him a sober nod. "Catastrophe, yes."

"So, the Teutonics all share this vision—that there's going to be war and strife, a full-on catastrophe? But in spite of it, your people are going to rise up?"

Elan's expression was grave. "Not in spite of it. Because of it."

Malvius laughed, trying to lighten their darkening mood. "Count me in. Just when and where is this party going to start?"

Vahldan suddenly stood, looming over him. Malvius had only seen his expression so hard, so full of malice, once before. From the wall, when he'd threatened the magister of Akasas.

"It begins here. In Pontea. Soon."

"Here? War?" Malvius's voice hadn't cracked like that since puberty. But once again, he couldn't resist asking, "Who will we be fighting?"

Vahldan's eyes narrowed. "*We* will be fighting *your* people."

"My people?"

"You know, those who buy and sell my people as if we were sheep."

Vahldan twitched, causing his shoulder to pop. Malvius thought he was swinging a punch and nearly fell over backward to avoid what was sure to be extremely painful—he'd witnessed the aftereffects of the man's punches. Vahldan burst out laughing. It was a feint. He was holding out his cup for more. The rest of the Gottari laughed, too. But not Elan, Malvius noticed. She looked out over the water.

Malvius opened the second bottle and poured. "It is but a joke, of course," Vahldan said as Malvius poured. "You are always to be our partner, our friend." Vahldan's grin grew sly as he added, "A jumpy friend, alas. But a friend." The Gottari laughed.

When both bottles were empty, Vahldan raised his cup in a toast. "To victory," he said.

Malvius had no choice but to hoist his cup. As they both tilted their heads to drink, Malvius thought he saw a trace of the malice he'd seen earlier flash in Vahldan's eyes. But when he looked again, his Gottari friend was smiling warmly.

"I suppose it'll be for the best," Malvius finally conceded. Vahldan sighed and nodded to his team. They would have it their way. He realized he was gripping the hilt of the sword in question and released it. The captain forced a carefree laugh. "Yes, it'll be fine. After all, Nicomedya has no law prohibiting openly carrying weapons—Isidros himself has seen to that. And we do want to convey the right impression. Besides, things should be calm here, now that the garrison's been fully restored." Malvius sounded like he was still trying to convince himself.

"We mean only to make clear the downside of discourtesy," Vahldan said, giving his partner one of his own lines. Before Malvius could start second-guessing again, he nodded for Teavar and Jhannas to climb down to the waiting rowboat, wearing their swords, same as he and Elan.

This was their first foray into Isidros's home turf, and Vahldan was not about to venture forth unarmed. If Malvius was going to insist on such a small delegation, this was an aspect on which he would not compromise. There was too much else to worry about to wonder how such a small group of them might defend themselves and their captain should trouble arise. They'd sailed Gullwing into the Nicomedyan harbor alone and still had not been granted a quay. The rower ferrying them ashore was a hired local, as both giants were too much for the ship's dingy. Vahldan hated that they didn't have an exit strategy he could control.

Everyone, including Malvius, kept telling him how impressed he'd be with Nicomedya. So far he was unconvinced, and he doubted his feelings would change. Enthusiasts spoke of the amazing breadth of the market and how plentiful and crowded it would be this time of the season, right before hiatus. The Amalus had been in Pontea for nearly five years, and Vahldan still wasn't used to the sorts of crowds that were typical in imperial cities. Indeed, he had a growing aversion to them. For a number of reasons, but the main reason was the increased threat—the additional diligence that was required of being surrounded by strangers.

Outside of Thrakius, every imperial city was someone else's home turf. They could never know who among the crowd meant them harm. Most every competing trader wished them ill fortune at the least. Financial ruin and bodily harm at the worst. And they all had their own guardians and strongmen. Some were former warriors or soldiers, some were mere street thugs. Most were employed for protection, but many were also utilized in more nefarious ways. Sabotage, fraud, and theft were routine occurrences. Violence was an ever-present possibility, and though their skirmishes were mostly bloodless, often earning them bruises and black eyes, serious woundings and even death were not uncommon—mostly among those they opposed, thankfully.

He could handle all of it when he had his entire host. His team was sharp, and they all had one another's backs. Here they were but four. His companions were his three best, but he still felt terribly vulnerable.

Once ashore, they fell into the flow of traffic, all heading toward the recently opened gates and the market within. The press only increased once they were inside and on Nicomedya's narrow lanes.

The march to the city center felt endless, one plodding step at a time. The lane became like two rivers of people and wagons, side by side and moving in opposite directions, most heading the same way as them. Vahldan nearly made himself dizzy, head swiveling, watching for potential threats and traps. Even putting Teavar and Jhannas in front of their little group didn't speed their progress much. City folk normally gave the giants a wide and wary berth, but not here. Not today, anyway.

The deeper they went into the city, the less Vahldan liked it. Most every building had a terrace overhead, and even those were crowded. Finally, the rows of brick structures that loomed over them gave way to the open sky above the city's commons, allowing the rising sun to beat down on them. Summer's grip remained here, and Vahldan and his crew were in full armor. He was already sweating.

Finally Malvius pointed to the side and led them out of the flow of traffic and up a wide set of stone steps. Happily the spot was in the shade. At the top of the steps, under the pillars of a temple to some foreign god, the sea captain turned back and spread his arms, smiling down.

Vahldan looked back out over the massive square, filled with the cloth pavilions of vendors, its aisles like rolling rivers of humanity. His dizziness returned as he stared into the dazzling blur of color and motion. The color was not due to the exotic clothing alone, but also the pavilions, awnings, laden tables, and covered wagons. There were more hues and tones than he'd imagined possible. It reminded him, not for the first time, of how muted and dull Danihem seemed in comparison to Pontean cities.

The view only enhanced the feeling that they might be trapped or ambushed. Besides that, he doubted he'd ever get used to the smell of large imperial cities that rose to choke him—a pungent blend of spices, perfumes, meats cooking, fermented drinks brewing, and perspiring human bodies. Not to mention the open trenches of sewage that invariably flowed through most Pontean cities. At least spending time ashore helped him to better appreciate their time at sea.

"How about this?" Malvius proclaimed. His partner was beaming.

"It's something," Elan said with an edge of scorn in her tone.

She disliked crowds as much as Vahldan did. Also, Elan was hard to impress. It wasn't that Malvius had never shown her anything that made her smile. Elan had smiled when they'd ventured into the forest of towering, red-bark conifers in Labassas. She'd laughed in delight when she stood in the spray of a thundering waterfall cascading from a soaring ridge into a clear pool just off the rocky coast of Sassanada. He shared her fondness for the deserted soft-sand beaches of the islands beyond the Straits in the Tibairyan Sea and the hospitable little inns and seafood and produce markets of the fishing villages that dotted their coasts. Malvius had hidden them away in such spots during the last few hiatuses. He seemed to dislike leaving the Gottari to roam the streets of Thrakius over the winter and because the alternative was so pleasant none of them minded what might be considered a slight.

Malvius seemed oblivious to Elan's tone. "Terrific, isn't it? Ever seen anything like it, Vahldan? It's one of the largest markets in the eastern empire. Larger than the one at Efusium."

Vahldan drew a deep breath and sighed it out. "Terrific," he said, forcing a smile. "I can hardly wait to get a closer look." No need to mention the unavoidable stronger whiff. Or the fact that the sooner they got to their destination, the sooner they could leave.

"Oh, come on. Cheer up, my fine Gottari friends. You'll be more amazed once we get in there. Follow me." Malvius beckoned and started skipping down the steps.

Halfway down, before they even rejoined the milling crowd, Malvius encountered an acquaintance—an occurrence so common, his Gottari guardians had a running joke about how Malvius would never get clear of Hel's bridge after he died, due to all of the old friends he'd stop to chat up along the way. As Malvius and his friend exchanged pleasantries, Vahldan positioned the giants on their flank and surveyed the square below. In a nearby busy corner, a barking merchant stood on a platform alongside a nude young man. The youth was tall but thin, with the light bronze skin of the Sassanada. The lad wore a placard around his neck, and the merchant rapidly touted his *product* amid a flurry of bidding from the crowd.

Elan followed his gaze. "Another slave auction?"

Vahldan grimaced. "They say this city is the worst for it. I'll never get used to it."

"It's an affront to the gods," she said. The Gottari held no slaves, but the Skolani abhorred the very concept of it. Elan had explained that in the tales of their foremothers, the Spali often sought to capture and enslave Skolani, deeming them a prized commodity. A Blade-Wielder was honor-bound to die, and even to mercy kill a sister, before enduring such a fate.

The thin Sassanada youth was sold and led away. In his place, two children were pulled up to the platform. Both had fair hair and skin, their shoulders and cheeks red with sunburn. The boy was perhaps ten and the girl around six. The girl's chest heaved. She was crying. The boy clung to her hand—likely her brother. The hawker started the bidding and moved to separate them. The slaver pushed the girl to the fore and held up a fistful of her hair, praising her appearance.

The girl's mouth fell open, and the sound of her bawling drifted to them. "Áithei!" she cried. It was a Gottari endearment; the girl was calling for her mother.

Stinging tears sprang to Vahldan's eyes, and Thunar's Blessing surged through him.

"They're Gottari," he said, impulsively setting out for the stage, hand on his hilt. He sensed Elan and the giants coming right behind him.

Malvius appeared in front of them, arms wide to halt them. "Please. Remember what I told you," Malvius pleaded in a low voice. "There can be no trouble today. We must not draw attention to ourselves here. Especially from the likes of them." He nodded toward a pair of imperial soldiers, standing at the far side of the slaver's platform.

"They are selling Gottari children," Elan spat. "Likely stolen from their parents."

Malvius shook his head and tsked. "You're right. It's terrible. In another place and time, perhaps we can do something about such atrocities. Perhaps even bid on them."

Vahldan was stunned. "Bid on them?" He'd thought only to seize back stolen children.

"Only if we could find a safe way to set them free, of course," Malvius hastened to add.

The bright flare of Thunar's Blessing fell away, leaving the smolder of the ugliness in its void. "Good idea," he said and started to push past Malvius. "I'll buy them."

"Too late." Malvius held a palm to his chest and pointed. The children were being led from the stage, already purchased. Vahldan glowered down on Malvius till he removed his hand. It seemed like their partner was relieved that it was too late.

Vahldan couldn't let it go. "Then I'll buy them from whoever purchased them." He started toward the auction stage again.

Once again Malvius rushed to block him. "Please, my friend. We're not safe here. There are imperial officials in this city who would love to see us fined, or even to have our charter revoked. Most are in the purse of our biggest rival." Vahldan resisted the impulses that danced through his thoughts. Malvius gave him an apologetic smile. As he often did, Vahldan sensed the underlying fear that Malvius veiled. "Come now. Let it go. The day will come when we can do something meaningful to protest this despicable practice. But it cannot be this day. Not here. Come now, Vahldan. Let's finish our business and get clear of this den of jackals. Our success today will provide a big step toward earning the fortune we need to really change things."

Vahldan hissed out a sigh, seeking to release the ugliness that had crawled up from his belly to the top of his throat. Malvius didn't keep slaves, and he spoke a fine fight. But he never truly seemed as outraged as Vahldan felt about it. Some of the things Malvius said about slavery made Vahldan suspect he secretly believed that a slave's circumstances were somehow their own fault. Which made him wonder if Malvius considered those of the races and tribes who were frequently enslaved to somehow be less-than, as so many high-born Hellains seemed to.

Malvius pointed in the opposite direction. "Isidros's pavilion is at the far end of the market. But I'm sure his men are already all around us, watching. They're looking for leverage—ways to gain an advantage. We can't afford to give it to them. Showing them that this upsets you so much would do just that. Please, lead on, my guardians. To our destination. I need you to protect this deal. I need you to help me avoid spectacles, not to create them."

They were being reminded of their duty, but also of their station. Although the Amalus shared a financial partnership with Malvius, he was reminding them that he was the fleet's captain. Vahldan couldn't even look at him. He gestured for Teavar and Jhannas to lead, and he and Elan fell in behind Malvius. Due to the giants' sly shoves and scowls, the group moved more quickly through the press.

Vahldan scanned their trading rival's pavilion as they drew near. It took up the entire end of the aisle adjacent to the anax's palace gate. "Why is Isidros willing to make this trading pact with us now?" he asked, trying to banish the remains of the ugliness.

"Because he's fond of gold." Malvius winked over his shoulder.

The rivalry between Malvius's and Isidros's families was generational. Because of Nicomedya's strategic position at the mouth of the Straits, an important hub on the most vital trade route in the imperial world, Malvius's family had fallen into a secondary status. It seemed similar to what had become of the rivalry between the Amalus and Wulthus. Since their first fight with them, the Amalus had been in more scuffles and brawls with Isidros's thugs than any other trader's force. Isidros only hired experienced fighters, gathered from across the Pontean. Thus far, the lions had always prevailed, but their conflicts were never easy and rarely bloodless.

"I just find it suspicious," Vahldan said.

"Why?" Malvius asked. "Now that we've secured our deal with Bhadran, our charter is as tight as a tick on the Sassanada hound. Isidros needs us more than we need him, and he knows it. We're only talking because of the additional markets we might gain access to."

"I understand that. I just don't like that he insisted on completing the deal on their turf. Especially after what happened in Trazonia last spring."

"Yes," Malvius said, "but we won, remember? And not just the fight for dock position, but the trading pact we were both vying for. I assure you, they remember. They know who has the upper hand. Meeting here is a concession, but it won't hurt our position."

Their last skirmish had left one of Isidros's men dead and a dozen more wounded. The Amalus had suffered several serious injuries, too. The city watch had stood by, waiting to see which force would be paying to haul the other away. It was getting to be a tiresome routine.

One of Isidros's lead thugs—the grizzled Illyrican named Encho—walked toward them wearing a smirk. Vahldan felt the ugliness flair back to life. All four Amalus gripped their hilts and slowed their steps.

"Nice sword, Teuto," Encho said as he brushed by. "Too bad about those slave pups. Kin of yours?" The Illyrican laughed as he disappeared into the crowd.

Malvius glanced back. "I told you they'd do this. And I told you not to let them get to you. Remember?"

"I remember," he said, forcing himself to release the hilt. He could at least take solace in the fact that he'd made the Illyrican's broken beak even uglier than it was before they met.

Malvius smiled. "Then stop looking so intense."

"It's my job to look intense." Seemed it was also essential to keeping the ugliness at bay.

Malvius gave a dismissive wave. "Don't worry. They won't touch us here. Not with the imperials back in charge. I heard the new garrison commander and Isidros have a tense relationship. Serves him right, for trying to swing his cock around here like he does. Besides, it's like I told you: They need us. We're his only route back into the spice game. He's been caught twice this year with unstamped goods, and the Tiberians are watching his fleet like a mother seahawk watches her fledglings. The poor bastard owes almost as much as his ships are worth in fines. There's nobody else left with a connection to a legitimate charter from the Sassanada. We're the only skiff in the race."

"The only skiff we can see," Vahldan retorted. "I recall the days of trading with the Peshtari without a charter. Wasn't it you who said that the Sassanada prefer gold to rules?"

Malvius shrugged. "True. But most of the sailors that used to call themselves traders seem to have misplaced their balls these days. Hades' furies, most of them are scared even to scoot through the Straits."

Vahldan kept scanning their surroundings. He spotted Isidros's fighters, one after another, scattered in an array, loitering among the throng. Isidros even had men lining the palace walls above his pavilion. As they neared their destination, Vahldan's gaze landed on Isidros, who was looking right at him. The man actually smiled.

Malvius waved to his fellow son of an anax. "See? I told you he'd be happy to see us."

"I still say coming here was risky."

"You're not wrong," Malvius said. "Out here on the fringes of the empire, men must consider their common foes, in spite of their rivalry. While it's true that the Tiberians present their own sort of risk, they also present an opportunity. They tend to level the stakes, even here. Isidros has as much or more to lose with them than we do." Malvius offered up his famous grin. "Trust me, my friend—the best is yet to come. The greater the risk—"

"The greater the reward," Vahldan finished another of Malvius's oft repeated lines.

"Opa! Especially for men like Vahldan the Bold!" Malvius turned and patted his chest. "By the way, excellent conversation. Your Hellainic just keeps getting better."

"Better than your Gottari, I think," Vahldan said in his own tongue.

"I doubt not," the captain managed in Gottari. Vahldan suppressed a laugh over Malvius's accent. He knew his Tutona accent in Hellainic was also funny to those who were fluent.

They arrived at Isidros's pavilion, its front lined with bins of spices and tables of exotic jewelry and perfumes. Isidros stepped through a gap in the displays and opened his arms to Malvius. The rivals embraced as brothers, slapping one another's backs when Vahldan was sure they'd as soon stab them. Very strange, these Hellains.

Isidros faced Vahldan. "Ah, I see you've brought the finest of your fine Teutonics."

Isidros's slick smile grew as he appraised Elan from head to toe. "Including your gorgeous, if deadly, Hippomache." Malvius had explained to them about the Hellainic legend of the Hippomache warrior women who rode out of the mountains. Vahldan secretly liked to believe the region's legend was born of actual encounters with Elan's Skolani ancestors. "Welcome, my beauty." The panderer took Elan's hand and kissed it. Vahldan pressed down the resurgence of the ugliness the man provoked.

Elan coldly stared as she pointedly wiped her hand on her tunic sleeve. She'd abandoned her old Skolani breastplate for fitted mail. She'd chosen a cuirass rather than a hauberk, as it left her arms free. Elan joked that having her hair cut to chin length kept it from snagging in the mail, but Vahldan suspected she considered it a symbol of her break with her Skolani heritage. She never admitted it, but he knew that her hard feelings over her banishment lingered—and perhaps even festered.

Isidros shrugged off her cold response. "When are you all going to accept that you should be working for me? How much is he paying you?"

"More than you can afford, believe me," Malvius interjected.

Isidros raised his eyebrows to Vahldan. "It's true," Vahldan said.

Isidros barked in laughter. "Ah well. You're clearly worth my trying. Keep me in mind if you ever tire of this one." He threw a thumb at Malvius. "Come, Malvius, tell me about something I *can* afford." The trader wrapped an arm around Malvius and led him to a lavish sitting area at the center of his pavilion.

Vahldan nodded for Teavar and Jhannas to circle around and take positions where they could see the far side of the pavilion. He spotted Encho hovering among the passersby, exchanging words and nods with each of his comrades. Vahldan stepped away from Isidros's customers and employees, out to the edge of the bustling market aisle. He sought to make note of all those to whom Encho spoke. He momentarily lost track of Encho and then spotted him lurking behind a pair of Tibairyan soldiers. The soldiers were standing vigil at the nearest intersection of market aisles. Their eyes met, and the Illyrican gave Vahldan a snarling grin, revealing a gap in his teeth that he was fairly sure he himself had provided. Vahldan shook his head and looked away, refusing to be goaded.

Elan appeared at his side, shielding her eyes and scanning their surroundings. "Oh, look at the colors," she exclaimed. "Is that all wool?"

Vahldan followed her gaze to a nearby cloth merchant with their wares laid out in tiered bolts. He laughed and her head snapped around. "What?"

"I've never heard you even mention cloth, let alone its color or type."

"So?"

"So, it's funny."

She frowned. "What's so funny about it?"

"I don't know. What would you want with colored cloth?"

"If you must know, Neveka is going to make me a Bafranii shift."

Elan was clearly annoyed, so he didn't dare mention that he couldn't imagine her in anything except leggings and a tunic. For her, dressing up had only ever meant donning her best armor and the knee-high Saurian boots she'd taken to wearing.

Elan glanced back at Isidros's pavilion, then to the cloth merchant again. "Go," he said. "Malvius is right—they'd never try anything here. The giants and I have this."

"No, it's you who's right. It's silly." She turned away. Her veiled sadness made him sad.

"It's not silly if you really want a Bafranii shift." Her mouth quirked in a feigned smile. He leaned and whispered, "On second thought, maybe I should be begging you to wear a Bafranii shift."

She tilted her head back, her smile growing sly. "Oh? Suddenly you can picture it?"

He made his own grin wicked. "Maybe I'm picturing it bunched around your waist."

Elan's apparent delight was reward enough. "Naughty boy." She started for the cloth vendor's display. "I'll be right back."

Malvius's laughter rang behind him. Vahldan returned to watching over his little Hellainic treasure-maker. It seemed Malvius was right—perhaps having the imperial garrisons back to full strength really would create new opportunities.

There was hooting and commotion behind him. Vahldan spun, hand on his hilt. The crowd had cleared away from a squad of a half-dozen Tibairyan soldiers near the cloth merchant's stall. The moment he saw her auburn head surrounded by soldiers' helms, Vahldan was in motion, Thunar's Blessing flashing through him like a bolt. He pushed people out of the way to get to her, but there were so many. One soldier held Elan from behind and another held the steel point of a spear-length pilum at her throat. A third, wearing a crested helm, had his face right in hers. He seemed to be the leader. The leader drew Elan's daggers from her belt sheaths and slid them under his own belt. The man sneered, grasped her jutting chin with one hand, and reached down to grope her crotch.

Vahldan roared and shoved through the onlookers, drawing his sword as he arrived.

With astonishing speed, four of the Tibairya rounded on him, their pilums all about him, ready to jab. His survival instincts came through with the clean burn of Thunar's Blessing, halting his momentum. He dropped into a defensive crouch, calculating which of them to attack first. Their crest-helmed leader instantly had one of Elan's own daggers at her throat. The leader got behind Elan and barked an order. His soldiers swiftly encircled Vahldan, keeping their weapons poised throughout. Even through his outrage, he saw that any attack was suicide. Worse, he had increased the danger to Elan.

Vahldan was utterly helpless.

The pulse of Thunar's Blessing fell to a surge of fear. Then humiliation. The ugliness roiled beneath it all. A thousand thoughts flashed through his mind, arriving on the question that broke his will: If he died and Elan didn't, what would happen to her? He lowered his sword, emasculated. "Keep your hands off of her," he growled in Hellainic.

Elan suddenly twisted, freeing one hand. She was going for her sword. Fear and rage fuzzed his reaction. Before Vahldan could decide how to best support her effort, the brute behind her snatched her wrist and wrenched her arm, tightening his hold. She grimaced but refused to cry out.

The leader's sneer returned. "Ah, my fine Hippomache, I see you've brought a beau to market. He looks to be a dangerous upstart, same as you." His accent was thick, but his delight in debasing others was perfectly conveyed. The man's gaze drifted to Vahldan's lowered sword. "That's quite a blade, Teuton. I already had my eye on your wench's sword, but yours looks even finer. How sad for you that we shall have to confiscate them both."

"Here you both are!" Malvius burst through the crowd with Teavar and Jhannas at either shoulder. "I hope they've not caused you any trouble, Centurion. I'll gladly take them off of your hands now and remove them from the city."

The centurion squinted. "And who might you be?"

"Malvius, son of Anax Decebius—Magister of Thrakius and liaison to Prefect Sabinus." Malvius turned to Vahldan. "Sheath that blade," he scolded. Malvius's eye twitched in a veiled version of his habitual wink. His partner was asking him to play along. Malvius turned back to the stocky soldier. "Trust me, they shall be punished for troubling you." Vahldan could hardly breathe. He swallowed back the battle cry that longed to erupt from him and slowly did as bidden. Gods, he wanted to lash out. Letting go of the sword hilt felt like cutting off his hand.

Malvius waved to the giants to stay put and stepped closer to the soldiers, speaking rapidly in the Tibairyan tongue. Even now, Vahldan recognized his captain's air of authority. It only fueled Vahldan's outrage. How was it that a man Vahldan could so easily defeat, in any sort of contest, could seize such command in a situation that had rendered him impotent?

Malvius smiled as he produced a small cloth sack and held it out to the centurion. The ugliness flared. This was what it came to. Wealth. These imperials and Hellains actually valued it more than battle prowess, let alone honor. Through the murk of his fuzzy impulse to lash out, he vowed that one day he would teach these pigs the truth of such matters.

The glaring centurion only paused a moment before snatching the sack with a grunt of concession. Malvius spoke brightly as he casually approached Elan and took her by the elbow. The brutes reluctantly released her and Malvius slowly led her away. Elan's face was pinched with fury, but she raised her chin and allowed Malvius to compel her steps.

"Come now, all of you." Malvius switched back to Hellainic as he led them into the parting crowd. With his every muscle clenched, Vahldan managed to turn and follow. Someone shoved his back. He spun around, only to find their pilum tips back in his face. He silently growled, turned, and stumbled into motion, following Malvius. Their laughter rang behind him.

The centurion called, "I don't care who your father is, coin man. If ever I see them here again, those swords are mine. Understood?"

Malvius waved without looking and sped his step. The group formed up as they had coming in, with the giants leading and he and Elan following. As they fell in with the flow of traffic, Encho passed going the opposite direction. "Almost lost it, eh, Teuton?"

Vahldan's hand was instantly in motion, grasping his hilt. A hand clenched his wrist, preventing him from drawing. The forge flared with unvented heat.

He looked down, surprised to find Elan's hand holding him. She stared ahead, but her grip was firm. Her expression and posture instantly brought him back to himself. He sensed the humiliation beneath her simmering outrage. Which made him feel impotent again. "Encho sent them," he muttered in Gottari. She gave a single nod. "I'll kill him. I'll kill all of them."

"Not today," Elan said softly, also in Gottari but with a growl in her voice.

Malvius said, "I knew I should've forbidden those blades."

Rather than barking *Just try it!* as he dearly wanted, Vahldan said, "The only way a Tibairya will ever get this sword is by robbing a corpse."

"Which will be likely if you ever pull anything like that again." Malvius had that bedamned air of superiority again.

"You shouldn't have paid them," Vahldan groused.

"You'd still be in custody if I hadn't. Either that or dead."

"How much did you give them? I'll pay you." He hated the thought of owing Malvius on top of it all.

Malvius waved him off. "Forget it. It's more than you can afford."

He just couldn't let it go. "Dammit, why did you give them so much?"

Malvius looked over his shoulder. "Because it was easier, faster, and safer to pay a rogue soldier twice the amount of the fine a legatus would've levied in order to avoid the risk of having my imperial charter revoked. If they'd taken us into custody, you would've lost more than your precious swords. We could've lost everything. All of us. Did you not believe me when I said we shouldn't draw attention to ourselves?"

Elan elbowed Vahldan, who was wearing a scowl. "I believe you now," he conceded.

"Good. Then it was worth the price." Malvius turned to look. His smile was forced, smug.

In light of the man's infernal superiority, Vahldan needed to know. "So how did you convince him? To take the money?"

"I told him the swords were my family's property. Same as those who bore them."

"You told him we are slaves?" Vahldan asked, the ugliness instantly flaring again.

Malvius nodded. "And you should thank me for it. I know you hate slavery. But this time, the sanctity of a slave owner's rights saved your damned skins. Not to mention your swords."

It made it all the harder to bear, being saved by the gods bedamned slave trade.

CHAPTER 5
WANTS AND NEEDS

"*I have always had the sense that my father's goals did not become grander during his experience with Malvius, they became grander because of that experience. Sometimes it is through the discovery of the means that we find the goals those means provide.*"—*Brin Bright Eyes, Saga of Dania*

MALVIUS LEAPT to his feet when Neveka started to clear the table. "I'll get it," he said.

Neveka gently pushed him back. "It's my turn," she said. Her smile was warm. It was the one Malvius loved most. She was usually so canny, nigh impossible to read. Except when she wore this particular smile. He never wanted her to feel like she was here to serve him. After all, theirs was still a partnership. One she had established at that dark tavern in Akasas all those years ago. If he'd wanted a maid—or a whore, for that matter—he would've hired one.

It still surprised him. Malvius had never felt like this about another human being.

He scooted back from the table, giving her ample space to clear away their bowls. Elan sat staring into her cup across from him. She almost seemed as sullen as Vahldan had been since they left Nicomedya. "Well, we're sorry that your beau was unable to join us. But we're graced to have you in his stead."

Elan's expression remained dour. "I doubt I provided any grace, but I do not doubt that we are all better off. *My beau* has been in a shitty mood."

She evidently disapproved of Malvius's choice of words. But what else were she and Vahldan to one another? They shared a bed. And neither of them seemed romantically or sexually interested in anyone else. Ah well. Teutons. Best to steer well clear of their grumpiness. "Trust me, I'm aware of our friend's mood. I've been seeking the breeze that'll clear away the fog that's settled between us."

She took a sip and shook her head. "Don't bother. Sometimes he just likes fog."

Malvius hadn't noticed a phase that had lasted this long, but indeed, Vahldan could be a moody one. "Why is that, do you think?" She knew him better than anyone.

Elan's stare grew distant. He'd started to think she'd simply ignore him (as it wasn't uncommon) when she said, "He's always carried a lot in his saddlebags. He's sulking now because he thought he could fit all of Pontea in there, too."

"All of Pontea?" Malvius scratched at the stubble on his chin. "I don't understand."

Elan raised her eyebrows. "So he could take it home. You know, to flaunt it to those who doubted him."

This was new. Vahldan the Bold had something to prove? "Why would he need to? He's got his own host. Not to mention that he's the Bringer of your prophecy."

Elan's wry smile didn't reach her eyes. "First, it is *not* my prophecy. But, yes, you have a point. Because should not the Bringer of Urrinan be able to remake the world in his own image of it? Silly as it sounds, there are some at home who will say it."

Malvius poured a bit in both their cups. "Seems to me he's making a damn fine start."

She stared into her cup. "Still, he's always needed to make others believe before he could convince himself. Never mind that he should avoid caring, let alone trying. Most of these moods are really more about whether or not he feels he's convincing his dead father of something or other."

Ouch. That sounded familiar. "Convincing his father, eh? Of what this time? That he's right or wrong? That he's done things just like Poppa would have? Completely differently? That he's as good? Better?"

Elan took a long drink and swallowed. "Yes," she said.

Malvius laughed. "Ah. I see."

Her gaze narrowed. "Do you?"

"Yes. Because I have the same father. Well, except mine's not dead. Yet." He gave her a wry grin. "Though some days it's hard to be sure."

Elan's dour expression finally broke. "It depends on the day with Vahldan and his father as well. I never really thought much about the name his father's enemies had for him. It makes more sense to me now than ever."

"What was it?"

"Long Shadow." Elan released one of her huffing laughs, which made him laugh louder. Elan's smile lit her from within, a rare glimpse of the real woman he wished he knew better.

Neveka came to take away the last of their dinner wares. "Since you claim to know so much about sons and fathers, you ought to go set him back on course."

Malvius didn't think he deserved the scolding tone. "Hey, it would be rude to leave our guest."

Neveka and Elan shared a look. Neveka tsked. "Poor man. Can't even see that he's been smothering the conversation all evening." His beautiful Bafranii partner looked back at him, her smile growing warm again. "Must I say it?"

"What?" Malvius asked defensively.

"Get out of here and give us girls some space, would you?" She shooed him with the snap of a hand cloth.

He held up his hands. "It's not the first time I've failed to notice a change in the wind." He stood and snatched up the half-full flagon and then went to grab an extra cup.

Neveka went to the cabin door. She opened it and waited, hand on hip, silently scolding him even as he left.

"For toasting the long shadows of fathers," Malvius pleaded, hoisting the flagon. She rolled her eyes and he hurried out, trying not to be too curious about what these two very different women had suddenly found in common.

ELAN STOOD at the foot of the surprisingly large and cushy bed in the captain's quarters, feeling awkward as Neveka rummaged through a trunk full of colored cloth. So many colors! It was like the merchant's entire stall, except it was all in a rumple.

"How many shifts do you own?" Elan asked.

Neveka shrugged. "Dressing well was essential to my former work. It was the only part of it I liked. And now Malvius indulges me. Ah, here's the one I was thinking of. The cloth is from the Peshtari. They shear it from their mountain goats, when they're not fucking them." The woman extracted a long strip of blue cloth from the pile. Neveka leapt onto the bed, kneeling to hold it against Elan's frontside. Her smile grew. "Yes, perfect. Well, it's not quite long enough, but it makes those eyes of yours even bluer. I'd give anything to have those eyes."

Till then Elan had never noticed that the woman had eyes the color of burnished leather. "I think yours are beautiful. They're so unique. Everybody has blue eyes."

Neveka scrunched her face in an exaggerated frown. "Maybe where you come from. But that doesn't matter. Believe me, if you wear this, yours will stun even someone who's seen a thousand blue eyes." Neveka held the garment out to her. "You'll see. Try it on." As soon as Elan took it, Neveka flopped onto the bed, waiting.

Elan glanced at the door, shrugged, and pulled off her tunic. She started untying the cording on her leggings, feeling even more awkward. Neveka was so curvy, so soft. So feminine.

Elan got down to her woolen underpants and breast thong. She held the shift out, trying to figure out how to put it on. "Oh no you don't. You won't need this." Neveka sprang up to unfasten her breast thong. "Unless you plan on getting in another scrum tonight, that is." The woman grinned at her own quip. "Who knew?" Neveka said, leaning back on the bed, appraising Elan's body.

Elan crossed her arms, hiding herself. "What?"

"That you have those!" Neveka took Elan's hands and gently pulled them to her sides, openly ogling her breasts. "Oh, my dear. You should let them loose more often."

In spite of her intrusiveness, Neveka seemed sincere. Elan fought the impulse to cover up again and instead raised her chin. "They're loose as often as I like."

Neveka's smile became sly. "Let's see how you like them in this." She gathered the shift in her hands and eased it over Elan's head. "The cut is sure to remind your man what you've been hiding." Neveka smoothed the cloth over her hips. It felt so soft and sleek. And airy!

The Bafranii woman reached to touch Elan's kestrel necklace. "And now your beautiful talisman shows as well." Elan grasped it protectively. "It means much, I see," Neveka said. "Between you and him?" Elan nodded and Neveka gave her a nod. "All the better."

Neveka dug in the trunk and pulled out a rectangular looking glass, about as long as her forearm. Looking glasses were not so rare in Pontea as they were in Dania. Elan avoided them, though. She found they made her overly self-conscious. And who needed that?

Neveka held the glass up so that Elan's reflection was lit in the lamplight. The blue of the shift was the color of the deep sea on a cloudless day. It made a sharp contrast with her auburn hair and pale skin. And yes, it seemed to make her eyes even bluer. How odd.

Elan ran her hands over the slippery cloth, from her waist to her hips, surprised by the look of her own shape. "You really *are* a woman," Neveka said. There was laughter in her voice.

Elan knew she was joking, but... "That Tibairyan chieftain in the city... When he grabbed me, he said it was to see if I had a cock or not."

Neveka's smile faded. "Men are such asses. I'd say they're fools, but all too often they know just how to hurt us." She folded each of the short sleeves up over Elan's biceps. "No, there can be no doubt, Elan of Dania. You are a woman. A fierce and beautiful woman." Neveka stood back, clearly admiring her. She reached for a small vial, pulled the stopper, and tipped it to her finger over the top. "A dab of this, and my work is done. There is no way your man will be able to keep his hands off of you tonight." The potion smelled both musky and floral at once. "In fact," Neveka added, "if he sees you in this, he'll marry you just to keep the rest of them away."

Elan's smile faded. "No. That he will not do."

"Don't be so doubtful. I mean, I understand why Malvius won't marry me. In fact, he won't even force his family to acknowledge me, even when I'm in the same room as them. But you? I can't imagine a better match than you and Vahldan."

Elan felt herself flushing. She grasped the kestrel again and turned away. "Our destinies are entwined. But Vahldan will never bond with me."

"How can you be so sure?"

"Because of the prophecy. The seeress who foretold his destiny also foretold a son." Neveka raised her brows, looking hopeful. "Another woman's son," Elan added.

Neveka's expression fell. "Oh. Let me guess—the seeress?"

"No. Her daughter. One who had yet to be born when this was foretold."

"And Vahldan bought into an unseen cargo like that? One that may never ship?"

"If you asked him, he would deny it. Especially now, since the supposed mother of his foretold son is still a girl. But he won't rule it out."

"Why don't you give him a son in the meantime?" Neveka's eyes gave her the once over again. "I mean, you're clearly ready to breed."

Elan pressed her lips tightly. "Vahldan hates it when I speak of having a child. He hates it because if he is the Bringer, his son must be the scion of his people's two greatest clans. We never speak of it, but we both know my father was born of the rival clan."

Neveka frowned. "I don't get it. Isn't that all good? Your child could bypass the girl of the seeress, right?"

Elan hated the topic, but she'd come too far to leave Neveka confused. "In theory. But any child of mine would be far from an ideal candidate. It's why we don't speak of it."

"Whyever not?"

"His ambition." She huffed a laugh. "Although they would never say it to the face of one of my people's warriors, the Gottari consider my existence to be the result of a sex ritual to a heathen goddess. I am a bastard, left to a mother's tribe by a father who is long dead. On the other hand, this girl who is the daughter of the seeress is also the daughter of the rival clan's chieftain. Not to mention that the rival clan is the more powerful of the two. Such a union would be a first and very momentous. It would restore much prestige for Vahldan's clan, and even the rival clansmen would sense the glory in it. Theirs would be the sort of match that makes for songs. More than that, it could serve to raise our moody shipmate to become the most powerful chieftain in Gottari history. It's what those who believe in the bedamned prophecy expect of him, and he knows it. Meanwhile, though we never speak of her, this girl-child is always there between us. The very thought of my having a child first can only complicate things."

Neveka took up their wine cups and handed Elan hers. "It all sounds terribly unfair."

Elan forced herself to smile and shrugged. "Fair or not, we are many things to one another, Vahldan and I. Among them, we are friends who fuck. And you're right. I'm ready to breed. The dreamers—myself included—have never foreseen that I will have a son. But I will have my daughter. She has been foreseen, and in her I believe. Whether or not it's fair to Vahldan, my daughter will be his."

Neveka raised an eyebrow. "A daughter, eh?"

"Yes. I know it. I feel it deep inside. It's as if she already exists. My grandmother says so, too, and she is a vaunted dreamer and very wise. My daughter shall come. I have but to bring her into this world. And once she is here, I will see to it that she remains free of the shackles of this bedamned prophecy that imprisons me. This, too, I know."

Rather than question her, Neveka gave her another emphatic nod and clicked her cup to Elan's. "Wearing this, you will make a good start on her arrival tonight. This *I* know. Although you will remain the only one to feel it deep inside." They both giggled like protégés.

As their laughter faded, Neveka's expression grew concerned. "What is it?" Elan asked.

Neveka's tone was sober. "Tell me, my friend. What is it you seek?"

"As I said. A daughter."

Neveka's gaze narrowed. "But what do you hope will then happen?"

Why should that question startle Elan? She searched her mind, seeking an answer that didn't come easily. "That Vahldan will come to see, I suppose. That he'll look beyond the prophecy; see what he already has." It sounded weak, voicing it. But it had to be so. Elan had no other plan. "Yes," she affirmed. "Once our daughter is born, he'll see."

Neveka rocked back, cradling her cup, releasing Elan from scrutiny. "I have known more men than I have cared to," Neveka said, "and I can assure you that they rarely see any farther than they wish to look." The Bafranii woman's sly smile reappeared. "In fact, they rarely see beyond their cocks. And an ambition like the one you say he holds is like an overlarge cock. Those who own them cannot help but to indulge the urges they instill."

GULLWING HAD PASSED through the Straits without challenge. Which meant the danger of imperial intervention was greatly diminished. For now. Vahldan was relieved. He'd had enough of imperials. For now. Someday the encounters with them would be on his terms. By the gods, he swore to it.

The winds were light as they headed southeast, following the Pontean Sea coastline toward Bafrana. He sat at the stern, legs dangling under the rail, watching the sun set on the Megarian hills. His hands were carving by rote, the shavings floating in the ships draft, scattering in the churn of its wake.

Vahldan had started the carving session by laying into the chunk of firewood coarsely, almost violently. It helped to release the heat from the forge. In spite of his lack of intention for the wood itself, the form of the piece began to emerge—calling him to task. He began to truly feel his carving knife and the wood in his hands, up his arms and on into his chest. The feeling settled as a drive in his belly and created an unbidden picture in his mind. He had no choice but to remove the excess.

As it so often did, the very process took him, mind and spirit.

It wasn't just that the forge had cooled. His muscles had loosened. His shoulders fell slack. Each breath released a bit more of what had been trapped within. With each swipe of the blade, each released breath, the ugliness that had been simmering in his belly settled to stillness.

"Another bird?"

Vahldan stopped. He looked to find Malvius proffering a cup, peeking over his shoulder at his work-in-progress. He set the knife aside and took the cup. "It's looking that way." He held the wood out to give it a look as he took a drink. It was good wine, at least. Malvius always brought out the good wine when he wanted something. Vahldan supposed he wanted what he'd been after since the incident in Nicomedya. His partner wanted things to go back to the way they were before.

Too bad. Vahldan knew Nicomedya was another of those moments when things could never be the same again. Same as when the wing burned. Same as when he plunged the sword into his father's flesh. Same as when he retrieved the futhark sword from the muddy battlefield. Same as when he first saw the ships in the harbor at Akasas. All he could do was recognize it and accept it.

Malvius sat with a groan, dangling his feet under the rail in imitation. "You're not sure?"

"I never am at first," Vahldan admitted with a shrug. "Eventually the wood lets me know what's in there."

Malvius waggled his eyebrows. "Seems like the wood's been hiding a lot of birds."

"I suppose so."

Malvius looked out to sea. "Makes sense, I guess. Maybe birds are in the wood because they spend so much time in trees."

Vahldan laughed. "I think, for me, it's because birds have always had a lot to say."

"What's this one saying?"

Vahldan held the piece up again. The body was still unformed. He wasn't sure if it was standing or roosting. Or maybe it was a waterfowl swimming. "Something about being patient, I suppose."

Malvius squinted at it. "That so?"

"Yeah. He wants to fly, to hunt, but he understands that he can't. Not just yet."

Malvius grinned. "I must admit, I'm glad to see it's not in flight. I mean, there's no fire to burn a broken wing." He laughed but Vahldan found he couldn't make himself join in.

Malvius squirmed and looked off again. "Vahldan, about the other day, in the market—"

"I won't let it happen again," he interjected.

"I know that. What I'm steering toward is that I can see how what happened has put your lines in a tangle. But we all lose track of the boom. We all take a thump now and again. We just have to sail on. Oh, it'll leave your bell humming for a bit. But, if we're willing to learn from it, over the long haul a good thump can sharpen our wits."

Vahldan could never stay angry with him. Very little of what kept Vahldan simmering inside was actually Malvius's fault. It wasn't his partner's fault he'd been born one of them. And he had a point—it had sharpened his wits in regard to what he must do. It showed him what—and who—he would be up against if he were to fully embrace his destiny.

Vahldan took a drink, savored the flavor a moment, and swallowed. Before coming to Pontea, he'd never tasted the like of such fine wine. This place was so restrictive and yet so expansive. "Funny, I was just thinking about what I learned from... you know, the incident."

Malvius clinked his cup to Vahldan's. "Ha, see there? Should've known you'd have already cast the nets. What're you hauling up?"

Vahldan set the cup aside, picked up the knife, and idly shaved the excess. "I guess the biggest thing it showed me is how so many of the folks I hope to lead have felt for years."

"Which is how?"

"Powerless. Abused and furious about it. Unable to resist or retaliate."

The sun had set, but the confusion in Malvius's frown was apparent even in the twilight. "Who makes those you seek to lead feel like this? I thought you were their long-awaited Bringer?"

"My being proclaimed as the Bringer certainly hasn't helped anyone. It's not like I'm the only chieftain in my homeland. There are forces there more powerful than any chieftain. More powerful and far more abusive."

"Such as?"

Vahldan stopped carving. "Most of my followers are simple herdsmen. They're beholden to those who control the land for grazing. They're also at the whim of the wool markets. The men who control those two things have a guild. The guild is bigger than any one of its members. It seems almost to have gained a will of its own. An evil will. The guild has become the most powerful force in the lives of most Danians. And it's corrupt to the core."

Malvius chuckled. "Sounds like the imperial bureaucracy." Vahldan turned to him, waiting. "Oh. I see. Hence, the abuse you and Elan experienced showed you how they feel."

Vahldan tapped his temple with the flat of the blade. "I knew you'd get there."

Malvius grinned. "I actually think I am getting there. This is why you're so intent on collecting such a trove—why you're tighter than a tar-sealed barrel, never leaking a drop of what you've accumulated."

"Hey, I'm not that tight."

"Vahldan, please. You are. And I'm beginning to see why. You want to go back and be a real force."

"I suppose I am pretty tight," Vahldan admitted, mostly to avoid confirming the astute guess. He hated the thought of being so transparent.

"So," Malvius began. "Are you looking to buy your way into this guild?"

He felt his face contort. "No! I don't want to be one of them. I want to beat them."

Malvius took his pique in stride. "All right. That's easy enough."

"Easy?" He harrumphed. "It's not like paying off a centurion."

"Actually, it should be just like that." Malvius was serious. "Dealing with imperials is easy, once you split them off from the system. Trust me, if these guild members are human men, they'll be just like bureaucrats. Even Teutonics are humans, right?" He laughed again.

Once again Vahldan couldn't join him. "Very funny," he deadpanned.

"Sorry, I just mean that you folks have a reputation for being tough—unbreakable, even. But I guarantee you that each of these tough Teutons has one thing they're more concerned about than what's best for their precious guild. You can guess, right?"

Vahldan could. "What's best for themselves."

Malvius raised his cup in salute. "Precisely! All you need to do is separate them and make yourself indispensable to each of them."

"Indispen...?" It was a word he'd yet to learn.

"Indispensable. It means making yourself vital to their self-interest."

"How am I supposed to do that? They all hate everything about me."

"Simple. You find the thing they want more than they need and be the man who can give it to them."

"Want more than they need? That doesn't sound right."

"Ah, but that's the trick. You see, my boy, wants are much more powerful than needs. And so few people realize it. You offer a man the choice between what he needs and what he wants, trust me, he'll choose what he wants every time. Even if it ends up killing him."

"Like what? I mean, I would guess they all want more wealth. But I can't just pay each one off. Can I?"

"Sometimes treasure works. Especially if each one thinks he's getting more than the others. But beware. The others always find out. Then each one feels cheated and wants more. It never ends. But there's more to it than payoffs. You have to dive deeper. Take the centurion. I immediately saw what he wanted: esteem. He's the sort who degrades others to make himself feel less degraded. He delights in being the one who makes others afraid, probably because he's afraid himself. It wasn't just that I gave him more than a month's worth of pay. I made him the most important man there—more important even than the son of an anax. You know I don't throw that title around lightly. Hades' realm, I only told you after you visited the ole' family homestead. I pulled it out for the bully because I knew what my status would mean to him. I sweetened the pot by making you two into slaves, which made you less than human— beneath him, unworthy of the effort it would take to continue your degradation. See what I mean?"

Vahldan felt a mild stirring of the ugliness. "I do see." He still hated what had happened, but he did indeed see it in a new light. He tried to swallow but his throat had gone dry. He held out his cup.

Malvius poured for him. "Good. Now be sure to look closely at how this works. I separated the centurion from the imperial bureaucracy that both empowers him and keeps him bound. I made myself, and thereby my wishes, indispensable to him. I freed him from his bindings but left him with the power he feels he's already earned from his station. By doing so, I gave him what he wanted rather than what he needed. You can do the same with these guildsmen back home. Alliances are difficult things to defeat. But they're also difficult to maintain. Even if every ally feels they need the alliance, they all have wants. And wants win out over needs every time. They can be the wedge that pries them apart."

Vahldan thought about the centurion, imagined his smug face. "But couldn't he just have continued to do what he wanted? I mean, if he really wanted power more than coin, what did you have to do with it?"

Malvius smiled. "Ah, a clever observation. The coin I offered provided him with the way out of what was becoming a tricky situation. You have to realize that when I revealed myself as the Thrakian anax's son, I showed him not only that I could leave him with the power he wanted, but that I also had a fairly solid means to take it away. Or at least diminish it. He might have gambled that I wouldn't try, but he knew I could've sought to expose how beholden to his superiors he truly is. Instead, he was able to take the coin and keep the power I left him holding. A double victory."

Vahldan studied his face. "Do you think the centurion knew you?"

"Only by reputation," Malvius said, sounding self-satisfied. "To make this work, at some point you've got to do something ruthless. It tends to leave a lasting impression." Vahldan suspected Malvius was referring to what he'd done to his father and sister when he'd stolen their fleet and returned successful enough to pay his way out of their retribution. It had certainly cemented his partner's reputation. He'd been bold, and the gods had rewarded him for it.

"Capisce?" Malvius said.

"Capeese?" Another new word.

Malvius's grin shone in the lingering light. "Sorry, that one's something the Tiberians say. It just means, do we understand one another?"

It reminded him of someone—someone who also left a lasting impression. "Back in Dania there's a woman I admire—a queen, actually. She just says, *'Understood?'*" He barked it in his best imitation of Keisella.

Malvius laughed. "Ooo, I bet that gets results."

Vahldan felt himself grinning. "It does."

"A queen, eh? You really do know people in high places. I'll bet she knows that wants win out over needs, doesn't she?"

His words struck Vahldan like a swinging boom. "Huh. Now that you mention it, I'm certain she does."

"I see you do now, too." Malvius raised his cup. "Understood?"

"Understood," he rushed to reply as he would've to Keisella. They clinked cups and drank.

Vahldan took the point position, walking ahead of Neveka's donkey, which was struggling to pull the creaking old wagon that they'd purchased just for this delivery. The rest of the squad was arrayed along either side of their cargo. No one else could lead this mission; it had to be him. His crew had to be led by their Lion Lord, for this was to be an Amalus mission. More so than any other since they had set sail on the Pontean.

In spite of the cold, Vahldan threw his cloak behind his shoulders, making it apparent that he wasn't wearing a sword. He hated how naked he felt without it. The lack of a hilt to grab did nothing to quieten the stirrings of the ugliness.

He wasn't sure if it was a boon or a curse, but the gibbous moon fully illuminated the dusty road. The rut beside the road stank with the sewage it carried from Nicomedya to the Straits. He hoped they weren't too late. It had taken several trips from ship to shore in the fishing boat they'd hired to get the spice barrels to the beach and loaded on the wagon.

He glanced back at Teavar and Jhannas, marching stiffly, cloaks held closed, leading the flanking lines of warriors on either side of their valuable goods. He'd brought a score—likely enough to put the odds in his favor. Still, Vahldan had sent Herodes and Ermanaric to scout the meeting site, just in case. If the situation looked at all fraught, he could still abort the mission.

Vahldan had all but commanded Elan to stay behind, which had left her sulking. It wasn't much of a change in her typical mood, though he knew she was more annoyed than usual. Of late she was often quiet and pensive, and he worried that she was growing more distant by the week.

He hoped that asking her to don the blue Bafranii shift when he returned would help to dispel her anger. A surprising side effect of her recent moodiness was how fond she'd become of their lovemaking. It seemed to have started when Neveka gave her the shift. She seemed either to be feeling sulky or sexy, and there was little in between. Given the choice, he had to keep seeking the latter mood.

Vahldan had avoided telling her what he'd planned for tonight because he knew she wouldn't approve. Mostly because she hated it when he was at risk and she wasn't able to provide guardianship. She was still devoted to her original duty, if to little else about their lives abroad. He was starting to wonder if she was losing sight of their shared goals. She grew moody when he discussed the means to achieving them, and tonight's mission was that, first and foremost. She also hated it when he reminded her that they needed to achieve something big in order to change things. And gods forbid any mention of *the bedamned Urrinan,* as she always called it. He'd told her time and again that the prophecy would be an important part of the means to the ends they had sought when they had first set sail. As would putting themselves in harm's way. Of course, pursuing a goal so big as theirs—challenging those who controlled the very means to wealth and power—would require no small amount of risk. She alone among his host seemed opposed to such talk. The goal required risk, but what sort of life would they have without it?

"The greater the risk..." he whispered to himself.

He glanced at the man who'd taught him the mantra seated on the front bench of the cart. Unfortunately, Vahldan hadn't been able to command Malvius to stay behind. His partner was too damned excited about receiving this first payment from Isidros for the first shipment of their new pact.

Nicomedya's walls loomed over them, casting them in shadow, before they saw the glow of the archway in a culvert at the wall's base. Vahldan scanned the wall top above, looking for sentries. It seemed ridiculous that the Tibairya would leave such an obvious breach point unguarded, but Malvius had assured him that the Tibairya posed little risk. Most every sentry in the city accepted some form of graft from Isidros. Apparently Malvius himself had been party to other transactions via this same sewer exit.

Making trades in sewers to avoid paying tariffs. This from his nobly-born partner and their esteemed new trading counterpart. Ah, Pontean traders—so refined, so dignified.

Several of Isidros's men loitered near the torchlit archway. He saw no more than a dozen, though there were likely some hidden nearby, as were his own scouts. Still, it seemed the Amalus had superior numbers. He scanned the interior, his eyes adjusting to the torchlight. He was happy to see that Encho stood front and center, hands on hips. He was even happier that he didn't see Isidros. Malvius had assured him that Isidros would send others to do his dirty work. If only Malvius had done the same.

Ah well. Malvius would've learned of his plan soon enough. He suspected that in the long run it would be for the best to have him witness this encounter firsthand.

Encho appraised him as they approached. Vahldan didn't try to suppress the ugliness as it began to flow through him. For this, he doubted he'd be able to find his way to the clean burn of Thunar's Blessing. This night's work would be ugly, after all. He would simply have to trust his men to keep him safe.

The Illyrican's scowl became a sneer. Gods, the man was ugly—inside and out. "No sword this time, eh, Teuton?"

This wasn't going to be so difficult after all.

Vahldan forced his lips to imitate a smile. "Not this time. A lesson well-learned. Very cute of you—the way you pointed out our swords to the centurion."

Encho snorted. "Ha—you should've seen the look on your face when that walking stump grabbed your Hippomache's muff."

The ugliness rose like a fog from a bog, clouding his senses and cramping his limbs. Vahldan fought through the murk, checking to make sure his men slowly drifted into position. The rest of Isidros's thugs remained at ease. Most of them hadn't even bothered to stand, let alone take a defensive position.

"Enough of this," Malvius called, climbing from the front bench. "You brought a donkey, didn't you?"

Encho frowned. "Naw. No donkey's coming down the sewer where we comes and goes."

"Well, you're getting the wagon, but you're not taking my donkey. He's an old friend." Malvius started undoing the straps to the wagon's breeching.

"We don't want your stinking donkey, your anaxship." Encho dipped in a mocking bow.

Really? He thought the donkey stank? An unwashed thug loitering in a sewer? Within the fog, the forge flared. As the heat rose, the edges of Vahldan's vision blurred. "I'm sure you'll want to take a look before you pay," Vahldan offered, beckoning the Illyrican to the wagon bed.

Encho made a couple of nodding motions, and two of his men finally bothered to stir. The pair began a flanking stroll as Encho headed for the tarped barrels. Vahldan recognized the closer one as Encho's second-in-command, a curly-headed Saurian. Teavar was on that one's side. Good.

Vahldan felt like he was visibly vibrating, that he'd give the plan away before his target arrived in position. Gods, it looked like Encho would get to the wagon first. Would the man dare to pull the tarp back? He sought to keep from rushing.

As they'd presumed, the Illyrican stopped at the back of the cart and stood awaiting him. Vahldan reached for the tarp, his head reeling. "I must admit, you really got me last time." The ugliness lurched as Vahldan flipped the tarp back. His hand instantly found its missing appendage. As soon as the sword hilt was in his grip, he swung.

"But it looks like I got you this time."

He barely noticed the impact, so clean was the cut. Encho's hands flew to his throat and blood instantly oozed through his fingers to dribble down onto his tunic. The gods had indeed made Vahldan an efficient killer. The ugly Illyrican's eyes bulged and he gasped as he collapsed to his knees. Encho's awareness of his fate was clearly written upon him.

Vahldan couldn't find any focus but on his bloody victim as commotion swirled around him. It was everything he could do to keep from striking again and again. As he fought the ugliness, his surroundings were a blur. With effort, he scanned the scene. Each of his magnificent lions now brandished their hidden swords. Teavar was nearest, with the tip of his broadsword at the chin of Encho's second. Teavar calmly nodded. All was in hand.

Better still, he'd managed to kill and then to regain himself. Without Elan's presence.

Encho was still on his knees, making horrible wheezing sounds. Vahldan held the futhark sword up before the thug's staring eyes. "It *is* a nice sword, isn't it? In fact, generations of my forefathers used it to make sure that pigs like you found their way to the mud they deserve." Encho drooped, falling to his side in the slop, wordlessly dying. Vahldan pushed his victim's filthy tunic up with the sword. He cut the tie to Encho's purse with a flick and bent for it. It was heavy with his employer's coin. Blood formed a rivulet, rolling through the mud to the sewer.

"What have you done?"

It was Malvius. His captain was in shock, gaping at the body.

"I did what needed to be done." Vahldan tried to veil his labored breath, hide his trembling hands, and avert the eyes that he knew were still crazed.

"Dammit, Vahldan! Isidros and I had a truce. This is the first shipment in a trading pact, for the gods' sake!"

Vahldan drew a deep breath and released it. The ugliness was still receding. He turned to face Malvius and shrugged. "Encho and I had no truce. I'm sure the pact will be fine. In fact, I think it'll be more secure and profitable than ever."

Malvius surveyed the scene with wide eyes. His lions remained perfectly positioned to cover Isidros's men. "How could you? You killed his lead man." Malvius's voice was tremulous.

Malvius's observation nudged him to the next step in the process—dealing with the number-two man. Vahldan presumed it was the Saurian.

"A wise man once gave me some advice," he said to Malvius as he moved. "He said that at some point you've got to do something ruthless. He said it tends to leave a lasting impression. I'd say Isidros will now understand what it costs to cross us. I'm sure others will gain an impression as well."

Malvius leaned on the donkey, looking too weak to stand

without aid. "Gods, man, we're in their territory. Do you really think they're going to just let us walk away?"

Vahldan smiled at the kneeling form of Encho's second. The Saurian was scowling, muscles straining, still poised for action. "Oh, I'm quite sure we'll walk away," he said to Malvius. "In fact, if these men don't swear to allow it, there's going to be a lot more blood flowing into that sewer."

He bent to the Saurian. "That would be a waste, now, wouldn't it?" Teavar's blade tickled the apple of the man's throat. Vahldan stooped to face the man. "You'll be taking Encho's lead, correct? You will swear to our safe passage from here, will you not?"

The Saurian's lip curled, and he suddenly spat. Vahldan's hand instantly grasped Teavar's wrist and thrusted. The giant's sword was apparently very sharp. As the man choked on his own blood and flopped to the dusty track, Vahldan said, "I guess not." He turned to the others in Isidros's band. "Who's next?" He strode to the man who'd flanked Encho's other side. Jhannas had him covered. This one was older, his cheeks pudgy and veiny. Sort of like an old babe, if babes could be drunks. Babe Cheeks had a pathetic expression, trying to harden his watery eyes, failing to veil his terror. "You seem wiser than your friend. I'm sure you'll be willing to swear to our safe departure and to deliver a message to Isidros for me. Won't you?"

Vahldan leaned in, staring the old man down. The man's babe cheeks trembled, his eyes scanning the scene. Apparently he didn't like what he saw. The old sod nodded. "Aye. Just let the others go."

"Good. Tell your anax that we look forward to continuing the trading pact that he and Malvius have agreed to. Also tell him that Vahldan of the Gottari will not be crossed. Ever." He looked into the shadowy recesses of the cavern. "Now, all of you get back. Face the back of the cavern with your hands flat on the wall overhead. Stay that way until we're gone or pay the price in blood. Or should I say in more blood?"

Once they had all shuffled toward the back, Vahldan nodded to Teavar. The Amalus slowly withdrew. Vahldan threw the coin purse to Malvius. Suddenly and magically regaining his spine, Malvius not only caught it, but he also opened it and checked the contents.

His crew walked briskly but did not run, heading back along the swale without speaking, the chorus of frogs drowning out their footsteps. Vahldan turned to glance at Malvius riding the donkey. The Hellain captain rocked with the little creature's gait, and even in the moonlight Vahldan gleaned Malvius's lingering dismay. It reminded him of when he'd first laid eyes on the Hellain, riding out from Akasas to confront those who'd taken his ships—terrified but brave.

Vahldan was certain all could be made well between them again. Malvius tended to swiftly recover to adjust to new circumstances. Especially if there was coin in it for him to do so.

Once they were all aboard the fishing boat, his men helping to row them into the mild chop of the Straits, Vahldan moved to the prow, where Malvius sat gazing at his anchored fleet. He took a seat a span away. "Why?" Malvius said without looking.

"As I said, it needed to be done."

Malvius turned to him. "How could you take such a step without speaking to me?"

Vahldan heard the hurt in his voice. "Would you have agreed to it?"

Malvius shook his head. "To that? How could I? No."

"Then I kept the two of us from a confrontation. One that might not have ended well."

Malvius's smile was a twisted frown. "And you're sure it will end well this way?"

Vahldan shrugged. "No. But at least the deed is done. And we got paid."

Malvius looked out to his ships growing closer. "I trusted you as a business partner."

Vahldan softly laughed. "I'm all but certain there was a moment, not so long ago, when your sister and your father said the same of you."

Malvius's head snapped around. He wore a bitter scowl. "I don't need this. I could have hired any gang of thugs in Pontea for half of what I pay you."

Vahldan leaned back on the gunwale. "You still can. But you won't."

"Won't I?"

He shook his head. "It's true that you need protection. You need muscle. Any gang of thugs in Pontea can provide those things. And most would be thrilled with half of our take." Malvius's scowl faded, his puzzlement apparent. Vahldan smiled. "Muscle is what you need, but it's not what you want."

Malvius nodded in recognition. "Ah. And you presume to know what I want."

"I do." He nodded toward the anchored fleet bobbing just ahead. "You want not just to captain your own ship, but to own an entire fleet. And once you do, it won't be enough. You want to command a shipping empire. The finest and fastest ships, the best warehousing, the most famous and notorious name in all of Pontean trading. Which means that you *want* the most renowned and lethal fighting force in all of Pontea. A force that everyone knows by their reputation."

Malvius looked away and said, "You think so, eh?"

"I know so. I know exactly what you want, because it's exactly what I want. You want to beat your father. Not just to win a few battles, but to emerge as the clear victor from the war everyone knows you two have long waged. You want Decebius to know that he was wrong, and you want everyone to know not just that you outdid him, but that you've become greater than he ever dreamed you could be."

They drew alongside Gullwing and the crew hauled in the oars. Two rope ladders dropped from the deck above. Vahldan grasped one and beckoned Malvius to climb first with a bow of his head. "After you, partner."

Before he started to climb, Malvius turned to him and said, "Tell me you won't ever surprise me like that again."

Vahldan didn't hesitate. "I won't ever surprise you like that again."

Malvius paused and pursed his lips. "Don't tell me if you're lying to me."

Vahldan smirked. "I would never."

ARNEGERN CLIMBED THE ROCKY RIDGE. She came into view on the crest, just as he'd suspected. Mara faced away, overlooking the road to Danihem, outlined by the setting sun, hugging her knees against the chill wind. He came up beside her. Mara didn't bother to look. She knew he was coming.

The eldest daughter of the Outcast was an alert girl, unsurprisingly.

"I thought I'd find you here." She shivered, silent. He took off his cloak, dropped it onto her shoulders, and sat down next to her. She pulled his cloak tight and nodded her thanks. "Mother and Father were worried. Mother in particular. She says you're too thin to be missing meals. Especially heading into winter."

Mara kept staring west. "It's been five years." She spoke softly, as if to herself.

"Even at the onset he said it would be that or more," Arnegern said.

Mara gazed into the snow-capped mountains. "The passes will be closed now."

Arnegern nodded. "Most likely."

She drew a deep breath and sighed it out. "Spring will come and they'll sail again."

Arnegern nodded. "It's unlikely they would ever leave before autumn."

"Another year," Mara said, choking back emotion.

"Vahldan is doing well, you know. Elan, too. They all are. You'll see."

For the first time, Mara looked at him. "I know you're right." Her words belied the sadness in her eyes.

She was still a girl, but she had a certain grace. Her eyes were sad now, but they were keen. Mara never missed a thing. She was calm, serene. And without a trace of the awkwardness of most girls her age. Arnegern had never known her mother, but his father often spoke of how much Mara reminded him of Frisanna.

Mara was imbued by the spirits of her ancestors and wiser than her years. She would be a beautiful woman. Soon. She would be old enough to betroth in four short years. No, wait—it was only three now. How had that happened? She sensed him staring again. Rather than look away, she gazed back—deeply into him, as if she saw his soul. Gods, those eyes of hers.

As if she sensed his growing admiration and wanted to rein it back in, she looked away. "Sometimes I feel useless, just waiting like this," she said.

"Vahldan bid you to take care of Kemella, and the gods know you've done that."

Mara smiled into the sunset. "Kemella hardly needs to be taken care of."

Arnegern laughed. "She's growing faster than a birch on a bank. She'll need a bed of her own soon. And you deserve some space for yourself."

"Oh, I don't mind. I'd probably never get to sleep without her tossing around all night." Mara shook her head, her smile fading. "Funny, I feel like it's she who comforts me."

Arnegern knew what she meant. "Kemella is sort of like an adult in a child's body. Mother says she has an ancient soul."

Mara looked up at the sky, her eyes shining with unshed tears. "It's just... I miss him. Kemella doesn't even remember him. She never knew Mother and Father. Eldavar misses all of them, too. More than he lets on."

Indeed, with every hand he grew in height, Eldavar seemed to grow more somber. "I'm sure you know this, Mara, but trust me.

Your brother will only stay away as long as he must. Every message we get reassures us of his success. He knows what he's doing."

"I know it's so." She wiped her eyes.

"Remember, too, that even now good things are happening. Our cousins are out there, singing his praises. Many heed their songs. With each passing season, more herdsmen pledge to bend the knee to our new Lion Lord. Many have committed their sons to his service. The more the guild tightens their grip, the more strength they provide to the host that will soon rival them. Our day is coming. The Amalus clan ascends once again. Just as your father foretold."

"As it shall be." Mara hugged her knees again, her face lit by the orange glow of the sunset. "For the Bringer has indeed come."

She seemed so certain. Arnegern's faith waxed and waned, but Vahldan's sisters were ardent believers. Mara faced him. As if reading his thoughts, she said, "We all have our parts to play in Urrinan. You, too, Arnegern. I've dreamed of it." Mara turned away, suddenly flushed and coy. He didn't dare hope over what she might be thinking.

Arnegern stood. "You're right. We have but to abide in our duty. We must keep our resolve and lend each other strength for what comes. And Mother's right—you're too thin to be missing meals. Come." He offered his hand to help her up.

She put her hand in his. It was warm, strong. He pulled her to her feet, and she was instantly leaning against him, her head tucked under his chin, her ear to his chest. He couldn't resist wrapping her in his arms. Her golden hair smelled of the rosemary and honey soap his mother made. Nothing could possibly feel more perfect... and yet inappropriate.

They lingered like that as long as they dared. Arnegern only released her when the sun had completely disappeared over the horizon. He held Mara's hand, helping her down the rocky slope. She would not relinquish his hand until they'd made it back to Hrith-varra. He helped her into the saddle. Mara looked down at him. He briefly saw the longing that he felt—the one that they both hid away. "Hrithvarra can bear us both." Her words were just above a whisper.

Arnegern shook his head and took the reins as a lead, walking the mare back. He knew that if they rode to his father's house together, even if no one saw them arrive, his affection and shame would be apparent.

He had but to abide in his duty. Their reward would one day come.

CHAPTER 6
THE NEXT INEVITABLE CHANGE

"I have gathered many things about my birth. Foremost among them, my coming offered strife, which led to dissonant change. But there are other things I have learned. My arrival had been foretold. My mother strove for me for a long while. I was finally conceived on a remote island with sandy beaches.

More vitally, I was conceived in love, at the height of my parents' adoration for one another. From these additions I take solace."—Brin Bright Eyes, Saga of Dania

THE COLD WIND that blew down from the north added urgency to their work as the Gottari gathered their gear on the docks of Thrakius, making ready for their annual sequestering through the impending hiatus. Vahldan was glad to have the wind at his back as he and Teavar made their way downhill from the market. The giant carried the crate they'd filled with crocks of sea salt, black pepper, and seasoned vinegar. The island they would winter on had an ample supply of fresh fish and produce available in the market of the primary village, but over seven years in Pontea, the Gottari had grown fond of well-seasoned food. Vahldan was particularly fond of black pepper and couldn't imagine going through hiatus without it.

Having Teavar carry the load allowed Vahldan to keep his hands wrapped inside his cloak as he held it closed. Any guilt he might have felt for having someone else do all of the work was lost on Teavar. His second oldest friend and guardian never seemed to tire or grow cold and arguing with him about such things was like arguing with the sea for being green.

They arrived to find that none of their supplies and gear, gathered from all four ships and piled on pallets on the docks, had been loaded. Herodes and Belgar stood at the center of the milling host. It seemed they had come between two arguing sides. Everyone looked cold and grumpy. It was no way to start a season of respite. When Vahldan arrived and inquired, both of his cousins rounded on him. "Herodes says Malvius is taking us aboard Gullwing," Belgar began. "But Dex told us that Malvius was not yet ready to leave, and that we were all to sail on Wavebreaker."

"It's the first I've heard of it," Vahldan said. "I presumed we would all sail on Gullwing. Where's Malvius?"

"I saw him and the other captains heading toward the warehouse." It was Elan. She was nestled in a pile of grain sacks, hugging herself in her Gottari wool cloak with the hood up. He hadn't even seen her. She'd been moody for days but now she looked truly miserable.

"I'll go and get this straightened out. Whichever ship it is, we need to get the men aboard and out of this cold."

Even as he started off toward the lane that led to the warehouse, he heard their bickering restart. He knew that there was more behind the disharmony than the question of which ship to load. Many of the men had expressed an interest in going home to Dania this autumn rather than staying on for another year. Vahldan had argued for staying on, simply due to the fact that it would likely be their most profitable year yet. Malvius had secured a source for an exclusive on a new spice called saffron. Vahldan didn't know much about it except that it was rare, fairly lightweight, and all the rage in Tibairyan cities. They could continue with their other regular contracts and add a commodity in high demand with relative ease.

In spite of his position on the matter, Vahldan did indeed sense that the time to return was drawing near. The rumors they received from Dania said it was so. With this last season of profit, he could afford to really shake things up on his return. If it went as well as he hoped, they could make an impact that would be felt throughout the civilized world. Success wouldn't just change the hierarchy in Dania, it would smash it. Perhaps in a way befitting of the Bringer.

The vote had been close, but those who wished to stay one last season had prevailed. The hard feelings over it continued to linger, which was why he had to get them out to the island, and quickly. Once everyone had a chance to rest and eat and drink, maybe find a temporary mate—all mostly enjoyed on a warm, sandy beach—the bitterness and homesickness would fade.

Vahldan turned from the docks and hurried down the lane. He arrived at the warehouse doors only to find them locked, which was strange for this time of day. Especially if Malvius and the captains were inside. He went to the side door that led to the office Malvius had partitioned from the cavernous structure. He leaned to look through the blurry glass window Neveka had insisted Malvius add to lighten the space. He spotted Sabas heading through the door that led out onto the warehouse floor. He tried the door to find it unlocked, which was also not typical; the alley on this side led to a row of brothels, and no few of those using the lane were drunken revelers.

He entered the warm office and strode to the inner door, which Sabas had left ajar. The office door led into the space Sabas used as his residence, and Vahldan heard voices before he reached for the door. "Not this time, Cap. Something has to be done, and soon."

Vahldan stopped short. It was one of the captains. Seemed he'd stumbled into another dispute.

"There's no need to overreact. Nothing has changed." It was

Malvius, his tone pitched to soothe. "They still provide more upside than the downside you keep predicting. A downside that has yet to come to fruition, I might add."

"You know it's coming. They're savages led by a murderer. You can't deny it. It's only a matter of time, Cap. They grow bolder by the season." It was a second captain. The others were all murmuring in agreement.

They were talking about him and his host, and it seemed they were unanimous in confronting his partner.

A third captain piped up. "They're dirty, often drunken, and lazy. None of them will lift a finger to clean up after themselves." The muttering in agreement grew.

"Now hold on," Malvius interjected. "The Gottari are drunk no more or less than any of our sailors. That's just part of life at sea."

"You aren't hearing us, Cap," the first captain said. "Dealing with the drunken and slothful behavior could be tolerated. It's their volatility. What happens when one of them throws the wrong punch? Or worse, spills the wrong blood? The entire imperial apparatus would come down on us. On all of us. We've come too far to invite that kind of disaster. We'd lose every last charter. Maybe every last ship. Rumor already speaks of prominent merchants looking for ways to trade around us. It's just the beginning."

"We only have those charters because of Vahldan and the Gottari. Gods, man, we only own any ships at all because of them. We're everybody's biggest rival because they put us on top." At least Malvius was defending them.

"That may be so, but things are changing. The war's over, and the Tibes are back in force. Things aren't as loose and wild as they once were. Times are changing, Cap. If we don't change with them, things could get ugly."

Vahldan waited for Malvius to respond but the silence stretched.

The first captain spoke again. "Let's face facts. They are brutes. Barbarians. Murderers. Yes, it's why they're good at what we once needed them for. But surely you sense what we all do. They've come to consider themselves our betters. What will you do when they turn on us, Cap?" Vahldan felt the stirring of the ugliness rising up from his gut.

When Malvius finally spoke, his voice was low and firm. "First, I'm not sure I sense what you do. They've changed, just as anyone enjoying a hot streak would. I'm not as sure they're going to turn on us as you are. But if it were to happen, I do have a plan."

"What sort of plan?" one of them asked.

"I've already made a few inquiries and received some assurances. If and when we need to, I will deal with such a situation."

"Gods, Cap, there are forty of them. Line them up and each one is more lethal than the last. How in the gods' names would we ever deal with that?"

Vahldan leaned toward the backside of the open door, straining to hear. Finally, "It has been noted that, as highly competent combatants, our Gottari friends would make very valuable slaves. They would make a fortune for any wrangler who introduced them to the fighting pits."

The ugliness surged up into his chest, flushing his face and blurring his vision. Malvius's voice brightened. "But as I said, I don't quite sense the need for panic. Not yet. Next year we are sure to have the best year yet, and Vahldan knows it as well as you and I. I have anonymous bids in on two of my father's ships, and I've commissioned another new ship. Sabas and I are going to look at another warehouse this very afternoon. Trust me when I say that all is well."

The sounds of boots shuffling closer came through the buzz of the ugliness in his ears. Vahldan turned and staggered to the outer door. He burst out into the cold and hurried back down the alley toward the docks. "We will *never* be slaves," he vowed, and he knew then. There was no turning back. The course he and a select few Rekkrs only dared speak of in whispers or in jest had become the only course.

The Bringer of Urrinan would always be the one to strike first. "As Thunar is my witness," he swore aloud.

ELAN KNEW she was experiencing a dream. But oh, such a dream it was—filled with bright sunshine and joy. She was warm and cozy. And happy. The happiest she'd been in years. The light of it filled her and surrounded her.

She woke up to the actual sunrise shining into her eyes. The delirium of the dream lingered. She was nestled in the crook of Vahldan's arm, her head rose and fell with his breathing. The sound wasn't quite in rhythm with the lapping waves on the nearby shore and yet the two worked in harmony. She shivered when a gust blew in off of the sea, ruffling the drapes she'd left open all night for exactly this moment. Their bodies were entwined under the softest fleece blanket she'd ever owned—a gift from Neveka. The shanty's wool-stuffed mattress held them like baby birds in a nest.

Gods, she loved everything about this moment. Not for the first time, she wished they could just stay like this forever. The Amalus had committed to another year aboard the fleet, but she wanted many more moments like this in their lives once their sailing days were over. Making it so was nearly all she thought about these days.

The past few weeks had been the happiest she'd had since she left the Skolani tribe. Bliss filled her and imbued her and continued to grow. Indeed, a primary source of it was something growing inside her. She'd suspected for weeks, and the change in her cycle had made it all but certain. But in the dream from which she'd just woken, Horsella had confirmed her most cherished hope.

She was finally pregnant.

Elan would have her daughter, and Vahldan would be the father. "As it shall be," she whispered.

The possibility had always been a source of tension between them. But Elan had to wonder. She sensed things were about to change. She sensed *he* might be ready to change, and that the right reason for it might have arrived. They'd accomplished so much.

More than any of them had dreamed possible when they set out after the Paralatoe.

Vahldan had been so angry at the start of hiatus. Elan considered his anger over what he had overheard in the warehouse to be a waste. She'd never trusted Malvius, and to hear that their Hellain partner was prepared to betray them was utterly unsurprising to her. Vahldan had brooded for weeks. He and his inner circle had often gathered by the evening fires, muttering and cursing. They fell to silence whenever she approached, only because they knew she would be the voice of reason in any open discussion. Men could be so childish, clinging to their resentments. She thought it best to let them grouse and scheme till they'd worked through it.

Besides, she'd done some scheming of her own. Elan could perfectly picture living here with Vahldan, raising their daughter together. There had been a time when she had dreamed of having her daughter take her place among the Skolani. But once this new image came to her—of both of them bringing her up in such a beautiful, peaceful place—Elan had been unable to shake it. She'd even looked into the possibility by chatting with a few of the locals.

The Amalus had been talking about going back to Dania for several years now. It was only reasonable to gather as much treasure as possible before leaving behind what was likely a growing risk of being betrayed by the Hellains. Once they did, any scheme Malvius had in place became a moot point. She continued to argue that leaving at any time the threat was sensed was reasonable. Vahldan had already led them to earning enough treasure to make good on his vows to really change things. They'd already won. There was no need to live in risk.

Once they left the fleet, their commitments would be near to being met. Her duty was to him, and he'd vowed to change things in Dania. Vahldan himself needn't wait around once change had been set in motion. He'd often vowed to never submit to sitting beside Thadmeir in the longhouse, listening to haranguing wolves all day.

He'd earned his reprieve from such a life, and returning here was the perfect alternative to it. Elan had but to make him see.

She had the clearest vision of how perfect their lives could be here. Surely he would see it, too. Here, unburdened by the weight of duty, Vahldan smiled often and laughed easily. Their time together this hiatus had—for the first time—felt like an amorous coupling. One that was meant to last a lifetime. Their lovemaking was languorous and playful. He'd become so attentive, which made her realize how distracted he had been during their first years together. Ever had his ambition been his top priority. After returning from Dania, he could let it all go.

How could he not recognize that here he was his truest and best self? He seemed so happy, so relaxed. He went fishing and they cooked and swam and walked the beaches. Here he prioritized carving again, setting time aside nearly every day. He had readily embraced the largest projects he'd ever undertaken. Including a life-size owl, to keep the seagulls away from their fish bucket before dinnertime. It didn't always work anymore, but the bird was still lovely and lifelike.

Her man was finally in a position to commit to a lifetime of love. It was something they often alluded to but had never actually committed to. She felt like the time was right. The feeling grew as she lay there, listening to his steady breathing. Her body was vibrating with this feeling. It was beyond intoxicating. It had to be right, had to be shared.

Elan sensed the gods' approval. She would talk to him this very morning. Before they got out of bed.

Once she decided, she wanted him to wake. She slowly draped her leg over his and pressed her form against him, subtly moving her weight onto him, snuggling and sliding, relishing how well their bodies fit together. His eyes cracked and a small smile crept to his lips. "Good morning," she whispered, running her hand down over his chest and stomach, unsurprised to discover the tip of his morning stiffness.

"Good, indeed," he said, his voice still scratchy. His hands snaked around her, pulling her the rest of the way onto him. Their skin-to-skin contact was warm but smooth and dry. It felt delicious.

She kissed him and slid back off, seeking to slow things down. "I want this to last forever," she said.

His smile grew lopsided. "With someone as gorgeous and inviting as you, I doubt that forever is a realistic goal. Indeed, I doubt I'll last the morning. I am merely a man, my dear."

Of course he was right, that if they continued on the current trajectory, this moment would end far too soon. But she meant so much more. "I mean, I want every morning to be like this. I want us to grow old with hundreds of mornings just like this. We could do that here."

He sighed and it turned into a laugh. "If only," he said. It sounded like appeasement. He wasn't taking her seriously.

"Think about it. We really could. I spoke to Naissa, at the market. She said her husband would gladly sell this place to us."

"How kind of her to speak for him. Why wouldn't he want to sell a seasonal shanty?" His mouth was smiling but his eyes looked puzzled—maybe even worried.

"Think about it," she said. "The markets for fish are better than ever these days. We could fix this place up, buy a boat, and—"

"Whoa." He sat up and rubbed his face. "What are you talking about?"

"Moving here," she said. There could be no tiptoeing around it anymore. "Just us. I'm only asking you to think about it. We could start a new life. Here. Away from the wolves, from the empire—all of it."

Vahldan continued to smile, but his countenance said he thought she was daft. "What about all that we've worked for? We can't just walk away, after everything we've been through. We finally have the means to really change things." His tone was cautious. He sought to make her see reality without inciting her.

She thought her version of reality was better. "We do. And we can. Walk away, I mean. You can do so much good back in Dania now. You can pay off enough debt for your kinfolk to break the stranglehold of the guild. Those who want to stay on can continue your work there. But you've never really wanted to sit the dais chair. You hate politics. You can set things on the right path, and then be free of it."

His incredulous smile faded. He stood and started dressing. "I can't believe you're saying this." He kept shaking his head but wouldn't look at her. "We're only just beginning. We've painstakingly set ourselves in position to shake things up in Dania. But that's only the beginning. How can you not know this? We're going to change the world!"

He finished dressing and faced her again. "Where is this coming from, Elan?"

She sat up straighter. She would have to tell him and hope it would help him to see. "I'm pregnant," she said. She instantly regretted the abruptness of it.

Before her eyes, his surprise morphed into outrage. "We talked about this," he said.

"No, we didn't."

He started pacing. "We agreed—"

"No," she interjected. "We didn't agree. Not ever. Not about this. Every time I tried to talk to you, you changed the subject. But now it's happened. Can you not be happy about it?"

Vahldan pushed his way through the drapes and thumped down the steps to the beach. By the time she rose and looked out, he was storming down the shore, heading for the gods knew where. Elan's hopes shattered. She couldn't catch her breath, couldn't swallow.

No. She couldn't let this stand. Her vision had been so clear. She had to keep trying to make him see. She hurriedly dressed and started after him.

When she caught him, he was standing at the edge of the waves, staring at the rising sun across the water. She made the final approach in silence. Without looking at her, he said, "Does none of it mean anything to you?"

He sounded hurt. It made her angry. She was the injured party here. Not only had he not listened, he'd dismissed what should've been the happiest news she'd ever shared with him. In doing so, he hadn't offered the slightest consideration for her feelings.

Elan drew and released a deep breath. There was still a chance. "Of course it does. You most of all. You mean the world to me. It's why I came. It's why I stay. It's why having your daughter makes me so happy. It's why I want you all to myself."

He shook his head. "Then you've missed it."

"Missed what?" she snapped, her anger finally showing.

"Missed what it should mean. I'm supposed to do more," he said. "You should know it as well as I do. I can't just walk away. I'm meant to change things. The gods have shown me the path to glory. It's the path that my people expect me to take. They all see it." He stood rigid. When he glanced back at her, his eyes were hard. "Why can't you?" He was formed of stone, resolute and unchangeable.

The last spark of her hope was snuffed. All that mattered was his ambition. It meant more to him than she did. More to him than their daughter. Indeed, he couldn't be bothered to consider either of them.

Elan suddenly saw that he was right. Why hadn't she seen it? She'd felt like the gods had given her a gift—the way to finish his transformation. She thought she could be the one to lead him to his true self. But he was still his father's son. He was still his clan's savior, his people's Bringer. He'd completely surrendered to it and couldn't be broken free.

The change she imagined was folly. The one he sought was inevitable.

Vahldan turned to look at her again. A surprising change had come over him. He looked furtive, almost apologetic. "Who can know?" he said. "Perhaps this is the work of the gods. You've said it yourself. Your father—he was of the Wulthus, right?"

Now it was her turn; the outrage he'd displayed earlier seized her entire being. She would never let her daughter suffer the curse of being a part of this charade—to be a puppet, dancing on the strings of zealotry and ambition. "No!"

Elan spun and headed to the shanty. He followed. "It could be a son, you know," he said.

It wouldn't have made a difference, but she knew it wasn't possible. Her babe was a daughter. She would be of the Skolani. She'd known it for years. How could she have lost sight of it?

Elan had made all the wrong choices, but about this she was certain. "It doesn't matter," she called over her shoulder. "No child of mine will be a pawn in your games. Not ever!"

Vahldan stopped following her. "Fine! Stay here, then! Have your babe alone and live on an island." He stood raving on, calling after her. "I'm going back to Dania. With or without you, I'm going to do my duty and meet my destiny head on."

The reality of his words assaulted her. She couldn't stay here alone. The gods were toying with her. Again.

She had chosen him, had chosen this life. She'd chosen his bedamned destiny. But she saw now that her choices were running out. She had always known the gods were fickle, but now it seemed they'd taken to tormenting her to entertain themselves. She was a prisoner of fate, but she would make sure her daughter was not.

"I'm going back to Dania, too," she said. Under her breath, she added, "It's where Brin will be born. So help me."

PART TWO
GAINING STRENGTH

CHAPTER 7
SISTERS OF FATE

"Having glimpsed her veiled insecurity and witnessed her undeniably palpable response to touching others, I always sensed the burden of Amaga's profound gifts. It's said that Amaseila had seemed at ease with her prescience. Though many considered the daughter more imposing, and perhaps even more powerful than the mother, unlike Amaseila, Amaga seemed never to be at ease.

Many feared Amaga throughout her life—at times even those she loved. And no few loathed her, including my mother. But I neither feared nor hated her. Though Amaga's role in Dania's destiny was great, her lot always seemed more a curse than a blessing. I came to pity her for the unfairness of what the gods bestowed upon her."—Brin Bright Eyes, Saga of Dania

AMAGA LEFT the longhouse by way of the stables rather than through the main door, which led straight onto the village commons. It was sunny and warm for being so close to winter, but she still pulled her hood over her pure white tresses—so recognizable—and hurried through the shadows. As she often did, Amaga planned to weave her way to the market by the back lanes. It took longer and today it would be muddier, but it might spare her being noticed. The herbalist's stall was at the far end of the market, allowing her to avoid walking the main aisle.

Amaga hated going out. She hated the way they all stared. She read their fear without even touching them. It was a joke. Oh, how they all revered her mother. She didn't begrudge them that—Amaseila's connection to Freya was beyond compare. But when it came to Amaga's gifts, they all scoffed. She knew why. They shunned her to maintain their willful ignorance. It was self-preservation.

The villagers didn't want what she had to offer. No one here wanted the truth.

Her mother had tricked Amaga into this trip to the market. Amaga's father would've gladly fetched the herbs. Thadmeir would do anything his wife or daughter asked of him. But it was only after Father had left Danihem for the day that her mother had suddenly realized she needed these particular herbs. Amaga knew Amaseila meant well. She wanted her daughter to be a little girl—wanted her to be the kind of child who wanted to play outside, to run with a group of friends. The problem was, Amaga had no interest in play. Besides that, she had no friends. Well, unless she counted her father. Her mother wanted Amaga to love the trees and the fresh air, as Amaseila had when she was a girl.

Amaga had no love of trees—their spirits were so solemn, foreboding. She disliked squinting in the sun and shivering in the cold. And she was almost always cold, even when others claimed they were too warm. Her father claimed it was because she was too thin. But Amaga knew otherwise. She felt cold because of her connection to the spirit world—as if the great door to the other side stood ajar within her, emitting a chill from the realm of the dead.

But today it seemed there was no way to avoid the exposure. The herbs really would bring comfort to her mother—ease her pain, help her rest. Fetching the source of Amaseila's reprieve from suffering, however temporary, was the least Amaga could do, since her mother's condition was all her fault.

It was Amaga's greatest regret. Her mother was dying, and Amaga was responsible for it.

Amaseila had never fully recovered from childbirth. Something inside her had been broken by Amaga's entry into this world. No healer could explain it, but her condition had steadily worsened since. It was as if Amaga had stolen something vital from her merely by being. Through all the eight years of Amaga's life, she'd witnessed her mother slide toward death.

Becoming aware of this awful truth through touch was Amaga's first recognition of her gift. Or did that make it a curse?

Amaga arrived at the end of the lane and hurried to the side of the herbalist's stall. She waited for the sole patron to pay and leave. The herbalist, a nosy woman with chin whiskers named Sáiwala, spotted Amaga lurking in the shadows. "Ah, Danihem's youngest priestess." The woman's tone was sarcastic. Amaga wouldn't give her the satisfaction of a retort. "To what do I owe the honor, your reverence? Your mother is wanting more of the lemon balm and white willow bark for tea, no doubt."

"No," she snapped, although the willow bark had eased her mother's inflammation. "I came for barberry root. And I'll take some dried birch and sage."

Sáiwala frowned. "Barberry root? Too much is poison, you know."

"Of course I know." Though even in the smallest doses, it led to delirium, barberry was the only thing that offered a deep sleep, utterly free of pain. Amaga had only to lay hands on her mother after dosing her to perceive the relief it provided.

The woman pressed her lips together and turned to fill the order. When she was nearly finished tying the bundles, Amaga said, "And a bit of the white willow bark as well."

Sáiwala smirked and inclined her head. "As you wish, your reverence."

The sarcastic cow was taking forever. Amaga glanced down the lane, into the crowded market. A pair of herdsmen's wives were looking directly at her. "I think it's her," the heavier one said to the other. The pair came rushing over. "Beg your pardon, Miss. But you are her—the young priestess—are you not?"

Amaga tried to act confused and turned away. "What do I owe?" Amaga asked Sáiwala.

"A half skatt, Priestess Amaga." The cow had done that on purpose. Sáiwala wore a smug smile as she filled Amaga's basket with the bundled herbs.

"Amaga, yes. You *are* her!" the herdsman's wife exclaimed, grabbing Amaga's arm.

Amaga yanked away from the woman's touch, afraid of what she might feel in it. Before she could reply, the woman fell to her knees. "Please, Priestess, will you offer a blessing from your goddess for my boy? He's taken a fever. I can't stop his cough. I fear for him, what with the nights growing colder."

Did this stupid hen not realize that if Amaga were able to dispense blessings from Freya for the sick, she'd be home, focusing herself in prayer for her own mother? "Sáiwala here can help you. Ask *her* how to heal your son." She tried not to smile. These two deserved one another.

"Oh, please, Miss. We've already tried every remedy." When their gazes locked, the woman drew a soft gasp and hastily bowed her head, averting her eyes. Amaga knew people feared gazing into her eyes. They thought she could see into their souls, or worse. It wasn't true, but Amaga never denied it. Let them wonder!

She knew if it weren't for the woman's sick boy, this simpleton would recoil and slink away. She also knew that if she offered any sort of blessing, and the boy worsened or, Freya forbid, died, she would be vilified.

The pathetic wretch bent to Amaga's feet, groveling right there on the plankway, attracting more godsforsaken attention. The hen reached to grasp her hand. To avoid touching her, Amaga held one hand up, feigning some vague otherworldly singing. "Oh, great Freya, goddess of motherhood and love. I know myself unworthy of your heeding. But, if you deem this woman worthy of your grace, please bless her child."

Rising, the herdswoman made a face. "You have my fitting gratitude, Priestess," the hen said in a tone meant to convey that she thought the fitting amount was none. "Please deliver our best wishes to your mother. The village would be lost without her." In other words, the hen thought Amaga unworthy of replacing her mother. Well, on that Amaga couldn't disagree.

Anxious to be away, Amaga spun to leave, instantly bumping into the hen's companion. She stumbled and dropped her basket, sending bundles of herbs rolling across the plankway. She bent to collect them. The pair of hens moved off and yet her head was buzzing in that bedamned portending way. Someone else was near and focused on her. Amaga kept her head down, trying to shut out the dreaded feeling and ignore the attention she had attracted.

Young female hands appeared, helping to gather her things. Her head still buzzing, Amaga rose to come eye to eye with a fair-haired girl. The girl was about her age, only slightly taller, with fierce blue eyes, high cheeks, and a strong chin. She wore a fine pale gray cloak with bright red embroidery over a clean white tunic. The girl's eyes were inquisitive but not unkind. And, unlike everyone else, she held Amaga's gaze, unafraid—intrigued even. Amaga backed up a step, wanting to flee but somehow unable to.

The girl boldly reached to place the bundles into her basket, coming far too close. "That was quite a collision. Are you unhurt?" She seemed sincerely concerned as she touched Amaga's arm. A warm current pulsed from the girl's touch. The buzzing in her head became the resonant drone of an ethereal bell. Amaga's whole body shuddered as she took another step back.

The girl's concern turned to alarm. "Oh dear. Are you well?"

The dizziness receded and the bell's hum faded. Amaga found her voice. "Yes, I am well, thank you." She tried to force a smile.

"I apologize, but I couldn't help but overhear that you are the daughter of the Priestess Amaseila." Amaga stared dumbly. "My sister and I had hoped to see her, but we're told she's too ill to receive visitors. Is that still so?"

"Yes, I'm afraid so." Amaga was both relieved and irritated by the hearsay.

"I'm sorry. Please convey our best wishes. I have long heard of her gifts. This is my first visit to Danihem—well, the first I recall. My sister and I had wanted to inquire of her as to my brother's return. You know, whether the goddess would confer her auspices for it. My sister even had hopes of petitioning your mother to perform her bonding ritual. She is recently betrothed, you see."

Amaga wanted to look away, to turn and leave. But she stood gaping.

The girl misread her stunned silence. "I'm sorry. I must sound so selfish. We would never trouble the priestess, knowing she's unwell. It's just that I have heard tell of her all my life."

"Of my mother," Amaga said.

"Yes. She's part of our family legend. It's said that years ago, when my brother was last here, your mother foresaw his destiny. Much of what she said that day has come to pass."

"Your... brother." Realization bloomed. Amaga knew.

"That's right. And we just hoped to learn more. About what's yet to come. So much is changing. These are such exciting times, are they not?"

Amaga's head swam. She could hardly assemble her spiraling thoughts. Clearly, Freya held forth here. This was no chance meeting. Amaga refocused as the girl prattled on. "You must think me rude. Forgive me for that as well... Amaga, is it? I am Kemella, and the sister I spoke of is called Mara. We are the daughters of Angavar, sisters to the Lion Lord of the Amalus clan."

"I know," Amaga said, still sounding stunned.

The girl grinned. "Freya's grace, you already knew?"

Amaga gathered herself. "I mean, I figured as much, once I saw the stitching of your cloak." She pointed at the little lions that now leapt from the elaborate embroidery.

Kemella glanced down at the garment. "Ah. Clever. Well, had you heard? My brother is on his way home to Dania."

"Vahldan is coming." It wasn't a question. Amaga would soon face this ominous and vital piece of her own destiny. As she'd long known she must.

"Yes. He's been abroad for the last eight years. And he's coming here, to Danihem. It's why we came. I can't even remember him. I was only a babe when he left. But oh, I've heard so many wonderful tales. I'm so excited. I've waited all my life for this."

Amaga drew a deep breath and sighed it out. "As have I. All my life." Kemella offered her a curious smile, and Amaga returned it. "And I'm very glad to have met you, Kemella. For we are to be as sisters."

To her credit, Kemella straightened, holding Amaga's gaze, and extended her hand. "As it has been shown."

"As it shall be," Amaga said in refrain. She warily took Kemella's hand. The familiar sensation surged. Mercifully, along with the upheaval of the Urrinan she knew she'd encounter through touch, Amaga found warmth and beauty in her connection to this girl, her sister of fate.

Amaga led Kemella to the longhouse residence through the stables. Her father's and uncle's horses were being unsaddled by the grooms. There had been other horses tied outside in the commons, which meant there was a meeting on the chamber floor.

"Are you sure your mother won't mind being surprised?" Kemella asked.

Amaga had to stop and consider it. Her mother would never say so, but Amaga would know how she felt. Even without touching her. She supposed it would depend on how Amaseila was feeling. And she'd been feeling poorly for days. But Amaga sensed that this was something Mother would want to know about right away. To see for herself.

Amaga looked down at her basket. She'd brought the means to make her mother feel better. "I'll make her some tea first."

Rather than seeming confused or questioning her, Kemella nodded, which Amaga appreciated. So fast and firm was their connection, they needed not waste words in explanation. She led her new sister in and peeked through the sleeping chamber door, relieved to see her mother hadn't tried to get out of bed. Amaga went to the kettle over the glowing coals of the residence hearth, happy to find hot water on hand. She added the birch bark and a tiny bit of the barberry root, along with some sage and a chunk of dried apple to cover the bitterness.

While it steeped, she turned to her guest. Kemella stood fidgeting. Amaga realized how rude she was being. In her defense, she'd never brought home a visitor before. "Please, sit. May I take your cloak?" Kemella nodded and undid the clasp at her neck—a snarling lion's head pendant. Amaga shed her own and hung both garments on the pegs by the door.

Kemella hadn't sat, but Amaga could already smell the tea. "That should do," she said and strained the steaming liquid into a cup. Amaga beckoned Kemella into the sleeping chamber. The air was stale and smelled of illness. She opened the shutter a bit to let in some air and light.

Her mother's eyes opened a crack. Amaseila forced a smile. "You're back. How was it?"

"You won't believe it until I tell you. But first I want you to drink some of this."

Amaga helped Amaseila to lean up and held the cup for her. Her mother's eyes went to their guest as she drank. Amaga sensed a stirring in her mother's soul through their contact. As always, touching her mother initiated a series of colorful, fast-changing images. Today the feeling conveyed was profound but not frightening, as it occasionally was when it flared like this. This was different—calm but shimmering with joy. This girl affected her mother in a way Amaga had never before witnessed. For both of them, Kemella's mere presence seemed to stir and bend their connection to the spirit world.

For her part, Kemella stood at the foot of the bed, shoulders square, hands clasped before her—alert and respectful, wary but unafraid. Amaga's admiration of her continued to grow.

Amaseila finished drinking and nodded for Amaga to take the tea away. She wiped her mother's chin. "I bid you welcome, Young Lioness," Amaseila said. Her voice was still hoarse, but the power of the goddess lay within it.

Kemella's eyes widened and she swiftly bowed. "Thank you, Wise One. I am honored and grateful to meet you. I was telling Amaga that you are revered among my family."

Amaseila extracted her bony white hands from her blankets and extended them across the bed. "Come, both of you. Take my hands."

Amaga did as bidden and nodded to Kemella to follow suit. Amaga squeezed her eyes shut as she surrendered to the touch. This time she saw clearer images—lion banners and armies and stone ramparts—all in quick succession. Then she saw an adult version of Kemella standing over her, clutching her hand and smiling. The image morphed into an adult Kemella inside a grand stone and timbered chamber, holding a swaddled babe, rocking and humming to the child. The stone halls shook, as if with the coming of the gods. Finally, the image faded to blood red—always these visions ended with blood, or with fire. Or both.

Amaga slammed her protective door shut—a mental image she'd modeled on the great wooden door of the longhouse—and all went white and still. Mentally she went to her safe space—her bed in the loft. Eyes still closed, she lay there, catching her breath. She reminded herself that none of it was sure to happen—that these were only things that *could* come to be.

The thudding of her heart settled. Amaga released her mother's hand, opened her eyes, and returned to the here and now. Kemella was still holding the other hand. Both her mother and her guest were smiling at one another. Amaga always wondered how much time passed during her visions, but this one seemed to have been brief.

"I've been waiting for you," Amaseila said to Kemella, and a tear ran down her cheek. "I've been... so very tired. I've been waiting for your promise. I need it. Say that it's true."

"That what's true, Wise One?" Kemella calmly asked.

"Promise me that you'll stay with her. Promise you will look after my beloved, through blood and fire and death." A steady stream of tears flowed down her mother's cheeks. "Promise me you'll never betray her, even when they speak against her. Even when they speak against you for defending her. Promise me you'll be as sisters, that you'll see her through to the end—into the hands of those who will carry her and the One to safety. Even when all seems lost."

Amaga opened her mouth but she couldn't speak. She wanted to stop it from happening... She was terrified that this was all too much, that her mother had gone too far. She feared that this would send her guest—a potential dear friend, even a sister—fleeing before their connection had a chance to grow firm.

To Amaga's shock, Kemella dropped to her knees beside the bed, holding Amaseila's hand in both of hers. "I swear it, Wise One. I will stay by my new sister's side and keep her safe and love her."

"And my grandson."

"Yes, him too."

"Until the end," her mother implored.

"Yes," Kemella confirmed. "Until the end. I promise. As it has been shown."

"As it shall be." Amaseila sighed and closed her eyes. "And now I can rest."

How had this happened? How had this young girl, so knowing, so strong, come into Amaga's life? Did Kemella know her mother was talking about the Urrinan? Did she know her brother was the Bringer? Did Kemella have any idea who Amaga's son was to become?

Amaga took her mother's hand. She shut her eyes and focused and cracked open the big wooden door. Warmth and love and gratitude flowed, to her and to Kemella. But she also saw the ever-present shadows. They were growing now, closing in, faster than ever. Her mother had been fighting them, so very valiantly. But Amaseila was giving up—surrendering to death. Soon she would be gone. Too soon.

Amaga's eyes sprang open. Her face crumpled. "Áithei, don't leave me," she managed.

Amaseila smiled again. "Not just yet, my beloved. Not yet. Now go, both of you. Leave me to rest until your father comes." Her mother swiftly slid into the steady breathing of slumber. Amaga laid down her hand, and Kemella followed suit. She stood staring at her mother; Amaseila looked so thin, so pale. So beautiful. Amaga could not stop the tears from flowing.

Kemella came around to her and enveloped her in her arms, holding her in the most comforting embrace she'd had since her mother had become bedridden. Actually, the only embrace since then.

Amaga surrendered to the strength of her sister. Not for the last time, she knew.

HOMECOMING OR INSURGENCY?

"*There can be no doubt that upon his return, the new Lion Lord sought to rankle the Wulthus clan leadership during his travels through Dania. And although Vahldan openly worked to undermine the wool guild, I believe he knew he could not simply buy his way to his goals. In order to break the guild's stranglehold on Dania's most essential marketplace, he needed more than mere treasure.*

By then he had learned the power of playing the outsider. He portrayed himself as the victim, ostracized and deprived of justice. He used his status to proclaim himself the champion of the oppressed. He willingly forwent any semblance of striving for clan unity, much to the wolves' distress. Although his behavior was inarguably divisive, it's difficult to argue that his plan was fruitless. For many common folk swiftly and gladly proclaimed him their sole hope."—Brin Bright Eyes, Saga of Dania

Urias suspected he knew, but he asked anyway. "Why wouldn't he come straight here? Surely he'd have the votes to claim this." He thumped the high seat of the Amalus chieftain. The chair had sat empty on the longhouse dais since Queen Keisella had led them against the Spali in Oium. Desdrusan had never once returned to seek to reclaim it.

Ulfhamr shrugged. "He's in no hurry. Vahldan clearly wants to win over more than just a chamber full of aging Amalus councilmen. Rumor says he won't come to Danihem until the solstice session. Others say he won't bother coming at all."

Thadmeir leapt to his feet and stepped from the dais. Urias knew his brother's anxiety was getting beyond containment. The Wolf Lord didn't often straighten the longhouse in front of guests, but Thadmeir was willing to do so today. To their cousin's credit, Ulfhamr pretended not to notice as his lord lowered himself to aligning the benches and picking up empty cups and plates left scattered from the prior night. It was a reflexive way for Thadmeir to soothe himself.

"Tell me again—just how has he come into so much gold?" Thadmeir asked as he worked.

Ulfhamr sought a prosaic tone. "None of our sources is quite sure. And the lions who know stubbornly refuse to be clear. It's long been rumored that he was involved in piracy. But cooler heads tell of his host being hired on as mercenary guardsmen for a wealthy Hellain trading family. All we're certain of is that he spent much of the past eight years at sea."

Thadmeir's frown deepened. "Mercenaries don't earn these sorts of sums, do they?"

"Not for guarding trade caravans. But I know nothing of ships and sailing, my lord." Their cousin shrugged. "Perhaps the lad did stoop to piracy. He's never shied from being ruthless. Nor from ambition."

Urias had to speak up. "Oh, come now. Vahldan wouldn't go that low. He values his reputation too much. His father's old guard Rekkrs would be appalled, and Vahldan knows it."

Thadmeir picked up four cups in each hand and took them to the wash basin. He turned back, frowning. "However he got it, you're telling me that Vahldan is using his newfound wealth to pay the debts of those he visits? Are those he favors the kin of his host?"

"Not only them, my lord. That's just it—seems he's paying the debts of any who ask it of him. Most are just common herdsmen. Many have never been aligned with the lions. Or at least not beforehand."

"So that's it? He's merely buying loyalty? I mean, how much is the goodwill of a herdsman worth? Does he ask for anything in return? Are these loans? Does he charge interest?"

"It seems not," Ulfhamr said. "Though I *have* heard that many who've received his gifts have pledged sons or younger brothers to his host. I don't know whether this is a condition, my lord. But those we've questioned say it was not asked of them. They claim to be repaying generosity with allegiance."

Thadmeir bent to lift the end of a crooked bench and slammed it back down. "Damn him! Does he presume to gather an army to march against the seat of the nation? He's already sundered our warriors. Would he dare use threats against his own people? Is that not treason?"

Urias went to him. "Come, Brother. You're upsetting yourself. We have no reason to believe Vahldan holds such ill intent." He led Thadmeir to the dais chair. "Sit and rest. I'll go and ask Amaga to make you some of her mulled wine."

Thadmeir dropped into his chair. "No, stay. It's quiet in there. If Amaga's returned, I don't want her to disturb her mother."

They sat in silence for a time. Thadmeir looked up at him. "What's he about, Urias?"

Urias didn't want to rile him again. But he knew his brother well. He didn't want to hear the truth, but events were pushing things to a head. Urias had to get his brother to face facts. It was a fraught situation that—given an indelicate response—could easily get out of hand. "Vahldan's always been clever. He should never be underestimated. He is not just gathering a following but a force. I don't believe he'd be so crass as to threaten the Rekkr's council or the guild. At least not overtly. He wouldn't risk the backlash that it would incite."

"Why, then?"

Urias had mixed emotions about what he suspected Vahldan was up to. He continued to hope for the restoration of balance to the futhark. In the aftermath of the Spali war, it had only become clearer that things weren't right. Even with Desdrusan out of the picture, things were not fair or just for those beholden to the wool guild and the landowning Rekkrs who controlled it. The imbalance was part of the truth his brother refused to face. Urias knew that balance could never be achieved in Dania as things stood. He'd admitted as much to Vahldan himself. The liberties taken by guildsmen had only grown more egregious since Queen Keisella's War. Which had only made Vahldan more popular in his absence.

He knew Vahldan sought prestige, but he suspected it went deeper. He sought dramatic change. Indeed, he'd all but promised as much, and his most ardent supporters were depending on it. Urias knew things had to change, but he also knew the contentious sort of shift Vahldan was stoking might very well be harmful to the Gottari nation. Outside of the guild, the rank-and-file Wulthus Rekkrs would likely suffer most for any success Vahldan achieved. The more impactful Vahldan's moves became, the more dramatic their response would be. And these were the very men Urias's family had pledged to serve and protect.

Most were good men—men who had helped to shape Dania's prosperity and stability. Reprisal by the resentful would only breed new resentments, which would incite retribution. Which meant things could swiftly escalate. This could easily get beyond Vahldan's current intentions, even if they were justified.

"My lord, think about to whom these men were indebted," Urias ventured.

"Their grazing landlords, most likely. Either that or they've taken advances from merchants." Thadmeir's eyes narrowed. "So it's merely an attempt to break the guild?"

Urias shrugged. "Perhaps not to break them. But at least to gain leverage against them. He's clearly building a coalition."

Ulfhamr grunted in agreement. "Folks who've sat at Vahldan's fires say he speaks openly of finding other markets for the spring shearing. And by some accounts, he's allowing several hard-put herdsmen to graze on Desdrusan's former lands."

Thadmeir sat up straight. "His *former* lands? By what rights? Where is Desdrusan?"

Ulfhamr shrugged. "Depends on who's telling the tale. Desdrusan's Wulthus neighbors claim Vahldan seized Desdrusan's lands and took the man captive. Some folks say Vahldan exiled him, by pain of death upon his return. The same sentence Desdrusan handed down to the father. But those with Amalus leanings say Vahldan simply bought him off and sent him packing. They say Desdrusan chose exile. I've also heard that Desdrusan ran off to Illyrica the day after the Skolani scouts reported that Vahldan was coming up through the Pontean Pass. It's said Desdrusan got wind that his nephew was coming for him and that he up and fled. Regardless of the reason, most say Desdrusan left everything behind when he departed."

Thadmeir leaned back. "Hmph. The Skolani sent *me* no reports of Vahldan's return. Nor has anyone sent word of Desdrusan leaving."

Urias silently sighed. Supposed Skolani favoritism was an old contention. His brother labored to read it into most everything the Skolani said or did. "In fairness, my lord, Vahldan is rightfully one of the lords of Dania. His return to his homeland would hardly call for a warning."

"At the moment," Ulfhamr went on, "Vahldan's host is camped closer to the Skolani Jabitka than to Danihem. Though I'm sure he'll work back this way before it snows. A man with a host that large has to consider both his supplies and the roads that deliver them."

"I'd guess their location has as much to do with Badagis as the Skolani," Urias said.

Thadmeir gripped the arms of his chair. "Badagis has always

been more loyal to Keisella than to his own people. It's the same with all of the unaligned herdsmen in the eastern marches. They'd rather bow to a Skolani queen than answer to a council of their peers. And Keisella has always favored Vahldan. Just as she did his father before him. You say he's building a coalition. Sounds like he's out there to whisper in Keisella's ear. They're all plotting against me."

Urias resisted rolling his eyes. "I'm sure that's not true."

"That woman deceived me in Oium. Vahldan's Skolani wench stayed with him, in spite of Keisella's assurances otherwise. What ever came of that one? Is she still with him?"

Urias had been wondering about Elan, too, but he'd been afraid to ask.

Ulfhamr nodded. "Oh, she's still with him. More than that, she's great with child."

Urias heard a soft gasp from above. He covertly glanced up to spot movement through the slats to the loft. Amaga was listening. She'd likely deny it, especially around her father, but he suspected his niece harbored fantasies about a destiny shared with Vahldan the Bringer.

"Is it his?" Thadmeir asked. Urias felt a jolt of defensiveness but kept silent.

"I presume," Ulfhamr said. "I doubt he'd keep the wench with him if it wasn't." Urias felt another jolt. He'd never told his brother of learning that Elan was his sister, nor anyone else. "Some say the nearness of her birthing time is the real reason the lions have settled down out east as they have. I doubt he's that sensitive," Ulfhamr added.

Thadmeir stroked his beard. "We need to find out what he's up to. Vahldan's clearly maneuvering for some power play at the solstice. When it comes, I need to be ready. Perhaps there's an opportunity here." He gave Urias an arch look. "If he *is* scheming to gain Skolani support for whatever he's about to pull—and I'm sure he is —perhaps you could persuade your *dear friend*, the princess, to share what she knows with us, Brother."

Urias hated his brother's paranoia. But experience told him that arguing made it worse.

He also hated that Thadmeir had gleaned his feelings for Icannes. More than that, Urias hated how his heart accelerated at the mere mention of her name. It was foolish. Icannes had made her own feelings clear after their last liaison, when she'd invited him to the Skolani fertility ceremony. Icannes had spoken plainly. That night was to be their one and only chance to enjoy being a couple. She'd even promised when they parted to never forget their moment together. And though Urias hoped some version of their friendship remained intact, he'd seen her only once since, several years ago, in an official capacity. His one-time lover had been cordial but devastatingly formal. To this day he had to fight the impulse to dwell on her.

And now this.

Beyond all of it, Urias knew he was one of the few who could keep Thadmeir calm these days, especially with Amaseila being as ill as she was. If Urias left his brother to go east, he'd be gone at least a fortnight. At a critical time. It would feel like leaving a volatile teenager alone.

He straightened. "I'd have no way of getting word to Icannes, let alone speak with her."

Thadmeir smiled. "Nonsense. You're the clever one, Urias, remember? And that princess is a sly one, too. Brash, but not without wit. If you ride out there, I'm sure the two of you could manage a rendezvous." His brother waggled his eyebrows.

Urias glared. Thadmeir's sardonic and suggestive tone morphed into pleading. "Please, Brother. Can you, this once, do something for me? Without all of your diplomacy and fret over appearances. I swear, my intentions are pure. I need this."

"*You* need this?"

"*We* need this," Thadmeir amended. "Please. Help me to keep our people whole. I know you believe in restoring the futhark. And you must trust me when I say that I do, too. But surely you can see that it cannot be accomplished through bullying. It will take finesse and patience. Only we can ensure such a course. The task is up to us now."

Urias inwardly slumped. He turned to Ulfhamr. "Would you and your men escort me?"

"No," Thadmeir interjected. Urias frowned. His brother's demeanor had flipped so swiftly. "I mean, the best odds for achieving quiet success lie in approaching alone. We don't want to stir things up with the Amalus. Besides, I have other duties for our cousin."

Urias felt annoyed. It was a daunting enough task without having to face it alone. And yet... The thought of having a reason to see Icannes had spurred his yearning. Being alone with her made the thought all the more thrilling. Still, riding into the Skolani hunting grounds without permission didn't seem wise. He could be summarily shot for his trouble. Beyond that, what if she refused to see him?

But what if she didn't? And, if he refused, how long would his brother hold a grudge? What if a conflict with Vahldan escalated? Was there really a chance he could avert it?

The arguments for going won out. "As you wish, my lord," he said.

"YOU THINK we're already being watched?" Urias asked. He'd known it would happen but he hadn't supposed it would begin so soon.

"I don't think it, I know it," his guide said. "The scouts will keep a close watch on us from here on."

"Are we in danger?" Urias asked, trying to sound unruffled.

His guide, a young trapper named Haidegern, shrugged. "Depends."

"On what?"

"On our manners, mostly."

That didn't help. Who knew what constituted proper manners to the Skolani? "Will heading for their village uninvited be considered good manners?"

"That's the right question," the young man said. Again, it was unhelpful.

"Surely they'll glean I intend only to convey my lord's best wishes for the maintenance of the alliance."

Haidegern squinted. "I doubt they'll bother reading that much into it. Besides, Skolani don't much care for intentions. For them, actions are what matter most. The closer you get to the Jabitka, or to one of the royals, the more dangerous they'll become." The man grinned as if he knew an inside joke. "Intentions aside, I'm guessing you'll be safer than most." For the first time, young Haidegern turned to him, eyes sparkling with mirth. Urias felt like the joke was on him. "Not sure what they'll glean 'bout you. But from what I've heard, you've already been the best sort of friend a male can be. And with one of the best who could've picked you."

Where had the lad heard that? Who was this trapper, anyway? The tanner in Danihem who had introduced them had been as evasive as the young man himself continued to be. Haidegern was ruggedly handsome and well-built. His full beard matched his tussled mop of golden hair. He was younger than Urias had originally thought, perhaps still in his late teens. He seemed oddly wise and mysterious for his age.

Urias had been looking for clues and hints as to his identity since they had left Danihem. Everything from Haidegern's doeskin tunic to the torcs on his arms and the way he wore an axe harnessed on his back was reminiscent of the Skolani. Beyond his curious attire, he seemed foreign and yet somehow familiar.

"You seem to know a lot about the Skolani," Urias said, probing again.

The young man's smile faded. "You could say." Evasive as ever.

"Mind if I ask how that is?"

Haidegern gave a shrug. "Don't mind if you ask."

"Does that mean I won't get an answer?"

Another shrug. "Not much to tell. I suppose it's because I live so close."

"You grew up near the Jabitka?"

"You could say." Haidegern's smirk returned. "'Bout as close as any outsider could."

Realization struck. "You've never said who your father is," Urias ventured.

The lad's smile faded again. "No. I didn't."

They rode on in silence. It didn't matter. Urias had a good guess now. And if his guess was correct, perhaps the lad himself was unsure. Either way, pressing him seemed unwise.

Urias recalled Icannes telling him about what became of male children born to the Skolani—how they most often went to the households of the fathers. But she had also said half-jokingly that this was the way it was handled *most of the time*, implying there were exceptions. Urias had gathered that Icannes was skirting a secret about her own family.

The conversation had come about because she'd made it clear that she sought a result from their coupling. She'd then assured him he would be left unencumbered, come what may. Of course Icannes had noticed his distress. She was sharp and observant—particularly with those for whom she cared. Plus, she had been with him when he had learned of his own Skolani mother—a woman of which he'd known nothing till that moment, not even her name. Icannes was also well aware of how lucky Urias had been, ending up in a stable and loving home. She'd reassured him that a potential male child would be as cared for as the sought-after daughter.

As much as he'd relished their moment together, the thought of leaving her with child had left him troubled. That this odd Skolani custom held sway over what might have come of their pairing left him with a lingering discontent. She hadn't even offered him a vote.

Which brought him to his suspicion about his guide, who seemed as close to looking like a male Skolani as he could imagine.

The lad also bore a strong resemblance to a man long rumored to have carried on a lasting relationship with another royal. A man whose life was well-entwined with Dania's divisive past.

Urias found himself comforted by the thought. If he had to endure riding into increasing danger under the watch of merciless Skolani sentinels so near to an Amalus host's camp, at least there was a good chance he was doing so in the company of the son of the Skolani queen and a vaunted Amalus captain.

AT THE END of a travel day of intense listening and watching, Urias had yet to detect the Skolani scouts' presence. It only made him more nervous. Tonight his young guide made matters worse by setting out after dark, leaving him alone in the depths of a pine forest. Though Haidegern had told him that he was simply checking on a hunch, and that it was fine for Urias to leave the fire burning and to rest easy beside it, the young man had clearly been provoked by something; the lad had been unable to mask his wariness.

It was windy and cold. The sky was clear, but the evergreens were tall and dense here. What little moonlight came through the swaying boughs only cast moving shadows that kept him on edge. Urias knew building up the fire wasn't exactly the wisest thing to do. It could only make his presence more apparent. Not to mention making him all the more night blind. It didn't necessarily make him safer, and yet he found comfort in the blaze. He also felt what he knew to be false security in having a bare blade leaning against the log he used as his seat.

Only moments after he'd fed the fire and settled again, the brush stirred alarmingly close by. Urias leapt to his feet, spilling his mead and clutching his sword. "Who's there?"

"I wouldn't call that resting easy, Captain." Haidegern flashed his bedamned grin as he appeared. Urias hated when he did that—the lad was always sneaking up on him.

Haidegern strode to his gear and spoke over his shoulder as he began saddling his mount. "I ran into some folks. They're moving at their own pace, but they should be here fairly soon."

Urias was befuddled. "What? Who? Are you leaving?"

"Yes, I'm riding ahead to deliver a message. Turns out these folks are looking for you."

"For me?"

Haidegern nodded. "Asked after you right off. I offered to stay and make the introductions, but they said there was no need." The young man finished buckling the girth and started on the harness.

"How will I find the rest of the way?"

Haidegern laughed. "It won't be a problem." He unstrung his bow, strapped it over his shoulder, and buckled his quiver to his saddle. "I'll have to leave some of my gear with you. I need to travel light."

"How will you retrieve it?" Urias also wondered how in the gods' names he'd carry it.

"Just leave it with the Skolani."

Before he could ask the next question, Haidegern extended his hand. "Well, it's been fine getting to know you, Captain." Urias had no choice but to grasp the lad's forearm. "At first I didn't, but I've come to see what she sees in you." Haidegern grinned. "I'm happy. For both of you." Urias realized then—he'd guessed correctly. Icannes was this young man's big sister. It was as close to an admission as he would get. He felt himself flushing.

The young man released his arm and mounted. From the saddle, Haidegern said, "I hope to see you again someday. Seems likely. Be well." The lad reined and vanished into the darkness.

Urias didn't know what to do with himself, so he repoured his mead. Before he sat, horses approached at a walk. He didn't suppose a naked blade was very welcoming. In spite of his apprehension, he convinced himself to sheath it. He had no reason to mistrust Haidegern.

"Ah, my favorite wolf. How convenient, running across you out here."

When the speaker came into the firelight, Urias could nearly have sworn that Angavar the Outcast had returned from across Hel's bridge. "By the gods. Vahldan the Bold, right here in Dania. Or should I say, *Lord* Vahldan the Bold?" He bowed his head.

"Bah, we've known each other too long for titles. And I've never been too fond of having accusations attached to my name." Vahldan grinned. "May we join you?"

"Yes, yes, by all means. I'd love the company."

Vahldan strode into the firelight, tall and looking much more like the rightful Lion Lord than the youth Urias had last seen in Oium. He wore a fine crimson cloak with a fur collar. His flaxen hair was tied behind his head, and his futhark sword's hilt rose from over his shoulder. He led two horses, and Urias not only recognized the sorrel mare but her rider, too. "Gods be kind, this night keeps getting better." Elan rode awkwardly, holding her great belly with one hand and the reins with the other. Urias bowed. "I'm truly delighted to see you again, Blade-Wielder."

She groaned as Vahldan helped her from the saddle. Elan stood, hands on hips, stretching her back and appraising Urias. "There should be several ways for someone as clever as you to deduce that I am no longer a Blade-Wielder, Captain. And none of them have to do with my not bearing a sword at the moment."

Elan had never been girlish, but it had been some time since he last saw her. Only now did he realize how young she'd been then. She was clearly a woman now. Her handsome face was etched by experience. Her gaze was knowing and her countenance assured. Most surprising was her hair. It was the same color, but it was unbraided and cut just below the jawline, with bangs swept from her forehead and tucked behind an ear. It was shorter than most men kept their hair. She wore fine boots, a simple frock of spun cloth, and a woolen cloak over her shoulders.

"Please, sit. May I offer you both mead? There's plenty to share."

Vahldan helped Elan to sit by the fire and said, "Yes, please."

Urias found the skin, wiped his spare cup, and poured. He turned to Elan. "You?"

She shook her head. "No, thank you. Makes me queasy these days." She leaned on one hand and held her cloak tight with the other. She looked less than comfortable.

Once they were all seated, Urias raised his cup to Vahldan. "Welcome back, my lord, and my... lady." He lifted his cup to Elan, too. She frowned.

They drank. "You're surprised?" Vahldan asked.

Urias raised a brow. "To meet you in the middle of the forest, after dark? Undeniably."

Vahldan smiled. "You mentioned our being in Dania. You're surprised by our return?"

"Gods, no. I never doubted that you'd one day come home. And your coming has stirred much too large a commotion for me to have not heard about it by now."

"A commotion, you say? Even in Danihem?"

"Oh yes. These days, few topics can rival that of your presence."

"I can't imagine why. There was never any other intention."

Clearly Vahldan's combative nature hadn't faded with maturity. "That's just it. It's been long enough that few can guess at your intentions, my lord. However long you've kept them."

Vahldan turned to Elan. "Seems strange to have our intentions questioned simply for coming home, doesn't it, darling?" He smiled wryly but Elan only stared at the fire.

Urias saw no reason to be evasive. "Most in Danihem would claim that you're the one making it strange. For those of us who live there, it's you who maintains the mystery."

"*I'm* maintaining a mystery?" Vahldan laid a hand on his chest, play-acting at shock.

"Most would presume a man hailed as a royal clan chieftain would come to Danihem to claim his seat on the dais before a council of his peers. Instead, they hear you've been roaming the countryside, mustering a host at a time when most Danians attend to harvesting crops. I must admit, even I consider it a bit mysterious."

Vahldan shook his head. "Ah, you wolves. You never change. Don't you see? I feel no need to claim a chair. I came to be with my people, Captain. And the folks out here don't seem to see it as a mystery. They gather to me for the same reason I came to them. This is a homecoming—something to be celebrated. There's nothing to be debated or claimed. Seems to me that harvest time is perfect for celebrating. And yet your brother and his lot see only that my host is growing. I suppose it's not the first time that their willful refusal to try to understand others has led to mistrust. Mistrust has caused so much hardship over the years, don't you think?"

Urias saw it then. The whole thing was a game to him. He was merely checking on the game's status. Urias figured he may as well play along. "Since you understand mistrust so well, you must understand how your methods have left many wondering if it's a homecoming or an insurgency."

"Insurgency?" Vahldan spat. "Dania is my home, Captain. Same as it's yours and your brother's. If you wish to speak of the causes of mistrust, please remember that it wasn't me or any of my followers who perpetuated the farce that Desdrusan thrust upon us. Just as it wasn't me that set the conditions that led to the murder of your brother and the wrongful banishment of my father. Now *that* was an insurgency. Do you deny it?"

He remembered that he was here to avert an escalating conflict. He shook his head. "No, I can't deny it. All of that was wrongful. And many of those who stood by while it happened are now the most worried. Does this surprise you, my lord?"

Vahldan drew a deep breath and released it. "No. I'm sure it's true."

"I ask you to please remember that I am an advocate of balance. I hope you recognize by now that I seek the restoration of the futhark."

Vahldan nodded. "Of course you do. Forgive me, Urias. I know you're not one of them." That quickly, Vahldan's demeanor had flipped again. He was as volatile as ever. But he still hadn't admitted that his own behavior was fostering division.

"If you continue to badger our host," Elan said, "he'll never agree to the favor we've come to ask."

Urias raised his brows. "Favor?" He was the one who'd traveled east seeking favor. He wondered what he could possibly do for them.

Vahldan grinned. "Ah, yes. A very important one. And speaking of trust—you, Captain, are not only one of the few who can accomplish it, but one of the very few I would trust for it."

"Please, don't leave me in suspense."

"Will you consider watching over something very precious to me, Urias?"

"I'm happy to be of service. But I think it would be wise to have you tell me more about this precious possession before I answer."

Vahldan took Elan's hand. "Oddly, I need you to become the guardian of my guardian."

"Me? A guardian?"

Vahldan cocked his head. "Yes, you. I want you to take Elan with you to the Jabitka. I'm asking you to see to her safety until you're sure another can take your place."

Urias watched Elan. She glanced, then turned to the fire, furtive. Was she blushing? "Again, I am happy to serve. But I am quite sure Elan would more easily find her way to the Jabitka than I ever could. Besides, she's always been the more capable guardian."

"I will hardly be welcome in the Jabitka, Captain," Elan said. "Whereas you will be happily anticipated. And I'm hardly in the condition to be considered a capable guardian."

Urias was still worried. "Just the two of us, then? What if... I know nothing of—"

"Men," she spat. "If the babe comes, I'll be in no better circumstances with you than I am now. Don't concern yourself. I'll handle it."

He gave in. "I'd be honored, my lord. My... lady." He still didn't know what to call her.

She gave a stolid nod. "Excellent," Vahldan said. "You've eased my mind, old friend."

Urias felt he had to try a final time. "As a return favor, perhaps you'd consider going to Danihem to speak with my brother?"

Vahldan smiled. "Urias of the Wulthus, I intend to do exactly that."

CHAPTER 9
A GHOST'S MOTIVES

"Powerful superstitions remain among the Skolani in regard to the banished, or 'ghosts' as they're henceforth known. Legends and campfire tales warn of ghosts' devious intentions and of their corrupting influence on a warrior's resolve. But a more potent force exists—a powerful and enduring force that makes any contact with the Skolani very dangerous for the banished: resentment.*

No small part of its power resides in the knowledge that, through surrender to weakness, the banished have access to aspects of life which are denied to the diligent Skolani warrior. It's a resentment fueled by the volatile combination of envy and a sense of betrayal."—Brin Bright Eyes, Saga of Dania

AT DAWN, Urias was already mounted and waiting for her. Elan made a face at him. To his credit, realization swiftly struck. Urias looked away and walked his mount off a few steps, giving them the privacy she'd wordlessly demanded. She had thought of Urias often over the years. She couldn't help but feel pleased that Vahldan had so readily agreed to utilize him like this. Even though she knew his agreement was partly rooted in his desire to take the next steps free from the presence of her judgement.

Vahldan came to help her into the saddle. She lunged to hug him. When he sought to draw back, she refused to let go. Elan knew things were about to change. She knew that a major part of their life together was ending. She'd never been one to shy away from change. But this felt different—as though nothing would be in her control again.

She clung to him, feeling the strength in his limbs, the breadth of his shoulders. Elan put her nose into his chest and breathed him in. The next time she'd see him, she will have given birth. It made her mourn their choices and the life that might have been for them.

"You don't have to do this," she whispered.

"You know I do."

There it was. Just for an instant, his rage flashed in his eyes. It was part of what frightened her. He seemed to have recently come to believe that what he called the ugliness could be tolerated, even useful. Their bond had originally been formed through her ability to anchor him and keep him from losing himself.

What would come of them if he no longer cared whether or not he lost himself?

"I'm frightened," she admitted. "I want to be there with you. Please. Wait for me."

He shook his head. "We've been over this. It can't wait. This is it. The time is now. This may be the only chance we get."

Gods, it couldn't be true. "There'll always be other chances. For now, we can go away, just us. And be like we were. For just a while longer. We could be a real couple, like we were on the island. Alone."

Vahldan sighed and gently kissed her lips. "You know how much I loved those days. And you also know that I can't."

"I still think we can. We could be a family, just us and our daughter. Just for a while more." Long enough for his true self to appraise a better path forward.

He put his hands on the sides of her face and tilted her head, forcing her to look at him. "You know I was born to be more. Our people depend on it. I've never misled you. You've known this since the beginning, my love."

Elan was tired of fighting, tired of trying to change him—tired of living for the bedamned Urrinan. It was like running a race in which the finish line was their doom. She looked away. She withdrew from his embrace and reluctantly nodded. It was done. He'd won.

She belonged to him, and he belonged to destiny. She'd already made her choice. All was forgone now. The day she'd walked away from her old life, she'd willingly bound herself to this fate. But she still had one last choice—the choice to shield her daughter from that fate. It was time to take her own next steps.

No one, not even the bedamned gods, would dare to take this from Elan. Not after all she'd endured, all she'd sacrificed. She would see to it that her daughter got to live the life Elan had walked away from in the name of his forsaken destiny.

He held onto her waist, keeping her near. "I understand how you feel here. You know this is not my home, either. We are both banished. *You* are my home. Come what may."

Elan nodded to acquiesce and put her hands on his shoulders to indicate she was ready to mount. He lifted and she managed to get one foot in the stirrup and the other leg up and over. Gods, so gracefully done. No wonder Blade-Wielders hid themselves away during this obscene joke the gods played on women. She balanced in the saddle, waiting for a dizzy spell to pass. She felt the precariousness of her daughter resting against Hrithvarra's neck. Only her dearest and oldest friend could be trusted with such a precious cargo. Both she and the mare were still relishing being reunited. At least it was clear that Mara had not just taken good care of Hrithvarra but had loved her. Learning of it had eased Elan's guilt over leaving her dear friend.

"Shall we, then?" Urias flashed his bedamned charming smile. The man seemed perpetually cheerful. At the moment it was getting on her nerves.

She nodded. He didn't set out. "Well?" she said to prompt him.

"Forgive me, my lady, but I was guided to this point. I don't know which way to go."

"First, don't call me that."

"What shall I call you?"

"How about Elan?" She was being snappish, but it couldn't be helped.

And yet, there was that smile again. "Fine. Elan it is. Please call me Urias."

She nodded toward the path. "Fine. Go east, Urias."

He moved in compliance. She turned to Vahldan. He waved. In the morning sunlight, he looked so innocent and young. The very image of the young man she'd fallen in love with, all those years ago. Back then she would never have guessed at the curse their love would become. Worse, she'd never have guessed at the ruthlessness he'd one day be capable of envisioning, all in service to a foretold doom.

Elan turned from him to face the rising sun, stroking her daughter in her belly with one hand and twining her fingers through her friend's mane with the other, heading toward a home that was no longer hers, away from a love and a life that could never again be the same.

ELAN RODE BEHIND URIAS, both of them in silence as the sun rose and stole the chill from the autumn air. She longed to distract herself from the hopelessness of parting with Vahldan and of what it might bring. She tried to look ahead, but that frightened her almost as much as what she was leaving behind. The man riding before her was practically a stranger. She hadn't seen him in years. She felt so alone, and it was of her own doing. How could she have placed herself into the hands of a stranger at such a critical moment?

They were riding into the hunting grounds of her former people, fully aware that they were being monitored. Ironically, those who kept these lands safe posed the most imminent of the many threats Elan now faced. She tried to set them all from her mind. One hope remained for her mission. She had to believe. This one aspect of her life might yet end well.

At least her fret distracted her from her bedamned physical discomfort.

Rocking along in the saddle soon caused Elan to flush again. The brisk air felt good on her skin. The pine-covered foothills gave way to the oaks, beeches, and meadows that surrounded the Jabitka. The path broadened and Urias slowed and beckoned her to ride up beside him. She really didn't want to talk. Still, he was doing her a favor. She nudged Hrithvarra ahead and they proceeded abreast. She faced forward, trying to make it clear she was fine with silence.

"It seems like Vahldan has come to believe in Amaseila's foretelling." Elan tried ignoring him. "I mean, it seems he's come to believe he might really be the Bringer."

Ignoring him hadn't worked. Perhaps shaming him. "It's not polite to pry," she said.

"Sorry, I couldn't help but overhear. But I only heard a bit."

Elan finally looked at him. "Most everything Vahldan does, he does in the name of Urrinan." Urias lifted both eyebrows. "It's a burden, you know. He feels he must."

"Or what?" There was his bedamned smile again.

"Or his people—our people—will fail to ascend," she said. "As has been foretold."

"So he does it all for others—no advantage to himself?"

"Is that a question or an accusation, Captain?" That wiped the smile off his mouth.

"Sorry, but I'm honestly curious. And you agreed to call me Urias."

"Well, Urias," she pointedly said. "I would say that many if not most deeds done for others have a benefit for those who do them. Even if the doer does not recognize them. I would call it human nature. And Vahldan is no less human." She looked at him again. "Are you?"

"Me? Gods, no." Once again, Urias smiled his smile. "Just look at me now—taking advantage of the deed of escorting you by pestering you with questions." He finally broke her mood. She couldn't help but chuckle. He inclined his head and went on. "It's just that, last Vahldan and I spoke of the prophecy, he seemed much more doubtful. He seemed wary of its effect, on himself and on others. I suppose that was a long time ago."

The man actually seemed worried. He was either a good actor or truly concerned. Still, a question remained: Was Urias concerned *for* Vahldan, or *about* him?

"Vahldan realizes it's not his to know whether his circumstances are divine or contrived. He faces his fate squarely." She thought about it for a moment. "From where I stand, he faces it mostly selflessly. I sometimes wonder how those who judge him would react to such a legacy and fate." Elan gave him an arch glance. Urias had the decency to look abashed.

"So the two of you never bonded, or married—whatever they call it in Pontea?"

"To do so would not be fitting to the prophecy." She officially hated this conversation.

"Why do you stay with him?" Elan turned to him wearing her best scowl. "I mean, he won't take you as a wife. And it's not as though he continues to need a Blade-Wielder guardian. Besides, you said yourself, you're no longer one of those."

Again, Elan considered ignoring him. "Feel free to ignore me," he offered. Gods, he was charming *and* perceptive.

"I can never leave him," she admitted, to Urias and to herself. "Not really." Even while being apart from him for her current mission, he was a part of her.

"Never? That's a long time," he observed.

Elan raised a brow. "Maybe." And maybe not, she thought. "He needs me. He will till..." She bowed her head and held her belly. "I belong to him," she said, just above a whisper. "There's nothing for it." Whatever came of them as a couple, he would change the world. For better or worse, she was a part of it. They were both beyond turning back.

Elan glanced at Urias, who seemed rattled. Maybe that was a good place to leave it. She found she couldn't. For some reason, she wanted Urias to understand. She turned in the saddle to face him squarely. "Look, I chose this. I knew then what I was choosing. I've always known what it will require of me. Which is the very reason that I need to go with you. I won't subject my daughter to my fate. She should be given the chance to choose, just as I did."

"I see." He really did seem to.

They rode in silence for a time. A view opened to the river to their left, the maples and birches lining its banks offering shocks of yellow and red among the green oaks. She reined in, halting Hrithvarra to take it in. She'd only seen the river in snatches since they'd returned to Dania. The water was high on the banks and muddy. The current looked swift and treacherous. Gods, it was beautiful. Her back ached, and her daughter was getting restless.

The day had started out in hopelessness, in resignation. But the river was eternal. Always changing but never really different. The sight reminded her of how much she missed this land—her old life. It reminded her of the promise she once felt in the future.

"Tell me about her," Urias said from behind.

Strangely, Elan instantly knew to whom he referred. She'd wondered if they would, or should, acknowledge the rummaging beast in the tent of their fellowship. But, she had to admit, it was a big part of why she'd chosen him.

"Her name was Ellasan," Elan softly said.

"That much I've heard. But little else."

"Our mother was a healer. She had a touch. One that always made others feel special."

"Special?"

"Maybe worthy is a better word." Elan smiled.

"Tell me," he prodded.

"The first time the elders turned aside my petition to be trained, I went to her, sulking and feeling defeated. Ellasan said, 'You may as well go and sit with the menials.' These are the Skolani who grind corn and work leather. She knew just what to say. We both knew I wasn't cut out for sitting. She made sure I never gave up—that I knew I had a special purpose in this life. Something worth striving for." Elan bowed to the river in unspoken thanks.

"She sounds wise," Urias said.

Elan nodded. "Loving, too. She held me for as long as I needed it —without saying a word. This may not sound odd to you, but believe me, it is rare among Skolani mothers."

"She was sensitive."

"Sensitive, yes. But brave, also. She died rushing to the service of a fallen companion during a Spali attack."

"Icannes told me. It's much the same as our father, you know. I never knew him, but his final act was very brave, by all accounts. Lord Theudaric's brother—who was our father's dear friend—had been overrun in battle, wounded and surrounded, at the whim of the foe. Usshvar rallied his fellows, reversing their retreat. He all but singlehandedly fought his way back and held off the foe while his friend was carried to safety. He stayed behind and fought to the death so that another might live."

Elan took that in, staring at the endless flow of the river. "Our mother was no warrior, but she was fierce—a force to be reckoned with. She was determined and true to her convictions. When she was censored over her inappropriate relationship with our father, she stood her ground. She defied the elders, risking her status as a healer. After you were born, she was determined to have me. Grandmother Sael had dreamed she and our father would have a daughter of destiny. Ellasan broke with an ancient decree to lay with him again. When she became pregnant, and the elders gleaned by whom, she was to be dosed, to rid her of me. She ran—went away and lived on her own until she had me. She brought me into this world alone, without aid. Only our grandmother's prestige and her own skill as a healer allowed Ellasan to eventually return to the Jabitka with me. After earning their disfavor, she bravely petitioned the elders again and again to have me trained. As you can imagine, I was anything but a favored child. I owe everything to our mother. She not only fought to ensure I gained my status, she fought for my very existence."

"Brave, fierce, determined, loyal, true to herself... Sounds familiar." She frowned, puzzled. Urias laughed. "You do realize how well you fit the legacy, do you not?"

"I don't know, Brother. Do you?"

His smile faded but his eyes shone, blue as the autumn sky. "Brother. I like the sound of that. I heard that Skolani don't recognize brothers. I wondered if I'd ever earn the right to be called that by you. Or to think of you as my sister."

Gods, he really was adorable when he wanted to be. "Let's just say you're earning it today. By being my guardian."

"I feel I must remind you that I really don't know the way." He winked.

"It doesn't matter. What matters is that bringing me along is not going to be a boon to your goals here. Far from it. I may even ruin your chances."

"Oh? How is it you presume to know my goals?" He was toying with her.

"I think I have a pretty good idea. About both the goals you discussed with your lord and those you didn't." She winked back.

Urias had the decency to blush. "Perhaps we'd best get to it, then. No time like the present to find out whether we're in or out." He reined back to the path.

She turned Hrithvarra to follow. "It may be too soon for me," she grumbled, wondering once again what she'd do if she were rebuffed —something that seemed more and more likely as they grew nearer without any sign of contact.

It seemed more and more likely she'd soon be alone when her

daughter came, just as her mother had been. She'd known the story of her birth for many years. Now the thought terrified her and made her admire and miss Ellasan all the more.

Elan's sense of unease only grew. She kept Urias ahead of her and on the trail that led to the old visitors' campsite—the spot where she'd first taken Vahldan almost a decade before. As they neared the camp, the signs grew, becoming more frequent and overt. They had attracted the attention of more than a few sentinels. Indeed, they were utterly surrounded. It did not bode well.

Finally the taunts started. "Go back!" was the first. Urias twisted in the saddle. She nodded for him to continue. "Ghosts are not welcome," came next, acknowledging her identity. Elan didn't recognize the voice. Then, "Ghost-whore, begone!" That one prompted cruel laughter. The guttural calls came from all sides, nearer each time.

It got worse. "Take your filth from here, ghost-whore!" And, "Go whelp your beastie elsewhere."

Urias's face reddened, and his hand drifted to his hilt. "No. Hands off," Elan said. He pointedly held the reins. "Eyes forward; keep moving."

An arrow grazed Urias's horse's rear fetlock, causing the animal to bolt. This was worse than she had dared imagine. They were separating her from him. She'd purposely come unarmed—a decision she now regretted. The surrounding foliage boiled with activity. She had to act fast. She pulled her leg over and slid from the saddle. She landed with a jolt and swatted her friend into flight. "Fluga, Hrithvarra. Go!" The mare obeyed. No Skolani would harm a riderless horse.

Elan knew she should hold her hands clear, but she couldn't keep from cradling her belly, her every instinct screaming for her to protect her babe.

A group of a half-dozen appeared, all painted and smeared for stealth work. They were young—likely senior protégés or newly risen Blade-Wielders. Thankfully, none of them had drawn bows or bared blades. Instead, they held switches. The worst of it was, Elan didn't recognize any of them. She heard Urias pleading in the distance. He was being kept from her. She was in for a beating. Elan broke into a cold sweat.

She knew better than to beg or show weakness. She decided to try to reason with them. "Listen, I mean no insult," she began.

"You *are* the insult, ghost-whore," the tallest snarled. They closed in. The first to charge slashed at her belly as she passed. The switch mostly hit the backs of Elan's hands, drawing bloody welts. She dropped to her knees. It would earn her more hits, and possibly some kicks, but she had to protect her daughter.

She bent over her belly and braced. The next hit was to her back, which was padded by her cloak. She was less fortunate when the third hit on the side of her head—it felt like it tore her earlobe off. Elan dropped onto her forearms and hunched into a ball. They gathered to stand over her, raining stinging slashes all over her. She felt hoofbeats drumming the forest floor and then heard the battle cry filled with an ungodly rage. It felt like a dream from her youth.

Once again, her savior had come.

Elan glanced up just as the boots hit the turf between her and her startled attackers. Icannes was a whirling demon from the underworld, raging and thrashing the youths with a wooden practice sword, same as the first time.

The attackers shrieked and fled. It was over in mere moments. Icannes tossed aside the wooden sword and dropped to her knees beside her. "Oh, dear one, are you hurt?"

Elan sat up, flexing her bloody hands, then gingerly touching her stinging ear to find it still attached and in one piece. "I think I'll survive," she managed. Elan felt the babe kick, and relief flowed through her.

Icannes took her hands, gently wiping the blood with her cloak, then bringing the welts to her lips. Their eyes met. And the gods' own magic struck Elan like a thunderbolt, sending a surge of love she'd thought long faded gushing through her, straight to her heart.

Icannes clearly felt it, too. Her goddess of the mortal realm seized her and pulled her in, hugging Elan tight and rocking her. They stayed like that for what seemed both an instant and a lifetime. "I'll kill the little bitches," Icannes finally growled. "And I'll thrash Anallya for putting them up to it."

Elan drew herself back. "The blood-bitch was behind this?"

Icannes clenched her jaw and nodded. "She's been given her own host. Of course she collects the most vicious she-demons. Then she makes them worse in training."

In spite of it all, Elan laughed. "She deserves them. Maybe one day they'll turn on her."

Icannes's harsh glare melted to a grin. She hugged Elan again. "Oh, my dear heart. How I've missed you."

"And I you, my love."

Icannes tenderly held her face and appraised her. "By Horsella's tits, your hair!" She ran her fingers through Elan's short locks. "It's adorable." Before Elan could reply, Icannes bent and laid her hands upon Elan's round belly. "And this has finally happened. Your first, right?" Elan nodded. Icannes bent and spoke to her belly. "Hello in there, Baby Brin. Are you ready to come out and meet your Aunt Icannes?"

Fresh tears sprang to Elan's eyes. "You remember her name."

"Of course I do. I helped to pick it, didn't I?"

Urias appeared on foot. Without turning to him, Icannes said, "Welcome, Captain. Thank you for delivering our momma-to-be safely to me."

"Well, most of the way, at least," he said. "Are you all right, Elan?"

"I'll be fine," she assured him.

"You brought her farther than most could have, I assure you," Icannes said.

Urias bowed. "Up till a moment ago, it was a pleasure and an honor, my princess."

Icannes stood and helped Elan to her feet. She spoke over her shoulder to Urias. "You are to be rewarded. With an audience with my mother."

"Princess?"

Icannes's smile was wry. "It is why you've come, is it not?"

"That's only partly true, Princess Icannes. It *is* what my lord would wish of me."

Icannes's smile became sly. "I'm quite interested in the other true parts. But for now we have to get our sister away from here, before my mother comes."

"Away?" Elan exclaimed. "I'd hoped to see the queen—to petition her on Brin's behalf."

Icannes's eyes grew sad and she slowly shook her head. "I'm sorry, dear heart. It's not to be. Not yet, anyway."

Elan crumpled. Everything she'd come for—the final hope she'd clung to—was beyond reach. Her connection to Vahldan was fading. He was embarking on a course toward their doom. Her daughter would have no home, no people of her own—same as Elan.

Elan really was just a ghost.

All was lost. She slumped, unable to hold back her sobs. Icannes lifted her and held her and said, "Stay strong, my dear heart. And be patient. One day, things will change. I promise."

"But how? And how will I...? My babe... I can't do this... Not alone." Elan gulped for air between sobs. She was useless. She didn't even know how to have a babe.

"Alone? Oh no, my darling. You will have help. And not just from me."

Icannes took Elan under her arm and turned her, pointing off into the clearing beyond. Cackling laughter rode the breeze to her ears. She staggered toward the familiar sound with Icannes's help. The crone was propped up, wrapped in a blanket next to their tethered horses. She looked so small. Her wispy hair was even whiter, the lenses of her upward-staring eyes all the more clouded. But she looked as vibrant as ever. Elan fell into her bony, outstretched arms.

"Grandmother! Thank the gods, you're still alive."

Sael rocked her and laughed. "Ah, child. You didn't dream you'd be rid of me so easily, did you? After all, I've yet to meet this fierce daughter of yours."

CHAPTER 10
THE PROPER FOOTING

"I have already spoken of the resentment directed at the banished. But there was also much resentment felt by the banished themselves, and my mother was no exception.

I know little of Elan's aspirations and hopes for my birth. To me she never spoke of such things, but over the years I have come to understand that some of her hopes were dashed upon my arrival. It is not so difficult to grasp how new resentments could have been born along with me.

From a very young age, I sensed a distance between us. It was a distance I myself came to resent, which created a barrier all the more difficult for us to overcome. I once found a certain irony in the realization that my resentment was born of hers. I have come to appreciate how this same condition lies at the core of most human conflict, and how often strife is incited by it."—Brin Bright Eyes, Saga of Dania

"I'M sorry I killed you, Mother." There was no reply. Not even a whisper on the wind.

The thing that alarmed Amaga the most was the complete severance death had imposed. She felt absolutely nothing of her mother.

Amaga hadn't expected that. Her mother had assured her death was but a veil. Apparently one through which Amaga could not yet perceive.

She couldn't help but to resent that she was unable to hear the voice of the goddess as Amaseila did. Her mother always said she shouldn't question Freya's gifts, that she should be happy with her visions. But since her mother's passing, there had been nothing—no voice, no vision. No dream or sensation.

She ran her hand over the cold stones stacked over Amaseila's grave. Well, she did feel *something*. Was it mere memory? "I know you never liked me to put it that way. So I suppose I'm sorry that my birth eventually led to your death." Amaga often wondered if it would have been better if she'd never been born. But there was much to be done. She resented that so much of it had landed on her shoulders. The absence of her mother left a heavy burden for Amaga to bear. It was no surprise to her. She'd been born to bear it. But that didn't make acceptance any easier.

"I don't know how I'll do this without you." Amaga turned to face the southerly wind and looked out across the Danian River, toward her impending fate. "He's here, Mother. Finally. I'm afraid."

Still they came, more and more folk, amassing in the meadows outside Danihem's walls. So many! Some had set up pavilions and many built makeshift tents, but most simply slept out in the cold, huddled beside one of a hundred fires. The camp of Vahldan's followers virtually engulfed the village, surrounding it and fanning out to the very edges of the foothill forests. They'd churned the meadows to mud and had dug astonishingly long trenches, latrines, that emptied into the river. Their stench and the eye-stinging smoke of their cookfires assaulted the village.

Amaga shook her head. "It never occurred to me that you wouldn't be here with me when I imagined facing this." How could it be that Amaga had never grasped the power of her mother's presence, and the comfort and sustenance she'd drawn from it, until she was gone?

"She'll always be with you," Kemella said. Her new sister had climbed the rocky path from the rowboat. "She stayed as long as she could, Amaga. There was so much pain. Besides, it's why I'm here. Freya brought me to stand by you in her absence."

Amaga knew she was right. Kemella often was. Not to mention that she was utterly at ease in her skin. Kemella was beautiful and confident—strong in so many ways. Everything Amaga was not. Meeting the man of Amaga's destiny was terrifying. And yet, meeting him with their shared sister seemed less so. Amaga wondered, not for the first time, how she deserved Kemella's devotion.

"It's time," Kemella said and held out her hand. The vista beyond the river revealed to Amaga that her sister was right again. A procession of mounted men was forming on the open ground beyond Dani-hem's south gate. The eve of the solstice had finally come. Vahldan was about to make his grand entrance. Amaga knew she had to be there when he arrived.

She reluctantly put her hand in Kemella's. Amaga avoided touching others, but she knew she would need her new sister's steadying aid in order to keep her footing on the treacherous path ahead. Amaga normally kept the big wooden door to the spirit world shut tight when touching others was inevitable. And although she'd seen Kemella's demise and the pain that would accompany it in snatches, the warmth of her new friend's feelings kept Amaga from examining that terrible distant day too closely. So far she'd been able to restrain herself from looking to see when it would arrive.

Besides the steadying aid, Amaga found she was also able to draw on Kemella's bravery through their contact. It was a new dimension to what Freya had bestowed upon Amaga. Each time Amaga had called it a curse, her mother had shushed her and told her that she could not yet grasp the benefits and the curses she embodied—that both would continue to unfold throughout her life. Amaseila had always assured her daughter that her life served a greater purpose than it was possible to perceive.

Amaga had been surprised to discover another blessing through

Kemella's touch: She could clearly see and feel how devoted Kemella would be to her son. All told, there was more than enough to make the contact worthwhile. Her new sister was teaching Amaga how to love someone other than her parents.

It provided Amaga with a hope that she might find similar blessings in her contact with Kemella's brother.

The girls hurried down to the rowboat and Kemella, being the larger and stronger of them, insisted on rowing once again. Evening turned to twilight as the prow struck the opposite shore. Together they dragged the little boat onto the bank. Kemella started to head around the riverside corral, but Amaga pulled her to the gate. They'd have to hurry to make it. They skipped through, hopping over the manure piles, and Amaga clapped her hands and scolded a stubborn ram from blocking the far gate. She'd long ago learned that many animals were wary of her. Today that too was a benefit rather than a curse.

The village gate stood open, and the lane that led to the commons was deserted, allowing the girls to run most of the distance. As the commons came into view, their way was blocked, mostly by women and children craning to see from the edges of the crowd.

The tension of the crowd was palpable. Amaga started to duck and weave, working her way through the press, pulling Kemella behind her. Horns blew outside the walls, and the gatehouse bell clanged. Vahldan's procession was about to enter the village. Amaga made it to the plank walkway under the longhouse eaves, her heart trilling. Her panic swelled in realizing she couldn't see the arrivals from her usual spot.

A hand grasped her shoulder from behind. She turned to find Kemella standing on the bench alongside the longhouse entrance. Amaga took Kemella's hand, and her friend pulled her up, causing the bench to rock. Their perch was a bit shaky, but if they leaned against the log wall to keep it stable, they had a perfect view over the heads of the crowd.

The gates remained open, as her father had ordered. And yet the gateway was blocked by a line of men. A few wore helms, but all wore hauberks and the green kerchiefs of the Wolf clan. They were the defiant young bannermen of Wulthus Rekkrs. None of the Rekkrs themselves were among them, but they hadn't forbidden the display, either. The young men were obviously spoiling for a fight, seeking any means available to ruin Vahldan's show. This in spite of the fact that Amaga's father had pledged to allow the Amalus delegation unimpeded access to the seat of Gottari governance.

A gang of herdsmen toughs on foot came toward the roadblock, rushing ahead of the mounted Amalus column. The young lions came chest to swollen chest with the line of young wolves, and the din of the crowd escalated as the two sides began to bluster and shove. A few punches were thrown, and the crowd surged forward from within and without. The standoff was swiftly becoming a riot.

It wasn't supposed to be Like this. This would ruin everything.

"You see?" Kemella said, pointing. "The guild put the young wolves up to this. They want nothing to do with restoring the futhark. Why else would they block their brethren? They oppose us at every step."

Amaga knew she was right. Again. But this time the situation was more complicated than Kemella made it seem. Vahldan certainly could've come to Danihem in a much less provocative way. He could've waited, backed off, rather than allowing the Amalus toughs to rush in to confront the young wolves. Amaga held her tongue and calmed herself in the knowledge that this era of clan conflict was part of the gods-intended path toward the inevitable. Indeed, her mother's visions had shown that the strife would grow worse before things got better.

After all, Urrinan was to be born of chaos and calamity.

Amaseila had foreseen that one day, Amaga's unborn son would become the Gottari's one true hope for the full restoration of the futhark. Beyond the darkness that lay before them, there was yet hope for a guiding light to come. Amaga would be central to providing it. She had but to fortify her belief and stay the course.

As the brawling spread, horns blew again, this time blaring inside the village walls. Vahldan's mounted retinue rode right through the melee, knocking no few to the ground. The Lion Lord dismounted and called for order. A squad of huge Amalus warriors, fully armed and armored, shoved the tussling youths aside, wolves and herdsmen alike. He was surrounded by a score of the lions, and they were the largest men Amaga had ever seen—as thick and broad as her father's cousin Ulfhamr, but tall and long of limb. Thank the gods, none of them had yet drawn the broadswords they all wore at their hips or on their backs.

Once the sides parted, the way through was clear. Flanked by his protectors, Vahldan strode to the longhouse. The young toughs yielded to the power and pageantry of the Amalus intervention. The crowd followed at a wary distance. Amaga strained on tiptoes, trying to get a better look at her future husband as he came on.

The nearby onlookers parted for Vahldan to approach the long-house entrance. He came into the torchlight and halted, surveying the scene. His eyes found hers, as if by instinct. Amaga froze, her heart pounding against her ribs. Gods, he was even more beautiful than in her dreams. But in such a manly way. He smiled, radiating kindness. It was clear that he knew her, that he felt their connection through the goddess, same as she did. The whole world went still and silent.

Amaga memorized his face, knowing this was a moment that would remain etched in memory for a lifetime.

"Vahldan!" Kemella cried, breaking the spell. The crowd noise and activity resumed. Vahldan waved to Kemella, but then looked back to Amaga. The Bringer offered her a respectful tilt of his head. His giant Amalus guardians fanned out, clearing the area in front of the longhouse door, and Vahldan went to it and pulled. It didn't budge. The door was barred.

Vahldan's face filled with fury. Amaga cringed. Her father was behind this.

Vahldan knew it, too. "Thadmeir!" He thumped on the door. "You can't do this!"

"Go ahead. Break the door." Amaga's father's voice came from behind her. He'd come through the stables and circled around.

Vahldan rounded on Thadmeir. "You can't keep us out. That seat is rightfully mine."

The knot of Vahldan's warriors fanned in a semicircle behind him. Their glares made Amaga fear for her father, who faced them alone.

Thadmeir was undaunted. "Threats and intimidation are no way to seek your legitimacy, Vahldan. Don't you remember? I once invited you to come and do things lawfully—to change things by working within the system."

Vahldan pointed. "Don't *you* remember? I said then that I would return when I controlled my own destiny. That day has come. The Amalus clan will no longer heel to the whip. The guildsmen who own you will never own us." His lions grunted and nodded in concurrence.

Thadmeir's voice rose. "Gathering an army to march on our nation's ruling seat is no way to control destiny. Our people cannot be bullied to change simply because you dislike our customs." The mostly Wulthus crowd surrounding the cluster of lions cheered in support. The fighting had abated but Amaga knew the return of violence was the snap of a brittle twig away.

Vahldan smiled and spoke out to the crowd. "I come here not to bully. I come to restore the futhark. Our two clans have long pledged to maintain balance between us. It is one of our people's oldest customs." Jeers and cheers rose again, and Vahldan spoke over them. "I come to reclaim the balance stolen from all of us. I come to lift the yoke of repression from the backs of my fellows, whether you are lion or wolf or neither. For we are all one people, are we not?" The loudest cheer yet rose in reply. He went on. "I come to speak for those with no voice, for those who toil to no avail. I've come to make your voices heard by those who collect coins on the sweat of their kinsmen. I come that you might be heard by those who would starve your flocks even as they stuff their own soft bellies full. I come to open the door that has been shut to the ordinary Gottari, keeping us from a market that should be free to all, rather than being rigged to favor those few who hold sway here. I've come to say that we, the Gottari people, shall be robbed no more!"

Most of the Wulthus scowled, and yet the overall cheering swelled. Scores of herdsmen had entered behind the Amalus column, and they were joined by no few of the villagers in applauding Vahldan. Amaga saw the fervor in their faces. His words seemed to be what many longed to hear.

Vahldan raised his hands for quiet. "These few—they think they can keep you all in your place by keeping me from entering this pile of logs. But they are wrong, my friends. It matters not whether the guild keeps me from a lesser wooden chair on a dais. We all know who is really in charge here. They seek to tame the lions just as they've tamed the wolves. But I will not be tamed!" The cheers rose again. Vahldan went on. "Lord Thadmeir chose long ago to heed the snap of their crop. But I choose to stand with *you*! *This* is how we will restore balance, my friends." The acclaim became a deafening roar.

Amaga's father moved closer, his hands raised for quiet. He'd gone pale. Amaga doubted anyone else could see just how incensed he was. Worse, Amaga could sense his rampant fear—most likely in response to the edge Vahldan had just gained. And to how close he'd pushed them to eruption. The cheering slowly abated.

"You dare to speak of balance?" Thadmeir asked. "You came here at the head of an army." Before Vahldan could respond, Thadmeir barked a laugh and went on. "You hold yourself out as a man of the people, but you only use them. You prop yourself above them even as you pander to them, by tossing around your ill-gotten coin, gained by selling yourself and your men as brutes—thugs who answer to foreign masters, in the service of foreign interests. You come here not for our people. You come as does a child throwing a tantrum—willing to make a spectacle on the village commons in order to get your way. We all know you'll abandon those you've gathered here as soon as you have it. You're even worse than your father was. At least he sought to veil his ambition from those he exploited."

Vahldan's grin twisted in rage. The Bringer started toward Amaga's father, fists clenched. Amaga shrieked and Thadmeir's eyes darted to her and widened; her father clearly hadn't seen her till then. Thadmeir rushed toward her. Vahldan's men shouted and lunged to impede the Wolf Lord. She knew her father was trying to protect her, but he latched onto Vahldan's tunic, bellowing. As the two lords tussled, Vahldan's elbow thumped Amaga in the chest, stealing her breath and knocking her off balance. The wobbly bench screeched, its legs giving way. Amaga lost her footing and plunged to the ground, landing hard on her back, her head bouncing on the plankway. She lay stunned, gasping for air.

Amaga's muscles twitched and spasmed. She spiraled, falling into one of her spells.

Strong hands gripped her, carefully lifting her head and shoulders. An incredible surge of warmth flowed to her, and her breathing came easier. Vahldan's handsome face filled her vision. "That's it. Just breathe." His voice was so kind, his eyes so full of concern.

"Get your hands off of her, you letch!" Behind Vahldan's shoulder, two huge men held the arms of Amaga's struggling father.

Vahldan glanced back. His expression grew dark, and his arms tensed. The warmth she'd felt ceased. Her breathing grew labored again, and her vision went fuzzy, then became tinged with oozing red, as if the world were being splashed and coated with blood. She started to convulse.

Vahldan's attention sprang back to her, his expression returning to concern. It was too late. Her face grew numb and her eyesight faded to a swirl. Her chest constricted and heaved, and her hands went from tingly to prickly. Her limbs locked and jerked. All she could do was listen to herself wheeze as the spell surged through her body and Freya seized her mind.

From the swirl came forth awful images, flashing into her mind's eye. Armies on the march morphed into men swarming and stabbing, crawling and shrieking. The horror of battle was replaced with an image of herself as a young woman, sobbing in a cell-like stone chamber, so cold, so lonely. She then saw a babe crying in another woman's arms and knew the child was her son. Next she saw her son as a toddler, looking terrified in a dank, torch-lit corridor. Her son cried out for her. A harsh-looking woman glared and clamped a filthy hand over the poor boy's mouth. The awful woman cursed and ran away into the darkness, holding her son.

"Get back, all of you! Get away from her, damn you." Her father's voice. From the world outside. Amaga was jostled. Her vision started to clear. Precious breath came to her in gasps and gulps. Thadmeir held her, snarling at those surrounding them, backing away with her still-limp body in his arms. He turned and fled, heading around the longhouse to the stable door.

"Give the poor girl a moment." It was Vahldan, his tone pleading. He'd followed them into the alley.

Her father spun to face him. "Stay back," he barked. "You will never have her."

"She's just a child. I mean her no—"

Amaga's vision cleared. She found focus on Thadmeir. She'd never seen him look so savage. "She is my daughter! You think her a gaming stone to be cast. But she will never be a part of your games. I swear, you will never touch her again. I promise you I'll make sure of it." Amaga had never heard her gentle father speak with such venom, such hatred.

"Come, Thadmeir," Vahldan said, his tone conciliatory. "You know I mean no harm."

"I know exactly what you want. And I will do whatever it takes to keep you from seizing it." Thadmeir spun and hurried to the stable doors.

Vahldan's voice echoed down the alley behind them. "There you have it! The words of a man who promised me a fair hearing. This is Wulthus justice for you!"

The crowd laughed and began to cheer again.

ELAN WASN'T SLEEPING when the babe started crying again, but it still made her jump. The bedamned pitch of it! It seemed like something she'd never get used to. Indeed, it became more jarring each time. She didn't move—didn't even roll over to check on her babe. She never knew what to do, anyway, which only served to make her more certain that she was a terrible mother.

She just lay there, jaw clenched, staring at the embers in the fire. She couldn't believe that another day had passed. She felt paralyzed, and she didn't know how much time she had left. She would soon have to move again. Somehow.

Elan wasn't welcome here. There was only so much a ghost could ask, even of a princess. In time, staying would become more than awkward. It could become dangerous.

But the facts begged the question: Where would she go? The countryside was patrolled by those who didn't think she had a right to exist. Among the Gottari she would be seen as an insurrectionist to those loyal to the Wulthus and the guild, and a traitor to those who supported Vahldan. She could try to get back to the island, but she couldn't think of a single woman there who lived without a man.

Elan didn't even know who she was anymore, let alone where she was supposed to be.

Everything had turned to shit. She'd failed.

Becoming a mother only further complicated an already uncertain future. Elan had no one to blame but herself. She'd tricked Vahldan into getting her pregnant. She'd sworn to his face that she would keep their daughter from suffering their shared destiny and doom. As trapped as she felt, she still ardently held to that vow.

Vahldan had clearly signaled not just his willingness to move on, but his preference to start the next phase of his life without the burden of an infant daughter. As often as he denied it, Elan sensed he would be content to move on without her as well. She'd clearly become as much a burden as a boon to his aspirations.

The realization felt like a blow. Elan had gone from absorbing that one to pushing the queen into striking the next.

By coming here, she'd forced Keisella to confirm that Elan's daughter was not welcome among the Skolani. It was as had been promised, all those years ago. Her daughter was as banished as she was. How could she have so willfully chosen to not believe them?

All of the glowing fantasies Elan had so eagerly kindled and carefully tended had been snuffed. She saw them now for the self-delusions they had always been.

The babe's bawling grew so fierce it made Elan wonder if the child sensed her own plight, to be left in the care of such an aimless and reckless parent.

Light spilled into the pavilion. A silhouette filled the open flap. "Your daughter is hungry." Alela moved to stand over Elan, gravely impassive as ever. Elan closed her eyes, wanting it all to go away. The woman actually nudged Elan with her boot. "You should try feeding her again," Alela gruffly added.

Elan raised up onto an elbow. "Why should I? You're here."

Alela harrumphed and shrugged off her cloak. The nurse scooped up the babe, rocking and shushing her. She gracefully sank to sit on crossed legs, lifted her tunic, drew out her breast, and held Brin to it. The crying instantly ceased.

Ah. A result so much more satisfying than it would've been had Elan tried again.

"Fine for now," Alela said. "But soon you won't have me to rely on." As if Elan needed reminding.

The condemning silence that followed became almost as unbearable as the bawling had been. Elan threw off her blanket, rose, and tugged her tunic straight. Gods, she hated the sight of them, so peaceful. Alela was everything her babe needed. Which was the opposite of herself.

Elan snatched up her own cloak and pushed through the flap into the shocking glare of the risen sun. The frigid air burned her throat and lungs. She wrapped herself tight and blew steam into her cupped hands. Her whole body shivered. She started for the fire, crackling in the nearby pit. A figure was already sitting there, facing away. Elan shielded her eyes.

She froze. The white hair and hunched back brought instant recognition. Elan considered flight. She scanned the campground. Her eyes alighted on the horses in the adjacent corral. The warhorse that had delivered the visitor was there, along with Kukida, who stood waiting, looking less than content. The royal guardian had evidently carried her visitor to sit by the fire. Elan offered the big warrior an awkward wave. She should've expected it, but it still hurt when Kukida seemed to look right through her and turned away.

Elan sighed. There was no way to avoid this. She went to the fire and sat beside her grandmother. "You came back," she said.

Sael's unseeing eyes stared into the fire. "I sensed your need."

As if there was any way to fix what she needed. "Alela is here," she said.

Sael didn't acknowledge that. Silence lingered. Finally: "You know what Urrinan is?"

Elan frowned. Gods, she existed at Urrinan's spinning vortex. Such a silly question. She sighed again, knowing there was some sort of trick or twist. All in service to conveying another bedamned lesson. Elan wasn't in the mood.

"Please, child—indulge an old woman," Sael prompted.

At least Elan could openly roll her eyes. "The tumult that leads to the breaking of the civilized world, through which the Tutona will rise, with the Gottari to lead them."

Sael chuckled and shook her head. "Just as we are led to believe."

Elan studied her grandmother, wondering where this might lead.

She was tempted to leave it at that, but she was too annoyed by Sael's mirth. "You're saying it's not so?"

Sael put a hand to her chest. "Oh no. I would never deny what the gods have long intended for us to believe. Nor even that it shall be so, in the end. Of course the gods would have us perceive Urrinan in the best possible light. Makes us all the more pliant, more easily steered to calamity's horrors."

Just as she'd guessed—more riddles. "Pliant," she repeated. It felt like a personal insult.

"Indeed," the old woman concurred with a nod. "But I see how you suffer, child. I've decided it's best I let you in on a little secret."

Elan huffed a laugh. "Ah. So there's a little secret." Why wasn't she surprised?

"Yes." Sael leaned toward her, lowering her voice conspiratorially. "The gods made a few small mistakes, you see. First, they left me living for far too long."

Elan raised her brows. "That's a mistake?"

"In regard to this, yes. Because they left me with a bit of wit as well. For I am a Dreamer, able to see beyond the enticements that most happily accept."

"Enticements?"

Sael nodded. "Revelations, meant to pacify as well as to steer."

"Such as?" Elan asked.

"Such as the fact that the Tutona shall rise from the ashes of the tumult that comes."

Elan tried to keep the chagrin from her tone. "And just what have you *seen* beyond that?"

"What Urrinan truly is, of course!" Sael squinted into the fire.

Another bedamned riddle. Elan played along. "All right, then— let's have it. What is Urrinan, truly?"

Sael closed her rheumy eyes. "A thing so simple, it breaks my heart to think about all you shall live to see, even though it cannot be avoided."

The old woman opened her eyes, and Elan noticed her tears.

Gods, her sorrow was real. And deeply felt. Elan grasped her hand. "It's going to be all right, Grandmother."

Sael shook her head. "No, it won't be. So much death. So much sorrow. And yet, it is as it shall be. As it must be. For Urrinan is nothing more than a path, from the old world to the new."

"A path?" Elan had never heard her grandmother talk like this.

"Yes, one that must be forged. Through war. Through bloodshed and hatred, bitterness and grief. It is a path upon which you and the Bringer have already begun. And yet, even as you forge it, you have thus far only to perceive the symptoms of what you carry—the chill and the sweat, the delirium that must precede the fever's breaking."

Elan's innards twitched. "Grandmother, why are you telling this to me now?"

"Because now is the time to face it," Sael sternly said. "You must now, because your daughter soon will. I am telling you now because you are lost. Lost, and you must regain your footing. For your daughter shall become the guide upon this path—the path of her parents' wreaking. The path their actions shall bind her to trek."

Elan had thought that having her daughter was the end of it— the mistake she'd made that had diverted her from destiny, ended her role in the curse of prophecy. "I still don't understand."

Sael patted her hand. "I know, child. I know doubt has seized you. I know you question whether the Bringer still needs you. I know you both resent and cherish that your daughter is not to be the prophesied leader—born of the wolf and the lion."

Elan gasped. "How did you...?"

Sael's expression brightened. "How could I not? Know that your instincts are correct, if not for the reasons you cling to. For Brin is meant for so much more. Our girl will be so much more than a mere leader. Indeed, she shall guide several leaders—be their most trusted council. Few will know it, but Brin shall ever be at the forefront of change, holding the reins of Urrinan's turnings. She shall best know the path from the old world to the new. As such, she shall be the lodestar, guiding those who must navigate what comes of calamity."

Elan squeezed her eyes shut. She saw images of Spali and Gottari, lying dead, scattered across the plains. She saw Sochana, bent over the Spali, saw the Spali Elan had thought to be fleeing who had then killed her friend instead. She saw Vahldan, filled with what he called the ugliness, bloodlust in his eyes. She shook her head, saw him wearing that boyish smile and little else in a nest-like bed in a shanty on the shore—love for her written upon him. She thought of her old dream, of them riding together through a city of stone, cheered by the crowd.

Ellasan's daughter had now seen dozens of stone cities. But Elan could no longer imagine her dream coming true. Not as it had felt. Not as she'd been led to believe. Had it all been a ruse? All she was supposed to be, to achieve, naught but a trick—to entice her to calamity? Now the gods would entice her to believe in some special status and role for her daughter?

Frustration turned to annoyance. Now, after all that had happened, there was this new thread in the fabric? Now Elan was supposed to raise a guide, leading Brin to believe she would be— what was it—a lodestar? In the end, would all they'd striven for be thrown away? Would her daughter live to learn how futile her lot had been, just as Elan had?

Was all of this mortal life a trick, to keep her, and everyone she loved, blindly enduring blood and mayhem, in a slow march toward an inevitable doom?

She looked to her grandmother. Sael stared into the fire wearing a placid expression. No. If anyone was deceiving her, it was not Sael. It was as Elan had long known. The gods were fickle. Not only did they want her to dance on, they wanted her daughter, too.

Elan glanced back at the silent pavilion, where another woman nursed her babe. A babe she'd basically neglected since her birth. A babe she'd longed for but now resented. Her anger melted. She really was lost.

A sob escaped her, tears running down her cheeks.

Sael gripped her hand. "Are my tidings not cause for hope?"

"They could be, I suppose. It's just…"

"Tell me," Sael commanded.

Elan shook her head. It seemed so foolish, so selfish. "So that's all, then?" she blurted. "All that's left to me? To be a mother?" It seemed so unfair. After all she'd been through, all she'd been led to believe. About herself, her role.

"By Horsella's light, no!" Sael cried. "You have much more to do."

"Then why can't I see what it is?" she wailed.

Sael closed her eyes again. "Perhaps because it shall be so difficult. The gods well know that a mortal can only bear so much. Few will ever grasp how much has already been laid upon you, child. Perhaps the gods protect you as you protect yourself. But I see you here, hiding. And there can be no hiding from what comes."

Damn, that sounded ominous. But at least it sounded like a purpose. "Please, Grandmother. Just tell me where to begin. What do I do next?"

Sael opened her eyes and turned them toward her. It was as if her grandmother could actually see her again as she stared into Elan's eyes. "Take your daughter. Go to him," Sael said softly. "There is much she shall need to gather. And he may not yet realize it, but he still needs you."

CHAPTER II
SEIZING DESTINY

"There were many forces of change at work during the autumn of Vahldan's return to Dania. The previous summer had seen a drought and was followed by flooding. Crops were poor. Many failed outright, others were washed away. The ready availability of silks and other fabrics in imperial cities, due to the cessation of hostilities with the Sassanada, caused a glut in the wool markets. Non-aligned herdsmen were summarily turned away by the wool guild. Wulthus land-holders sought to staunch their losses by raising grazing tariffs. Planters quailed and grew desperate as autumn fell to an uncommon cold snap, ruining unharvested crops and portending a bitter winter to come.

Understanding the times makes it easier to see how Vahldan's return could be hailed as portentous. His personal magnetism and astounding generosity lifted the flagging spirits of those in dire need. Then came his call for a return to the days of Gottari glory, a renewed self-reliance, and the promise of retaliation against the forces that oppressed those who suffered most.

It was the autumn of my birth, but everyone who lived it recalls the feeling of change in the frigid air that beset them. No few recall the feeling being an ominous one. Wolves and lions agree that Dania was perfectly *kindled, dry fuel, laid up and waiting for Vahldan's spark, and the Amalus flame that would soon consume it."—Brin Bright Eyes, Saga of Dania*

THE TORCHES LOOKED like a swarm of fireflies, filling the meadows between the foothill forests and the village. So many that together they illuminated the encircling trees at the edge of the forest and cast shadows onto the walls of Danihem below.

Vahldan stood behind the wagon they'd set up on the high ground at the meadow's southern edge to use as a stage. It was strange—they'd all come for him, but few had noticed him. He wasn't hiding, but for the moment, in the festive atmosphere that had blossomed, only his guardians and inner circle were paying him any heed. His family and all of the prominent Amalus Rekkrs and their bannermen were nearest, arrayed at the fore.

They would've been enough. But so many more had come. More than he'd dreamed possible.

Many wore odd bits of armor or assorted weapons, and no few carried red shields on their backs that featured the golden roaring lion. It had been his father's sigil, but most of them looked freshly painted. More still had simply donned red kerchiefs around their necks. In spite of the finery of the Rekkrs, the vast majority of the crowd wore dun work clothes and boots, their women wrapped in roughspun blankets against the cold. Most were herdsmen, huntsmen, and planters. But there were quite a few villagers—crofters or traders—among them. Only the Wulthus elite and the guild were unrepresented, he knew.

These were his people. Their noble spirit, their belief, their loyalty—it humbled him.

Vahldan stood staring, hardly able to absorb it all. He'd done it. Well, he'd managed the first important step—he'd drawn the bulk of the Gottari nation together as one.

Arnegern came up beside him. "What is it? You look troubled."

"Not troubled. More like... astonished, I suppose. And a bit nervous."

"No need for nerves. They came for you, my lord. They're here because of what you've already provided."

Vahldan raised a brow. "Which is?"

"Hope, of course."

Vahldan chuckled. He knew there was much more he'd have to provide. Success, first and foremost. Tangible achievement. For some of these who'd come, success meant as little as having food for the winter. But others expected much more. Many hungered for the glory he'd bandied about. If they followed him, as he hoped, he'd have to provide more than food. He had to lead them to victory, and swiftly.

Although the situation abroad wasn't ideal, things would only become more adverse. Vahldan was more certain than ever that waiting was not an option.

Still, it would be a struggle. He would be asking much of those who joined his cause. Some of them would have to walk away from planting or sell or slaughter their herds. Those who committed their sons were offering more than any man had the right to ask. But this was it. Vahldan had to succeed tonight, and then again as a battle commander, or his chance was lost. Failure would not be forgiven— nor easily forgotten. Failure would result in a status quo that was even more entrenched, both in Dania and in Pontea. Everything relied on what he hoped to unleash this very night.

In spite of the pressure, what he beheld exceeded his wildest dreams. "They all brought torches."

Arnegern glanced. "Of course they did. You asked it of them."

"They did it because I asked," Vahldan said, still marveling.

"Best get used to it."

"What's that?"

"A willingness to do your bidding." Vahldan sighed and Arnegern grinned. "This is a bit more than... What is it the wolves are calling it? An Amalus temper tantrum?"

"I'm not sure I really believed it would all come together. And so fast. I'm not sure if it makes the rest of what we planned more or less likely."

Arnegern laughed. "It's never really mattered whether or not you believe."

Vahldan gave him an arch glance. "Why is that?"

"Because *they* do." His captain waved to indicate the entire crowd. "They believe that you're the man who can lead them to change. Finally. It's change that's overdo. It must come. Deep down everyone knows it—even the wolves. It's why they're so afraid. All you have to do is call your people to action. They are already yours, my lord."

"They're mine," he repeated. It was something Elan had often said. It always made him uncomfortable. It could feel more like a burden than a boon. "I hope I'm worthy."

Arnegern gripped his shoulder. "Of course you are. You're the Bringer. In fact, that gives me an idea. Call on me first when you ask for pledges."

Vahldan scanned his Amalus followers in the front rows. His little brother's face shone among them. Eldavar looked so happy, so fervent—an exemplar of devotion. "Fine, but why?"

"I'd like to try to set a trend. You'll see what I mean."

Mara stepped to Arnegern's side and handed him a cup of mead. "Come," his sister said to her betrothed. "Kemella and Eldavar are saving us a spot."

Vahldan was beginning to get used to the idea of Mara and Arnegern as a couple. Finding out had been a bit of a shock. Mara swiftly banished any notion that his friend had taken advantage of his little sister in his absence. Even the verbal thrashing she'd given Vahldan the first time he'd implied it had demonstrated a more important truth—his little sister was a woman grown! And very much their mother's daughter. Beyond that, seeing not only how genuine their love was, but how much they lifted and supported one another, made him happy.

Mara pulled Vahldan's most trusted captain away by the arm. "I trust your sense of timing, my lord," Arnegern said over his shoulder. "But they seem to be getting restless."

Vahldan knew he was right. It was past time to start. What held him back? For some reason, facing this was harder on his nerves than facing a battle.

He suddenly realized what was different. He'd never faced a battle without Elan by his side. Gods, he needed her, now more than ever. She was his safe haven. He always felt alone in the cold without her. Vahldan wondered again, as he often had since their return to Dania, whether he'd grown too dependent on her. Had she become a point of weakness for him? After all, his father's weakness had been exposed by his love for Frisanna. Must he forsake love to become what had been preordained and to avoid his father's fate?

Vahldan reminded himself that he'd dealt with Isidros's man Encho without her. And now she seemed set upon opposing him at every turn. Plus, she'd willfully sought pregnancy against his wishes. To top it off, when he needed her most, she wasn't with him.

He knew she didn't actually intend to oppose him—not exactly. She simply refused to grasp what needed to be done in order for them to fulfill their shared destiny. It wasn't just that she considered his plan a gamble. He easily perceived her veiled disapproval. He suspected she'd secretly hoped her condition would stop or delay this night from happening. He also sensed that she was glad she wouldn't be a part of the mission that success tonight would lead to.

Perhaps their destinies were no longer entwined, as they once had been. Perhaps she'd already performed her role in what was to be. Perhaps her stepping back was as the gods intended. He sensed her caution could only hold him back.

Her stance didn't make him mad. It made him sad. She longed for a life that he'd never promised her. But his feelings went beyond sadness. The thought of her moving on, having her babe, suddenly disinterested in destiny—it made him... resentful. Another word sprang to mind. Maybe he was jealous. Even the thought made the ugliness stir in his belly.

Now that he sensed its waning, Vahldan yearned for Elan's devotion. He fed on it, thrived on it. If they were doomed, he wanted her devotion until their final day.

The realization made him feel foolish. She'd given herself to him, but he'd always known he didn't deserve her. He owed her everything. Without her, none of this would be happening.

Gods damn the twisty feelings he had for that woman. He loved her, but if he had to, he could do what needed to be done without her. He'd proved it before, and he would again.

The ugliness couldn't stop the Bringer. If needed, he could harness it and use it.

In fact, the heat in his belly, ignited by pondering her, felt like just the fuel he needed this very night. Indeed, it was high time he got on with it. "After all, the gods favor the bold," he said aloud and pulled himself up onto the bed of the wagon.

The cheering began up front with his lions, raucous but tinny, like the plucking of strings in preamble. They all held their torches high to illuminate him. He raised a fist in salute, and the cheering spread through the crowd, becoming an uneven melody and then rolling across the hillsides like a thunderous chorus, bouncing from the village walls to echo back in refrain.

Vahldan basked for a moment before he held up his hands, and the crowd gradually fell to silence. It became so quiet he heard the wind through the trees. Their faces tilted to him, expectant. He saw their hope written upon them. It was as Arnegern had said: They were already his.

THE CROWD'S roar turned Arnegern's skin to gooseflesh. Vahldan still chided Arnegern for addressing him as his lord when they weren't in public, but they both knew how much things had changed. They remained close, but their relationship had changed, too. During Vahldan's eight years away in Pontea, Arnegern's old friend had truly become the Lion Lord of the Amalus.

Of course it was partly a physical change. Vahldan looked splendid—the image of his father, if not more handsome. Surely he weighed half again what he had when Arnegern had first met him. On the stage, Vahldan gripped Bairtah-Urrin's hilt at his hip. The Lion Lord had his finely embroidered crimson cloak thrown behind his broad shoulders. His beard was trimmed close, and he'd combed his flaxen hair and tied it behind his head. And yet, his hauberk was unpolished, dingy and gashed, and his boots were worn and scuffed.

His appeal was due to more than his appearance, of course. It was his bearing. Vahldan was poised and assured. In his years away he'd achieved the perfect combination of nobility and approachability. Any herdsman could easily imagine hoisting an ale with him. But he'd also become a man that any herdsman would follow into the fires of battle.

Vahldan raised his hands for quiet, and the elated crowd rushed to obey. The Lion Lord stood appraising his audience as the hush fell to the sound of wind in the pines.

"You are great." Vahldan spoke audibly but without shouting. "Each of you—every man, woman, and child here tonight—is great. But greatness aside, you have been wronged."

A murmur swept through the crowd. Vahldan raised his voice. "It's true, my brothers. The Wulthus clan has failed you. Oh, some of the wolves may mean well, but the clan that sits the dais chair has offered you up as chattel."

Scattered boos sounded. Vahldan continued. "It's tragic, because you are the opposite of chattel. You are Gottari! Greatness flows in your blood—passed down to you by our mighty sires. Still, those you've trusted have allowed the greediest among them to steal your greatness. They withhold from you the glory that is our people's legacy. Why? Because they don't want you to know.

"They don't want you to know that you don't need them. They

don't want you to see the great bounty that lies just beyond your reach. They tether you, to collect a toll from what you manage to reap from the meager patch of dirt to which they've tied you." The boos and jeers increased and became louder.

Vahldan's tone brightened. "But fear not, my brothers. For I have seen what they seek to hide. I have seen the bounty of the world beyond their tethers. I have come to know those who conspire with the guildsmen and the landowners. I have witnessed what has been withheld from you, the givers, only to be hoarded by the takers. Takers with soft hands, round bellies, and limp pricks." The crowd laughed. Vahldan grinned. "The imperials name us barbarians. Well, I say we show them just how barbarous we can be."

The cheering rose again. Vahldan raised his hands. "My fellow Gottari! The guildsmen and the landowners are in league with the imperials—men who scoff at us and think us beneath them. Men who buy and sell your stolen children." That incited the loudest booing yet. "The lot of them would like nothing better than to continue to reap the profits of your toil. But I have seen, and I know. Given the chance, I would no longer allow them to abuse my people. Their era of injustice can begin to end, this very night!" The crowd clapped and stomped their approval.

Vahldan waited a moment, then raised his hand again. "In order to begin it—in order to set us free from this injustice—I need *you*." He pointed and swept his arm over the crowd. "Each and every one of you can give me that chance. Together, we have but to embrace the glory that is the lifeblood of our sires, beating in our hearts this night. The bounty of our effort is rightfully ours! And we can take it back."

Vahldan drew the futhark sword and pointed it down at the cheering crowd. "This sacred relic was stained with the blood of the futhark. Stained by those who've conspired to rob you. They say that I sundered the futhark—that I am the one who created imbalance. But do you feel balance when they keep you from trading freely?" In unison they cried, "No!"

"Do you feel balance when they keep you from open grazing? When they raise your fees while they offer you less and less for your shearing?"

They bellowed, "No!" in unison, then cursed and shook their fists.

The Lion Lord raised Bairtah-Urrin overhead. "You and I know the way to restore balance. With this sword—the very sword they thought to stain with the blood of the futhark—we shall cut the ties that have kept us tethered. Will you join me in restoring balance?"

Vahldan put a hand to his ear, and the crowd shouted, "Yes!" Arnegern's dearest friend was grinning. Vahldan knew he'd won them, and he relished it.

He cupped his hand to his mouth. "Will you let me lead you to our rightful greatness?"

"Yes!" They were even louder this time.

"Will you let me lead you to glory?"

The reply thundered forth. "Yes!" Vahldan slashed the air with the futhark blade, and the cheering rose to its loudest yet.

The Lion Lord pointed down, scanning the front row with the sword's tip. "It starts here, with my captains—my brother and my cousins." The pointing sword stopped on Arnegern. "Captain Arnegern—what say you! Will you let me lead you to glory?"

A thrill sped through Arnegern as the crowd hushed. He stepped to the wagon, drew his blade, and laid it on his palms, proffering it to his lord with a bowed head. Carefully annunciating, he called, "I belong to you, my lord!"

Vahldan ran the flat of the sacred sword across Arnegern's blade with an audible scrape. "Thank you, my brother. Now they may claim our blades are both stained. But with these stained blades we shall restore the futhark."

"Who else?" He pointed to young Eldavar next, repeating the ritual. His brother looked nervous but repeated Arnegern's pledge. As Vahldan bent to rub their two blades together, he lowered his voice and said, "Father would be proud." Eldavar beamed.

Vahldan then called to Belgar, Herodes, Teavar, and Jhannas. In turn, each of his oldest followers proclaimed, "I belong to you, my lord." And Vahldan *stained* each of their blades, same as Bairtah-Urrin had been, and assured them that their glory would soon erase the stain.

After he had called upon his inner circle, he pointed the sacred relic and swept it over the hushed crowd, repeating, "Will you—each and every one of you—let me lead you to glory?"

As one came the thunderous cry. "We belong to you!"

Vahldan raised the sword overhead. "On to glory, my Gottari brothers!"

The refrain became a chant. "We belong to you, we belong to you, we belong to you…"

As the chant echoed into the cold night air, Arnegern saw it written upon his lord's face—it was the Gottari people who'd convinced him, not the other way around. Vahldan believed them, and he reveled in his newfound possessions.

KEEPING LIONS AS PETS

"*Although the empire had slowly restored the garrisons to most Pontean outposts after The War of Two Empires, the units assigned to the region were downsized and stretched thin. Years of war had depleted imperial ranks and diminished the reach of its power. Making the problem worse, the Tiberian elite often sought and received exemption from service for their sons. Hence, the priority was to reinforce the cities and areas most vital to trade, such as Megaria and Nicomedya on the Straits, and Trazonia, the gateway to the Peshtari trade routes. The Hellainic cities of the northern coast, such as Thrakius and Akasas, were far less vital to commerce. Once these secondary cities were finally garrisoned, it was with less than adequate numbers, consisting of ineffective officers and unseasoned soldiers.*

In spite of Malvius's rivalry with his father and sister, the lack of imperial scrutiny made his home city of Thrakius an ideal port of operations. Over the years, Malvius had paid his debts and bought up much of his family's aging fleet—saving his father and sister the burdensome expense of upkeep in a volatile market. At the same time, with property values plummeting, Malvius secretly bought much of the warehouse district. Utilizing veiled bribes, he also forged agreements with the imperial harbormaster for preferred access to the best quays. Too late, his father and sister realized that their rogue kinsman had maneuvered the family business to the brink of bankruptcy.

Malvius had played a long and patient game and was clearly winning as the end of Vahldan's tenure with him drew near. It was a situation his family found outrageous, which seemed to delight Malvius all the more."
—Brin Bright Eyes, Saga of Dania

A GUST of frigid wind blew in through the open seagates of Thrakius, sweeping across the harbor and docks and up the alley. Malvius pulled his cloak closed and held down the fluttering ledgers that he was studying. At least the cold kept the whores from lounging on the terraces across the alley from his warehouse office, eliminating the annoying catcalls he often received. Still, spring was in the air. The sun was warm and the quiet made Malvius love sitting at his outdoor table all the more.

Hiatus was nearly over, but not quite. With almost no ships coming or going, the docks and the adjacent alleys and markets were all but empty. Which made it easy enough to spot her coming. Even from fifty paces away Malvius saw the rage on Ligaia's face. His old instincts seized him, and he nearly fled. He could simply lock the office door and wait his sister out. After all, Ligaia actually hated the docks, despite the fact that these very ships and men were the source of her luxurious lifestyle. Ligaia rarely ventured down here. He suspected he knew what had pried her out of her precious top-floor residence in the palace. If he hid, Ligaia would pound on the door and shout curses, but she'd soon give up and leave.

Ligaia marched forth with two of her lackeys in tow. He recognized them. Both men counted coins for his father, which bolstered Malvius's suspicion. Someone in his father's company had gotten wind of Malvius's latest shipping contract.

Even as she approached, Malvius sought an amicable tone. "Well, if it isn't my big sister come to call. Greetings, Anax Ligaia." He bowed his head with a mocking flourish of the hand. "You're looking well. Such a healthy glow in those high-blood cheeks."

"Shut up, Malvius," Ligaia snarled. So much for amicability.

"What, the title doesn't fit? Is father still determined to pass our family legacy on to that winsome husband of yours? Oh well. It'll only be until you two manage to come up with a son. By that I mean a legitimate one, of course."

Ligaia's eyes narrowed like a predator's. "You never fail to be a little shit."

"Such ugly talk for such a pretty girl." She hated being reminded of her femininity even more than being accused of being masculine. He was juggling torches in a pitch pit, but something about Ligaia had always sparked an irrepressible urge to seek to infuriate her.

"You willfully undercut us," she spat. "You stole the provincial Trazonian run."

Malvius held up both palms. "Whoa. The contract was fair game. It was up for renewal, and we were invited to bid by Rector Horius himself."

"Fair? You underbid us by almost half! Father's held that contract all of our lives. What you did wasn't just spiteful, it was stupid. You left money on the table, Brother. It's so unlike you, unless..."

Malvius raised his brows, repressing a smile. "Unless what?"

"It's true—you're actually trying to bankrupt us. You're willing to operate at a loss just to watch it happen." Ligaia made a show of looking shocked. "Your own family." The disapproving scowls and shaking heads of Ligaia's coin counters were a fine addition to the act.

"I'm hurt," Malvius said, joining Ligaia's mummery, hand to his chest. "You make an unfair allegation. First, as you'll recall, I have been wrongfully disinherited. Which means, strictly speaking, you and Father are no longer family. Second, in spite of my wrongful treatment, I have been exceedingly supportive of the house of the anax of Thrakius. May I remind you who has been paying top prices for the ships you folks continue to sell off?"

"You know you're forcing those sales by stealing our contracts."

"Oh, come now. Even your coin pinchers here must see that this contract makes far more sense for us. My ships are already running the route. I'm merely trying to improve our fine city's reputation among the imperial bureaucracy in Megaria. That's all there is to it."

Ligaia moved in till their noses nearly touched. He had to admit, she was an intimidating woman when she wanted to be. "You expect me to believe that after a lifetime of skirting the law, you suddenly want to be taken to the imperial bed?" She threw a thumb over her shoulder at the brothels across the street. "Even your whores would see that you're up to more than that."

"I suppose you would know, Sister. After all, you've been bedding imperials since you were barely out of play leggings."

Malvius braced himself for a slap. Ligaia growled but managed to resist lowering herself to violence. "You're a pig," she said instead. "I hope you choke on Horius's cock," she added as she stomped away. Her heel dogs each gave him a snarl before scurrying after their master.

"Maybe you could offer a few tips?" he called after her. She didn't slow or look back. "Seriously, Ligaia, you've obviously got skills. That last Tiberian snake you charmed belonged to an officer, didn't it? Too bad he slipped away. What happened, anyway? Did he find the swelling belly distasteful?"

Ligaia made an obscene gesture over her shoulder and kept walking.

Neveka stuck her head out of the office door. "What was that all about?"

"She heard about the new contract," Malvius told her.

"I suppose that was inevitable." Neveka disappeared inside for a moment and returned with two steaming cups of tea. She set one before him. "Since you're determined to sit out in the cold." She sat across from him, hugging herself in the fox fur wrap Malvius had given her.

"Why wouldn't I sit out here? It's not snowing or raining."

"Aye, but the visitors you seem to attract aren't so pleasant."

Malvius waved off the departing trio. "It's still her city. If we're both going to live here, best to keep the air clear." He drew in a deep breath and blew it out. "And now that she's gone, I can smell spring in the air again. And spring smells like money."

Neveka lifted her nose and frowned. "All I smell is the sewer. The warmer it gets, the greater the stench."

Malvius wouldn't let her spoil his mood. He'd soon be sailing again, heading for the eastern markets. After the record profits from the prior year, he'd been able to afford more improvements and repairs than ever before, to both ship and shore. Not to mention commissioning the building of two new vessels. His crews would be sailing in class, no matter which of his ships they served on. Even if Vahldan chose not to return with his host, as Malvius feared, he could still afford to hire the next-best guardsmen in the Pontean.

To top it off, during hiatus, Neveka had wisely allocated part of her acquired earnings from the deal they'd made back in Akasas all those years ago. His astute partner had paid off the Bafranii sadhu, freeing her brother from the indentured service that Neveka herself had fled in their youth. The newly freed and enterprising young man had immediately formed a partnership (also with Neveka's financing) with one of the most prominent Bafranii pirate captains. The lad was now able to give his dear sister assurances that Malvius's ships would be much safer from future larcenous encounters.

"Never mind the smell," he told her. "Just enjoy having the sun warm your skin."

She lifted her copper eyes to the partly cloudy sky. "I will. On the rare occasion."

"This weather must make you miss Bafrana."

Neveka arched a brow. "Hardly. Besides, I can handle the cold. Haven't I proven that?"

She had. Malvius knew she meant more than the weather. Though he knew she didn't have fond memories of Bafrana, Thrakian society had hardly embraced her, either. His own family went so far as to pretend she didn't exist, even when Neveka ventured to speak to them. But then, Anax Decebius, Imperial Magister of Thrakius, scarcely even spoke to his own son. Judging by Ligaia's reaction to his new contract, at the moment that was probably for the best.

Neveka leaned to look down the alley. "Your plaster man comes."

Malvius turned. The mason he'd hired was splattered with plaster. He even had globs of it in his hair. Plaster man, indeed. The mason held out a key. "It's done, then?" Malvius asked.

"It's done." Plaster Man smiled proudly. "My men are taking down the scaffolding. Come and see, if you like."

"No need. I trust you." Malvius put the key in his belt pouch. "Do you have a tally ready? We can pay you straight away. Neveka, go and open the strongbox."

The mason held up a halting hand. "And I trust you, Captain. I'll bring a tally by tomorrow." He bowed and left.

"I wonder what that'll cost," Neveka said, watching him go, suspicious as always.

"Whatever it costs, it'll be worth it. We now have the only fireproof warehouse in all of Pontea. When we don't have goods of our own to fill it, we can rent out the extra space. Furriers, silk merchants, carpet weavers—they'll all gladly pay a premium for the peace of mind."

The bells of the city began to ring, including the harbor bell. "Now what?" Malvius stood and looked out the seagates as they groaned into motion, closing against some perceived threat. "More jitters over a passing caravan of your kinfolk, no doubt."

Neveka scowled. "Someone should explain to the watchmen that Bafranii would never risk a raid on a port this large. Not even during hiatus."

"I fear someone is telling them the opposite. Namely my father." Since Decebius had resurrected the city militia, he seemed intent on making the whole city as paranoid as he'd become.

"Perhaps your gambling partner can tell us what's happening." Neveka nodded to a chariot speeding down the alley toward them.

The driver was indeed Porcius, the imperial centurion with whom Malvius occasionally wagered on tumbling stones. Malvius always over-served the man, and he usually let him win. The thirsty Tiberian had consistently proven a great source of inside information. Indeed, Porcius had been the source of the tip about the contract renewal for the Trazonian run that Malvius had stolen from his father's firm.

Mercifully, the seagates boomed closed and the harbor bell stopped tolling. And yet, the *all-clear* blast of the horn had yet to sound. All of the gates of the city—to those coming and going via land and sea—would remain closed until the horn blew.

"Viricus requests your presence at the north gate," Porcius said as he reined in his horses. Captain Viricus was the imperial garrison commander. It was strange, as Viricus rarely left his lush suite in the armory. The few times Malvius had spoken to the man, Viricus had made his disdain apparent.

"At the north gate? What's going on up there?"

"Your friend has arrived. The Northman."

"Vahldan is here?" The centurion nodded. A wave of happy relief flowed through Malvius. The Gottari had come to their senses. How could they not return, when the prior year had been their most profitable yet? "What of it? Vahldan is well-known here."

"Your father was on the parade grounds and overheard a sentinel announcing his approach. The anax took one look at them and ordered the gates closed and the alarm sounded."

"For the gods' sakes, why?"

"Your father says that your man has more men with him than usual. He also claims they're more heavily armed than they should be. He demanded the captain be called, and now Viricus wants you to come and claim responsibility for them. I sense Viricus is trying to appease your father. Tempers are running hot up there."

Malvius rolled his eyes. "Just what I need. Another needless fight with my father."

Porcius gestured for Malvius to board the chariot. As soon as he stepped on, the centurion cracked the reins and they were in motion. Porcius rolled out onto the docks to turn around and urged his team to an uphill gallop. They sped through the market, shouting pedestrians out of the way as street vendors and shops closed up their stalls and shuttered their storefronts—a wasted effort as they'd just have to reopen in mere moments, once the *all-clear* signal came.

Porcius nodded to a group of men on foot, trotting up the palace road. "Your father took it upon himself to call up his militia. Viricus is none too pleased." Malvius could see why. Most of the restored order of Thrakian militiamen were either idealistic young hotheads or graybeards with delusions of bygone grandeur. The lot of them were ill-equipped and undisciplined.

Malvius sighed. These days his father relished this sort of drama. With Decebius's business in its death throes, holding the title of magister was the only pretense left with which the old prick could fluff up his flaccid stature. Anax Decebius's fall from grace was his own damn fault. He'd been a fool for casting Malvius aside over their first needless tiff, and now the old man was just too proud to admit it. Decebius had deluded himself into thinking things would be fine with Ligaia and Kluctus, his sister's doltish husband, running things. By now even his father recognized that the joke was on him. Too bad Decebius had neither the stamina nor the lucidity left to do much about it. All he had left was his hemorrhaging pride. Hence his new penchant for spiteful roleplaying.

The chariot clattered across the pavers of the martialing courtyard between the palace and the north gate. Porcius pulled the reins to halt the team and pointed up the stairs to the wall-walk. A group of men stood at the top alongside the gatehouse. Among them were his father and Viricus. The Tiberian officer beckoned Malvius. His father turned to sourly glare.

Malvius took the stairs two at a time. He reached the top and brushed past his father on his way to the parapet. The person whose feelings he most cared about was still outside.

Below him, Vahldan sat ahorse looking cross. Teavar and Jhannas sat their mounts at Vahldan's flanks. Malvius spotted Ermanaric and Herodes among several strange faces. There were perhaps a score of Gottari, but not enough to stir such a fuss. The men sat well within bowshot, their shields hanging on their saddles or slung over their backs. They looked more bored than dangerous. "What's this about, Captain? These men work for me."

"You know exactly what this is about," his father interjected. "They are hired killers, regardless of who's hired them. We don't allow armed killers to come and go as they please."

Viricus looked pained. "They claim to have business with you. Is it true?"

"Of course," he said, though he hadn't been expecting them. Malvius had hoped to get them back, but as he left for Dania the prior autumn, Vahldan had made that seem unlikely. Malvius turned to call down. "Greetings, Vahldan! Where is Elan?"

Vahldan shielded his eyes. "Not here." He didn't dare ask about the result of her pregnancy, and Vahldan's tone made it clear he was beyond annoyed.

Malvius pushed past it. "You're here early. Had you sent word, I'd have been here to meet you."

Vahldan's eyes narrowed. "Shall we turn back, then?"

"No, no—earlier is much better than later."

"You'll vouch for them?" Viricus asked again.

"Yes, of course."

"This is a mistake," Decebius hissed.

Viricus called to the guards. "Open the gate!" The Tiberian turned back to Malvius. "I want you to personally escort them to the docks, Captain, and keep them there. I won't tolerate drunken Teutonics causing havoc in the upper markets, understood?"

"Of course." Now Malvius was getting annoyed. They certainly didn't seem drunk, and the Amalus hadn't caused havoc before.

Well, not often, and mainly not in Thrakius. It wasn't as if he'd hired tattooed Kaukazari. This was clearly a case of prejudice.

The portcullis clanged as it rose, and the Tiberian headed downstairs. Malvius followed. He heard the old man rushing to keep up. "You're playing with fire, Malvius. These men will betray you the moment they see a way to profit by it."

At the bottom of the stairs, Malvius faced him. "This isn't about their trustworthiness. This is about your bitterness—your envy of our success. You lost your boldness, Anax. And it happened just as we found ours."

Decebius's eyes widened. "Boldness? You stole my ships and my men."

"I prefer to call it borrowing. And you forced my hand. I did what I had to do, after you stole my inheritance. Besides, you had your chance to press charges. Instead, you chose to take a share of the profit I earned. What's done is done. You can relax now, Father. Sit back and enjoy watching your bumbling son-in-law fritter away what remains of your fortune. Perhaps before it's too late, Ligaia will produce a legitimate heir—of the type you seem so sure will come to rescue your fantasies of legacy. You still won't be sure Kluctus is the father, of course. But as I've long said, if the next one's not his either, it'll be for the best."

Malvius briefly wondered if he ought to also mention that it seemed likely Neveka was pregnant with Decebius's grandchild. No, Malvius wasn't sure how he felt about fatherhood, and his father would sense his uncertainty and target it. He'd save that news for another fight. Ideally one that he wasn't already winning.

Instead, he walked away, heading across the courtyard to meet his Gottari friends. His father followed on his heels, refusing to concede. "This has nothing to do with me, or with Ligaia. This is about your disregard for everyone and everything that doesn't serve to fill your purse. You could have easily told your brutes to camp outside the walls and picked them up elsewhere. Parading them through the city armed will only serve to embolden them."

"Too late." Malvius waved him off and kept walking.

"Maybe this time, but you heard Viricus. You take them straight to the docks. The citizens of this city won't tolerate their carousing and brawling, sullying our markets and terrorizing our women. Do you hear me, Malvius? I'm speaking to you!"

He rounded on his father. "How can I help but hear you? But it makes me wonder if you have ever heard me. Whether you approve of him or not, whether you dislike his race or his looks or his smell, Vahldan is largely responsible for saving this city from poverty. The Tiberians all but threw us to the whim of the pirates. If not for these Teutonics, few Thrakian ships would have made it to the eastern markets and back over the last eight years. Vahldan and his men kept us all sailing when no one else could. Without them, you and your city would be destitute, your precious markets and inns empty. Are *you* hearing *me* now, Father?"

Malvius held his father's tight-lipped glare as the Gottari horses clip-clopped from the arched gateway out onto the brick-paved courtyard. Decebius looked away first.

Malvius turned from his father, grinning. He relished finally managing to stare the old man down. In spite of the win, he sensed his father ghosting behind. The Gottari moved to form a cluster at the center of the courtyard. The Hellain militia still lingered but kept their distance. Vahldan steered his towering warhorse toward Malvius's approach.

Malvius raised a hand in salute. "Again, I offer my greetings and apologies, my friend."

Vahldan nodded but made no move to dismount. Teavar and Jhannas drew their horses up on either side of their leader. All three wore stony expressions. Vahldan raised up in the saddle, looking back over his men. The last of the Gottari column cleared the archway, bunching together on the martialing courtyard. The riders scowled at their surroundings on restless horses, looking out of place. Malvius took in the encircling Tiberians and militiamen. This was obviously not the reception the Amalus had expected; Malvius's father had made sure of it.

Vahldan pointed at his father. "This is the magister?"

It was an odd question. "Of course. Surely you remember my father, Anax Decebius."

Vahldan raised his voice, his words clipped and formal. "We mean your citizens no harm. Order your militia to drop their weapons and disperse. Quickly! Or we will not be at fault for what comes of it."

Decebius turned to Malvius. "I told you this would lead to trouble," his father seethed.

Vahldan raised a hand. Malvius took another step. "Look, this is a simple mis—"

"Time's up!" Vahldan dropped his arm, initiating a torrent of activity.

The Gottari in the interior of their formation raised bows, arrows already nocked. Their volley of shots clearly targeted the Tiberians on the wall and in the archway to the gate. At the same time, horses on the perimeter were in motion, swords were drawn, and shields raised. In a few heartbeats nearly every Tiberian soldier was down or scurrying for cover. Most of the Hellain militiamen leapt into flight too, many dropping their weapons as they ran for safety.

Decebius drew his ancient sword and shouted, "For Thrakius! Militia, attack!"

"Father, no!" Malvius lunged for him.

His father had advanced no more than three steps when Jhannas's broadsword swooped. The blade struck at the apogee of the giant's mighty swing, cracking against Decebius's skull and splattering Malvius with blood. His father's body slumped into his arms, slack and lifeless.

Malvius frantically pulled his father's body back from the fray. He tripped and hit the cobbles with Decebius landing on top. His ears filled with thudding hooves and the screams of men and horses.

"Father?" He rolled his father onto his back and knelt over him. The side of Decebius's head was smashed, his gray hair soaked with gore.

His father's eyes were wide with fear and rage, unblinking—a stare-down Malvius could never win.

Gods, this was embarrassing. The stubborn old prick was right. How could Malvius have thought these men were his friends? He'd never had friends. Vahldan had pulled stunts like this before, and Malvius had refused to see the truth. These men were killers who were led by a killer. And they'd played a long game. Malvius had swallowed a ruse.

Mockery of the gods, he was pathetic. Just as the old man had always said.

"Stay down, Malvius!" Vahldan was shouting at him. Why? To make him an easier target? To continue to use him? No. He launched into a hunched run, scrabbling with his hands, hurrying to the shadow of the palace keep wall. He spotted Porcius's chariot and made for it.

He arrived and flung himself onto the chariot's deck. Porcius was slumped inside, both hands gripping an arrow protruding from his neck. Malvius braced his back on the front of the box and kicked the Tiberian's body off the deck. He pulled himself up to peek out at the chaotic scene. He instantly wished he hadn't looked. Bodies littered the courtyard, their clothing and faces smeared with blood.

The Gottari had seized the element of surprise, but surely there would be a way to overcome this. The assailants were so few. Surely the entire Tiberian garrison would be called out. As amazing as he knew the Amalus host's fighting skill to be, this madness stood no chance of success. Even Vahldan couldn't win against an entire city.

And yet the Gottari were clearly having their way. Not one raider had been unhorsed. Every city defender was either down or in panicked flight.

Malvius's gaze drifted beyond the slaughter to the open gateway, and his remaining hopes fizzled.

Outside the city, on the open road from the Pontean Pass, he saw them. Hundreds—no, maybe thousands—of barbarians galloping toward the city, their banners flapping overhead, their shields and swords glinting in the spring sunshine. They would arrive in mere moments.

He scanned the gatehouse and wall-walk for someone to warn. But there was no one left.

An urgent voice inside Malvius called for flight. He looked to the entrance to the palace keep, but it was too late. He saw Gottari riders chasing Hellains into the inner keep. He briefly thought of Ligaia. Had his sister gone straight back to the palace after their spat? Even if she had, what could he do for her?

What could he do for anybody? What about Neveka? He had to stop them from getting to the docks and get himself and his love onto a ship. An idea formed from his panicked thoughts: He had to rouse the garrison—alert someone who could stand up to this onslaught. What had become of Viricus? Surely the captain had gotten clear before the attack. Surely he would call his men to action. Malvius had to find out. The armory was along the way to the docks.

A nearby crash drew his attention to Teavar riding down a young Hellainic militiaman. Teavar felled his fleeing victim with a single slash. Malvius recognized the poor lad, a former dockworker who was now apprenticing for a cloth merchant. The pursuit brought the Gottari giant nearly close enough for Malvius to smell him. Malvius dropped flat onto the chariot's deck. He landed in Porcius's sticky blood. His whole body shook, waiting for the giant's sword to chop him from above. But the hoofbeats of Teavar's warhorse melted into the cacophony of battle.

Malvius cautiously raised up, wiping his bloody hands on his bloody tunic. The endless Gottari column was already streaming in through the archway. Groups of Gottari were sweeping across the martialing courtyard, heading around the palace on the east side into the broad roadway between the wall of the keep and the stadium. The warriors who rode in front bore pike-like spears, jabbing those who fled before them. And still the Gottari came, their horses' hoofbeats growing to an unending thunder with only the occasional sharp scream able to pierce it.

Malvius felt unable to move. He wanted to wake up from this nightmare. But he knew he had to act. He had to get to the armory. He forced himself to stand, grabbed the reins, and cracked them on the team's backs. The horses lurched ahead, happy to flee the raucous courtyard. He headed for the narrow lane on the west side of the palace keep wall. He came around to the front gates and got to the top of the market avenue ahead of the Gottari. He yanked the reins to turn the team and rumbled downhill, shouting panicking townsfolk out of the way.

The avenue ahead became choked by the frenzied mob. Malvius steered into a side lane. The route wouldn't lead him directly to the armory, but it kept him moving.

Renewed tolling of the palace bells echoed over the battle noise. Another blocked lane forced Malvius to turn back out to the market avenue. He whipped the horses to greater speed as he approached more fleeing townsfolk jamming the way. He bellowed like a mad man, and the crowd actually parted. Some cursed him and others pleaded to be taken to safety. One woman held up her small child, almost in his path, begging for him to save her babe. He rumbled past them all. He knew the chariot would be mobbed if he stopped.

He approached the armory walls to find that a crowd had already gathered at the compound's closed gates, clamoring to be let inside. A small group of Tiberian soldiers stood wielding poleaxes inside iron bars. It seemed the Tiberian soldiers that remained were not willing to risk compromising the armory by opening the gates. Little good it would do them to wait and become trapped. The heartless bastards.

Realization struck him. There was no one else who could save the city.

Malvius's next thought was for the only other person besides himself that he truly cared to save. "Neveka. I've got to get her onto a ship."

The lane ahead had filled again, everyone fleeing to the docks. Malvius had slowed the chariot too much and a man was able to jump onto the deck behind him, grabbing his shoulders to stay on. "Get us out of here!" the man shouted, his eyes wild. "They're coming!"

Malvius shrugged out of the man's grip and shoved him with one hand as he cracked the reins with the other. The chariot lurched and the intruder tumbled off. Another man leapt from the crowd to grab the harness of one of the horses. Malvius snapped the whip, slashing the man's cheek and causing him to fall—apparently clear of the chariot wheel.

"Make way! All of you! I have imperial business." Malvius cracked the whip again, and folk backed away. The horses moved through the gap and onto open ground again. He turned to see men chasing and cursing him.

Behind the fleeing mob, the Gottari raiders crested the hill. The murderous horde swept downhill, crashing through market stalls and riding down scrambling townsfolk with their pikes. The sight was surreal.

Malvius turned toward the docks and another crowd loomed into view. Men and women were pressed tight, inching their way toward the quays, all hoping to get aboard a ship—any ship. It seemed he was sliding to the base of a pestle with the mortar rolling his way. Out in the harbor he saw that most of his docked ships had successfully cast off. A few were already making for the reopened seagates. Malvius cursed under his breath. His captains had done the right thing, of course. Except for one minor detail. They'd left without their employer!

He had to get to his office to make sure Neveka had gotten on one of the ships. He drove straight into the chaotic crowd. He cracked the whip to frighten those ahead or too near his sides and pushed the team on through the gathering throng. He was soon surrounded and making little progress. He jumped from the deck, and no sooner than he was off, others took his place. He heard a man snapping the reins in vain. The mob's distraction with the chariot provided an opening, enabling Malvius to slide through the press to an alley between the tavern and the warehouses that lined the edge of the docks.

He ran to his office and found it locked up. The entire area looked deserted. He had to be sure. "Neveka!" He pounded on the door. "You in there?" He turned to look down the alley to the harbor, crowded with rowboats, barges, and just about every other type of vessel damn near overflowing with frantic townsfolk.

He stood craning and trying to catch his breath, trying to think. "Where is she? Where would she go?" Could one of the captains have sent for them and found only her? Would she have left without him? He doubted it. It wasn't just that Neveka was more loyal than most. It was more that she couldn't be rattled. The woman was nigh fearless. Leaving without him seemed too rash for her.

Horns blew, and the roar and clatter grew louder. The Gottari were closing in. The frantic crowd cried in renewed terror. Malvius ran down the gap between two warehouses. A bit of his plaster workers' scaffolding remained alongside the wall to his newly refurbished warehouse. He climbed partway up to scan the crowd. As he watched, a panicked surge caused dozens to fall into the harbor. The brown water churned like a stream overfull with spawning fish.

Across the sea of heads on the docks at the far side of the throng, just outside the harbormaster's cottage, he spotted the fox fur, then the black hair. "Neveka!" There was no way she'd hear him. He often met his captains in that spot. She must've gone looking for him. She wasn't in danger of being pushed into the water, but she was far too close to the end of the fishmonger's lane—one of the main ways by which the Gottari would surely come.

He jumped to the ground and weaved his way across the current of the crowd. Before he was even halfway to her, the lead Gottari chargers burst into view, their mounts rearing as they slashed and jabbed. The crowd surged again, squeezing Malvius into the inexorable press toward the water. Placing his hands on the shoulders of the two men nearest him, he pushed himself up, stretching to see. He caught sight of Neveka just as the riders crashed down on those gathered around her, the pikes of a trio of lead chargers tilted down in an inescapable trident of death.

Her black head of hair simply disappeared from view, lost in the turmoil of the scene. Malvius helplessly watched while the only woman he'd ever actually loved fell before charging pikes. If she'd survived their deadly tips, she was sure to be crushed under the hooves of the host that followed through the space in which she'd been standing.

The only person he loved had been trampled by the raiders under the command of the only man Malvius had ever foolishly called a friend.

Tears flooded his eyes. For a moment, Malvius gave in to the momentum of the crowd carrying him toward the churning water and probable drowning. What did it matter?

His legs felt weak and he fell against the nearest human body. A fist hit the side of his head, and his anger flared. It woke him from his stupor. Malvius was not about to die with this herd of panicked fools. He punched back, surprising the young man behind him, who reared away. The reaction gave him the space to take a step laterally, back toward his warehouses.

Malvius mercilessly repeated the feat again and again, slugging at faces and midsections—male and female, young and old—to slide by his shocked victims as they recoiled. As he neared the building, the press of the crowd lessened, and he was able to spare his now aching hand and bleeding knuckles.

As he arrived at his office door, flaming arrows clattered onto the cobblestones and then began to thunk into wooden walls and stacked barrels. The Gottari were burning the warehouse district. The aging timber frame building that housed his office immediately ignited. Rather than going inside, Malvius turned and ran to the alley he'd emerged from earlier, a thought instantly dawning upon him: He now owned a locked, fireproof warehouse!

Malvius beat to a halt in front of the smallest door on the far end and fished in his belt pouch. "Follow him!" someone shouted. He glanced to see a group of townsfolk in flight from the docks, heading right for him. He finally felt the key the mason had given him. He fumbled with trembling, bloody fingers to insert and turn it. A woman's scream pierced the din. He resisted looking and finally felt the latch release. The door swung open. He heard their pounding footsteps grow near. One cried, "Hold that door!"

Malvius slammed the door shut, slapped the bar into place, and collapsed against it. He leaned there, catching his breath and letting his eyes adjust. The handle rattled, followed by pounding and calls to be let in.

Malvius pressed his hands over his ears and moved away from the door into the cavernous space. It seemed the frantic dance of his heart would not relent, and his eyes refused to adjust to the darkness. He wandered until his shin hit something soft. He bent to touch it. A pile of sails. The masons had worked around some of the items he had intended to store here. He let his hands fall from his ears. The muffled thumps and screams from outside continued to intensify. If they got in, he was as doomed as them. As doomed as his dear, sweet Neveka.

He wondered if he should care anymore. He suddenly felt so damn tired.

Malvius grabbed a handful of cloth from the top of the pile of canvases and drew it back. He crawled between the folds of the sails as if they were his bed. He lay there under the heavy cloth, trying not to listen to the desperate pounding and pleading. Trying not to think.

It wasn't working. Lying there in the dark, the images of horror returned. His father's broken head. Neveka disappearing from view beneath the stomping hooves of warhorses. He squeezed his eyes tight. Tears rolled into his ears, but they didn't block the awful sounds.

If he survived, what would be left of his world? He wondered how he could've allowed himself to love Neveka, let alone to consider Vahldan a friend. He'd learned so long ago—love and friendship only led to betrayal, to heartache. Just as when his mother had betrayed him as a boy by returning him to his father and then leaving again—this time without him. Just as his sister had betrayed him as a teen to go off with Tiberian soldiers and let them have their way with her, leaving him to deal with their father's spiraling bitterness and wrath.

Just as his father had later betrayed him as a man, spitefully snatching away his inheritance after all he had endured to earn it.

His mind reeled, playing scenes from the past unbidden. He recalled how many times Vahldan had questioned him about the Tiberians. Malvius himself had taught Vahldan their weaknesses and vulnerabilities. Now he was being punished for revealing his own weakness. He'd laid himself bare to a barbarian. How could he have been so desperate for the approval of such a man? The shame of it burned on his cheeks.

He forced it down, coerced it to rage. Never again. If he survived, he would be strong. Those who'd done this would burn in humiliation on their way to death.

The smell of smoke seeped in. Malvius scanned the roof. Cracks of light glowed through the clay tiles. He realized that the roof was held in place by wooden timbers. Had it been folly to imagine he could withstand the forces of the natural world? Had he really believed getting richer than his father would save him from the decadent descent of his family? Had it been hubris to imagine himself beyond the whim of the gods? He wondered, for all his touting of this building as fireproof, if the intense flames of a burning city would bring the roof and walls he had ordered to be made so heavy down to crush him.

Malvius vowed to himself aloud, "If I survive this, I swear that Vahldan and all of his kin, all his followers, will suffer the same fate as those who suffer and perish on this day. Gods, spare me and I vow to be the hand of your tricks and whims. No matter what part I must play or price I must pay. No matter what it takes."

CHAPTER 13
HOME INVASION

"Many of the servants working in the palace of Thrakius at the time of Vahldan's invasion were slaves in all but name—indentured to service to repay debt or as penance for transgressions against anax or empire. Some even for the debts or offenses of sires. Around half were from other realms around the Pontean, most of these having spent long years far from ancestral homes. The rest were Hellains, but most of these felt no special kinship or allegiance to the Hellains of the city.

Hence it is unsurprising that when the Gottari seized control and most servants found themselves spared and uninjured, no few left Thrakius upon learning they were absolved of past obligation. More surprising were the dozens who chose to stay in their roles and serve the palace's new occupants. Likely as they had nowhere else to go."—Brin Bright Eyes, Saga of Dania

A THUMP JOLTED LIGAIA AWAKE. It had been a fitful sleep. Gods spare her, she had been dreaming that the barbarians had already broken in. Such a horrible dream, in which she had been pummeled and pushed, stripped nude and dragged through the palace, only to then be thrown into one of several crowded cage-wagons, all hitched to teams and lined up to depart the palace keep. She had found herself in a parade, displayed among the spoils of victory, hauled through her own city's streets that were lined with jeering barbarians. The awful spectators had spat on her and thrown awful projectiles that, even now, made her wince.

Ligaia still felt dirty, defiled, and, oddly, a lingering shame.

In spite of those horrors, the worst part of the dream was when she had spotted the boy clinging to the bars of the wagon ahead. His filthy face had been streaked with tears and his servant's tunic had been ripped and bloodied. The boy had often haunted her dreams, but she'd never been as devastated by any dream of him as this one.

But no, she was still in the residence. "Thank the gods," she murmured aloud. The reality of her circumstance sank in. She grimaced and shook her head. It was far too soon to be thanking the gods. In fact, she suspected she might soon be cursing them. Her dream was still far too likely to come true. Her city had already been invaded, her home already breached. She had no idea if the boy was safe or not. Worse, Ligaia was sure she was only aware of a fraction of the horror that had already occurred.

Perhaps the worst horror was that the gods had allowed it to happen.

Ligaia was lying on the floor between the bed and the wall, her frock clinging to her, sweat-soaked. She was amazed that she'd slept at all. The air was still thick with smoke, even indoors. She had drifted off to the echo of screams and cries that often incited drunken laughter. Even now, the drone of distant voices was punctuated by bangs and shrieks.

She pushed herself to a sitting position. Daylight flooded the bedchamber. Morning had actually come. After one of the longest nights of her life. It seemed unnatural that the routine cycles of life could still go on. The world had been warped, normality despoiled. The Gottari had pillaged and burnt her city—a city deemed unconquerable for centuries. Not even mighty Tiberia had breached Thrakius; that transition had only come through the negotiated surrender of her forebearers, almost four hundred years ago.

Not only had Ligaia lived to see the unthinkable, she had somehow survived it. Well, the first day and night of it. Not only did she wonder how long survival might last, but whether she should even strive to maintain it.

Another louder thump caused her to bolt upright. Ligaia clambered to her feet, tugged her twisted frock straight, and crept to peek out the bedchamber door. Kluctus was still propped on his stool in the sitting chamber, facing the barricaded residence door. Her husband seemed not to have moved since she'd left him, his father's old sword still lying across his lap.

The voices and commotion emanating from the corridor grew louder. Ligaia tucked her tangled hair behind her ears and moved into the sitting chamber. Kluctus glanced over and said, "This is finally it. They're coming now. Time to get out to the terrace, as we agreed."

"As you decided, you mean."

"There's no time to argue, Ligaia. I told you, you'll survive a jump to the terrace below."

"To what end? If they're up here, they're damn certain to be down there."

A rhythmic pounding began. The brutes were chopping at their door with axes. "You can't know that!" Kluctus stood, still staring at the door, gripping the sword hilt but letting the blade hang flaccid at his side. "They'll know the top floor is the anax's residence. Down there, you may still have a chance to hide, until..."

Ligaia actually laughed. "Until what? Until the Tiberians arrive to save us? You know Horius won't risk intervention. Not as long as Megaria is safe. He'll wait."

"The empire will send someone," Kluctus exclaimed, sounding desperate.

"Ha! From where? On ships from Cispadaena? Shall I hide till then?"

Her husband finally looked at her. "Well... Is he still there?" He'd lowered his voice.

Ligaia knew to whom he referred. Though they never spoke Vernius's name aloud, the imperial general had been a constant presence in their marriage. "Last I heard," she admitted. "But even so, Cispadaena is how many days away, even in good weather?"

Kluctus couldn't hold her gaze. "Never mind that. Get to the boy. Get him into hiding. The man may or may not be willing to come for you, but he's certain to come for the boy. Just stay alive."

Ligaia knew he meant well. These were some of the bravest words she'd ever heard from her husband. They'd rarely spoken of the boy. She didn't have the heart to tell him that Vernius didn't even know of his son's existence. It made her sad that it took till now for Kluctus to show a bit of character. Even in the midst of near-paralyzing terror—after all she'd endured from him, after all he'd proven to lack—she had to admire it.

Perhaps it was never too late for redemption, even if it came mere moments before death.

The sounds of splintering came from behind the furniture they'd piled against the door. Maybe he was worth clinging to after all. "We both will. We'll make it through this together."

Kluctus shook his head and faced the door. "No, we won't. But they're likely to let a woman live. Just stay strong—survive! Obey me for once and go out to the terrace and jump."

She rushed to the terrace doors and looked back. The door was torn from the hinges. Voices grew louder, speaking their harsh Teutonic gibberish. The furniture screeched as it was pushed aside and toppled with ease. The fear that had burned within Ligaia since the bells rang the prior day leapt to a flame. The three men who filed in through their breached barricade were huge. One even had to duck his head under the lintel. They all wore armor and had long hair.

The biggest two held naked blades. The shortest of the three wore his sword sheathed at his hip. This one spoke in accented Hellainic. "Why did you make us destroy that door?" The speaker scanned the space. "Just as I thought. This will be our lord's chambers." He turned to Kluctus and his gaze hardened. "And now its door needs replacing. Such a pity." The scolding barbarian tilted his head toward Kluctus. "Seize him." The man's towering companions calmly stepped forward.

Kluctus awkwardly raised the ancient sword with his bony arm. "Go, Ligaia—jump!"

"Kluctus, no!" she shrieked. "Don't try to fight!"

The brutes moved with swift assurance. The first swung his blade and chopped Kluctus's hand off at the wrist while the second slashed higher, opening her husband's throat with casual but deadly precision. Kluctus fell to his knees, clutching his throat with his remaining hand, his stump of a wrist spraying blood onto his face and chest.

Ligaia stood gaping, one hand over her mouth, holding back the scream that would do her no good. Oddly, through the terror, she felt... resigned. Kluctus was dead. The waiting was over. Death would end all of this, and it had finally arrived.

The scolding brute turned his gaze on Ligaia. "Damn. Another pity. And another mess to clean. Seems your man was poor at making decisions. I hope you're better at it, my lady."

The brute spoke perfect Hellainic. It seemed so odd that this awful intruder was a striking, even handsome, individual. He seemed more intelligent than she'd imagined a pillaging barbarian could be. It sickened her. How could someone like this be part of such horror?

She backed away, stumbling across the terrace. Her backside struck the parapet. Ligaia turned and looked down. Her head swam. Perhaps Kluctus was right. Perhaps she really should at least try to get to the boy. And maybe try to get a message out to Vernius. And yet, the tiles of the terrace below looked incredibly hard. She leaned over. The parapet was only waist-high. She could just vault it. Easy. However she landed, she'd be better off than if she did nothing. Even if it was on her head.

Ligaia looked back. The trio strolled toward her. "Jumping was not the sort of good decision-making I had in mind," the leader said prosaically. He shrugged. "But it matters not. Broken legs can heal. Either way, you will likely make a good slave yet."

Ligaia turned from them and leaned over the parapet. Perhaps she should *try* to dive headfirst. As she gathered her resolve, a group of barbarians appeared on the terrace below. She gasped, drawing the attention of one of them. The brute called to his mates and pointed. The men below hooted and laughed, inciting the trio behind her to join in. The first one spread his arms wide, grinning and nodding, inviting her to jump to him.

Her slim hopes of escape, even the escape of death, evaporated amidst the uproarious laughter of barbarians.

Vernius reclined till the water touched his chin, savoring the warmth of the last bath he would have for the gods knew how long. Well, the last decent bath, anyway. He felt his muscles uncoiling and tilted his head back to wet his newly shorn hair. He devotedly kept his prematurely gray and balding pate closely cropped and his face clean-shaven. He'd done so since becoming an officer, same as his father before him. To Vernius, his father had seemed ageless—hardly changing from Vernius's earliest boyhood memories till his passing.

Though Vernius knew he'd never be the soldier his father had been, he hoped he'd at least inherited his enduring appearance. Constancy was affirming to those in his command.

He sought to calm his mind, to enjoy the bath. All was in place. The augurs had foretold good weather. His men were ready to march. It was time. Not that anyone had dictated the moment of his departure. The coming mission was a broad objective—one that had come from His Highness himself. No one but Vernius would enumerate and articulate the steps to achieving it. But dallying in Cispadaena would gain him nothing. His Highness expected results, and everyone knew what resulted from failing to please him—particularly Vernius.

Vernius spent the better part of every day in certainty that his status was undeserved. Every day he waited for others to realize he was hopelessly underqualified. Every night he prayed to his Equites ancestors to keep him from the blunder that would compromise his men, dishonor his emperor, or complete the ruination of his family's reputation. He'd long accepted his fears and doubts and used them as motivation. Beyond prayer, his only real means of ensuring his shortcomings stayed in their place, hidden away, was through rigorous training and study. That and maintaining a strict schedule. He ever sought to take persistent and definitive steps toward clearly defined objectives.

His objective for the last hours before dinner? Bathing. And relaxing. His mind and muscles needed this. There was one minor nuisance: Vernius had always had trouble letting go.

He had to focus in order to let go—which seemed ironic and ridiculous but had proven necessary.

A man entered the otherwise empty bathhouse. Vernius eyed the figure, seeking to will the intrusion to fade. Damn, Vernius recognized him. The man was one of the naval captains wintering in port. Vernius could only hope the recognition didn't work both ways. The intruder stripped off his robe, stretched his lean body, and stepped into the steaming water. Only once the man had settled in did he notice Vernius. Vernius felt his gaze and returned it with a purposefully hard glare. The man quickly averted his eyes. Success.

Vernius closed his eyes, hoping they could properly ignore one another. "It's good and hot today," the man said. "Don't you think?" Shit. The seaman couldn't contain himself.

Vernius kept his eyes closed. "It's a fucking bath," he growled.

The man sloshed, bolting up as if Vernius had pointed out a water snake. "Forgive me?"

He couldn't forgive pointless blathering. "Baths are either hot or deficient," Vernius said in his best commander's voice, still hoping to end it.

"Indeed." The man settled slightly but kept glancing. "Forgive me, but you *are* General Vernius Stallicus, are you not?"

"Depends on who's asking." He cracked open one glaring eye.

"Oh, er... well, no one was. Or is. Just my own curiosity." Vernius gave a nod and closed his eye. "It's an honor, is all." The seaman was utterly lacking in self-control. Typical. "Your victories are legendary. Not to mention your father."

Vernius opened both eyes this time. "Ah. Finally. A good suggestion."

The seaman goggled. "What's that?" Realization finally struck. "Oh, of course. Not mentioning your father. Forgive me again, my lord."

"I'd like to," he said and put a finger to his lips. Vernius had been taught that apology was nothing to be offered lightly or without sincere regret that informs reparation. At the very least it should come with concession. The seaman could earn his pardon by shutting up.

"After all, there is no need to mention a famous father when the tales of the son's deeds are equally worthy of renown. I mean, if they're all true." Vernius felt his jaw clenching, the relaxation of his muscles being reversed. Indeed, he felt more tense than when he arrived. Clearly this man was incapable of taking hints. The seaman hurried on. "As I'm sure they are, if only perhaps slightly embellished." Incapable of shutting up as well.

"Embellished." Vernius repeated the word, not bothering to veil his growing ire.

"I mean, for example, it seems unlikely that, upon your army's deep thrust into the Sassanada territory and finding yourself surrounded, you slayed every man, woman, and child in the nearest village, burnt the bodies, and then used their bones and skulls as mortar spacing for a swiftly constructed fortification, built from the rubble of their destroyed homes. Why, I have even heard it told that you withstood five times as many besieging foes until your rescue. Seems the original tale must have begged for embellishment in the retelling." In the silence that followed, the seaman's smile faded.

Vernius finally forced a smile. "I find myself at a loss."

The man slunk down in the water. "A loss, my lord?"

"You are...?"

"Oh, Neptune swallow me—I can't believe I haven't..." Thankfully, the man stopped himself from apologizing a fourth time. "I am Evandas, captain of the Saturn's Scythe. Do you know her? She's a quin, in the eastern command."

Vernius had never heard of the ship. "Her reputation credits you, Captain."

"Oh. Thank you. I am—"

"In answer to your speculation, Captain Evandas," Vernius interrupted. "One of the biggest problems in a land battle is finding sanitary means of dealing with the corpses of the foe. We bury our own, of course, but... Well, it's something that seamen, like you, need not trouble yourselves over. I've found that some solutions are not only sanitary but also provide a morale boost to our own men and a biding inhibition to the remaining foe."

The man swallowed noticeably. "I see."

Indeed, it seemed Evandas did see Vernius's solution anew. Even in the hot bath, his cheeks had lost their color.

The seaman seemed to remember something and regathered his pluck. "If you don't mind my inquiring, my lord, I see your men are mustering. Some of my fellow captains and I are wondering if we will be sent out during winter hiatus."

Vernius narrowed his eyes. "We are indeed mustering, but I have no idea when you'll sail again. Nor do I see what the two issues have in common."

"So... you're not going to Pontea?"

"Gods, I pray not." Vernius had already done his time there and was doing his best to forget it. Particularly the people of Pontea. Or at least one of them. He'd been doing much better at forgetting lately, and this was no time to stop practicing.

Evandas looked genuinely startled. "I suppose I just presumed that we—I mean the eastern fleet—would ferry the mobile reserve to Pontea. I simply wondered how soon—whether we would be ordered to break hiatus."

His Highness's orders had nothing to do with Pontea. The mobile reserve was marching overland, to Ostium. From there they'd sail west to put down a tribal uprising among the Breccae of Iberica. Vernius knew the seaman was simply casting nets. But being the ranking officer, Vernius decided he could take the bait without fear of getting too tangled. "And just why would you take us to Pontea?"

"Surely you've heard of the trouble there before the likes of me."

Vernius rolled his eyes. "Apparently your sources and connections are superior to mine, Captain." Despite the fact that Vernius routinely met with the Emperor himself. "But I suppose I would be grateful if you'd share your bounty." Grateful for an end to the guessing game.

"Forgive me, my lord." Another damn apology. "It's just that I happened to be on the docks when the arrival of a Hellain fishing boat surprised us all. They'd risked skirting the shores all the way from the Pontean Straits to bring urgent tidings. Their captain hurried off to the palace, but in his absence we enticed his first mate to offer a glimpse of their cargo, if you see my meaning."

Vernius stood, utterly done with wading through blather. "Tell me. Now," he growled. "What's happened in Pontea?"

Evandas cowered beneath him. "Barbarians. They stormed Thrakius and hold it still."

"Barbarians? Thrakius? What sort of barbarians would dare such an attack?"

"Teutonics from the northlands, by all accounts. The mate says he heard it was the same chieftain who laid siege to Akasas several years ago. Seems this chieftain since took up with pirates. Made himself rich enough to buy an army. Made up for his failure at Akasas by rampaging through Thrakius. Chased everyone down to the docks. They're saying the harbor was red with the blood of the innocent—women and children included."

Vernius was up and out of the water. He donned his robe as he headed toward the changing room, leaving the man gaping. His attendant Nicandros came in as he donned his underclothes and tunica. "There are tidings, General. The palace sent a runner."

"Yes. Pontea. I heard." Nicandros took his commander's advance knowledge in stride and helped him to don his belt, boots, and cloak.

Vernius exited the bathhouse and stopped. He needed to go straight to the palace. "I presume our orders will change," he said to Nico. "Head back to camp and tell the officers we're preparing to sail rather than march." The lad nodded and parted at a trot.

The palace guards saluted as Vernius hurried past. In the corridor, Vernius ran into Facerius, the Magister Militum—chief commander of both His Highness's armies and navies. Vernius snapped to attention. "Magister. I came as soon as I heard."

Facerius nodded to release him from attention. "Were you summoned?"

"No. I just presumed that Emperor Mycanius would wish to see me."

"He hasn't asked for you, and you should be grateful. He's in a shitty mood. Besides, there's little that can be done at the moment."

Facerius kept on walking in the direction he had been, and Vernius followed. "Still, I presume my orders will change."

Facerius sighed. "Not likely. The Straits are still safe. As is Trazonia. The trade council has all but talked Mycanius into settling this through diplomacy."

"But... This is Pontea we're talking about. You and I fought a long and bloody war to maintain those trade routes."

Facerius grunted. "Hm. How could I forget?" They arrived at the doors to Facerius's chambers and halted. "Come now, Vernius.

Having been stationed there, you know better than most. These days Thrakius is little more than a Pontean sideshow. Even the anax's family has fallen on hard times. And we're talking about a petty Teutonic chieftain. His warriors will get bored once they've fucked all the Thrakian maids." Vernius winced. "Trust me—the brutes will leave as soon as the coffers have been looted and the cellars run dry."

Vernius lifted his chin. "So my orders remain unchanged?"

Facerius raised an incredulous brow. "I hear Iberica is lovely in springtime."

Vernius grimaced and bowed his head. "Magister."

Facerius laid a sympathetic hand on his shoulder. "Get the Iberican job done, my friend. Come home soon. We'll speak of Pontea again then." His commander turned to open the door to his chambers.

"Facerius, you mentioned the anax. Is there word of him or of his family's wellbeing?"

The Magister paused and shook his head. "Nothing specific. But it was a slaughter, by all accounts. Particularly in the palace. I'm sorry, old friend. Will you be all right?"

He snapped to attention and saluted. "I am but a soldier in His Highness's service."

Facerius returned the salute, offered a sad little smile, and left him. Vernius stood in the corridor, thinking about all of the death in his life. His mother had succumbed to the black fly plague, as had his sister. He'd lost uncountable friends and comrades to war. He'd watched men die—men that he'd sent into the situations that led to their bloody deaths. And he'd killed more than his fair share, some in retribution. Most whose only crime was being on the wrong side of the battle lines—lines often drawn in the name of an unclear agenda. Usually in the supposed name of some god, while actually in service to the purses of the lofty.

His father had died in disgrace, in the vain pursuit of a sort of honor that seemed to have lost meaning in this world. Vernius struggled to continue to believe any sense of true purpose could exist, let alone honor.

In spite of it all, his heart ached for a woman he hadn't seen in what felt like half a lifetime. A woman who had a husband. She had likely died a horrific death. Could he have prevented it if he'd pursued honor? Would tragedy have come to pass if he'd stayed—if he'd chosen love rather than ambition? "Ligaia," he whispered.

Vernius felt a deep, festering anger. A yearning to avenge her as well. But there wasn't a thing he could do about it. Not if he were to avoid the folly of his father. "Lovely Ligaia. Rest well." He strode out the palace doors, heading back to camp. Then it was off to distant Iberica, on the far side of the world from Pontea.

He would pursue more death in service to an unknowable agenda, trying to convince himself his life had purpose. He would carry with him yet another death on his conscience. And he would carry his anger, knowing it would be more useful than his regrets.

ONE OF THE three Teutonic thugs who'd broken into Ligaia's residence appeared at the barred window of the cell door. It was the one who'd chopped off Kluctus's hand, right before his companion sliced open her husband's throat. This huge brute had also been the one to rush to Ligaia and sweep her up with one arm to keep her from jumping from the terrace. Ligaia had to admit, the giant was more agile than she'd have imagined possible.

The thug was so tall he had to stoop to peer in, scowling in the torchlight. "You are Ligaia, sister to Malvius?" He sounded like an ornery ox. How shocking, that such a beast spoke at all, let alone in Hellainic, however comical the accent.

Ligaia hugged her knees to her chest and stared at the opposing stone wall. Of course they'd surmised who she was. But the last thing she wanted was any sort of clemency due to her traitorous brother. The longer she thought about it, the more certain she was.

This was all Malvius's fault. He'd hired Gottari, brought them into her city, shown them what they lacked, what to covet. He'd set them into position to strike. She was starting to wonder if he'd at least condoned it. Or maybe even planned it. She couldn't put it past him.

She would rather die than claim that greedy little shit as a blood relation.

"Come, come," the ox prodded. She pressed her lips tight and bowed her head to her knees. "Please yourself," he said. "If you speak yes, you are let out. If you speak none, or false, you stay in." Ligaia gave him her most hateful glare. The thug's laughter was a low, deep rumble. He sounded and looked like a villainous puppet in a mummery. "If you think to die, there is to wait. Long time. You stay until you are being so weak and uncaring, you no more have a will to chase away rats who come to bite at your flesh."

She looked at the black corner behind the pail, which was half-full of her excrement—the spot in which she'd seen the rat's eyes, glowing in the dim light, watching her when she woke. The gods only knew how long ago that had been or how much time had passed down here. She hadn't a clue whether it was day or night anymore.

"Bah." The brute waved her off and disappeared from the window.

"Wait," she cried. Her leg muscles shrilled in complaint as she forced them to straighten and lift her. She limped to the door. The thug reappeared wearing a smug grin. "First tell me," she said. "Is Malvius up there?"

The ox shook his gigantic head. "No."

"Is he behind this?" The brute squinted. "I mean, are you here because of him?"

"Malvius comes to palace early this day. Though he comes not for you. As he goes, Lord Vahldan offers you to him. Your brother, he says no. He is gone now. So, because of him?" The brute shrugged. "Is for you to decide."

She raised her chin. "Yes, I am Ligaia, daughter of Anax Decebius, wife of Kyrios Kluctus—both of whom you people murdered during your outrageous invasion of my home." She bit back her venom and straightened her snarl. If released, she might gain a chance to see to the boy's safety. Or at least learn of his fate. Perhaps she might even get a message to Vernius.

Though she couldn't imagine how she'd accomplish any of those. Still, playing along might provide a chance. A chance without rats staring at her.

Without replying, the brute produced a key and the lock clanked. Screeching on ancient hinges, the door swung open. "Come," he grunted and stood aside.

She stepped into the corridor. Gods, the brute was half again her height. She felt like a child next to him. His sheathed sword was as long as her leg. He gestured for her to lead. Ligaia only vaguely recalled being carried down here like a sack of laundry. She peered into the other cells as she moved down the dank corridor. The barred windows were dark, but she knew the cells weren't empty. She didn't know who else was being held down here, but the corridors incessantly sang with soft crying and moaning.

They came to the torch-lit stone stairwell. By the top of the steep steps, Ligaia's legs felt weak. The brute reached past her to open the massive door. She squinted against light that flooded in from high windows. It was daytime. She was in the corridor that connected the kitchens to the larder and the wine cellars. Ligaia had lived in the palace all her life but had never been beyond this intimidating door. She'd rarely set foot in the kitchens since she was a girl, running and playing with the servants' children.

"That way." The brute pointed to the servants' stairwell.

The clank of pots and kettles echoed from the adjacent archway. Ligaia craned, hoping for a sign of the boy. She didn't see him, but she spotted Apontia lingering near the washtubs—likely busy avoiding work. So they'd not only spared the servants, they'd kept at least some of them working. Made sense, she supposed. Who else would keep the palace running? Certainly not the barbarians. The gods knew sly servants like Apontia had no loyalty.

The brute pushed at the center of her back with a finger. "Up," he said. The firmness of it made her sure that he could've toppled her with just that one finger.

More stairs. Gods, provide relief to her wobbly legs. When she slowed, the brute made a growling noise. Recalling the powerful finger, she obligingly carried on. When they came to the entry hall, Ligaia stopped short. The destruction brought tears to her eyes. All of the tapestries were gone, and the statue of her great-grandfather was a pile of rubble. There were scorch marks on the pale marble, and she knew the numerous stains on the floors were bloodstains.

"Move," the brute commanded.

Ligaia rounded on him. "Where are you taking me?" She used her most imperious tone, the one that had always caused Kluctus to back down or sent servants scurrying.

"There." He pointed up to the terrace leading to the high hall. "Lord Vahldan is waiting."

"May I at least wash and change my clothes?" She was still wearing the filthy frock from the day of the attack.

The giant appraised her sullenly. "Change into what?"

His words struck like a blow. Gods, they were in her home. They'd taken everything. What had become of her clothes? All of her beautiful things, her jewelry, her art—all would be gone, she knew. Gone like her father, like her husband. She slumped inwardly. But she would not let this brute see her despair. She raised her chin again. "Fine. Lead on."

Ligaia willed her legs to keep her ahead of the giant as she ascended the final flight. She stopped before the doors, trying to subtly catch her breath. The brute rapped but didn't wait for a response. He held the door for her, commanding her in with a casual tilt of his massive head. Midday sun streamed through the windows. She supposed she'd been expecting the new lord to be sitting in the high seat, waiting to pass judgment. As it would've been with her father.

But the hall was set up for dinner, with the long table centered. At its far end, a half-dozen barbarians sat speaking in their own tongue.

The giant led her to the near end of the table and halted her. They waited in silence.

Ligaia would've expected drunken revelry. But their conversation was quiet—almost solemn. They seemed respectful of one another. She would've expected them to be wearing battle gear and weaponry, or finery stolen from those they'd murdered. Instead, they wore unadorned woolen tunics in soft earthy colors over leggings tucked into worn leather boots. She would've expected tangled hair and unkempt beards, but their hair was combed and tied back, their beards trimmed. All this in spite of the hall's stench, testifying to their lack of a recent bath.

Ligaia would've expected a table filled with decadent platters of food and bountiful drink. Instead, they spoke over a scattering of maps, scrolls, and bound books. She recognized some items as being from the palace library. Others she presumed to have been brought from the armory. The youngest and thinnest of them read a passage in their tongue from a Tiberian book.

She had to admit, the man at the head of the table—Lord Vahldan, she presumed—was striking. And young! He had full lips, gaunt cheeks, and sky-blue eyes. His light brown hair was streaked with gold, same as his short beard. He listened attentively, had a pensive air about him.

Ligaia reminded herself that these men had taken her home by force. They had murdered her husband and father as well as the gods knew how many others.

She felt herself grimace, and the thug lord's eyes snapped to hers. She resisted the impulse to look away as he appraised her. Gods, his judgmental gaze made her feel like a girl—especially standing before the giant as she was. When the thin one paused in his reading, the thug lord raised a halting hand. "This is she?" he asked in accented Hellainic.

"Yes, my lord," her giant guard said. "Here is Ligaia, daughter of Decebius." The brute gave her back another firm nudge with that finger of his and bowed, obviously intending for her to follow suit. She stumbled a step forward but remained staunchly upright.

"Thank you, Teavar." The giant kept his head bowed and backed away.

"I extend my apologies, Lady Ligaia, for the loss of your husband." Vahldan nodded toward the man at his right. "Captain Arnegern here says he was offered surrender but chose to attack." This was the man who'd so jauntily spoken to her right after they'd murdered Kluctus.

"Really? I doubt you actually care," she said. "Beyond the blood-stain his murder left on your newly stolen rug."

Vahldan's eyes momentarily flared. He quickly recovered, and a small smile appeared on his lips. "You don't disappoint. I have heard you are fierce." The brazen man leaned back in her father's dining chair. "And perhaps you're right—that I do not grieve the loss of your husband. I have also heard he was generally useless—fawning and weak when it came to dealing with the imperials. But I do regret that your losses have put you and I at odds, my lady. For I should have welcomed your council as we take the reins and get this city back to work."

"Why in the gods' names would I have ever helped you?"

"For the same reasons I do as I do. For the benefit of our people, of course. And in the certainty that we will all be better off once we're freed of Tibairyan tyranny."

Ligaia huffed a laugh. Was he serious? Tyranny? "This city has prospered, free of tyrannous conquerors for over four hundred years. Until you managed to ruin the streak."

"Four hundred years?" Vahldan smiled archly. "Ah, since your family arrived and seized the city, you mean."

She frowned and shrugged. Even if he had a point, why should she stoop to debating a thug? Ligaia was growing sick of standing before a table full of gawking Teutonics. Seriously, she felt ill—mostly due to the smell of them. "So you've apologized. And?"

The thug lord sipped his wine. "And so you are free to go, Lady Ligaia. Though I know not where. It sounds as though you prefer Tibairyan tyranny to freedom. Perhaps once the ships begin to sail again, we can arrange for your passage from Thrakius. Is that to your liking?"

Ligaia was about to seize on the offer. If she could get to Cispadaena and Vernius... But then, he may or may not be there. And what could he really do? Vernius led the imperial mobile reserve, for the gods' sakes. He was at the beck of the Emperor. It was doubtful that Mycanius would allocate such a vaunted force to this minor setback. Even if this invasion came to his attention, it'd be like sending a pack of prized hounds after an already trapped badger.

Besides, Vernius had left her. Worse, Ligaia had made a fool of herself, thinking he'd actually want her—that he'd come back for her. Vernius had taught her what a guppy an anax's daughter was in the vast imperial sea.

If anything, she was even smaller now, with no wardrobe, no jewels, no title.

None of it mattered. Not since she'd seen Apontia. If that harlot was not only alive but still working in the kitchens, there was an excellent chance that the boy had lived and was still in the palace, too.

"No. This is my home. Not just Thrakius, but this palace. I have lived here all my life."

The captain who'd broken into her residence spoke. "If I may, my lord, it seems Malvius had guessed right. He predicted Lady Ligaia would not wish to leave. Perhaps her brother's suggestion is the solution."

Oh gods, what villainy had the little shit put in their heads?

Vahldan narrowed his gaze. "Your brother suggested that you might be willing to stay on as a servant here, perhaps in charge of the housekeeping in the residences. He claims you have always held high standards for those who are already serving up there and would likely be very thorough. But I will not force such a life upon you. The choice is yours."

Malvius was probably still laughing about planting this seed. But... It actually made some sense. It offered not only access to the boy but time. Time to figure things out. And perhaps the chance to be a part, however small, in taking back her home and bringing these murderers to justice. Including her dear, treacherous brother.

She took her filthy skirts in both hands and curtsied into a bow, holding it with all the grace her aching legs could manage. She made her tone as pleasant as she thought might still be believable. "It would be my honor to serve, Lord Vahldan."

ON HER THIRD day as a servant, Ligaia patiently waited until she was sure her hulking shadow had left the residences of the palace. She needed to make a start. Doing so involved risk. The time had come to seek the will and the hope she would need to carry this through.

Before he left, Teavar had checked on her during her Gottari language lesson with the thug lord's sister. Kemella was her tutor's name. The girl was tall for her age—Ligaia had gleaned Kemella was the youngest of the family. The cursed girl was exceptionally beautiful, even among the thug's admittedly attractive family. Through signing, facial expressions, and a few shared words, Kemella had begun teaching her their barbarous, harsh tongue. Kemella was actually kind enough to be patient with her. It surprised Ligaia, as it was the first real kindness any of the intruders had shown her.

In the name of efficiency, Ligaia was also teaching the girl Hellainic. Kemella was a clever girl and a fast learner. She was actually picking up the new tongue faster than Ligaia. In fairness, the girl was learning a classic language, rather than a backward one.

Still, these people continually challenged all of Ligaia's presumptions about Teutonics. None of it changed the fact that they were invaders and murderers, of course. Regardless of any trait she found that resembled their humanity, they were clearly still backward brutes.

For three days, Ligaia had silently sought to transform herself into the best version of a housekeeper she could imagine. Mostly by recalling the details that had annoyed her about her staff before the underworld had burst open and these beautiful-yet-wretched murderers had crawled forth into her world. To think—the former mistress of the house not only washed stinking and stained bedding but scrubbed the privies of those who'd displaced her. She hadn't sewn since she was a girl, but she'd even managed to alter the servant's frock they'd given her to a better fit. So many things she'd never dreamed necessary, let alone possible.

It had been crushing to clean her former chambers for the first time—to see how they'd stripped her rooms of all of their beauty, to futilely scrub the stain left by her husband's blood, absorbed and set in cold stone forever. On a good note, however, she had recovered her secret jewelry box. The first time she was sure she was alone there, she'd lifted the loose stone on the bed chamber's window ledge, and there it still was. Ligaia swiftly spirited it back to her windowless chamber, at first considering it a link to her former self. In a mere few days of keeping it hidden, knowing its contents could never be worn and realizing they only reminded her of a life she could never fully return to, she'd made a decision.

Ligaia gave almost all of the jewelry to Kemella. All but one item that was too precious to part with. The girl had already become useful. She needed to build on their tentative shared trust. But the gesture had provided a surprise benefit: a distraction.

As Kemella tried on each piece, checking herself in the looking glass—also something new and fascinating to the Teutonic girl—Ligaia let herself out, quietly latching Kemella's chambers' door to find no one in the corridor. She hurried to the servants' stairwell to find that also empty.

This was really it. The opportunity to begin pursuing her own goals. She vowed to start small. She would sneak down to the kitchens to quickly look around. She'd draw no attention to herself. If she didn't succeed, she would make sure there would be future chances to try again.

Ligaia grabbed a water jug from the servant's storage closet and tiptoed down the stairs. If she was caught, she was simply fetching wash water for the lord's basin. As she neared the bottom, a scolding voice echoed to the stairwell from the kitchens. Ligaia peeked out. The cooks were cleaning up before starting the evening meal. No one was looking Ligaia's way. She set the jug on the steps and hurried to the adjacent larder—dim aisles lined with shelves through which she could observe the corridor and a portion of the kitchens without being seen.

Ligaia crept along the shelves, peering through the jars and baskets into the more brightly lit work area. The round-bellied head cook, Heliopa, was scolding three minions for their lack of effort in cleaning the worktables. "It was Apontia's turn," one of the girls whined.

Ligaia froze and held her breath.

"Where is that girl?" Heliopa grumbled.

"Probably upstairs, figuring out which of these Teutonics to fuck," a second minion suggested. Ligaia nodded in silent agreement with the guess.

The third minion chimed in. "Yes, since she's bound to start fucking at least one of them, she's sure to be seeking the one who'll provide the most benefit."

"That's enough of that," Heliopa said halfheartedly.

"Why? Everyone knows it's true," the first girl said. "It'll be the same as before."

"Who could doubt it? I mean, *no one* would choose to fuck that shrivel-dick Kluctus for his charm or good looks." They all tittered. Even Heliopa bit her lip and turned from them.

Ligaia stiffened. Rage raced through her, suffusing her from chest to cheeks. As the cook and the girls argued on, she stayed very still, focusing on taking small, even breaths and restraining the impulse to either charge out screaming or to turn and run.

Her rage wasn't born of any sort of disbelief or of newly realized injustice. She never imagined Kluctus to be virtuous, let alone faithful. And she knew Apontia was a slut. No, her gut told her it was true and that she could've known about the pairing if she'd cared to look. As bitter as she was over the thought of all of the servants knowing of her husband's humiliation of her, that wasn't what fueled this intense anger, either.

Ligaia was outraged that—for years—she'd felt ashamed and guilty about her own affair with Vernius. And that she'd let Kluctus and her father, and even Malvius, use it against her—to weaken her and keep her in her place. They'd not only perpetuated her shame, they'd used it to preserve her loveless marriage. Worse, they used it to force her to give up her babe. She'd even allowed them to give her babe to her husband's concubine. For five long years, she'd willingly lived the lie they'd conspired to impose upon her.

All the while, Malvius had played a deeper game—stealing her ships, her legacy, and her very future from her.

Ligaia was outraged by the invasion of her home. But in truth, her life had been invaded long before the arrival of Teutonic barbarians.

Heliopa left to find Apontia while the minions reluctantly got busy rescrubbing the worktables. Ligaia had seen enough for one day. She slowly backed up to gain some distance. When she turned from the chattering girls to go, she gasped, nearly tripping over the waist-high presence lurking behind her. "Who are you spying on?" the boy whispered.

Ligaia looked back through the shelves. The girls hadn't heard. She bent to him. His eyes were gray and his disposition was solemn, scrutinizing. Tears of joy sprang to her eyes. He was alive! And, gods, he was the very image of his father. "No one in particular," she whispered shakily, blinking away her tears. "Who are *you* spying on?"

"You," he said, his mouth set in a flat line.

"Do you know who I am?" Ligaia brightened her smile.

He nodded. "You're the witch queen."

Apontia's voice echoed down the corridor. "I told you, I already did it, fatso!"

The boy's eyes widened. "Maaman is coming. I'm not supposed to talk to you." He dropped down and scurried through a low empty space on the shelves.

"Vernouthus," she whispered, trying his name on her tongue for the first time in years. "Don't go," she added as she bent to look for him. He'd disappeared into the depths of the larder. The tears over-filled Ligaia's eyes and ran down her cheeks. "Please don't hate me, my son."

PART THREE
IMPERIAL ASPIRATIONS

THE APPEASEMENT OF CONQUERORS

"Vahldan preferred to consider himself a liberator in Pontea. He had convinced himself of the corrupt nature of the imperial system and of the decadence of the Tiberian people and thereby presumed he would find support among those living under Tiberian rule. It never materialized.

Throughout his time in Pontea, Vahldan felt unappreciated and considered particularly the Hellains of Thrakius to be ingrates. He clung to this view and chose to ignore the resentments born of the casualties, persecutions, and shunning that the Hellains suffered during his own rule."—*Brin Bright Eyes, Saga of Dania*

VAHLDAN STOOD on the terrace of his residence on the top floor of the palace, looking down the market avenue toward the docks. He lifted his face to the brisk spring wind, drawing in the fresh air to calm himself. The sunshine lit the splendid sight of his new city and the blue sea beyond. He reminded himself that the view represented his boyhood dream *and* keeping his vow to his dying father. He was in an exotic city by the sea, seizing his destiny by winning glory.

He could do this. He'd won this city. He had conquered what the civilized world had deemed unconquerable. This was only the beginning.

Vahldan would never forget his first time seeing the palace. He'd never seen anything like it. It was the day he'd learned that Malvius was an heir to the decadence that had made the imperial cities of the Pontean coast the corrupt outposts of the slave trade that they were. He'd never forget how casually Malvius had mentioned that the palace was his childhood home, how his tyrannical father and scheming sister lived here still.

As they returned to the docks at dusk that evening, Vahldan had taken in the hurrying citizens, filing by rote through the maze of their stout stone dwellings, traversing on cobbled lanes to and from markets brimming with the bounty of being at the crossroads of imperial trading routes. It was then that he fully recognized that Ponteans were oblivious to the immense privilege of their existence. Privilege due solely to the place of their birth.

Over the course of centuries of living with such privilege, these people had lost their appreciation for what they had. Along with it, they lost their will to master their own destinies. Vahldan knew then that it was his destiny to seize what the Hellains had come to callously disregard. He still hoped his actions might awaken the pride of these indolent Ponteans—that they might become allies as he and the Amalus strove for what came next.

Come what may of this day, Vahldan was becoming something his father had never dreamed possible. He was finally making himself worthy of Angavar's sacrifice.

At last, he spotted the imperial procession traveling toward him. It had been a gamble, letting the Tibairyan ships into the harbor. He kept waiting for their duplicity to be revealed. But so far, there was none. The imperials were behaving as they'd pledged. Seemed they actually sought a diplomatic solution. The best possible scenario.

He wouldn't admit it—not to his inner circle, not even to Elan— but he felt enormous relief that the imperials were arriving in the form of a diplomatic delegation rather than a besieging army or a naval blockade. He'd gambled and won.

After taking the city, all through the remainder of hiatus, he'd both dreaded and anticipated this day. It was time to show the world that the Gottari were a force to be reckoned with. But for the Amalus, that meant putting themselves onto the world stage.

It was time to show every Danian who had doubted him, who mocked him behind his back, who'd tried to keep him and his clan down, that he was meant to lead the Gottari people to heights beyond anything they'd imagined possible.

They had offered the premier quays to the Tibairyan delegation's three ships. The meager imperial retinue—perhaps thirty members in all—approached the palace at a tortoise's pace. Still, it was a humbling uphill walk for such soft men, even through empty streets. Vahldan had imagined the return of the imperials would have resulted in jeering crowds lining their route, but once again the Hellains were proving meek and yet standoffish. It had been weeks since he'd declared a return to trade as usual, and now the imperial shipping hiatus was over. He'd been forced to issue a decree that shopkeepers and vendors must reopen. It seemed no matter what they tried, sea trade and city commerce remained sluggish. Thrakius's lauded bustling markets seemed remarkably resistant to decree. It was frustrating, but his advisors assured him that having a signed treaty with Tibairya would ignite the city's recovery.

If these damned bureaucrats had actually come to sign one.

"The captains have gathered in the throne room, as you requested, my lord." Attasar stood at the terrace door. "Shall I go down and greet the ambassador at the palace gate?"

"That'll be fine, Attasar. But no Tibairya..." He caught himself. "I mean, allow the *Tiberian soldiers* access to the entry hall but not beyond it." Attasar had been tutoring him to speak more formally. "Leave their men surrounded by twice as many of ours. I want Rekkrs in full battle gear. Have Teavar and Jhannas escort the ambassador up to the high hall." A smile quirked at the thought. "That ought to make an impression."

"It will be done." Attasar bowed his head and turned to go.

"Oh, and Attasar." His younger cousin turned back. "Remember, Hellainic only. Don't let on that you speak Tiberian. Maybe they'll be arrogant enough to speak freely among themselves."

"Yes, my lord." Attasar bowed again and left.

A few moments afterward, there was movement in the outer chamber. "Elan, is that you?" No answer. At dawn he'd sent word to her of the day's schedule, and he'd still heard nothing back. Vahldan went to look inside to see if she'd finally bothered to stir herself.

Standing in front of the water basin, Ligaia spun to face him. She looked solemn and stern, as usual, though her cheeks were flushed. "It's only me," she said. "I brought fresh water."

As fitting as Vahldan found the symbolism of having the former lady of the palace as a servant, he was far from trusting her. As with the brother, he was confident he could trust her to always act in her own interest. Which left her worthy of keeping an eye on. Same as Malvius.

"Thank you, Ligaia. Have you seen Elan?"

"No." The woman looked like she'd swallowed a bug. Unlike Malvius, Vahldan suspected Ligaia disliked Elan. At least Vahldan could be sure of one thing—they both feared her. Which had its uses. At least it would if Elan ever returned to her normal self.

"If there is nothing else," Ligaia said. She was as clever as her brother, too. Her phrasing was always twisting toward her desired outcome. Although she was careful to avoid being disrespectful, she never addressed him by name. She clearly loathed using an honorific. When she had no other choice, the words dripped with disdain. He often felt as though Ligaia was spying, or at least keenly monitoring the palace's goings on. He had to admit, Ligaia was swiftly learning the Gottari tongue. Something Malvius had never really bothered to do.

"Yes, that'll be all," he said. Ligaia tilted her head and left. She was stealthy, that one.

He checked each of the adjoining chambers for Elan. It was a cavernous set of rooms and not at all cozy or homey. As stunning as the outside appeared, the palace interior only pretended at lavishness. But it was a thin gilding. The austere space echoed. The residence had been stuffed with scores of tapestries and carpets, but they'd all felt foreign and fusty. So he had them removed. Still, nearly every bedamned surface was padded with dusty cushions or worn leather. Worse, he'd seen a greater variety of spiders, beetles, and centipedes living here than in all of his years in the forests and mountains of Dania.

Turned out he liked the idea of residing in the highest residence in the city much more than actually living here. He refused to consider how long they may need to remain.

Any inconvenience was worth it, though. Living here was vital to his goals. An Amalus lord had attained the highest heights of the civilized world, literally and figuratively. He made sure that every visiting merchant from Dania was treated to a tour and, whenever possible, an extravagant feast—a tale to tell upon their return home.

Besides, it beat sleeping on the ground or in a hammock in a swaying ship's hold.

Unsurprisingly, Elan was nowhere to be found. She should be at his side at a time like this as a rival entered his hall. He never let it show, but it still annoyed him that she'd taken her own residence on the floor below his. Vahldan practically begged her to spend more time in his lonely quarters, to no avail. It wasn't just her scarceness that annoyed him. Since Elan's arrival from Dania, even when she was present, she seemed distant. Even her usual diligence over his safety had become an afterthought.

Elan claimed she came back to be there for Vahldan as his guardian. If it was true, it was difficult to tell by her behavior. She'd returned as a mother, but she'd changed beyond that.

Elan's hatred of the city and the palace was palpable, but she also seemed scornful of his pursuits and goals. She seemed annoyed but resigned to everything that related not just to governing, but to the Urrinan itself. She longed for Dania, he knew, but she grew peevish whenever the subject arose. He'd assigned the most esteemed manservant to her personally, and she had still complained about needing help with the babe. Thankfully, the manservant, Hesiod, knew the staff well enough to find her a wetnurse and a housemaid. Even fully staffed as she was, she often missed dinners and was almost always unavailable for the strategy meetings he invited her to attend. No one ever seemed to know where she was. The gods only knew what she did with herself all day every day.

The worst part was that she often seemed lost in thought. Vahldan sensed a deep sadness in her. He wondered if she was sad that things had changed between them or if things had changed between them because of her sadness.

It seemed motherhood was the likely source of Elan's malaise, which he found ironic considering how long she'd nagged and pined for it. She'd even tricked him into playing along. Mara and the other womenfolk just kept telling him to give her all the time and space she needed. He'd done his best. But on a day like today, her inattention was beyond irritating.

Vahldan supposed he would eventually have to go and deal with her personally. As if he had nothing else to worry about.

As soon as Nia the wetnurse took Brin out into the sitting quarters to feed her, Elan closed the bedchamber door behind them and got to work. She threw her saddlebags onto the bed and then started digging through her trunk. She didn't have a lot of clothing, not by the standards of most Pontean women, but where she was going she'd need even less of it than she owned.

Through the door she heard Brin fussing. Her whole body tensed. She stood waiting until her baby girl made a mewling sound and then fell back to silence, likely suckling. Elan drew in a breath and hissed it out. She could hardly bear the thought of leaving her. But she'd been up all night and could think of no recourse. She couldn't take her—not this time, not without the wetnurse. It wasn't just that Elan had trouble feeding her daughter. She simply couldn't stand the thought of putting her in harm's way again—an outcome she couldn't rule out for the initial journey. If experience had taught her one thing, going all the way back to baby Kemella, it was how difficult it was to travel with an infant.

She vowed to herself that she would come for her daughter once she got herself established. Now that she'd found Nia, she could rest assured that Brin would be in capable hands. It went beyond ensuring she was fed and changed; Mara and Kemella doted on the babe, too. Vahldan may be uninterested in his daughter, but she had to believe that he would see to it that no harm came to her. Brin would be well cared for until Elan was able to come for her.

She rolled the clothing she'd selected to take and started stuffing it into the saddlebags. She was still in her nightfrock, but she'd already laid out her cuirass, leathers, leggings, and undertunic on the bed. She intended to wash herself before she dressed, as it might be the last thorough washing she would get for some time.

A soft knock on the door preceded the manservant's haughty voice. "Lady Elan? I brought you up some breakfast."

"Take it away," she called, allowing her annoyance to be heard. How many times had she told the man that she didn't want his bedamned breakfasts?

"I brought the tea that you like." Elan did like the tea. After a sleepless night, she could use the energy boost the stuff seemed to supply.

"Leave it," she called.

Less than a heartbeat later, and before she could do anything to stop him, the latch clicked and Hesiod appeared carrying a tray. "*Excuse me,*" she scolded.

"I'll leave all of it, just in case you change your..." As he bent to set the tray on her bedside table, the manservant's prying eyes scanned the bed, taking in her travel gear and warrior's garments. He stood straight as a soldier, clasping his chubby hands before him. "Are we planning another journey, my lady?"

Elan straightened to tower over him. Gods, she found the man annoying. It didn't help that she suspected he was spying for Vahldan. Beyond that, she was annoyed by his softness, his round belly, and his perfectly trimmed little beard, which barely disguised his double chin. She was annoyed by his silk servant's clothing, which was as fine and impractical as the attire of a highborn lady. And everyone with a nose had to be annoyed by his perfuming of himself to cover the odor of his tendency to flop-sweat. More than any of it, she was annoyed by his condescension, which was ever at war with his pathetic wariness of her, both of which were barely masked by false fawning.

As her assigned keeper, Hesiod was the perfect embodiment of this shithole prison of a palace, its opulence veiling its crumbling antiquity, its cookfires masking the odor of its decay.

"First," she began, "*we* aren't doing anything. Second, it's none of your concern. Third, I've asked you repeatedly not to call me that."

The Hellain had the decency to drop his gaze to the floor. "Might I inquire as to where?"

Elan bent to fasten her bag buckles. "To the docks, if knowing will make your day. And I suspect it will. I'll be leaving by ship, you see. Which means you'll be free of me."

"Oh, Lady Elan. That simply isn't so. It has been my honor to serve you."

She smirked. "Kind of you to deny the obvious. Regardless, I fear I must be off."

The pudgy Hellain made himself meet her gaze. "I fear that if you intend to take along Nia once again, I must intervene. The girl was terrified by what came of your last venture. It took some convincing to have her return to your service."

In her mind's eye, Elan clearly saw the bloody arrow embedded in the tree trunk a mere arm's length away. She shuddered. It had whizzed by a hand's width in front of her nose, but the shooter had purposefully missed. The shot had been preceded by the agonized wail of a wounded hare, also purposefully not killed by the shot that bloodied the arrow—specifically so that they would hear its cry, so closely resembling the sound of a human infant.

She'd never seen a single Skolani scout on the way south through the Pontean Pass. They'd obviously been happy to watch a ghost leaving Dania. But when Elan had attempted to leave Thrakius for the first time, less than a fortnight after her arrival, the Blade-Wielders guarding the pass had made it clear she was not welcome to come back through.

Which is why she had to sail to get away. Leaving her baby girl behind.

Gods, could she really do this? She had to.

Anyone could see that Elan was lost. Even this haughty Hellain spy, staring at her with pity in his eyes. She'd lost her purpose. Everyone knew that a lost purpose made for a lost soul. Ellasan had told her so before she had even earned her blade. The only home she could imagine was the shanty on the island. Since her banishment, it was the last place she'd felt like herself.

"I know she can't," Elan snipped, resuming her buckling of her bags. "I've already told the girl that she's not coming."

"I see," Hesiod said. The man was fairly good at feigning concern, at least. "Might I ask about the arrangements for your passage? What ship shall bear you?"

Elan harrumphed. Her fingers refused to finish their task. She stooped over the bed, staring at her unmoving hands. "I haven't found one yet," she admitted. She stood to face him. "Malvius will help me. I'll find him first."

Hesiod momentarily pressed his lips tight. "May I inform you as to why the timing might not be right for this trip, my..." He stopped himself from naming her a lady, so she reluctantly nodded for him to proceed. "The harbor is closed at the moment due to the arrival of a

Tiberian diplomatic fleet." He studied her for a moment, seeming to be deciding how much to say. "In addition to the imperial visitation, the city beyond the palace keep may not be so safe for those of you who are from Dania. You see, there are those who wish your people ill. There are bound to be resentments after... ah, what happened. Resentments that might lead some to act. And I fear that the presence of the imperials might embolden those prone to such action."

Elan stopped trying to secure the last straining buckle and plopped onto the bed. She stared at her hands again. They weren't a mother's hands. They were a warrior's hands. There was blood on them, regardless of whether or not she'd participated in the sacking of this city.

"Might I add another bit of advice, Lady Elan?"

She felt spent, defeated. "Why not?"

"Speaking of resentment that has arisen, having known Captain Malvius since he was a boy, I would advise you to give him some time and space, too. Perhaps he'll come around to a willingness to help you once the circumstances..."

"Once he sees how the circumstances might benefit him," she provided.

Hesiod's smile was genuine. "Precisely so. I see you really do know him."

Hesiod started to let himself out. He stopped in the bedchamber doorway. "Lady Elan, would you mind doing me a small favor?"

She scowled up at him. "What?"

He beckoned her. "Could you please come and look at this?"

Elan harrumphed again, stood, and went to the door. Hesiod stepped back and gestured toward the cushioned chaise. Nia had dozed off, sitting upright, cradling the sleeping babe. The morning sun shone through the terrace door's panes, bathing the pair in golden warmth. Brin's round cheeks were flush with the satisfaction of her recent meal.

"Beautiful, isn't she?" Hesiod offered. Her baby girl was beyond beautiful. She had no idea how to be a mother, and yet she'd given birth to this earthly goddess. Sometimes Elan couldn't believe she and Vahldan could've made such a glorious creature. "I thought it would be a shame if you missed such a moment," the manservant softly said.

She looked to find him wearing a sly, contented smile. At the moment, the man seemed less like a spy and more like a kind, doting uncle. His haughtiness had disappeared entirely. She returned the smile.

"Perhaps I could bring you some of that late harvest wine that you like," he suggested. She raised a brow. "Well-watered, of course. It might relax you. Now that you're staying, I mean." He headed for the exit.

She followed him to the archway of the entry hall. "Hesiod." He stopped at the door and turned back to her. "Why?" He gave her a puzzled look. "Why help me? You said it yourself. There are bound to be resentments."

The manservant offered her a sad little smile. "I have cause to recognize another troubled soul. One with limited options. Looks as though we're in this together, my..." He chuckled. "Forgive me, but given our limited options, I hope you'll reconsider allowing me to name you a lady, Lady Elan."

Elan huffed a laugh. "Since we're in this together, all we can do is cling to the few hopes that remain to us." He bowed his head and left, the door softly clicking behind him.

Vahldan was done waiting. He had to get moving. Slow as they were, the imperial delegation would be at the gates all too soon. He buckled his sword belt and left his residence. He hurried down the steps to the floor below. Elan's manservant was just about to enter her residence, bearing a tray with a wine decanter and cups. "Hesiod," he called to the man. "Has Elan already gone down?"

The manservant seemed nervous to answer. "I believe she's still within, my lord."

Vahldan swept past Hesiod and flung the door open. He strode through the entry hall into the sitting chambers. The wetnurse startled. She sat on a chaise holding the babe. He spotted his objective, out on the terrace, and went out. Elan sat staring out at the horizon. She was wearing a nightfrock, one bare shoulder jutting from the top. She had a blanket across her lap, as a crone would. The morning was almost gone and she'd yet to dress herself. She absently fondled the kestrel charm hanging around her neck. Hesiod went to Elan, set down the tray, and poured a cup of wine. She took the cup with a whispered thanks. The man bowed his head and left them.

"Why aren't you ready?" Vahldan asked.

Elan jumped. She hadn't even noticed his arrival. "Ready for what?"

"The Tiberians are on their way up the hill. They'll be here in moments."

"And?" She raised her cup and sipped.

It was a new tactic of hers—being willfully obtuse. Vahldan had learned that shouting only made these incidents worse. He kept his expression pleasant and spoke softly. "*And* I want you to be with me during this crucial meeting."

She raised her brows in a plea. "Must I? Brin has been cranky all morning. Neither of us slept well last night."

Vahldan craned to look in at the babe, now nursing contentedly. Elan sipped again. She seemed more interested in the wine than the babe, but pointing that out wouldn't help, either.

He drew in a calming breath and released it. "You've said it yourself. Our destinies are entwined, my love. I can't imagine a first meeting with our people's greatest rivals—those who are certain to be at the very core of our shared destiny—without having you at my side."

Elan's chin dropped and she closed her eyes. Was she blinking away tears? What had gotten into her? She opened her eyes and nodded as if in self-affirmation. "You're right. You are still my duty. I am a guardian. It's what I am here to do. It's my destiny." She cast off the blanket, stood, and tucked the kestrel into her frock. "I'll be right back with you."

Vahldan smiled. She already looked more like herself. "Thank you. Please hurry, darling." She padded into the sleeping chamber in stockinged feet, a far sight from the Blade-Wielder he'd once known. He hoped she'd find the rest of her old self. And quickly. If she could, it would be something worth making the Tiberians wait for.

VAHLDAN TRIED to keep a straight face as the visitors were led in. The Tiberian delegation was puny—and not just in number. All three men were small, two of them balding and all of them graying. None of them was armed, and they wore what appeared to be glorified bathing robes and sandals. And yet, all three followed Attasar toward the throne dais with their clean-shaven chins held high, their contempt etched upon them.

They halted before the dais. Rightfully, they should bow. They didn't.

Attasar introduced the one in the center as Legatus Avitus. Everything about the man was gray—his face, his hair, even his lips. All but his dark eyes, which shone with hatred. His sashes and cloak were of the most ridiculous reds and purples, his paunch pushing them tight at the belt. His hateful eyes seemed to be lined with paint, same as a dock whore's. He looked more like a sickly minstrel than a diplomat. The other two, whom Attasar named as *adiutors*, were apparently the minstrel's aides. One rubbed his hands together as if perpetually washing them, and the other's eyes darted around the hall as if studying all of the possible escape routes.

These were the chosen emissaries of the great Tiberian Empire. Vahldan didn't know whether it showed how pathetic they'd become or if it was an insult. Likely both.

After an awkward silence, Vahldan said, "Attasar, bring them the proposal we drew up."

Vahldan's young scholar produced the scroll and offered it to Avitus as he spoke. "My lord has outlined the advantages to the empire of our holding of Thrakius—in Tiberia's name, of course—including the savings to your government on troop costs as well as an increase in tariff revenues due to my lord's more diligent monitoring of what are often smuggled goods traded and warehoused illegally here. In addition, ships' captains who use Thrakius as a home port will be more likely to maintain contracts with the brokers of eastern goods, as they shall have access to onboard Gottari guardsmen—ensuring fewer losses to both piracy and Sassanada seizure."

Attasar gestured with the rolled parchment, but Avitus made no move to take it. Finally, the envoy nodded to his handwringing aide, who stepped forth and took it. The aide put it in a shouldered bag without a glance. Seemingly so he could get back to wringing his hands.

Another uncomfortable silence. Attasar spoke again. "My lord hopes you'll find the agreement not only acceptable but advantageous to your emperor and his government."

Avitus's smile became a sneer as he stepped by Attasar, eyes locked on Vahldan. At Vahldan's either side, both Elan's and Teavar's hands went to their hilts. The derisive look this fop gave to Vahldan's guardians caused the ugliness to stir within him.

The Legatus spoke up in Hellainic, enunciating as if he were a player in a mummery. "Should you allow me to speak freely, *Lord Vahldan*," the Tiberian said, making his title a mockery, "I might offer clarity you will find useful in all of your future interactions with His Eminence's government."

For his tone alone, Vahldan considered having the man thrown in the dungeon. He could hold the entire delegation as hostages. Or perhaps he should have them publicly tried and executed. Or at least flogged. Surely he could come up with the charges. The ugliness was urging him to bypass all of it and simply slice their throats right here and now. They could formalize the charges afterward.

The Tiberian waited with a raised chin and curled lip. Vahldan's vision blurred at the peripheral and his ears rang. The forge in his belly grew hot. Attasar gave Vahldan a look, reminding him that he had but to get through this. He forced himself to nod, giving the insolent Tiberian permission to speak freely.

Avitus cocked his head and began. "Since I am reasonably certain that there is a limit to your grasp of world affairs, allow me to bestow a historical summary as a preface to my promised advice. The Tiberian Empire has flourished here in Pontea for over four centuries, in part because of the robust benefits to the region's citizenry, but also due to the might of the militum each emperor has at his disposal. Throughout an era defined by Tiberian supremacy, literally scores of barbarian strongmen have attempted to seize imperial territory or pillage its wealth. You are but the latest."

Teavar stepped toward the man, starting to draw his blade. The gods knew Vahldan wanted to draw his own. "Hold," he made himself say in Gottari. "Let the goose honk." The giant's blade slapped back into place. Though the minstrel seemed unfazed, Vahldan noticed beads of sweat forming on his forehead. The sight actually helped Vahldan to push down the ugliness. Of course this was nothing more than a show. After all, the emperor had sent a painted minstrel. He should've expected nothing less.

Vahldan played along by giving the man an impatient wave. Avitus barked a single laugh. "I am told that your father was reckoned a vaunted chieftain. In appraising you today, I rest assured that the progeny shall never surpass the sire." The ugliness reignited, sending a hot tingling through his limbs. The man grinned. "Do you wish to know how I know?" Vahldan kept himself very still. He knew if he moved or spoke, he might lose himself. "It is evident, as your father had the wisdom to never tread foot on imperial soil."

Were they trying to provoke an incident? As if Attasar had guessed his thoughts, the scholar gave him a reassuring nod. His scribe was telling him to wait it out. The empire would grant the treaty or else they would've sent an army instead. This was but a final trial. The thought released him to breathe again. Vahldan glanced to Elan. She had been watching him closely. She nodded and smiled slightly. She recognized that he was holding the ugliness in check.

He fixed the man with his own haughty glare. "And?" It was the same obstinate response Elan had given him earlier.

"I say so merely to point out that there have been many others who weren't so wise. Besides you, I mean. May I tell you how many of these incursions came to an end that did not include the execution of the offender and the death, suffering, or enslavement of his or her followers?" The Legatus paused for only a moment. "Exactly one. Yours. Thus far, that is. You have the benevolence of Emperor Mycanius to thank for this rare exception. I am not here to explain His Eminence's reasoning for it. Suffice to say he considers your tenure in this stinking backwater bilge to be the equivalent of allowing a maggot to eat the rot from his foot sores."

When his hand went to his hilt again, Elan's hand grasped his wrist. His eyes darted to meet her steady gaze. They held the look while he drew and released a breath, and she released him with a nod.

The emperor's minstrel droned on. "For as long as the status quo suits Emperor Mycanius, you may stay. But I assure you, the moment he finds himself displeased, for whatever reason, the situation here shall be dealt with. In a way unpleasant enough to make a worthy example to others of your ilk. Until then, I would avoid making a nuisance of yourself, which would only serve to expedite this nearly inevitable outcome. This includes the harm of any of His Eminence's emissaries, agents, or allies—starting with present company. It shall also include an imperial harbormaster, appointed by the rector in Megaria, who is to be left to do his duty without the slightest encumbrance. These are His Eminence's generous terms. In other words, this is your only chance at becoming half the man that dear papa had been." The minstrel paused for effect. "Before you murdered him."

Everything blurred and the flames flared. In a flash, the futhark blade was out and at the man's throat, the tip of the blade nudging his whiskerless chin. The ugliness pulsed in response to the man's evident terror. It would be so easy, so satisfying, to thrust that tip into his flesh.

His sword arm was now gripped by two strong hands. "Hear me?" It was Elan. He nodded without looking. "Good," she said in Gottari. "This one is not worth the trouble. He is nothing—a mere puppet for those too frightened to face you. Look beyond the slurs. The Tibairya are admitting that you have already won. They might even prefer the puppet's death to allowing your victory to stand. Don't let them take it from you. From us."

Vahldan's vision started to clear, his racing pulse to slacken. "Almost inevitable, is it?" he said to the minstrel in Hellainic. The puppet's eyes bulged, sweat streaking his face paint. The man looked utterly ridiculous. Vahldan lowered the sword and grinned. "I'm afraid I only murder men worthy of the bother. So I suppose we'll have to test your forecast on another day."

He sheathed the blade and Avitus staggered back. "But don't give up hope," Vahldan added. Avitus's assistants cowered like whipped hounds, afraid to flee for the lash that would be earned by turning tail. He laughed and bowed to the trio. "Do come again. I often feel lust for blood. Next time I may indulge it."

Vahldan turned from them and started out. He spoke carefully to Attasar, who ghosted behind. "Please escort our guests back to their ships. See to it that they set sail immediately."

Attasar turned back to do his bidding. Vahldan found focus on Elan walking alongside. He expected her to scold him. Instead, she narrowed her gaze. "See me?" she asked.

"I do."

"Good," she said and took his elbow with a satisfied smile. "I was afraid I'd lost my touch."

LIGAIA EXITED the servant's corridor into the palace's entry hall. She stood hidden in the shadows under the staircase to the high hall's terrace, surveying the scene. She held a pail of clear water and a dipper. She had no idea how long the three Tiberian emissaries would be upstairs, but she'd already surmised she had no real chance of speaking with any of them.

She studied the waiting Tiberian guardsmen formed up in the entry hall. The one closest to the stairs had a colorful crest on his helm that ran from ear to ear rather than front to back. Ligaia knew nothing of uniforms or insignias, but she knew enough about Tiberians to know that ostentation usually indicated status. The nearest man was not only the showiest, he seemed the most indignant about being surrounded by barbarians and unable to do a thing about it.

Ligaia was determined to make contact. For the twentieth time, she shook her arm, allowing the papyrus tucked up her sleeve to fall into the hand holding the dipper, practicing its smooth removal. Besides getting it to the showy one without notice, Ligaia had to convey both its secrecy and importance.

She would only have one chance. If one of the Gottari warriors questioned her before she reached the target, her mission would fail. The only advantage she had was her ability to speak Tiberian, however poorly—a language she was all but certain none of the Gottari spoke.

Her window of opportunity would soon close. There was nothing to be gained by waiting. Ligaia took a deep breath and started for her target. Before she'd taken two steps, a hand clutched her wrist, crinkling the papyrus under her sleeve. "Do not do this thing."

Ligaia instantly recognized that accent. Seething, she spun to face Apontia. She tried to yank her arm free but couldn't. Rather than bothering with denial or playing dumb, Ligaia snapped, "Why not?"

The Sass woman's grip tightened. Ligaia had never actually been this close to her. Apontia's brown eyes blazed with passion. Her tan skin was flawless. She really was stunning. Small wonder that Kluctus had been fucking her. "Trust that if you do, I will make you regret it," Apontia said through clenched teeth. Damn, even her teeth were straight and white.

Ligaia glanced at the Tiberians and the score of Gottari thugs that surrounded them. She knew it would take very little for Apontia to ruin her attempt. She looked back, and the woman's broad mouth curled into a victorious smile. "You see that I can do this, yes?"

Rather than argue, Ligaia asked, "Why? They are heathens. Murderers. Monsters."

Apontia tipped her head toward the servant's door and pulled her toward it. Ligaia glanced back, but realized it was over. She'd lost. For now. She allowed Apontia to lead her out.

When the door closed behind them, Apontia rounded on her. "The Gotars, they are murderers, yes. But they tell me I am free to go. Though I stay for now, I may go when I wish. Not one of them has even tried to rape me."

"Not yet, eh?" Ligaia archly said. "Such a high standard to hold them to."

Apontia's gaze grew fierce again. "It is more than I can say for your precious Tibairya." The woman raised her chin. "Even your beloved general—he is more monster than any Gotar."

Ligaia yanked her arm free. "Vernius is no rapist," she snapped.

"Maybe not. But I wonder. In your culture, what do you call someone who stands back, allowing crimes to happen? In my culture, that man too, we name a criminal."

"Shut up. What do you know of it?" Ligaia started back toward the stairs to the kitchen.

"A lot is what I know," Apontia called after her. "Why do you think they brought me here?"

Ligaia stopped but did not turn back. "Brought you?" It started to make sense. Ligaia had never questioned why Apontia had come.

"The troops—they captured you?" She looked over her shoulder. Apontia gave a single nod.

Ligaia realized she had arrived in the palace at about the same time that Vernius's legion arrived to be stationed here. She also knew that his legion was fresh from the Sassanada front.

Ligaia had also heard that they'd brought dozens of slaves to sell.

Ligaia stood very still. "They... hurt you?"

Apontia's expression softened. She nodded again. "Not just me. When the Tibairya came to my village, they cared not that we did not bow to the Xah. They cared not that we once hoped the invaders would win their war. They cared only that we have brown skin, like those they fought. For this crime, the Tibairya showed us what true monsters can do." Ligaia turned to her. Apontia's eyes shone with unshed tears.

"I... I didn't know," Ligaia said.

Apontia shook her head. "And if you had?"

Ligaia didn't know the answer. Would it have changed things?

Apontia averted her gaze and barked a bitter laugh. "It doesn't matter. You and I—we are much the same, yes? When I watched my people die—everyone I ever knew—at first I thought like you, that murder was the worst the Tibairya can do. I wanted to live. I begged them to spare me." Apontia turned her sad eyes to Ligaia. "But you must trust me when I tell you—murder is not the worst a monster can do."

Ligaia had to look away. "I didn't know," she repeated lamely.

Apontia forced a smile. "But now we have both seen. We have both suffered. For me, I know I can no longer have a babe of my own. But you—you gave birth to one of them." Apontia tilted her head toward the chamber full of Tiberian soldiers. "But because of it, you gave me the chance to know what it is to be a mother. And we both now see that monsters are not born but made, yes?"

Shaken, Ligaia started toward the stairs. "Housemaid!" Ligaia stopped again. "I warn you. Do not try to take him from me. Agoraki is all I have. I earned him."

"I gave birth to him," Ligaia said without looking.

"And then you gave him away. You needed me to take him, yes?"

"Things are different now."

"Different yes, it's true. Before, if you had come to take him, I could do nothing. Now, if you try it, I will tell the Gotars who he is."

Ligaia rounded on her, glaring.

"Yes, things are very different," Apontia said, narrowing her beautiful eyes. "You will not make a monster of him. On this I think we can now be of one mind, yes?"

Ligaia had no response. She felt drained, disarmed, and defeated. She had no idea what direction to take, so she turned and headed down the stairs to the kitchens. Her world had turned upside-down for the second time in but a whirlwind of days.

CHAPTER 15
A BRINGER HAS TO BRING

"*When I was young, Dania seemed distant and wild. A place fondly recalled by many around me but beyond my reach. A place of dire striving that rewarded its survivors with simple pleasures never to be known in Pontea. Though I remained enthralled by Danian tales, in my imagination my parents' homeland somehow became frightening. As much as I longed to see and know Dania and explore my heritage there, the thought of facing up to that part of myself was a secret source of dread.*

In hindsight, I see that my conflicted perception was fueled by my mother's ambivalence."—Brin Bright Eyes, *Saga of Dania*

EIGHT YEARS **since Vahldan's conquest of Thrakius.**

VAHLDAN WENT DOWN to dinner in the palace's high hall as usual but swiftly excused himself under the pretense that he felt ill. He returned to his residence, and as he finished changing into riding clothing, the soft knock arrived. "Come," he called, buckling his sword belt.

Teavar stepped in. "She just left for the stables."

Vahldan swept past the giant and into the corridor. Teavar fell in behind him. "I'm going with you," Teavar said.

"Not this time, my friend."

"What if she leads you into danger?"

Vahldan hurried to the stairs. "Danger? Just where do you think she'll lead me?"

Teavar kept up. "You could find yourself surrounded by..."

Vahldan stopped on the first landing and turned to him. "By what?"

"You know. Dissenters."

When would his Gottari followers drop their suspicion of his new subjects? Vahldan knew he had to break the cycle. How could his people take their rightful place in the civilized world if they continued to keep themselves so isolated and insular?

"Are you really proposing that she rides out to be among these dissenters you all imagine to be lurking outside the palace walls?"

His old friend looked down, abashed. "Well, how can we be sure that—"

"Teavar." Vahldan leaned in, forcing eye contact. "Can you find it in your heart to believe that Elan would ever do anything disloyal or put herself in any situation that might compromise our people's destiny?"

Teavar drew a deep breath and released it. "No, my lord. I cannot."

Vahldan gave a single nod. "Good. Because I have no friends that I trust more than you and her. I'd hate to think that either of you did not share my trust in our triad." He started down the stairs again. "If I'm not back before the city gates close," he called over his shoulder, "*then* you can worry."

Vahldan strode to the palace stables and peered in before entering. Elan was already gone, and the stable boy had Gadöf saddled and waiting, as Vahldan had arranged. He flipped the boy an imperial silver and mounted. The lad's eyes lit up. He bobbed a hasty bow and ran off with the prized coin. It was an unfortunate reality, but they were so much more versatile than a Gottari skatt.

The gray gelding was Vahldan's new favorite, in spite of his humble breeding. Also despite the stable of fine warhorses his Rekkrs kept urging him to ride. Gadöf remained calm as Vahldan rode at a trot down the busy lane to the east gate. The even temperament he displayed here was part of the reason he'd grown fond of the young horse.

Vahldan knew he needed every advantage this evening. It was no small undertaking—to successfully track a former Skolani Blade-Wielder.

He slowed Gadöf to a walk at the city gate and made it through without attracting a second look from the guards. As he came clear of the wall onto the road, he caught a glimpse of the roan mare just as Elan rode out of view. The road here was carved into the base of the mountain range as it plunged to the churning sea. He kicked the gray to a canter, riding at the faster pace until he rounded an outcrop and Hrithvarra came into view again. He rode along like that, cautiously moving at an unhurried pace, with her appearing in the early evening sunlight then disappearing into the shadows or around the road's bends. Elan showed no sign of being aware she was being followed.

All the while, Vahldan scolded himself. How had it come to this? It had been months since she had deigned to share a meal with him. And, Freya help him, even longer since she'd stooped to sharing his bed. It had been several weeks since Vahldan had heard that she often left the city alone, but no one seemed to know where she went or why. Only that she always rode east on the coastal road. The one time he'd had her followed, she'd never left the city walls and had swiftly returned to the stables and then to her bedchamber. She'd obviously detected the tail.

Vahldan rode a section of the roadway that ran along the base of a cliff that jutted into the sea, afraid to gallop but anxious about how long it had been since he'd had her in sight. When he swung back northward, he could see a long swath of the coastal road. But not Elan.

She'd disappeared.

He felt foolish. He'd never been a scout, and it dawned on him that he had no idea how to track her. A thought occurred to him, and the back of his neck prickled. He scanned the rocky heights above, half expecting that he'd find that she'd gotten behind him. There was nothing.

The entire endeavor had been ridiculous. If she wanted to keep her secrets, why should he care? Just as Vahldan convinced himself to turn back, the heartsickness struck. Gods, how could she do this to him? How could she abandon their connection, their commitment to a shared destiny? The questions led to a surge of anger, which threatened to summon the ugliness.

"No, dammit," Vahldan said aloud. He slapped the reins, urging Gadöf into a canter, continuing the pursuit. He nearly rode past the rocky gap. He turned back for a closer look. Sure enough, there was a path. It was green beyond the encroaching rock, although the path itself was little more than mud and sea-spray puddles. Even without dismounting he spotted the fresh hoofprints. Which meant she still didn't suspect she was being followed.

Once Vahldan rode through the gap, the canyon opened up before him. The pathway wound up along the base of a gorge. The hillsides became forested, and soon the firs and hemlocks leaned over the trail, plunging him into shadow. The rhythmic drone of the sea faded and was replaced by birdsong. Spring breezes stirred the boughs. It felt much like the Pontean Pass. He wondered where it led. Could it be followed all the way to Dania?

The path steepened and narrowed, the forest crowding the way. He was forced to dismount. He found himself fretful, his head swiveling at every stirring bird or squirrel. The footing became rockier—almost stair-like. He came to a plateau covered with evergreens. The trail seemed to end, but the sound of rushing water drew him on. As he moved through the trees, the shushing became a dull roar.

Vahldan spotted Hrithvarra first, untethered, munching sprigs of lush grass from between the rocks. The mare regarded his approach calmly. He left Gadöf with her and moved into the low-hanging branches of two entangled firs. He parted the final boughs to see sunshine glinting off a waterfall that fell into the canyon, its water rushing to the sea. He stopped short, lingering in the shadows, struck by the vision before him.

Elan sat in partial profile on the bank, about a stone's throw away. She'd taken off her boots and leggings and dangled her feet from the rocky bank into the spray. Her head was bowed as if in prayer. She held her kestrel charm in her hand.

He suddenly felt ashamed. How could he spy on her like this? The rushing water seemed to have drowned out his approach. He could pretend he'd never been there. He turned to go.

"It's about time."

Vahldan stopped and turned to her, his heart thudding. "For what?"

Elan kept her face to the water. "That you came out here to talk to me. I've been waiting. For months."

His cheeks grew hot. He stepped from the boughs into the sunlight. "We've lived under the same roof for years. You could've spoken to me at any time."

Elan finally looked up, shaking her head. "Not so. In there I can only speak to Lord Vahldan of the Amalus—Conqueror of Thrakius, Bringer of Urrinan. No, I wanted to speak with the man who carved this." She held up the kestrel, her smile mischievous but radiant.

Gods, she was right—he hadn't carved in years. Why not? He knew as well as she did how it brought him back to himself. It provided peace, and he'd been feeling everything but peaceful.

Ah, Freya's grace... that smile. She was still the loveliest being in all the nine worlds.

Vahldan went to her and fell to his knees before her. "I'm here now."

She took his face in both hands and cocked her head. "Ah, there you are." She kissed him, featherlight. "I've missed you, my darling."

"What has happened to us?" His eyes grew itchy.

"Nothing. Those people living in that stuffy old palace, they aren't us. That's why we need this." Elan gestured to the waterfall.

"How did you find it?"

"I'm not sure. It's like I was drawn here." She gazed about her, eyes alight. "It feels like a little piece of Dania." She drew a deep breath and sighed it out.

"I miss it, too, you know."

Elan's gaze darted back to him and narrowed. "You said we'd go back—that all of this was the way to make things right. You said coming to Pontea would restore the futhark."

"And so it will."

"When? All I ever hear about is war and empires and Urrinan."

Vahldan drew back from her, sitting on his haunches. She'd gone to all this trouble to restart the same old argument? "Actually, we're discussing the plans to return to Dania soon. This summer, in fact. And I intend to restore the futhark while I'm there."

She narrowed her eyes. "Why now?" A moment ago, he'd have guessed she'd be thrilled.

"Many reasons."

"Such as?"

"It's time for the next step. The imperial mobile reserve is as far from Pontea as can be, but rumor speaks of peace in the west. And there is trouble brewing between the Bafranii pirates and their sadhu, who is pledged to the empire. The imperial focus will shift eastward, to Pontea. Thankfully, my sources say things are finally coming together for us in Dania. And just in time."

Elan stood. She backed away a step. "Things?"

Vahldan rose to face her. "Things."

"Such as?" she asked.

"Such as wool prices. They remain extremely low. There's a glut of supply. Even though the wolves still retain their hold in the long-house, several of their key supporters have left the guild to seek markets of their own. Their stranglehold is weakening." Elan turned away, crossing her arms to hug herself and staring at the waterfall. He went on. "On top of that, some say the Elli-Frodei are as scarce as ever. Their numbers are falling, and—"

"It's because of her," she said.

Vahldan closed his eyes. She really *did* want to argue. "Who?"

Elan faced him, eyes blazing. "You know damn well who. She's come of age. You waited all of these years. For her."

He straightened, seeking courage. "I've waited for the workings of destiny to align."

"Don't patronize me. You've been waiting for what was foretold. At least have the honor to admit it." Still bootless and bare-legged, Elan stormed past him toward the horses.

"Gods curse me. All right!" He rushed to grab her shoulder, spinning her back. "Yes, among other things, I waited to see what would happen with Amaseila's daughter. She's a part of this, dammit. What am I supposed to do? If I'm to be the Bringer, how can I ignore the foretold means to Urrinan?"

Her face was incredulous. "If I'm to be the Bringer?" she mimicked. "Did you really just say that? So you've finally gone there. You actually believe it."

"Oh, come on. You know what I mean."

Elan's laugh was full of scorn. "I don't think I do. Not anymore."

"I meant, if I'm going to play the role of the Bringer, of course. Same as ever."

Her lip curled. "I may not be sure what you mean, but I know that I hate this."

He fought the urge to roll his eyes. "You hate what?"

"This forsaken place, the bloody empire, the cursed prophecy. The gods bedamned Urrinan. All of it!"

Vahldan held up his hands in surrender. "You think I don't?"

Elan's expression fell from angry to sad. "Honestly? No. I think you love it. You're obsessed. And for that, I hate what you've become most of all."

She spun to leave again. He grabbed her again. "You don't get to walk away. I've told you over and over that I can't do this without you."

"Seems like you're doing just fine."

Freya's vengeance, was that actual hate in her eyes? "You... you can't hate me. You belong to me."

Tears filled her eyes and rolled down her cheeks. She shook her head. "I do hate you. I hate you." She suddenly swung and hit the side of his shoulder. Hard. He grabbed both of her wrists, but she shook loose, swinging both fists now. He raised his forearms defensively. "I hate you, I hate you, I hate you," she ranted as she rained punches on him.

He seized her and drew her in, too close to keep hitting him. She collapsed against him, her raging tirade flipping to sobbing. "Horsella help me," she said, gasping for air. "I pray, and I try, with all my might. And I can't stop. I don't want to, but I can't stop loving you." Her legs seemed to give way in his embrace.

Vahldan eased her down till they were kneeling. He drew her from the crook of his neck and gazed deeply into her wet, red eyes. She was right—they were no longer the lord and the guardian who lived separate lives in a palace. In that moment, she was the young warrior who'd taken in a lost man-child and protected him and propped him up. And loved him. And he was the young man who'd carved the kestrel—who was sure he'd already lost her as he did it but knew he'd love her forever, no matter what. And he'd hurt her. And, gods, how that pierced him.

"I once told you I had no home, and I still don't. Not in Pontea, not in Dania. *You* are my home. It's always been you."

Elan tilted her face to him, parting her lips. Their mouths collided in passion, tongues seeking. His hands roved, groping, clutching, squeezing.

As she always did, Elan slowed him down and took control. She touched his face, meeting his gaze, her eyes smoldering. Her mouth found his again, tenderly, expressive. She pulled him down on top of her, wrapping him in her arms and legs. Once again, they tumbled toward passion. Without disengaging from their kissing, she fumbled to undo his sword belt. He tossed it aside even as she tugged on his leggings, trying in vain to get them down before they'd been untied. He pulled her underpants down onto her bare thighs even as she finally freed him.

They both gasped as he entered her. Gods, it had been so long—how could they allow so many precious days to go by between these blessed moments? He drew back to look at her. Woden's halls, she was beautiful. She bit her lip and shook her head. Their connection was renewed, and he knew they were as close to the divine as was possible in this life. Freya's Blessing could never be cast aside—could never be broken. He knew it, and she knew it, too.

She kissed him again and pulled on his hips, urging him on, speeding him to climax.

He released and collapsed on top of her, panting for breath into her tangled hair. Elan clutched him to her and inside of her. Her breath was hot in his ear. "Hear me?" He nodded, unable to speak. "Good. Because I need you to hear me. Really hear me."

He raised up and looked down on her. "I'm listening."

A steady stream of tears flowed again. She rarely looked so vulnerable, but gods, she was so beautiful. "I have searched my heart, and I simply can't believe that there is no deep meaning in the connection I feel with you—that what we share is simply animalistic attraction."

"That's because it's real. I feel it too. It can't be denied, ever."

She drew a shaky breath and released it. "Then I am asking you, in the name of that connection, to at least try."

"Try what?"

"Try to restore the futhark without any of it. Let it all go—Amaseila, the foretelling, the bedamned girl, the forsaken prophecy

—all of it. Promise me you'll try and unite us, and then you can have your war. You'll have your war and me beside you throughout it. Together we can seek the glory that will lift our people. Can you do that?"

Vahldan's heart was pounding against his ribs. There simply wasn't a chance he could deceive her, even if he wished to try. Why should this be a difficult decision? Had he really come to believe in the prophecy, that he was playing an actual role in such divine mischief?

He loved Elan, more than anything. And she was offering him a rational recourse. She was only asking him to vow to try. He could do that. If the gods were, indeed, utilizing him, surely they would reveal it. Or he would be free of it. Either way, he would know for sure.

"I promise," he said to his one true love. "I will try, with all my heart."

THE RISING crescent moon cleared the mountaintops as Malvius made his approach. A warm, almost summer-like breeze provided the vessel with the perfect speed. Still under sail, he steered Gullwing into the gap between the looming dark shapes of the Thrakian seagates rising on either side. He gave the signal as soon as they were inside the harbor. Without a word, the sails collapsed and sailors scurried. He signaled again, and the anchor splashed. The sleek vessel glided to just shy of the quay, halting at the end of the anchor chain. Ropes were thrown and the anchor was raised. His shore hands drew the ship the rest of the way to the deserted docks.

Malvius's heartrate remained high as his men tethered the ship broadside to the quay and lowered the gangplank. In spite of the ongoing risk, he was beaming. He hadn't lost his touch.

Such undertakings made him feel alive again—a rare feeling these past years. Nights like tonight made Malvius feel like he was finally making progress on the path to winning his life back. Though ventures such as this were a trifle, perhaps even a sideline to the ultimate goal.

Malvius had paid dearly to ensure those gates remained open after dark, but success tonight would be worth the investment. He had to admit, the arrangement Vahldan had somehow managed to negotiate with the imperials offered many interesting prospects for additional profit. Other than the imperial harbormaster and his meager handful of tariff officials, there was little imperial oversight in Thrakius these days. Malvius's current cargo was an excellent example. He'd mostly filled the hold with cheap silks and a few dozen slabs of colored marble, which—come morning—he'd happily have tallied, taxed, and dutifully stamped. All that before shipping them on, enabling him to circumvent the more stringent oversight that came with first reentering the empire via Nicomedya. The laxity alone was worth the stopover in his home port. But this arrival after dark allowed for an even more profitable aside.

Malvius carried a veiled lantern down the gangway and onto the docks. His chief dockman Sabas stood waiting. "The harbormaster?" Malvius asked.

"Long abed, Cap."

"Any Gottari?"

"Two came by on patrol at dusk. They're in the fishmonger's tavern now. I slipped Dion enough coin to offer them a few pints on the house. Ought to keep them busy a while."

"Perfect." Malvius waved to Dexicos at the top of the gangway, who gave a soft whistle. The hoist creaked up from the hold to the deck. As soon as the wooden crates were in sight, two pairs of sailors carried the goods down the gangway onto the dock and slid them onto the hand-wagon. Since Sabas had only one good arm, Malvius gave him the lantern. "Lead on." He and Dex put their shoulders to the load and pushed it swiftly to the main warehouse. Rumbling across the planking and onto the cobbles caused the little vials in the crates to make a pleasant tinkling sound, reminiscent of gold coins clinking in his purse.

The imperial ban on trading in Pharsisi exports made the perfumes in these four crates more profitable than the rest of the shipload. Particularly since his customer was willing to pay up front before hauling the illegal but wildly popular product overland to the clamoring black markets in the west. Not only was Malvius avoiding trying to slip through the Straits, someone else was willing to take the risk of passing through the Thrakian city gates. As soon as he had the crates into the warehouse, his risk was all but gone.

Sabas set the lantern down outside the warehouse doors and unlocked the building. He and Dex pushed the wagon in and Sabas closed the doors behind them.

"Ah. Made it," he said.

"I've a nice bottle of Saurian," Sabas said, gesturing toward the living quarters.

"None for me, thanks. But you two go ahead." His two key employees both bid him goodnight and Malvius headed for his little shipping office. The space was oddly cool compared to the warehouse—almost the same as the night air outside. He set the lantern on the table, closed the door, and turned to check the window shutters.

His nose bumped into a chainmail-covered chest. "Hello, Malvius," said a voice from the depths of the underworld and yet from overhead.

He gasped and leapt back, nearly knocking the lantern over. "Gods be cruel!" Malvius clutched his chest theatrically. "You scared the very warmth from my blood, man."

Teavar took a step closer, head looming at the rafters. "Rather late to be docking, no?"

"Early, actually. We weren't supposed to dock till morn. But you know what a nocturnal beast I am," he joked. Teavar didn't smile. "I pressed on for the sake of my men," he added. "They just wanted to be home, you see. So I sent word ahead—made some special arrangements."

Teavar finally smiled, but it didn't reach his unblinking eyes. "I *do* see. We always see your *special arrangements.*" What was the giant implying? Was Vahldan having him watched?

"I can explain. I came across an opportunity. In fact, I'm going to head up to the palace to talk to Lord Vahldan about it come daylight."

"No need. We're going now." Teavar opened the door to the alley and held it wide.

"Oh no, I wouldn't want to bother our lord so late."

"No bother. He's waiting." The giant gestured for Malvius to lead. There was a carriage up the alley, sitting in the shadows.

AFTER ONE OF the longest and most awkwardly silent carriage trips to the palace of his life, Malvius was led up the stairwell to the high hall. It seemed he was about to stand before the court of judgment.

But the high hall's massive doors stood open, revealing a dim, empty room.

Without a word, Teavar led him through to the far end and to a familiar side door. The cozy little chamber had likely been built for the use of servants. Malvius's father had repurposed the rectangular space as a study. It was secluded but still near to the high seat on the dais. The only windows were overhead and barred, but the space tended to stay warmer in winter and cooler in summer. Decebius had often held one-on-one meetings in here, particularly if he wanted to intimidate his counterpart.

Malvius hated the spot.

Vahldan had pulled one of the cushioned chairs which normally sat beside the hearth over to the round table. The warlord was studying his maps again. Malvius remembered giving Vahldan his first look at a real map and teaching him to read it. Vahldan had been fascinated then and seemed near obsessed with maps now.

Once he stepped inside, Teavar closed Malvius inside and himself out. Malvius would've guessed having the giant on the other side of a door would make him feel safer. It didn't. He found himself assessing the situation—noting Vahldan's sheathed sword leaning in the corner, just out of the thug's reach. Little good that did, as there was no other way out. Malvius stood waiting, almost afraid to breathe.

Without looking up, Vahldan said, "You've been busy."

"My lord?" Malvius's voice squeaked like a pubescent teen's. He cleared his throat.

"Your name has come up in most every conversation I've had since the end of the shipping hiatus." Vahldan finally looked up. "Seems you've dipped your fingers in a lot of pots, old friend." Same as with Teavar, Vahldan's smile didn't lighten his countenance.

Malvius shrugged. "It's already been a busy season."

"And a profitable one, I take it."

"I suppose I've been fortunate, my lord."

Vahldan leaned back. He didn't invite Malvius to sit. "So your perfume is safely ashore?"

"Yes, my lord. As I told Teavar, I intended to—"

"How long have we known one another now?" Vahldan interjected.

His first thought was that it'd been long enough to know that Vahldan wouldn't hesitate to kill him. Rather than voicing it, he said, "Gods sustain us, fast approaching a score of years."

"And do you really believe, as well as we've come to know one another, that I would ever seek to change you? Or that I'd be foolish enough to even try?"

Malvius reminded himself to breathe normally again. "I suppose not."

"It would go as well as you trying to change me. We're both too stubborn. And too busy to waste our time on folly."

"I suppose so," Malvius admitted.

"I've received word that your sly trading partner is safely inside the city. And once he has your goods, he'll be allowed to leave.

Unhampered." Vahldan smiled, this time a bit more warmly. "So come. Sit. Stop your spinning and be of use for a change."

Malvius sat across the table from a man much more recognizable. Vahldan had always possessed no small amount of charm. He could light up his magnetism like a lamp. Damn, Malvius hated himself for wishing they were still the friends he'd once imagined they were.

Vahldan poured him a cup of wine. "Now, tell me. What do you hear from Bafrana?"

Blood rushed to Malvius's face and pounded in his ears. Every muscle clenched as images of Neveka flashed before his eyes. Was the thug trying to provoke him? Rattle him?

Malvius drew a breath and took in Vahldan's demeanor. He dismissed the notion. Since her murder, the murderer and his victim's loved one never spoke of this mountain-sized grievance between them. The man didn't care enough about anyone else to use such a thing as a tactic. Malvius sought to gather himself and to swiftly surmise what Vahldan really wanted and why. As always, he would look for ways to steer the thug lord to his own advantage. Starting with Bafrana caused him to stumble, but he could recover as he went along. "The captains' uprising continues," he began. "They're as angry as ever, having heard about the sadhu's deal with Rector Horius."

"Not the deal so much as being cut out of it." Vahldan was still sharp.

Malvius reminded himself to never underestimate his partner-turned-nemesis. Vahldan had his delusions and his issues with rage, but it couldn't be denied—he was clever. Not to mention observant. "True enough. Horius should've known not to restart the tribute payments before the Bafranii had settled their little internal conflict. The captains have besieged the sadhu in his own palace. It was a bad deal from the start, and vowing to hold to it only made things worse for the imperials. The captains have returned to their pirating ways. With a gusto! Worse, they're specifically targeting the very ships that

Horius continues to pay the sadhu to keep safe. Which has angered Hellain merchants and taxpayers alike. Our sage rector has managed to rile most everyone."

Vahldan nodded as though he'd heard nothing new. "How will the Tiberians react?"

Malvius glanced down at the top map on the table. It showed the Pontean but also the eastern half of the empire. He had a sudden suspicion, perhaps even a tiller to grasp. "His Eminence won't have much choice. Particularly if the pirate problem continues to make his sanctioned traders cautious. He could get rid of Horius, but the deal with the sadhu is a trickier knot to untie. The longer he tries to save face, the higher the importers will raise prices. Which has crofters and shopkeepers crying foul to bureaucrats, and so on. Mycanius has always relied on the favor of the merchant class in order to control the senate. His Eminence will feel great pressure to respond in some way, regardless of the militum's concerns."

"Which are?"

Malvius paused. "The militum's concerns?" Vahldan nodded. "In a word, grave." He laughed and took a drink. It was the good stuff— some of the distilled Saurian he'd brought back.

The thug drank, too. "Tell me," Vahldan prompted.

Malvius's thoughts continued to whirl. He had to find the right tack, and he wasn't quite sure of the wind just yet. "The scenario with the Bafranii insurrection only serves to lure the Sassanada back into Trazonia. The Sass will claim they're only seeking to protect the eastern trade routes, of course. If Tiberia follows suit and sends troops, tensions are bound to escalate. Again. Even if Tiberia only sends troops into Bafrana, it could give the Xah the excuse he needs to seize Trazonia."

Vahldan shrugged. "Why don't the Tiberians just send the navy after the pirates? You know, out on the water, as navies do. Without marching into Bafrana."

"They'd be chasing them till next hiatus, likely with little to show for it. The Tiberians need to address the root of the problem, which is the insurrection in Bafrana itself. No matter what they do, tensions are bound to rise in the region. The militum is cursed no matter which course they choose. All they know for certain is that choose they must. And while Mycanius knows he too must do something, he will do most anything to avoid restarting the war with the Xah. The emperor and his generals well recall what war with the Sassanada costs."

"What can be done?" Vahldan asked, looking innocent.

Malvius was growing more certain. He just had to hoist the sail and watch for turbulence. "Well, besides placating pirates, Mycanius will be looking for ways to protect Horius. In spite of Horius having blundered into his pile of Bafranii excrement. The rector's family is well-tied to the palace, after all. I suppose Mycanius could grant Horius the funding to hire someone else to do the imperial dirty work."

Vahldan looked down into his cup and sipped, but Malvius saw it. He'd harnessed the right wind. Now he just had to ride it. "You mean a hired army," Vahldan suggested.

"Of course," Malvius said. "Let someone else be the muscle. Preferably someone who won't make the Xah nervous." Malvius allowed himself to grin. "Why? Know anyone?"

Vahldan, too, gave up a grin. "I used to," he said. The thug straightened his expression. "Why wouldn't they use the mobile reserve? What news of them?"

Now Malvius was certain. The thug lord still had his grand ambitions. Indeed, very grand ambitions. But he shouldn't be surprised. Malvius had already reminded himself not to underestimate Vahldan the Bold. Nor to deny that he tended toward delusion—particularly if the delusion flattered him. The proclivity to rage could become a useful tool, too.

Many years prior—in fact, on the day after Malvius's city was invaded and his father, his woman, and his unborn child were killed —Malvius had made a decision. If he was going to have his vengeance, it had to be complete. No half measures would do. Not only must the Gottari be driven from his home, Vahldan and all of his murderous Amalus cult must be completely destroyed. The Gottari must be ruined as a people—devastated in battle or calamity, their remnants scattered, their national identity lost. What had happened here must never happen again.

It had taken years of thought. It took time to determine the means to achieve such a feat. But he'd finally landed on the only solution. He had to let someone else—someone powerful enough to decisively achieve the feat—strike them down for him. And the most powerful entity in the Pontean world? Without question, it was still the Tiberian Empire.

The best part was, Vahldan's ambitions, paired with Gottari superstition, had always pointed him directly to Malvius's solution. The thug lord would willingly walk right into it. With the correct prodding and guidance, of course.

Malvius had always loved hearing the Gottari tales of the Bringer and the Urrinan. He had grown certain that Vahldan felt beholden to play the role his people had laid upon him. In order to be what Vahldan thought his father had wanted of him and what his followers believed about him, Vahldan had to bring about this war of upheaval. If he did nothing, he would become just that in the eyes of his people: nothing. After all, if he really was the Bringer, he was going to have to bring... something. And it had to be something big. Seizing Thrakius had only been the first step. The thug was still determined to start the war that would be his and his people's demise. It was the reason Malvius was sitting across from him right now.

Malvius wasn't sure whether Vahldan had actually come to believe he was destined to play a role in their ridiculous prophecy. It didn't matter. All Malvius had to do was play along—provide his aid and support, cautiously craft the setup, then sit back and watch his two worst enemies battle it out.

Malvius sipped his wine. "Funny you should ask. I just heard that the mobile reserve is being recalled to Tiberia. Likely they'll soon be stationed in Cispadaena again." He sipped and watched over the cup's rim as Vahldan studied the maps.

"Do you think there's a chance Mycanius would send them to deal with Bafrana?"

"If the situation becomes dire, I suppose," he said and sipped again. He chuckled. "And the way things are going, dire seems inevitable."

"How soon would they come?"

"I'm sure they'll wait till the rector tries a few rolls of the stones. But for better or worse, Mycanius knows the situation will have to be resolved before the next hiatus."

Vahldan's concern was clear. Malvius had successfully raised the stakes. For the thug, it was now or who knew when.

It was time to cast his own stones. It was a risk, but one that would eventually have to be taken. "You know, I have a few connections to Horius," he said as casually as he could manage.

"And?"

"Well, you said you used to know someone who could get the job done. As did I." Malvius raised a brow and Vahldan pursed his lips. The thug was sorely tempted. Malvius figured he'd gone this far, might as well go all the way. After all, he could be charming, too.

He leaned in. "You're thinking this is it, aren't you?"

Vahldan narrowed his gaze. "This is what?"

"Your moment. You could seize it now. Before the mobile reserve is near enough to be a factor."

He appraised the storm on Vahldan's face while he sought to calm the rippling of his own sails. There was no glazing of the thug's eyes as so often happened when he was enraged. The veteran warlord stared at his precious maps, pensive. Vahldan slowly raised his gaze. "Starting with Nicomedya?"

He had him. His nemesis had opened the gates to him. It was on.

He'd done it. It had taken eight long years—years of mostly keeping his distance but of also pretending he'd been unfazed by the murderous treachery of a man he'd considered a friend. It hadn't been easy, but his patience was being rewarded. Vahldan finally trusted Malvius again.

Malvius solemnly stroked the whiskers he'd neglected while at sea. He had to pretend things were just occurring to him. "If you're set on going all the way, taking Nicomedya would be a stunning first thrust." Malvius leaned in. "But I'll let you in on a little secret. The key to Nicomedya is Efusium." He reached to point to the port on the map. "It's got the larger garrison, a substantial naval presence, and it's close. Close enough to strike if they get the slightest tip that Nicomedya is in danger. It's the reason Nicomedya hasn't fallen in... Well, almost as long as Thrakius. Taking Efusium first wouldn't just be stunning. It would be decisive."

Vahldan looked startled. Or maybe he found the reality of discussing it aloud daunting. "Efusium is one of the largest cities in the empire, isn't it?"

"The third largest, actually. That's the beauty of it. *No one* would see it coming."

Vahldan frowned. "It would force a major response."

Malvius laughed. "You don't think seizing the Straits would force a major response?"

"I have no interest in Efusium." Indeed, Vahldan the Bold was actually daunted.

"Good," Malvius said. "Because a city that large would be all but impossible to hold, anyway. But once you've eliminated the threat of the garrison and naval yard there, you could simply leave and move on to Nicomedya."

"You really think it's possible?"

Malvius stroked his whiskers again. "Oh, it's possible. I even have an idea how. It would be difficult, but very possible. And there's really only one way to find out. Which is what's kept it from happening all of these years. No one's been bold enough to try."

Vahldan eyed him. Was he suspicious? Too wary? Finally, "Tell me, my friend. What will it take?"

Malvius leaned back in his chair. The man was ambitious, vain, desperate to prove himself, full of rage, and delusional. It was the perfect combination. Allowing Malvius to successfully prod the first step. "For starters, what I have in mind will take excellent, loyal, and disciplined warriors."

One side of Vahldan's mouth quirked. "That's foregone and you know it. What else?"

Malvius smiled. "The man who's bold enough to lead them in the attempt."

Vahldan actually laughed. "You're such a little shit." Gods, had he been talking to Ligaia? He snatched up the flagon and poured for them both. "But you do find the best damn wines." The man really did love his wine—the stronger the better. Which gave Malvius an idea. Maybe he could give those delusions a nudge. He'd recently heard about a particularly ominous fortified wine, laced with the gods only knew what. The broker had actually joked that it would make a fine gift... for an enemy. Said it would bend an upright man into a twisted fool.

Malvius raised his cup. "To Vahldan the Bold." Vahldan rolled his eyes but reached to click cups. The delusional soon-to-be fool then willingly drank to Malvius's impending triumph.

ANOTHER SORT OF HOMECOMING

"*Most scholars agree that the order of the Elli-Frodei was not founded as a religious one. It was created by the Arrivals— the Gottari who migrated to the Danian River Valley under the rule of the Amalus kings. The Arrivals swiftly realized that Dania's neighboring peoples were, in many ways, more advanced than their own, who were mostly poor herdsmen. The early kings and their Rekkrs set the order's mission: to collect knowledge, through study and travel, for the betterment of the nation. Vigs-Utan, the fortified gateway to Dania at the head of the path that leads to the more cultured cities of the Pontean coast, seemed the natural place to house the scholars and their written findings.*

It was only later, after the kingship had ended, that the order was tasked more and more often with religious matters as well as the settling of theological questions and disagreements. Their stature as holy men, as being closer to the divine, only grew—particularly among the common herdsmen. As there was no established hierarchy among the priestesses of the countryside, the presence of an Elli-Frodei came to lend godly legitimacy to appointments, adoptions, bonding and funeral ceremonies, and contractual agreements."—Brin Bright Eyes, *Saga of Dania*

· · ·

Urias was strolling from the market back to the longhouse when the gatehouse bell rang. Visitors came regularly to Danihem this time of year: farmers bringing their first grain reaping and berry harvests as well as Rekkrs arriving for the summer solstice council session. He stopped on the gangway, shading his eyes against the midday sun. Two riders appeared in the distance through the gateway. The glint from the fair hair of the lead rider spurred Urias's heart to a fast trot. Could it be? The pair were clearly Skolani. But he told himself it wasn't like her, not without a full retinue.

Urias was sure before they cleared the gate. No one sat quite so proudly in the saddle and yet rode so fluidly as Icannes. And the sheer size of her companion confirmed that this was Kukida—perhaps the largest, and most laconic, woman in all of Dania.

They crossed the commons before a crowd could gather and reined in at the trough. Urias tried not to hurry over. He stepped from the walkway and stopped a span away. She looked and he bowed at the waist. "Welcome to Danihem, my princess." He sounded ridiculously excited. He sought to calm himself. Her expression was pleasant but reserved.

The pair dismounted and Kukida took both sets of reins. Icannes stepped close enough to tempt him to reach out and touch her. She wore scouting attire. The close-fitting doeskin revealed a still-slim waist and the curve of her hips. The torcs on her bare arms emphasized her still-toned muscles. Her face was already quite tan. She wore a few new but healed scars, and the creases around her eyes and at the corners of her smile were perhaps a bit deeper.

If anything, she was more beautiful than ever. And certainly more regal.

A small smile finally formed on Icannes's face. "I'm even more pleased to see you than I'd imagined, Captain." A crowd of curious onlookers gathered but kept their distance. Icannes lowered her voice. "So pleased that I long for a hug and a kiss." She leaned in, and as he was about to comply, she added, "But that wouldn't be fitting for a princess, would it?" She winked.

"I suppose not."

"Perhaps later, then?"

"Later, my princess?" Was she toying with him again?

Icannes raised her chin. "Do you mind if I ask you a personal question, Captain?"

"Ask me anything." His heart was trotting again.

"Have you ever bonded?"

He looked at his feet. "No, my princess."

"Really? A man so handsome and eligible as you?"

Urias felt himself flushing. Damn. He'd spent years convincing himself he was over her. And just like that... "Well, I haven't felt strongly about a woman in some time. I think it's because I'm afraid that a new one would suffer by comparison to the last."

"Is that so?" Was she the one now blushing? He was fairly certain.

Being certain did nothing to calm him. "It is. In fact, she's beyond compare."

"Handsome *and* charming." Gods, her eyes were full of the same longing he felt. "Ever the bachelor, then?"

"I suppose."

"It's got to be hard." Icannes glanced down and grinned. "Difficult, I mean."

Urias laughed. "I contend with my lot by serving the realm, my princess. Helps to keep busy."

"I see. Speaking of which, I came with tidings for your lord. Perhaps you could join me later. We could discuss your predicament. Maybe seek a means to relieve all of that contending. That is, if you're not too busy."

"I would gladly set aside everything for even a chance to have more of your insight."

Her smile was almost girlish. She leaned in again. "My camp is on the meadow at the west end of the green lake. You know the spot?"

"I do."

"Dine with me at sunset?"

"I'd be delighted, my princess." Urias bowed.

"Perfect. Perhaps in the meantime, you can arrange for an audience with your brother."

"I was just on my way to meet him. I'm sure he'll be well-pleased if you join me."

Icannes huffed a laugh. "I wouldn't be so sure."

"I'll remind him to at least pretend." He opened the longhouse door and held it for her.

ICANNES WAS RELIEVED. At least it was clear that Urias was happy to see her. Too much time had passed for her to be certain the connection she'd felt between them would last for him. It was crucial, as she would be asking much of him. Much more than she led him to believe by flirting. She almost felt bad about misleading him. Although Icannes was confident that even if he refused to help with her hidden agenda, he would still leave satisfied. Actually, she was sure they'd both find no small measure of satisfaction.

The thought made her feel wicked, made her want to smile. But smiling at a formal greeting was not her style, so she had to set her wickedness aside. For a while.

Upon entering the cool, dim interior of the longhouse, Urias proceeded to chase out a trio of gossiping crones drinking tea near the hearth and a handful of sojourners at the rear tables—including a guardsman who had to carry his bowl of porridge with him. Urias invited her to sit on the front bench while he fetched Thadmeir from the residence.

Thadmeir parted the drapes. His frown became a strained smile as he led Urias across the dais. Another figure came behind the brothers—a crone in a finely woven frock, walking with her hands folded before her and her head bowed. The crone's face was curtained by lank, white hair. Icannes stood.

"Welcome to Danihem, Princess Icannes." Thadmeir looked and sounded as suspicious of her as ever. Some things never changed.

Urias stepped aside and indicated the woman hovering in his shadow. "I'm sure you'll remember my niece, Amaga. Since you've last seen her, Amaga has been ordained as Danihem's priestess to Freya, same as her mother before her."

The crone who was actually a girl bowed. Amaga raised her face to reveal smooth skin nearly as white as her hair, though her lips were red and sensuous. Her nose was prominent and her cheeks gaunt. At a glance she resembled one of those painted dolls the traders brought from the Pontean markets. But her eyes! Icannes had always thought the mother's eyes to be among the strangest she'd seen, but the daughter had surpassed her. Amaga's were large with irises of the palest gray and pupils large and black—almost bird-like. They were seeking, delving eyes. Worse, they seemed to be boring into Icannes's very thoughts and feelings.

"An honor, fierce princess." Amaga's voice was poised and melodious. It did not fit her.

Icannes tilted her head. "The honor is mine, Priestess."

Amaga leaned in. "After so long merely hearing, it is good to finally see, to be sure." She extended a thin hand. "May I?... No, forgive me." She withdrew her hand and looked down.

Icannes had heard about her gift. "You wish to touch me?"

Amaga glanced up, furtive. "Please, if you are willing."

"Let us grasp forearms as warriors do." Icannes extended her hand.

They grasped each other, her skin cool and dry. Amaga's arm was slender but surprisingly firm. Amaga closed her eyes and her breathing came audibly. Her eyelids quivered as though beetles scurried beneath them.

The young woman released her with a gasp. Amaga kept her eyes closed and laughed as if in relief. "Yes, it shall be as I have dreamed. You shall provide for him. You will continue to play a role in it. As you have nigh from the start." The priestess opened her raptor-like eyes. "Thank you. Thank you for your true heart."

Icannes felt unsettled. She longed to ask for clarification, but Sael had long warned her of the dangers of prodding a seeress. Better to simply be satisfied that she was not deceiving herself—that she would serve the Urrinan well. Icannes inclined her head and held her tongue.

The Great Wolf plopped into his high seat with a huff. "Please, be seated, Princess. Urias, fetch Princess Icannes some mead. Or better still, there's Illyrican wine back in the residence."

Icannes raised a staying hand. "No, thank you, Lord Thadmeir. I came to deliver tidings, which will take but a moment of your day. Then I must be off. I have a nearby camp, with companions whose needs I must attend."

Thadmeir nodded. "As you wish. Go on."

"I came to tell you that Lord Vahldan is on his way here."

The Wolf Lord gripped the arms of his chair. "To Danihem?"

"Yes."

"When? Why?"

"He is more than halfway through the Pontean Pass. With continued good weather, he'll arrive at Vigs-Utan tomorrow by nightfall. I would guess he will halt for the night and come to Danihem the morning after."

Thadmeir scowled. "Why would he not send word, seek permission?"

"It's the same as before," Urias said. "The lord of one of the ruling clans hardly needs permission to return to his homeland."

Thadmeir turned to glare at Urias. Icannes rushed on. "We have Blade-Wielders patrolling the pass, of course. He sent a request with a scout to me. In it, he asked that I pass these tidings along to you. Hence my visit."

The Wolf Lord's lip curled. "You're telling me Vahldan sought Skolani permission but not that of his own people?"

She raised her chin. "Permission, no. He sought our guardianship, actually. Considering his last visit to Danihem, and the accusations it provoked, Lord Vahldan thought it best to approach without a host. He comes with his close kin and a few Rekkr companions. In the absence of a host, he asked the Blade-Wielders to watch over his family's passage to Danihem. As a courtesy to our Gottari allies, I have agreed to provide him this boon."

Thadmeir harrumphed. "A courtesy to the Gottari, you say? Queen Keisella knows of this... *boon* you provide to the man who sundered our nation?"

"Mother is aware of Vahldan's coming, yes." Technically true, as her mother remained confident in the prophecy which foretold the necessity of Vahldan's return. Semantics.

Thadmeir stood and paced the dais. "So, Vahldan seeks Skolani aid and receives it. Vahldan sends the Skolani to inform the seat of his people's governance that he is coming. Has he also deemed us worthy of knowing why he comes? Did he pass that bit along with his Skolani friends as well?" The Wulthus lord stopped before her, his face red and his jaw clenched.

Urias came up behind his brother, looking worried. Icannes offered Urias a reassuring nod. "He did not, Lord Thadmeir. But I presume that Lord Vahldan hopes that he will be welcome. I'm sure he hopes for suitable accommodations for his family and that he might consider the longhouse a safe haven. Perhaps he wished for me to forewarn you that you might better provide these things."

Thadmeir's face twisted. "That *I* might provide. For him. When he is not willing to provide even a hint as to why he comes."

Amaga pitched her voice to soothe. "Oh, Father. We know why Vahldan comes. We have long known he must. This cannot be avoided." The young priestess took her father's hand in one of hers and put the other on his cheek, gently coaxing him to look into her eyes. "Father. We know."

Icannes once met an aging Wulthus Wise One who lived in the eastern marches. The old man had claimed he communed with wolves. Indeed, the night the Skolani spent camped at his homestead, a pack came to the edge of his fire's light, eyes aglow and growling. Though many Skolani nocked their bows in response, the old man had merely stood and walked to face the alpha. The Wise One then tilted his head and gazed in much the same way as Amaga did now. The wolf had swiftly seemed mollified and had turned to lead his pack away into the darkness.

The Wolf Lord's face went slack and he sat with a sigh. Amaga knelt beside him, holding his hand and petting it. "This has been ordained. It's no cause for fret. It is as it shall be."

Thadmeir's eyes found focus on his daughter. Something snapped. His face contorted to a snarl. He snatched his hand away and leapt up. "No! He cannot have you!" The Wolf Lord turned and kicked the empty but smaller Amalus chair onto its backside. "Destiny be damned! That man can have his bloody seat. He can sunder our nation, take our finest warriors. He can have his fine palace in his stone city. But the Severing Son will not have my daughter!" He bent nose to nose with Amaga. "Do you hear me?"

Amaga's face crumpled. She ran to Urias and fell into his arms, burying her face on his chest. Thadmeir stood, fists clenching and unclenching. The Wolf Lord dropped a hasty bow to Icannes. "Forgive me, Princess," he said and hurried out through the residence drapes.

Vahldan had his camp set up a respectful distance from the Danian border. He waited just beyond a bowshot from Vigs-Utan as his company's Blade-Wielder guides scouted the ramparts at the entryway to his homeland.

The sun dropped below the steep slope to their west, casting the canyon into shadow but leaving the top of the ancient watchtower bathed in gold. The ramparts looked even more lichen-covered and decayed than the last time he saw them. Vahldan spotted the faded scraps of a torn banner above the open archway. "It must have been glorious, once," he said.

"All through the days of the Arrivals," Attasar began, "the lords of the ruling clans would select their most esteemed warriors to man the gates. So, too, did the Elli-Frodei select the cleverest children to be trained as acolytes. It was considered an honor. So yes, Vigs-Utan was considered almost sacred and maintained with pride, that it might befit the glory of the Gottari."

"Father had a hundred stories about this place," Eldavar added wistfully.

Vahldan gripped his brother's shoulder. "Of course he did. He sought the stories from his sires, just as we did. It was once the pinnacle of Gottari learning and martial training."

"What happened?" Teavar gestured toward the broken gate, rotting on the ground.

"It's said that the host stationed here was diminished over time as the threats changed," Attasar said. "Spali incursions from the east became the more pressing threat. It was eventually abandoned as a guard posting. Though they've dwindled, the Elli-Frodei have lingered on. Thank the gods. It still houses the largest archive of our nation's scrolls and written records. Without the Wise Ones here to keep it, I don't know what would come of our written word. To lose it would be to lose a piece of our history—of who we are. Which I would consider tragic."

"Beyond tragic," Eldavar said.

"Damned foolish," Vahldan added. "In some ways it feels like we've gone backward as a people rather than forward."

"What happened to the acolytes?" Teavar asked. "I've passed here often, but never have I seen children. Only hunched and cranky graybeards."

Arnegern harrumphed. "It's the wolves that put an end to that."

"More accurate to say it was the guild," Attasar said.

"Same difference," Vahldan said.

"Not that I'm surprised," Eldavar said. "But how so?"

"The chieftains of the clans used to supply the candidates," Attasar said. "In appreciation, the ruling clans compensated the acolytes' families for being left shorthanded. But as the guild's influence grew and the Amalus coffers diminished, the Wulthus declared an end to the system and refused to pay. In response, the nonaligned clans refused to send their children."

"They ended it in the full knowledge that only the Wulthus guildsmen would be able to afford to send a son here," Arnegern added.

Vahldan knew his cousin's bitterness was rooted in the knowledge that he once was to have been sent to the tower. But his father had fallen on hard times before he was old enough.

It made Vahldan consider Eldavar's circumstances. The family's focus had become mining when Eldavar was but a babe. In their isolation and needing to tend to flock and field while her husband and eldest worked the mine, his mother had struggled to teach her younger children. Eldavar had a limited knowledge of runes, and he'd only recently begun to learn to speak and write Hellainic. He had lived a life of hardship and struggle. It was unfair, but Eldavar's young son Rohdric was already growing up with two languages. And Rohdric would surely learn to write faster and better, simply by virtue of starting younger. It seemed as though Angavar's grandchildren might actually lead richer lives than his children.

The thought made Vahldan wonder if the same could be said of Brin. He supposed so. Elan had said something about enlisting a tutor for her. Vahldan had been cross about it. He had mixed emotions about the girl being so exposed to Hellains. Brin seemed to prefer the company of the manservant Hesiod over her own parents. Well, over that of her father in particular. But Vahldan spent so little time around her. The girl was so damn silent—stealthy, even. Although Brin often slipped away moments after Vahldan entered a room, he felt like she was always lurking on the fringes—watching, judging. He hadn't been surprised when Brin had adamantly refused to come along on this journey. Nor had he been surprised when Elan had acquiesced to the girl's wishes. Elan seemed not to have the will to assert any sort of discipline with the child.

Arnegern said, "As far as I know, my uncle was among the last of the lions sent. And he passed on before I came of age."

"Do you think there's a lion left?" Teavar asked.

Vahldan shrugged. "We can only hope."

"What will you do if there isn't?"

The Blade-Wielder Sakaria appeared in the archway. She beckoned to them, signaling that someone in the tower was willing to see them. "If there are no lions left, we'll simply have to install our own." Vahldan turned back to the still bustling camp. "Give me a moment."

He went to the fire already blazing. The evening air had only begun to cool, but Elan was already huddled there. She'd been sullen since the Skolani took over the scouting duties. He knew her last dealings with her former tribeswomen had been less than pleasant, but he needed their favor. Elan's mere presence in their party risked damaging his relationship with them. Mara, who was visibly pregnant, sat with her. Kemella and Eldavar's wife Sairsa had started preparing the evening meal. Belgar and Herodes had gone to haul water and collect firewood.

"Are you sure you won't join us?" Having Elan at his side for this encounter would be a plus. The Elli-Frodei revered the Skolani, and seeing her could remind them that she had been Keisella's gift to the Bringer.

Elan gave him one of her best scowls. "You've already chosen your scouts and guardians. I'd rather be left out of your schemes."

Vahldan wanted to ask why she'd insisted on coming if she didn't want anything to do with his plans. He knew it was best not to start. Not if he wanted any peace during the coming evening. "As you wish." He bowed his head and strode back to his waiting team.

∽

THE SKOLANI GUIDES led them to a rickety wooden door on the Danian side of the stone tower, then took up positions to either side. Clearly the women would not be leading them inside. The door was ajar and the interior was dark. Vahldan beckoned Arnegern, who brought his torch to the fore. Teavar and Jhannas both drew their blades. Arnegern pushed the door wide and led the giants inside. Vahldan followed, flanked by Attasar and Eldavar.

Vahldan was startled to find that the entire first floor of the tower was a barn. A rather shabby barn, at that. Though most of the stalls seemed empty, there were bales haphazardly stacked against the outer walls. It stank of urine, manure, and mildew. As his group moved inside, he saw the source of the stench. Adjacent to a wooden platform was a turnstile apparatus with an aging donkey hitched to it. The platform hung from four chains, attached in each corner. The ceiling above the platform was open to allow access when it was raised, presumably by the donkey's rotation. Soft light shone from the opening above.

The silhouette of a head appeared in the opening. "Just two," a voice commanded.

Teavar frowned. "Two what?"

"Only two of you can be raised. And not you." The speaker pointed at Teavar. "Or that one." He pointed at Jhannas.

The speaker was evidently an elderly male. "Why not them? They are his guardians," Eldavar complained.

The old man cackled. "Ha. Spinner is almost as old as some of us. He can't lift the likes of those two. But fret not, cub. Your master has nothing to fear up here. If any of you believe he does, perhaps he'd do better to stay down there."

Vahldan held up his palms. "Fine. Just Attasar and I, then." He had no fear for his safety, but he wasn't about to spar with a chamber full of scholars without bringing along his own.

No one seemed pleased, but Vahldan stepped onto the platform and beckoned his youngest cousin to join him. The gray head above let out a piercing whistle and the donkey started walking. The chains snapped and the contraption creaked and groaned.

The platform lurched and swung from side to side as it slowly ascended. They came into a circular chamber that encompassed the entire second floor, with a stone stairway that coiled along the wall on one side and a large stone hearth on the other. The smell of the barn manure was replaced with the comingled odors of sour milk and rancid lamp oil riding on a blast of warm, stale air. Too warm. A fire blazed in the hearth. The place was lit by several lamps hanging on chains from pulleys on the overhead beams. It was starkly furnished. The benches lining the walls had worn, cushioned seats and slat backs. Those flanking a long table had neither cushions nor backs.

A dozen graybeards in shabby, matching robes stood fidgeting, though mostly with pronounced stoops. A few were leaning on canes. For many, standing looked not only challenging but painful. Not a single one bowed or even tilted their head.

Though most frowned, the one standing the most upright and at the fore wore an amused grin. Vahldan recognized him from his judgment before the council after his trial against Teavar had resulted in a draw. The man had at least ruled that Vahldan had the right to speak that night. That had been the better part of a score of years ago, but the old wolf hadn't aged a bit.

"Gods beguiling. It is indeed Vahldan, son of Angavar the Outcast. What in Freya's frock brings you up here? Do you imagine you need our leave to enter Dania?"

To his credit, Attasar ignored the quip. His cousin stepped off the platform, bowed, and said, "Greetings, Wise Ones. I am Attasar, son of Halasar of the Amalus. I beg your indulgence, as you clearly seem unknowing of my lord's station. Allow me to introduce Lord Vahldan, imperial regent of Thrakius in Pontea and Lion Lord of the Amalus of Dania."

Vahldan stepped off after him. "Wise One Gizar, isn't it? Of the Wulthus, as I recall."

Without replying to or taking his steady gaze from Vahldan, Gizar said, "I confess, I am unknowing. We know naught of Pontea, and the last we heard here, the dais chair of the Amalus remained vacant and unclaimed in Danihem."

Vahldan gave a carefree laugh. "I care nothing for chairs in Danihem. Though I do not begrudge them. I suppose they're fine for those who enjoy sitting. It's the consensus of the Amalus Rekkrs that matters to us, Wise One. But I didn't come to quibble."

Gizar finally spoke directly to Vahldan. "Do tell, then. Why have you come?"

Vahldan raised his gaze to appraise the whole of them. "Thank you for the formal greeting, Wise Ones. But trouble yourselves no more. Please, sit and be at ease." Gizar looked both amused and annoyed to be invited by a visitor to take a seat in his own home, but several of the eldest among them sighed and sought respite. One of the oldest and heaviest loudly broke wind as he sat. Vahldan stifled a laugh. Within moments, most of them were seated and talking amongst themselves.

Gizar rolled his eyes and gestured for Vahldan and Attasar to sit at the table. Vahldan took the seat at the head of the table. Besides Gizar, only two other Elli-Frodei sat at the table with them. Once all were seated, the wolf refixed his amused grin, his gaze still stern. "And so?"

Vahldan smiled back. "I'm guessing you get very few visitors."

"Why do you say so?"

"Mainly it's your curiosity as to why anyone would come. Which I'm guessing is central to the issue."

He'd caught Gizar flat-footed. "What issue?"

"Your lack of visitors. You're not exactly a welcoming bunch."

Gizar sighed. "Are you here merely to insult us, Young Lion?"

Vahldan shrugged. "Not merely that. But it's a start." He glanced around the mostly empty chamber. "Seems your membership is dwindling, is it not?"

Gizar frowned as though he had heartburn. "These days there are fewer willing to submit to such a life. We are indeed fewer than when I arrived."

Vahldan nodded. "In answer to your question, I mostly came with my own. Questions, that is."

Gizar rolled his eyes again. Seemed so natural to him. "Such as?" the old wolf prompted.

"Let's start with your stance on the futhark. What is it? As a collective, I mean."

Gizar scrunched his bushy eyebrows. "The futhark? We are for it, of course. Or we were, until you sundered our people, rendering the oath broken. Seems a moot point nowadays, don't you think?"

"Hmm. I'm not so sure. I'm more interested in finding a way forward. I desire nothing more than to see our people reunited. I'm simply exploring ways to go about it."

Gizar leaned on the table. "Son, the way to go about it is to go to the longhouse and subject yourself to the will of the many. Offer a plea to the council to claim your seat on the dais. Bring our people home and be a part of our governance, rather than a pariah to it."

Vahldan shook his head. "Thanks for the advice, but that's not what I had in mind. Nor would those who followed me to a more prosperous life ever wish to return to life under the system that once repressed them. No, what you suggest would be moving backward. Seems endemic to this order's thinking. I'm more interested in moving forward. In that spirit, it occurs to me that one virtue both of our clans can embrace, in spite of our differences, is the pursuit of knowledge. Gathering it with the aim of advancing our nation. It's what your order was founded upon, after all. And yet here you are, no longer gathering and admittedly shrinking." Vahldan leaned on the table, mirroring Gizar. "Let's face it, basically you're dying off. I'd suggest it's due to your backward thinking, which can only be a result of the abandonment of your founding principles."

Gizar's grin grew wry. "And what remedy might you propose?"

"Get out there! Infuse some youth! Bring in more acolytes."

"We are not without acolytes. But there are reasons they are fewer than in the past. In difficult times such as these, few herdsmen can afford to part with a son."

"How about seeking some women, then?"

Now the man was definitely taken aback. "Women? You can't be serious."

"Why not? Women are almost always the most renowned religious leaders. They're usually the best healers, the best herbalists. And you must trust me when I tell you that they always make the most prudent warriors." If Elan wouldn't stand with him, he'd at least remind the old wolf of her presence.

"I can't imagine a woman willing to come and live among the likes of us." Gizar gestured toward the wizened faces, glowering. Vahldan thought of young Brin, tried to imagine her here. He hated to admit it, but the wolf had a point.

It was beside the point. "Then I can't imagine how you'll survive. You know—since you're shrinking."

"As I said," Gizar began, "these are difficult days, and—"

"So you'll just sit back, sequestering yourselves, unwilling to embrace forward thinking, and watch your order die out?"

"Gods, no. But—"

"If you're going to survive, you've got to step outside. And not merely to go to Danihem. Travel to the homesteads, as you once did. Offer yourselves as healers, perform ceremonial services, be willing to help solve problems. Visit the far flung homesteads of this land. And go abroad along with those who venture forth into the world, in the pursuit of wisdom."

Gizar shook his head. "The order has precious few resources for travel these days."

"Simply solved. While you're out in the world, ask for support. Perhaps folks would be willing to fund you if they felt they were receiving something in return. And for Freya's sake, bring in some lions. Most Amalus supporters consider your order to be ridiculously biased toward the wolves. Who can blame them? I mean, do you even have any Amalus left among you?"

Gizar sat back in his chair and narrowed his gaze. "Ah, I think I'm beginning to see. You want to know our stance on the futhark. You wonder if we have any Amalus members left. Are you next going to inquire on the order's stance on the prophecy of the Urrinan?" The old wolf stroked his gray whiskers. "Next you'll be asking whether we believe the coming calamity will begin abroad. Say, in Pontea?"

Attasar's eyes went round and his face lost its color. Vahldan laughed, but he knew it sounded hollow. "I'm sure men as wise as you all have more interesting topics to study than superstition."

Gizar's smile became mocking. "If you wish members of our order to travel forth with you, would you also have us publicly sanction your conquest?"

He kept smiling. "You're mistaken, Wise One. I need no sanction from you."

"Perhaps not. But it would undoubtedly sanctify the senseless death and destruction that your foreign wars cause, would it not? Since you're aiming at restoring the futhark, I'm sure having the blessing of our order might even help you to recruit warriors from among the nonaligned clans, and even those pledged to the Wulthus, to carry out your future ambitions." The old man smiled at the ceiling. "Ah, the advantages of unity."

Vahldan turned to Attasar. "It seems our good intentions have been misread. I suppose we'd best be on our way."

"Must you? Please forgive my misreading, Young Lion. Before you go, in answer to your very direct—if also leading—question, there is indeed one from your clan among us, in this very room. Wise One Mundelan." Gizar pointed at the fat one who'd farted. The man's chins were on his chest. Mundelan let out a snore that nearly woke him and resettled himself. "Shall we rouse him for you? Please bear in mind, he's one of our oldest members, so he does need his rest."

He stood. "That won't be necessary. I can see that our ideas are unlikely to be given serious consideration at the moment. Still, I remain hopeful that you'll ponder them in the days to come. You know, try out a bit of forward thinking. Before it grows too late. Know that I'm pulling for your survival."

Gizar stayed seated. "Oh, I'm quite sure we'll be discussing your visit, Young Lion. For quite some time. I'm sure the Rekkr's council in Danihem will even take interest."

Vahldan beckoned Attasar onto the platform. "If you're planning on passing a message, don't trouble yourself. I'm heading there next. I'll be sure to share the tale of our time together." He stomped a boot on the platform and called, "Arnegern, we're coming down!"

The platform creaked into motion. Vahldan stared down the old wolves at the table until he disappeared through the floor. "Come," he said as he stepped off the platform. "Let's get away from this stench." He strode to the door, leading them out.

Arnegern hurried at his shoulder with the torch. "It didn't go well, I presume?"

"I never had high hopes. But they're considerably lower now."

"No lions among them, then?" Eldavar probed.

"Apparently there's one," he admitted. "But he's too old and fat to be of service."

"What will we do now?" Teavar asked.

"Since this den is full of wolves, I suppose we'll have to dig a lion's den of our own."

As they reached the door, Jhannas drew his blade and spun to face a shady corner. "Who's there?" Someone was climbing stealthily down a ladder beyond the stalls.

"I mean no harm." A man stepped into the torchlight, palms raised. "My lord." The man bowed. "I am but a humble apprentice to Wise One Mundelan. My name is Sueridas."

He was young—at least by the standards of the tower—perhaps only a bit older than Vahldan. He was so thin that his robe hung slack on him. His face was thin, too, which was emphasized by his lack of a beard and his cropped brown hair. "You're an apprentice to the flatulent lion?"

"I am, my lord." Sueridas spoke in a hush.

"Where were you during our visit?" Vahldan asked.

"Forgive me, but I was listening. From upstairs. We were told to stay out of sight."

"Why?"

Sueridas put his finger to his lips and beckoned them outside. He led them along the wall in its shadows and finally stopped. "None of the acolytes were allowed to appear. But I am an apprentice. It should've been allowed. I believe I was singled out because of my leanings."

Vahldan raised a brow. "What sort of leanings would single you out?"

Sueridas smiled. "Although my family can claim only distant blood ties, we are steadfastly loyal to the Amalus. I am a lion, born and raised."

"Why did you come down now? Do you risk being disciplined?"

"I do. But they can hardly treat me much worse. And I felt you should know, my lord, that not all of us would treat you with such disrespect as Wise One Gizar and his ilk. When we heard you were coming, there was some debate as to the... *tone* of your reception. Gizar holds sway now. But there are those keeping an eye to the Urri-nan. A few will admit to your resemblance to the Bringer. I believe several members are willing to be of service to your ideals. In addition, Wise One Mundelan is particularly amenable to my persuasion. He... Well, let's just say he owes me."

Vahldan studied the man. He seemed earnest. "I still wonder. Why risk coming to me?"

Sueridas lowered his gaze. "It's just, I've heard of the glories you've wrought in Pontea. How you continue to bring our people back to greatness—some say even to the glory of the Amalus kings of old. And I think we—I mean, the Elli-Frodei—should be a part of it all. We shouldn't be hiding away in this decrepit tower while the world changes around us. I believe you're right, my lord. We should represent all the Gottari clans. Instead, we are a pack of gray wolves with rotting teeth."

Vahldan smiled. The young man had aspirations. He knew the feeling. "You really wish to serve me, Apprentice Sueridas?"

"I do, my lord."

"What if it meant traveling to Pontea to do so?"

Sueridas beamed. "I would love it all the more. I long to see Pontea, my lord."

Vahldan gripped his shoulder. "Then go back inside. Remain diligent and obedient to your elders. For now. I will call upon you very soon."

"Yes, my lord." The young man bowed, his excitement palpable.

"Do not let me down, Sueridas."

"I won't."

"Then you shall be rewarded. Our time has come—we lions. The longhouse in Dania, and even the tower of Vigs-Utan, will soon be forced to reckon it."

CHAPTER 17
EXCHANGING FAVORS

"*There can be no doubt that Icannes felt sure of her ascendency, even as she came of age with her mother still in her prime. Icannes's stature grew to match her confidence as her victories accumulated and her mother's vigor declined. Though she remained at odds with the elders throughout her years as a princess, Icannes garnered ever strengthening support from her fellow Blade-Wielders. Although I know of no one who heard her admit it, I believe that Icannes considered herself divinely ordained. She believed herself central to the Skolani's destined role in Urrinan.*

I also believe her conviction was rooted in her love for both my mother and my uncle. Icannes gave her whole heart to very few humans in her lifetime. It would seem she considered feeling so deeply for a brother and sister who were so intricately tied to destiny to be a sure sign that she too was fated. And since Icannes often found herself holding the strings of destiny, she never hesitated to tug."—Brin Bright Eyes, Saga of Dania

After Icannes left Danihem, the rest of the day felt to Urias like the longest of the year. But evening finally arrived. Urias cantered south-

311

ward as the sun slipped toward the western mountaintops, hoping not to appear too anxious. He wondered how many Skolani sentries ghosted his progress. Which made him wonder if any had arrow-nocked bows trained upon him. He was too excited to indulge the usual trepidation over it.

He never saw a soul until the small circle of Icannes's pavilions came into view. A stranger walked across the meadow to greet him. It was a woman, wearing a loose, flowing frock of pale blue. Only when she swept her arm overhead in greeting did he realize it was Icannes herself. He goggled at the sight of her unbound hair, fair and full, thrown behind her shoulders to cascade down her back. Without braids, her hair was much longer—nearly to her waist. He hadn't seen a Skolani with unbraided hair since Queen Keisella had scandalously invited him into her pavilion after the battle in Oium.

He'd never seen Icannes like this. It wasn't just the hair. She was... so feminine, so casual and carefree. So radiant.

Urias dismounted and she came to him. Her strong arms immediately wrapped him into her spicy glamour. She drew back, appraised him briefly, laid a hand on his cheek, and kissed him. The first kiss was brief, soft. There was a spark in her eye as she came in again. The second kiss was firm and lingering. More passionate than he'd dared hope for.

"Well. I believe that's the warmest welcome I've ever received."

"As promised." She offered a lopsided grin and took him by the arm, pulling him to the camp. Kukida appeared out of nowhere to lead his horse away. Icannes ignored her guardian and led him to the center of four pavilions. She gently pushed him down onto a cushion by the fire. He saw no one else, but there were five horses plus his corralled nearby.

A hen was roasting on a spit near the fire, already perfectly browned. Icannes disappeared behind him and reappeared with two goblets, handing him one. It was filled with golden wine that smelled of freshly scythed hay and tasted of barely ripened gooseberries.

"Relax a moment, Captain. Dinner will be ready soon."

Urias leaned back on the log behind him—obviously placed there for exactly that purpose. Icannes gathered the hem of her frock and dropped to her knees at his feet, pulling off one boot then the other. She crawled up to recline beside him, twining a bare leg between his outstretched legs. She tucked herself into the crook of his arm. "Damn, I'm hungry," she purred.

Urias felt like he'd fallen into one of his dreams. "Me too." He didn't dare hope she meant more.

She reached to give him another soft, wet kiss. "But I suppose we really should eat first," she whispered. Gods' grace, she definitely meant more. She extricated herself and rose gracefully. "Alela, could you help me serve the captain his dinner, please?"

The nursemaid who'd accompanied Vahldan and Elan to Danihem all those years ago appeared with a platter. She was a bit grayer but looked remarkably unchanged. The two women bent to collect the hen from the spit. Urias had just taken a sip of his wine when two tiny arms wrapped around his neck from behind. With a squeal, a curly-haired toddler landed in his lap, spilling his wine. He swallowed wrong and started to cough.

"Haelya!" Icannes scolded as she hurried to scoop the girl from his lap. "Haven't I told you not to sneak up on people like that?" The child giggled in response, clearly unrepentant. "I'm sorry. I should've introduced you two right away. Captain Urias of the Wulthus, please meet Haelya, Princess of the Skolani." Icannes lowered the child to her feet but held her by both arms. Urias suspected if the wriggly girl was let loose, she would launch herself at him again.

"It's an honor, Princess." Urias offered his hand, but the fair-haired girl suddenly became coy, her round cheeks glowing. She slipped from her mother's grip and ran laughing back to the pavilion with Alela hurrying after.

"Yours?" Icannes nodded. She looked slightly annoyed, and Urias regretted asking such a stupid question. He avoided another by surmising that the child could be no older than three, and it had been eight years since... Well, the girl wasn't his. "She's gorgeous."

"Yes, and she's a real handful." Icannes huffed a laugh. "I suppose I deserve it. Her father was impetuous, and so was I to have invited him to the rites. Sometimes Haelya feels like penance for my poor impulse control."

He didn't know how to respond to that, and Icannes prepared their dining platters in silence. Besides the perfectly cooked hen, she fed him fresh peas steamed in the pod, plums steeped in mulled wine, and that famous chewy Skolani bread with clotted cream and honey.

The twilit sky turned purple then starry, and their conversation turned to reminiscences. Urias learned that Elan would be accompanying Vahldan upon his arrival, but that their eight-year-old daughter Brin would not. Apparently, his niece had grown quite close to Elan's manservant. It seemed the servant was nanny, mother, and father, all in one. Telling him of Elan seemed to sadden Icannes. The feeling was growing mutual, so he let the topic go.

The moon had risen when they set aside their empty platters. A cool summer breeze blew across the meadow, carrying the scent of clover. Urias had rarely felt so serene. Icannes refilled their goblets, tucked a blanket under her arm, and held out her hand. "Come, walk with me."

They set out across the meadow. They meandered along the lakeshore. Urias found himself mesmerized by the moon's reflection on the rumpled surface of the lake as Icannes laid out the blanket and reclined on it. Realization dawned. "The moon is full," he said.

"So it is." Icannes smiled slyly and patted the blanket.

"You're missing your people's ceremony." He sat beside her.

She lay back, pulling him down with her and wrapping her arms around him. "I thought we could have our own." She kissed his ear. "Would that please you?"

"How could it not? But the last time, I understood you were only... Well, that this wasn't supposed to happen again."

One of her hands slipped under his tunic and snaked up to stroke his chest. "There have to be some advantages to being a royal. Plus…"

Urias brushed a strand of hair from her face. It was too dark to be sure, but he thought she was blushing. "Plus what?"

"Our daughter, she's been foreseen. When it didn't happen last time, I was devastated. I almost gave up on the idea. But I couldn't."

"But… you *have* a daughter."

"Of course. But Haelya is not *our* daughter." Her gaze met his, girlish and coy.

"Our daughter? You sound so sure."

"Of course. Our daughter will be… Well, let's just say that she haunts my dreams. Same as you. And the timing is right—I can feel it. This time it'll happen. I've grown wiser about such things, you know." Urias drew a deep breath and sighed it out. Icannes leaned into him, eyes averted. "I hope that's all right. If it's not, I…"

He took her face in both hands and kissed her, long and deeply. He moved from her mouth to her ear. "I am honored, my princess."

Icannes eased him back and straddled his thighs. Silhouetted by the night sky, she reached and pulled her frock over her head, then flipped her tousled hair behind her shoulders. She grabbed the hem of his tunic, and he raised up to allow her to pull it off. She tossed the garment aside, wearing a mischievous grin. She leaned down and slid her breasts across the skin of his torso. "As I recall, I made you do all of the work last time. This time, you shall play the royal, and I shall be your serving girl."

She kissed him, exploring his lips with her tongue before moving down to kiss the apple of his throat, then his chest and stomach. Her nipples tickled his skin as she progressed downward. She sat up and teasingly undid the laces of his leggings before tugging them off.

Icannes kissed and tickled back up his legs from his ankles. He'd heard about it before, but he'd come nowhere near to imagining the sensation when she drew him into her mouth. The sky was beautiful enough without the additional stars he saw as she worked her magic, using hands, lips, and tongue in concert. Urias ran his fingers through her silken hair and groaned. Far too quickly, his stomach tightened and his toes curled.

She sensed the impending outcome and stopped, pinching his shaft at the base. "Oh no you don't. You don't release until I say. And only inside of me. Got it?"

How could he argue? He made a sound that he hoped resembled agreement. She moved up and kissed his ear again. "Here, work on this while you cool back down a bit." She took his hand and put it on her sex, pushing his middle finger into her slickness, wiggling his hand with hers until she was writhing and groaning just as he had.

Urias hadn't exactly *cooled back down* yet when Icannes climbed atop him. She lowered herself onto him and pulled his face to her breasts. She rode him slowly at first, then gained speed. Icannes must've sensed him nearing release again and abruptly dismounted and pulled him on top of her. She grabbed her legs behind her knees and held them back while he galloped to the finish.

Urias groaned as he released. "Yes," she urged. "That's it—give it all to me, my love."

She held him there afterward, and he felt his whole being growing limp. Icannes finally let him loose, and he withdrew and flopped onto his back beside her. The night breeze cooled his sweaty skin. "Sorry about the abrupt change of positions," she said. "The Wise Ones say it helps to produce a girl if the man is on top." Urias briefly marveled not only that she'd had the presence of mind, but that there were those who bothered to study such things. But it seemed fitting that if anyone had, it would be the Skolani.

He rolled onto his side, facing her. Icannes was still on her back, holding her legs up, arms under her knees and hands clasped. "Is everything all right?" he asked.

"Of course. More than all right." She smiled, then followed his gaze to her legs, dangling above them. "Oh. The Wise Ones say it gives your seed the best possible chance to work its magic. Do me a favor and hand me my wine, would you?"

Urias did as bidden, trying to ignore how all of this made him feel a bit used. She'd clearly warned him that she sought a daughter —his daughter—beforehand. "So did you…?" He shook his head. "Never mind."

"No, please. Did I what?"

"You… enjoyed it at least, didn't you?"

Her bright smile made his heart sing. She reached for his hand and pulled him to her for a fulsome kiss. "More than you can know. More than any other time. With anyone. Ever."

Urias chuckled. "You don't have to coddle me."

"No, really. You want to know why?" He nodded. "Because it was with you. You and I, my darling, can never be bound. But we have something so special, so precious. Our connection—it's something few couples actually share. We are entwined by Freya's Blessing. Our souls yearn for one another's. I will never forget tonight. Come what may. I cherish each moment with you, dear heart. For the rest of my days. Please never forget that. Nor me."

Urias leaned to kiss his beautiful, fierce princess. "How could I?" he asked and meant it.

Icannes held Urias's hand as they strolled back to the firelight, trying not to worry about how she would ask him or how he might react. Did she even have the right to ask so much of him? She tried to reassure herself that however Urias answered, the results would be as they were meant to be. But she couldn't quite convince herself. Sure, she believed in their destiny. But she also knew that destiny was a matter of choice. A series of choices, actually.

Icannes took a deep breath, ready to blurt it. Instead, at the last moment, she said, "Will you stay with me tonight?" Maybe it would be easier in the morning.

Urias smiled. "I'd like that."

This wasn't fair. She should've asked him at dinner, before he might feel any sort of obligation. Asking in the morning might be even less fair. It would only make it harder. Plus, how would she sleep? "I have a favor to ask," she said and drew to a halt. He turned to her. "I should have asked it earlier."

"No matter. Ask it now." Icannes sensed his apprehension. How could he not be?

"It is much to ask. You don't have to answer tonight. Just promise that you'll think on it."

Urias laughed. "Now I'm frightened."

"Don't be." Icannes forced a smile. "Know that however you answer, it changes nothing between us. Tonight will always be as special as we both know it to be."

"All right, I promise. Ask already."

"It has to do with our sister," she said. "And her daughter."

His brow furrowed. "Elan? And Brin?" Icannes nodded. Urias sighed and smiled. "For a moment there, I thought this was going to be about our... well, the child you hope we've made."

"In a way, it is. Come, let's walk some more. There is a tale to tell in order for you to understand what I'll be asking of you." Icannes pulled her kind and loving man back toward the lakeshore, knowing there was no going back. She reminded herself that he would be just as kind and loving, no matter how he answered.

LION AND WOLF, CHANGED AND UNCHANGED

"Even publicly, Elan was a skeptic of the prophecy of the Urrinan. In private, she openly scoffed it. My mother made no attempt to hide how she frequently sought to shake my father from his obsession with the prophecy. In fact, it was through my parents' private quarreling in response to Elan's public assertions that I first gleaned not just her scorn, but her deeper, masked feelings.

I came to see that Elan was both torn and terrified by the prophecy. Torn between the destiny she'd seen in her dreams—which incited her longing to create a better world for her people—and all that she had, and yet would, sacrifice for it. Terrified not just of what she felt certain she'd lose, including my father's love, but that her role in destiny may have already been played. Elan had come to fear that her own doom was to languor and bide merely to witness his.

Perhaps more than all of the rest, she feared that there was more she was supposed to do, but she hadn't a clue what it was."—Brin Bright Eyes, Saga of Dania

* * *

THE RAIN finally ended at dawn, and Amaga slipped out through the longhouse stables and made her way to her little hiding spot on the village wall-walk, a nook between a support beam and a corner where the parapet didn't quite meet the wall of the gatehouse. She waited all through the morning without being questioned by the guardsmen or seen by anyone who might tattle on her. Just as the sun broke through the clouds, her diligence was finally rewarded.

Vahldan's retinue emerged from the treeline on the road from Vigs-Utan. Amaga slipped past one of the guardsmen on the wall, almost tripping him. The man scolded her as she hurried down the ladder-like steps, barely in control of her descent.

She gave a cursory glance across the already teeming commons toward the longhouse. Amaga wasn't about to be called back. Thankfully, she saw no sign of her father or uncle. As far as she knew, her father presumed she was still up in her loft sulking, which she'd admittedly spent most of her time doing since hearing of Vahldan's coming. But Amaga wouldn't simply sulk over Thadmeir forbidding her to be among the receiving party. She was willing to take any sort of punishment for disobeying that unfair pronouncement. After all, it would be the last time her father would punish her.

The Lion Lord had come for her—to ask for her hand in marriage. At last.

Amaga would soon be a chieftain's qeins rather than a resented priestess and a disobedient daughter. Once he had received a formal request, there was no way her father could refuse. He would come to his senses, realize what was at stake. When the time arrived, Thadmeir would remember his promises to her dying mother.

Yes, she had to believe. Amaga gathered her skirts in her fists and ran out across the gateway. She'd forgone wearing her priestess robes in favor of a more feminine frock. But she'd stayed with white, out of respect for Freya. She ran out onto the southbound road, ignoring the mud that splattered her pristine hem.

The delegation was made up of perhaps a dozen riders escorting two of the strangest wagons she'd ever seen. She ascertained from the tales of Pontea that these were carriages—designed not to haul goods but to carry passengers. The first was enclosed but lined with windows. Although the other had protective sides, it was open to the sky. The riders at the fore were mostly Blade-Wielders, but she spotted whom she sought among them, raised her arm, and cried, "Kemella!"

Amaga's dearest friend squealed and kicked her mount to canter out into the lead. One of the Skolani scolded her, but Kemella paid no heed. Amaga had seen Kemella relatively recently. Two summers earlier, Kemella's brother had allowed her to accompany the sons of the Amalus Rekkr Fritigast, who'd honorably fallen in some sort of fight in Pontea. The sons had returned to Dania to take their father's body back to be buried alongside his ancestors on the Isle of the Valiant Slain. The sons had left Kemella in Danihem for a fortnight as they made their solemn journey to the far eastern edge of the realm and back. She and Kemella had instantly rekindled their sisterly bond during the visit, and Amaga had confirmed that they would remain as sisters until one of them passed from this world—though she kept herself from looking farther, dreading the distant darkness she foresaw in their touch.

That their parting would be tragic was all Amaga allowed herself to glean.

Kemella reined in before Amaga with a grin and ruddy cheeks. Her sister wore a shiny crimson sash over a lovely pale blue tunic. And leggings! She wore the most beautifully fitted brown leather leggings and boots. Kemella's golden hair was trussed into a loaf behind her head, held there by a shiny silver clasp that encircled her head.

"Gods, you're beautiful," Amaga breathed. They'd lived the same sixteen years, and yet Kemella not only looked more womanly but more worldly. Amaga worried that she'd never have that sort of grace, let alone the curves that her dear friend had already gained. Even if she grew into either or both, Amaga knew she'd never look so fetching or carry herself with such confidence.

Kemella laughed and leapt from the saddle. They collided in embrace. The touch delivered a dazzling array of images: colorful clothing, banners and tapestries, lovely tables filled with marvelously strange food and drink—snatches of the many pleasant, shared moments to come. Tears welled in Amaga's eyes. She buried her face on Kemella's shoulder. "And you smell wonderful," Amaga added.

Kemella drew back with a sly smile. "It's perfume, all the way from Medicia."

"Perfume? For what?"

Kemella's smile crinkled her sun-freckled nose. "To make us smell nice, silly. They say it makes us ladies irresistible to suitors. I brought two kinds. Later we'll try them both on you."

Amaga blushed and dropped her chin to her chest. "My father... He—"

"Shhh. Don't worry, Sister. All will be well. It is as it shall be."

Amaga sighed. "As it shall be," she sang in refrain. Kemella had always been able to read her and calm her like no one else could. Welcoming bells clanged in the gatehouse above.

Kemella's eyes sparkled. "I can't believe we're finally here! It's so wonderful to see you." She held Amaga at arm's length to appraise her. "Hardly the right sort of finery for our future qeins. But you mustn't worry about that, either. I brought some garments for you to try on. And some jewelry." Kemella raised Amaga's hand overhead and beckoned her to twirl. Amaga did as bidden. Kemella tsked. "So thin. But with a few weeks of eating Pontean foods, we'll have you looking like the mother to our future heir."

"Young lioness—you promised to stay with your guardians." A scowling Blade-Wielder rode up adjacent to them, just ahead of the wagons heading to the village gates.

"Forgive me, Sakaria. I'm simply too excited."

The woman sighed. "Best remount before your brother sees. Your friend, too—before the mud swallows her whole."

"Good idea." Kemella lifted her leg startlingly high to get a foot in the stirrup and was up and seated in the saddle in a flash. Kemella reached for her hand. Amaga was always nervous around horses and hated riding. Perhaps it was because she so often sensed the huge beasts' resentment. She took Kemella's hand and somehow found her way to getting a foot in the dangling stirrup. Kemella pulled Amaga up to sit before her, wrapping her strong arms around her. Their height made Amaga slightly dizzy, and yet she had never felt so at ease on a horse.

They started toward the gate just as the lead carriage came alongside. The carriage itself was a marvel. It was elaborately carved from wood, lavishly painted and polished. Even the spoked wheels were gilded. "Greetings, sage priestess." Amaga looked to find a handsome and highborn lady leaning out the side window, smiling warmly.

It startled Amaga when she realized who this elegant creature was. "Oh, Mara," she cried. "You look amazing! So lovely. Greetings and welcome."

Kemella sped their pace, and they joined the Skolani as the entourage approached the village gateway. "Your sister looks so happy," Amaga said.

"She's finally expecting. Arnegern didn't want her to come, but Mara insisted. She said no unborn Amalus son was so fragile as to keep his mother in bed."

Amaga sat up straighter. "Mara thinks it's a boy?"

"She's as sure as Eldavar's wife Sairsa was when she was expecting."

She looked back over her shoulder. "Eldavar has a son?"

"Indeed. He's with us! His name is Rohdric. You'll meet him soon. He's only three, but he already considers himself a Rekkr. I must admit, he's already got the attitude for it."

Amaga's face grew hot. A son. Perhaps two sons. Amalus sons. An Amalus heir as well as a backup already on the way. They came through the gateway and the stunned and silent crowd parted before the Skolani. All eyes seemed drawn to Amaga. She sensed the crowd beginning to seethe. Soon there were even scattered hisses and barely audible jeers. Amaga hadn't considered this. She could hardly breathe. The feelings of Wulthus supporters remained raw over the scene Vahldan had created during his last visit to Danihem. And her father had only fostered their spite. Thadmeir was forever harping upon how it was the Amalus who had sundered the nation and broken the futhark.

Amaga suddenly wished she had stayed in her loft sulking.

"I told you not to worry, Sister." Kemella's arms tightened around her. "Your son is the Amalus heir that we all await, and his cousins will serve him well. He who is born of the wolf and the lion shall restore the futhark. Our glory lies ahead. All of their bitterness will soon be forgotten." Amaga blinked away tears of gratitude for her fierce sister.

A chorus of horns blared. The delegation drew to a halt on the commons. The Skolani remained mounted, riding the perimeter of the carriage line, scowling and grunting commands to the crowd to stay back. The longhouse door opened. Amaga's uncle emerged, finely arrayed and squinting in the sunshine as he led the Wulthus procession out to the carriages.

Kemella dismounted and held out her hands for Amaga. She cautiously drew her leg from sitting astride and slid down to Kemella's waiting hands. Her uncle spotted Amaga as she straightened her frock. Urias frowned and shook his head. She scanned the Wulthus delegates and found her father. Thadmeir hadn't seen her. Not yet anyway.

Amaga squeezed Kemella's hand. "I have to go."

"What? Go where?"

"I'll explain later." Amaga left her and crept through the crowd, which was pressing in toward the backside of the carriages as the passengers disembarked. Most villagers focused their hostility on the visiting lions. A few offered Amaga glares of disapproval, but they kept their distance. There were some advantages to being feared.

Weaving her way behind the carriages, Amaga sought to cross behind the one that was open to the sky before making a dash to the longhouse stables. She came clear of the crowd at the back end of the carriage. The occupants all stood, waiting to disembark and meet the greeters. Amaga slowed, staring. The man closest to her had his back turned, but her eye was drawn to his flaxen hair, splayed over broad shoulders. His cream-colored tunic had a sheen, as did a mantle of crimson, inlaid with golden crests of roaring lions, hanging down his back.

As if drawn by her stare, the man turned. Vahldan smiled.

His face had aged some, but it only made him more impossibly handsome. He clearly knew her. His eyes radiated kindness—perhaps even fondness. Had Freya whispered to him of Amaga in his dreams, as the goddess did of him in hers?

"Lord Vahldan, welcome." Her father's greeting drew Vahldan's attention. Amaga knew she should leave before her father spotted her, but she stood gaping, longing for Vahldan to look at her again.

Amaga's view was suddenly blocked. A large sorrel warhorse had stepped between her and the carriage. "Stay back." The command was curt—not so unusual for a Skolani. But something was different here. Amaga sensed hostility. The rider's leather leggings were cord-wrapped as the Skolani wore them, but the boots were finely-made and knee-high. And rather than Skolani armor, the rider wore a fine chain cuirass, belted and accented with leather. Amaga looked up, squinting into the brilliant sky at the silhouetted figure. Indeed, a Blade-Wielder's hilt rose from over the woman's shoulder. But rather than Skolani braids, the rider's auburn hair was cut bluntly at the jawline, her bangs partially obscuring her glare.

"I *said* get back," she snarled. The crowd had obeyed and had left Amaga standing alone.

"I intend him no harm," Amaga said. She hated how girlish and petulant she sounded.

"I know what you intend." Scorn radiated from the woman. "I am still his guardian. I will always protect him. Even from the likes of you." Realization dawned—this was Vahldan's Skolani lover. He'd fathered a child with her. A girl, thank Freya. It had taken Amaga weeks to secretly uncover the child's gender, ensuring that the bastard would not be a rival to her son.

"Elan!" The awful woman turned to the call. Urias was coming toward them wearing a warm smile. "I heard you were coming along. It's wonderful to see you, Sister."

Sister? Her uncle considered this she-demon a sister? Stunned, Amaga backed away.

"Hello, Brother," the woman replied.

Freya's light, how could this be? Not Uncle Urias. He was her confidant, her comfort, her only friend in Dania. Her fortress. This felt like such a betrayal. How could he have not told her? With whom would she now commiserate over this awful woman?

Could someone so loving be the sibling of someone this hateful? Amaga didn't want to know. She pushed through the crowd, many conceding her passage with curled lips and muttered curses. Gods, *everyone* hated her. She hurried to the stables, anxious to hide away in her loft and collect herself. She needed to pray to Freya for strength and guidance through the newly revealed morass that was her future.

THADMEIR MADE HIMSELF SIT. He hated to wait, but waiting for this was even worse. He glanced up into the shadowy recesses of the long-house rafters. There was no light, no sign of his daughter in her loft. Urias had promised to make sure she remained outside. Amaga could be devious, particularly when it came to a meeting like this one. His headstrong daughter hated being excluded, probably more than he hated waiting. Thankfully, the girl was smitten—both with her fancy friend and with the many visiting storytellers at the bonfire out on the commons.

Thadmeir looked back to the fire, then to the other chair. He leapt up to readjust both chairs again. He wanted the correct angle, partly facing the center hearth of the longhouse, partly turned to one another. He didn't want to feel compelled to maintain eye contact with his guest. But he also didn't want to appear to be openly standoffish.

He certainly wasn't willing to have the man sit on the dais!

He just had to get through this... And without surrendering anything of substance.

Thadmeir sat again. He wiped his hands on his leggings. He remembered that he'd planned on having two cups of mead poured. Just as he stood to fetch the cups, he heard voices outside. He sat back down, trying to appear relaxed but with an air of impatience.

"After you, my lord." Urias pulled the door open and held it wide.

"Gods be praised! It's not barred this time." Vahldan swept in carrying a flagon and a cup, unable to hide a satisfied grin. Always the witty one. And every jest a dart. This was going to be even worse than Thadmeir had imagined.

"Of course. And as requested"—Urias gestured toward the empty chair across from Thadmeir—"Just the two lords of the ruling clans."

Vahldan glanced at the dais. Thadmeir detected a flicker of annoyance, but the showoff quickly recovered and strode to gallantly bow before him. "Lord Thadmeir. Thank you for receiving me."

Thadmeir nodded for him to be seated. Vahldan went to the chair, but before he sat he turned his false gladness to Urias. "Might I trouble you for another cup for our Wolf Lord, Captain?"

Urias went to the sideboard at the far end of the chamber as Vahldan sat with an exaggerated groan. "So, what did you think of Heliopa's creations?" The pompous fop had actually brought his rotund Hellain cook as well as an abundance of oddities and delicacies, all the way from Thrakius. Thadmeir had to admit, it was impressive. And the Severing Son had spared no expense—feeding the entire village at scores of tables brought out onto the commons. The Amalus upstart had made quite a show of it. Of this entire visit, come to think of it.

Thadmeir's stomach churned at the thought of all that he'd eaten. He'd been getting gassier by the moment since.

Urias arrived with Thadmeir's cup. His brother spared Thadmeir having to discuss his ominous dinner by interceding. "I'd heard of oysters," Urias said, "but hadn't actually tried them. The texture was... interesting. Tell us, how did you come to have so much ice this time of year?"

Vahldan leaned forward in his chair, brimming with eagerness. "Now *that* is a fascinating tale. It all starts in midwinter, when the Thrakians cut huge squares of ice from a small, clear lake, high above the city in the Pontean Mountains. They then slide these massive slabs down to the city on sleighs made just for the job. Beneath the city lies a series of tunnels. It's a maze and a marvel; some are manmade and some are natural caves, all interconnected. Near the palace there is a massive door, which opens onto a ramp. They tie up and lower the chunks to a chamber beneath the palace for storage. Through the summer, the chunks slowly melt, of course. But it's quite cool down there, and the pieces are so large. Well, suffice to say we have ice year 'round." Vahldan indicated with the flagon. "May I?"

Thadmeir held out his cup. "I must say, the wines you've brought are the most exceptional I've had." This new one was golden in color and smelled of ripe melon. Might as well admit it—give the fop a pat on his finely groomed head.

Vahldan poured his own. "And I've saved this best one for just this moment, my lord. It comes all the way from the highlands of the Tiberian homeland. The grapes used to make it can only be harvested after the first particularly cold night of the season, when the dew on the grapes freezes for the first and only time. I understand it's a delicate and fraught process."

Thadmeir swallowed back a belch. "Must be expensive."

Vahldan waved the issue off. "Just an example of the fine things available due to the success of our little venture on the coast."

Thadmeir raised his brows. "Little venture? I'd hardly name it—"

"Well," Urias interrupted. Again. "I'll leave you to your privacy." His brother gave him that scolding face of his as he bowed and started for the exit. Urias stopped at the door. "Please remember to be patient with one another. And that your people are counting on you both."

"*I* would never forget such a thing," Thadmeir grumbled.

"It's just that the last time I left you two alone, things didn't turn out so well."

Vahldan smiled. "Ah, but that was half a lifetime ago, Captain."

"True," Urias conceded. "But has anything changed since?"

Vahldan flashed his buoyant false grin. "Surely Lord Thadmeir and I have grown wiser."

"I am sure it's so. My lords." Urias tilted his head and left them.

With Urias gone, they fell to silence. Thadmeir put his fist to his chest, swallowed back another belch, and sighed. Gods, this stuff was sweet! And stronger than it first seemed.

Vahldan looked down at the flagon and cup in his hands. "May I just..." The lion revealed himself by setting the items right on the filthy floor. Vahldan stood and went to the nearest bench, stooped, and dragged it noisily to their chairs, leaving it askew. Then the pariah set the now dirty flagon on the bench. Vahldan sat back down and retrieved his cup. "There. That's better." Vahldan's smile revealed even more.

The man had done it on purpose. Everyone knew Thadmeir hated when his benches were out of place. At least the scheming lion hadn't put his feet up on it. The gods knew he yet might. Thadmeir grimaced as he spotted moisture wicking and dripping from the sides of the flagon to pool at its base. He forced himself to look away. "I'm surprised, Vahldan."

"Surprised? By what?"

"That you wanted to meet alone. Rather than waiting for an audience with the Rekkrs and the elders. I had presumed the annual gathering was your reason for picking the solstice."

"I thought that perhaps, if things go well tonight, we could approach the councils together."

"Together? To what end?"

"To announce that we're restoring the futhark, of course." Vahldan drank, eyes smiling over the top of his cup.

Thadmeir leaned back. "So, you're ready to face them, at last? Ready to ask them to overturn your banishment and to name you the rightful Lion Lord?"

Vahldan rolled his eyes. "No need. I already *am* the rightful Lion Lord."

"I suppose you are in Pontea. But this is Dania. And Danian law still holds sway here."

"You mean the guild still holds sway." Vahldan grabbed the flagon and refilled his cup.

Thadmeir put his hand over his cup to refuse the gestured offer to refill. "Well, yes. Unfortunately. Surely you understand that by sundering us, you only postponed their decline."

Vahldan shook his head and gazed into the fire. "I suppose I'm starting to." The admission startled Thadmeir. "But to be honest, when I left, I had no idea what would come of it." Vahldan glanced up. "Back then, I believed what the guild has long wanted us to believe—that we are a nation of simple herdsmen and warriors— that our identity is tied only to those two things. I thought to exploit the one the guild didn't control. But I've since seen beyond their illusion."

"Are you saying you believe that the guild has held sway over our decisions about war?"

"No, not that." Thadmeir found that he'd turned to face him after all. Vahldan followed suit, facing him with eyes alight. "You should see Pontea, my lord—how our people prosper there. We are so much more than just herdsmen. Or warriors, for that matter. Our people are artisans and craftsmen. We are traders and sailors, jewelers and woodworkers, innkeepers and winemakers. And, yes, we are wool experts. And fine warriors too, of course. We have carved a place in the wider world. A world of plenty that had been kept from us."

Thadmeir frowned. "Kept from us? By the guild?"

"Perhaps indirectly, but yes. Even moreso was it kept from us by the imperials. But the guild played along. All in the name of profit. An exclusive profit, at that. Our people were but the toiling shepherds for the lords of cloth—those who make and sell what Dania produces. The profits of that toil have ever been withheld from us by those who seek to limit our access to their world, to their markets. The guildsmen are but impotent gatekeepers. Now that we Amalus stand in their way, holding the very city that serves as the gateway to the imperial world, they can only cling to their ever-shrinking slice."

Vahldan gestured with the flask again. This time Thadmeir let him pour. "So, you intend to stay. In Pontea."

"Yes, of course."

"If you have all you sought, why bother with talk of restoring the futhark?"

Vahldan gave an incredulous look. "Because it's rightful! You really think I have all I sought? Please, you must know that I never sought to keep us divided. We are one people. Don't you see? The guild would love to keep us sundered. But they can't compel us anymore. Our two great families are beyond their petty hold on markets and land." Vahldan slapped his cup down, sloshing wine on the bench, and stood. He began to pace. "The Wulthus and Amalus have ruled our people since the days before any Gottari man or woman had a care for the price of wool or who presumed to lay claim to a grazing pasture. We led our people forth from the frozen north. Together we took Dania and made it our own. Just as we can take our place in the wider world."

Thadmeir rose and stood eye to eye with the Severing Son. "I agree. Now please sit."

Vahldan huffed but did as bidden. Sweet wine was the makings of a sticky mess. Thadmeir went to the sideboard. He dipped and wrung out a wet wiping fleece and brought it back. He lifted the cup, wiped the bottom, and handed it to his smirking guest. He then wiped the bench, including the filthy bottom of the drippy flagon. He took the fleece back to the wash pail, rinsed and dried his hands, and returned to his seat. Thadmeir sat with a sigh. "I grow weary, Lord Vahldan. Perhaps it's your fine wine. So please, tell me exactly what it is you want of me?"

Vahldan wiped away his smirk and lowered his voice. "They're weak, Thadmeir. Weak and decadent men. Never moreso than now. Our time has come."

"You mean the guild? Of course they are. Prices have never been lower. Is that what you mean by *our time*?"

"No, I speak not of the guild."

"Who then?"

Vahldan leaned forward. "The Tiberians."

"Tibairya? What have they to do with this?"

"Everything. The empire's grip on Pontea is failing. I see it all so clearly now. It's as if the gods have revealed what this has all been about. This is it. This is how the Urrinan begins."

The Outcast's son had a gleam in his eyes. Those same eyes had so often been crazed, revealing that he was on the brink of rage. But this was something different—something Thadmeir had known of him, and of his father, but had nearly forgotten. The lion's eyes were lit with predatory ambition. "And exactly how does that play out?" he deadpanned, going along to see where it led.

"It begins with our rising—together. We can make the futhark's restoration the start of it. Join us, Lord Thadmeir. It can be ours. Together we can seize it from them."

"Gods afire. Seize what?"

"Pontea. I feel it. I know it." His voice was drenched with fervor. "Fighting together, wolf and lion, side by side, we would easily prevail. In Pontea we can create the first and highest kingdom of a hundred that shall be wrought by Urrinan. Think of it. The richest trade routes, the crossroads of east and west. It can be ours. It can be the beginning of the end, the shattering of the Tiberian Empire and the creation of a great Gottari Empire. The high kingdom our progeny shall rule—as was foreseen."

There it was, laid bare. Within this bombastic admission was the pariah's unveiled objective. Not merely that he still sought to present himself as the Bringer. He wished for the Bringer to restore the Amalus kingship of old, same as the father had. Oh sure, he would gladly lead young Wulthus men to their deaths in an unwinnable war. But Thadmeir knew that wasn't what he was truly after. No, there was something else he actually needed. He had an agenda even more hidden than this alarming bluster. To fulfill his massive ambition—to convince people that he could start the Urrinan, Vahldan needed Thadmeir's daughter. Or at least a son by her. As the prophecy foretold, the progeny of wolf and lion, first king of a hundred kingdoms.

Vahldan had revealed what was at the rotten core of this visit, no matter how he dressed it up. Now it was Thadmeir's turn to stand and pace.

"I am indebted to you, Vahldan. For I have been troubled. For long years now, actually. But you have finally freed me from my torment." Thadmeir turned, delighted to find his rival looking perplexed. "You see, I'd been torn between my belief in my beloved, departed qeins and her visions of your part in Urrinan and what I knew to be best not just for our people but for my family's future.

"But now, thanks to you, I can see clearly. I well recall how even my wise Amaseila used to say that only the folly of men can spurn the glory of the gods' intentions."

Thadmeir strode to the sideboard and threw his half-full cup into the wash water. "And tonight you've clearly shown me your folly. For you have gone mad. Ambition has gotten the best of you, Vahldan, just as it did your father. And yet, I think it's driven you to excesses that would have appalled even Angavar."

Vahldan glowered, red spots blooming on his cheeks. Thadmeir went on as he strode back toward him. "I now grasp that the futhark can never be restored through the likes of you." He stopped, standing directly over the young Outcast. Thadmeir kept his voice low but filled with his newfound conviction. "I told you before that you will never have her, and now you've assured us both that you won't. You'll leave this longhouse now, and you'll leave this village at first light. May the gods forgive you for what you've done to our people."

Vahldan actually erupted in laughter and stood catching his breath. "Ah, you poor little man. You actually think this is about your precious daughter. You are small. Smaller than even I had dared conceive. And now you've shown your desperate need to keep your followers just as small." Vahldan walked to the door slowly and stopped. "For the record, not only did I have no such intention, I made a vow to avoid it. But at least I now grasp something about you, Thadmeir. It's clear you can never be made to comprehend how the gods favor the bold. You and your ilk are doomed to cower here in your precious valley with your precious sheep. Please bide in the knowledge that you will be lost to history."

"Happily," Thadmeir said. He rushed to open the door and held it for his despicable guest. "Better to be forgotten than to be remembered as a fiend. Goodbye, Vahldan." The pariah stepped out and started to turn back, opening his mouth, seeking the last word. Thadmeir slammed the door and barred it. He leaned against it and sighed, trying to slow his racing heart.

CHAPTER 19
DESTINY'S DAWN

"Some scholars choose to focus on studying the ways that people change a place, such as the ways that the Gottari changed Dania over the generations. I have always found it equally interesting to consider the ways that places change people.

A few of the ways Dania changed the Gottari are obvious, such as their adoption of the wool economy and a growing dependency on shared settlements and a division of labor. The effects that Pontea— particularly the city of Thrakius—had on the Gottari who migrated there were more subtle, as they were only just beginning. Yet they existed. Effects that changed the whole of the nation and the course of history.

Certainly, my parents were changed. And though I now consider the forest to be my heart's home, I, too, was undeniably shaped by my years in Thrakius."—Brin Bright Eyes, Saga of Dania

WHEN SHE'D GONE to bed, Amaga hadn't supposed she would get any sleep. She'd slept, but what little she'd managed had been fitful, filled with tedious dreams of angry Wulthus town folk cursing and chasing her. There had been little distinction between slumber and wakefulness.

Amaga was grateful when the soft knock on her window shutter finally came. She'd gone to bed fully dressed and had even thought to wrap her hair in a scarf to keep it from tangling. She rose, unwrapped her hair, smoothed her white priestess robes, and pulled the packed bag from her trunk to set it beside the window.

She donned her mother's old gray hooded cloak, opened the shutters, and handed her bag out to Kemella, silently waiting there. Kemella started down the short ladder ahead of her. Amaga climbed atop her trunk, turned to face her bedchamber—perhaps for the last time—and stuck her leg through the window. Kemella guided her foot to the top step of the ladder. They managed to get to the ground in silence. She tried to take her bag back, but Kemella had already shouldered the strap. Her co-conspirator strode out ahead, beckoning her toward the alley that led to the north gate. On the previous evening, Amaga had wished aloud for a better moon, but Kemella had reminded her how darkness would better shroud their flight.

Amaga froze. The way forward looked impossibly dark.

Amaga only knew so much about the future. Mainly because there was much she refused to see. But this was different. This went beyond her avoidance. Tonight's mission reminded her how little she actually could know of what lie in store for her. She'd never felt so frightened. Until Kemella came back and took her hand, pulling her into the inky night and the unknown.

Amaga told herself that escaping Danihem would be the worst leg of her journey. Being caught by nearly any villager could lead to as much trouble as being caught by her father. Gods, how these people hated her. If she and Kemella failed, a second attempt would become all but impossible. She'd be trapped among them for the rest of her days, and the prophesy would go unfulfilled. Her people would unknowingly doom themselves to a crude decline.

A dog barked from inside one of the adjacent homes, causing her to stop short and gasp. Kemella pulled her along through the white noise of her terror and suddenly they were at the end of the lane, a stone's throw from the gate. Kemella stopped at the edge of the last shadow, scanning the top of the wall. Her sister nodded and pulled her on, hurrying across the clearing. Kemella had left the small gate's bar out of its bracket late the prior evening, after the new guard shift had made their rounds. She had returned via this route, fetched Amaga, and still no one had noticed the breach.

Once outside, they kept to the base of the wall, heading for the northeast corner of the village. Kemella stole out into the meadow and scanned the tops of the walls again, then beckoned Amaga. They rushed to the deep shadows of the mill on the riverbank. From there they trudged through the muck of the Shepherds' Alley, heading east before turning south. Kemella had assured her this route offered the most cover, and she'd been right. Each time Amaga looked back, she could only see the walls of Danihem in snatches.

They finally started the climb into the foothills, skirting the meadows surrounding the village. Kemella's pace soon had Amaga huffing. They made it to the road that led up to Vigs-Utan, and Kemella led her straight to a copse of pines off the road. The carriage and team looked so strange, sitting empty in the dark but for a hunched driver in a hooded cloak on the bench.

Kemella opened the carriage door, climbed in, and pulled Amaga up behind her. Their driver turned. Even in the dimness, Amaga recognized Mara's grin. Mara clearly relished the adventure. Amaga admired her pregnant soon-to-be sister-in-law all the more for it.

"Ready?" Mara asked softly.

"As I'll ever be," Amaga replied.

With a soft slap of the reins, they were in motion. As soon as they were on the road, they were climbing. Amaga turned and saw a few winks of light in the otherwise dark village. She faced forward again, wondering if it was the last she'd see of the only home she'd ever known. She wondered how long it would take for her father's anger to turn to sorrow. Would he feel betrayed? Would he always resent her? If she found her way back, would she be welcome? Would her son ever know his grandfather?

She hoped so. But it didn't matter. She would soon show them all. Amaga was the one who'd been betrayed. Destiny summoned, and Thadmeir would have had her ignore it. In urging her to do so, her father had betrayed not just Amaga but her mother, the love of his life.

How could he, when he'd known all of Amaga's life that this was what she was born for?

Amaga of the Wulthus, priestess to Freya, would soon be the qeins of the Bringer. And her son would be the king that would forge the greatest of a hundred Tutona kingdoms that rose from the rubble of the shattered empire. Then they would all see.

THE SUN HAD YET to rise above the eastern ridge and the sky was filled with low, foreboding clouds as the carriage rumbled without slowing through the open gateway at Vigs-Utan. Amaga stared at the dark windows of the tower that rose over the ramparts, wondering whether their passage was being marked by the Elli-Frodei. If they learned of her presence in the nearby Amalus camp, would any of her father's allies among them come after her? She doubted it. Such a move would require actual courage.

Vahldan's camp was nestled at the mouth of the narrowing Pontean Pass, just beyond the sight of the tower. A steep, gray cliff rose behind dun pavilions. Against the dull backdrop, the flapping crimson banners of the Amalus stood out like smears of blood on a pristine tunic.

It would soon be her banner. Amaga had officially left the lush green of Dania. Just as she would soon leave behind the green of the Wulthus clan banner.

Did Vahldan know of his sisters' plan? Was he expecting her? Would her father's denial of Freya's will offer Vahldan the justification for taking her in? Would he still be accused of kidnapping if she left Dania on her own?

Amaga wondered if her father had yet found the birch stick with the runic inscription that she'd left in her bedchamber. To the original futhark, "*Two become one, Together to stand, Forever to lead, Brothers unto Urrinan,*" she had only added, "*I must go,*" and signed it with the rune for love and her initial.

Two young guardsmen came to receive the horses as Mara reined the team to a halt. Both men openly stared at Amaga but said nothing. Kemella hopped to the ground and turned to help both Amaga and Mara down from the carriage. Her dearest friend hoisted her bag and blithely led her into the camp. A tough-looking group of about a dozen young warriors sat around a fire, holding steaming cups. They, too, openly gaped. Amaga didn't recognize a single one. Evidently these men had been left here during Vahldan's family's visit to Danihem. Icannes had cited Vahldan's lack of accompanying warriors in defense of her assignation of Blade-Wielder guardians for his delegation. Amaga scanned the surrounding hillsides. There wasn't a Blade-Wielder in sight.

The Amalus warriors' presence made Amaga wonder if her father had been intentionally misled, and if so, by whom.

Kemella bid Amaga to wait and then headed for one of the larger pavilions. Without saying goodbye, Mara walked to another pavilion —likely her own. Amaga wished she'd thought to thank her. She surveyed the camp and spotted Vahldan's brother's wife, Sairsa, in front of one of the pavilions, swinging her little boy by his outstretched arms.

Sairsa caught Amaga watching. Rather than waving, she merely frowned. Amaga hurriedly looked away. Which brought her back to the warriors. Amaga sought for one of her ominous scowls. They didn't look away. Amaga was used to people staring but this felt almost cruel. Did they disapprove of her? Consider her a burden? Fear that she'd bring trouble?

Would she ever be welcome among the Amalus? Or would her life be the same as it was in Danihem?

Just as she determined to speak to them, the warriors all looked away. Sairsa swept up her son to hurry into her pavilion. Evidently they had all seen something beyond Amaga so she turned to look. Vahldan's ex-Skolani whore strode straight for her. The awful woman held a bow in one hand and a pair of dead rabbits by the ears in the other.

The ex-Skolani spotted Amaga and stopped short. "You," the woman hissed. She dropped the bow and rabbits and came on, speeding her step. "I warned you, you cursed little bitch!" Amaga stood frozen with terror, unable to flee or even to utter a sound. The horrible creature reached over her shoulder, grasping her hilt and drawing her sword as she came. "I told you I would protect him from you!"

The ex-Skolani raised her blade and smoothly stepped into a swinging motion, bringing the blade whizzing toward her neck. Of their own accord, Amaga's hands flew up to block it.

"Hold!" The male voice carried command, and somehow the blade stopped. The gleaming steel edge was so close to Amaga's palms, she could've closed her fingers on it.

"Elan, no!" Kemella shrieked and came running. Amaga released a pathetic mewling sound and crumpled to the ground. Sitting in her rumpled robes, she realized the cry wasn't the only thing she'd involuntarily released. Her white skirts were soaked, warm with urine.

Kemella bent to her, her arms enfolding her. "Are you hurt, dear one?"

"I'm... alive," Amaga managed.

Vahldan had somehow gotten Elan's sword away from her. He wrapped an arm around the vicious woman and pulled her away. "Elan, how could you? Come away now." His voice was soothing, as one would speak to a willful but prized horse.

"You lied to me," the woman seethed.

"No," Vahldan told her firmly. "I kept my vow. This is clearly the work of the gods. She is imbued by Freya—anyone can see it."

"No, it's her doing. She's evil. We were clear. I thought we'd made it." The ex-Skolani looked and sounded as if she were on the verge of a breakdown. "We were free of her, of this whole awful curse. And now..."

"Amaga is not evil. Her father is the one to blame. It's Thadmeir who keeps us from reuniting our people. Amaga has only done as she must, in the name of the futhark—of the Urrinan. Of course the daughter of Amaseila would sense our impending glory and the means to grasp it. The way forth has been revealed, and Amaga shares our destiny." Vahldan gently compelled the crazed beast to move off. "This is as it shall be," he said with finality. "I kept my vow, and yet the goddess has spoken."

Elan looked back, shaking her head. The hate in the woman's eyes had turned to sorrow. "No. It didn't have to be. She is cursed, same as her mother. And now she curses us. She will revel in our doom."

Amaga found that the savage's final assertion did not sound farfetched.

Urias entered the longhouse through the empty stables, stepped into the residence, and called out. No answer. He headed into the public chamber for breakfast only to find it empty. Which was odd on any morning but extremely unusual with so many visitors in the village. Something had happened while he slept.

Urias hurried to the main door and flung it open. Outside, the village commons was bustling with Rekkrs, some mounted, some making the final adjustments to their tack and gear. All of them wore their full gear and arms. Women brought supplies and boys loaded pack horses.

This wasn't any routine patrol. This was a mustering for a campaign.

One of Ulfhamr's young bannerman trotted to the longhouse walkway to retrieve his saddle bags. "Sisbert," Urias called. "What's happening? Who's called for muster?"

"Lord Thadmeir! His daughter has been stolen away in the night by the Outcast. The gods well know what that beast has in mind." It seemed to dawn on the lad that he was referring to Urias's niece. Looking abashed, the young man bobbed in a shallow bow and fled.

"It can't be," Urias said aloud. Vahldan wouldn't take such a risk. Would he?

Urias went back inside and rushed into the residence to retrieve his own gear, wondering why Thadmeir hadn't woken him. Urias stopped short. Something about Amaga's bedchamber grabbed him. Her bed was neatly made. Who makes their bed when they're being stolen away?

He stepped inside. Amaga's trunk had been pushed under the shuttered window. He opened the trunk. Many of her clothes were missing. He turned to go and spotted a smooth birch branch, ends neatly cut. He snatched it up. As he'd suspected—a rune stick. He instantly recognized the futhark, then saw Amaga's final words: "I must go."

His niece hadn't been stolen. She'd run away. Urias should've predicted it. Rather than gathering his gear, he took the rune stick and ran for the commons. The mounted column was forming up as Urias arrived.

At the column's front, a squire worked to fasten Thadmeir's gauntlets while a stableboy held his horse. His brother faced away, already wearing his helm. Urias hurried to his side. "What's this about, my lord?"

Thadmeir scowled, refusing to look. "Your services are not required here, Captain."

"You mean you'd rather not be talked out of what you're about to do."

"Even you can't keep me from rescuing my daughter, Brother."

Urias held up the rune stick. "She left. Of her own accord."

"You know as well as I that he's behind this." The lad finished with his gauntlets and Thadmeir clapped them together and mounted.

"And you know as well as I that this is her will, her wish," Urias said. "Whether Vahldan encouraged her or not, this has long been something your daughter has felt she must do. You can't pretend you don't know how strongly Amaga feels about this."

"Urias, I am going for my daughter!" Thadmeir thundered. His lads stood with eyes wide but averted. All of the waiting Rekkrs turned in the saddle, gaping.

Urias moderated his tone. "You're willing to risk open warfare— to shed the blood of our own people—to bring back a woman who's old enough to bond, who has willfully left to do so? Do you imagine that any chance of restoring the futhark would then remain?" Thadmeir said nothing. Nor did he start out. He sat in the saddle, staring out the open gateway. "Amaga will be humiliated," Urias gently added.

Thadmeir raised his chin. "I can live with that."

"She'll never forgive you. Can you live with that, Brother?"

Thadmeir slumped a bit. "If I must."

"You recognize that Amaga is doing what she believes your qeins foresaw and beseeched of her, right? You understand that she feels she is sacrificing for the good of our people? You can see that Amaga, and many others, will take what you're about to do as a forsaking of all that Amaseila strove for, the very change she felt she lived to see begun?"

Thadmeir's lower lip quivered. "What am I to do, Urias? He's taken everything from me. My little girl is all I had left. Am I to just let this happen?"

Urias laid a hand on his forearm. "Send me, my lord."

Thadmeir finally looked down. "To lead in my stead?"

He shook his head. "No. Send me alone, to Pontea."

His brother's bloodshot eyes grew sadder still. "What good would it do?"

"I can watch over her. I've been thinking, since this all went awry. I've been thinking that the only chance we have at reuniting our people is to keep a connection between us. We need someone in Thrakius. An emissary in residence. Vahldan trusts me, I think. I could watch over Amaga, make sure she's safe and happy. And I would do everything in my power to ensure that she returns to you—that you and I remain in her life. And in her son's life."

Thadmeir's brow furrowed. His brother gazed up into the Pontean Mountains. "Send me, my lord," Urias repeated. "Please. This feels right, like a providence. I feel it in my heart. This is what I am meant to do—the role I am intended to play."

Thadmeir looked back to him, his eyes wet. "When you see her, tell her I love her. And that she's broken my heart." The Wolf Lord slumped and, without a word to his baffled men, reined and walked his mount back toward the stables.

VAHLDAN FINALLY DISAPPEARED into one of the pavilions with his ex-Skolani wench. Only then could Amaga finally breathe again.

"Come. Let's get you into some fresh clothes," Kemella whispered. She helped Amaga up and guided her, in much the same manner as Vahldan had the disarmed savage, toward a different pavilion. Those who'd gathered to gawk solemnly parted to allow their passage.

Kemella led her through the flap and to a cot with bedding. She helped Amaga out of her wet robe and sat her down in her underclothing on the cot. "I'll be right back with your bag," Kemella said.

Amaga snatched Kemella's hand and clutched it. "You're leaving me?"

"All's well, Sister. No harm will come to you here. I promise."

Kemella eased her hand from Amaga's grip and slipped out through the flap.

Amaga couldn't draw a satisfying breath. She focused on breathing in slowly and releasing it as she surveyed the dimly lit space. She suddenly knew it was Vahldan's pavilion. His folded leathers were lying beside the bed, with an under-tunic at the top of the pile. She picked up the tunic and drew in a breath. It smelled manly, not at all foul. She hugged the soft wool to her chest, and the edges of her vision blurred. Her breathing grew labored again. Before she could set it aside, she fell into one of the goddess's trances—her own world clouding and morphing.

Looking down at her lap, a babe materialized. She knew it was hers—her son. Amaga pulled him to her chest and cuddled him as she took in her changed surroundings. She was in a stone building, but this was a cozy chamber—a nursery with bright tapestries and a window made up of various colored panes in a geometric pattern. Her son was warm, so tiny, so peaceful. Amaga's heart swelled and joyful tears sprang to her eyes. It was all still going to happen. Her father would not alter her destiny. Nor would the horrible Skolani wench. In her vision, Amaga laid the swaddled boy into a finely-carved wooden crib.

The moment she broke contact, Amaga was back in the pavilion, standing now. She'd set the tunic on a dressing table. Before her lay a sheathed sword, a rune ring dangling from its hilt. Bairtah-Urrin, the futhark blade of the Amalus. Amaga reached out tentatively and paused, fearful. No—she had to know. She willed herself to grasp the hilt.

And the world around her was instantly aswirl.

Amaga found herself outside, under a vast blue sky dotted with fluffy clouds. She stood on a terrace overlooking an expansive courtyard of smooth silver stone. A broad lane descended from the courtyard into a city filled with clay-tiled roofs. On either side of her were grassy lawns lined with manicured greenery, blooming with flowers. Up the lane and through the courtyard rode a proud Gottari host, resplendent in their polished mail. Banners snapped over their heads. On their backs, their bright crimson shields were emblazoned with golden snarling lions.

As each row passed the terrace, the riders turned and offered a fist raised in salute, then pulled it back to their heart as they rode on. Glory was written upon them, for glory they had earned. Though they were lions, her heart filled with pride and gratitude. For she knew—an Amalus army would begin it. The shattering of the empire had come. Urrinan was nigh.

"Are you well?" The concerned voice brought her instantly back to the pavilion. Vahldan stood before her. She backed away a step. "May I?" He reached for the forgotten hilt in her hand.

Amaga gave it over and her cheeks grew warm. "I'm sorry. I just—"

"All is well. What's mine will soon be yours." He smiled.

She followed his eyes as he glanced down. She was in her small clothes—the front stained yellow. Her legs were mostly bare. Even to her they looked pathetic—thin and pale. Vahldan must've sensed her distress. He snatched up a cloak and held it open for her, averting his gaze. She let him wrap her in its scratchy warmth. It too smelled of him.

"Please, sit." Amaga sat, leaning over her tightly pressed knees and clutching the cloak closed. "You must forgive Elan," he said. "She's not been herself of late. Rest assured that she is committed to our cause." Vahldan implored her with his impossibly blue eyes.

"I understand," Amaga found herself saying, though she didn't. How could she possibly understand someone trying to murder her? How could he forgive or even skim past such behavior? Evidently her future husband's murderous ex-Skolani's presence was something she'd have to grow accustomed to. As long as the savage didn't kill her before she could.

Kemella entered with Amaga's bag. "Oh. I'm sorry." Amaga couldn't imagine what she was apologizing for. If anyone should be sorry, it was Vahldan, though he hadn't apologized.

"Come, Kemella," Vahldan curtly said. "Help the priestess to make ready. I came to tell you both that we're setting out today. I'd like to get some distance between us and the border before sundown." Amaga's shock must have been apparent, because he added, "If that's all right with you, Priestess."

"Of course," Amaga murmured. She realized that moving away from the border was probably wise, but it still felt so final, so severing. Would it look as though they were fleeing?

Vahldan knelt before her. "Please know that I'm humbled, and that my heart is full of joy. And gratitude." Before she knew it, he'd taken both of her clammy hands in his.

This time Amaga plunged into a trance. She was standing on the same terrace as before, but this time stormy skies roiled overhead. Thunder rumbled ominously, without relent. No, it wasn't thunder. She looked down to find the courtyard filled with writhing, battling soldiers, some afoot and others ahorse. They roared and screeched and grunted and sobbed, their swords and spears stabbing and slicing. The grass was churned to mud and gore, and they were all coated in it, the gray stone walls and alleys splattered with it. Men swarmed toward a shield-grinding scrum at the battle's center, boots pushing and sliding, trampling the writhing men who'd fallen at their feet.

Amaga had never seen a battle, but this was more horrific than anything her mind could have conjured. As she watched in fascinated horror, blood flew up from the carnage, spattering her face and arms like wind-blown rain. Was it actually raining blood? She tilted her face to the sky, now glowing red. Down the red droplets fell, covering all the kingdom they'd founded, until even the distant paved courtyard and roads, and flowers that lined them, were stained red.

"The Urrinan is here!" The Bringer's voice boomed and echoed, deep and frightening. Horns blared and Vahldan towered over the mayhem that he'd wreaked, arms outstretched with pride, reveling in his masterwork. His shining glory and his bloody doom had entwined, and they embodied Urrinan.

Amaga saw and knew it as never before: Only from such horror could true change be wrought. The power of the gods was both terror and joy, decay and nourishment, death and rebirth. She quailed in realization.

"I'm sorry if I've upset you." His voice was soft and warm again. The horror of battle was snuffed. Bright light flooded her awareness. "I can see that there's no avoiding it. Our destinies are entwined, yours and mine. Although I've rarely admitted it, even to myself, I've known it for truth, all of your life." His voice was all she knew for what seemed a long while.

Amaga blinked as the pavilion returned. She found focus on Vahldan's face again. He had released her hands, but he still knelt before her. She nodded. "No, you couldn't upset me. Because I've known it, too. All of my life." What upset her was so much bigger than that.

Her future husband, the man who would gloriously break an empire and rain blood upon his own kingdom, bowed to her and left the pavilion.

CHAPTER 20
EMISSARY WOLF

*"*T*hough their Amalus lord may have preferred to imagine their situation to be elsewise, I think most of the Gottari who dwelled in Thrakius lived in the full awareness that they were conquerors living among the conquered—an elite minority dependent upon an often resentful and exploited populace.*

While living there in my youth, every Gottari accepted that the safety of the palace did not extend for us to the streets, alleys, and docks of the city. Gottari women did often walk the markets but never unescorted. And Gottari men almost never ventured beyond the palace keep unarmed.

Such was the state of things when my uncle arrived as the Wulthus emissary to my father's Thrakian court. Uncle Urias told me how grand the life of a Gottari in Pontea seemed before experiencing it for himself. His sarcasm could not be missed."—Brin Bright Eyes, Saga of Dania

URIAS FOUND it odd that he was alone on the road approaching the imposing arched gateway at the center of the city's vast northern wall. The late morning grew warm, but he was instantly chilled by the shadow of the towering palace that rose before him. The place was obviously old—the stone walls were pitted, cracked, and splotched with drab lichen.

The gate was open, but two aging Hellains stepped out to block Urias's entry. One of them spoke in a blasé monotone, presumably inquiring of his intentions. Once Urias managed to convey that he spoke no Hellain, the disdain of the pair was apparent. The one who'd questioned him stuck his head through a doorway cut into the wall just beyond the rusty portcullis and shouted up a stairwell. The pair then indicated Urias should wait outside the gateway.

He dismounted to stretch his legs, and both his horse and the packhorse grazed on the weeds growing between the ancient cobbles. He was about to try to ask the guards to send word to the palace when a voice called in Gottari from above, "What's ya' business, rover?"

Urias didn't recognize the young man leaning over the parapet of the wall. His long hair was tussled, and his accent was that of a herdsman of the eastern march of Dania. He looked about sixteen. "I am Urias, son of Theudaric, brother to Lord Thadmeir of the Wulthus. I come as an emissary. At the invitation of Lord Vahldan." That last bit wasn't technically true. He hoped it would aid his cause but didn't seem like something he'd be challenged over.

The lad's demeanor instantly changed. "Apologies, Captain. A moment." He held up a finger before he disappeared. A girl's face then appeared. Based on her dark hair bound by an ornate head-dress, he suspected she was a local. Urias waved to her. She covered her mouth, laughed, and fled. Her presence suggested a cause for the delay.

The Gottari lad appeared at the bottom of the stairs, still straightening his disheveled tunic and vest. "Again, I apologize, Captain. May I escort you to the palace?"

"Actually, I was thinking of finding a cup and a bite first. Maybe have a look around before going to the palace. Can you point me to a good spot?"

The lad was taken aback. "I suppose so. Long as it's Hellain food you're wanting. Or maybe some of that Baffy grub. Good here has much to do with the courage of the eater, if you take my meaning."

"I suppose I'm feeling brave enough. Sampling the local fare ought to begin to tell the tale of the place."

"Suppose so, if you like foreign tales. Mind, you'll have to have the right coin, too. Most here won't take Gottari skatts. Seems no decree from the palace will force 'em to, either."

"I do. I changed a bit with one of the wool merchants before leaving Dania."

The young man's judgmental gaze fell upon Urias's horses and gear. "It might be best if I take your horses to the palace stables. The market is no place for them this time of day."

The lad led him across a courtyard of pavers to another elaborate gate. The palace itself was enclosed by yet another wall. It soared over both the inner and outer walls. Urias wondered how many stairs there must be within. After giving him directions, the young man nodded at the sheathed sword on his saddle. "I'd recommend carrying your blade, Captain."

"Oh? To the market? Is it unsafe?"

The lad squinted. "Well, not exactly unsafe. But most of us have found it's best to keep reminding them who we are. Some of 'em seem to love hugging their hard feelings close." The youth gripped his own hilt. "Seeing a handy blade seems to keep 'em hugging, rather than letting those feelings loose."

The lad was a lion, all right. Urias decided to appease him and donned his sword belt. He set out around the palace. As he came around the inner keep to the sea side, he stopped short. The view, opening down the broad lane before him to the enclosed harbor below, stunned him to stillness. It took time to absorb as it was beyond anything he'd imagined seeing all at once. His vista included hundreds of rooftops, dozens of lanes, scores of ships, and thousands of people. The roadway was festooned with banners and awnings in a dozen bold colors, but none of those gaudy colors could compare with the dazzling blue of the vast Pontean Sea beyond.

The hilltop was open, seemingly like the village commons in Danihem. In the center was one, lone, ancient tree. Below the tree was a stone carving of a man—seemingly a scholar—on a pedestal amid a perfectly circular pool of water, with clear water trickling at the stone man's feet. It was four times as tall as a man. He presumed it to be a rendering of one of their leaders—perhaps a priest or a Wise One, like the Elli-Frodei.

Gaping at the sea again, he forced himself to move on, trying not to stumble across the cobbles of a courtyard as large as the Danihem commons, till he was moving downhill on the center lane. The gorgeous vista was blocked by the equally dazzling bustle. He found himself in the damp shade of narrow stone buildings, lined shoulder-to-shoulder and leaning over the street, like crows lining a stream to hunt crayfish. His eyes seemed to be adjusting to the change of light slowly, probably due to the confusion he felt. The lane was busy here, and he couldn't help but notice the wide berth he was being given. He first sensed the hostility, then noted the openly disdainful glares. A few of the locals even seemed to be muttering curses as they passed.

The crisp but briny breeze he'd been enjoying grew tainted. Urias averted his gaze from a glowering woman and found focus on the filthy trenches running alongside the lane. Danihem was not exactly sweet-smelling—and often the smoke of a thousand smoldering cookfires was enough to sting the eyes and parch the throat—but at least the sewage canals that emptied into the river were located outside the walls. The stench of Thrakius was nearly overwhelming until he turned on the adjacent alley that the wall guard had directed him to, lined with a dozen or more food vendors. Though his senses were still overwhelmed, at least the smells here were pleasant— exotic but appetizing.

The first few vendors he approached seemed to purposefully

ignore him. Urias's nose led him on to a counter under a striped awning with several open tables arrayed nearby and out of the sun. The vendor actually made eye contact. Together Urias and this affable Hellain found just enough common words and hand gestures for the man to begin assembling a plate. Before he was settled at his seat, a bustling woman in a headscarf placed the full platter and a brimming cup on the table before him. The berry-colored wine was watered but brightly flavored and refreshing. The fish was cut into square cubes—firm but moist, obviously from a large fish—and drizzled with a tangy vinegar sauce, served alongside crunchy green vegetables mixed with a heap of long starchy grains. The white cheese at the platter's edge was flaky and almost had a nutty quality. But the bread was his favorite part of the meal—flat, round, and spotted brown, it was warm and chewy. It reminded him of Skolani bread.

Urias watched the pedestrian traffic as he ate. He was still garnering the occasional baleful stare, but most passersby just hurried their step. From a distance, he spotted a cluster of Gottari—a middle-aged couple and two matrons with their armed servants in tow. He not only noticed how the crowd offered his kinsmen the same wide berth, but he was in a position to also see the rolled eyes, snarls, and even crude hand gestures his oblivious kinfolk evoked behind their backs.

Quite a place to call home. At least the food was good.

Urias hadn't slept well during the journey through the pass. He'd been told the Skolani sentinels would watch over his passage even if he never saw them. He hadn't. And knowing about them without seeing them had failed to reassure him. He had felt cranky and out of sorts all morning, and the subtly menacing atmosphere of the city did nothing to raise his spirits. He was starting to second-guess his decision to come.

He knew he needed some rest. Preferably in a place that felt safe.

On the way back up to the palace, Urias studied its unique stair-like façade—a series of cascading terraces, giving the appearance of stair steps down from a tower at the rear. The building was unlike anything he'd seen. His eye was drawn to a curious green splotch among the gray stone. It seemed to be a small forest of plants sprouting from one of the higher terraces.

Before he made it through the palace archway, a young man stepped from the gatehouse, halting him. "Welcome, Captain. I am Hunulf, son of Hunigeld." This was a different lad than the one who'd taken his horses. Hunulf's tone was more formal than friendly. His back was spear-straight and his chin high. "If you're up to it, I would take you to your chambers now." They'd sent a Rekkr's son to greet him and get him settled. The lions considered him a chore rather than a visitor from home. Would they keep him at arm's length? The lad's stare lingered. "Are you?"

"Am I up to following you to my chambers?" The lad inclined his head. "I'll do my best to keep up."

Hunulf seemed satisfied. Or maybe it was relief that his chore would soon be done. "This way, Captain."

"If it's possible, I'd like to present myself to Lord Vahldan," Urias said, his voice echoing in the stone archway.

"Unfortunately our lord has pressing issues to attend to," Hunulf said over his shoulder. "But you may trust that he is aware of your arrival. I'm sure he'll receive you quite soon. Many are curious about your visit."

Did the lions think that his intentions were devious? Urias supposed it was inevitable. To the Amalus, conflict was everything. Which meant that everything was conflict. "I look forward to the opportunity to enlighten," he offered.

Hunulf seemed on the verge of a harrumph but said nothing. The gardens that lined the flagstone path were overgrown and choked with weeds, and another circlet of water at the center of a pair of flanking stairs to the palace was green with scum. On the matted meadow to the west, a dozen young Rekkrs sparred in pairs on patches of mud between various stone carvings of men. To the east, several grooms lunged horses in muddy circles outside the stables.

They climbed broad stone steps to enter the palace through sturdy double-doors that were twice the height of a man. They crossed an echoing hall with soaring ceilings. The elaborate candle holders that hung over the space held only drippy remains. Instead of with candles, the otherwise austere hall was lit with torches in makeshift holders set low along the walls. They passed a cracked pedestal, carved with foreign letters. Urias guessed it once must have held another stone carving.

Hunulf grabbed one of the torches and led the way up a dimly-lit stone staircase. After two more flights up smaller wooden stairwells, Urias was led down an unlit corridor to an elaborately carved panel door. His young guide opened the door to a cheery chamber flooded with light.

Urias blinked, feeling dazzled. It wasn't what he'd expected. The furnishings were dusty and ornate but appeared cozy and comfortable. The place was hung with vibrant tapestries, and at least a half dozen colorful rugs covered most of the floors of polished stone. His saddlebags already sat on a padded bench at the foot of the largest bed he'd ever seen.

His guide opened double doors set with glass panes, and even more light beamed into the space. Beyond the doors was a terrace that overlooked the city and the sea. That such a space had been allocated just for him was beyond his wildest dreams. "Beats a bench for a bed in the longhouse, don't you think?" Hunulf asked.

It felt a bit smug, but... "Undeniably," he said.

"A serving woman will bring you wash water shortly, Captain. She can also bring you anything else you require. Dinner is served at sundown, if you think you'll be up to attending."

Again, as much a challenge as an invitation. "How could I refuse?" Wearing a satisfied smirk, the lad gave a shallow bow and left.

The lions hadn't turned him away, at least. Far from it. Seemed they wanted to impress him. Urias couldn't help but wonder how long he'd be allowed to stay. If he were to have a chance at achieving everything he'd come for, it would take time. Which was something he may or may not be granted. Or perhaps not in such luxury as this.

The serving woman showed up with a bowl and a wiping cloth just after the Rekkr's son left. The Hellain woman gave him a cold glare as she crossed the room and set the basin on a sideboard that seemed tailored for the purpose. Although the woman wore a simple frock, she had a haughty manner. She was more intimidating than Hunulf, to be sure. Her combed black hair was shiny and pulled tight and secured behind her head, revealing a handsome, stern profile.

"Thank you," he said.

Her nostrils flared as if she were smelling him. "Is there elsewise you need?" Her Gottari was heavily accented but serviceable.

"Not at the moment. But I'll let you know." Urias smiled. Rather than returning it, she set out for the door. "And your name?" She turned back, scowling. "You know, in case I need you."

"I am Ligaia." He half-expected her to bow or blush. Instead, she stared defiantly into his eyes. Another challenge? Clearly, serving others did not come naturally to her.

"Thank you, Ligaia. It's a lovely set of rooms."

Ligaia appraised the space and gave a single nod. "Yes, it still is." She finally tilted her head. "Thank you, Captain. For noticing." She spun and left.

Urias was relieved to be alone. He stripped off his outerwear and washed. With his face and hair still wet, he walked out onto the terrace and leaned over the rail, relishing both the sunshine and the breeze. He marveled again at the view. He scanned the marketplace below, now less crowded. A ship was rowing through the massive seagates into the green harbor. The docks were lined with vessels. He counted at least a half-dozen sets of sails out on the rolling surface of the sea, both coming and going from the bustling port.

He'd never felt so far from the forests of Dania and the stout timbers of the longhouse.

The thought reminded him of the greenery on the terrace he'd seen from below. He turned and leaned back against the ledge, craning to survey the higher tiers. The plants drooped over the parapet of the terrace two floors directly above. Among them was what appeared to be a sizeable fir tree.

Also hanging over the same parapet was a pair of forearms, with hands cradling a cup. He glimpsed one of the hands lifting to brush aside wisps of auburn hair. Could it be? He cupped his hands around his mouth and called, "Elan? Is that you?"

His sister's face appeared. Her puzzled expression was swiftly transformed into a broad grin. Before he knew it, Elan was at one end of her terrace and over the parapet, climbing down the jutting stonework—barefoot, no less. Halfway down from the terrace above, she leapt, causing her loose frock to billow. She landed, cat-like, and lunged to embrace him. "How can this be? Are you really here?"

She smelled of wine, but her delight was intoxicating. Urias laughed. "Of course."

"Why? For how long?"

"I am the Danian emissary to the Thrakian court, my lady." He bowed with a flourish. "So I hope you're stuck with me for quite some time. At least until I'm expelled."

"That's wonderful. I was just wondering if I was going to die of boredom here."

Elan's slight slur convinced him that the cup he'd seen her holding wasn't her first.

"You? Bored? With all this?" He waved an arm, indicating the view. "I can't imagine it."

"Give it a few days," she muttered. "The prison will be revealed."

"Prison?" He made a point of gazing out at the view and the sea beyond. "Have you already seen so much of the world that you choose to remain here?"

"Much of it, yes," she said. "But staying is no choice. I would leave tomorrow, but..."

"But what?" he prompted.

Elan turned to him. "But there is nowhere to go. In Dania, I am a ghost. Even entering the forest at the mouth of the pass is a death sentence. Out there," she nodded toward the sea, "is no safer. I have gained a reputation."

He thought he knew but had to ask. "What sort of reputation?"

His sister gazed at the sea. "In Pontea, I am known as the Hippomache. It is a name from a legend of Hellain. A legend that tells of killer warrior women from the hinterlands. Now that Vahldan has named us raiders and pillagers, we are all marked." Her laugh sounded sardonic. "Ironically, even though I was not here when this city fell, I am the most infamous among us. I can take care of myself, of course. But I cannot leave my daughter. And I cannot put her in such danger as leaving would entail."

He didn't dare push the topic. "Speaking of whom, I also came to get to know my niece. When can I come and meet her?"

Elan continued facing the sea. "Whenever you like," she said, sounding oddly aloof. "Or I should say, if you can catch her in. She's always off with her tutor or her manservant or the other servants' urchins. I have no guess as to which she's with now."

"Ah, right. Her manservant." Icannes had told him of the manservant. It still sounded so odd that a child would have a servant.

Elan shook her head. "Hesiod was originally assigned to me. But he and the girl are nigh inseparable. I never took to the man, but we came to an understanding, so he stayed. And then Brin never took to her nannies, so I suppose it worked out. When she's not sleeping or being tutored, she spends her time traipsing the grounds of the keep or prowling the cellars. Seems I rarely see her."

"Perhaps I could stop by in the morning."

"Morning? Tomorrow?" Elan shrugged, still unwilling to meet his gaze. "I don't know."

"Someday soon, then. I could come early, before she's left for the day."

Elan shrugged again. "As you wish. But I warn you, the girl is cranky most mornings."

Urias watched her, puzzling over her upended disposition.

"Uncle? Are you here?" The call came from the entryway inside.

"Ah, there's the other niece." He smiled. "We're out here, Amaga!"

Amaga appeared at the terrace door, beaming. "I just heard…" She stopped short and her expression instantly fell.

Urias took a step toward her, but Amaga backed away. "It's wonderful to see you," he said. Amaga didn't reply. Her face was etched in fret. Another disposition he'd unintentionally upended. What was going on here? "Your father sends his love," he added, seeking the solution.

It was when her gaze focused on him that he realized she'd been looking beyond him. "Father said that? You're not here to take me back?"

"Of course not." Urias looked back at Elan. His sister's icy glare would've made him back away, too. "You two are acquainted by now, are you not?"

"We've met," Elan spat and shouldered past him. "I have to go." Amaga flattened her back to the wall as Elan strode through the terrace doors.

"Will I see you at dinner, then?" Urias called after Elan.

"These days I have little appetite for dinner."

He followed her inside. "See you tomorrow, then?"

Elan didn't even pause or look back. "Perhaps." She didn't actually slam the door, but neither was it gently closed.

Urias turned to Amaga. He had a guess but had to ask. "What was that all about?"

Amaga shuddered. "She wants to kill me. Please, you have to help me."

"What? That's ridiculous."

"It's true! I swear. You have to convince Vahldan to send her away. I've tried, but he's forbidden me to speak of her. Either that, or take me back to Dania until Vahldan comes to his senses."

Urias shook his head. "We're not going anywhere. She's my sister. There's no way that—"

"Please, Uncle." She clutched his hand. "You must believe me. You've got to help before she succeeds."

Gods' guidance, being the Wulthus emissary was already far more complicated than he'd dreamed possible. And Urias had yet to speak to the famously temperamental Amalus lord.

CHAPTER 21
MUTUAL MISTRUST

"*I have never claimed any special knowledge of the Tiberian Empire nor its militum, but I suspect few would refute my assertions about the impact of Tiberia's mobile reserve on the events of the Gottari era in Pontea. Their importance was nothing new, nor surprising. During the years leading up to my father's arrival in Pontea, the empire's commitment to the broad deployment of standing armies had flagged and the size of local garrisons had dwindled, causing the Tiberian reliance on the mobile reserve to continue to grow.*

This elite force's position was vital to the politics of the day, even when it was far away. Perhaps especially when it was far away."—*Brin Bright Eyes, Saga of Dania*

URIAS WANDERED THROUGH THE EMPTY, echoing entry hall, hoping to ascertain where dinner was being served. No one had invited him— not exactly. The Rekkr's son who'd taken him to his chambers had mentioned offhandedly that dinner was served at sundown. The sun had gone down, the smell of cooking filled the lower levels of the palace, and no one had come for him.

He finally spotted a pair of servants carrying trays up on the second-floor balcony. He was arriving at the top of the steps as the pair stepped through a large double doorway. One door was falling closed as he approached, emitting the drone of crowd conversation. The door clicked closed before he could catch up. Although it was clear there were many within, and that food was being delivered, he felt it best to try knocking first. No response.

Urias sought to quietly turn the latch. It was impossible—the latch clicked loudly. He opened the door far enough to peek inside. Indeed, it was another large hall. There was a long table, lined with dozens of diners. At the far end there was an empty dais, reminiscent of the longhouse. He couldn't see anyone he knew. He leaned through, scanning the space.

"Good evening, Captain."

Urias jumped back into the corridor, heart thudding. The voice had been so close. And it was so low. He swiftly realized it could only belong to one man. Urias pushed the door wider and looked behind it. "Ah. Good evening, Teavar."

"Sorry to startle you." The giant narrowed his gaze. "I wondered if you would come."

Every utterance from the lions resembled a challenge. "Wouldn't miss it. Had a bit of trouble finding you, is all."

"Allow me to show you to your seat, then." Teavar set out for the near end of the lengthy table. The big man pulled out and proffered a chair among what seemed a group of teenage boys who were already ravenously eating. Vahldan's seat was at the opposite end, with his family. Amaga was nowhere in sight. It was clear that the senior Amalus Rekkrs were seated by rank, from the old guard and cousins down to the Rekkrs' sons and the secondary bannermen at Urias's end. There wasn't a Rekkr he knew within earshot. No one acknowledged him. Indeed, no one seemed inclined to spare him a glance.

He was being snubbed.

Teavar left him there without another word. Urias had decided to simply settle in and accept the shitty circumstance when Vahldan's gaze met his. Rather than even offering a nod, the Lion Lord swiftly looked away. Urias bristled. He'd known Vahldan for twenty years. And how often had he been the only Wulthus who sought to understand Vahldan's point of view?

He pushed back his chair and strode to the far end. With every step, the dull roar of conversation faded until nearly every eye tracked his approach. It felt like an uphill slog through mud in the hot sun, but he finally arrived before Vahldan in hushed silence.

Urias formally bowed. "My Lord Vahldan, I wish to present myself and offer my gratitude for welcoming me to your hall and hearth." He glanced around, relieved to see there was indeed a hearth along one stone wall.

Vahldan leaned back in his chair. "Captain," he said in gruff acknowledgment. "We were just talking about you."

"About me, my lord?" Odd, then, that no one would speak *to* him once he arrived. "I'm flattered." Urias surveyed the hard stares, all focused on him. "Nothing bad, I hope," he added.

"Well, certainly nothing personal." Vahldan dropped his utensils with a clang. "May I speak bluntly?"

Urias bowed his head. "I'd be honored to have you speak to me however you see fit." May as well blow the smoke from the chamber, no matter how brisk the cleansing air.

"Why have you come?"

The bluntness still startled him. "As an emissary, my lord."

"Yes, but to what end?"

"To maintain the brotherhood of our nation's two royal clans, of course."

Vahldan put his elbows on the table, folded his hands before him, and laughed. "If you wolves really wanted to play at maintaining brotherhood, you should've come at the head of a column of Rekkrs, ready to join our cause. As I pleaded for your brother to do. As our Bafranii guest of honor, Captain Zafan here, has willingly pledged." Vahldan tipped his head to a man Urias hadn't noticed. "This man— a foreigner—has more courage and loyalty than our own kin."

The Bafranii was dressed in bright, shiny fabrics, and his skin and hair were as brown as any Urias had seen. If it was true that he was a sea captain from Bafrana, and if what they said of Bafranii sailors was true as well, it meant the man was a pirate. Seemed about right. Zafan's countenance was fierce as Vahldan spoke Hellainic to him, presumably translating what had transpired. The man's tension eased. The pirate offered a sly grin and a cursory tilt of his head.

"Forgive me, my lord, but I confess I do not even know what your cause is."

Vahldan's smile became an angry grimace. "To bring an end to tyranny. Of course," he added, clearly imitating Urias.

"Of course," Urias said in concession. "But I fear that whether or not I came at the head of a column was not mine to decide, my lord. Knowing that I've disappointed you makes me all the more appreciative of your hospitality and of the bounty of your table."

"Now that we've established why you're here," Vahldan said, sounding sardonic, "perhaps we can get back to the bounty you mention." The lord of the hall gestured with his hand, dismissing him to return to his seat. Urias turned and strode back, avoiding the smirks and stares of his tablemates. Before he sat again, the roar of conversation had returned, only louder and punctuated by laughter. Mostly at his expense, he supposed.

Soon after he sat, a server offered him wine from a large flagon. Then another proffered sliced meat from a platter. It had been cut from a trussed, roasted bird of some sort, with its colorful plumage displayed on the platter. "Is it a rooster?" he asked.

The server cocked her head. She didn't understand. One of the Rekkrs' sons said, "It's called peacock, Captain. Comes from south of the sea. The Tibairya consider it a delicacy."

Urias put a slice on his plate, along with some of the pickled turnips that accompanied it. He cut a bite and put it in his mouth. The lad who'd identified it for him watched for his reaction. "Perfect," he said with a smile.

He hadn't lied. The bird was perfect for this crowd: pretentious, overhyped, and tasteless.

~

THE WULTHUS EMISSARY entered his study just moments after Vahldan had sent Teavar to fetch him. The high hall was still loud with those who lingered to drink. Vahldan signaled Teavar to close the door behind their guest.

"You asked to see me, my lord?" Urias bowed his head again. The man was adept at playing the respectful guest, at least.

Urias glanced at the chair across from him, but Vahldan thought it might be best to leave him standing for this. "We've known one another a long time," he said.

Urias clasped his hands behind his back. "Fast approaching half a lifetime."

"Then I'm sure you'll understand my hanging a target 'round your neck. So to speak."

"It was for them?" The wolf gestured toward the lingering revelers outside the door.

"For them, yes. But also for me. And I still haven't scored the hit I'm looking for."

Urias offered Vahldan one of his charming wry smiles. "Shoot."

May as well try bluntness again. "I need to know if your brother sent you."

"Well..." Urias paused. "He approved, of course. But my coming wasn't his idea."

"I see you're still intent on dancing away. Perhaps you'll grant me another try?" Urias furrowed his brow but nodded his ascent. "Did you come to take the girl—to stop the bonding?"

Understanding eased Urias's fraught brow. "Ah. Now *that* is a very direct shot, so I'll reward it with a direct response: No. Amaga came of her own, very determined, will. Even my brother has come to accept that truth. He sees that, much as he'd like to, it's not his place to interfere. She is her own woman, same as her mother was."

Vahldan leaned back, appraising him. He'd always liked Urias. Probably more than was wise. He wasn't willing to completely trust him, and he presumed that Urias felt the same of him. But he was as trustworthy a wolf as there ever was. "Am I to believe that you're not here to seek some loose chink to pry at?"

Urias looked puzzled. "A loose chink in...?"

"In the Amalus armor. You know—a means of exposing our efforts here as folly. Some way to reassure everyone at home that the rogue Lion Lord is a fraud?"

"A fraud?" Urias seemed genuinely surprised. "I can't imagine myself ever trying to convince anyone that you are a fraud. I've considered you many things, Vahldan, but never that."

Vahldan sighed. "Forgive me, then. Your brother and I have exchanged harsh words. And I know our position here has affected the guild's profits. I just can't help but wonder about their bidding of you."

More of Urias's tension melted. "I suppose I can see why you would wonder. But did you ever consider that those in power might have bid me not to come at all? Or that I bid my brother to send me anyway? Did you ever consider that I was the one who prevailed on Thadmeir to allow his daughter to pursue her own destiny? Or that I might have been the one who kept him from mounting an armed pursuit the morning she left?" Urias's smile became more earnest. "As well as we know one another, did you not have cause to suspect that I still wish to see the futhark restored?"

Vahldan didn't want to believe him, didn't want to feel abashed. But he found the man an irresistible force, as usual. "I can see that I should have considered those possibilities."

"Have I ever truly given you reason to suspect otherwise?"

"Truly? You have not. So either you're very clever and I am gullible, or you have ever been honest with me."

Urias laughed. "Well, I'm certain you're not gullible." The

Wulthus emissary leaned in with a conspiratorial look. "Speaking of cleverness—did you ever consider that I have an agenda that has nothing whatsoever to do with my brother, the guild, or the Wulthus clan? Maybe I am acting in the confidence of someone you'd never suspect, who only wishes you and yours well. Someone who is always striving to advance the Urrinan."

"I certainly hadn't considered that." Was the wolf playing games now?

"Can you find it in your heart to consider that I mean you no harm? At the very least?"

"I suppose I can search my heart." He chuckled. "Hadn't thought to look there." Vahldan stood. "But out of respect for our long years together, please consider this. As fond as I am of you, if I ever suspect that you are acting contrary to what you are implying now, sentiment will not keep me from expelling you from this city." He leaned in. "At the very least."

"Consider the point taken. My lord." Urias bowed his head and turned to leave. The Wulthus Captain stopped at the door. "Please remember, Vahldan, that Elan and Amaga are my sister and niece. I care deeply for them. They are not mere playthings in some game of destiny. As challenging as I now see it to be, please promise me that you'll do your best to see to their wellbeing."

It was overly familiar, verging on disrespectful, but Vahldan found he couldn't be angry with him. "I'll promise to try. But I fear we are all just the playthings of the gods." His guest stiffened. "Good night, Urias," he added with finality, and the door latch clacked behind the wolf's departure.

THE KNOCKING SOUNDED ALMOST as urgent as Arnegern's voice through the door. "He's here, my lord!"

Vahldan leapt to his feet, then caught himself. "Come," he said as calmly as possible.

The door sprang open to reveal Arnegern's grin. "Word has arrived from the docks. The anax was indeed on his flagship. He's hired a carriage. Seems he's on his way."

"Here?" He realized it was a stupid question. Arnegern nodded enthusiastically. "Maybe he's taken the bait after all."

Vahldan hurried past Arnegern, heading out. He stopped at the door, turned back for his sword belt, then stopped again before donning it. "Probably not the most welcoming."

"I doubt it would set the proper tone," Arnegern added. "Swords make poor invitations to alliance." His first captain went to the hooks, grabbed the ceremonial robe, and held it out for him. "Maybe this instead?"

Vahldan was fond of presenting himself as a warrior, but he saw the wisdom in the choice for this. He turned to allow Arnegern to help him into the brocaded silk garment.

They left the residence and hurried down the stairs. "Teavar and Jhannas?"

"Already sent for them," Arnegern said. "Shall I send for Eldavar? Or Belgar?"

"Let's wait to see how many he's bringing in."

They arrived on the balcony level outside the high hall just as Herodes came up from the main hall. "The carriage is almost to the main gate, my lord."

"How many are with him?"

"He brought only two guardians, my lord," Herodes said.

"Both of you, go back to greet them with two more of ours. Give them a bit of space and a lot of respect. Lead them up, then leave us." Vahldan turned to the giants just arriving. "Teavar and Jhannas, both of you will stay. Just you two. And out here. I take him into the high hall alone. No rough stuff. No scowls or growls. I want him wary, but I don't want his hackles up."

All of them murmured their assent, and Herodes and Arnegern hurried down the stairs.

He went into the high hall and gathered all of the maps and

scrolls from the table in his arms. He hurried to the study, opened the door, and flung them to the floor inside. He turned to the sideboard to make sure there was wine and clean cups.

"They're on the stairs," Teavar discretely warned from the doorway.

Not enough time to make sure the cups were clean. He found two that matched and set them out front. They would have to do. He straightened his robes, drew a deep breath, and blew it out. His hand sought the missing hilt. He clasped his hands together instead. Vahldan thought about the men he'd killed. Isidros's men. The ugliness stirred, low in his belly. The treacherous thug Encho's face sprang to mind. He saw it twisting with pain, eyes wide with surprise, realizing that Vahldan had cut his throat.

Vahldan reminded himself how necessary it had been—how disrespectful the foreign thugs had been, how smoothly the trading pact with Isidros had gone since.

He didn't dare hope this meeting would lead to an alliance. But other good outcomes were possible. His plan would still work, whatever came of this.

Vahldan forced his mouth to a smile and strode to the stairway. It was perfectly timed; their guests were almost to the top. "Ah, Anax Isidros. Welcome to Thrakius. What fortunate circumstances have led to this pleasure?" He hadn't seen the anax face to face since they met in Nicomedya, over a decade ago. The Hellain was a bit grayer but otherwise unchanged.

Isidros moved with assurance and a warm smile. "Does one need a reason to visit an old friend when one happens near to that friend's port?" Whether his cheer was genuine or not, he preferred Isidros as a fake friend to a real enemy.

He led his *old friend* to the high hall ahead of Isidros's guardians —one of whom was the fat-cheeked man Vahldan had spared that night in the sewer. Fat Cheeks was huffing from taking the steps. Teavar and Jhannas stepped into the space between the leaders and his visitor's guardians, blocking them out. Isidros raised his eyebrows. "What's this? Surely you don't fear a mere pair of guardsmen, my lord."

Vahldan opened both palms. "Of course not. My own guardsmen mean no insult. I was merely hoping we could speak privately. Man to man. As old friends would."

Isidros's smile returned. "Of course we can. Neither my men nor yours then, eh, friend?"

Vahldan tipped his head for Teavar and Jhannas to close all four guardians out. Once the doors closed, Vahldan drew out the chair at the head of the long table. Isidros plopped down without hesitation. The man was well-used to such treatment. Vahldan sat to his right.

"And so. What brings you to Thrakius?"

"As I said, merely passing by. Nothing but a boring trade mission, I fear. But I could not miss the opportunity to congratulate you, my lord. The topic of your impending nuptials is the main course at every public house in Pontea, whether it's served with tea or wine."

"Thank you, Anax. It truly seems a destined union."

Vahldan knew the man considered him a Tutona brute. Hellains of noble blood thought themselves superior even to their own commoners, let alone the *lesser races*. Isidros probably imagined Vahldan's bonding entailed carrying the bride in tied hand and foot. Or worse.

"Speaking of wine, may I serve you some?" he asked.

"I don't have long, but how can I refuse?" The anax was putting on quite a show. Considering the stretch Vahldan knew it required of him made it all the more entertaining.

Vahldan went to the sideboard and checked the matching cups he'd selected. One looked dirtier than the other. He filled them both, handed the dirtier one off, and raised the other. "To friendship, then?"

"To friendship." Isidros kept his smiling eyes on Vahldan as he drank. "Rumor has it that this marriage will make you a king in your homeland. Is it so?"

Where in the nine worlds had he heard that? "Even if it were so, the title would mean nothing here. After all, in Pontea I am but a mercenary thug who once worked for a prosperous pirate, who then sacked a city." It suited him for now. By the time they learned differently, it would be too late.

"Ah, I take exception to that appraisal. Malvius is no mere pirate, and clearly you have never been a mere thug. You were the envy of every trader on either side of the Straits. But speaking of mercenary work, I hear you've corresponded with our imperial friend in Megaria."

Indeed, Isidros had taken the bait. It had been Malvius's idea. When Vahldan had speculated about seeking a meeting with Isidros, it had been Malvius who insisted that Isidros should come to them. Malvius had also suggested that even the thought of closer relations between the Gottari and the imperial government would drive Isidros to distraction. "The Rector?" Isidros nodded. "Seems wise to seek to keep our regional bureaucrats content."

"Oh, I agree. Eases their urge to be meddlesome." Isidros smirked.

"Exactly."

"Some say you've gone so far as to offer your aid in settling their Bafranii problem."

Vahldan probably shouldn't be surprised by how well the ruse had worked. Like most astute traders, Isidros made a tidy profit by dealing with both sides of any regional conflict, and the one in Bafrana would be no exception. "A small gesture. And somewhat self-serving. After all, putting down upstart pirates can only promote prosperous trade." Not so desirable for those who carry out secret deals with pirates, but still.

"Have a care, my friend," Isidros said. "It will be no small risk, inserting your men in Bafrana. They say the sadhu himself is afraid of his own subjects. It's become a very dangerous place, by all accounts."

Vahldan leaned back. "My men are used to danger. I have a feeling it will work out."

"Makes me wonder when you might send them. Certainly not before your upcoming wedding?"

The man never stopped digging. Vahldan wondered how much to reveal, and how fast to reveal it. Today might be his only chance. If there was a chance Isidros could be made an ally, it might be worth the risk of oversharing. Depending on to whom Isidros then revealed what he learned. "Of course not."

"And then comes hiatus. Certainly you don't mean to wait till spring."

"Of course not," he repeated.

"I see." Isidros sipped his wine. "And whenever you do sail, you will use Malvius's fleet to transport your army?"

"Of course. Why would I seek elsewhere than my own harbor for ships?" Was it just his rivalry with Malvius that had Isidros's blood up? Did using Malvius make things look better or worse for the rival anax?

Isidros stared into his wine. "No reason. I mean, after his father's death, I presumed... Ah, forget I spoke of it."

Vahldan frowned. "You of all people should know that Malvius is a realist. He would never allow sentiment to keep him from profit. Even when a bit of bloodshed is one of the costs of the transaction."

Isidros's eyes flashed with anger, and the ugliness fluttered in Vahldan's belly. "We three are much alike in that way," the anax calmly stated. "And the gods know there is much profit yet to be reaped." The Hellain's grin returned, but it was not so warm as it had been.

"I can argue with neither statement," Vahldan said. "Though I also wish only for what is best for Pontea. Or at least what's beneficial for us all."

Isidros ignored the addition. "I am merely glad for both you and our mutual friend that after all that's happened you can trust him so well."

"Malvius and I have always understood one another. I know I can trust him well enough to always do what's best for Malvius."

Isidros's smile warmed again. "Just as he can trust you. And just as you and I can trust one another." Vahldan supposed the sentiment was nothing new here in Pontea.

He tilted his head in concurrence. "As I hope it always remains, Anax Isidros."

"As do I. But enough about our mutual friendship. Besides conveying my well-wishes for your marriage, I also came in the hopes we can be of service to one another."

Ah, now they were getting to it. "How so?"

"I have a sense, old friend, that you are on the verge of an endeavor."

"In Bafrana? As I said—"

"My sense is that you have something larger in mind. Perhaps much larger." Vahldan opened his mouth to speak, but Isidros held up a halting hand, saving him the trouble of dissembling. "No need to confirm my suspicions, for they are merely that—suspicions. But just in case I am right, I merely wish to avail myself. I've come to trust that any endeavor of Lord Vahldan the Bold is worthy of my betting on its success."

"I'm... flattered." He still hated the moniker, but maybe it was serving him well.

"I am willing to offer more than flattery. I image that you already have substantial chits in your possession—certainly one from Malvius. And I would venture you hope to collect a chit from one side or the other in Bafrana as well, regardless of whatever deal you may have made with the rector. In any case, your collection of chits bodes well for your position in Pontea's future. And, since I fancy myself a wise bettor, I wish not to be left out when it comes time for you to collect."

Vahldan finished his wine. "You seem confident about my chits. What of yours?"

Isidros raised his cup in salute and finished it. "I suppose the chit I've held longest would be the one which would interest you most: my city. The reason I hold that chit is because my city needs my ships and my men. Regardless of any imperial presence. Or lack of it. If you see my meaning." Isidros's smile was the oiliest yet. "I came to lay my chit on the table, old friend."

"It's an impressive offer. Mind if I ask why you would extend it?"

"Because I know you, Lord Vahldan. I know you well enough to sense you're about to make one of your bold moves. And I sense that when you do, there will be an unprecedented potential for profit in the offing. Knowing me as you do, you can be sure I am not likely to pass on the chance to reap a percentage. But perhaps even more importantly, I sense that someone's blood is about to be spilled. And I dearly wish to ensure it is not mine."

Vahldan leaned in. "What a coincidence. For some time now, I've been considering asking you to help me make sure it's not mine."

AFTER LINGERING SULLENLY, scrubbing halfheartedly at her husband's bloodstain, Ligaia gave up on its removal once again. She worked backward from the spot, hand mopping the final section of the floors to the entryway of her stolen residence. Still on her hands and knees, she opened the door and backed her way into the corridor, pulling the wash bucket with her. Though the thug lord had banished most of her beautiful things from the space, Ligaia still prided herself on keeping it spotless. After all, one day it would be hers again.

She finished and turned to wring out the fleece. She gasped and lurched back. The little witch had snuck up on her again. The white-haired waif was standing behind her in what appeared to be a sleeping shift, holding a bundle of white woolens under one arm and a flagon in the other hand. "Gods, you startled me."

"Didn't you claim to have washed these?" The nasty little creature threw the bundle on the floor before Ligaia. "Or did I mishear you?"

The bundle was the waif's robes. Ligaia stood to face her. "You heard right, Lady Amaga." She refused to refer to the waif as a priestess. And although she was as tall as Ligaia, she was as thin as a swamp reed. Amaga seemed small to Ligaia, regardless of the size of her bluster. It was preposterous that a teenager just arrived from the wilderness could claim any real knowledge of life or death, let alone the nature of the gods.

"Anyone can see how dingy they are, even in this forsaken cave of stone." Amaga relished voicing her disdain for the palace. Ligaia longed for the day when the nasty little creature was well-gone from it. "Try again with this." Amaga thrust the flagon toward Ligaia.

Ligaia had no choice but to take it. Their hands momentarily touched on the handle, and the waif jerked her hand back as if she'd been burned. In the process, the liquid inside sloshed and spattered onto Ligaia's hand and wrist. The overreaction made Ligaia hate her all the more.

The smell from the flagon instantly assailed her. "This is…"

"My piss." The waif smirked, her unblinking reptilian eyes becoming even more malicious. "Seems yours isn't strong enough to get the job done. You *are* stomping it with your bare feet, are you not?"

Ligaia longed to wipe her splashed hand. "Of course, Lady Amaga." Of course, Ligaia had *not* used urine or stomped on the nasty garment. Gods, no wonder the girl stank so badly. And of course, this wasn't about dinginess. It was about little Amaga making herself seem worthy of a status no one in the palace but the servants seemed willing to give her. Apparently, the girl had been brought here to marry the thug lord. The marriage was obviously for purely political purposes. Amaga spent most of her days alone in Ligaia's former servants' quarters. This sad little creature dwelled adjacent to the life of a future husband who barely acknowledged her.

It seemed the only friend the wretched girl had in the palace was Kemella. Which put it far beyond doubt that Kemella was the kindest of all of her kind. Amaga's unacknowledged status and her terrible treatment at the hands of the Gottari brutes were the only things Ligaia had in common with her. So Ligaia didn't begrudge the waif her little victories too much. Beyond the nuisance, Amaga hardly mattered to Ligaia. There was no chance she'd ever gain the spiteful creature's trust. Not even enough to be ignored, as Ligaia was by most of the other Gottari. Even that had its uses. But bitter little Amaga was beyond usefulness.

Ligaia gathered up the robes and tucked them under her arm, picked up her bucket, and bowed. "I shall seek to do better this time."

"And make it quick. My uncle has arrived, and I'd like to wear them to dinner."

A ridiculous assertion. It would only be possible if Amaga wore them wet. "Yes, Lady Amaga." The waif needed to learn that she didn't need excuses to order around the servants. In fact, having none could make it all the more delicious.

Without making eye contact, Ligaia headed for the servants' staircase, holding the flagon as far away from her body as possible. The last thing she needed was to slop more of the waif's piss on herself. As soon as she was out of Amaga's sight, she set the bucket down, rinsed her splattered hand in the dirty wash water, and dried herself on the robes before setting out again.

On her way down, Ligaia came across Hesiod rushing up. "Oh, here you are, my lady," he said, huffing. In spite of her constant reminders not to, Hesiod persisted in addressing her as he always had. "You asked me to help keep watch for the visit of Anax Isidros. He is here."

"Where? In the palace?"

"Yes, he's in the high hall with Lord Vahldan."

"For how long? Never mind, it doesn't matter." She had to get to the stables. She hurried by the baffled manservant. In her haste, the piss sloshed onto not just her hand but her skirt, too.

Before the last set of stairs to the kitchens, Ligaia came to the servants' exit. She set the little witch's piss and her bucket on the landing. Once again, she rinsed her hand and wiped herself off with the waif's robes before flinging aside the nasty bundle of cloth. She slipped out and hurried through the gardens, keeping to the shadows and behind the hedges, making her way to the stables in stealth. Ligaia peeked inside. The stable boy on duty was a son of one of the kitchen servants. No Gottari were in sight. "Where is the anax's carriage?" she asked the lad.

"Waiting out in front of the palace, my lady."

Damn. Isidros hadn't followed her instructions. Had he even received her missive? Was he simply here by chance? Could she trust him? They'd always been fierce trading competitors. What if Isidros was in league with Malvius? Could an anax be allied with the Gottari brutes who slayed another anax? It seemed unlikely. In that regard, Malvius had to be an anomaly. As her twisted brother so often was.

Ligaia had to take a chance. She slipped one of her arms inside of her frock, to the purse she kept under the sash at her waist, and produced an imperial silver. She showed it to the boy. "Would you like to have this?" The boy's eyes sprang wide and he nodded. "It has to be earned. Which includes keeping this a secret. Can you do that?" The boy's gaze stayed locked on the valuable coin as he nodded again. "Good. Besides keeping it a secret, I need you to wait for the anax to come out. Tell him you noticed one of his horses needs a shoe. Say that you'd be glad to change it for him if he'd have his driver come by the stables. Tell him it will only take a moment and that the horse needn't be unhitched."

The stable boy frowned. "Won't he know if he needs a shoe? I'm not sure I should—"

"It doesn't matter whether he'll know or not. If he tries to turn you away, you must find a way to tell him that it was I who sent you."

The lad squinted. "I thought it was a secret."

Ligaia reined in her annoyance. "It is. You must tell the anax without letting anyone else hear our secret. Do you understand?"

The boy nodded and departed wearing a fretful expression, which made her feel the same. Ligaia couldn't quite see the palace doors from the stables without standing in the open, so she paced. It would only be a matter of time before the waif sent someone looking for her. Or before the boy flubbed and the Gottari guards came for her.

It was all such a risk. She could be waiting to be taken back to her cell. To live her remaining days with the rat in the corner.

Finally, the carriage came rolling to the stables, with the boy hurrying out ahead. Ligaia hastily straightened her loose strands of hair. Why hadn't she thought of it sooner? It was no use. Once inside, the carriage rolled to a halt. Ligaia pulled her neckline onto her shoulders, yanked her frock down, and stuck out her tits. Her chin held high, she moved into the light.

Isidros instantly saw her and stepped from the carriage. He didn't seem surprised. Ligaia hitched up the piss-splashed skirts with her pruned fingers and bowed, just deep enough to reveal her assets. "I bid you welcome, Anax."

Isidros grinned but tsked and shook his head. "Such a tragedy, Lady Ligaia. To see one so beautiful, so gracious, reduced to this."

Did she really look so bad? Feigning a lack of concern, she changed the subject. "Thank you for coming."

"How could I not?" Isidros turned to his men. "Watch both doors. No one approaches without warning." The pair nodded and parted.

The stable boy wrung his hands. Ligaia flipped him the coin, bid him to fetch water for the horses, and led Isidros into the tack room. Isidros leaned against the workbench, appraising her from head to toe. She felt herself flushing. Isidros was at least a decade older. His head was a bit grayer than she remembered. He'd always been a bit too weasel-like to be called handsome, but he did have a commanding presence, a certain masculine allure. "Seriously, my lady. How has it come to this? These brutes compel you to serve?"

Ligaia lifted her chin. "No. I was offered my freedom. Even passage to another city. I chose this." That took him aback. "Would you have me leave my home, my city, my ships, to these murderous thieves?"

Isidros raised his brows. "I'm impressed. Although I suppose I shouldn't be surprised. You always had a fire inside. More so than your brother."

"Don't speak of him," she spat. "And please, don't speak to him of this meeting. Malvius is the one who brought them here. This is all his fault."

The anax inclined his head. "As you wish."

He seemed sincere. At this point she could only press on.

"So what did you learn from the thug? Do you sense that I'm right?"

"I more than sense it. He all but told me. That madman is actually conspiring against the imperial crown."

Ligaia glanced out the tack room door. The stable boy was alone, watering the horses. She turned back to Isidros and lowered her voice. "They don't even think to try to hide it, even when they know I am in the room. They consider everything they've done and plan to do to be a part of some dire prophecy, foretold by their religious zealots."

"But to actually attack the empire? I had no idea Vahldan could be so stupid."

"No—not stupid. He should never be underestimated. It's his arrogance. His ambition." The anax's expression grew concerned. "What did you tell him?"

Isidros gave a little shrug. "I pretended I was with him. What else?"

"Did he believe you?"

"He seemed to. Although I'm not sure. You're right—the man has ever been crafty."

"The thug will believe what he wants to believe, of that I am sure. He already believes a gang of Bafranii pirates are with him. The gods know they'll turn on him the moment it suits them. The hubris among the lot of them is monumental. It's sure to be their fatal flaw."

Isidros still seemed wary. "You honestly believe Vahldan will sail off with his entire army on such a venture?"

"He's been trying to lure more warriors from his homeland, but thus far he's failed. I've heard him brag that a mere dozen of his loyal warriors could hold this city in his absence. Yes, I'm all but certain he will take the bulk of them to war, leaving Thrakius ready to be plucked like a ripe plum."

Isidros narrowed his eyes. "Even still, what you suggest entails a substantial risk."

"A risk, yes. But not a substantial one. If anything goes awry, you merely claim you came to aid Vahldan in his absence. He's so sure of himself that he's sure everyone else must feel the same about him. A little groveling and he'd send you on your way with his gratitude."

"What of the imperials?"

"The same. We wait for their return and tell them we were holding the city for them. In fact, I think we should send a message to the rector to that effect as soon as it begins."

Isidros turned from her, running his hand over a saddle. "And so, what's in it for me?"

Ligaia knew sacrificing now would offer her the opportunity to take a step toward regaining her city and her ships. And one day, perhaps Vernius would come for her. She needed time. Whatever was done now could be undone. She would do whatever it took to regain her family's legacy for her son. "In return for retaking the city, we jointly petition the imperials to name you magister of Thrakius."

Isidros rounded on her wearing a grin. "I am already magister of Nicomedya."

"Thrakius is the bigger port. And you can keep your title and ties in Nicomedya. Plus you gain another share of the imperial tariff. In addition, if you aid me in reclaiming my ships and my trading contracts, I will give you one in five on all of my future profits."

"Two in five."

Ligaia drew a deep breath. She just needed time. "Done."

She extended her hand, trying not to frown. Isidros grasped her fingers—how she hated it when men refused to offer a woman a normal handshake. "Done. And you know, we could take this alliance a step further." His grip tightened. The anax pulled her so close she feared he intended to kiss her. His nostrils flared and he blanched. He swiftly released her and backed away. Perhaps smelling of piss had its advantages.

"I am still in mourning, you know," she said.

"Of course. I lost myself for a moment."

"What else did you have in mind?"

Isidros backed away another step. "I'm sure we can work something out. Once you have your ships back, of course."

"Of course," she repeated. Isidros looked even more nervous now. But she thought what he had committed to was enough. Even if he ended up trying to out-maneuver her. Couldn't hurt to leave him with an image of what more might come. He must realize that she would bathe as soon as she could. "I can't thank you enough." She curtsied, again pulling her frock tight and pushing out her tits. "For coming to my rescue. For your willingness to insert yourself in my moment of desperate need."

The anax regained his sly grin and bowed. "It shall be a pleasure, my lady." He strode back to the carriage and whistled for his men.

As the driver slapped the reins and the carriage rolled out, Ligaia remembered the waif's washing. She spun and headed down the aisle of stalls toward the garden-side door. Movement caught her eye through the slats of the first stall, just on the backside of the tack room. She stopped short and peered in.

The boy darted to the back corner and rushed to lift a straw-covered trap door. "Agoraki?" He continued to climb in. "Wait." Halfway in, her son stopped. He was covered in soot. Lately he'd been tasked with hauling coal for the kitchens and tending the ovens. But oh, how he'd grown! He had the square chin and broad shoulders of his father and her round dark eyes. He was beautiful.

Gods, he was twelve already. Her fine son. He would be a man soon.

"You heard?" Ligaia ventured. Those dark eyes stared, wary but clever. Ligaia wanted to tell him that everything she did—all she was about to do—was for him. She wanted him to know that he was the embodiment of her remaining hope. Instead, she said, "Keep it between us? Please?"

Without answering, Vernouthus started to climb down. "Wait!" He stopped, eyeing her solemnly. "Know that your father will come for us. I will see to it. And once he does, trust that your rightful place will be restored." The boy narrowed his gaze. "Your estate, your inheritance. Your legacy. It shall be yours. I'm just asking you to be patient."

Without word or gesture, her son disappeared, the trap door softly closing over him.

THE MAKINGS OF A WARRIOR

"I have very few memories of my childhood years in Thrakius that are as clear or as powerful as those of the time spent with my uncle."—Brin Bright Eyes, Saga of Dania

THE DAMP CHILL reminded Urias that autumn was approaching. And with it, Amaga's bonding ceremony. So far he had spent much of his time in Thrakius calming one niece's jittery nerves and reassuring her that she was safe. But Urias had yet to even seek connection with the other. It weighed upon him, to have neglected such a vital aspect of his mission here.

The palace was quiet at dawn. Other than servants carrying trays, Urias saw no one. He arrived and knocked on the door, hoping he'd calculated correctly. He'd met the niece he sought, but he'd never been invited to her residence. Elan's manservant Hesiod answered, so his first step was a success—he'd knocked on the right door.

"I am sorry, Captain, but Lady Elan, she sleeps. May I gift her your words?" The manservant's Gottari was a bit off and heavily accented but serviceable.

"Actually, I came to see my niece. Is Brin available for a visit?"

Hesiod was clearly startled and seemed reluctant, but he opened the door. "Come, be indoors, Captain. The girl eats at her morning food."

Knowing Elan, Urias shouldn't have been as surprised as he was by the greenery within. Elan's chambers were filled with dozens of potted plants, some reaching to the ceiling. It was a complete departure from the rest of the palace. Indeed, the rest of the city.

The nervous Hellain led Urias out onto the chilly terrace, lined with even larger potted plants and small trees. A tarp draped between poles provided an overhead cover for a small table and chairs. The cozy spot almost felt like an open-sided pavilion in the Danian forest, but with a view of the sea. Brin sat at the table wrapped in an adult's woolen cloak, her profile lit by the sunrise. Her orange curls were the perfect blend of her mother's auburn and her father's flaxen locks. Her head was bowed to a scroll. Urias was impressed. He could read runes but had yet to master Hellainic letters. He was having a tough enough time with the spoken language.

Hesiod sighed. "Well, Bright Eyes should be at her food. Instead, she works hard at not eating, as is common." On a plate beside her were an untouched round of buttered bread and some dates. She had yet to so much as glance up from her reading. Hesiod clapped his hands, scolding her in Hellainic. The manservant switched back to Gottari. "Be of courtesy. Your uncle, he visits."

The girl's alert gaze snapped up to meet his. Urias had heard the manservant's nickname for her before, but it made all the more sense in that moment. Yes, Brin's namesake orbs were wide and bright blue, but it was more than that. The child's regard was keen and curious. "Uncle," she said. It was halfway from a greeting to a query.

"Good morning. I've come to ask if you'll join me on my morning walk."

Brin frowned. "Your walk? To where?"

"Just around the palace grounds."

"For what purpose?" Her Gottari had more of a Hellain accent than a Skolani one.

"The morning air! Exercise invigorates the blood and clears the mind. Plus, it would provide a chance for us to get better acquainted."

Hesiod cleared his throat. "Mistress Brin's tutor, she comes. At the bell."

The manservant referred to the midmorning tolling of the bell in the Seagate tower, signaling when vessels from other ports could enter the harbor and queue for unloading. "If we hurry, I can have you back by then. Come. I've already spoken to your mother, and she considers it a good idea." A slight stretch of the truth, but he doubted Elan would bother to refute it.

Brin stood and shrugged the overly large cloak from her shoulders. Fortunately, she was already dressed to go. She even had on the ankle-strapped sandals so many Thrakians wore. She popped one of the dates into her mouth and headed straight for the door. The girl was tall for her age, lean as a colt, but she moved with the assurance and grace of a well-bred filly.

Hesiod followed them to the door, nervously babbling, "It is well if Lady Elan has said yes. Remember, Bright Eyes, before bell you must come. I make no excuse for you."

"Don't worry, she's in good hands," Urias assured him.

Urias had been wise to have Brin lead the way—she took a route that he'd never taken, down a narrow back stair that he had assumed, due to the growing aroma of baking bread, led to the kitchens. At ground level, there was an exit to the garden right from the stairwell.

They walked abreast through the empty gardens. It felt awkward. Urias had no idea how to begin his mission. "So. How old are you now?" he asked. Anything to get her talking.

"I'll be nine at the solstice." The silence stretched as Urias searched for the next question. The girl broke it. "What else would you like to know, Uncle?"

She was perceptive. "Oh, I don't know. Everything about you, I guess."

She crinkled her nose. "Well, that narrows it down."

Sarcasm. And so young. At least she was witty. "Tell me about your studies."

"I've mostly been mastering my letters and learning sums and tallying, but of late Mistress Despoina has been teaching me the philosophies of the scholars and the histories of the peoples of Pontea."

Urias pointed toward the north gate. "Let's go this way. What about the history of your own people?"

"All she's told me is that the Gottari migrated from the frozen north, that they are warlike and prone to drink. But I've heard my father speak of the Amalus kings, of the wolves and their wool, and of wars with the Spali and others. I like to listen, but when he's talking with those who know more than I do, it can be hard to follow."

"And what of your mother's people?"

Brin shot him a side glance. "Mother *never* speaks of the past. I overheard something about how she was banished by her tribe. I think it's part of her sadness."

Her sadness? Urias pondered that for a moment. There was indeed a sadness, always lurking just beneath the surface.

"It's true, then?" Brin was studying his reaction.

"That she was banished? Yes." She nodded, self-satisfied. "What else do you know about her tribe?"

"I've heard mention of a queen. I think she was the one who assigned my mother to be my father's guardian. I take it Mother's people are warriors. They seem a lot like the Gottari."

Urias pointed through the open gate from the palace keep to the city's northern gatehouse. "Let's head out there. There's something I'd like to show you."

Brin stopped short, well inside the gateway. "I'm not allowed to leave the keep."

"I'll be with you." Brin looked worried. Urias said, "If we're caught, I'll take the blame."

They crossed the empty martialing court and Urias led her up the stairs to the wall-walk. The young Gottari sentinel did a double take. Urias waved and the lad nodded and turned back to his duty. Urias went to the parapet and leaned on it. Brin was tall enough to see through the lower half of the crenels. Urias pointed out across the lush vale to the mouth of the pass. Steep wooded ridges rose to either side of the roadway that disappeared into the mountain mists.

"Do you know what that is?" Brin shook her head. "It's the Pontean Pass—one of the few roadways that lead to our homeland, Dania. Do you know that your mother's tribemates, the Skolani, have guarded that roadway for many, many generations?" She shook her head again. "In fact, there are likely Skolani Blade-Wielders patrolling in those trees, within sight of the city." She laughed. "What's so funny?"

"Really? They're called Blade-Wielders?"

"Bit of an obvious name, I suppose. But at home, we're used to it. It's an esteemed title."

"So... why?" Brin asked, staring out.

"Why are they called that?"

"No, why are they guarding a road?"

"Against intrusion. They guard the entire realm."

"They watch every road?"

"Pretty much. There aren't that many of them."

"What's so special about them?"

"The Blade-Wielders?" he asked. Brin nodded. "They're only the fiercest and most skilled warriors in Dania. All Skolani train to ride and fight and scout from when they are little girls, and only the fittest among them are chosen. When they receive their blade, they swear an oath, to protect those who can't protect themselves."

Brin squinted and shielded her eyes. "I don't see any."

"You wouldn't even if you were traveling up that road. They could be just a few spans away, and still you wouldn't. Blade-Wielders are masters of stealth. They say that a mere trio of them is able not just to warn the realm of intrusion, but to either delay or decimate an entire host, such is their swiftness and prowess."

"Decimate?"

He nodded. "Yes."

"You mean they kill them?" Urias nodded again. She shuddered. "They sound horrible."

Well, that backfired. "I see what you mean. They are a bit scary. When I was a boy, they terrified me. But I always admired them. All Danians do. We're glad they're on our side."

"You're not scared of them anymore?"

He shook his head. "Especially not since I've gotten to know some of them." Urias watched her. "Your mother was once a Blade-Wielder, you know."

Brin's eyes widened, but she quickly veiled her reaction. "That figures." She glanced his way. "So my mother has killed people?"

He saw no way around it. "Our enemies, yes."

"A lot?"

"I suppose many people would say so."

"How many?"

"I'm not sure. But in war, it's kill or be killed." Brin looked away. This wasn't going as well as he'd hoped. He reminded himself that he wasn't dealing with a Gottari lad. She was a city girl. Palace life was the only life she knew. He wondered if he could steer this back on course. Brin was so damned perceptive. Perhaps a bit more openness would help.

"There is another Blade-Wielder I know—a princess. She's a dear old friend of your mother's. This princess has played a big part in taking away my fear of them. And she's part of the reason I asked you out here this morning. She asked me to send her regards to you."

"To me? How does she know about me?"

"Come." Urias led her to the lower inside parapet. He sat and patted the stone beside him. Brin hopped up and sat. "I know we're just getting to know one another, Brin. But I'd like to share a secret with you. Would that be all right?"

She looked away again. "I suppose." She felt awkward, reluctant.

"I'd like to keep it just between us, whether you decide you're interested in what I'm about to propose or not. If I tell you, you have to promise not to tell anyone—not your mother, not even Hesiod. Agreed?"

Brin considered for a moment. "Is it about the Skolani?"

"It is."

"All right. I promise." He'd succeeded in arousing her curiosity, at least.

"It has to do with the princess I mentioned. Her name is Icannes. You see, Icannes believes that someone can either be born with the skills that make them into a warrior, or—if they work hard and long enough—they can be trained to become one. But Icannes believes that a warrior who is born to her skills and who also has the dedication to pursue a lifetime of training—these few she considers a very special sort. They're the sort that become the leaders, the inspirations, the world-changers. Icannes believes these few are destined to great things."

Urias paused. Brin looked up at him, squinting against the rising sun. He lowered his voice. "Princess Icannes believes you can be one of these few, Brin."

The girl's eyes widened. "Me? She doesn't even know me."

"Icannes knows both of your parents. And their parents."

Brin turned away. "Whatever." Did she roll her eyes? "I could never kill anyone."

"I'm not talking about killing people. This is about commitment."

"Commitment to what?"

"Commitment to strengthening one's mind and body and to overcoming one's fears. For an honorable warrior, taking another human life is a last resort." His niece stared off into the distance, processing. "Brin, your parents are two of the finest warriors Dania has ever produced."

Again, she scrunched her nose. "Says who?"

Urias smiled. "Oh, most everyone agrees. Even their enemies." On this there was no need to exaggerate.

She continued to stare off into the mountains. "Were they born to it or trained?"

Good—she was paying attention. "Both," he said.

"So a princess I've never met wants me to train to kill people?"

"No. She's not interested in having you kill people. Not exactly. But yes—she believes, as I do, that focused daily training makes each of us the best we can be. It's part of why I still walk every morning. And I've been thinking that I should add more focused training to my morning routine. Something that engages all of me, body and mind."

"You mean pretend fighting, like my father's bully-boys do?"

Uh-oh. Bad example. "No, not like them." He had to be careful—she was clever. "Well, not exactly like them. Anyway, I was thinking it would be nice if you could join me as I add focus. Every day."

Brin shot him a sidelong glance. "This princess wants me to, or you want me to?"

"Both of us," Urias swiftly answered. "I admit, it was Icannes's idea. But I think it's a fine one." She gazed into the mountains again, biting her cheek. "Look, Brin, I'm not going to try to talk you into this. I'll only ask once. After this, I'll let it drop. But I promised my friend that I would at least ask."

She hopped down and faced him. "Why? I mean, what's the real reason? Why me?"

"Honestly, it's because we both want you to be the best you can be. We want you to find your own true purpose in life. And..."

"And what?" Brin glared. "Look, there's no way I'm doing this if you won't tell me the whole truth."

"All right, here's the whole truth. Princess Icannes and I—we both love your mother very much. And we think there are things you could be taught about your people and your heritage that will make you a more complete person. We think there's a chance you could play an important role in what comes next for our people. That's partly because of who your parents are. But we suspect that your mother has, well... We think your mother may have lost sight of that."

Brin snorted. "Most days I think my mother would just as soon forget I was ever born, let alone tell me about her past."

"Oh Brin, that's not true."

"Isn't it? If you didn't believe it wasn't at least partly true, we wouldn't be here, would we, Uncle Urias?"

Perceptive and clever. And brutally blunt. "I'll admit that you have a point. A little one. But still, I really do want to get to know you better. I honestly thought it would be good for both of us to—"

"When do we start?" Brin interjected, wearing her mother's pugnacious stubbornness.

Urias decided to quit while he was ahead. "Tomorrow. At first light."

PART FOUR
BRINGER OF WAR

CHAPTER 23
BONDED BY PROPHESY, BOUND BY FATE

"*It was from my mother that Vahldan first learned about the song of the Skolani Dreamers. 'And a king shall rise from among the kingless, born of exile, bound by prophesy. Forth he shall come, but back he must lead. To an age when the gods' own light shone from their favored few. In glory shall he rise, and glory shall be his song; calling to the faithful, echoing across the ages. Even in his doom shall he call them forth and lead them back, unto Urrinan. Such is the fate of the Bringer.'*

The song never strayed far from my father's thoughts. If it was the sundering of the Gottari tribe that set my parents' fate in motion, it was the bonding of Vahldan of the Amalus to Amaga of the Wulthus—along with the false restoration of the futhark that their union suggested—that bound them to it."—Brin Bright Eyes, Saga of Dania

As soon as Vahldan received word that the column had been spotted coming through the Pontean Pass, he hurried to the gate to meet them. He stood in the swirling snow, with the sea roaring through the canyon. Gods, even if Arnegern and Eldavar had succeeded,

Vahldan knew his plans could still be ruined if this weather didn't improve. Timing was everything.

"There," said Teavar, pointing. Vahldan couldn't help but smile. He'd been so anxious, for weeks. Even the giant grinned. "Hey ho!" Teavar cried and waved a massive arm. "Seems they've done it, my lord."

It certainly looked as though they had accomplished at least part of their mission. Vahldan hurried down the stairs from the wall to the marshalling courtyard with Teavar close behind. Arnegern and Eldavar led a lengthy column of riders through the gates, and behind the carriage and the supply wagon came rows of marchers as well. Arnegern raised a fist, calling the arrivals to a halt.

"We grew worried," Vahldan said.

"Apologies, my lord," Arnegern replied. "The delay couldn't be avoided."

"But you'll be pleased when you learn why," Vahldan's brother added.

"How many?" Vahldan asked.

"Twenty score," Arnegern said. "Though nearly half are in need of gear."

"Gear we have. It's men we need."

"You were right. Once we started telling the tale of the upcoming bonding of the royal clans, many were moved to join us. Even a few who'd been aligned with the wolves. Word spread, and many came to meet us as we moved from homestead to homestead."

"What of the acolyte, Sueridas?"

Arnegern nodded. "In the carriage. It's what delayed us."

Eldavar grinned. "We did one better. It's the extra bit that will please you."

A KNOCK at the bedchamber door finally ended Vahldan's ridiculous fussing over his beard. He'd botched the trimming of it. It was still uneven. Gods, why were his hands so shaky? "Come," he called, and Arnegern entered.

"Everything is in order, my lord. All are present, gathered around the circle. As soon as we arrive, he'll begin."

"Thank the gods," he said. "I can't wait to get this over and done." Vahldan brushed the whiskers from his tunic and pulled on his silk ceremonial robe. "I'll be out in a moment," he added. Arnegern tilted his head and stepped out. Vahldan drew the drinking skin from his robe pocket and swigged the distilled wine. He gasped out the vapors and blinked away the sting in his eyes. The stuff was a gift from Malvius, from faraway Iberica. It was the only thing that seemed to calm his jitters. Something about an herbal infusion, or some such. Malvius had given him some over the summer, and as soon as it had been gone, Vahldan had asked him if there was more. Malvius had seemed delighted to be asked and had brought him a small cask of the stuff a few weeks prior. Plenty to get him through these nerve-wracking days. He took a second slug, tucked it away, and stepped into the entry chamber.

"Does the old goat understand his role?" Eldavar was asking.

Arnegern nodded. "Well enough. Sueridas will be there if he gets confused."

"Sueridas has his own part to play," Vahldan pointed out.

"I'm not worried," Arnegern said. He chuckled. "Mundelan may seem feeble, but I think he's glad for the chance to twist the Wulthus teat, so to speak."

"Understandable, after spending most of his life trapped in that moldering tower with all of those mangy old wolves," Eldavar said.

"Let's hope his resentment keeps him motivated till this is done," Vahldan said. He was grateful that the young acolyte had convinced the seniormost Amalus Wise One to travel so far. But the man's dotage kept the outcome uncertain. At a rehearsal the prior evening, Mundelan had seemed to forget where he was, let alone what he was supposed to do or say.

"Do you each have your items?" Vahldan asked them.

"I do, my lord." Arnegern patted his chest reassuringly.

He turned to his brother. "Of course," Eldavar said.

"Let's be done with this, then." Vahldan knocked on the door to the adjacent servants' chambers. There was no answer. "Amaga," Vahldan called. "They're ready for us."

His betrothed opened the door. Her white priestess robes were tied with garlands of tiny flowers, as was the wreath in her hair. Where she'd gotten fresh flowers in this weather was beyond him. Vahldan's sisters had been a godsend in getting her ready. And in keeping her from falling apart, by all reports. Her attire was lovely. It was Amaga's face that took him aback. If she was normally pallid, she was utterly chalky now. Except her eyes, which were perpetually startling. They were downright scary now—puffy and ringed red, with dark bags underneath.

Vahldan actually felt for her. A bride should have her mother beside her. It was tragic that neither of their mothers would witness this. And honestly, he was feeling overwrought himself. He'd hardly slept in a fortnight.

"Promise me," Amaga croaked.

Vahldan smiled. "It's precisely what we're on our way to do, my dear."

Amaga shook her head. "No. Promise me that you still feel it— that we are meant to do this. That you are the Bringer. That we're doing this for our son." She sounded near to hysteria. Her hands were shaking worse than his, and her voice was shaky, too.

She looked so childlike. Gods, she was half his age. She needed reassurance.

"Of course," he declared. "This day has been ordained since before you were born. I'll never forget the moment your mother told me of you and of our son." Indeed, it haunted his dreams often. Sometimes he wondered if the dreams were divine reassurances or nightmares. "Believe me, no one who witnessed it could doubt Amaseila's connection to the goddess. I felt the truth of it then, and I still do. I promise, this is meant to be. Our son is depending on us."

"Is it?" she asked, her odd eyes pleading now. "Is he?"

Vahldan drew a shaky breath. "All that I have striven for since that day is about to begin. I made a promise, long ago. I intend to keep it. Same as my promise to you. I will see to the greatness and the glory of our son's destiny. As it shall be."

Amaga squeezed her eyes tight and sighed. Tears leaked from the corners. Behind her Eldavar rolled his eyes. His brother had little patience for Amaga. For that matter, other than her Uncle Urias and Kemella, few did. Vahldan probably should've had Kemella stay with her all the way through the ceremony.

"Come," he said and held out his hand.

Amaga wiped her eyes and took his hand. Hers was as cold and damp as melting snow. As usual, she grimaced, as if Vahldan's touch pained her. She looked like she was surrendering to be led to a dungeon cell. It made him feel the same. Once they were in the corridor, Vahldan beckoned Arnegern and Eldavar to lead the way.

The four of them started down the stairs in silence, Amaga fiercely gripping his hand. Vahldan felt as though he was forgetting something. He couldn't shake the feeling. At the first turn of the stairs, he glanced back. Vahldan thought he saw a flash of movement on the stairs above. He stopped and stared. There was nothing there.

Vahldan turned to head downstairs again. He became lightheaded. Flashes of light burst in the periphery of his vision. He slowed his step, gulping for air.

Amaga drew him on, oblivious. The dull roar of voices grew as they descended. The crowd fell silent when they came into view. The terrace outside the high hall was packed. Indeed, the entire palace below seemed filled with faces, all turned to appraise him and his bride.

Vahldan stopped on the stairs. "Hold on a moment." He reached inside his robe, turned to face the stairs, and slipped the stopper off of the skin. He took a long pull. Amaga stared at him, aghast. He proffered it. "Might help," he suggested. His bride turned away, her lips pressed tight. Vahldan took her hand again and she stiffened. At least she didn't try to pull away.

"Lead on," Vahldan called to his groomsmen. Arnegern and Eldavar started into the crowd, folks stepping clear of their way into the cavernous entry hall.

Familiar faces stood out from the crowd, so many Vahldan couldn't put names to them all. It was bewildering. He felt like he should sort them out, pay heed. It was impossible.

The circle came into view. His family and most loyal followers lined the first row, holding hands a few steps back from the newly sanctified space. His sisters, Kemella and Mara, stood at the western end, along with Amaga's Uncle Urias. Mara held her infant son, Ragnavar. Standing along the south circumference behind the Elli-Frodei were Eldavar's pregnant wife, Sairsa, and their toddler son, Rohdric. Beside them, his cousins Belgar and Herodes stood with their growing families. Teavar and Jhannas stood flanking the empty space left for the betrothed. Just behind his family, his scribe Attasar stood with dignitaries from throughout Pontea as well as dozens of prominent Hellains of the city of Thrakius.

Not for the first time, Vahldan wished his parents were alive to see this. His father would be so proud. All of Angavar's hopes would soon be realized. Today would mark the death of Wulthus dominion and the beginning of the end of the guild's oppression of the Gottari.

The hum of conversation receded as he and Amaga reached the circle. Vahldan gave his betrothed's clammy hand to her uncle at the western end of the circle. Then he and his groomsmen circumvented to the far end. Anxiety seized him anew. The feeling of having forgotten something returned. He was drawn to look up. The railings of the two floors above were lined with staring faces. Dizziness spiraled to nausea. He looked down, gulping for air.

He forced himself to look to the far side of the circle. Freya's grace, was that scrawny, bug-eyed girl really his betrothed? Could she really give birth to his prophesied son?

At Sueridas's prodding, Mundelan stepped into the circle. The hunched and aging Amalus Elli-Frodei thumped his rune staff three times. The packed hall went silent. The old man grunted and wheezed, and Vahldan hoped he wouldn't break wind. "I call upon Amaga of the Wulthus and Vahldan of the Amalus." Mundelan's voice was surprisingly strong. "If you both seek a sacred and binding union, step forth. Present yourselves before both Freya and those who shall witness your oaths of binding. Will you both freely enter the portal of this sacred circle?"

Vahldan was pleased. Mundelan actually sounded like a spiritual authority.

Both he and Amaga replied that they would. The old lion indicated for them to take up their candles and beckoned them to him. Vahldan bent to retrieve the candle. His head swam. He stumbled forward, barely managing to catch himself. The room swirled around him. The faces blurred and spun. Everything seemed to shift. Had he really stepped into the spirit world?

Mundelan's concerned face appeared in Vahldan's field of vision. "All is well, my lord?"

"All is well, Wise One," Vahldan said. Amaga stood stiff, eyes boring into him. "Please, let us continue."

The old man softly slapped his and Amaga's shoulders with cedar boughs. He then sprinkled them with salted water. Sueridas handed Mundelan a horn of strong mead. The old man poured a bit on the floor at the circle's center and waved for them to step closer. As one, he and Amaga stooped with their candles. Vahldan's world spun again. He stumbled again, and this time he fell to his knees. His candle hit the floor, the wick touching the liquid, which burst into flame. He yanked his hand back and got his feet back under him.

He'd lit the fire without her. They were supposed to have lit it in unison. He'd botched the ceremony. She scowled and he shrugged. He motioned for Mundelan to continue. They just had to get through this.

As the fire he'd set burned down, Mundelan continued, "The past is now aflame. You are forever changed on this day. Nothing remains behind you. There is only your future path to one another and the journey you will henceforth make together." The flames sputtered out and the Elli-Frodei pulled them onto the scorched spot. "You step into this new world not as Vahldan, not as Amaga, but as one— a pair consecrated by Freya. Together you shall..."

Vahldan's mind drifted as the old man blathered on about the need for love and devotion and loyalty in forming an enduring union. The unease—the feeling that he'd neglected something vital —returned, stronger than ever. It pressed against him, threatening to steal his breath. The feeling emanated from a presence above him, urgently beckoning. Vahldan ventured looking up again, seeking that which would not relent. This time, his eyes were drawn right to her. A numbing shudder jolted him and his throat constricted.

Elan stood at the rail, her auburn hair aglow in the torchlight.

He hadn't seen her in weeks. All they'd done since they'd returned from Dania was fight. So, of course, he'd been avoiding her. But at the end of their last fight, he'd told her in no uncertain terms. The gods had demanded this union, and their people expected it. There was no choice in the matter. But he'd also told her that it would never change his feelings for her.

She hadn't spoken another word. But her seething rage had been palpable.

His ability to breathe returned, and he gasped. The rest of the world fell away. Ah gods. He found himself wishing he still sensed rage from her. Instead, the depths of her sadness and pain pressed down upon him. Mother's mercy, she was beautiful. An awareness hit him. Vahldan suddenly knew he would never love another. It felt like his soul had converged with hers, to jointly mourn their loss.

"Who has brought the tie that binds?" Mundelan's voice boomed, drawing him back.

"I have." Arnegern drew the red rope from his robes, and Mundelan shuffled to fetch it.

Vahldan looked back up, but it was too late. Elan was gone. His head spun again.

He nearly left to chase after her. A hand grasped his wrist.

"The time has come to face your future," Mundelan said forebodingly, and Vahldan knew it for the truth.

BRIN FOLLOWED MORE CAREFULLY after her father nearly spotted her on the stairway as he headed down. She stayed back and tried to keep quiet. She had no choice but to spy. Her mother had forbidden her from even mentioning tonight's party. Hesiod finally let it slip that it was some sort of a ceremony for her father. When Brin had pestered Hesiod for more, even *he* became cross, which was rare.

Hesiod said that what was happening was something that only a parent could—and should—explain to a child. Which meant that no one would explain it to her. It also made her suspect that it wasn't good. Or at least that he thought it would upset her.

All of it made Brin more curious.

Once her father and the others got to the floor above the high hall, Brin stopped. The landing below was too crowded for her to go on without being caught. She crawled along the railing on the terrace above. From here she could see the landing outside the high hall and down into a portion of the entry hall. She peered through the balusters as she went, trying to see. Her father led Whitey Frog-Eyes to the circle Brin had seen the servants setting up in the entry hall. The rest of Brin's family stood next to the circle in front of a crowd of others. From where she was, Brin could only see half of the circle. Her uncle stood at the far end, facing her. Father walked arm-in-arm through the crowd and left Whitey with Uncle Urias. Her father moved on to the opposite end. It seemed the ceremony was beginning, but from here Brin couldn't tell what it was all about.

The droning voice of the fat old priest (or at least that's what she thought he was) echoed up to her. He sort of ran all of his words together, so she only caught about half of what he was saying. The priest brought Whitey Frog-Eyes and Brin's father together in the center of the circle. Whitey and her father had candles. Her father bent but stumbled. His candle lit a fire on the floor between them. It smelled like the burnt stuff Heliopa made the serving girls scrape out of the ovens once a month.

The priest was mumbling again. Whitey and Father stood face to face. She strained to hear but still couldn't. It seemed so serious. Not knowing made Brin's belly all fluttery, like when the bully-boys teased her. Brin crawled along the railing to the stairway and peeked down.

Right below her, Brin's mother was at the railing on the terrace outside the high hall, looking down on the circle below. Her mother suddenly went stiff, her back snapping straight and her hands flying to her chest. From behind, it looked like she'd been hit in the chest with an arrow. Her mother turned from the rail, her mouth gaping like a fish spilled onto the dock.

An icy wave crashed over Brin, and she shivered all over. Her mother was hurting.

It was like seeing her mother naked, but instead of seeing too much skin, Brin could see Elan's sadness stripped naked. Brin knew it was always there, but her mother kept it covered up. Until now.

Brin always suspected that her mother's sadness came from her father. Now she saw that it had something to do with Whitey, too. Seeing her mother suffering like this made Brin feel ashamed. Elan wouldn't want her to see it. Which made Brin sad, too. It felt unfair. She couldn't even try to comfort her own mother. Elan wouldn't have it. Trying would get ugly.

The whole thing made Brin mad. The fluttering in her belly came back.

Her mother staggered from the railing like a sleepwalker. Elan was coming toward the stairs, moving fast now. Brin scurried to huddle in the shadows alongside the next stairway. Elan ran right past to continue up the stairs, taking two at a time.

Brin sighed and was briefly seized by another shiver. Then she heard it. "Psst." She jumped and turned to the sound coming from behind her. The door to the servants' corridor was cracked, revealing a face. A boy's face. It wasn't one of the bully-boys, thank the gods. This was the boy who hauled coal for the kitchens. He never spoke to her, but she caught him looking all the time. He usually looked away when she stared back. This time he waved her over. She shook her head, pointing to the ceremony below. The boy rolled his eyes, nodded, and waved again.

Brin stood and tiptoed closer. "I want to see what happens," she whispered.

"Then come with me." He held the door wider.

She tentatively stepped inside, and Coal Boy was off, hurrying down the dark corridor, holding a lamp. The door closed behind her. His was the only light. Brin could either follow, stand in the dark, or go back out. She followed.

VAHLDAN FELT dazed and stared into the ancient Elli-Frodei's shadowy face. He gasped as it morphed into his father's. "The time has come to seize your destiny."

He squeezed his eyes shut. When he opened them, Mundelan reappeared. The old man held Amaga's wrist as well as his. Mundelan tugged his hand toward hers. The old fool sought to tie them together. It seemed ridiculous—unfair even. Vahldan realized that Arnegern had an arm around him, holding him in place. There would be no escape from this future. A future that now seemed so hastily chosen. Was he doing this for the right reasons?

He gazed around the circle. Everyone smiled, but he could feel the tension in their faces. He looked at Eldavar last. His brother nodded, eyes hard. Eldavar looked so much like their father. Again, he heard Angavar's final command echoing through the hall. *'Seize your destiny.'*

Vahldan relented. His hand touched Amaga's. Energy surged from the connection, searing without burning. A current flowed from his hand up his arm. He longed to yank away, to run to Elan. His legs went limp, but Arnegern held him firmly. Mundelan looped the rope around their hands, drawing it tight. Sweat dripped into his eyes and he couldn't catch his breath.

"I bind you in the name of Freya, our patron goddess," Mundelan boomed. Vahldan could hardly see the old man. Trying was like peering through amber. Then he felt like he was falling, dangling in a vacuum from his bound hand. The faces of the onlookers blurred and fell away. There was only Amaga, glaring. Now she began to morph. Only her eyes remained unchanged. Her white hair became a wreath of flame, swept by a wind that didn't exist. Her face grew beautiful and yet terrible, smooth and yet ancient, angry and yet rapturous.

"Freya, help me," Vahldan gasped. He wanted to flee but couldn't move.

"*I am here, Bringer.*" The voice resonated, filling his head, reverberating in his chest. "*Long years have passed since you made your pledge. **The time has come.**"*

"What is it you want of me?" His own voice sounded so weak, so timid.

"*Urrinan! Urrinan for my people.*"

"I am trying, oh goddess."

"*You falter. Do you seek to escape destiny?*"

He bristled, the ugliness surging to rise from his belly. "No."

Her smile grew, wicked and yet approving. "*Ah, there it is. Fear it no longer. Use it.*"

"Use what?" He suddenly knew. "Use the ugliness? For what?"

"*To feed! For you are the lion! Feed and sacrifice in my name.*"

"What sacrifice do you require?"

"***Blood!***" The resound of Her voice became a force, driving him to his knees. She towered over him. "*Take what is yours. Heedless, without regret. Give yourself over to it. Feed and revel in the glory that shall live in your name, your legacy, unto the ages. Know that the price has already been set.*"

"What price?"

*"Doom, lion. **Doooom**."* As the final word echoed, the image faded. The terrible presence morphed into a scrawny, pale girl. Amaga was cowering beside the Wise One, rubbing her wrist and looking terrified.

Vahldan was still on his knees. Everyone was staring. He had the cord clenched in his fist. Arnegern was kneeling beside him, an arm around him. "Are you well, my lord?"

"Did you not see it?"

"Of course," Arnegern said, his brow creased. "I tried to catch you, but you fell."

"But did you hear her?"

Arnegern bent to whisper, "I think she cried out like that because you hurt her wrist." Amaga visibly trembled, rubbing her wrist. Vahldan turned to appraise Arnegern. "When you dropped down, you yanked the tie from her wrist. I'm sure it was an accident, my lord."

"How long has it been?"

Arnegern looked puzzled. "You merely blacked out. Just a moment ago."

"So, you didn't see or hear any of it?"

Arnegern frowned. "I'm not sure what you mean, my lord. But come now. Everyone is waiting. Here, let me help you." Arnegern pulled him to his feet. Vahldan looked around the hushed hall. Every face was full of concern or shock. Many even looked fearful. Particularly Amaga, who was clutching Mundelan. "Ready to carry on?" Arnegern asked. Without waiting for a response, his friend nodded to Eldavar, who gently brought Amaga back into position. Then both his brother and Arnegern nodded to the Wise One.

Mundelan seemed relieved and raised his voice to the crowd. "My fellow Gottari, I present to you the long-foretold union of wolf and lion. The futhark is restored in this fine coupling. With their bonding comes a return to what once was pure and true for our people." The Elli-Frodei turned to Eldavar. "Do you have them?" Vahldan's little brother nodded and reached into his robe.

His brother handed the iron circlets to Mundelan. Arnegern kept an arm around his lower back, urging him to stand tall. Mundelan held the circlets high and stepped to him. Eldavar put his hands on Amaga's shoulders, guiding the baffled-looking bride to Vahldan's side. "And now, my lord and qeins, I bid you both to kneel." With Arnegern's aid, Vahldan sunk back to his knees. Amaga stood there, her expression moving from confusion to anger. Eldavar glowered, hissing for her to obey, pressing her shoulders. Amaga finally lowered to her knees, looking rattled and belligerent.

Mundelan held the circlets over their heads. "In the name of the futhark and of the Urrinan that hereby arrives, I proclaim Vahldan, the son of Angavar, who is the blood of the Amalus kings of old, and Amaga, who is the blood of the Wulthus of the Arrivals, as the rightful sovereigns of all the descendants of those who once pledged themselves to their royal ancestors. May you reign in wisdom and strength for long years to come. And may the gods grant you a line of heirs to lead us from Urrinan unto its promised glory."

The old man placed the circlets on his and Amaga's heads and beckoned them to rise. Jhannas let out a whoop as Arnegern helped Vahldan to his feet. The Amalus faithful cheered while the rest of the crowd politely applauded.

Sueridas stepped into the circle, holding up his hands for quiet. "You heard the Wise One," the acolyte called over the lingering applause. The hall fell silent. "This ceremony bonds two who are of the blood of the Arrivals. We, the Gottari people, are made whole again by their union. All who have pledged to the two clans of the futhark shall now name them sovereign. Let none forget the revelation of our nation's destiny, foretold by this woman's own mother. 'And a king shall arise from among the kingless, born in exile, bonded by prophesy.'"

A murmur ran through the crowd. Amaga's cheeks became scarlet. Vahldan's new qeins gasped for breath like a runner after a race.

Sueridas went on. "This man is the blood of the Amalus kings of old. Already has he led us back to glory. That he is the Bringer is beyond all doubt. We who pledge ourselves to this union, to this restoration of the futhark, can now proclaim it so. What say you?"

The Amalus cheering ran back through the cavernous space and only seemed to grow as Eldavar took Vahldan by the wrist and raised his hand overhead. "All hail King Vahldan!" his brother bellowed. Vahldan's head started to spin again.

"Hail King Vahldan!" came the echoing refrain.

Gods, it was done. Vahldan knew what he needed. He reached into his robes, pulled out the skin, turned, and grasped the stopper. He tipped it up and looked into the face of Amaga. She held the circlet in her hands. Tears streaked the cheeks of a face contorted to an animalistic snarl. "How could you?" Amaga cried. "You promised me."

"I promised this was meant to be." Vahldan put the stopper back and took a step toward her. "I promised you a son."

"And you've already supplanted him," she spat and threw the circlet at his feet. Vahldan's new qeins spun to scurry into the crowd, disappearing from view.

BRIN HURRIED after Coal Boy's light, following him through the maze of dark servants' corridors. She turned a corner to find him kneeling near a low stone arch. She thought arches like that were old drains of some sort. The boy went to his elbows and knees and slithered through, pushing the lamp ahead of him. Again, Brin was left in the dark. How had she gotten herself into this? The boy's head popped back through. "This way," he said and disappeared again. Brin still hesitated. "Don't worry," his voice echoed from the depths. "It gets bigger." She frowned. His arm snaked out and waved for her to follow. "Hurry," he urged.

Brin wasn't sure why, but she obeyed, dropping down to crawl to the light. The stone was cold and felt grimy with old dust. The space beyond smelled of damp and moss, with a faint whiff of piss. The boy hadn't misled her—on the far side she was soon able to stand, but only just. The gap between the stone walls wouldn't easily accommodate an adult. He started moving, straddle-stepping, keeping his chest turned sideways as he went. There was nothing to do but follow. Brin looked back to find the little drain arch fading from view. She wondered if she should go back, but remembered how dark the corridor had been. On she followed.

Brin was glad when the space between the walls grew wider and taller. The boy led her to what seemed like a narrow stairwell that ran around the outside edge of a pitch black hole before them. It was impossible to know how deep it was. When Coal Boy started hopping down, Brin got so scared it was hard to breathe. He whisper-called for her to follow, and even that echoed. Again, he was leaving her in darkness. She went to the edge. There was no handrail, and each stair was tall. The only way she could follow was to sit on her butt on each step till her feet touched, then scooch to the next step and do it again, keeping herself as close to the outer wall as possible.

The boy got far ahead of her again, but he stopped at the bottom and waited. As soon as she was down, he started again. They moved through another corridor. She kept having to wipe away cobwebs that touched her face. The stuff between the big square stones in here had oozed out and dried that way, never to be wiped. At least this part had plenty of headroom. The air seemed fresher here, too.

The gap between the walls suddenly widened, and Coal Boy stopped next to a wooden trap door at the crest of the curving rise in the stone floor. The corridor ahead was bigger—it seemed made for adults. He pointed down. "The entry tunnel to the main hall is right below. I heard they made this door to pour boiling oil on invaders." His eyes were lit up, like the thought excited him. It chilled her. He sat his lamp at the top of the curving stone floor, turned, and scrambled right down the far side. He waved her down. "Hurry. You can see everything from over here."

Brin's sandals slipped and she braced herself with her hands on either side. Coal Boy grabbed her elbow and pulled her closer than she liked. He smelled of the ovens. He nodded for her to look toward the wall before them. There were narrow slots between the stones, about as long as her forearm and as wide as her fist. She peered out, startled to find a view looking right over the heads of the guests.

There, directly ahead and incredibly near, was the circle. The ceremony.

She spotted a cord connecting her father to Whitey Bug-Eyes by their wrists. The fat priest was droning on again. The scene felt like a weird dream. She could see her father's face now. He looked upset, almost like the cord was causing him pain. Her father's legs suddenly gave out. "Freya!" he cried, and he dropped to his knees, hard. Everyone gasped, and Brin realized she had, too. Captain Arnegern lunged to get an arm under him, but too late. He fell sideways, pulling Arnegern over with him. The cord was yanked from Whitey's wrist and she fell against the old priest. Whitey's shriek sounded more like she was scared than hurt. She huddled by the priest, who didn't bother to comfort her. She stared wide-eyed at Brin's father, who stared back. They both seemed horrified by the other. Her father looked like a rabbit caught in the open, watching a raptor swoop down to seize him. Arnegern struggled to lift her father and Whitey clung to the priest, like a child clutching a distracted nanny's robes. She looked like she thought Vahldan was about to come after her, even though he seemed just as scared as her.

The old priest didn't seem to know what to do as Arnegern spoke softly to her father, who was gasping for air. Her father finally seemed more himself. Vahldan whispered to Arnegern and pointed at Whitey. Arnegern shook his head and spoke like Hesiod did to Brin when she woke from a nightmare. Arnegern held on to her father and Uncle Eldavar wrapped an arm around Whitey and coaxed her away from the priest. The two helpers nodded for the old priest to carry on. He did, as if nothing weird had happened.

The priest droned on a bit, and then Brin was shocked again when he pronounced them a bonded couple. How could he bond with someone in addition to Brin's mother? Was that even allowed? Then Brin knew: This was what they'd all been hiding from her—why her mother was in such pain. A renewed current of resentment morphed into the purest hatred and flowed through her. How could he hurt her mother like this? Why would he be doing this with Whitey? A moment before he had looked scared of her. And Whitey had felt the same about him! Why was this happening?

Brin's mind kept whirling as the old priest bid her father and Whitey to kneel and he put metal rings on their heads. The old man said something about an heir, about the Bringer and the Urrinan. Adults talked about this stuff all of the time, but Brin still didn't quite know what it was all about. When they stood and the priest raised their hands overhead, the crowd cheered.

The shocks continued when the younger priest that had been hovering as near as he could to her father stepped into the circle. The young priest shouted a bunch of stuff like he was in charge, and at the end, he called her father a king. More than once, her father had said he didn't want to be a king, but even before now, Brin had known that he'd been lying. She could always tell with him. For someone who lied as much as Vahldan did, he wasn't very good at it. Even now, the look on his face told her that this whole thing was nothing but a big lie.

Brin knew her father thought Whitey was gross just like she did. He could barely stand the sight of her. Whenever he had to deal with her, he looked like he was being forced to drink his milk, and that it was beginning to spoil.

Uncle Eldavar called, "All hail King Vahldan!"

They all cheered and it echoed through the boy's secret corridor. Even as the crowd carried on, Whitey Frog-Eyes said something mean to Vahldan. Brin could tell. Whitey said mean things all of the time. She was good at it. Whatever she said, it stopped him cold—shocked him, even. Good. He deserved it. They deserved each other.

Whitey ran off and no one even seemed to care. The cheering faded to a bunch of talking over other talking. She watched her father as his men slapped his back and patted his shoulders. They always pretended he was the best thing that ever happened, but most of them seemed to actually believe it tonight. Someone handed him a goblet. He smiled, but Brin saw he was rattled. Maybe even sad. Maybe as sad as her mother. Good. He deserved it.

Coal Boy said, "Looks like we gained a king and a queen, all in one day."

Brin drew back from the slot to look at him. "A queen? Whitey?"

"Yep. Seems it's just as they've been saying."

Brin had no idea what he meant. "What have they been saying?"

"That he brought her here to marry her. That he had to marry her so he could name himself a king. Something about clans in the old country."

"Gods, he married her," she said, realizing it was true. "So he could be a king." It made perfect sense. Brin leaned against the wall, then slid down till she was sitting.

The boy snorted. "Why else would he marry *her*?"

Brin hugged her knees. "It's why she came," she said. "To be a queen."

"Why else?" he asked. "She seems to hate it here."

Brin knew Coal Boy was right. It finally all made sense. It was why her father had gone to Dania, why he'd brought Whitey back. And it was all tangled up with her mother's sadness.

Brin felt the tears dripping from her chin before she realized she was crying. The boy was staring at her, his smile gone. She turned from him and wiped her face with her tunic sleeve.

"Look, I get it, Brin," Coal Boy said, sounding awkward. She shot him a look. His cheeks had gone pink. He seemed to actually care how she felt, same as Hesiod or Uncle Urias. "It is Brin, right?" She nodded. "You know me?" He pointed to himself. Unable to speak, she shrugged. "Call me Ago," he said, patting his chest, putting on a fake smile.

Ago slid down to sit, leaning against the opposite wall. "Anyway, I get it. He's your father, right?" She scowled and looked away, but he kept talking. "I can see it in you. Some say you're not his, that he lets your maaman say it's so just to keep the old hens quiet. But I can see it's true. He's your pap, all right." Brin met his gaze, trying to convey her fury.

"Hey," he said, holding up open palms, "it's the same with me. I hear them whisper. Except with me it's true. I know my maaman isn't my real one. I mean, look at me. Anyone can see I'm no Sass. I'm way too pale. Anyway, I finally figured out who my real one is. But Maaman says my real one is evil. She says I should want naught to do with her. And plenty say your pap is evil, too. So I get how stuff like this makes you feel. Like you swallowed ash, and it makes you a little sick. And sometimes it gets blown into a swirl inside. And sometimes when it blows, there's a few sparks in there, and it all starts to glow and even burn. And you wish it'd just go out, but it won't."

Brin realized she was staring, amazed by how wise he suddenly seemed. Ago smiled. "It doesn't mean you and I are evil. We're not them, Brin." The flickering lamplight lit half of his face, and he almost looked like a beardless adult.

"I don't know who I am," she blurted, and the fullness of her own words hit her like another wave, pushing her over and pulling her back out to sea.

He reached out, his hand thicker than a boy's should be. "Neither do I," he said softly. "So we should stick together." He gestured to get her to take his hand. She did. It was rough, scratchier than Hesiod's or her uncle's. And strong. It held her from being swept away.

Ago stood holding her hand and they listened to the happy voices below. She wondered how much older Ago was than her. Not too much. She'd seen his mother, and what he was saying was now as obvious as could be. Funny but it had never occurred to her before.

Ago finally said, "Bad things are coming, you know. Worse than this."

Brin pulled her hand from his. "What's that supposed to mean?"

He leaned to her. "I hear things. I'm not sure what, but it's going to be bad. Maybe as bad as when your father first came. Maybe worse. But don't worry. This time I know lots more places to hide. I know how to get around. I even know a few ways to get out. All the way out."

"Out of where?"

Ago indicated their surroundings. "The palace. Even out of the city, if we need to. So don't worry. When the bad stuff happens, I'll come for you."

"You will?" she asked, feeling surprisingly relieved and grateful.

"Of course. We're not them."

CHAPTER 24
TRYING BINDS

THE CELEBRATION WENT on into the night. The flask in the pocket of Vahldan's ceremonial robe—with the special wine Malvius had gifted him—was empty. It hardly mattered. He couldn't recall the last time the jeweled goblet someone had put into his hand had been less than half-full. Every time he turned, someone was refilling it. His Rekkrs had all insisted on toasting him with their newest and most potent alcoholic finds. Most of them had either passed out on the tables and chaises or disappeared. Even Mighty Teavar was face down on the high hall's long table, snoring. Vahldan's siblings and first cousins and their families had been among the first to retire.

Amazingly, after the dizzying ceremony, Vahldan had drifted into a second wind. He had no idea how far off dawn was, but he had no desire to return to his residence.

It might have been partly due to the dread he had for facing his angry little qeins.

That was beside the point. Vahldan had been waiting for this day for so long, he wasn't about to let his spooky, scrawny wolf priestess spoil it. Everyone else seemed happy. Everyone else seemed to rejoice in having him as their king. Rightfully, Amaga should've been smiling quietly at his side. Nothing about bonding with her was as it should be.

He should've known. The girl was Thadmeir's offspring, after all. After all of these years, the stickler and the wolves were still finding ways to ruin all that was good. For Vahldan, and for their people. He refused to let them. This was his night, his triumph.

None of them had believed he could pull it off. No one had believed he would live up to his father. He'd already surpassed Angavar's wildest dreams. And he was only getting started.

Vahldan stood to mingle but then stopped short. His head was swimming again. He leaned on a table and fixed his gaze on the stairwell outside the high hall's doors. He held his half-full goblet to his chest and wove through the remaining revelers. He made it to the banister without stumbling or spilling. Ah—another spot to lean. He held the rail, waiting for the spinning to subside. In the hall below, dozens of servants still circulated with flagons of his favorite wines and trays of his favorite delicacies. Maybe food would help. He set out again.

For staying upright and mobile he relied heavily on the handrail. Somehow he made it down the stairs. Fewer of the faces down here were familiar. Still, the revelers made way for him, some even bowing as he wandered past, searching for a servant with a food tray. The Hellain merchants and foreign dignitaries greeted him with a sort of reverence. They praised and toasted him as he floated through. It felt better than he'd dared to imagine. Turns out, being addressed as *my king* or *Your Highness* was easy on the ears.

His fixation on food was interrupted by an urgent pressure in his bladder. He suspected that a bit of fresh, cold air would do him some good as well and headed for the terrace over the garden to relieve himself. But as he came to the rail, a cheer rose from below. More revelers mingled in the garden. They nearly filled the entire torch-lit keep, actually. Seemed the whole damn city had come. He raised his cup in salute, and the cheering crested. Seemed no one was leaving until the food and wine ran out. Vahldan supposed he couldn't blame them. The fact that it hadn't yet was likely the reason they were cheering him.

Their enthusiasm didn't solve his pressing problem, however. It wouldn't do to piss on his new subjects. At least not on his first day of kingship. He spun away, heading back inside. Time to find a privy. Vahldan was sure there must be privies down in the kitchens and larders, but he didn't know the way to any. He was only sure of the location of one. Much as he hated the thought, he supposed he'd have to go up to his residence—at least briefly. Perhaps he could slip in and back out without being noticed. Perhaps Amaga was in her own quarters. Surely she would be more rational in the morning.

Vahldan made his way back through the crowded entry hall, heading for the stairs. He rounded the balustrade, focused on the first step, and collided with a young woman coming down. He put his hand out to keep himself from falling and it landed on her breast. It wasn't just any breast. It was an ample one, well-displayed by the low cut of a fine Bafranii frock.

"Forgive my clumsiness, my king," she said.

His gaze rose to a pretty face with full lips and rosy cheeks. She was obviously Gottari; she had no accent and her hair was a brighter shade of red than Elan's. Her eyes sparkled with mirth. And perhaps other secrets as well. "Nonsense. Your lovely breast has saved me from falling. I feel lucky to have stumbled onto it."

To her credit, not only did she seem unoffended, she leaned in to give him a better view. "If ever a whim occurs for which the rest of me can be put to service, my king, I beg you to indulge it." Her breath was warm and laden with wine. This beauty was obviously as drunk as he was. Well, that might be an overstatement. He doubted anyone was as drunk as he was.

"Funny you should say. A number of whims have already occurred to me. But I fear there is an issue that overrules them all. I must hurry on my way."

"Must you? May I join you?"

Could kingship really be this wonderful? Of course it was. And he deserved every bit of the decadence the position provided. He'd earned this. "Only if you also need the privy. And soon. It wouldn't do for a new king to piss himself on the night of his being risen."

She smiled slyly, took his hand, and slid under his arm, pulling his hand over her shoulder and laying it on her breast with a pat. "Then allow me to start by serving as a prop. I'm sure I can keep you erect, my king."

Had she really said that? All Vahldan could do was grin in response. By the time they reached the high hall terrace, he realized just how much he needed her to navigate the way. By the fourth stairway, he realized he'd never have made it alone. She was tall but shapely, soft yet muscular. She smelled nice, too. All very pleasant things, in the moment, but she was more than pleasant and useful. She was all but essential, practically carrying him by the time they arrived outside his residence.

Vahldan didn't recall the names of either of the young guards outside his residence. Thankfully they averted their eyes and said nothing as one opened the door. His savior helped him in and the guard pulled the door shut behind them. She led him to the privy and directly to the shoot. He looked around for somewhere to set down his cup. She said, "Allow me, my king." He thought she would take the cup. Instead, she reached round to draw back his robe, gathering up his tunic and bunching it above his waist. "Hold that," she said.

He realized she meant the wadded fabric. He did as he was bidden, clasping it to his stomach with his free hand. She pulled down his leggings, then nestled up behind him, pressing her form against his back as her arms snaked around his torso. One cool hand grasped his manhood, aiming it into the shoot, while the other stroked his stomach, sending a shiver through him. "Go on," she whispered. He released his stream, and she cooed. "Ahh, that's a good king."

He finished, and—chin on his shoulder—she peeked over to shake off the lingering drips. "All done?" She smiled, still holding him and continuing to stroke his stomach. Vahldan felt himself stiffening in her hand. She giggled. "Oooh. My king is ascending once again."

Vahldan turned, wondering if he should kiss those lush lips. He didn't need to bother. Her lips locked onto his even as she continued to stroke him to fullness. He reached to embrace her, pulling up her frock, finding his way to bare skin. He eagerly groped her wonderfully soft-yet-firm buttocks.

She explored his lips with her tongue while expertly continuing her ministrations. He leaned against her, his eyes closed, lost in dizzying lust. The gasp of a newcomer only fully registered when his savior ceased her efforts and drew back from him.

Vahldan opened his eyes to his new qeins standing in the privy doorway. Amaga wore a loose sleeping frock. Her hair was down and brushed, and her bare arms and shoulders shone with oil. She'd clearly prepared for something other than quarreling. And she was clearly shocked. But shock was swiftly morphing to rage. Apparently it was an easy switch for her.

His savior gave Amaga a cheeky grin. "Your husband has a fine cock, my qeins. You are a lucky woman."

Amaga's fists clenched and her skin flushed to fire. Vahldan feared she might come in swinging. Instead, she spun to leave, then stopped. Turning back, she pointed and said, "You. Out!" The command carried enough threat to propel his savior to disengage herself, straighten her frock, and stride out, brazenly brushing past Amaga.

"Wait!" Vahldan called. "You never gave me your name."

She halted in the outer chamber and feigned a pouty face. "You really don't recognize me? You've known me all my life." Her pout became a sly smile. "I am Harma, daughter of Herodes, my king. At your service, always." Harma bowed, swishing her skirts with a flourish. She then threw back her shoulders, raised her chin, and strode out.

Gods, could this really be the daughter of Herodes? Damn, he remembered the day of her birth. He really was getting old.

"How could you?" Amaga couldn't believe Vahldan was actually still smiling, gazing wistfully after the trollop's departure. And he'd just learned she was his cousin's daughter!

"How could I not? She started it."

Did he really think this was *funny*? Amaga was beyond anger, felt beyond humiliation. She was so disappointed. All of her dreams of him, her hopes for their lives together, shattered. "This is the worst night of my life."

"Oh, come now, darling." Vahldan tried to take a step toward her, but his leggings were bunched at his knees. He nearly fell. Rather than pulling them up, he kicked his feet free and left them on the floor.

"Don't you dare call me that. You used me!" Amaga hurried through the living chamber, heading for her adjacent quarters.

Vahldan followed. "I used you?" He threw his goblet, spraying wine across the carpets.

He had her by the shoulder before she reached the door. Amaga faced him. "Yes, you, oh mighty king. The long-foretold union of wolf and lion, eh? What a barrel of sheep shit."

She tried to leave, but he held her. "Please don't forget, my dear, that you came to me. Isn't it lovely, being central to destiny? And living in luxury isn't so awful either, is it?"

"It *is* awful. I hate it here." She jerked away, got through the door, and tried to slam it.

Vahldan blocked it open and came inside. "Do you have any idea what I gave up for you? I deserve so much more than this! Your bedamned clan never gave me a chance. Your father and the wolves tried to block me at every turn, and yet I have done as the gods have willed." He was hoarse and wild-eyed and staggering. She backed away. He laughed and it sounded bitter. "And here we are. Admit it, Amaga, you relish being at the center of it all. You're just like me— here in spite of your actual feelings. You never wanted me. You wanted this!" He gestured at their surroundings. "This and your precious son."

Once again, outrage pierced her fear. Yes, her son. He was all that mattered now. She'd decided it before he came upstairs. Nothing had really changed. Only that this man that she'd idealized had revealed even more of his true self. The only change was that he was even drunker, more pathetic. Oddly, knowing precisely where they stood felt empowering. The man suddenly looked so foolish, ranting about what he deserved in shoes with no leggings. His words were slurred, his hair was tousled, and his tunic was askew—and draped over the top of his still-hard cock.

Some king. Such a farce.

As if the goddess had spoken, she knew it for the divine joke that it was. It all made sense. Of course the Bringer would be a buffoon— one who would gladly lead those willingly vexed to calamity. She could still see to it that what was important came of it.

Amaga had never actually seen an erect penis before, but she knew of them. She knew how it all worked. She'd seen sojourning couples copulating on the longhouse floor in the dim glow of the hearth. In the moment, she had an epiphany. She knew why her so-called husband remained hard.

It was more proof—the will of the goddess. Freya was revealing the way for her son to exist, even in the midst of this farce of a bonding night. It was rightful. After all, Amaga had already used the teachings of her mother—bestowed by Freya herself—to calculate the exact date of this bonding.

This was meant to be. No matter what else came of their marriage or of the buffoon's crude joke on his clan.

Amaga gathered her courage and faced him. "All right. I *do* admit it," she said. "I do want to fulfill the prophecy. I want to have our son. I have only ever wanted your seed." Amaga forced herself to curl half of her mouth into a smile and pointedly looked down. "Slim chance I'll get it. Even your busty trollop couldn't get it out of you. You're obviously too drunk to fulfill your..." She raised an eyebrow. "*Husbandly duty.*"

Vahldan looked down at himself and then up at her. He suddenly looked more like a naughty boy than a king. Was he actually embarrassed?

Amaga laughed and backed toward the bed, trying her best impression of the few seductions she'd witnessed. "It's a shame, really," she said. "After all the trouble I went to." She grabbed her skirts and pulled them partway up. "That Sassan servant woman gave me a fine, smooth oil mixture." She kept backing up and lowered her voice to a husky whisper. "The smell is supposed to drive men wild. I've already applied it where it would make for the perfect slippery sliding." The backs of her legs hit the bed. She flounced her skirt and it billowed as she plopped down, hopefully providing a glimpse of her nakedness beneath it. "If only there was something worthy of sliding on."

Vahldan stepped toward her. "I see what you're up to, witch. You don't even understand the game you're playing." The rising arc of his manhood said she understood it pretty well. Still, her fear crept back. Amaga summoned back her anger, her determination.

She pulled the frock over her head. Cold air rushed to her skin. She laid back on her elbows, trying not to shiver. "Maybe I'd understand it better if you were man enough to show me how to play."

Vahldan flung his tunic over his head as he strode to her. In a heartbeat, he seized her by the waist, pulling her toward him. Fear won out over anger. She squealed and tried to roll away.

Facedown on the mattress was as far as she got. Strong hands gripped her hips and hauled her back. She got to her knees and tried to crawl. He held her firm and slid himself against the oil between her thighs. Amaga made herself stop. In this, the goddess would side with her rival. Her face grew hot. She refocused on her goal—on her son. This was the only way.

Vahldan pulled her back a bit till her calves were dangling off of the mattress. He put a knee between them. Amaga didn't resist when he parted her thighs. His fingers probed a moment, surprisingly gently. She scrunched up her face as he entered. She gritted her teeth and reared back against him, wanting to be done with it. There was a tearing sensation. A squeak escaped her.

"Does it hurt?" he asked, sounding like a boy again.

Really? Now he was concerned? "No. Get on with it." Her so-called husband obeyed, slowly at first, then thrusting and grunting. Amaga had just begun to breathe again when he groaned and convulsed.

Just like that, it was over. Thank Freya.

Vahldan collapsed on the bed beside her, his skin slick with sweat. She crawled to the top of the bed, as far from him as she could get, to lie on her back. She hugged her knees. "I'm sorry," Vahldan said, still breathless. "About all of it. It can be better."

"It doesn't matter," she said softly, hating that he was so different now.

"It does," he said. "I can be a better husband."

Amaga barked out a lone laugh. "I doubt it. Besides, I've already admitted that you were right. All I want is my son. Hopefully it's already done. If it's so, we never have to do this again."

Vahldan sat up on the edge of the bed. "Amaga, don't."

"Don't what? You used me. Now I'm using you. You have your precious kingship, and I will have my son."

Vahldan stood. "I told you, I've sacrificed for this. Our son will be mine, too."

Amaga turned her head from him. "Not if I can help it."

"What's that supposed to mean?"

Her anger surged. She turned her glare back to him. "It means that if I can help it, he'll have nothing to do with you. I despise you, and I'll see that he does too. Now get out."

Vahldan stood, scowling. "I said get out!" she shrieked. "Guards!"

He shook his head, snatched up his tunic, and slammed the door behind him.

CHAPTER 25
A KING'S POSSESSION

"I remember King Vahldan the Bold of Pontea quite well. I have fewer memories of my father. I don't recall us ever being alone together. Although he must've known my name, he seemed to have trouble recalling it. Instead, he usually called me Daughter and referred to me as 'the girl.'

There was a time when I blamed my mother for my father's distance. But his bonding day changed everything between the three of us. After that, I realized that his interests and concerns did not include a bastard daughter. From my mother, I learned that caring about it only led to heartache. Without seeking to, Elan also taught me that heartache would gain me nothing."—Brin Bright Eyes, Saga of Dania

RHYTHMIC THUMPING JARRED ELAN AWAKE. Her mouth was beyond dry, leaving her tongue stuck to the roof of her mouth. Her eyes were crusty, too. She wondered if Hesiod had left water at her bedside. Raising her head only revealed the scope of her headache. She reached to feel for a cup instead. Thank the gods, he had. Eyes still shut, she drew the cup to her lips and swallowed, hoping it would stay down.

The bedamned thumping recommenced. Someone at the door. Hesiod answered it. Surely he'd send whoever was there away. Instead, he knocked on her bedchamber door. "My lady?"

"What is it?"

Lamplight spilled in. Hesiod's head appeared in the doorway. "Forgive me, Lady Elan, but the king is here. He insisted I wake you."

The king? It took her a moment. Realization came... and dread. "Shit," she said. She doubted he'd accept being sent away. "Tell him I need a moment."

Hesiod stepped in and checked the bowl he'd left at her bedside. "Do you need to vomit?"

She wasn't sure yet but she shook her head. "I'll brew you some tea, my lady," he said.

"No, I'll be fine," Elan said, hoping it was so. "What of the girl? She's back?"

"Yes, Bright Eyes is long abed. Fear not. A sound sleeper, that one."

"Go back to bed, Hesiod."

"Yes, my lady." He bowed his head and left. Elan sat on the edge of the bed and shivered. She'd gone to bed naked. Better than in her clothes again. She wrapped herself in a robe, her head pounding. She drank the remains of the cup. It quelled the nausea. She took a deep breath and rose. Her head swam.

Elan ventured the three steps to the chamber door and stopped, leaning against it. She let go, pushing her hair from her face and hooking it behind her ears. She rubbed her swollen eyes, cinched her robe tight, and went out.

Vahldan stood near the entryway, disheveled and slumped, looking lost. In the soft light of the lamp Hesiod had left burning he almost looked like the young man she'd fallen in love with all those years ago. "You left," he said.

"I'd seen enough. You went through with it?"

"Yes, it's done."

"Then you should be with her."

He took an unsteady step toward her. Gods, he was in worse shape than she was. "I tried," he whined, "but she's awful. I don't think we'll be spending much time together."

Elan shuffled back a step. "Seems like something you should've noticed beforehand."

Vahldan shuffled another step closer. "You know I had to do it."

She raised her brows. "Had to?"

"Of course. You know this better than anyone. You were there."

"I *was* there. I've always been there for you. And I know better than most that you've had choices. I offered you some of them."

He shook his head. "With this, there was no other choice. Not if I believe there's a chance of fulfilling the prophecy. And I do."

Elan huffed a laugh. "Ah, a confession."

He scowled. "Confession?"

"Yes. You say it now like you've always bought into it. You do recall how we used to speak of it, don't you? Or have you deluded yourself completely?"

He closed his eyes and shook his head. "In spite of our skepticism, I've always said that I need to believe in the possibilities. Just as you once believed in your dream, Elan. It's all tied up in what we want for our people."

"Mine was due to the folly of youth. What's your excuse?"

"I hate this," he said. He kept moving toward her. "What's happened to us?"

"We grew up!" she snapped. "Or at least one of us did." She backed away from him until her legs hit the chaise.

"Don't you see, Elan? We won. The wolves, the guild, we beat them all. This lifts us above it all. We finally did it."

"*This* lifts *us*?"

He sighed and gave a dismissive wave. "The bonding means nothing. Nothing."

How could he be telling her this? Elan hated that she had to swallow back tears. "It may mean nothing to you. And you may feel like you've won, but I certainly don't. Your actions and words—they mean something." She would not cry. Not in front of him. She moved to get past him to her bedchamber door.

Vahldan stepped in her way and wrapped her in his arms. He buried his face in her robe. She reflexively put her arms around him.

Damn, it felt good, having him against her, breathing him in, feeling his hands on her. It was an old battle, and she was losing.

His mouth found hers, his tongue pushing past her lips. His breath was laden with strong spirits and she didn't even mind. "How's this for actions and words? I've missed you. I want you." His breath was hot on her ear. He kissed his way down her neck and pulled back her robe to kiss her bare shoulder.

He missed her? She'd been right here. Now he wanted her? It rekindled her anger. She fought. Her instincts and him. "It's not right. You can't treat me like this."

"Shhh." One hand found its way inside her robe to cup a breast while the other slid to the small of her back, pulling her tighter.

The gods knew how badly her body called to his. He'd all but won. Till she remembered the image. They'd locked eyes, just before he vowed to another. She'd used their old connection, pleaded with him. And he'd looked away, severing the connection. Severing them.

"I said I won't be treated like this!" Elan pushed him off and pulled her robe closed. "You made your choice. You can't have us both." He looked stunned, even hurt. A pang of remorse gripped her. "I... I can't do this," she said. "Please. It's too painful."

Vahldan reached out and brushed his fingers over the kestrel hanging around her neck. "You always said you belonged to me."

Elan tucked the kestrel charm into her robe and took a step back. "There was a time when it was true. But—"

"No buts. I need you, Elan." When he grabbed her again, years of training prompted an instinctive reaction. She gripped his hand, peeled free, threw out her hip, and rolled until she was behind him, wrenching his sword arm.

Vahldan yelped. She released him, but she knew she'd inflicted pain. Pain that would last. Same as she'd done all those years ago in Oium. That time he'd looked forlorn, but this time he turned on her with an expression contorted in rage. She saw the ugliness behind it.

He was losing himself. Worse than ever. His former anchor had become his target.

Dangerous as it was, Elan dropped her arms and raised her chin. If he was going to hit her, so be it. A tiny part of her almost hoped he would. Maybe that would free her from the bedamned longing he inflicted upon her. He shook his head, seeking to banish the ugliness. "Enough of this. It's not what I want. Take me to your bed. Now."

Vahldan was fighting for self-control. But he'd picked the wrong recourse. She kept her chin up and her eyes on his. "No, my lord."

"You just agreed that you once belonged to me. Well, now I am your king." His eyes were still crazed.

Elan drew an even breath. She knew what she had to do. She also knew it could push him past the brink. But it might bring him back to himself. "No," she said softly. "When I said that, you already were my king. More than that. You were my all: my world, my life. But it wasn't enough for you. Tonight you chose to be her king, their king." His red eyes narrowed and his jaw worked behind closed lips. "I won't defy you if you compel me against my will. Yes, you've succeeded at pushing me into this trap as you seized your power. Yes, you have the power to partake of my flesh. But you no longer own my heart."

He massaged the hand she'd twisted. His eyes were clearing. "You can't mean that."

"I do. And now you must choose again. Be a king and take me against my will, or be a man and leave."

Vahldan returned to himself. She'd brought him back. And the hurt in his eyes almost broke her. But she held firm until he turned and strode out, slamming the door behind him.

The moment he was gone her legs gave way. She sunk to the floor and released the tears she'd managed to dam.

~

LIGAIA LINGERED in the entry chamber, wiping down the basin and then the wine cups, one by one. She stood facing away from the thug lord and his captain. Although, as absurd as it was, she supposed she ought to think of him as the thug king now. Ligaia suspected that the ludicrous assertion would end up being a boon to her cause.

It used to make her nervous, eavesdropping on the Gottari. But no more. Ligaia the housemaid was all but invisible to these ruffians. They had not the slightest concern over her. They were obviously still unaccustomed to having servants. That, and fantastically hubristic.

"It's just that, well, everyone is wondering, my king," Arnegern said. "The seas are calm, and the men are ready. The supplies have been procured, the new recruits are outfitted. And you've scarcely left your chambers in days. Nor has your qeins. Where is she, by the way?"

"I haven't the slightest idea," the thug king replied.

"Maybe you could make an appearance? Perhaps at dinner. If only to reassure them."

Ligaia furtively glanced at the pair. Vahldan lay prone on the chaise, massaging his right hand with his left. He was still scowling, same as every time she'd seen him since his obvious farce of a wedding ceremony. As far as Ligaia knew, the door that separated the new couple's quarters hadn't opened since then. They'd taken their meals separately and on their own schedules. Based on what she'd seen the morning after, he'd been banished from the little witch's bed. She doubted the couple had exchanged a word since.

The captain was clearly at a loss. As was Ligaia. The Gottari army was supposed to have sailed for Bafrana by now. Malvius was waiting. The thug's pirate allies were waiting. All of Ligaia's plans relied on their departure. Vahldan's sudden inertia made her frantic with worry.

The thug king broke the silence. "I'm not so sure about this anymore."

"Sure about what?"

"All of it. There's just so much... risk."

Arnegern sat up straighter. Ligaia's fret surged toward panic. "My king, we've been planning this for years. You said yourself that the time had come—that you sensed the gods' approval. The harbormaster is waiting to send word to the rector that we've set sail. Captain Zafan will wonder if we've abandoned him and his fellow rebel captains. If we don't at least follow through in Bafrana—"

"All right, all right. I'll come down to dinner. Just leave me to think, please." Ligaia quietly made for the door to leave ahead of Arnegern.

Arnegern stood. Too late. She slipped into the privy and started cleaning there. The captain said, "My king. My dear friend. Is there anything I can—?"

"I'm fine," Vahldan insisted. "Be at ease, Brother. I just need a little time and space." The thug king groaned. She peeked out. He'd stood to see his guest out.

"Is that foot still swollen?" Arnegern asked.

"It'll be fine," Vahldan reassured. "I'll see you at dinner."

The door thumped closed. Ligaia listened as he shuffled back to his chaise. She headed for the door. When the latch clicked, Vahldan spun to her. "Oh, it's you. Fetch me a glass of wine, would you, Ligaia?"

Ligaia went to the sideboard and poured from the flagon. Gods, the stuff reeked. Obviously it was the distilled dreck that Malvius kept giving him. It had some awful herbal infusion, the gods only knew what. Vahldan groaned again as he lowered himself. Wearing a grimace, he propped his left foot up on a pillow while she waited to hand him the cup.

"You really should have that foot looked at," she ventured in Hellainic.

He glared and she instantly regretted it. But she had to try something. She couldn't just let him back out of his plans. It would ruin everything. "Sorry," she offered, this time in Gottari. She still couldn't bring herself to address him as a king. But then she'd never been good about calling him a lord, either.

He sighed, accepted the cup, and took a drink. "Apology accepted. I'm not even sure how it happened."

Ligaia was pretty certain that both the hand and the foot injuries had happened during the drunken rage, the aftermath of which she'd cleaned up the morning after his so-called wedding. The inebriated fool had broken one of Ligaia's favorite Saurian vases—she presumed by kicking it. He'd slept through much of the following day, leaving the cuts to fester in his usual filth.

"Perhaps the wiseman you brought from your homeland could take a look." She gritted her teeth and spat the farcical honorific in Gottari. "*My king.*"

"That old farter? The man can hardly see." At least he was speaking Hellainic to her now.

She rolled her eyes behind him. "No, the younger one. Surely he's had some sort of training as a healer." Ligaia could sense an ambitious rogue when she saw one, and that younger priestly poser fit the mold. "Shall I fetch him for you... my king?" With a plan forming, calling him a king was getting easier.

Ligaia held her breath. "I suppose it's not a terrible idea," he finally replied. She released it and headed for the door.

Within moments, Ligaia was leading the poser back up the stairs to her stolen residence. "It's the left foot," she explained. "And maybe the right hand."

"His hand, too?" The heathen priest was huffing to keep up with her.

"Yes, but please do not tell him that I spoke of the hand." Ligaia stopped outside her stolen residence. "And perhaps you could... No, never mind. It's not my place."

The priest frowned. "What is it? Speak."

She switched to Hellainic and lowered her voice. "Well, it's just that I noticed he seems to be questioning himself. He's usually so... resolved. It makes me fear something is amiss. I thought that perhaps you could offer some solace."

The poser raised his eyebrows. "That seems a very personal observation for a housemaid to make." Ligaia was stunned. And impressed. His Hellainic was actually quite good.

Had she taken it too far? She really had nothing to lose but the opportunity to attempt her plan. She demurely dropped her gaze. "My apologies. It's just, I can't help but notice such an obvious truth. It's much like the trust and admiration the king has for you, Wise One."

"Yes, well, lead me to him, then." An ambitious rogue, indeed.

"As you wish." Ligaia kept her head down and led him inside wearing a secret smile.

VAHLDAN HAD RESISTED but he had to admit, the acolyte had a deft touch. Sueridas had presented it as the mere application of the ointment, but the man had been rubbing his foot for far longer than application required. Vahldan also hated to admit that he didn't want him to stop.

Sueridas glanced up. "You are pleased, my king?"

Vahldan's cheeks grew hot. "Well, the damn thing hurts less than it has in days. You have skilled hands, Sueridas."

"Gained through experience. Wise One Mundelan's feet swell nearly daily." The acolyte gently lowered Vahldan's foot to the chaise and wiped his hands on a fleece. "Now, let's have a look at that hand."

"My hand?" Vahldan instinctively grabbed his right hand with his left. "How did you know about that?"

"Never mind how," Sueridas said, beckoning him to show it. Vahldan reluctantly laid his hand in both of the acolyte's hands. Sueridas gently probed his fingers and knuckles. Vahldan winced and pulled away when he hit the spot between his thumb and fore-finger. Sueridas took it again. "I'll be careful." The man felt it more gently, massaging the sore area. Vahldan sighed. "Well, it's not broken, at least," Sueridas said.

The acolyte applied some of the same ointment and rubbed it in. Sueridas glanced up again. "If it pleases you, my king, I'm happy to listen."

"Listen to what?"

"Forgive me, but it's clear that you're troubled. And your injuries... Well, they seem like those that arise from an altercation. I'd be honored by the chance to unburden you."

Vahldan nearly yanked his hand away and ordered him out. But damn, the man did have talented hands. He sighed again. "I suppose you could call it that." Sueridas raised his brows. "An altercation." The man nodded, waiting. "It's just... The woman is infuriating." The acolyte's eyes widened. "It was she who attacked me, you under-stand. I did nothing to her."

"You speak of your qeins, my king?" Sueridas's voice had gone squeaky.

"No! Gods, no." Vahldan wondered how he'd gotten into such a conversation. But now he had to offer some sort of explanation. "This was with Elan. I mean, my guardian."

"Ah, your ex-Blade-Wielder. I understand, my king." The man actually did seem to understand. Sueridas took another fleece and wiped the excess ointment away.

Vahldan shook his head, recalling the night. "I simply never imagined doing this without her. I mean, Elan has been there from the beginning. It's like she's a part of me. And now... I'm not sure I want it anymore."

"Want it?" Sueridas frowned.

"Kingship. Urrinan. Any of it."

Sueridas rocked back and sat on his haunches. "Tell me, my king. Do you recall what she said exactly?"

"Who, Elan?"

"No. The priestess Amaseila, on the day of your trial, when she named you the Bringer."

Vahldan laughed. "Of course I do. As though it were yesterday."

"Would you mind sharing your recollection?"

"She said, 'You are he. The Bringer.' She seemed to recognize me, but we'd never laid eyes on one another before."

"What else?"

He dropped his chin to his chest. "She said that I would bring great pain to our people."

"But also glory," the acolyte added. "She said that through you, we would all be changed forever. As it shall be. Did she not?"

Vahldan studied the man. "You were there?"

Sueridas smiled. "I was. And I, for one, have already been changed. It was on that day that I realized I must go to Vigs-Utan, to begin my study. You inspired me to seek my destiny."

"Then you'll also remember Amaseila saying that upon my doom, Urrinan shall ride."

Sueridas took his hand again. "My king, we are all doomed. It is as it shall be. No man lives forever. But only the rarest few change the world forever while they are here."

The goddess's voice echoed in Vahldan's head. *"Blood! Take what is yours. Heedless, without regret."*

Freya's image had become a recurring nightmare since—often a waking one. The horror was especially vivid when he'd been drinking from the cask. Vahldan glanced at it and looked away. Indulging in it dulled the pain, but, oh, the images that came afterward. He shook his head. "Many will die. And so young."

"That is in the hands of the gods. Change comes from upheaval. The Urrinan will be a great change. Hence, born of great upheaval."

"But who am I? I am no god."

"Give yourself over to it and feed."

Could the goddess really be urging him to give over to the ugliness? Confronting Elan had reminded him how much he hated losing himself to it. How much harm he could cause. Even to himself. Or worse, to those he loved.

"Close your eyes, my king." Vahldan hesitated, afraid of what he might see. "Please," Sueridas pleaded, "indulge me." Vahldan closed his eyes. "Now, focus on the moment the priestess came to you to offer the prayers at your trial."

Amaseila's face sprang to mind—her strange beauty, her odd gray eyes, so incisive. Gods afire! Those eyes. Realization struck. They were Freya's own eyes. "I remember," he said.

"Can you feel her touch?" Sueridas asked.

Vahldan saw Amaseila's hands grasping his, the strange surge of energy that flowed through the contact—same as during the cere-mony with Amaga. He remembered Amaseila's convulsing, the strength of her grip when he had tried to pull away, the calmness that had come through after the initial surge. "I do," he said.

"Can you still doubt, my king? Can you deny Amaseila's commu-nion with blessed Freya in that moment? Can you reject the future the goddess saw in you—for our people, for all of the Tutona? For our glory? For your son—the progeny of lion and wolf, first king of a hundred kingdoms?"

"Feed and revel in the glory that shall live in your name, your legacy, unto the ages. Know that the price has already been set."

Vahldan opened his eyes and looked out over the terrace, to the gray skies and the green sea. His cheeks were wet. "I can't," he whispered.

Sueridas stood and smiled down at him. "Then you know what you must do." The acolyte gathered his ointment and fleece and bowed. "My king," he said and turned for the door.

The pain between Vahldan's thumb and forefinger flared. "Gods, help me. There's no going back. I've lost her."

Sueridas stopped. "Your Skolani? What makes you think you've lost her?"

"She hates me now. They both do."

The acolyte Elli-Frodei turned back to him. "And yet their

destinies depend on yours. Never forget: Hate is often just love that has been enflamed by passion. Remember, too, that your people must come first. Now more than ever. Staying true to them demands that you stay on the path to glory. The one the priestess Amaseila set you upon. However much they mean to you, neither of these women can justly take precedence over that." Sueridas paused, watching him. "Does that sound rightful to you, my king?"

Vahldan shrugged. "It doesn't sound wrong."

"Perhaps you should also remember that neither of these women can deny that they belong to you, King Vahldan. As do we all. I have a hunch that in the absence of your attention, once each of them searches their heart, both of them will come around. Given time, both of them will recall who you are to our people and who you really are to them."

Vahldan flexed his hand before making a painful fist. "Thank you, Sueridas."

The acolyte bowed again and left Vahldan with a newfound respect for him.

~

ELAN RUSHED BACK into her chambers and slammed the door. "Hesiod? Who's home?"

Silence. It figured. "The bedamned man is never around when I actually need him," she muttered. She went to her chambers and stripped off her frock. She opened her trunk and pulled out her leathers, her cuirass, and Biter—still in the sheath bound to the harness—and threw them onto the bed. "Bastard thinks he can just sneak off without facing me? Oh no."

She hurriedly donned her gear. It'd been a while. The leathers were stiff, as were her boots. Worse, both felt a bit snug. In her haste, she got tangled in Biter's harness. Once she finally wrested herself into shape, she went to the looking glass. Yes, she was still a warrior.

Her bangs were a bit too long. She'd have to cut them during the voyage.

Gods, she needed more time to properly pack. Elan threw her wrist guards, a comb, and a half-full wine skin into a shoulder bag. What else? Her saddle bags in the stables should have most of the essentials. She slung the bag on her shoulder and turned to go.

And almost ran the girl over. "Gods, you startled me. How long have you been lurking there?" Elan had to admit, the girl had mastered stealth.

Brin's eyes were wide—bigger than usual. "What's happening?"

"I have to leave. I'm not sure how long I'll be gone. Hesiod will be here for you. As will your Uncle Urias." Elan headed for the residence door.

"Go where? Why are you wearing a sword?" Brin's fretful tone caught her by surprise.

"Why else? I'm your father's guardian. You know this." Elan strode through the foyer.

"But... he's going to Bafrana. Everyone says it's dangerous."

Elan stopped at the door. "Of course it is. War is dangerous. You know this, too."

"Will you kill people?" The girl's voice had become tremulous.

Hand on the latch, she turned back. "If I have to. As I said, I'm going to protect your father. It's my duty. Which means I have to leave now, Brin." She opened the door.

"Why you? I mean, he has Teavar. And Jhannas. And he..."

"He what? Married another woman? Named himself a king?" Eyes downcast, Brin nodded. "None of that matters," Elan said.

The girl looked up at her. "How can it not?" She'd inherited Elan's pugnacious streak.

"Because I made a promise a long, long time ago."

"Isn't what he's done the same as breaking a promise to you? To us?"

Elan thought about it. "I suppose so. But even that doesn't

matter. He can break his promises. That's up to him. But I won't break mine. That's mine to decide." She wondered if it was the last remnant of her Skolani heritage. "Our choices are our own," she told her.

She turned to go again.

"Mother?"

Elan halted, exasperated. "What is it?" she huffed.

"Who will protect *you*?" Her daughter's eyes shone with unshed tears.

Elan sighed. "I always forget how young you really are." She forced herself to smile. "You don't need to worry. Trust me, I am *very* good at this. I protect myself. I'll be back before you know it. Safe and sound."

A lone tear rolled down Brin's cheek. "Promise?" Clever child!

Elan suddenly realized how long it had been since she had held her baby girl. She bent down and opened her arms. Her daughter ran to her and Elan wrapped her tight. "All right, you got me. I promise." Gods, the girl was so thin. But there was strength in those arms clinging to her.

"Ha. Now you have to come back," Brin whispered.

"Oh, my beautiful baby girl. Don't grow up too much before I get back."

Elan drew her daughter back, holding her shoulders. She remembered what Sael had said, about how this beautiful child would grow to become the link between the old world and the new. Elan hated the thought of it. But she already sensed how special Brin was. She wanted her baby girl to be free—free of all of it. She didn't know what to say. "Take care of Hesiod, all right?" she managed. Brin nodded. Elan wiped her daughter's tears with her thumbs. "And eat something. You're too thin."

Elan stood and went out the door. "I know you have to go," Brin said, following her out into the corridor. "And I know we don't say these things. But I love you."

Elan stopped at the top of the stairs. She felt her face flushing. Gods, how had she raised a child who so clearly saw her shortcomings and was still willing to overlook them? That feat alone should be enough. She should just stay with her daughter, let the rest of it go. But even Brin knew that was impossible. "I love you, too, baby girl," she said softly, then put a finger to her lips. "Shhh. I won't tell if you don't." Brin beamed.

Elan hurried downstairs with her daughter's beautiful smiling face fixed in her memory.

ARNEGERN ROAMED the docks in the brisk morning air, overseeing the bustling efforts of the dockworkers loading the holds of the fleet among the loitering soldiers making ready to board. Two of Malvius's ships bobbed at anchor in the harbor, already loaded, and four ships lined the prime quays. He'd hoped to load and dispatch the fleet over several days, to try to disguise the sheer size of the undertaking for the handful of Tibairya who recorded the comings and goings of the harbor and operated the seagates. His plans had been dashed by the strange reluctance of their new king to initiate the campaign they'd planned for years.

Any semblance of disguise was gone. Once Vahldan had given Arnegern the go-ahead, he threw caution to the winter winds. Let the bureaucratic tongues flap.

No more delay. The Gottari would launch the entire fleet carrying their entire army, all in one day. Indeed, he hoped to be seaborne by the high sun. The loading process was humming along now. All of the warehouse space Malvius had allotted him was emptied. Everything was either on the docks or already loaded. Malvius's sailors worked alongside Gottari soldiers, in most cases smoothly. But an undertaking like this was never without a degree of conflict and chaos. Which had kept Arnegern scurrying from one issue to another through the morning.

In spite of the challenges, Arnegern was filled with vim. He'd spent months planning the details of the campaign and weeks procuring supplies and gear. Much of the work had been done in secret, hiding his purchases in Malvius's various warehouses. It was a relief to have it all out in the open. The entire Amalus army—including the newly arrived Danian volunteers—was mustered, and it was glorious to behold. They looked splendid, all decked in their finest armor and gear. It filled Arnegern with pride.

His plan for their departure was all but complete. Arnegern had only one last troublesome issue to attend to. One that had the potential to disrupt all that had been accomplished.

In spite of that concern, he couldn't stop smiling as he moved along the dock, heading for the waiting vanguard. Vahldan and his inner circle would board Gullwing, the fleet's flagship, last. Arnegern's smile wilted when he spotted the hunched and berobed Tibairya snooping among the final pallets and crates waiting to be loaded.

The withered imperial harbormaster was frowning down on a pallet of grain sacks, a Tibairyan guard scowling over the snoop's shoulder. Arnegern hurried over. "We should be ready to sail before your midday meal, Excellency. Please forgive the delay." He'd told the man's apprentice they'd be through the open gates by the midmorning bell. A deadline they'd missed.

The harbormaster crinkled his gray brow. "By Neptune's balls, man—what is all of this?"

"Grain, Excellency."

Even without his hunched back, the Tibairya barely stood to Arnegern's shoulder. He puckered as he glared up, his eyes puffy with the prior night's drink. "Of course it's grain. I mean all of this." He waved his bony arm.

"This is an expedition to Bafrana. To quell the uprising. In the name of His Eminence, Emperor Mycanius. We did submit documents. And I presumed the rector had sent word—"

The man's haggard face grew ruddy and his jowls shook. "I know it's supposed to be a bloody expedition to Bafrana. You're telling me that a bloody expedition to bloody Bafrana requires *all of this*?" He gestured more emphatically, indicating the extensive activity and freight.

Arnegern lowered his gaze demurely. "One cannot know what one might encounter in a foreign land. Particularly one in the grips of a civil war. We intend to be prepared."

"Have you been to godsforsaken Bafrana, Captain?"

"No, Excellency. Hence our preparing for the worst."

The harbormaster rolled his eyes. "The entire realm is a shit-filled latrine."

"From what we understand, their high priest is besieged within his own palace. Or temple. We are prepared to encircle those who encircle the seat of government."

"Those who encircle their palace are either dirt poor or they are sailors. And if they are sailors, they are pirates. The moment the pirates hear that our emperor has dispatched you, they will flee. You shall never see them. You could quell this so-called uprising with a score of well-trained men. None of this"—the grouch dismissively fluttered a hand—"extravagance is necessary."

"Well then, I suppose much of our effort will be in vain. But as my father used to say, better to be ready for all that is possible than to realize too late that you are unready for what actually arrives." Over the top of the harbormaster's head, Arnegern spotted his final issue of concern. "Regardless, if you'll forgive me, I shall see to it that we soon clear the quays and make haste through the gates." He bowed his head and walked away, leaving the man stammering. He strode toward the gathered vanguard sitting outside the fishmonger's tavern.

"I'm going to have to cite this in my report, Captain," the harbormaster called after him.

"As you must," Arnegern called back. "So be it," he muttered and sped his step. By the time the old crank's report reached the rector in Megaria, it would be too late. And even if the imperial bureaucrats got word of this before the Amalus army reached Bafrana—even if it made them suspicious—their bloated system would leave them unable to respond in time.

Arnegern hurried through the crowd, heading straight for the sorrel horse.

Before he arrived, Elan dismounted and led Hrithvarra to the edge of the bustling docks. She'd made it. He'd been trying to speak to her for days. She'd been elusive and had refused to see him even when he'd gone to her residence. When he'd inquired about her this morning, Teavar had merely shaken his big head. The sight of her revived Arnegern's spirits.

Arnegern weaved through the scores of soldiers milling near the food and spirits vendors lining the edge of the docks. The army's horses had already been loaded. Clearing the quays of livestock first had been vital to his plan.

Most of the original members of Vahldan's host loitered at the tables belonging to the tavern, and several more Rekkrs stood surrounding their king and his inner circle. Those who noticed Elan turned to her approach. She moved across the docks, the clomping of her friend's hooves on the wooden planks seemed to be demanding their attention and silence. The warriors hushed and parted to allow her passage.

Vahldan sat at a table between two of the ships' gangways with Eldavar and Malvius, all of them sipping from steaming cups of mulled wine. Teavar, Jhannas, Belgar, Herodes, and several others of his closest followers stood surrounding the table. Arnegern arrived before Elan did and stood among them. Malvius spotted her and whispered to Vahldan. The Hellain captain then stood and left—coward that he was. Arnegern frowned at him as he weaved his way clear.

THEY ALL TURNED TO HER—THE very host with whom Elan had originally ridden to Pontea. They stared as if she were an outsider.

Their collective gaze seemed to press the air from her chest, which caused her heart rate to soar. Gods, these men had been her fighting comrades for half of their lives. She had always stood with them, had never abandoned them. Indeed, she'd saved the lives of several of them, just as a few had saved hers. How had it come to this? What had he said to them?

Elan raised her chin and kept walking. The lions gave way but murmured in her wake.

Malvius leaned to whisper to Vahldan and then rose and fled. Typical. The coward.

Vahldan glanced and swiftly looked away, muttering a curse under his breath. Eldavar stared into his cup, flushing profusely. Teavar sat back from the table, arms crossed, unreadable.

She left Hrithvarra on the fringes of the gathering and strode to within a span of his table. She stopped and stood tall. The docks were silent but for the gulls crying and the groan of the loading winches beyond. Vahldan reclined in his chair and stretched out his feet. He gathered himself and took a sip. He donned a smug countenance as he would a chainmail hauberk.

Elan tilted her head. "May I speak?"

Vahldan imitated the gesture. "If you feel you must. But make it quick. As you can see, we're about to leave."

"As *you* can see, my lord, no one came for Hrithvarra. I'm not sure why I wasn't told we were so close to departing."

"The reason is simple, Elan. It's because you aren't invited."

He'd never sounded so cold. It froze her already aching heart. She shook her head. These men were her extended family. And they had been taken from her. This man was her duty. It was why she was here. It felt like being banished all over again.

"This isn't right," she said. "It's not as it's meant to be. I know it in my heart."

Vahldan smirked. "The heart that's no longer mine?" The flare in his eyes revealed that he was willfully indulging the ugliness.

"You know I wasn't talking about this." Elan swept a hand to indicate her place in the host.

"Oh, I think I know exactly what you were talking about. Is it wrong of me to want only those whose hearts I am sure are devoted to me, and to our cause, at my side?"

It was more complicated than that. He was the one who'd made it so. She didn't want to argue—not here and now, in front of everyone. But she simply could not let this stand. An impulse seized her. Elan reached up and Biter was out in a flash, gleaming in the winter sun. With no shield, she assumed a two-handed fighting stance.

Eldavar leapt to his feet and Arnegern sprang to Vahldan's shoulder. They and the giants, and at least a dozen others, drew their blades. Elan glanced to check her flanks and called, "Hear me first, my brothers!"

Vahldan sat bolt upright. "Hold," he said with a raised hand. All movement stopped.

"I am Elan, daughter of Ellasan! I am the sworn guardian of Vahldan, son of Angavar. So named by Mighty Keisella, Queen of the Skolani. So named by the Skolani Dreamers, who first foresaw his ascent. I was at his side on the day Priestess Amaseila named him Bringer. I alone was at his side when he reclaimed the futhark sword. I *chose* this. I have surrendered my all for this cause, this duty. This life. It cannot be taken from me. At my subject's side I shall remain. To my last day in this world or unto the coming of Urrinan."

Saying it revealed her core truth, even to her. This was her only constant. She saw that her words impacted all who heard them. Even Vahldan, though he sought to veil his emotions.

Elan went on. "I will yield my role only to the one who can best me with a blade, here and now." None of them stirred. "Well? Who among you believes himself more fit?"

The sole rumbling laugh that broke the silence could belong to no other. Teavar abandoned his fighting stance and sheathed his blade. "Not I." The giant bowed to her.

"Nor I." Jhannas said and sheathed his blade with a sigh. One by one, every Rekkr put away their sword and tilted their heads. It was written upon them, one and all. They were her brothers once more. By revealing her truth, she'd shaken them awake to theirs.

Teavar turned to Vahldan. "Forgive me, my king, but I beg you to reconsider. I can imagine no guardian to better serve you than Elan, daughter of Ellasan."

Vahldan stood. He walked to her with a noticeable limp. He stopped before her and stared down at his sword hand. He made a fist, then flexed it. She'd hurt him. Again. When his eyes rose to hers, she saw he was fighting his lifelong worst impulses—pushing down the ugliness. She used to be his anchor, tethering him to his true self.

Elan put herself in position to fill his field of vision. "See me?" He closed his eyes, resisting, even shaking his head slightly. "I chose this life because you told me our destinies are entwined. You promised me that nothing can undo it." He kept his eyes closed. "Hear me?" she softly implored. He finally nodded. "Good. Because I intend to hold you to your word. You are my duty. My duty is my life," she hissed. "It's all I have left. It is as it shall be."

When Vahldan opened his eyes, he was the boy she'd met in the mountains. "I don't deserve you," he whispered.

She huffed a laugh. "No. You don't. I guess we'll have to keep working on that."

He smiled, his eyes full of regret. She'd brought him back from the brink. For better or worse, their connection was not so easily severed. The joy and the grief of that undeniable truth passed between them.

"Captain Arnegern," Vahldan finally called, his gaze still locked on hers.

"Yes, my king."

"See to it that my guardian's horse is safely loaded and that her gear is stowed aboard Gullwing."

"With great pleasure, my king." Arnegern gave Elan a wink over Vahldan's shoulder and hurried off to do as he'd been bidden.

CHAPTER 26
REASONS TO FIGHT

"It was through the kitchen boy, Agoraki—or Ago, as he was called—that I came to know of the hidden ways within and beneath the palace. Indeed, beneath much of the city of Thrakius!

There were the manmade catacombs and connective tunnels, of course. But the original source of the system was an expansive network of natural caves. Some have speculated that the caves provided shelter to the area's original inhabitants.

Because of the trauma Ago experienced during the Gottari conquest of the city, he had made learning the hidden ways the mission of his childhood. When I met Ago, I would never have guessed that his knowledge would weigh so heavily on my future. More than once, his expertise and guidance made the difference between life and death."—Brin Bright Eyes, Saga of Dania

MALVIUS HAD THE HELM, steering Gullwing upstream in the shallow, muddy channel that led to the port at Bafrana. No small feat due to the shifting sands creating new shallows that were rarely marked, let alone dredged. Sails furled and under oars, they cleared the outer dunes. The wooden ramshackle buildings came into view, surrounding the walls of the stone city and leaning over the docks. More unsettling than the risky navigation was the virtual forest of masts that lined the docks and filled the harbor. Scores of ships were tied three and four deep, and more lay at anchor in the narrow bay. He'd never before seen half this many ships here.

"Those all rebel pirates?" Dex asked, climbing to the aftcastle.

"I'm not sure who else they'd be," Malvius said, studying the strange sight. "Not a single captain stayed loyal to the sadhu, as far as I know. Certainly not this many."

As they came nearer, what had to be the largest vessel in port drew his eye. The ship was tied fast to the main quay and boxed in on the other three sides by sleek but smaller single-mast pirate ships. "Oh shit," he muttered.

"What?" Dex asked.

"They're not all pirates," Malvius said and pointed.

"A bireme? Imperial?"

"Looks that way." Malvius scanned the vessel. "Not a warship, though."

"Towed in, you think?" Dexicos asked. "These pirates are getting bold."

"Maybe towed in. Maybe not. Check the flags on the rigging. Home port is Megaria. I'd say she's carrying diplomats."

"If the rest of these are pirates," Dex mused, "you suppose the imperials are being held against their will?"

"If that's true, may the gods spare us," he said. A cluster of men waited on the docks near the only empty space on the quay. A flagman waved Gullwing into the open slot. "Take the helm, Dex. Bring us in slowly. Leave us room to change course until I signal."

Malvius climbed to the main deck and moved through the milling Gottari to the prow. Vahldan and his inner circle were already gathered at the rail. Malvius spotted Zafan standing prominently among the waiting pirates. All of them wore their finest garments and gear.

Neveka's brother's finery bested them all. Zafan wore a feathered hat, a shiny purple sash, and a wide grin. A half-dozen bound figures were on their knees behind the raucous pirates, their heads covered in dark hoods. "Oh shit," Malvius said again, realizing who the prisoners must be. The sash Zafan wore was indeed that of a Tiberian royal diplomat. A high-ranking one, judging by the ornamentation affixed to it.

Malvius spun around to hurry back to Dex and nearly collided with Elan, who was blocking the way. She'd sneaked up on him. The woman was watching again, he realized, as she so often did. Elan was ever the keen observer, but lately she'd become this brooding, lurking presence. She didn't interact with anyone—particularly not Malvius—but she was never far from anything of import. She and Vahldan had always been inseparable, but now they were like a partially hewn, gristly steak, severed but unwilling to be fully divided. He supposed having the person you love, and had vowed to protect, marry someone else might inflict a deep cut into the meat and bone of a relationship. Added to that, anyone who'd known them for long would guess that their connective tissue was so sinewy as to be impossible to cut.

Malvius almost felt bad for her. Almost.

"Problem?" Elan asked.

"Not sure," he said. "Not yet, anyway." Malvius bowed his head as he carefully circumvented her.

"Ho there, Captain!" Before he made his getaway, a glowering Vahldan beckoned him over, demanding as ever. "What's this all about?" the thug king asked as he heeled like a dog.

"I'm as curious as you," Malvius said. Arnegern shot him a look. "My king," he added. Vahldan's inner circle insisted on adding an honorific to every utterance addressed to the thug. The rule applied to everyone but Elan, he noticed. Seemed Vahldan's cadre of manliness needed to constantly reaffirm that he matched up with their bold boy's self-proclaimed status.

Malvius scanned the rest of the quay as they neared the open slot. The trapped bireme's rails were lined with Tiberian sailors watching with concern. The decks of all the ships that pinned the bireme in were infested with pirates, most brandishing their finest stolen steel. "Whatever it is, I'd advise you to proceed with caution," he said to Vahldan. Arnegern shot another look. "My king." As if the lions weren't irksome enough before the ascension.

He supposed it was too late to meander into a position from which they could flee. Malvius would simply have to trust Zafan. He would go against his instincts in honor of Neveka's memory. He waved to Dex to steer them on in, and his first mate frowned but nodded. They had the angle and momentum to carry them in so he called for the oars to be banked. The pirates who caught their cast lines and hauled them dockside wore boyish grins. The gangway was lowered. Malvius bowed his head and indicated for Vahldan to lead the way.

For once the thug's insistence on primacy worked in Malvius's favor.

Zafan stood at the bottom of the gangway, hands on hips and chin held high. The young pirate had done quite well for himself since his sister had bought his freedom. Malvius had always kept his word to Neveka, paying her their agreed-on percentage of his profits. His admirable partner had gone from a whore in a backwater port to a very wealthy lady. And her brother, just a handful of years out of his teens, had reaped the benefits of having a loyal—and generous— older sister. Neveka had been both benefactor and advisor, he knew.

"Greetings, exalted one!" Zafan called as Vahldan descended.

Vahldan halted before the young man. "Captain," the thug replied with a curt nod. The pair looked awkward, unsure how to proceed. After all, they'd swiftly risen from ruffians to men of pres-tige. This was new to both of them. In spite of the awkwardness, there was a fierceness in Zafan's eyes that made Malvius nervous. He'd been wondering for months if Zafan could actually veil the hatred he felt for the murderer of his sister.

Teavar and the rest of Vahldan's inner circle spread out to face the line of pirates. Malvius sidled up to Elan's shoulder to stay close. Gods forbid, if trouble started and he had to choose one of these awful, violent humans to stand behind, it was her. Each side suspiciously eyed the other, and the awkwardness glided toward a standoff. "We thank you, Captain Zafan," Malvius interjected, "for the opportunity of this alliance." Elan gave him one of her scolding side glances, and he shrugged. Someone had to say something.

Zafan's intense gaze shifted to Malvius. "You brought the item?" he said in Bafranii.

Malvius nodded. Again, Elan was watching, ever suspicious. "We are made glad by the opportunity to benefit one another," he said loudly and in Hellainic. "We are ready to begin, as per our agreement," he added, seeking to reassure everyone.

Zafan grew a sly smile. "In that spirit, I have a wedding gift for the mighty king." The pirate stepped aside and gestured to those bound and kneeling behind them. Laughter rose from among the Bafranii, who also cleared the way to the captives.

"Remember, my king—caution," Malvius surreptitiously said to Vahldan in Gottari as they stepped over to the captives. In a flash, Zafan produced a dagger and bent to slice the rope that held the cloth sack on the center prisoner's head. The young pirate yanked off the cloth, pulling wispy, gray hair into a mess with it. The ruddy, veiny cheeks instantly identified the victim. It also marked the moment as Malvius's worst nightmare come to life. "Ah shit," Malvius muttered again, this time in resignation.

Pontea's leading diplomat blinked furiously, squinting against the daylight. Malvius backed into Elan's shadow. The old man's terror morphed into outrage as he found focus on Vahldan standing over him. "You!"

"Legatus Avitus." Vahldan gave a mocking bow. Malvius was surprised the thug had remembered the man's name. The other hoods were cut, revealing the diplomat's aides as well as the imperial harbormaster of Bafrana.

Malvius had to hand it to the wily old diplomat—even with his hands and feet bound, kneeling on a dock surrounded by outlaws, Avitus actually managed an impressively smug grin. "If it's not Vahldan the Bold," Avitus spat. "In league with pirates? And betraying the rector in the process? In spite of the moniker, even I'm surprised you have the nerve to be this bold."

Vahldan offered a wry smile. "I only promised the rector that I would settle the dispute in Bafrana. I still intend to."

Avitus shook his head and sighed. "Still seeking that inevitable doom, I see."

Vahldan's smile remained, but his tone grew as cold as a winter crypt. "I am, actually."

"Clearly you are well on your way. How pathetic. Don't tell me you actually believe the mystical claptrap you've been selling?" Vahldan's smile faded. "Oh yes, we in His Excellency's service know all about your catastrophic tales. A fine way to keep ignorant heathens in the dark, I suppose. But to keep oneself there as well?" Avitus tsked. "It seems even I thought too highly of you."

The thug king's grip tightened on his hilt. Malvius felt compelled to warn him. "Caution, my king," he repeated in Gottari. There was nothing quite like the murder of a diplomat to incite the imperial machine to swift and deadly reprisal. Even for what Vahldan had planned, such a move would not make for a good start.

Avitus's gaze snapped to Malvius as he ducked behind Elan. "Is that you, Anax?"

It was no use. Malvius stepped into view. "At your service, Legatus." He bowed formally.

"Ah, how perfect. Yet another wayward son. Still playing nice with your delinquent chum? Even after he murdered your father? I suppose I shouldn't be surprised. Such a pairing! At least your warlord friend here had the guts to commit the patricide you always aspired to."

Malvius painfully pulled up a smile. Perhaps he could still maintain some semblance of deniability. "I am but a humble ferrying service for the Gottari army." He could still keep Vahldan's mad schemes far enough off the beam to avoid a crash, even if there were scrapes in the passing.

Avitus raised a brow. "Come now, Anax. Surely there are motivations beyond a fee." The Legatus made a mocking face of deep thought. "What possible reason could there be for a barbarian and a smuggler to fight the battle of an insurgent pirate?" The diplomat leveled his gaze at Malvius and then Vahldan. "Unless, of course, they'd been promised immunity from the reign of terror that is sure to be unleashed upon our fair sea. Not to mention a slice of the profit." Malvius bit his cheek. "Forgive me, Anax. In your case, potential profit should always be mentioned first."

If the man only knew how much worse it was. Malvius turned to Vahldan. "My king, I would recommend that you release these men immediately. Have their ship towed from the harbor and be well-rid of them. With no disrespect intended toward Captain Zafan, of course."

Zafan shrugged. "None taken. His gift, his choice."

The crafty old diplomat's smirk grew more confident. "At least your chum has retained some of his wits, Lord Vahldan. Perhaps you two can find your way back to lawfulness yet."

"Get them up," Vahldan called. "Take them to their ship." Several of Vahldan's hulking supporters moved to lift the bound men to their feet. Malvius slouched in relief as Teavar took Avitus under the arms and yanked him to unsteady feet. Jeers and booing rained down from the surrounding pirates.

Even standing, Avitus still had to look up at Vahldan. The old man's chins waggled as he shook his head. "Such a waste. Wayward perfidy in the face of such leniency. We gave you such an opportunity. And it turned out precisely as I suspected. Just another heathen from the hinterlands—an errant boy spilling blood to raise his lacking self-esteem. Anything to prove his worth to his dead papa."

Elan stepped to Vahldan's side. "Hear me?" she said in Gottari, offering him a plea Malvius had heard from her before. But this time Vahldan didn't, or wouldn't. His gaze remained locked on the Tiberian. The thug had gained that baleful, distant stare—the one he'd worn when he'd ordered the murder of Decebius. Same as when he'd killed Isidros's henchmen. It was the look of the killer he kept locked up inside, and even Elan couldn't retrieve him.

Avitus leaned in conspiratorially. "I realize it's too late, but for the record, it's usually best if you prove yourself before you murder the man whose approval you so desperately need."

Elan grabbed Vahldan's arm. With stunning speed, the thug king pushed Elan aside, drew his sword, and lunged. His blade sank into the old man's gut, just below the ribcage. His weapon encased in flesh halfway to the hilt, Vahldan leaned in, nose-to-nose. "Guess I'll have to prove my worth to your precious emperor, then," he growled.

The old man gasped, his eyes bulging. "Inevitable… doom," Avitus wheezed.

Vahldan yanked out the blade and Avitus collapsed in Teavar's arms, a vast red bloom staining his fine silk robes. The other captives gasped, and a few began whimpering.

Zafan broke the crowd's stillness with hearty laughter. "Well, there'll be no turning back now," the young pirate said. Malvius's heart sank. Truer words had never been spoken. Zafan turned to his fellows, arms raised in triumph. "Hail King Vahldan of Thrakius— soon to be emperor of Pontea!" The pirates roared in approval.

"Oh shit," Malvius said yet again. Staring at the bloody robes, the body slumped in another's arms, he could almost recall the weight of Decebius in his own arms, with the spray of his father's blood wetting his face.

Another high-ranking man had been murdered, and Malvius would once again be named an accessory to it. This time it would be much more difficult to deny—even to himself.

Worse, he knew that this time around many more would die. There would be no way to keep himself at a distance from what came next. To bring such dangerous murderers to justice, he must be an accomplice to murder. Malvius was no longer just a scofflaw or a crooked trader. He was a genuine outlaw now. It made his goal all the more difficult and the endgame as tricky as could be. He knew he might end up imprisoned or exiled. He might not even survive it.

He firmed himself. He would do what had to be done. He would go through fire and blood to get to justice. "Forward is the only way," he whispered.

Vahldan wiped his sword. "Put them on their ship and tow it out," the thug ordered.

"What about him?" Teavar asked, nodding at the bleeding body.

"Especially him," Vahldan growled, sheathing his sword and storming back to Gullwing.

Elan paused next to Malvius. "Sure if it's a problem yet?" She didn't wait for an answer before following the betraying lover from whom she could not sever herself.

Click clack, click clack. Urias swung two practice swords to Brin's one, making her block high, then low, up, then down. The girl's arm wavered, but she didn't quit this time. He knew her muscles were burning. Reaction to changes in strokes would come later. This was about endurance, precision through repetitive contact, and hilt grip memory.

Brin's face flushed, but she hadn't whined since Urias questioned whether she was really the daughter of Vahldan and Elan. Based on her apparent anger, tactics rooted in shame might best be used sparingly. If she'd inherited any of Vahldan's volatility, he doubted it was wise to purposely tap into it. Besides, he needed this to have a fun side.

They'd strayed dangerously far from fun this morning. She'd started their session by complaining about the cold. Then it had been how her hands hurt and that she had a blister from the last session that still hadn't healed. But now there was sweat at her brow and a determined poise in her posture and movement.

Thus far she had responded well to most challenges. Urias knew he had to push, but he also knew this required caution and patience. He could lose her at any time. They'd only been at it a few weeks, and Brin's strength and wind were rapidly improving. His niece was agile and had good balance. Her frame was well-suited to blade work. She was long and lean. A bit too lean—he'd have to figure out how to get her to eat heartier; perhaps he'd approach that battle through Hesiod.

In spite of the progress, the girl remained reluctant and suspicious.

Urias began to glean that she wasn't just suspicious of his motives. Brin was suspect of her own heritage. He even sensed a bit of resentment for her legacy. This amazing child saw little to aspire to in the example of her parents. Their heroics predated her—hence were stodgy old tales, to be consumed with a generous dose of skepticism. And their more recent behavior wasn't exactly inspiring.

Brin's nose wrinkled. She was getting annoyed. Urias ended the drill and motioned for her to set aside the wooden practice sword. She rubbed her bicep. "That hurts."

"It'll hurt less the next time." She rolled her eyes, and then her gaze locked onto something behind him. He turned to look. "What is it?"

"Ligaia. She's watching us."

Urias caught a glimpse of the woman disappearing from one of the terraces. "The housekeeper? What of it?"

Brin frowned. "She's up to something."

"What? Cleaning? Not cleaning?"

"No, something else. I'm just not sure what... yet." Before he could probe any further, Brin's tone brightened. "So we're done for the day?"

"Not quite. Come. We'll do something that doesn't hurt." She rolled her eyes again. He'd have to broach her attitude over time. For now it was all about keeping her going while seeking her aptitudes and limitations. He led her to the short wall that surrounded the keep's east gardens. It was waist-high and flat on top.

"Hop up here." Urias patted the wall.

She eyed him. "To sit?"

"No, stand on it," he said.

"What now?" Gods, that attitude.

"You'll see. Come on, it'll be fun. And the sooner you start, the sooner we're done." She reluctantly climbed up. "Turn toward me. Now sidestep, all the way to the gate, like this." He demonstrated a straddle hop.

Looking down, Brin carefully hopped a few paces.

"Now without looking," he said. "Keep your eyes on me."

She frowned and stopped. "This is stupid."

"It's only stupid if it's too easy. Even if it is, doing it might improve your balance." He sensed a bit of fret. "I'll be right here," he added. "Even if you fall, it's not far." She sighed. He laughed and said, "You just have to trust—"

"I know," she interjected. "If I trust the training, it'll lead me to my best self."

"No. What I was going to say was that you just have to trust *yourself*."

Brin's scowl reminded him of Elan. "What makes you think I don't trust myself?"

"Oh, my dear niece. You have no idea what you'd be capable of if you trusted yourself. The key is having the confidence to truly seek to be your best."

"What? I'm here, aren't I?"

He had to give her that. "Come now. You're here, but you've only ever given me half an effort, at best. You don't like to be judged, even by yourself. By holding back, you can avoid it." Brin's face reddened. "You don't have to say I'm right but admit it to yourself at least." She looked furious. He'd already blundered past the limit he should've sought to avoid.

Urias waited for her to storm off. Instead, Brin lifted her chin, drew and released a breath, and set out again. There was her mother's stubborn streak—this time as a boon. His amazing pupil began to sidestep with agility and gracefulness. She was focused, but only on her feet.

"That's it." Urias walked alongside. "Feel your feet, visualize the wall, and scan your surroundings as you move. Be aware of all around you. Where is the nearest guard? Find him." She pointed to the sentinel on the wall-walk. "No, without slowing. Keep moving. Be mindful of everything: other people, animals and birds, the wind, the position of the sun. Trust your instincts and push yourself. Remember, you are the blood of warriors, with the heart of a Skolani."

Brin stopped at the garden gate and slumped. "Now back," he said. She sighed again but complied. "Where is the guard now?"

Without pause and with hardly a glance, she said, "Sunrise side, about to turn onto the front wall. And Ago the kitchen boy is watching us from the bushes on the path to the stables."

Urias turned and scanned the bushes, finally spotting the boy's silhouette in the shrubbery. "Good catch," he said, genuinely impressed.

They reached the starting point and he pointed to the ground. She leapt down, landing on the balls of her feet, flexing as she hit. Perfect. "That's enough for today." More than he'd dared hope for, in fact. Her physical progress was astonishing. The attitude was pliable. Improvement was all but assured.

Brin sighed in relief. He came up beside her. "Eyes forward. Tell me when you know how many fingers." He moved two fingers from behind her head around toward her cheek.

"Two," she said as he neared her ear.

He smiled. "Bright Eyes, eh? Perhaps we should call you Keen Eyes."

"I did well?"

"You did." The look on her face was his reward. She tried to veil it, but she was pleased, even a little proud. He tossed her a cloth to wipe her face and gathered the practice swords.

They started toward the door to the servants' stairwell. "So this is how a Skolani protégé is trained?" she asked.

"I have no idea."

Brin stopped short and gave him an incredulous look.

"They're very insular," Urias said. "Males are rarely allowed in the Jabitka. I can only guess how a Blade-Wielder might be trained."

"You've never been there?"

Urias couldn't keep from smiling. "Actually, I'm one of the few who has. My visits have been brief, though. The Skolani don't appreciate prying. But I have known several Blade-Wielders, including the queen. I've even fought beside them in battle."

"You've been in a battle?" Brin asked.

"Several."

"Did you kill people?"

"When it was necessary."

"You fought beside that princess, too—the one who thinks I'm destined for great things?"

"Yes. And trust me, she's impressive. I've not only seen her fight, she's allowed me to witness her morning drills. She's even told me a little about the training of her youth. These are all rare insights for a male to gain. So while I'm not exactly sure how Skolani protégés are trained, I do know a thing or two."

"They're really all women? No men at all?"

"None at all. A Skolani has no brothers, no husband... and no father." Urias watched her.

She gave him a sidelong glance. "I may be a child, but even I know that's not possible."

"Well, you're right. But the Skolani don't recognize those relationships, even if they exist by blood. Your mother only recognized me as her brother after she was banished." Brin's gaze was distant. "That troubles you?"

Brin's huffed little laugh reminded him of Elan. "I already told you that I know my mother is sad. And even though she thinks protecting my father is her duty, I know that he only makes her sadder. As for not recognizing a father, mine barely recognizes me. I have no brothers, and my cousins are all bully-boys. So to me, the no males thing doesn't sound so bad."

Urias had no idea what to say in response to such heartrending words from such a beautiful child. They walked in silence a moment before she said, "So is that all Skolani do—train and fight?"

He raised a brow. "Of course not."

"What else then?"

"Well, they're esteemed hunters and trackers. They breed and train prized mares. They grow their own vegetables and grain."

"But do they make things?"

"They tan their own leather and make beautiful tack and boots. Oh, and they make the most wonderful bread. It's one of my favorite things to eat. They even keep the bees that provide the honey that they serve it with."

"I mean, do they make things just for their beauty? Mistress Despoina says creating beauty is the key to a harmonious society."

"Hmmm. I suppose the Skolani find beauty in their devotion to the pureness of the warrior spirit." Urias glimpsed her familiar roll of the eyes. "Beyond that, I think they would consider the items they make to be beautiful in their simplicity, sturdiness, and usefulness. Through their traditions, they honor their ancestors, their goddess, and the natural world which surrounds them. Take their breast-plates. They're not only made entirely from horses, but from horses who've served in battle. They're faced with hooves, stitched with sinew of hide and straps of braided mane; even the awls they use to make them are from horse bone. The result is a beautiful and useful item that pays homage to their four-legged friends and to the past. Your mother used to have one."

"Still does. It's at the bottom of her trunk. Took me a while to figure out what it was."

"Well, first off, you shouldn't snoop. Also, I'm surprised she stopped wearing it. They're a highly-prized possession for a Blade-Wielder. They're often passed down from an elder. But they have to be earned, through valor and honor, even as a gift from mother to daughter. I'm not sure how your mother earned hers, but it must hold great value for her."

"I guess I'll never get it, then."

"Ah, don't be so sure," he said.

"I am sure. I don't want it. It smells funny." Urias shrugged. A moment later, she asked, "How many Blade-Wielders have one?"

"I can't guess a number. Some are older or more elaborate, but it seems most of the Blade-Wielders wear some version of one."

"So, a hundred?"

"Oh, many more than that."

"That many of their horses have served in battles? That's a lot of hooves!"

"Over the generations, yes. It's why having one means so much. The Blade-Wielders consider their primary warhorse to be their friend. Often, their best friend. It's one of the most important relationships in their lives."

Brin laughed again. "I'm positive my mother loves Hrithvarra more than me."

"Oh Brin, that's not true."

She raised her brows. "Have you seen her with Hrithvarra?"

"It's just that she's loved Hrithvarra longer. That's all."

"Well, I don't even like horses. They smell, too. And I can smell them on Mother when she's been in the stables. I don't want to smell like that."

There was the attitude again. "All right. I get it." He put a hand on her shoulder, drew her to a halt, and turned her to face him. "The life of a Skolani must seem completely foreign. Even a little ridiculous. I told you from the beginning that I won't think less of you if you don't want to do this. You can go back to your studies, and—"

"No," she interjected. She looked away, drew a deep breath, and sighed it out.

Urias feared she was going to cry. "It's all right. We'll keep going."

She shook her head, lips pressed tight. "It's just," she began, swallowed. "I've always felt out of place. And doing this... I don't know. My belly feels funny when I think about it. But after we train, my chest feels full. Does that make any sense?"

Urias smiled. "It does."

Her expression lightened. "I dread it, but then once I'm doing it, I like it. And I like being with you. It's just that..." Her brow furrowed. "I still can't imagine—"

"I know," he said. "You can't imagine killing someone. It's all right. No one can. Until they have to. But remember: Killing is not the point."

"I keep hearing that war can't be avoided. Even Mistress Despoina says so. Ago says his maaman's tribe didn't do anything. They didn't want to fight. But soldiers came anyway, and most of the people got killed. Except her, and they took her and brought her far away to work as a servant. That's awful. And now Mother is following him to war."

Him. Her father. "Come over and sit a moment." Urias pointed to a garden bench.

"I better go. Mistress will be expecting me."

"The bell hasn't rung yet. This won't take long." They sat side by side, but she looked away. "As a boy I was told that many, many generations ago, the Skolani were the wives of a mighty warrior tribe that had come south from the frozen northland. This tribe found the Danian River Valley and thought it a safe and fertile place to leave their women while they went off seeking conquest and riches in the desert kingdoms across the sea. Well, the warrior men never returned, and no one knows whether they were wiped out in battle or simply lost at sea.

"Anyway, at some point, the women realized they were alone in Dania. And soon winter was upon them. They had to build shelters and learn how to hunt and forage. If that wasn't trouble enough, spring came and along with it came raiders from the steppe tribes, seeking sheep and horses. The women were forced into hiding. Their livestock was taken, their shelters were burned. No few were captured and stolen away, or even killed."

Brin looked at him. Urias couldn't tell whether she was absorbed or annoyed.

He pressed on. "The women felt more alone and terrified than ever. Particularly at night, when the wolves howled and the raiders stalked their hidden camps. They prayed to their people's goddess of the moon, Horsella. The goddess offered to give them strength if they devoted themselves to her. The women toiled as Horsella demanded, and in return the goddess gifted them with warrior strength and hearts to match. The Skolani vowed never to trust outsiders, never to submit to men. When the raiders returned, rather than fleeing and hiding, the women fought. Rather than surrendering blood, they took it. In their ancient tongue, the name Skolani means, 'We fight to be free.' They have honored the warrior tradition that made them free ever since."

She looked down at her hands, studying her new calluses.

"Brin, I'm telling you all of this to help you understand. War is awful. It's never fair, and it almost never leads to anything good. But it is indeed unavoidable. And precious few warriors are honorable. But honor can be found. Indeed, there are warriors who strive for it.

"If you can envision being abandoned to a dark forest, terrorized by invaders who came again and again to steal your food, even to capture and kill your sisters, then maybe you can imagine wanting to be able to fight back and striving for justice. The way of the warrior, of the Blade-Wielder, is the Skolani's history—their legacy. It's rooted in duty. In justice. In honor. For them, honor is won through duty. Duty is a devotion to righting injustice, to preventing suffering, to protecting the weak. Not to mention ensuring their freedom. They still consider those things to be their purpose in this world. They are very proud people. And they are your ancestors. Their blood flows through your veins, Brin." He paused, watching her. "And through mine."

Her head snapped up. Urias smiled. "Remember, my mother is your grandmother."

"And the Skolani and the Gottari are friends, right? I mean, not like the raiders."

"Oh yes. Age-old allies. Although when the Gottari first came to Dania, the Skolani were already there. And at first, they fought. But both sides soon saw that it would be better to be friends. The first Blade-Wielders' swords were gifts from the skilled Gottari smiths of old. It's part of the pact they share. It's partly in return for Gottari blades that the Skolani have pledged themselves to guarding Dania's borders."

Brin gazed away, through the open gate of the keep to the sea beyond. "So the Skolani protect the Gottari?"

"Yes, from all foes," he confirmed. "Our foe is theirs, and theirs is ours." He thought he knew what was on her mind. "But their oath only applies to Dania. The Skolani loathe leaving their homeland, and they very rarely fight in a foreign land."

"So they won't help us if bad things happen here?"

"What do you mean by *bad things*?" he asked.

"Some of the servants say bad things are coming. They say my father is bound to bring darkness upon us."

It didn't surprise him. Urias knew that many of the servants resented the Gottari. He put his arm around her, drawing her near. She was shivering. "I'm sure your father knows what he's doing." Urias couldn't tell her that he suspected Vahldan's intentions were misguided.

"But when the bad things come, we can run away," Brin said. "You'll come with me, right?"

He frowned. It sounded like she already had something planned. "I suppose so. But I think we're safest here in the palace."

Brin gave him an arch look. "If raiders came and I ran into the Pontean Pass, would the Skolani protect me or would they kill me?"

"Of course they wouldn't kill you." At least he hoped not.

"But they'd probably take me and anyone who came with me captive, wouldn't they?"

Urias knew she'd sense a lie. "They may." She narrowed her eyes, studying him. He suspected if he were with her, it might help. But he wasn't sure if that's what she had in mind. And he shouldn't make promises he couldn't keep. He was saved by the harbor bell. "We can talk some more next time." He stood and offered her a hand up. "Let's get you to Mistress Despoina before both of us are in trouble."

Brin looked dissatisfied, but she let him pull her to her feet. "I suppose if Skolani have no brothers, husbands, or fathers, they also have no uncles."

Urias smiled. "Whether I'm your uncle or not, I'll always be your friend."

BRIN WAS in bed but hadn't fallen asleep yet when the knock at the residence door came. She instantly knew whose voice she heard talking to Hesiod. She slipped from bed and crept to her bedchamber door but still couldn't hear what was being said. She shivered in her night frock. She pulled her cloak over her shoulders and stepped into her sandals. She crept from her bedchamber, across the sitting area, to just outside the entry chamber. Brin stood perfectly still behind a potted plant, focused on the quiet conversation at the residence doorway.

"I told you, I am not comfortable..." Hesiod's voice faded to a whisper.

Ligaia's voice was clearer. "You are still one of us. Soon you will have to make a choice. I ask only that you come and hear the man out."

Hesiod said something that ended with, "...the child." Was he talking about her now?

Ligaia said, "She is the thug's daughter." Yes, it was about her, for sure.

Hesiod raised his voice, his tone sharp. "I have tasks to attend to before we retire, my lady. If you'll excuse me."

"Then at least promise to stand aside."

"Good night, Lady Ligaia." Hesiod closed the door on the sneak. Brin stood frozen as Hesiod walked right past her and into his own quarters.

Brin hurried to the door and worked the latch slowly. Once the door clicked closed behind her, she raced for the servants' stairwell. Brin took the stairs as fast as she dared in the dark, peeking ahead down each flight before descending, until she glimpsed the light of Ligaia's lamp. She'd stopped, so Brin did, too. Ligaia was at the garden door. Brin stood on the landing of the floor above. The latch clicked and the door opened. Brin watched Ligaia's shadow on the wall.

A cold breeze swept up the stairs. For a long moment, Ligaia stood holding the door partway open but not going out. Brin stood still, trying not to shiver. She pulled her cloak tighter about her. Finally, she heard shuffling and then the door closing. Ligaia kept her husky voice low. "You were unseen?"

"Yes." A male voice. "There was only one guard. He is paying little heed to the gate." The man sounded winded.

"Come," Ligaia said. Brin jumped up and started up the stairs. She stopped at the next landing to listen, her heart racing. Rather than coming her way, the light had disappeared, and their footsteps faded to silence. The pair had gone downstairs, into the larder.

Brin crept to the landing at the doorway and peered into the dimness below. They stood halfway to the kitchens, outlined in the lamplight, their voices an inaudible murmur. The man was taller than Ligaia but stood with a hunch. He had a thick head of curly dark hair, streaked with gray. Brin thought she'd seen him before. Maybe in the market.

She should just go back up to bed. Maybe confront Hesiod about what Ligaia was up to. What if Hesiod wouldn't tell her? What if he was angry at her for eavesdropping? Brin hated the idea of mistrust coming between her and her friend.

No. She had to know what that woman was up to.

Brin crept down the stairs, her body tight to the wall. At the bottom, she darted into the darkness of the larder, moving down the aisle, catching glances of the lamplight through the crocks and bowls on the shelves. "What about the harbormaster?"

Brin stopped. Ligaia's voice came clear now. Brin crouched behind a cask, focusing on hearing their voices over the thrumming haze of white noise in her head.

"He is the reason the anax decided to send a freighter. They'll signal him to open the gates, and then pay him a bribe to avoid the fine. They'll tell him that weather stranded them out east, and that they're making their way home empty. Such things are not uncommon, even in hiatus."

"The old man is no fool. He's sure to suspect."

"We'll have wagons ready, just up the warehouse lane. The anax's men will be off the boat and hidden in the wagons before the harbormaster arrives on the quay. Trust me, he'll be none the wiser. Until it's too late."

"Remember, straight to the palace. Both gates at once. Timing is everything."

"Of course, my lady. We shall see it done."

"Now go, before someone sees you here."

As Ligaia carried the lamp to the door, Brin backed onto her haunches to stay in the cask's shadow. She stepped on her cloak, causing her sandal to slip and audibly scrape the stone floor as she caught her balance. The lamp stopped. Brin held her breath. "What was that?" the man asked.

"Probably nothing. I'll check to be sure once you're gone." The lamp moved on.

Brin's escape route was blocked. Ligaia said she'd be back to check the area. Brin's only option was to make a break, flee through the kitchens. But Ligaia might see her before she made it to the stairs to the entry hall at the far end. She hurried to the kitchen end of the aisle, knelt, and peered back toward the stairs. The lamplight grew brighter. Ligaia was coming.

With her hands on the floor, Brin got her feet under her. Just as she was about to launch herself, a hand gripped her mouth from behind. Brin struggled to get away but she was forcefully turned to face her attacker. Even in the dimness she recognized the solemn face.

Ago put a finger over his lips and released her mouth. He took her hand and led her swiftly into the depths of the larder. Brin glanced to find the lamplight moving through the aisles toward them. Ago came to a spot, dropped to his hands and knees, and crawled through a gap on the wide bottom shelf. He beckoned and Brin dropped down to follow. At the back there was another arched drain, a bit larger than the one he'd led her through on the night of the bonding.

After she was through, Ago put his upper body back through the archway. Brin saw the light getting brighter until Ago slid a wooden box down the shelf, blocking the light out and plunging them into blackness. Brin heard Ligaia muttering to herself on the far side of the wall.

Ago took Brin's hand and pulled her to her feet. He slowly led her away from the drain. She held her free hand out, worried that she would hit her head. Gray light soon revealed that she was in a very similar corridor to the last time he'd led her through. His small lamp was burning ahead.

"Did she see you?" Ago asked.

"I don't think so."

"Good. She'll think it was me. She's always looking for me."

Ago didn't ask her what she heard but she read his concern. "You were right. Bad things are going to happen, aren't they?"

Ago nodded. "Soon now, I think."

"What can we do?" Brin whispered.

"I don't know. I'm not sure there's much anyone can do. There aren't enough of your father's men left to stop it." Brin bit her bottom lip. "I'll still come for you. I can get you out."

Brin thought about the morning's conversation. "What about my uncle?"

Ago rubbed his square chin. "I'm not sure. My maaman won't like it. But maybe we can get him out, too."

"If I tell him she's up to something, maybe he can think of a way to stop her."

Ago shook his head. "I doubt it. My maaman says there are too many of them now, and that they've grown bold. She says that boldness always begets trouble. She thinks we're only asking for woe if we help your people or try to run ourselves. She doesn't even think I should try to help you. But she won't forbid it."

"She won't?"

"No. I told her I made up my mind. She knows she can't stop me." Brin shuddered and pulled her cloak tighter. Ago noticed. "Let's get you back to your bed."

He started down the corridor. "Ago?" He looked back. "I'm scared."

He turned back to her. Brin could see he was trying to look brave. "Don't worry. I made you a promise. I'll keep you safe, Brin."

Brin wondered how she deserved such a gift. She used to think Hesiod was her only friend. Well, the only one that wasn't related by blood. But she supposed Ago was becoming a friend. She couldn't imagine why, and before she could thank him, Ago set out again, forcing her to hurry after.

NO GOING BACK

"Efusium is an ancient city and was founded long before even the Hellains made it a hub of trade. Its citizens are cultivated, prosperous, and diverse. At the time of Vahldan's ascent, it was the fifth largest city in the Tiberian Empire.

Efusium is situated near several trade routes on a well-protected delta at the eastern shore of the Tiberian Sea. It's said that the sprawling city has been both the home of a dozen kings and the domain of a dozen empires. Even the early Tiberians, who were originally welcomed without a fight, were thrown out for a time by another ambitious Pontean monarch, long before Vahldan's ascent. After almost three centuries of imperial rule, Efusium's citizens grew to feel invulnerable. Backed by nigh impassable mountains, the city's surrounding walls are among the longest in the imperial world, running up from its broad port to encompass not just the river basin that holds the city center but the mountainsides across which the city's residential districts sprawl. Efusium boasts not just a thriving harbor but a massive coliseum and one of the largest libraries in the civilized world.

As with most major imperial cities, the Tiberian militum was forbidden in the city proper, particularly near the forum square, a part of *the palace grounds used by the imperial bureaucracy as well as the location of the city's largest market and temple. The restrictive law was an old one, originally enacted to discourage the numerous internal coups of Tiberia's youth. It created a situation that suited Vahldan's ambitions well."*—Brin Bright Eyes, *Saga of Dania*

BAFRANA WAS OVERWHELMING to all of the senses. The sights and commotion were distracting but Vahldan had to focus on the task at hand. So many steps remained to achieving their goal, but none could be taken until this first mission was accomplished. The transport of the catapult from the docks to just outside the ancient fortress's walls, followed by its reassembly, had stoked the curiosity of the locals—pirate sailors and inhabitants alike. The work brought the newly allied groups—Gottari and Bafranii—together. There was much signaling and gesturing, punctuated with simple Hellainic words and phrases that most every Pontean knew. Thankfully their hosts seemed lighthearted and accommodating.

Vahldan was still fuming about the Tiberian captives that Zafan had foisted upon him. He knew he should let it go, that it didn't really change anything. He still needed the pirates but hated being deceived, let alone set up. It bothered him even more that he'd allowed himself to be goaded. Ugliness aside, he needed to rise above such behavior. It didn't befit his new station.

The worst part was that the incident had him questioning his new allies' intentions.

Their arrival at the site made those besieged inside the old temple and palace curious as well. Crowds had gathered to watch from the palace terraces and the fortress walls. Their would-be insurgency hadn't exactly seized the element of surprise. But if all went according to plan, the section of the wall which seemed to be holding the majority of their armed foes would soon be gone. Better still, it would occur while their side remained beyond a bowshot. That ought to be surprising enough.

They had left the shipyards at dawn. With any luck, the Gottari mission would be done and they'd be on their way from Bafrana by mid-afternoon. It couldn't be soon enough for Vahldan. They'd spent a rocky night on the ships, at anchor but far too close to the mouth of the harbor for the comfort of a steady ship. Malvius had insisted on keeping them clear of possible espionage or entrapment, and Vahldan hadn't argued.

The days were short, and the nights would only grow colder once they left the coast and started their trek into the mountains. Cold Vahldan could handle. He had no desire to stay another night in this bustling, muddy maze of a city with its endless leaning stacks of brown brick hovels. He hadn't forgotten his wonder when first visiting what he had once considered exotic foreign ports. How he'd longed for that sort of adventure in his youth. Back then, his imaginings hadn't included the cutthroats, whoremongers, purse thieves, swindlers, and beggars such places seemed to breed in droves. Here in Bafrana, every road, courtyard, and floor felt crooked. It was dizzying. Making the issue worse, at every turn they were assailed by a new stench. And the noise! Vendors called and horns squealed and bells rang. As that began to die down, the flutes and drums began. In the lower quarter, singers sang and dancers danced; the whine of relentlessly buoyant music echoed across the murky harbor long into the night.

Vahldan supposed that over the years—always posturing, ready to fight and often needing to—his wonder over exotic cities had gone as stale as a journey's last loaf.

As they got into position, the city's denizens swarmed around the position the Gottari and the pirates had taken, staying behind the siege lines near the main gate to the temple fortress. The Bafranii kept their distance, watching with suspicious frowns. Were they hopeful? Doubtful? Disapproving? It was impossible to tell.

It wasn't just the strange atmosphere that troubled him. Not a single Bafranii had done a single thing to make the Gottari feel welcome. Vahldan couldn't say they'd been at all hostile, he sensed their suspicion. You'd think he'd brought an occupying army rather than allies to fight for the people. It made him wonder if Zafan was being truthful about the will of the realm's common folk. The pirate had already shown he was not above deceit. Did the Bafranii people really want to overthrow their oppressors in the palace? Did they really wish for an end to imperial rule? Seeing them, Vahldan felt far from confident it was so.

With half of his force marching on the fortress, he'd left Arnegern to oversee the unloading of the horses and their gear and supplies. Malvius had elected to stay back as well, which was typical of him. Zafan had most of his men gathering, loading, and hauling rocks for use in the attack. The first wagonload arrived just as his men cranked back the contraption's arm for the first time.

"Almost ready?" Vahldan called to Attasar, who'd supervised the catapult's reassembly.

"We are, my king," the scholar replied. "We'll need strong backs to load these rocks."

"Jhannas, Ermanaric. Help them load the weapon." Teavar gave him a side glance. Of course the giant was the strongest of them. But Vahldan preferred to keep his guardians close. He mistrusted these people as much as they seemed to mistrust him.

The situation made him all the gladder that he'd ended up having Elan with him as well. She had barely spoken to him since their exchange on the docks in Thrakius, but she diligently maintained a perimeter around him. Today she'd even taken the unusual step of wearing Biter at her hip rather than on her back. Her hand had rarely strayed from the hilt since they had made shore. That and her fierce Skolani countenance made the Bafranii suitably wary of her.

The two big Rekkrs grunted and lifted one of the larger rocks from the wagon and shuffled to plop it into the sling. "When you're ready, my king," Attasar said.

"Let's try one," Vahldan said. "Go ahead."

The lever was thrown, the counterweight plunged, and the arm snapped. The entire contraption leapt against its restraints. The rock bounced a few spans short of the palace but still hit the base of the ancient brick wall with resound. The dust was quickly cleared by the brisk wind, revealing a series of cracks. A cheer went up, from pirate and Gottari alike. The wall above the damaged spot quickly cleared of spectators. It hadn't even been a direct hit.

An encouraging start.

Attasar calculated how much closer to move. The crew pulled the restraining lines and gathered to push the weapon into its new position. A paltry few arrows flew from the walls but fell laughably short. The palace's visible defenders were quickly thinning. The second shot scored a direct hit. The cracks gaped and those left on the walls mostly vanished.

Within five more shots, the wall had fallen into rubble.

"That was quick," Vahldan said. "Best not leave them time to recover," he said to his inner circle.

"That's a lot of rubble," Teavar noted.

"And right in our path," Belgar added.

"It'll take some climbing to get in," Elan added. "If I were them, I'd put every archer I had sighting down on that gap."

"Every archer who hasn't already fled," Vahldan amended. "The longer we wait, the worse it gets for us." Elan actually shrugged and nodded. He turned to the column. "Eldavar! Form them up!"

"Yes, my king," his brother called. "Lions! Battle lines! Blades and shields!"

Since the onset, it had been presumed that the Amalus would lead this attack. At least till the fortress was breached. The Gottari simply had the better gear. Still, a large percentage of the Bafranii pirates formed up behind his chargers. Perhaps it was a show for the rabble of city folk who raptly but silently watched.

Vahldan drew his own blade, slung his shield from his back, and headed to the fore.

A hand gripped his shoulder, stopping him. He spun, ready to berate the offender, only to find it was Elan. "You're not really thinking of leading this attack, are you?" Concern bordering on outrage radiated from her.

"Of course I am. Where else would I be?"

"You're our king now. Let the men have this one." Vahldan couldn't keep from grinning. "What?" she asked, annoyed.

"Nothing. It's just the first time you've voiced that."

Elan didn't crack a smile. "I'll say whatever it takes to keep you safe."

"I'm afraid you'll have to keep me safe from the front of the charge. That's where I'll be. It's the sort of king I intend to be." She studied him a long moment, reading him to see if he was near to imbuement. He knew he wasn't. Yet. He wasn't sure if he'd even find his way to it, or if he'd need to. It was difficult to seek Thunar's Blessing without knowing a thing about the foe. "I know this mission is different," he said. "It still has to be done. This is not our war but it's the first step of many. What I'm asking of our warriors will carry us to our destiny. But I should rightfully lead us there."

"Everything is different now," Elan grumbled. "Every step will be from here out." She was clearly unhappy about the realization. Vahldan couldn't really blame her.

"It'll be fine," he assured her. "This is as it shall be."

She nodded once and stepped back, farther than he preferred.

He moved to the fore. The Rekkrs gathered around him, looking grim but ready. He didn't know what to say, so he merely shouted, "For the glory of Urrinan!" Rather than cheering, most merely grunted, growled, or nodded and clanged blade to shield. They looked and acted like workmen with a job to put behind them. It seemed fitting.

With Teavar and Eldavar at his shoulders, he raised his sword overhead and shouted, "On, Gottari!" He leveled Bairtah-Urrin, pointing it at the gap in the fortress wall, and started running across the dusty field. The rumble of boots and the heaving breaths of his fellows were the only sounds. The ground became softer and the distance suddenly seemed annoyingly far. He hadn't run like this in years. Perhaps he should've done some training. Or maybe listened to Elan.

Not a single arrow fell until they reached the breach. Teavar got out in front of him, holding his massive shield high as they navigated the rubble. Vahldan was too winded to complain. Then, as if the giant had signaled the others, a core group of Rekkrs fanned into a crescent before him, shielding him as they all scrambled over the jagged hunks of the crumbled wall. Vahldan sensed Elan's presence. He glanced to find her at his shoulder, watching his back as usual.

As they crested the rubble, the arrows began to rain down. He heard a few cries from those hit, but most of the force hurtled over the last of the rubble and ran out into the fortress keep beyond, shields up, moving to regroup.

With his inner circle arrayed before him, Vahldan led them toward the inner buildings, scanning the lay of the field. The grounds were lush and green, especially in contrast to the dreary and barren city that surrounded them. This wasn't a soldiers' space. The temple and the palace stood adjacent to one another, connected by a two-story corridor. The structures were built of lavishly carved gray stone, inset with variously hued accent stones.

A host of perhaps two score of finely-clad warriors was arrayed in a shallow phalanx before the palace doors. In contrast, the temple doors stood open with no guard whatsoever. "Looks like the sadhu is in the palace. May as well hit these dandies straight on." He pointed and Eldavar nodded.

"Form up," his brother called. "Shields!" The Rekkrs hurried to do his bidding.

The sadhu's host wore matching silk tunics and blousy leggings, topped with a leather vest. Oddly, the individuals wore various bright colors. Those in the front row bore short spears and those behind had bows. Not a one wore armor or carried a shield. In unison, the foe's archers drew their bows. Without fanfare, Eldavar pointed and started for them. The rest of the Amalus host fell into a wedge, those with the biggest shields at the apex. They charged without a roar, which seemed odd to Vahldan. He fell in behind the leaders, scanning the windows and roofs, watching for a trap to spring. None came. This paltry, silk-clad squad of guards was the only visible resistance.

The Bafranii archers' first salvo only took out two of the chargers. The attack hit the foe before they could reload. It seemed half of the spearmen fell with their initial contact. Within heartbeats, the remnants scattered and fled. Many of those who fled were caught and cut down from behind. A few made it to the palace doors, instantly slamming them shut, leaving their fellows behind. Once the doors were shut, the cries of the Bafranii wounded were the only sound. The garden courtyard returned almost to what must be its typical serenity.

This was the strangest skirmish Vahldan had ever witnessed.

The Gottari gathered beyond the archway that led to the palace doors, and once again Vahldan scanned the walls above to find them empty. The archway seemed free of pouring holes. The host warily approached, shields up. Ermanaric rattled the door. "Barred," he said.

"Bring throwing rocks from the rubble pile," Vahldan called. Several youths ran to do his bidding, carrying rocks for the strongest Rekkrs to take turns hurling them at the center of the double doors until one of the dented metal panels popped off, exposing splintering wood beneath. A few well-aimed throws, and the spot became a hole as big as a helmed head. The bottom of the bar inside was revealed. A young bannerman unwisely rushed up and thrust his arm through to push the bar from its brackets. The lad screeched in agony, his arm caught on the far side. A group of his fellows hurried to his aid, but could do nothing to get him free. The lad grimaced and pulled until his hand came out gushing blood with a broken arrow shaft protruding through his palm.

A group of pirates had caught up to gather behind the Gottari now, and several with bows moved to take shots through the hole. After a dozen shots, the thuds of the return fire from within tapered off. Ermanaric nudged the pirates aside and pushed the bar from its brackets with a gauntlet-clad hand. The Gottari with the largest shields gathered and Ermanaric counted them down to charge. The doors burst open, and Rekkrs fanned out in the entry hall. Now it was a matter of searching the palace to find and capture the sadhu.

Zafan and his retinue appeared, striding across the garden grounds. "Huh," Elan scoffed. "Look who's right on time to avoid the fighting."

Eldavar returned to the entryway just as the pirate captain arrived. "No one in sight," his brother reported. "There are several sets of stairs. Looks like we'll have to clear the place room by room."

"Not to fret," Zafan said. "You and your brave men have played your promised role, great king. My men shall gladly finish this. We ask only that you stand by and guard the keep until we are certain this thing is finished."

Vahldan remained suspicious, but in truth he was relieved to step aside. As long as the sneak lived up to the remainder of the bargain. "As you wish." Vahldan inclined his head. He turned to Eldavar. "Get ours out. See to the breach and send squads to patrol the surrounding grounds."

Eldavar strode off, calling to gather the other captains.

The Gottari who'd led the charge milled in the garden, several taking a knee. Others filled their skins in a clear fountain. In mere moments, Zafan's men started leading out captives. Seemed most of the finely clad prisoners were female. The males were far from warrior-like. The captives were herded together in the cobblestone courtyard between the temple and the palace at spear point. Several of the pirates standing guard over the group began tearing off their clothing, forcing them to their knees, and binding their hands. The heads of some were covered with strips torn from their own garments. The lavish hair of some of the females was hastily sawed off with daggers by the fistful. The intent of the treatment seemed to be humiliation.

As the inbound wave of captives dwindled, screams of terror

rang through the palace and the courtyard. One particularly loud screech had the Gottari reaching for hilts. On a terrace above, two pirates held a bound captive over their heads. They unceremoniously flung the captive, forcing those below to scurry to stay clear. The screaming ended with a sickening thud.

Elan nudged the body with her boot. She shook her head. "Little more than a boy," she said. "There is evil afoot here."

"Revenge of the oppressed?" Teavar suggested. "Damn sight finer in here than out there." He threw a thumb to indicate the dockside slums.

Elan curled her lip. "Seems a bit sadistic, even for the deprived. I thought this uprising was over unfair tariffs. Hardly seems a just response to a half-full purse."

"Malvius tells me Zafan and many of his men are former slaves," Vahldan said. "I can only imagine how those Gottari children we saw on the block would react if they were freed as adults and given a chance to confront their captors."

Elan scowled at the pirate guards shoving and debasing the captives. "So cruelty answers cruelty? Slavery begets more slavery? Where does it end?"

Vahldan shook his head. "I haven't been here long, but I doubt that their struggles will end anytime soon. It's not really our problem, but by ending corrupt rule in the region, we may end up helping." Another piercing scream echoed from the palace—this one undeniably female.

"Not our problem, not our war." Elan met his gaze with a hard glare. "Maybe so. But these are not our ways, my lord."

The ugliness stirred within him. "Today's mission is but a means to an end."

Elan raised a brow. "Ah, so there *is* an end?"

"For us, there will be," he said.

"Which is?"

"Same as ever. Glory for our people. The futhark restored.

Urrinan for our progeny. The result of which brings an end to tyranny."

"Tyranny as we perceive it?" she asked.

"Would it not be better if all who perceived it then resisted, Elan?"

"Of course. That way war becomes ceaseless." Elan turned and sheathed her sword with a snap. "How glorious," she muttered.

Vahldan wondered if he should've left her behind after all. "A debate for another day," he conceded. "Come, everyone. Back to the docks. We need to get moving. I don't want to spend another night in this awful place."

"We're leaving without them?" Teavar pointed back at the palace, where Zafan and his men were spreading chaos and terror.

"This coup seems as close to done as I care to witness," Vahldan said. "We don't need these men and they no longer need us. Zafan left his squad of guides with Arnegern. I want to march the instant we're together. We've got enough daylight to get us well into those foothills." He nodded toward the base of the snow-capped mountain range to the southwest.

"I don't like it," Eldavar spat. "These pirates are going to march the sadhu and the rest of the captives through the city in triumph." His brother nodded toward the captors, chaining their pathetic charges together.

"Seems likely," Belgar agreed. "But who cares?"

Eldavar frowned. "They couldn't have done it without us. This Zafan character seems to be a master at doing little along the way to reaping the credit for all that's done."

Another shriek drew all of their gazes back to the balcony just as another bound captive was tossed to thump down next to the dead boy.

Vahldan hated to admit that Elan had a point, that, indeed, these were not their ways. "For this, Zafan can have all of the credit," he said and started toward the breach in the wall with his host falling in behind him.

BRIN'S ARM was starting to ache. But letting it show wouldn't help. Her uncle's sword drills always went until she was beyond aching, whether she showed it or not. He had a gift for pushing until her arm went all floppy and then letting up just before she had thoughts of telling him she would quit training. At least her sore arm made her forget the side ache he gave her during the stop-and-start sprints.

Indeed, her arm flopped down when Urias finally let her stop. But the parrying drill wasn't over. Instead, he had her switch hands. Doing the drill with her left was awkward and difficult, but Brin held her tongue. She tried to channel her crabbiness into useful angry energy. She'd learned that complaining only brought more pain. Some days she wondered how he'd talked her into this daily torture. Which made her wonder why she kept coming back.

Uncle Urias often said she could quit any time. Something about the way he said it always made her feel more like not quitting. The feeling was weird, like it was in her chest rather than her head. She supposed it was a trick he'd learned, but she didn't mind. It sort of felt good. Well, afterward it felt good. Not during their sessions. She'd figured out that she could get past the pain easier if she looked forward to the good.

Thankfully, the left-handed drill didn't last too long. "Let's get up on that wall," Urias called. "Twist jumps!" Brin groaned. The good news was that this was usually his last drill. The torture was almost over. Dancing on top of the wall required focus. More than that, she had to stay alert till the end. If she let herself slack off, it would cost her. The *twist* he'd added was calling out for her to switch from facing one way to the other. Worse, he had a knack for doing it when she wasn't expecting it. That was why she had to stay awake. She had the scrapes and bruises to remind her what happened when she got lazy.

On her way to the wall, she scanned the keep. Urias always quizzed her about her surroundings during this drill. The bully-boys were sparring in the training area. Before the army set sail, there would have been scores of Gottari males of all ages training in the sparring circles. Now there were only a few dozen boys, fifteen and younger.

The absence of the men brought Ligaia's scheming to mind again. Brin had tried to tell Urias what she'd overheard—about tricking the harbormaster, about the wagons, how Ligaia had asked Hesiod to stand aside. Urias had not only scolded her for spying, he'd accused her of leaping to conclusions. He'd said Brin had likely misunderstood. He'd said that Ligaia and her visitor might have been discussing a cultural celebration that normally would be frowned upon by the Gottari. Gods, how she'd wanted to roll her eyes. She knew better than to do that, too.

When Brin had tried to explain that Agoraki, and even his mother, knew that bad things were going to happen, Urias had shut her down again. He had said it was hearsay and alarmist. When she'd sulked, he'd said that he might be willing to discuss it further after her training, but only if she was ready to approach the topic with reason. It made her so annoyed, she doubted she'd try.

Brin spotted little Rohdric swinging his wooden sword with one of the other toddlers. Bully-boys in the making. Even toddler males were allowed to spar against one another. She was almost as old as the eldest boys there but had never sparred. "How will I ever learn to fight if I never get to do that?" She pointed her practice sword at the sparring grounds.

"What, spar?" She nodded. Just as Urias was about to reply, one of the larger boys knocked another to the ground. The bully stood over his opponent, puffed up like one of those fighting cocks in the alley pens down by the marketplace. The other lions cheered. "No need to worry about that," he said. "You'll soon be beating the likes of them. That'll come in no time."

It startled her. "What? *Beating* them? I've never even tried it."

Urias shrugged. "Doesn't matter. You'll be able to beat most anyone... *if* you stay focused on *your own* training and with your current level of dedication."

Brin's annoyance flared back to life. "That's ridiculous. I can't spar with boys."

"Why not?" It seemed like a dumb question, but Urias had that knowing little smile.

In that moment, Brin hated that smile. "They're bigger. And stronger."

"That's true. But unless you're Teavar, there's always going to be someone bigger and stronger."

Brin knew she should let it go. But... "The boys start so young. I just started."

"None of that matters." They arrived at the garden wall. Urias took her practice sword and laid their gear aside.

She refused to give in to his cheery little quips and his secret smile. "How could it not?"

Urias took Brin by the shoulders and compelled her to look at him. "Listen to me. If you don't quite feel it yet, you must trust me. You are gifted. If you keep this up, it's not just that you'll be faster, more flexible, more accurate, more alert, and far cleverer than every last one of them. If you stay on your own path, you'll be free of the mind games that plague most of them."

Brin tried but couldn't keep his words from getting into her chest and filling it up. It was his best trick, after all. This time it made her feel floaty and achy at the same time. She looked over at the boys and it made the achy part win out. "Well, they still get a big head start," she whined. "It's not fair."

Urias actually laughed. "Believe me, Amalus males are far from fair with one another. They pull brutal stunts and play cruel tricks—on their fellows and on themselves. Their culture focuses on competition rather than self-knowledge and improvement. They thrive on goading and obsess over saving face. The fear of losing is as debilitating as any other fear. All of that deprives the warriors of their most important attribute: clear thinking. I'm trying to provide you with the chance to avoid being bogged down by such things. If you stay on your current path, you won't have to worry about proving yourself or protecting your ego. You'll be conscious of your passions and your fears. Rather than hiding them away until they ambush your thinking, you'll have harnessed them for your own use."

Urias gently turned Brin by the shoulders to look back at the boys. "Yes, there will always be larger opponents. And, as with the ox, most of them will always be stronger. But, as is the ox keeper, you will be superior in ways that they will never quite grasp. Once your superiority is clearly demonstrated, they will simply accept it. Even if some of them will continue to resent it. Remember, every warrior respects a Blade-Wielder. Even if deep down they resent her. And respect provides advantages. Advantages that far exceed a mere head start. Understood?"

Brin watched the boys lurching and lunging. They did seem a bit slow. And obvious. She'd always known they were cocky brutes. She'd just never seen it as a drawback.

She sighed and looked back at Urias. Her uncle's lessons always came for more than the obvious reasons. "You think I'm allowing my fear to ambush my thinking about Ligaia, don't you?"

The corners of his mouth raised into his secret smile again. "Does it matter what I think?"

"I suppose not."

"Look, Brin, it's natural to have fears. Even suspicion can be useful. In regard to Ligaia, what would someone who'd mastered their passions and fears do next?"

"Remain mindful. Be cautious without overreacting. Seek a better understanding of the entire situation."

He crossed his arms over his chest. "A good start. What else?"

"Consider the worst outcomes and take steps to prevent them, or to at least reduce any harm."

"Such as?"

"Recruit allies. Look for ways to keep others safe. Especially loved ones."

Urias rubbed his beard. "Sounds like a reasonable plan. Keep me apprised." He smiled again, but this time he was sharing something with her—no smiley secrets. "But not before your twist jumps. Up on that wall. I want two round trips before the bell."

"Yes, Uncle." Brin hopped up onto the wall. He didn't *disbelieve* her, at least. And, unlike her absent parents, Urias would never ignore her.

ELAN WOKE WITH A START. She thought she had heard footfalls in the snow outside the tent. Had she dreamed it? She silently freed herself from the pile of blankets and gripped her knife. Biter lay beside her, but the tent was too small for a full-size blade.

Elan lay perfectly still, listening. All she heard was the steady breathing of Vahldan sleeping. Where was Teavar? The giant had assured her she could go inside and get some sleep. How long ago now? She'd begun this trek through the mountains sleeping outside Vahldan's tent, with Vahldan insisting she should sleep inside all the while. It was only when the snows grew deep and fell ceaselessly that she began taking him up on it. Still, she slipped in after he was long abed and slept on the ground across the entry flap.

A voice softly murmured outside, and the reply came in the familiar rich baritone. Teavar. Elan sighed and sheathed the knife.

"My king? Elan?" It was Herodes. Vahldan had put his cousin in charge of the scouting for the expedition. Elan had her reservations. Herodes was a good man, but she wondered if he was the best choice for the job. Especially now that things were growing ever more difficult.

"What is it?" Vahldan snapped. Elan rose and wrapped herself in a cloak.

"My king, I'm sorry to disturb, but I fear it's urgent." Herodes sounded distressed.

"Come," Vahldan said and Herodes slipped inside. "Well?"

Vahldan demanded, sitting up and putting a twig in the brazier to light the bedside lamp. Elan already had a guess.

"It's about our Bafranii guides," Herodes said, unwilling to look them in the eyes.

Elan knew. She would've wagered on it from the onset. "They're gone, aren't they?"

Herodes nodded. "Yes. They seem to have slipped away after nightfall. Their trail swings wide around the camp and heads back the way we came."

Vahldan stood. "Dammit."

Herodes bowed his head. "It gets worse, my king."

"Let's have it."

"They appear to have led us into a closed canyon," Herodes said.

Vahldan frowned. "What do you mean, closed?"

Herodes shook his head. "The way forward is unpassable. The only way out is back. And..." The captain of the Amalus scouts stared at his feet and his face flushed.

"And?" Vahldan prompted, his temper clearly flaring.

"I just got word from those I sent in pursuit of the Bafranii. It appears they've set off an avalanche. The way out is blocked." Herodes finally lifted his face. "We are trapped, my king."

ARNEGERN BLINDLY TRUDGED through a white world. As he moved, the swirling snow gave way to dark figures—first the tents and then men, loading a miserable-looking line of packhorses. As he approached the campsite's corral, a lone figure loomed. It was a young sentinel, huddled in what was likely every blanket he'd brought. Another dark shape, much larger, came into view—a pile outside the corral with protruding legs and lolling heads slowly being covered by snow.

Dead horses.

A pair of men struggled to drag another by its stiff hind legs to the growing pile. "A new one?" Arnegern asked the sentinel.

The lad nodded. "Over a dozen now, just from last night."

Arnegern moved on, heading to where he presumed the vanguard would be. His fellow captains' faces came into view, each one looking miserable. But no one looked worse than the king himself. The difference being that Vahldan looked more angry than cold.

"This is a matter of our reputation," Eldavar was heatedly saying. "We must go back and teach these slippery pirates the lesson they have coming. We must show the Bafranii—as well as the rest of Pontea—that the Amalus will not tolerate such treachery."

"If there is one thing we can guess of slippery pirates," Teavar prosaically began, "it is that they are not easily caught. Once they catch wind of our approach, they have but to sail away. Likely in as many directions as they have ships."

Vahldan's scowl swung to Arnegern. "Well? What's the situation?"

Arnegern hugged himself. "We lost four more men overnight— two to the coughing sickness and two frozen to death on watch duty. We also lost at least fourteen more horses, my king. The remaining packhorses are being reloaded as best we can, but the baggage train was hit hardest. The beasts we purchased in Bafrana are not as hardy as Gottari-bred horses."

"How soon before we can get moving?" Vahldan asked.

"Everyone is working at it, but it's going to take time. We have dozens of footmen who will need to ride due to frostbitten toes. The squad leaders are still sorting it out. Meanwhile, the snow we heated for water is beginning to refreeze, and our supply of firewood dwindles."

"Damn!" Vahldan's outburst shouldn't have been a surprise but it still made them jump. "And, of course, the longer we sit here, the worse our loses become."

"My king, I fear going back is our only option," Herodes bravely ventured. "Regardless of whether or not we can catch the pirates. My scouts can find no easy way forward. And the weather shows no sign of improving. Perhaps there is a way to punish the pirates once we're back in Bafrana, even if they flee the port. Maybe retake the fortress and await them? In any case, by going back we can cut our losses."

"We'd be waiting for imperial troops to arrive," Belgar suggested. "I'm not sure I relish the thought of becoming besieged in someone else's fortress."

"What else?" Herodes asked. "Back to Thrakius, then?"

"Presuming we can find our way there," Teavar said with a humorless smirk. "I doubt we can rely on Malvius to save us. Even if we got word to him."

"No, no, NO!" the king bellowed, his voice swallowed in the void of white. Vahldan spun back to face his captains. "We need no one to save us. We shall *not* go back to Thrakius. Not until we are victorious. In case you've all forgotten, the first blood of this war has already been spilled on the docks of Bafrana. By me! Do you know why?"

"He was insolent, my king," Eldavar offered. "The snake deserved it."

Vahldan began pacing before them. "It matters not whether that old shit deserved death. I killed him because *I am the Bringer!* And do you all remember who you are?" They exchanged glances. No one else dared speak. "Gods afire," Vahldan ranted. "This is our very problem. None of you do."

The king walked to each of his inner circle, staring into their eyes. He came to Arnegern last, his blazing glare locked on him. "After all we have been through together, Cousin, do you really not remember?"

"We are the Amalus, my king," Arnegern said, willing himself to look into his wild eyes.

Vahldan sighed. "Ah, at last." He began to pace again. "We are *Amalus!* We are the blood of the Gottari kings of old. We lions shall provide the first king of a hundred kingdoms of Urrinan. Did any of you believe that none of us would die when we left Dania? Can any of you imagine facing your families, to tell them that we've failed or retreated? Can you imagine us fleeing back to Dania, groveling to the wolves, resubmitting to the whim of the guild? Do any of you need to ask your men whether they would rather risk death or face such a certain disgrace?"

Arnegern's chest ached at the thought. Vahldan was right—this was a matter of honor.

The king kept pacing, breathing steam. "I damn well hope not. I damn well hope you all remember what we believe, for it's the reason that we are here. We believe that the old world shall quake at our coming and that a new world shall be made in our glory." Vahldan stopped in the center of them. "And I refuse to do anything but strive to win that glory, or die in the attempt. Now, which of you can offer me the solution to this puzzle?"

"I will."

They all turned to the only one of them who had yet to speak. Elan's blanket-wrapped head and shoulders were thick with snow; she had all but vanished into the storm. "You will what?" Vahldan demanded.

Elan stepped into the circle and stood nose to nose with him. "Solve it. Hrithvarra and I will find the way through. We will reveal the way for our army to cross this mountain range. Then you can have your war. Whether or not you are the Bringer, whether or not there's glory in it. Those will be your problems."

As she had so many times before, Elan seemed to waken her subject from his rage. "But you seemed so... Why, then?"

"Why risk venturing out in a blizzard so that you can lead us to war?" Vahldan nodded. Elan raised her chin. "Because we are doomed." The king opened his mouth to speak, but she went on before he could. "You're right. There's no going back. The first blood has been spilled. Ill-advised or not, destiny is in the making. If we stay, we die. And it seems we face dire hardship whether we go backward or forward. I would prefer to seek to lift our people up on the way to my foretold demise than to find it while slinking away from any challenge. Which leaves only going forward. Whether you are the Bringer or not, we must face the war you've already begun, or face dying without bringing about the reckoning we have all long since chosen."

Elan turned to Arnegern. "Captain, I'll be needing extra gear and supplies."

Arnegern glanced at Vahldan. The king nodded. Arnegern bowed his head. "You'll have whatever you need," he told her.

THE THRAKIAN GATEHOUSE bell rang at midmorning, echoing up through the mostly deserted lanes to the palace. The bell normally signaled permission for waiting ships to enter the harbor. Urias didn't think too much about it. He'd recently returned from his morning training session with Brin, so all the bell meant was that they'd beaten their deadline. It was a bit odd for it to toll during hiatus, but not an unheard-of occurrence.

Cold as it was, as long as it wasn't blowing wind, raining, or snowing, Urias preferred taking his breakfast and tea out on the terrace. Even with coal burning in every firebox, the palace was a drafty, bone-chilling place in winter. But his preference had more to do with winter's interior stench. The smell that permeated the closed-up palace was partly due to the scores of smoldering fires and poorly venting chimneys. Added to that, there were cooking odors from the kitchens, the mustiness of damp cushions and carpets, and —perhaps most egregiously—a score of privies and a hundred chamber pots. All of it mustered to carry out a unified assault on Urias's nose.

It made even the lowest temperatures on the terrace tolerable— particularly during meals. And today the sun was shining. Urias took a sip from his steaming cup. Somehow even the tea and sunshine failed to banish his anxious thoughts.

Although he ostensibly came to be the Wulthus liaison, Urias had additional—more personal—reasons for staying. First, he'd come to find a way to befriend and train his sister's daughter. Which was finally going well, thank the gods. There was always a chance of losing her interest or effort, but Brin's growth in strength, endurance, and skill continued to astonish.

A second reason was to keep his promise to his brother, to provide guardianship to his other niece. A third reason for staying had come to his attention since his arrival: keeping Amaga and Elan from harmful conflict. He'd learned that the goal was best achieved not only by keeping them apart, but by keeping them each in good spirits. In this last bit Urias was not doing as well. Even when kept apart, both women seemed miserable. The man one of them loved had married the other. Worse, that same man seemed intent upon shattering the dreams of both of them. At the moment, Urias could contribute to the safety of neither. One was at war, which was undeniably unsafe. The other was pregnant and seemed determined to take her unborn child away from his or her powerful father.

Urias had already talked Amaga out of fleeing to Danihem a half-dozen times, and yet he still wasn't at all sure that keeping her in Thrakius made her safer. Urias knew nothing about kingship, and he'd long ago learned not to predict anything about Vahldan. But he knew one thing: One does not steal away a king's heir. Not without repercussions.

Now, with the army abroad, he faced the addition of Brin's fears in regard to the remaining Gottari residents' state of vulnerability. The girl had a point. They lived in what remained a foreign city among a vastly more numerous conquered populace. And they were currently without the well-armed faction of their insular society. Urias was one of the few Gottari warriors left in the city.

Making all of his Thrakian problems even more troubling was the fact that a part of him longed for Dania, too. He poured the last of the teapot into his cup and stared at the sparkling sea as he sipped, wondering when he might see his princess again. He could imagine nothing better than to spend even a few days with

Icannes, if only to have her help him sort it out. Well, that and attending to a few other things that he'd been missing here in Pontea.

Urias popped the last boiled pigeon's egg into his mouth whole. As he chewed what turned out to be too large a bite, something curious caught his eye. The seagates had closed. The three ships that had arrived were docked at the quay. How long had he been lost in thought?

Commotion in the foreground pulled Urias's attention to the palace keep gatehouse. He nearly choked on the last of the egg as a column of armed men entered and trotted across the keep. Remembering Brin's hearsay, Urias leapt up and went to the parapet. He crouched and peered over. The arriving men seemed to be of various ethnicities, all decked in differing types of armor and weaponry. They appeared to be some sort of mercenary force.

This could not be good.

A dark-haired man with a brilliant blue cape and an elaborate hat with a brim and feathers led the column to the palace doors. Urias scanned the gatehouse and spotted a trio of the intruders who'd stayed behind in the archway. They had a Gottari guard at sword-point. One was binding the guard's hands behind him. As Urias watched, the guard tried to jerk his hands away and the one with the bare blade plunged it into the guard's throat. The pair of intruders ran to follow the others even as their victim slumped to the cobbles in the archway.

The sight jolted him. *Bad things are coming.*

"Damn it—why didn't I take her more seriously?" Urias muttered to himself as he rushed to grab his sword belt. He buckled it as he hurried out. He wondered if he should've donned his hauberk, or at least grabbed his shield. His instincts said it was too late. Going back was ill-advised. Speed was all. He flew up the servants' stairwell, taking two steps at a time to Elan's floor.

He drew the sword and burst into Elan's residence without knocking. Brin sat at a table and Despoina stood over her. Brin startled and the tutor gasped. Hesiod rushed in from the servants' quarters. "Captain, what is it?"

"Intruders. I think it's a coup. We've got to get the king's daughter to safety. Come, Brin. All of you, grab your cloaks and follow me." They all stood gaping. "Quickly!"

Hesiod rapidly translated to Despoina, and they finally started moving. Urias watched the corridor out the doorway until the trio joined him.

Urias took Brin's hand and started up the servants' stairs, holding the sword before him. Brin said, "Up, Uncle?"

"Yes, I have to get Amaga to safety, too."

Urias turned back when he realized that Hesiod and the tutor weren't following. They both stood on the stairs, looking forlorn. "Take Mistress Despoina down to the garden door. I'll bring the others and we'll leave the palace together." Hesiod nodded in confirmation.

Brin gripped his hand and resisted. "We can't just leave them. We all need to find Ago."

There wasn't time for this. "Brin, listen. I can't leave either you or Amaga behind."

"But Ago said—"

"Remember when we spoke of duty? Well, this is mine."

Brin flushed with irritation. Hesiod knelt and took her hand. He spoke to her in Hellainic, too rapidly for Urias to follow. Brin nodded. The man looked up. "Not to worry about us, Captain. I'll see to the mistress. Keep Bright Eyes safe." Hesiod gave Brin a pat. "Now go."

The foursome split into pairs, Hesiod leading Despoina down and Urias leading Brin up.

CHAPTER 28
THE CONTAGION OF WAR

"With the benefit of hindsight, many scholars have observed that Vahldan's attack upon the empire was pure overreach. They use its audacity to define his flawed legacy, cite its scale in decrying his ambition, his hubris.

I, however, consider such perspectives too narrow as they glaze over the simple fact that its vast scale lay at the very core of its success. No one expected anything like it because nothing like it had ever been attempted. Yes, my father's ambition caused no small amount of suffering and death. Still, it cannot be denied that his ambition led to a series of events that stunned the civilized world and changed the course of history."—Brin Bright Eyes, Saga of Dania

MORE THAN ANYTHING, Elan was glad to be out of the snow. She knew Hrithvarra felt the same. In spite of being led astray and abandoned in the mountains by their so-called guides, there was indeed a nearby pass through the mountains. Elan's instincts, honed in the mountains of Dania's eastern marches, had led her straight to it. The trail that descended from the heights led down to a series of shepherds' paths and tiered pastures directly above the sprawling imperial city of Efusium.

In spite of the Bafranii treachery, their crossing would only lose them a few days.

The sight of their destination was a marvel. The description they had heard, about hundreds of Efusium lanes being lit by thousands of lamps, turned out to be true. From on high, the canyon looked like an illuminated spider's web, spreading up from the harbor and fanning out to the massive city's surrounding walls. Many of the largest buildings seemed to be carved from white stone, shining like moonlit ice. Even the surrounding walls were impressive—the longest Elan had ever seen, following the contours of the foothills and running all the way to the harbor. She supposed the entirety of the Gottari nation could comfortably live inside of them.

The only problem Elan was having with her scouting mission was that the mountainsides above the city were barren. Other than the darkness, she had no real cover. Elan moved swiftly and silently, arriving at a lonely outcrop that provided a good vantage point. From here, the city was laid out to her like a map on a table. Efusium's walls were not as tall or formidable as those of Thrakius, but any wall might be deterrent enough. Especially from a surprise attack launched from these forsaken mountains. Few would willingly endure what the Gottari had to get here.

She spotted a closed gate at the base of an ancient, rutted cow path. The gate itself was wooden. It looked breakable. Better still, this entire top section of the city seemed deserted. There was no nearby gatehouse or bulwark, seemingly no sentinels at all. In fact, there wasn't a conscious soul as far as she could see. All of these lit lamps providing light for no one.

The place was undeniably beautiful. And peaceful.

The sick feeling in Elan's gut returned. She'd first felt it when the bastards the Gottari had been duped into aiding in insurrection had thrown a bound and terrified boy from a terrace to his death, right at her feet. Gods, she could still hear his screams and the thud that ended them. It only made her suspicion harder to stomach—suspicion that the war Vahldan was about to unleash was the sort she'd vowed to oppose when she'd taken her oath as a Blade-Wielder.

Elan reminded herself that she was no longer a Blade-Wielder, that she'd committed herself to the guardianship of the Bringer, that the war had already begun. As often as she'd thought of untangling herself from the life she had chosen all those years ago, there was no breaking free. Regret gained her nothing. There was no turning back.

To distract her troubled mind, she ran all the way back up the mountain to the army's position just over the ridge. Before going to him to report, she remounted. Vahldan and the Amalus leadership walked their horses to gather around her, waiting. She refused to reveal that she was still catching her breath. She let them wait. At least her success in leading them through the pass, saving an untold number of lives, had firmly reestablished the respect Vahldan had sought to strip from her back in Thrakius. For most of them, at least.

"Well?" On top of sounding impatient, Vahldan sounded smug. This was the persona he'd crafted for the Bringer—a role he now seemed determined to play.

"A shepherds' gate exists. It's wooden. There are no guards that I could see. It's quiet. The city sleeps. Or at least the top side of it does."

"We'll have to break the gate quickly," Teavar said. "Even lazy Tibairya might not sleep through that."

"The entire campaign relies on surprise," Vahldan said. "Remind everyone: We're seeking the fastest path through the city. No delays. Malvius said there should be fewer than two hundred in the armory barracks, but that's plenty. Even the escape of a handful of them could threaten the success of the campaign." He turned to Arnegern and Eldavar. "Remind them, too, that there's to be no pillaging. And no fires. Not yet. Assign just one squad to collect the lamps. We're not here for plunder. Our reward will come once we control the Straits. Remind them that our primary mission is to smash a corrupt regime." Vahldan smiled. "Getting rich will be a mere side benefit."

Elan only realized she'd harrumphed when Vahldan's head snapped to face her. "Something you'd like to add?"

"Not really." She drew a breath and released it. "Things have changed, is all."

"Not really," he mimicked. "This will be the same as the seizure of Thrakius. And look how well that's served our cause."

Elan wasn't sure how well she'd been served by his cause. "I wasn't there. But this all started with bringing murderers to justice. After that, we only fought against those seeking the same profit we wanted. Everyone in the game came willingly and agreed to its terms. I don't recall any talk of lofty causes, let alone their side benefits."

Vahldan bristled. "Are you saying our brave lions don't deserve reward, after their service, their sacrifice?"

She shrugged. "Not saying that. That just doesn't feel like what brought us together or what made us successful through all of our years at sea."

"Funny, but what it feels like to me is that we're three quick victories away from everything we've been fighting for since the beginning. And winning wealth will be a natural side effect. It's what builds empires and sustains the societies willing to seize upon the venture."

More lofty talk. Elan rolled her eyes. "I'm sure killing sleeping soldiers is a natural side effect as well."

Vahldan's scowl deepened. "Did you imagine that the Urrinan would just occur on its own, Elan? What would there be for the Bringer to do?"

This had gone too far. All of the captains and senior Rekkrs were staring. She could only whittle away at the respect she'd begun to rebuild. "Only a Bringer could know." She'd picked a futile fight at a terrible time. She tilted her head and softly added, "Your war is mine, my lord."

Vahldan hissed steam, then lifted his gaze to the group. "Remember, the gods favor the bold. We are lions! Never the prey. What our rivals cannot protect is rightfully ours. Our people's long-awaited feast lies before us. The Gottari shall be the spark, the Tutona the flame. Our people shall ascend amidst the ruin we shall wreak of this decadent empire."

Vahldan nodded to Jhannas. "Call up the ram. Let's break the gate."

In that moment, watching Vahldan lead them to war like this, Elan realized that—veracity of the prophecy aside—he was indeed the Bringer. He'd remade himself to fit the role. And she hardly recognized him.

The sick feeling surged anew, nearly overwhelming her. Was this necessary to the destiny she'd chosen? She'd known about the doom, and could accept it, but this?

This was harder to accept.

Their attack would achieve the surprise they sought. Dozens of men and scores of horses had died to get to this point. Scores more were ill or suffering the effects of frostbite. And that was just the Gottari. Untold more were about to suffer and die.

Now that all they'd striven for was laid before them, Elan felt sick with remorse. Perhaps the prophecy was indeed a sickness that had taken him, and now it had taken her. Perhaps Amaseila's voice had been the contagion, her augur left within them to fester and grow.

How could she be surprised by any of it? She'd watched as it all unfolded. If his inclusion in prophecy had led him—step by bloody step—to this, she too had long been infected.

Efusium's old shepherds' gate shattered on the second stroke of the ram. The Rekkrs chosen to ride with pikes swiftly filed in to lead the way. Next came the vanguard, with Elan on one side of Vahldan and Teavar on the other. Eldavar and Jhannas spurred their mounts out ahead of them, with Arnegern, Belgar, and Herodes just behind. The city of Efusium sprawled as the Gottari column penetrated deeper into it. The streets remained deserted, and the pike bearers held their long weapons upright and unused.

Elan continued to be impressed by the place. The upper city had rows of homes stacked in tiers rising from the street. Frightened faces peered from cracked drapes and over terrace parapets. Elan wondered how many must live there. The main roadway grew broader and was paved with increasingly smooth stone. The route to the waterfront was lined with columns on which sat large crockery lamps, perfectly lighting their way and leading them through the maze. The effect was dazzling; it sped this deadly invasion force toward its goal.

The echoing clatter of thousands of hooves on pavers had to be rousing every living soul within a bowshot, and yet they galloped through the city center without facing the slightest sign of resistance. She'd known Efusium's citizens were not warriors and yet it still amazed her. The vanguard entered what must be the market district lined with shuttered shops. Elan looked back at the column. The entire army had yet to clear the gate. Against the pale stone cityscape, Vahldan's army looked like muddy water flooding a dry ravine.

The main road turned to run parallel to the coast and into a broad, level court edged with grand colonnaded buildings, fronted by dozens of statues, all pristinely glowing in the lamplight. It looked to be the political and religious heart of the city, with one ornate structure seeming to be the palace opposite what looked like a massive temple.

On they rode, turning again to head downhill, straight for the harbor. The roadway began to level again and opened into a straight, broad raceway lined with low walls and tiered benches for seating. Elan imagined it was used for parades to welcome returning heroes. It made her wonder who these folk considered to be heroes. The surface here had changed from pavers to fine, packed gravel. The column picked up speed on the softer surface, and Hrithvarra wanted to fly. Elan had to admit, she felt as exhilarated as her friend, speeding through such a vast city among such an unstoppable force.

The squad who'd gathered the lamps were waved up to pass the vanguard and ride behind the pikemen. Their target came into view. It was exactly as she'd pictured, laid out exactly as Vahldan's maps and diagrams had foretold. The pikemen broke through the flimsy gate and stomped onto the armory grounds. The guards stationed there were mowed down in flight.

The barracks buildings remained dark. They'd achieved the surprise Vahldan had so diligently sought. His army had paid dearly for it. Now the Tibairya would suffer, too. More death was imminent.

Vahldan gave the command and the squad with the lamps fanned out to complete their deadly assignment. The rest of the column rode into position, surrounding the barracks. The pike-bearers smashed in the panes of the windows, and those carrying the lit crocks of oil slung them through to crash and explode into flames within. The shouting and screaming soon followed.

Tibairyan soldiers poured out in various states of dress, some jumping from the upper stories' windows. Many were afire and frantically rubbing themselves or rolling to snuff out the flames. Vahldan signaled and the first wave of Rekkrs rode in, cutting down the burning victims at will. Red blood splashed on white stone. The smell of cooking meat soon mingled with the stench of burning oil. Elan covered her nose and mouth and turned from the sickening slaughter.

Gods, it was despicable. It felt dishonorable. Her sickness grew, infecting her heart.

As the flames died down, a squad of remaining Tibairya emerged. Amazingly, the ragtag group sought to fight back. The first few held poleaxes and a few others had thrusting swords. None of them wore armor or bore shields. The survivors were brave enough to make a charge, but Gottari pikes quickly scattered their formation. The ensuing action had the feel of a romp, like a band of hunters who'd burst open a warren but had to compete for too few rabbits. Vahldan watched with a look of grim satisfaction, the flames reflecting in his unblinking eyes—eyes that were alarmingly familiar. The ugliness had him. And he was reveling in this. In war. In death.

The Bringer was pleased. This wasn't the crazed, raging ugliness. He was outwardly calm, still tethered to his functioning self. Elan saw him as never before. Realization struck. She saw that nothing she said or did this night would draw him back to himself. Playing the role of the Bringer had changed him. Accepting the ugliness as a necessity seemed to be cementing the change.

The ugliness frightened her as never before. It made her wonder if his true self had now been altered. Which chilled her to the core.

It hit her like a hoof to the head. This was the change she'd been sensing, since before his bonding ceremony. It was more than the acceptance of the ugliness. It was that he'd found his way to blocking her from interfering. This was a circumstance he had sought.

Corpses littered the grounds. Few of the defenders remained alive. Perhaps a score threw down their weapons, showed their hands, and pleaded to be spared. A group of Rekkrs rode in circles, herding them. "Your orders for these, my king?" Eldavar called.

"Eliminate them," Vahldan said. "No captives."

Elan recoiled, nearly vomited. "Yes, my king," Eldavar prosaically replied, and the little boy she'd watched grow to manhood called for his squad to dismount to perform the Bringer's gruesome bidding. The remaining Rekkrs rode in tightening rings around the victims, like carrion birds awaiting their chance to feed.

Elan opened her mouth to name it as murder, but before she could, Vahldan bellowed, "Herodes!"

"My king?" His cousin's horse trotted to them.

"Take your division now. Remember, target the warships first. Sink every vessel. No one escapes the harbor."

"Yes, my king." Herodes galloped off, calling to the archers who would shoot flaming arrows at the ships at anchor. Whether or not there would be sailors aboard them, no one knew.

Elan's stomach roiled. "We were told it's a lesser harbor," she said. "Malvius said there'd likely only be a handful of warships, that the rest will be fishing boats or belong to local traders."

Unlike her, Vahldan continued to watch the murder he'd ordered. "Boats and vessels that can be commandeered. We cannot afford even the chance that Nicomedya is warned."

"Oh right," Elan said. "I forgot. Natural side effects. This is how wars are won."

Vahldan turned to her and smiled, his eyes still cold and hard—the smile of the Bringer. "Now you're getting it," he said.

BRIN'S UNCLE pulled her along, keeping her running up the stairs as fast as her legs could carry her. They arrived on the top floor and Urias released her. "Stay here and listen. Call if you hear or see anything." Breathless, she nodded.

Urias went to her father's residence door and tried the latch. It was locked—probably to keep Ligaia out. Amaga and Ligaia despised one another. Urias knocked softly but urgently without stopping. Kemella finally opened it, looking annoyed.

"Where's Amaga?"

"She's inside."

"And your sister?

"We're all here. What is it?"

"We're under attack." Urias said, pushing past the king's sister to enter.

Urias left the door open. Voices questioning him and then full of alarm came from within. She detected a rumbling sound beyond the voices and her own heavy breathing and tiptoed from the servants' stairs to the main stairway. The rumbling grew. Boots on stone steps.

Brin ran back to the king's residence. Inside, Amaga and Kemella gathered around Mara holding the crying babe. "They're coming. Fast." They all turned to her.

"Come, ladies," Urias said. "There's no more time. Leave every-thing and follow me."

Mara was the first out into the corridor. Amaga complained even as Kemella pulled her out the door. "This is ridiculous. We don't even know what they want. We'll never outrun them."

"To the servant's stairway," Urias called, pointing with his blade. Brin was last, and he put a hand on her shoulder. "Run ahead and lead them. I'll be right behind." Brin nodded and hurried to do as bidden.

"Seize them!" The shouted command came in Hellainic from the top of the main stairwell. Urias turned to face the threat, waving for her to go without looking.

Four armored men emerged from the stairwell, warily approaching Urias. Brin hurried after the fleeing women. As the women started down the servants' stairs, another group of armed foreigners appeared, coming up. Ligaia was behind this squad of ruffians. "There they are!" Ligaia cried. "It's the thug's family. Don't let them escape!"

Brin instinctively spun and ran, leading the terrified women back to the residence. Urias had taken a defensive stance beyond the resi-dence doorway. The two invaders at the fore came on, slow and steady, swords held ready. Two more hung back, but only one had a blade. The unarmed fourth issued a string of hushed commands. Before Brin reached the door, one of Urias's attackers lunged. Her uncle's blade whirred, striking the man's blade so hard it was knocked from his hand. The attacker's companion was canny enough to strike before Urias could recover. Her uncle's reactive swipe clanged against the second blade, but too late. Urias growled in pain, obviously cut.

Urias staggered back, clutching at his left side, a red stain blos-soming on his pale tunic. "Uncle!" Brin cried.

Urias glanced but quickly refocused on the threat. "Go," he hissed. "Now!" The command set Amaga and Mara scurrying into the servants' quarters with the babe.

The unarmed one issuing the orders said, "He's hurt. End this." Brin stopped at the residence door, hoping to close out the invaders with her uncle inside. Urias backed away, hunched over his wound but with his defenses intact, and the three foes came on. Another lunging attack forced Urias to stop and swing. He knocked aside the thrust then slashed backhanded, scoring a hit on the attacker's shoulder. The struck man screeched and fell back. The other two armed men kept coming. Urias started to back away again, but he stumbled a bit and chaos ensued. The pair rushed in. Urias managed to shove one, but the other grabbed the wrist of his sword hand. Within moments, the pair had him by the arms. Urias's blade clattered to the floor, but he fought on. Her uncle was larger than both men and the struggle continued as Brin gaped in horror.

Urias pushed and grunted. His blade was behind the scuffle now. Brin could get to it, pick it up, help him. If she could get one of them, maybe hurt him, Urias could handle the other.

"Grab the girl! She's Vahldan's daughter!" It came from behind her. Ligaia!

Brin swiveled to find Ligaia and her ruffians coming down the corridor.

Brin glanced at the blade again. A squawk behind her made her whirl. Kemella had appeared in the corridor, struggling, her arms held behind her. One of Ligaia's ruffians had her. Brin's brave aunt must have come out to try to impede them. Brin stood frozen between the two struggles. Kemella was helplessly captured, Mara and Amaga would be trapped in the servant's quarters, and Urias seemed sure to be overpowered.

"Brin! This way!" The call came from inside her father's residence.

Through the doorway she saw Ago, standing at the terrace doors, wildly beckoning her.

Feeling helpless and terrified, impulse drove her. Brin ran to her friend.

When Brin got to the terrace, Ago was climbing over the end of the low wall and onto some gnarled vines. Ligaia was coming through the residence, pointing. "She's getting away!"

Brin's own residence was below. She looked down over the parapet. More armed men were already on the terrace. One of them spotted Ago, pointed, and called to his companions.

"Come on, Brin," Ago urged her. "Up!" He started to climb. There was nothing above but the tile roof. Boots thumping, running, coming. No choice. No thinking, just doing.

Brin scrambled up on the parapet and frantically grabbed for handholds in the vines. Her feet left the terrace wall, but she couldn't seem to find solid footing. She kept reaching and grasping higher holds. She looked down alongside all of the stacked terraces to the garden and was instantly dizzy. "Climb," Ago pleaded. She released her hand and her shaky foothold gave way. She gasped but her foot struck another branch that held. She was frozen, clinging for her life with one hand. She looked up to find Ago already on the roof. Her amazing friend hung over the edge upside down, holding out a hand to her.

Ago was only a span above. Just a span. Why couldn't she move?

"There she is," a male voice called from her father's terrace. "Get her!"

Brin's fear of falling disappeared. She reached and grabbed and pulled and stepped, reached and grabbed and pulled. In moments, Ago's strong hand latched onto her wrist. Before she knew it, she found herself on slanted tiles, crawling upward, following Ago. It was so steep! Brin was sure she would slip and fall to her death at any moment, and yet somehow her sandals and hands held to the gritty ceramic surface.

Ago led her all the way to the tiles of the peak, which were covered in pigeon poop. The far side's slope was less steep, and a big old chimney stood higher than their heads at the center of the span. Ago got on his butt and started scooting down to the peak of another roofline jutting from the slope and holding up the tall chimney. She followed. They held the jutting roof's edge to get around to the side facing out. The front side of the roof's extension was a metal cage stained with soot—some sort of vent. Ago pulled at the bottom and it opened upward, like a street vendor's awning. He climbed inside and held the vent open for her. She all but fell in and he closed it behind her, blocking out much of the light. Voices drifted to them on the cold air from outdoors.

The slats of the vent let in a bit of light. They were in a narrow walkway with a stone wall and a large metal door before them. "It's for the chimney sweeps," Ago told her. "Follow me. I know the way." He started down the walkway.

"To where?" Brin asked, suddenly shivering uncontrollably.

"I can get us all the way to the caves from here. They'll never catch us."

Brin was frozen in place again. "But my uncle! They have him. My whole family."

Ago came back to her. "I don't think they'll hurt them. My maaman said they want you all as hostages."

"Hostages? For what?"

"To exchange for their freedom, in case your father gets back before the imperials come."

Imperials? Coming here? She could hardly breathe. "I can't just leave them," she gasped.

Ago took her hand and gave it a squeeze. "Calm down. You'll be no good to your family if we get caught." He nodded, trying to look assuring. "Just breathe. We'll figure out something."

Brin couldn't imagine what that something might be, but she realized she could breathe again. Of course she had to avoid getting caught. It's what Uncle Urias would have her do. "All right," she said. "As long as we're not just leaving them."

"We're not," he said. "Not for long. Come." Still feeling caught in a riptide, she gave in to the pull as Ago led her down the corridor into the dark unknown.

THE PRICE OF CHANGE

"*Although I dared not ask at the time, I find myself wondering exactly when it was during the campaign to seize the Pontean Straits that my parents had learned of our plight back in Thrakius. Did either of them wish to return as swiftly as possible? Did my father ask his men to fight on in the knowledge of the danger their own families faced? Or was pressing ahead a foregone course, accepted by all? I suspect the latter, but, by all accounts, a dark pall lay upon the Amalus army, even in the war's early going.*

Even in the tales of it, the war seemed far from glorious to me. The Amalus had first been tricked into abetting a bloody coup by the pirate Zafan, after which they had been stranded in the frozen heights by their traitorous Bafranii guides. Many had died horrible deaths even before the campaign truly began. Soon after which the duplicity of Isidros was revealed. For those at home and abroad, it seemed misfortune only hardened an already grim spirit. For the Amalus faithful, if nothing else, hardship and trial served to confirm that the Urrinan was nigh.

For me, anticipation was ever tethered to dread. I recall it being in the very air we breathed. Yes, glory would eventually be won. And yes, dark-

ness loomed for those who were about to bring it forth."—*Brin Bright Eyes, Saga of Dania*

THIS WASN'T AT ALL what Elan had expected. Brutality aside, taking Efusium had been laughably easy. How could such luck continue? The gods were too fickle for it. After spilling blood so heedlessly, she had presumed taking the next city would be bloodier still, the odds near insurmountable. Nicomedya, after all, was the gateway to the famous Pontean Straits—the waterway of trading wealth for not one empire but two.

She certainly hadn't expected open city gates and cheering crowds inside them.

Teavar and Jhannas rode with long pikes bobbing before them, slowly clearing the way for the column of the Amalus army on the bustling narrow streets that led to the market square. Elan could already see that the square ahead was jammed with people, though the scouts had reported that the army would face no threat. It seemed no opposing warriors remained in the city, unless they were well-hidden. Which certainly remained a possibility. Although Elan felt as though no one else was concerned over it.

It seemed that hubris, too, was a contagion.

Vahldan, riding beside her, waved and the Nicomedyans cheered. Vahldan was beaming, and Elan hated it. She shouldn't, but she did. This smile was genuine, but it only reminded her of the Bringer's smile. She hated how he'd changed, and she resented how his changing had changed them all. She hated that she couldn't stop herself from loving him. It felt like trying to stop her hair from growing.

Even if it was only a part of him, how could she still have these feelings for someone who repulsed her like that? The fear that his true self was lost roared in her ears, louder than the cheering crowd.

He glanced over. "What?" he said.

"Nothing." Everything.

Vahldan harrumphed. "Even you have to admit it?"

"Admit what?"

"That this is pretty great. Come on, Elan. Look at them. They love us!"

Those who had made a show of their arrival, anyway. "There will always be those thrilled by war, I suppose," she said. Elan looked beyond the crowd lining the main street, down the alleys and into the courtyards. People were shouting, drinking, singing, laughing, crying, flirting, lounging, fighting. Just as Vahldan reveled in his ugliness, some of these folks reveled in the ugliness of war. She suspected she knew what they were about. "Those in the streets are the laborers, the debtors—the downtrodden. There are always folks with a reason to cheer any army that chases away their drudgery for a spell."

"Oh, Elan," he said, sounding like he felt sorry for her. "Do you really not recall? Folks cheering us in a stone city? It's your dream come to life."

She knew it wasn't true. Her dream had been of joy. Saying so would gain her nothing.

He chuckled. "Even so, this is better than a dream come to life. Remember how things used to be here?" He pointed. "Right over there is where those soldiers bullied you, groped you. All you were doing was shopping for cloth. Those soldiers are gone now, never to return."

"Perhaps," Elan admitted. She pointed to the edge of the market square. Beyond the gawkers lining their route, looters came and went through shutters torn from shops, weaving between over-turned merchants' carts strewn across the lanes. The raucous throng scurried for and fought over booty. "But now the merchants who were here can't even sell cloth."

Vahldan's frown flipped to a smirk. "What about over there?" As they entered the market square, he pointed to the slave traders' stages, stalls, and pavilion. Axe-wielding Gottari were among city folk—presumably former slaves—demolishing the entire apparatus of that dreadful segment of the market. The spectacle was surrounded by hooting and laughing onlookers passing stolen bottles of wine as they cheered on those dismantling their city's primary economic powerhouse.

Vahldan's smile was one of the smug sort that the Bringer preferred. She knew he'd sent men ahead to attend to this. He'd been waiting to impress her with it. "Before today, sanctioned merchants were selling Gottari children. The day will come when no child will be sold as chattel in Pontea."

She couldn't deny that it was rightful. But she suspected his motives, and, for her, the fact that he'd made a show of it tainted the achievement. He loved wielding his lofty goals. Not that she disapproved of them. But they were easier to bandy about than to bring to reality. "That will be a fine day, when it comes," she said, doubting it was possible in her lifetime. "All men deserve justice. As freed slaves seek a new start, many honest merchants and crofters—even those who never bought or sold a single slave—will have lost everything to war. In the aftermath, it will require a great effort to make things right for all of them."

In an instant, the arrival of the ugliness was revealed. His eyes crazed and his body went rigid. "All change comes at a price. We are making the world over. Nothing will be easy about it. Still, in the wake of our conquest, the world will be made a better place, one city at a time."

Elan bowed her head, silently conceding. Anything she said would be wrong.

"Do you doubt it?" It wasn't so long ago that Vahldan had sought the anchor she provided each and every time he fell to the ugliness. Of late he didn't seem to want to find his way back from it, which was alarming enough. Worse, now he was goading her, flaunting his rejection of their former roles. When she didn't answer quickly enough, he pressed. "Well?"

Elan chose her words carefully. "I do not doubt the change or the price, my lord."

"But?" Vahldan goaded again.

"But I suspect that there are winners and losers in every change."

"I'd say it's damn well time *our* people were winners."

He glared. She kept her eyes averted, her countenance impassive. "As it shall be."

"Believe me, it fucking shall." Gods, he was relentless. She had to wonder what would become of them now that he was casting their roles aside? The gods knew she'd tried to adapt as things had changed. She was already wary of sleeping so near to him, of sensing his resentment right up until he closed his eyes to sleep. She often found herself wishing she'd been left behind. If she had, what would've come of her duty? Had she only postponed confronting that question? Which only led to the next: What would then become of her destiny? She already knew she had nowhere to go. With the advent of war, it would only be truer.

They rode on in silence. If she was no longer his anchor, maybe she should at least point to the storm on the horizon. After all, she suspected she was one of the few who could. His acceptance of the ugliness made him unpredictable at best and dangerous at worst, but she didn't think he would actually attack her. Not physically, anyway. "This doesn't worry you?" she asked, gesturing at the chaos of the market square.

"What? A little looting?"

"Not just that. All of it. This city is the gateway to the Straits—a jewel of the empire. And the imperial garrison simply abandoned it."

"They weighed the odds and saw they were beaten. Foes flee from defeat all the time."

Elan sought a neutral tone. "So it's over? You think the war is won?"

"I didn't say that. But progress has been made. Our fortunes keep improving."

Horsella's grace, there were so many questions a prudent leader should be asking. "What about your shifty new friend?"

"Who, Isidros?" She nodded. Vahldan shrugged. "He promised he would deal with the garrison. The garrison is gone." His bedamned smirk reappeared.

It was fine that he wanted to put her in her place, but his people needed him to think. "And the man disappears with them? Doesn't that seem strange?"

"I don't know. Perhaps not. Perhaps he'll turn up. Just say what you mean." The ugliness was so close to the surface now—it flared back in an instant.

Elan composed herself. "I'm only saying that there is much to consider." They rode a few beats. His silence was a hopeful sign, but his expression remained stormy. She had to keep trying. "For instance, why would the harbor be so empty in hiatus?"

"Dammit, I don't know," he shouted. "What do you want from me?" Teavar and Jhannas swiveled in their saddles, both wearing concerned expressions. Were they concerned about him? Or for her? Likely both.

Elan drew a breath and cleared her head. She conjured an image of how they used to be together—searched for the feeling. She turned to him, cocked her head, and reached out, seeking their old connection. "Look at me." He turned, still fuming. "Hear me?" He pressed his lips tight but nodded. "I only want the best for you. For all of us."

"Do you?" Still snappish, but less hostile.

"Of course. I want to help you consider things—to help you see." She gestured to indicate the unrelenting chaos surrounding them as they turned toward the palace. "And hear." She put a hand to her ear, like an old woman glad to hear a granddaughter.

Vahldan actually smiled, the ugliness finally clearing from his gaze. "You want to know what I see? I see that this city is ours. I see that we took it without losing a drop of Gottari blood. I see walls that now protect *us*. For as long as we need them to. What I hear is that all of this irks you, Elan. Can you not just allow the rest of us to enjoy this for a moment?"

Sure, she'd managed to banish the ugliness, at least temporarily.

Still, his coldness stung. Gods, it made her realize how much she longed to reach him. The real him. "What will become of us?" she ventured. He shrugged. "Please, dear heart. What we had, I know it still exists. It must. Can you not seek it?"

"So the answer is no—you can't let anyone enjoy this?"

"Please," Elan said. "Don't do this. You used to hear *me*, see *me*. I need to know."

"Know what?" he snapped.

"If you intend to surrender to the ugliness. If you no longer..." She didn't dare finish.

He laughed. It sounded so bitter. Tears sprang to her eyes and she turned to hide them.

"Oh, come on," he said. "You can't possibly be so upset."

"Of course not," she said, wiping her face, straightening in the saddle, and raising her chin. "Forget I brought it up." She tapped Hrithvarra with her heels, speeding ahead.

The crowd thinned as they came to the gates of the Nicomedyan palace. Arnegern and his advance unit had formed a perimeter. The guards were already set. The palace was ready for their use. Elan only wished for a safe place to be alone.

She cleared the gate and slowed, scanning the grounds, looking for a place to go.

"I know this is hard," he said. It surprised her. He'd caught up. She thought he was done with her. His tone was soft, sympathetic. She turned to find the real Vahldan staring at her. Something had jolted him back to himself. "We were told, again and again, that Urrinan would be born of turmoil, of bloodshed. Who could have known how it would really feel? I sure didn't. And it doesn't seem to be getting any easier. But if I am the Bringer, then the Bringer is me." He looked away. Was he abashed? "It's not just that the gods chose me; they made me what I am. All of me."

It stunned her. Not only had he embraced the belief that he was the Bringer, he was using it to justify his acceptance of the ugliness. "So that's all we are? Tools of Urrinan? Playthings of the gods?"

Vahldan sighed. Stableboys scurried out to meet them. Before she could dismount, he laid a hand on her arm. "I don't know," he said. "Maybe so. But I need you to know that I'm still striving for our people. I have to keep believing. The prophecy says that the Tutona will rise from the ruins, and our people will rise to the fore. I have to strive to make it happen. Look around, Elan." He gestured at the debris and the mess, at the fine homes in shambles. "The civilized world is already in decline, and not because of us. Those who hold the reins of power—they're not going to willingly step aside." His expression grew pained. "People are going to die. There will be suffering. I fear none of us can avoid the ugliness of what's sure to come. If it's unavoidable, I want us to come out on top."

His earlier words came back to her. "All change comes at a price."

Vahldan lifted his hand from her arm and gave her a shy smile. "This has always been hardest on you. You don't deserve it. You've always been the best of us. I hope you can keep believing, too." He dismounted and came to her stirrup. "I've always said that I can't do this without you. But when you leave me to it—when you refuse to support my efforts—I have no choice but to try." He slumped, turned, and walked away, heading toward his loyal captains gathering at the bottom of the stairs to the palace doors.

Elan sat on Hrithvarra, processing. Gods, could she continue to stand by him if he left his true self behind forever? What efforts would she be required to support? What if those efforts grew crueler, darker? Could she be the guardian to a monster? Would she still love him? She already wished she could stop. She'd given herself to him— walked away from everything to do so. What would come of breaking that vow? Things were already darker and more painful than she'd imagined was possible on the day she had left her people. Could the goals remain the same amidst such darkness? Who could decide whether her duty was done? What would her life become without it? What else was left to her but Urrinan and its Bringer? Had the gods tricked her? If they had, who else was there to blame? She'd always known they were fickle.

Did any choice remain to her? Or had her only real choice already been made?

Elan's hand went to her chest, pressing on the kestrel under her cuirass. She felt her heart beating beneath it. She remembered what she had told him on the day she'd made her choice. That when a kestrel makes her choice, it's for life.

BRIN SHIVERED, and not just from the cold. She watched as Agoraki set aside his little lamp and pressed his hands against the opposing walls to nimbly climb up onto an overhead shelf of stone. The corridor they'd used to get here had continued to grow smaller. The space Ago had gotten to was barely tall enough for him to lift his head while on his hands and knees and only slightly wider than his shoulders. He somehow twisted around and reached down, holding his hands out to her. She reluctantly reached to put her hands in his and he pulled. Brin used her feet to clamber up, pushing off on the excess mortar between stones. He backed away as he pulled and she ended up stretched out on the cold stone.

Brin lay there, her nose full of ancient dust, letting the fear of the small space close in and press up against her. Till she got used to it and could move again. It was like everything else these days—if she really wanted not just to survive but to help others, she had to accept living with fear and discomfort.

Brin found it helped if she thought about her uncle. Urias had been so sure of her. He always reminded her that Skolani blood flowed in her veins, that her heritage was a gift, that her mother's mothers were strong and resolute. That she could be, too. Every moment of every day, she willed herself to remember it. Her uncle needed her to.

Ago had already set out again, crawling on hands and knees. She rubbed her itchy nose, hoping she wouldn't sneeze again. Making noise was one of the few things that truly seemed to annoy Ago.

More afraid of staying behind, she willed herself to get on her hands and knees and start crawling. She'd never realized how terrified she could feel about being left alone. Or finding herself in total darkness. She was about to experience one or the other. He'd left the lamp in the corridor and moved around a bend in the corridor. She willed herself to pass by the lamp and follow the shuffling sounds of Ago's crawling, fighting her rising panic. Just as she moved into complete blackness, a dim glow appeared ahead.

Ago's form was brightened by illuminated slots. He slid aside to make room for her. She slithered up next to him into a space not much larger than her shoulders' width, the light ahead her only small solace. They lay facing vertical blocks with venting slots between them, the same as those she'd watched her father's bonding ceremony through. Ago put a finger to his lips, then gave her arm a reassuring squeeze.

How had he found this place? Brin always marveled at his curiosity and fearlessness. He'd made it his mission to know every one of the hidden ways of the palace and every feature of the caves and catacombs beneath it.

Brin peered through the slots and instantly recognized the chamber below. The vent was above the double doors of the high hall, looking into the chamber. She heard their voices before she found them seated across from one another at the far end of the long dining table.

"You must be patient, my lady. You shall have your vengeance." It was the man with the cape who'd been directing those who fought with Urias. Ago had already told her that he was the anax of Nicomedya. She'd often heard her father and others mention his name: Isidros. "The punishment for crimes such as theirs is either enslavement or execution."

"Why wait?" Ligaia said. "If all is going as we'd hoped in the Straits, I don't understand the need for caution."

"We need only keep them captive until we are sure the Gottari are overcome," Isidros said dismissively, barely looking up from the papers lying before him. "Which is all but assured. Then your captives' trials can begin."

"We ought to at least throw the beasties into the dungeons with the men."

"The menfolk are different. The precaution is warranted. Vahldan's family is secure enough in the servants' quarters. As are the women and children we have under guard in the barracks. We mustn't stoop to their level of savagery. The imperial bureaucracy will demand a record of all that comes to pass."

"Stooping as low as them isn't possible," Ligaia spat. She rose and started pacing. "They're such hateful people, and we keep them in luxury. You should see how the she-beasts growl and glare. Even the youngest sister, whom I once thought almost human. But that little white-haired witch is the worst, hissing and spitting. I do believe she'd bite, given the chance."

"A good slap now and then should keep her in line. But no bruises. If the thug king somehow manages to get back before the imperials, there can be no evidence of abuse."

"She'd immediately rant to him of it. She loves nothing better than complaining."

"Her word against ours. If I guess right, Vahldan has little patience or pity for her. He only wants his heir."

Ligaia laughed. "Perhaps that's how we should discipline her. A few swift kicks to her swollen belly. Anything to ensure the thug's line is broken." Isidros made a tsking sound. Ligaia started pacing again. "Speaking of which, has there been any sign of that feral daughter?"

"Again, patience, my dear. My men will find them."

Ligaia spun back. "Remember, the boy is not to be harmed."

"Yes, yes—they know. The pair will be caught and secured, safe and sound. Just like the rest of the thug's family. In the meantime, they pose no real threat. They are but children."

"Ha. Don't be so sure. That girl is as slippery and crafty as a weasel."

The anax looked up from his reading. "And the boy?"

"The boy is clever, yes. But, as I said, he's of noble blood. He just doesn't realize it yet."

Brin glanced at Ago's profile. He didn't look surprised. Brin couldn't tell if he was just listening hard or if Ligaia was making him upset.

"Such a mystery," Isidros said. "One day you'll share the solution with me, yes?"

Ligaia lifted her chin. "One day. Which reminds me—you're certain my missive will be delivered?"

"For the fifth time, you may rest assured, my lady. I've been assured that the imperial ships from Megaria got clear of the Straits. They're well on their way to Cispadaena on smooth seas. We gave the Tiberians ample warning before we left, and the Nicomedyan garrison should be in Megaria by now, which doubles the size of the force there. I've also received confirmation that the Bafranii pirate Zafan has betrayed the Gottari, just as he boasted he would. The thug's army is all but trapped."

"Smooth seas," Ligaia muttered as she started pacing again. "Makes me wish I knew where my sly little brother has gotten to."

"Fear not. Malvius wouldn't dare go near the Straits right now. He'll stay well-hidden. You know Malvius better than I do. Deep down, he's little more than a coward. Your brother likes to let others start his fires, then he stands back and watches them burn. He'll keep plenty of distance until he figures out how the flames can serve his purposes."

"The traitorous weasel," she spat. "I thought the eastern fleet was tasked with hunting him down. Horius was supposed to have the little shit before he left Bafrana."

"Malvius is a canny one," Isidros said. "He must have sensed the trap. Perhaps they'll find him yet. But it really doesn't matter if Malvius is caught or not. If he manages to briefly elude imperial justice, once we're married, I'll see that it catches up to him. I'll petition Horius for a hearing and hunt him down myself. The rector owes my family many debts, which add up to considerable influence. In no time at all, we'll have your sly brother convicted of conspiring to murder not just your father but you and your former husband."

Ligaia stopped pacing but did not turn to him. "How can you be so sure?"

Isidros laughed. "Most of the imperials with power already suspect it's true." The anax stood and took his cup to the sideboard to refill it. "For many years now, the bureaucrats have simply looked the other way, thinking they needed your brother in order to maintain a viable shipping operation in Thrakius. Once you and I are a team, my dear, that will no longer be a concern. Soon enough, all of the ships Malvius stole from you and your father will be restored in your name. His entire fleet will become part of ours." The anax sidled over to put his hands on Ligaia's shoulders from behind. She startled and then stiffened. "Very soon now," Isidros said, massaging her shoulders, "we will have near total control over all of the trade crossing the Pontean. Things will be just as you have long wished them." He leaned to gaze at the side of her face. "Do you believe me?"

"Yes," Ligaia hissed, but the tension in her body and face remained.

Isidros gave up rubbing her shoulders. "There are no more petitioners today. My lady should retire, get some rest before dinner. If anything else arises, I will send for you."

"Perhaps I will go up for a time," Ligaia said. Brin recognized her tone. This was placating Ligaia, saying one thing but meaning another. The woman was always scheming. "They've very nearly gotten the stench out of my residence," she said as she left.

After Ligaia passed beneath them, Ago signaled and they crawled back. They got to the ledge and he dropped down, then helped her to the floor. They stood in the lamplight, staring at one another. "What'll we do?" Brin said.

Ago's brow creased. "I'm not sure. But at least we're sure your family is still safe. For the moment. Come on." He started off, heading back the way they'd come. Ago was always thinking, always on the go. It distracted her from being scared all of the time. Besides that, the way he kept moving forward gave Brin a good feeling deep down in her stomach.

MALVIUS LED the girl into his chamber at the inn. Dex had already lit a lamp and had a fire going in the firebox. He glanced at his guest as he poured two cups of wine from the flagon he'd had brought up from his special barrel on Gullwing. This one wasn't a girl but a woman, which was sort of the point. She didn't seem at all nervous, just curious as she intently looked the space over. She was a handsome woman, more sturdy than graceful, but she was by far the best he'd seen since he'd arrived. His guest shrugged off her woolen cloak and brushed aside a lock of gray-streaked but lustrous dark hair, tucking it behind an ear. Her eyes were full of wonder, which was perhaps the most attractive thing about her.

"You've never seen this one?"

Her gaze snapped to meet his. "My lord?"

"Sorry, I just assumed." She was still puzzled. He handed her a cup. "I assumed that, well, in your line of work, that you'd have seen every bedchamber for rent in town."

Her mouth quirked in a sly smile. "This is the nicest bedchamber for rent in Akasas, my lord."

Malvius looked around at the shabby space. "Don't remind me. But still…" He shrugged.

"Few men around here will pay for the finest chamber in town to bed a whore… my lord."

He raised his glass. "Here's to men who aren't from around here." She laughed, raised her cup, and sipped the wine. Her eyes widened in apparent delight. "You like it?" He paused. "Wait, what shall I call you?"

She regained the sly smile. "How about Raven?"

"Raven," he repeated. "It suits you."

"My hair," she said, running her hand through it, clearly proud of a fine feature.

"That," he conceded, "and you seem clever."

Raven's smile grew. "A compliment. I'll take it. Thank you."

"Undoubtedly the first of many you deserve." Malvius gave her a quick once-over.

Raven looked away, slightly flushed, and sipped again. "To answer your question, this is the best wine I have tasted in long years."

"Knowing this place, I don't doubt it. I had the same problem last time I was here. It's why I brought my own this time."

He sat in the lone chair. She stood fidgeting, then reached for the stays on the front of her frock. Her countenance switched from awkward to businesslike. "And how would my lord like me?" She instantly adopted the sexual persona her vocation relied on. It changed her expression, posture, voice—all of it. For him, not for the better. At least not at the moment.

Malvius waved for her to stop. "Leave it be. Perhaps we'll get to that later. For now I'd just like you sitting." She frowned, puzzled, and fidgeted again. "Please, sit. On the bed is fine." He started to rise. "Unless you'd prefer the chair."

"Oh no, my lord." Raven hurried to sit on the bed's edge. She sipped her wine, studying him. "So, if not this"—she flounced the frock's stays—"what else would my lord like?"

Raven was halfway back to businesslike. He had to admit, at the moment, she was alluring. It felt halfway to getting an invitation from the real woman rather than the actress. But still, his heart wasn't in it. "I'd just like to talk. I hate it here, and I enjoy talking to women. It's been some time since I have. I thought your company might help me endure this shithole."

"May I ask why me?"

Malvius shrugged. "You looked like you could use a break."

Raven surprised him by sighing and leaning back. "I can't argue with that." She was revealing another glimpse of her true self. Which continued to charm him.

Her gaze met his again. "Plus, there's a certain level of... shall we call it *maturity*?"

She dramatically arched a brow. "I beg your pardon?" Sarcasm. She was funny.

"I mean that in the most flattering way. As in, a mature conversationalist."

She softly laughed, crossed her legs, and leaned onto one elbow. "Honestly, I'm more thankful than you could know."

"How so?" She bit her cheek, obviously weighing how much to say. "Go ahead. We're here to talk, remember?"

"I was afraid you were going to say I look like your mama or some awful thing like that."

"Trust me," Malvius said, "that is *not* my sort of thing. I hardly knew my mother."

Raven's smile grew wry again. "Trust *me*, my lord. It's the distant mothers who create that sort of thing." Her smile faded. She looked at him. Really looked. "Since we've established why me, why here?"

He glanced around the chamber. "Where else? You said yourself, it's the best in town."

"Not the bedchamber. Why Akasas?"

Malvius hadn't counted on her questioning him in return. He was torn between enjoying and hating it. But that was true of most worthwhile pursuits. He shrugged. "Why not?"

Raven gave him a mocking scowl. "You hate it here, remember?"

Malvius reminded himself that he could tell this woman whatever he wanted, or nothing. He could lie if he wanted and end it whenever he wanted. It was the beauty of having hired her. But what was there to hide? Whom would she tell? "Let's just say that Akasas is out of the way."

Raven took a slug of wine and swallowed. "It's a fucking sheep shack."

"I can't argue with that." It was becoming the conversation's refrain.

"Which makes your arrival all the more curious." Her eyes lit with a new level of charm. "My lord," she added.

Hers was a devious charm. It was like she was teasing him with the potential of revealing her true self. Or was it something else? "You know who I am, don't you?"

Raven paused again. She was still being quite cautious. Finally: "You, my lord, are the disowned heir to the anax. The one who fell in with the barbarians who killed his papa. More specifically, the barbarians he met here, in Akasas." She waggled her eyebrows. "Is it not so?"

Malvius tipped his head. "Well done. It is so. Which means you'll understand that here is the last place that anyone would expect to find me. Which makes it a fine place to avoid the sort of scrutiny that someone like me tends to attract."

"So, you're hiding."

He shrugged. "Fine. I'm hiding."

"From?" Raven reset her charming gaze.

"No one and everyone." She rolled her eyes. "You could say that it's more that I'm waiting for a new circumstance to arrive. One I helped to set in motion."

She scrunched her nose. "Sounds miserable."

He grinned. "I can't argue with that."

Raven held out her empty cup. "The wine is good, though."

Malvius rose to retrieve the flagon and pour for her. "Perhaps temporary misery is the price of improving circumstance. Hopefully one that's actually pleasant. Maybe one that lasts for a while."

She laughed. "That is exactly what I tell myself before every customer." She started to drink and caught a glimpse of him. "I mean no offense, my lord," she added.

"I'll accept your admission as a temporary misery. And perhaps hope to become an exception."

"Oh, you're already that." She leaned back and looked at him again—the same sort of true looking she'd done earlier. "My I offer you some advice, Lord Malvius?"

She really did know him. It made him want to know her real name. "How could I refuse?"

"You mentioned your mother. My father is gone now, too. And though I often hated him when he was here, I find myself thinking of him most every day. He was a wagoner. After the amber was mined out of these hills, he hauled salt and tin ore down to the docks. It didn't pay. Well, not enough. Things went ill for him, but he did his best. Mostly by playing it safe. I knew I wasn't like him. So did he. He always told me that I was reckless. He said I was sure to one day set my wagon running rogue. It can happen, making daily runs down the mountain. The wrong runaway load can crush you if you're not willing to accept it as a loss. My father said that even if one is ill-fated, like me..." She narrowed her gaze. "Maybe even like both of us. Well, if we can keep our wits and accept our losses, when the right one comes along, we can at least ride it out—maybe even steer it to a favorable crash."

"I get it. You're saying my wagon is running rogue. But are you saying I should accept the loss? Or is this the right one to ride out?"

Raven raised her cup with a smile. "That is not mine to say. I mention it only because I sense a kindred spirit. I wish you well in your quest for the best landing."

"I appreciate the well-wishes," he said and raised his in salute. They drank.

Her countenance became earnest. "We can't go back, my lord. Once the wagon's running. We can only jump clear or crash." She met his gaze, and he saw her sorrow, knew that she saw his. "She's not here, and I'm not her," Raven whispered. "Remember, riding out the wrong load will crush you."

The images flashed: Neveka's face among the crowd, then disappearing in the crush of the Rekkr's lances, lost at the feet of stomping warhorses. Malvius blinked away the sting in his eyes. He opened his mouth to speak but couldn't.

Raven came to him and put a finger gently on his lips, silencing him. "I know how it hurts, how long it lasts," she said, her voice a soft melody. "But the pain can lend us strength. And sometimes, if we make ourselves strong enough, getting clear before the crash and taking the loss is the best path to the changes we truly seek."

He stood, suddenly longing to embrace her. But he knew it wouldn't be right. She deserved better than that. Instead, he grabbed the flagon and poured for them both. "Didn't I say? Only a mature conversationalist could be so wise."

There was a rap at the door. "Sorry, Cap," Dex called from the corridor.

Malvius strode to the door, glad for the diversion. Another young man lurked in the shadows behind his first mate. Dex threw a thumb over his shoulder. "He's Dallian's first mate. We used to sail together. Dallian snatched up the imperial courier contract from Megaria. They're here with an urgent dispatch from the rector."

"Get inside," Malvius said and ushered them in. "And?" he asked as he closed the door.

Dex glanced at Raven. "She can be trusted," Malvius said. "Can't you?" he asked her.

"I work for you, my lord," Raven said. "No one else."

"Tell him," Dex said to the sailor.

"The dispatch has orders from Rector Horius for the magister. He's to have you arrested, Captain." The lad looked down. "They say you're wanted for the murder of a legatus."

"You read an imperial dispatch?"

The lad bristled. "Wouldn't you?"

Malvius gave him a grin. "Of course. Has the magister seen it yet?"

"We arrived late, and our cap was feeling peckish. And parched, if you see my meaning." The sailor glanced at Raven then winked at Malvius. "It's why I ran into Dex. Anyway, the dispatch pouch won't be delivered till after he's sated. Which won't be before first light."

Malvius drew two gold pieces from his belt purse and pressed them into the lad's hand. "I'm grateful," he said. "Buy yourself and your cap another mug." He turned to Dex. "Round them all up. Everybody onboard, right away. Tell them to make ready for a night sail."

Both first mates bowed their heads and left.

Malvius turned to his guest. Raven rose and handed him the cup. "I guess we're not going to get to these." She flounced the still-tied laces of her frock.

"Sadly." He took her hand and put the rest of his gold coins in it. "Still, I consider our time together a bargain." He bowed as he forced her hand closed and kissed her wrist.

Her smile was as charming as any thus far. "You're running fast, my lord. Be sure to keep your wits."

"Perhaps we'll meet again, after the crash."

"I hope so," she said, offering a smile that gave him another glimpse of the real woman.

"Perhaps then I can convince you to share your real name?"

Raven's businesslike persona instantly returned. "Oh, your crash will really have to change things for you to earn that," she said. The smile that followed was her sexiest yet.

"From your lovely lips to the gods' ears, my dear," he said with a tilt of his head.

Brin rushed to keep up with Ago, following him through the frigid catacombs. The catacombs and caves felt so much different than the cramped passages inside the palace. At least down here she could stand and walk. And breathe. She didn't even have to tiptoe or whisper. Still, between the darkness and the uneven footing, she had to stay alert. Ago always pointed out the holes and open shafts. But there were also fallen beams and piles of rubble to navigate. Even being roomier and farther from the danger of being caught, the deep places below the city were far from pleasant. The cold down here was a special sort of bone-chilling. There were layers of ancient dust and more cobwebs than she'd dreamed could exist. Not to mention the constant dripping and trickling sounds. Which she supposed was what led to the slick-bottomed puddles of the gods knew what. The echo of every sound they made and word they spoke seemed out of place, like they might wake the grouchy ghosts who would linger in such places.

There seemed no end to Ago's ability to find his way in the vast labyrinth below the city. There was no sun or moon, mountains or sea. It all looked the same to her. Down here Brin was forever lost. Every step, every moment, she relied on Ago.

On today's quest, they finally came to something that actually looked different: an ancient wooden doorway with rusty iron bands and hinges. Ago slung his bag from his shoulder and handed it to Brin. "Hold this." He squatted, ducked his head, and disappeared. The lamplight revealed that one large piece of the door's wood had rotted away. Ago peeked back through, beckoning for the lamp. She handed it to him, and then the bag, which hardly fit through.

Brin was puzzled. Ago was quite a bit larger than her. "How'd you do that?" she asked.

"Squat down and put your back to the doorframe," Ago said softly, reaching a hand out to guide her. "That's it. Now put this foot through." He reached down and tapped it. "Duck your head through." He had her arm, keeping her steady. She ducked through. "Wait, your hair is caught." He carefully tugged her hair free and guided her head clear. He was so gentle.

She pulled her other leg through and he helped her up. She combed her hair with her fingers and shook her head to shed the bits of rotten wood. He set the lamp down inside the door and put his finger up to his lips. "Time to stay quiet again. If anyone speaks, say nothing. Just keep moving. If they make a fuss, it may bring the guards. Be ready to run."

Brin nodded. Ago slung the bag behind him and held out his hand. She took it. She was grateful. It made her feel safer. They moved into the deepening darkness. He slowed and a dim light appeared in the distance, revealing a corner. They turned to a long corridor with a scattering of wall-mounted torches. There were cell doors to either side. They tread carefully on the slippery, damp stone. The stench hit her. Sewage and rodents and rotting flesh. Each door had a barred window just above her head. Ago was just tall enough to peer into several of the cells as they progressed.

Brin heard a male voice muttering. Could it be? She tugged Ago's hand and pointed toward the sound. He went to the door and gaped through the bars. "Uncle?" Brin whispered.

The muttering stopped. Ago shook his head and pulled her away from the door. They started down the corridor again. "Brin?" The voice came not from the cell with the muttering, but one they had passed on the opposite side of the corridor.

They rushed back to find Urias peering through the bars, his face ghastly pale in the flickering torchlight. His hair hung in tangled ropes and his hands gripped the bars, brown with grim and dried blood. "How did you get here?" His voice was hoarse, frail.

"We're going to get you out," Brin said.

"Who's there?" All three of them started. The voice had come from down the corridor.

"Just another prisoner," Ago whispered.

Brin lowered her voice. "Ago says the keys are all locked in a cabinet in the guards' quarters. But we won't give up. We'll find a way to get you out."

Urias shook his head. "No. Leave me. Get away from here. Save yourselves."

"Never," Brin said. "This is all my fault."

Urias frowned. "What are you talking about?"

"There was a sword on the ground. I could've gotten it. I could've helped you."

Her uncle's gaze hardened. "No, Brin. You did the right thing."

"I didn't. I ran. I left you. I'm a coward." Brin swiped away the tears that sprang to her eyes.

"Listen to me. You did what a Blade-Wielder would have. You assessed the situation and took the path that avoided defeat. In the absence of victory, a Blade-Wielder seeks to live to fight again. You're alive and so am I."

"That's what I've been telling her," Ago said. "Now we come and go as we please. I can keep her safe. And fed. We may not know how to get you out yet, but we will."

"Yes, we're doing fine, thanks to Ago," Brin conceded.

Ago opened his shoulder bag and held out a leaf-covered mass. "We brought you this. To use on your wound."

Urias reached through the bars and took it. He smelled it. "What is it? Smells of pitch."

"It is. Pitch mixed with medicinal herbs. My maaman says it'll protect the wound and speed the healing. But you'll have to clean it with this first."

"How did you know—"

"I saw him stab you," Brin said. "I haven't stopped worrying since."

Ago pulled out the skin next. "We brought strong wine. Maaman says it's fortified, that it'll kill the infection. You can drink it, too. But not till the puss runs clear. Then use the black stuff. Here, we brought clean dressing. We have some bread and dried goat strips, too. You need strength to heal, so you need to eat." Ago handed the cloth pouch through the bars.

"Is someone there?" This time the voice spoke in Gottari. Gods, Brin hated that there were others. She couldn't spare the worry. "What's going on?" the voice said, louder.

"Quiet," Urias commanded, and the speaker fell silent. "Amaga?" Urias asked. "What's become of her?"

"She's safe, we think," Brin said. "She and the rest of the family are locked in the servants' quarters."

"Have you seen or spoken to them?"

"No," Brin said. "We overheard Ligaia talking to the anax. They're holding them as hostages." She couldn't bring herself to tell him about how Ligaia spoke of killing them the moment they were no longer of use.

"The chambers they're held in have small windows and no vents," Ago said. "They'll be tough to reach, let alone to get out. That'll be harder than getting you out."

"But we will," Brin insisted. "Once we have your help. First we need you to get healthy."

"What about Rekkrs? Have you seen any other Gottari?"

Ago shook his head. "Not a one. They're either captured, dead, or hiding."

Urias squeezed his eyes shut. "There's got to be someone." His eyes sprang open. "What about Malvius?"

"His ships carried father's army away," Brin reminded him.

"Which means he can get back to Vahldan. There's got to be someone loyal to Malvius at the docks. His sailors or warehouse workers. They might know a way to get word to him."

Ago nodded. "Maybe. Isidros's men control the palace and the marketplace, but I doubt they're trying to hold the whole city. I'm willing to bet the docks are still in the hands of the imperial harbor-master. I heard Ligaia talking with Isidros's man about slipping past him."

"Is there a way to check?" Urias asked. "Without putting your-selves in danger, that is."

"I think I can get us down there," Ago said. "Leave it to us."

"You can't trust the harbormaster either," Urias said. "And watch out for thieves. And slavers," he added. Her uncle was getting worked up. It frightened her.

"What's all of that racket?" another captive called, this time in Hellainic and louder.

"We'd best go," Ago whispered. Urias nodded in agreement.

Brin looked from Ago to Urias's worried face. Ago had kept her too busy to realize just how bleak things looked. Ligaia was winning. They faced so many dangers. But her uncle had just reminded her. A Blade-Wielder calmly assesses a situation, takes the path that avoids defeat, and lives to fight on. She had to be brave for him. "Don't worry, Uncle. We'll get to Malvius. Meanwhile you must heal yourself. Understood?"

A thump and a clang echoed from the far end of the corridor. Ago took her hand and pulled her back the way they had come.

"Be careful," Urias whispered.

"We'll come for you," Brin whispered back. Urias nodded and feigned a smile, but his eyes were windows to his pain and worry.

CHAPTER 30
A TEUTONIC TELL

"Training is vital to the life of a warrior. It strengthens the body and disciplines the mind. It provides the mechanical abilities that warriors need to summon and utilize by rote in the heat of a fight. But training can only take a warrior so far.

Nothing could have prepared me for the circumstances created by the invasion of the palace by Isidros and his mercenaries. Prior to it, I could never have dreamed of enduring the fear, the cold, and the isolation that came in its aftermath. But for me the worst aspect of the warrior's lot, by far, is the uncertainty. A warrior must withstand constant looming danger, sometimes over long durations. Throughout such periods, they never know what will be required of them. It pushes one beyond fear—even the fear of death. Every decision affects not just one's own chances of survival, but that of others. Often others for whom they care deeply. It is a condition for which there can be no real inurement.

In many ways, Ligaia's plot provided my first audition for a life I later chose to adopt."—Brin Bright Eyes, Saga of Dania

. . .

533

A HAND GRIPPED Brin's shoulder. She lurched awake, threw off her covers, and sat up, hitting her head on the low rock ceiling of the cave. "Ouch."

"Sorry," Ago said, stirring the nearby fire to life. "Guess I should've held you down."

Brin didn't like that idea any more than she liked the sore head. "If you had, I may have taken a swing at you," she said.

Ago laughed. "I don't doubt it."

Once again, Brin marveled at how the smoke was drawn out of their cozy sleeping nook and up the nearby crevice. Ago knew so much more than she did. He'd gotten this way all on his own. It made her want to be better—to know things and learn to do things for herself.

Brin settled back, reluctant to get up. She realized he'd put his cloak over her again. She unwrapped herself, scooted to the fire, and handed the cloak back to him. "It's my own fault. I was awake half the..." She had no idea what time of day or night it was. Darkness made everything harder. Seemed it was always pressing in. It kept her on edge. Their only salvation was Ago's lamp. Early on, he had sensed Brin's fear and hatred of the dark so he kept it burning all day and night. He always left it for her, using candles when he went off alone. He kept telling her not to worry, that he could easily get more oil, but he never told her where it was coming from. Which meant he was stealing it. Which meant he was risking being caught. So she did worry. But she still couldn't bring herself to have him snuff it.

There was another risk to always burning the lamp. Isidros's men were still hunting for them. Even recently, Ago had seen them in pairs, searching the cellars and catacombs. She and Ago didn't dare sleep in the palace or the catacombs. They always came here, which required crawling through small caves. Brin hated getting here. "Is it morning?" she asked.

"Midmorning, actually." Ago pulled off his shoulder bag and donned his cloak. He dug into the bag, produced half of a loaf of bread, and handed it to her. It was still warm. She tore it in two and started to give half back. "No, I already ate. Maaman says you should eat all of that and this." He pulled a wad of cloth from the bag and held it out to her. Brin tore off a bit of bread and popped it in her mouth before reaching for the cloth. She was ravenous. Inside the wrapper was a chunk of cheese and a strip of cold cooked meat. Probably goat, which she loathed. She set the cloth down beside her and pulled her own cloak tighter. "Maaman says you're too thin," he said. "She says you need some meat on your bones if you plan on making it through this mess."

Ago watched her, waiting. Brin bit the cheese. "She always says that." She went back to the bread, hoping he would let it go. Brin didn't think Apontia liked her much. She suspected Ago's mother disliked the idea of helping the king's daughter, let alone the rest of her family. But Ago had a way of getting what he wanted from her.

"She does. But I'm starting to agree with her. You're getting even bonier than usual."

He handed her his wine skin. As much as Brin hated the watered wine Apontia gave them, a swallow or two was necessary to get the bread down. Drinking it was both safer and easier than boiling their own water from the dirty streams in the caves. They were all tainted by the runoff from the city gutters above.

"Did she get to the market?"

Ago nodded. "She asked around as best she could. Says there's a man named Sabas who works for Malvius. He normally stays back when they sail, on account of a bad arm. He lives in one of the warehouses. Or he used to. Might've run off when Isidros came."

"How can we find out for sure?"

Ago took a swig from the skin. "We're going to have to go down there. I thought we should go after dark, but Maaman says we should go by daylight. Too many drunks about after dark, and Isidros sends out even fewer patrols than the Gottari did. She wants us to go in the early evening, while everyone is cooking or eating. Which means we're going to have to cover your face and head." He dug into his bag and threw her a scarf.

"My head?" She rubbed her new sore spot. She was growing a lump.

"It's bad enough you're so lanky. But then there's your orange hair and pale skin."

Bad enough? Her hair and skin were worse than bad? "Hey, I can't help how I look."

Ago laughed. "I know. But it's a tell. That and your accent."

"My accent? I don't have an accent. Do I?"

"I like it, but it'll give you away. Same as your hair. You've got to admit, there's nothing ordinary about you. You're bound to attract attention." She must've looked angry because he held up both hands. "Whoa. I can't help how you look, either. I mean, you do know how beautiful you are, right?"

Brin had a weird sort of heat growing in her belly. No one had ever said such a thing to her. He smiled and the heat in her belly flew to her cheeks and then to the top of her scalp. She couldn't bear to look at him, but when she turned away, he let out a little laugh.

His tone became prosaic. "Best you stay mindful of it. Beauty like yours will draw slavers like gutting a fish draws gulls. I was thinking I should go without you. But if I found this Sabas, he'd likely wonder why the likes of me would want to help the king. I'm guessing we'll have a much better chance of getting him to help if we're together."

Brin slyly glanced. "Think so?"

Ago grinned. "See? Being a Teutonic beauty is both a blessing and a curse."

Agoraki climbed the ladder first. The crack of daylight when he opened the trap door was blinding. Brin closed her eyes and turned away, seeing the crack of light everywhere. She squinted back up to find Ago peering out. He pushed the door farther open, letting in a gust of cold but refreshing air. He climbed until he was out to his waist, scanning the stables above.

Then Ago was up and out. He closed the door on her with a thud, and she was back in blackness. This had been the plan, but it still made her heart pound in her chest. He'd insisted on scouting the stables before bringing her out. What if he never came back? What if he was seen, and someone else came looking? After what seemed like forever, the trap door opened. Thank the gods, it was Ago, beckoning her up.

Although it was similar to the ladder that led to the stables inside the palace keep, this one led to the old city stables, outside the palace walls. They could only guess whether or not Isidros's men were guarding the building. It seemed likely. Even if not, Ago's mother had heard that there was a price on Brin's and Ago's heads. Now no one, including the other servants, would hesitate to turn them in for coin. It didn't matter how anyone felt about Isidros or Ligaia.

Ago led her from the tack room, walking swiftly but not running to the exit. Several grooms worked on horses tethered in the aisles, but no one paid any heed. She had her hood up and her head bowed, keeping her face in shadow. Sunlight streamed in through a crack between the doors ahead. They were almost out.

"Who's there?" one of the grooms called.

Ago pulled her along faster. "Keep going," he said under his breath. Brin waited for a hand to grab her by the shoulder. But the hand never came.

They emerged facing the sea at the top of the crowded marketplace. Ago strode directly into the foot traffic, pulling her along behind him. She was huffing to catch her breath when Ago made an abrupt turn to head down a nearly empty lane. The city's east wall loomed before them at the lane's end. He pulled her abreast of him and wrapped an arm around her. "Head down," he said softly. A pair of matronly women waddled toward them carrying baskets. "Look at me," he said. "We're lost in conversation."

"You mean like this?" she asked brightly. "Without a care in the world?"

He laughed. "Why, yes. And besides not having a care in the world, we are very amusing to one another." It made her laugh too.

The women passed without a glance. They came to the lane that ran alongside the east wall toward the sea. They started downhill. The road was lined with panhandlers and scruffy merchants selling oddities and used items, often on makeshift tables or simply laid out on the ground. "What is this place?"

"Beggars' Row," Ago said. "None of these merchants are sanctioned. Don't make eye-contact. If anyone hails us or tries to stop us, keep your head down and let me do the talking. Stay ready. We may have to run."

"It's that dangerous?" she asked.

"Not as dangerous as the other roads to the harbor would be. Folks here don't want to be seen or recognized, same as us."

Brin felt cold stares as they filed past. She was beginning to think they'd make it without incident when a tall man with a great black beard stepped in front of them. The man wore a shiny green robe. "You two wish to be far away from here, do you not?" he asked in a thick accent, blocking their way with his hands spread wide. "I can get you to sunny Trazonia. You will never be cold or want for food again."

"No, thank you," Ago said, pulling her tighter and seeking to steer her around the man.

The man hurried to stay in front of them. "I supply only for the noble class. You would do only housework, no difficult labor."

"No, thank you!" Ago repeated. His tone gained an edge she'd never heard from him.

"Ah, young lovers," the man said with a gap-toothed smile. Ago pushed past, holding her close. "This is a selling point." The man kept after them, staying so close Brin could smell his musky, smokey odor. "Some Sassanada seek breeding couples. Your children would be prized!"

"Run," Ago hissed. He dropped his arm and grabbed her hand, pulling her downhill as fast as her legs would carry her. Brin had to hold her hood to keep it from blowing off her head and revealing her hair.

The bearded man gave chase but they seemed to be gaining a lead. They wove through the crowd and it seemed the man had given up. The harbor loomed ahead as they beat to a halt. She glanced back and was startled to find their pursuer still coming. The road ahead looked like a dead end to her as the water lapped onto the stone foundation of what seemed to be a storehouse blocking its end. "Where are the docks?"

"This way," Ago said, pulling her to the right. "Come on. Through here." As they came around the last wooden structure, a narrow gap opened before them. An alley that looked like another dead end. "Keep going; don't look back," he said. He helped her step over two bodies wrapped up in cloaks blocking the way. They made a slight turn and a gap opened at the far end. Soon she could see the docks, still bustling as the evening deepened. They emerged and rushed right into heavy foot traffic, earning a curse from a man hauling a small crate on his shoulder. "Keep your head down," Ago reminded her as they scurried toward the warehouses at the west end. Ago glanced back as the crowd thinned. "I think we lost him."

Brin wondered if she'd ever catch her breath with Ago pulling her along so fast. Ships lined the quays, in spite of hiatus. Sailors and dockworkers were coming and going. Ago kept to the shadows of the warehouse eaves and slipped behind the food vendors lining the bottom of the lanes. They came to a muscled worker in a headscarf and tattered clothes sitting on a barrel and eating from a bowl of grain with his fingers. Ago approached him. "Excuse me. Could you tell me where Malvius's warehouse is?"

The man stared coldly as he chewed with his mouth open. Finally: "Cap's not here." He had a thick accent.

"I know, but I'm looking for the warehouse with his office."

"He's not there. Cap's at sea."

"I understand. But I have a message I'd like to leave for him."

The man grew a sly grin and held out his palm. "I give him your message."

"No, thank you." Ago pulled Brin on.

"You want to sell the girl?" the man called after them.

Ago sped their pace, continuing west along the warehouse fronts. Brin still hadn't caught her breath. It took some weaving, but they finally managed to cross the end of the bustling fishmonger's lane. Ago slowed and said, "I wonder if…" He steered her toward a man sitting alone at a table outside the tavern, nursing a cup. He was elderly and looked to be Hellain. He wore a workman's clothes, but they were clean. He cradled a cup close in a gloved hand and held his oiled cloak wrapped tight, gazing out the open seagates. Brin finally saw what Ago had seen. His free arm was in a sling.

"Sorry to bother," Ago began. The man's gaze shot to them and gave them a once-over. "We're looking for Captain Malvius's warehouse."

A lopsided grin twisted his weathered face. "Which one?"

"Actually, we're looking for a man named Sabas."

His grin instantly disappeared. "Sorry, don't know 'im." His tone was brusque.

"You looking to sell the girl?" They spun to find another hulking man with an unruly gray beard, a ragged brown tunic with a fur collar, and red leggings. He'd snuck up from behind.

"No, I'm not," Ago said. His voice was still a boy's, but his outrage was apparent.

Ago pulled her by the hand, leading them on. Graybeard grabbed Brin's shoulder with a filthy hand, spinning her back. "I know a man who'll outbid old Hunch. You'd do best not to deal with outlaws, anyhow."

Graybeard had a frightening gleam in his eyes as he swiftly yanked her cloak open, pulling her hood partway off her head. "Let me go!" Brin cried, tugging to get free.

The gleam in Graybeard's eyes grew. "Oh ho! A Teuton." The man gave a hard tug, pulling her cloak from one shoulder. "Just as I thought," Graybeard said. "Look here, Tash! A bloody Teuton!"

A smaller, round-bellied man dressed in similar tunic and leggings hurried toward them. "Could be the one from the palace," Tash said, his grin growing. "The thug's daughter. The anax will pay dearly for 'er!"

Brin slipped out of her cloak and started to run. Graybeard flicked her cloak like a whip, tripping her. Brin hit the docks hard, jarring her teeth to clack. The wooden planks burned her hands and pain jolted up through her arms to her shoulders. She rolled to face the pair looming over her. Suddenly Ago was there, his leg swinging as he hopped over her. His foot landed against Graybeard's shin with an audible crack, sending the big man sprawling into Tash.

Ago grabbed her arm and pulled her up. "Run!" he cried for the second time that day.

Again, they were chased. The vendor booths gave way to a long row of nothing but warehouses. Brin's knees felt like they were on fire and she couldn't get enough air. Ago gripped her stinging hand, leading her into another alley. This one was wider and empty.

The noise of the docks was muffled and their footfalls echoed in the passageway. Brin glanced back to find Graybeard and Tash striding after them. They looked smug and they weren't in a hurry. Ago took the first turn into another alley. This one was narrower. There was nowhere to go but into deeper shadows.

She glanced back at the silhouettes of the red-legged pair turning into the alley. Another gap between buildings appeared to their right. "Turn," she said, pulling Ago.

They rounded the corner and beat to a halt. A figure was blocking the narrow gap, one hand on a hip, the other holding a cloak closed. "Sorry," Ago said, backing away.

"Wait." The command was soft but urgent. "In here." The man nodded to a sliding door, open shoulder-width. The space within was black as a moonless sky. Brin shivered. "Quickly if you want to stay free," the dark figure hissed.

Footsteps echoed in the alleyway behind. Ago shrugged and led her into the darkness. The man followed them in and the door slid closed, shutting them into blackness. There was a shuffling sound followed by a soft thump. He'd barred the door. Brin stood shoulder to shoulder with Ago, her heart racing. She clung to his hand in spite of how it stung hers.

The man who was either their savior or a new threat stood at the door they'd entered for several long moments and then sighed. "They've gone." The figure moved past them, deeper into the unknown space behind. Metal clanked, and a stove door opened to red banked coals. A piece of straw flared and was drawn up. A lamp lit the space to reveal bales of cloth, stacks of crates, and rows of barrels.

The man came back toward them, holding the lamp high to appraise them. It was the elderly man from the table outside the tavern. He kept the arm in the sling under his cloak. "Now. Tell me what you two are about?" His tone was not unkind.

"I told you," Ago said, stepping in front of her. "We're looking for a man named Sabas."

The man squinted. "You must tell me what you want with him."

"We're hoping he can help us. We want to send a message."

The man sighed again and turned away. He went to the end of the aisle and beckoned them with a nod. They didn't move. "We're safe here," he said. Ago slowly started toward him. He led them toward the stove. "So tell me—what's this message?"

"You are him, then?" Ago asked. "You're Sabas."

"Aye. And you're down from the palace," Sabas said, moving past the stove. "Besides that, you're damn fools for showing yourselves. You think those two goons were a fright?" He nodded back at the exit. "There's a hundred more out there that'd happily club your soft noggins before they drag your tiny asses back up the hill for their reward."

Sabas's hard expression softened. "So, now that we've got that cleared up, best give me the whole tale." He led them around the corner of a brick chimney. Behind it was a table and a bed pallet, closed off on one side by more stacked crates and on the other by a plaster-covered wall with a wooden door. The warm space made a cozy bedchamber.

Sabas set the lamp down, pulled a cork from a bottle, and poured a bit of rusty brown liquid into a cup. He appraised them as he took a sip. "Out with it," he said. "Start by telling me who gave you my name. Then hoist that message from your hold."

Ago straightened and raised his chin. "My maaman got your name. She works in the kitchens, but she knows everyone in the marketplace. And the message isn't for you, it's for Captain Malvius. We're hoping you can get it to him."

Sabas gave a laugh. "You and a dozen others." He sat at the table, set the cup in front of himself, and stretched out one leg. "Sorry, lad. Would that I could."

Panic swelled inside of her. Getting word to Malvius was the only plan they had. Brin stepped to the table. "But we need his help. My family needs him. Lives depend on it."

Sabas shook his head. "Look, girlie—wouldn't matter if my own ma's life depended on it. I don't know where Cap is. No one does, not at the moment. That's the way Cap operates."

"When will he be back?" Ago asked. He sounded as upset as she felt.

"That's just it. If there's one thing I'm sure of, it's that this is the one place Cap won't be showing his face. Not till this damn war is in the wake."

A thumping sound came from behind the plastered wall. Sabas stiffened and held up a hand to still them. The man silently rose and retrieved a metal prybar half as long as Brin was tall. He moved to the wooden door. Ago put himself in front of her. Sabas stood waiting at the door, brandishing the bar.

The door burst open. The man entering saw Sabas and shrieked, causing Sabas to yowl. Ago pulled Brin back toward the chimney.

Sabas slumped, letting the bar slide through his hand to clank onto the stony floor.

"Gods ablaze, Cap. You scared my balls to my belly."

"*You're* scared? Poseidon's wrath, Sabas, you nearly killed me."

It was Malvius! Brin hurried back into the bedchamber area, her hope restored. "Gods be merciful," Brin whispered, even though she shared her mother's doubts about the gods.

"Sorry, Cap." Sabas closed the door and leaned on it. "Where'd you come from? How are you here?" He gave Malvius a once over. "And why are you covered in mud?"

Malvius was indeed slathered in mud, from hair to boots. The ship captain's keen gaze had already locked onto Brin. "It's a long tale. But before I tell it, you three have some explaining to do. You can start by telling me to what we owe the pleasure of the company of Brin Bright Eyes, daughter of King Vahldan the Bold."

DANCING WITH THE LION

"*Of course King Vahldan's march from Nicomedya to Megaria was made all the more fraught by the betrayal of the Nicomedyan anax, Isidros. Although I am uncertain how much my father knew before they set out, we can safely presume the Gottari were wary of what they would find, both along the way and once they arrived outside the city nestled on the shore of the more mountainous Pontean end of the Straits. With the benefit of hindsight, I have come to believe that the most impactful factor in the campaign's outcome was the lack of familiarity the two sides had with one another.*

It must be remembered, by the onset of the Bringer's War, both my father and the imperials had spent almost two decades denouncing and disdaining one another. And yet, until Megaria, they had never actually met on the field of battle."—Brin Bright Eyes, *Saga of Dania*

THROUGHOUT THE MARCH, the Gottari kept the shoreline of the choppy Straits on their right while increasingly rocky heights rose to their left. Elan was thankful that the brisk wind, funneled by the water's narrowing course, blew at their backs. The shore along the bedamned Straits was bone-chilling. She was starting to hate the landscape between the imperial cities as much as the cities themselves. The terrain was much like the trees that managed to survive it—sparse and coarse, ugly and lonely.

After three dull days, the vanguard finally rounded the last rocky bend and the towers and turrets of Megaria came into view. The road now crossed a broader plateau, edged on the north by sheer cliffs. To get to the city they would have to pass through a gap between the cliff and a jutting stack of rocks that tumbled to the water. Megaria's gates were visible through the gap, its banners and tiled roofs glinting in the winter sun. The city's stone walls looked stout, much like those of Thrakius, though it had no enclosed harbor. White smoke billowed from the distant chimneys, gathering like the warm breath of a giant beast to hang in the frigid skies.

"The foe," Teavar called and pointed. "There, at the pass."

Elan shielded her eyes. It was as the scouts had reported. A phalanx of men stood in perfect symmetry, blocking the gap. They were only six score in number, but each and every man wore the same crested helm and bore the same chin-to-knee rectangular shield. Long spears hovered half a span over the heads of those at the fore. She'd seen spears like that before. They would be braced to thwart a mounted charge. She absently reached to stroke Hrithvarra's mane.

"What's the matter?" Vahldan asked.

Elan shrugged. "Nothing." Except for an unavoidable battle to be fought. And maybe a wider war she considered ill-advised. Of course he'd married someone else. Oh, and perhaps the worst of it all, his acceptance of his ugliness. Nothing much.

"Give me a little more credit than that. You're still angry that I trusted Isidros. You hate that we've lost the element of surprise."

It was true—she had never trusted the anax. Just as she hadn't trusted the Bafranii. She even had her suspicions about Malvius. But actually, a part of her was relieved. They would finally face the sort of fight she recognized. War was always abhorrent, but at least this one was about to become more honorable. No more sneaking around in the dead of night, seeking an ambush, heedless of innocent civilians. They would now fight in the field, against soldiers.

Not that she clung to some false ideal about shared honor on the battlefield. She'd fought Spali long enough to grasp the absurdity of such a notion. How could those who sought to resolve conflict by killing one another ever share any code of conduct?

Rather than explain, Elan shrugged again. "No matter. The gods are fickle. Who can know? Perhaps this is our foretold doom."

Vahldan's smile was wry. "No, can't be. Fighting this lot? Can't possibly be epic enough to bring the Urrinan."

That was absurd reasoning, too. Elan had been fighting long enough to not underestimate any foe, and so had he. Large or small, who could know what a battle might lead to? A pebble could start an avalanche, after all.

The lay of the upcoming confrontation seemed straightforward enough. All of their scouting suggested that they faced only the two imperial garrisons—those who'd fled Nicomedya combined with Megaria's. There seemed not to be any hidden surprises. Nonetheless, these soldiers had to be faced. Still, she was suspicious about the foe's choice to face them out here. The relative safety of the city's stone walls was only a bowshot behind them.

The Tibairyan lines blocked the width of the gap, but they'd also constructed what appeared to be a new wooden stockade, also blocking more than half of the gap behind their phalanx. At the stockade's left end, at the base of the steepest cliff, they'd left an open gateway—likely to provide for their own flight. The length of the stockade was fronted by a freshly dug trench and out of the trench rose stout, sharpened pikes.

Apparently, the Tibairya knew about avalanches, too. In the steep incline above the open gateway they'd installed netting to hold a substantial fall of boulders. The Skolani had long utilized such devices to protect several of the Danian border passes. A well-crafted version could be initiated by a lone warrior.

The foe had put in a stunning amount of work. Elan presumed it was all intended to delay the Gottari's arrival outside Megaria's walls. To what end, she had no idea. It seemed worthy of discussion, and yet no one else seemed inclined to bother.

Elan was beginning to think that taking Megaria was going to be the greatest obstacle the Amalus had faced since the Battle of the Oium Plains.

People would die on this day.

The Rekkrs of the vanguard were joking and laughing. All around her, spirits were high. Elan reminded herself of her place in it all. She was a guardian. The only thing left to her was her duty, and that duty was to keep Vahldan alive until he fulfilled his destiny, whatever that might entail.

"You disagree?" Vahldan asked.

"With what?" She'd honestly forgotten.

He looked exasperated. "That this can't possibly be our foretold doom."

"As it shall be," she said.

Eldavar cantered up. "The scouts say we outnumber them by tenfold, my king!"

Elan couldn't hold her tongue. "What makes you so sure they've seen all of them?"

Vahldan's little brother lifted his chin. "Either way, we're mounted and they're not."

This time Vahldan retorted. "Horses will not win us this city, Brother. Only Amalus resolve will bring us victory." Eldavar sulked but stayed silent. Elan was relieved that Vahldan seemed to be keeping himself from submitting to the ugliness. It seemed a bit odd, so close to battle, but she considered it a plus.

As they started across the plateau, Vahldan led them off the road and onto the brown grasses. "Split off and form up," he called to Arnegern and Herodes. Both his captains nodded and set off back against the column, calling orders to their divisions.

Jhannas pointed across the field. "The foe's chieftains sit ahorse behind the lines."

Vahldan stood in the stirrups to see. "And not just a captain or two. I do believe that's Rector Horius with them." Elan spotted the man he referred to sitting among the crest-helmed officers. The rector was helmless and wearing a purple and gold cape. "Why would he risk coming out?"

"Maybe he's using himself as bait," she suggested.

"Bait?" Eldavar said. "For what? They're still outnumbered."

Before she could reply, cries from the rear drew them to turn in the saddle. With crimson sails billowing and oars in motion, a line of Tibairyan warships came speeding along the coastline toward the column's rear—at least a half-dozen of them. Commands rang out. Some captains were calling for their men to halt, to turn and face them, and others to move from the shore out onto the field. Confusion reigned.

Elan found herself face to face with Eldavar. "You were saying?"

Eldavar scowled, his cheeks turning scarlet as he kicked his mount to follow Arnegern.

The ships swept right alongside the Gottari column and the skies filled with arcing, fiery slashes. As the arrows dropped, horses screamed and men bellowed curses. Dozens fell from the saddle, mounts bolted, and the Gottari descended further into chaos. The grasslands began to burn, swiftly creating a smoky haze across the field. Some Gottari riders broke formation and galloped to escape the deadly rain of arrows. After each ship had fired as they passed, the fleet was coming about for another pass. Elan didn't think a single arrow had been fired in response. At the current rate, it didn't seem likely they would muster much of a response to a second pass.

Just as the disorder in the ranks was beginning to be quelled, new cries came from the landward side of the Gottari formation. Elan swiveled to find more arrows falling from the opposite direction. She scanned the horizon and pointed. "There! On the heights!"

Rows of archers lined the cliff tops, firing down on those who'd fled the barrage from the ships.

Vahldan roared in frustration. Elan recognized the sound. She spun to find him glaring at the Tibairyan phalanx with the crazed eyes and snarl of the ugliness. He was losing himself. "Cowards!" he cried. "Fight us man to man!"

As if he'd taken the honorable road to get here. "Hey!" Elan called. "Hear me?"

"No!" Vahldan cried. "Not this time. We're charging!" He drew Bairtah-Urrin.

Elan leaned to grab his arm. "See me?" He yanked away. "Listen! A rash reaction is exactly what they want."

"It's what they'll get!" Gadöf danced beneath his furious rider.

She tried to stay in his field of vision. "Vahldan, please! Come back to me!"

His crazed eyes fixed on her. "I said no! This time you come to me."

Vahldan jabbed Gadöf with his heels and cantered out across the open field, riding parallel to the unruly lines. He raised Bairtah-Urrin overhead and called to his men. "To me, Gottari! To me! On to glory! On to Urrinan!" He reined to face the foe and pointed. "Onward!"

Vahldan kicked Gadöf to a gallop, aiming right for the imperial command.

Teavar and Jhannas fell in right behind him, one on either flank. Elan cursed under her breath, slipped her arm through the straps on her buckler, and drew Biter. She leaned over Hrithvarra's neck. "Fluga fram, dear one," she urged her friend. "To duty. To destiny."

To say Malvius felt surprised was an understatement. Vahldan's daughter seemed surprised, too. The girl was always skulking nearby, but he and Brin had never exchanged a word. The boy with her looked slightly older. The lad wore a pugnacious frown and moved to stand protectively in front of her. Ah, young love. Well, at their age, maybe it was just a crush. And not without reason. Brin was lanky and gaunt, but it was clear that the girl would one day be a savage beauty, just like her mother. Maybe even more so.

Malvius hurriedly considered the possibilities. There had to be a dozen ways he might use her presence to his benefit. Why couldn't he think of one of them? To whom was she of value? Her parents, of course, but they were off to war—hopefully never to return. He simply needed more information to figure it out. Best to bide time, keep it friendly, open.

"They say they came looking for you, Cap," Sabas said. "Nearly got themselves snatched by a pair of Illyrican slavers in the process. Not that there aren't dozens of others that would've grabbed them, just for the price on their heads up at the palace."

Malvius turned to Sabas. "Price on their heads?"

Sabas laughed. "Not likely as high as the one I hear they put on yours, though."

"Mine? At the palace?"

"Aye. Actually, rumor says your bounty was set in Megaria. Which reminds me. Anyone see you coming, Cap? Harbormaster and his two goons been asking after you for days."

Malvius looked back at the children. He'd gathered the girl was quite clever. He'd have to tread carefully. "No one saw. I came in carefully and alone." He nodded down at his wet, muddy tunic. "It's how I earned the mud bath." Seemed he'd outgrown the gods bedamned caves along the shore. He couldn't recall the parts where one had to slither through narrow gaps from his days of sneaking off in his youth.

"Where's Gullwing?" Sabas asked.

"Anchored," he said, gathering his thoughts. "In the Isantris cove —far side of the horn."

"Good," Sabas said and moved past him to a chest next to his sleeping pallet. "The farther the better. I'll get you something dry to put on."

Malvius kept his eye on their guests and they on him. "Tell me about this bounty."

He'd been asking Sabas, but the thug's daughter shouldered past her young guardian and spoke up. "It's Isidros. They want Ago and me as hostages, just like the rest of my family."

"Isidros?" Malvius glanced to Sabas who was still digging through a box of clothing. "Isidros is supposed to be in Nicomedya. He was to have helped deliver the city to…" Malvius almost called Vahldan the thug. "The king," he finished.

Sabas looked up from digging through the chest with a grim expression. "I thought you'd have heard by now. Isidros abandoned Nicomedya. Snuck his men in here, and they took the palace. Word is he tipped off the imperial garrison at home, and they fled, too."

"Isidros? Here?" Sabas nodded. "Damn." The slimy fish had outmaneuvered everyone. He should've known. Sabas threw him a faded garment. It smelled like sunbaked clams.

"It was Ligaia's idea," the boy blurted. "She asked him here. I heard her. In the palace stables, before you and the king set sail. She told him it would be easy—that she'd learned that all the Gottari were going off to war."

"Ligaia," Malvius said. It actually made perfect sense. How could he have imagined she'd be harmless if they made her a servant? He supposed he had only himself to blame. It had just seemed such a fitting penance for her. "Damn, sister," he whispered. The more he thought about it, the cleverer it became. Should the imperials arrive, she could claim she'd seized the palace in the emperor's name. And she could even petition for some of the very favors he himself sought to claim at the end of this nightmare. If word came that the Gottari had won and were returning, Ligaia had gained an ally who could get her safely away.

Malvius had stupidly deemed his sister out of the game. When would he learn? Ligaia was like a skin rash. Just when you consider it gone and get busy ignoring it, a rash will come roaring back—likely at the most inopportune moment.

He noticed that the boy was all puffed up again. "Forgive me, lad, but who are you, and how did you overhear this meeting?"

"He's Agoraki, and he's my friend," Brin said, her tone as protective as the boy's posture. "He works in the kitchens, but he knows the palace better than anyone. He's the reason we escaped."

"I see," Malvius said. "Well met, Master Agoraki. Thank you for saving my friend's daughter." That seemed to mollify both of them. Malvius was beginning to sense a rising wind that, by taking the right tack, might be ridden to his benefit.

He spotted a corked bottle on the table and pointed. "Pour me some of that, would you, Sabas?" He tossed the fishy garment aside and plopped down on the man's only chair. He needed to figure out the next move.

The girl was studying him with those big eyes. "We heard them —Ligaia and Isidros. She wanted you to be trapped by some fleet. They sent a warning." Probably the eastern fleet, out of Trazonia. "Isidros said it didn't matter if they caught you, because once they got married, he was going to have you caught and tried."

"Married? My sister?" His recently-widowed sister? "And Isidros?"

Gods, they were both descendants of the anaxship. The imperial bureaucracy would love it. As would many Hellains—especially those in the merchant class. But it meant Ligaia was so desperate that she was willing to give it all away. And to their family's oldest rivals. She probably thought she could outmaneuver Isidros, too. Given time, she just might.

Brin was still studying him. "They plan on saying that you were in on your father's murder. And her husband's. And that you tried to murder her, too. He said they'd get all of your ships." The girl studied his reactions with a cold gaze that reminded him of Elan. "Isidros told Ligaia that once they got rid of you, they would control all the trading in Pontea."

He could almost hear Isidros saying the words, picture him near to drooling over it. Malvius hated to admire it, but their game was being brilliantly played. Even if they were each plotting to outlast the other, which was all but assured. Gods, they deserved each other.

He'd risked coming here to gather information, and he'd gotten it —mostly from these unlikely children. Since the murder of the legatus, he'd known things hadn't exactly been going his way. But it was much worse than he'd dreamed. Here he was, an imperial fugitive in a city controlled by his awful sister and his scheming rival. He had few, if any, allies left. Particularly if this girl's parents were defeated before they returned. Which seemed all too likely, given Isidros's betrayal of them.

Malvius recognized the irony. He'd been scheming, too. It was with his guidance and prodding that Vahldan had left the city wide open and blundered into his predicament. Now Malvius needed those he'd plotted against. The Amalus had gained the enemy that would eventually defeat and destroy them, but it couldn't happen yet. Because in the process of getting them set up, Malvius had implicated himself in the eyes of the same dangerous foe. And the more immediate threat was sitting in his palace, at the top of his city.

No matter how Malvius looked at it, his long game had just gotten longer. And his path thornier. But he had the thug king's daughter. And she'd come here seeking his help. It was something. He just had to figure out what.

Vahldan felt like a looming lightning bolt amidst the rolling thunder of his army charging behind him. He was powerful, lethal, invincible, and ready to strike. He'd rarely felt so alive!

He finally understood, better than ever, why Angavar had told him to never fear it. His father had been right—the glory was his to take. His people would laud him simply for embracing and then releasing what the gods had bestowed within him.

Vahldan felt it flow into his limbs. He was Thunar's hammer embodied.

A command echoed, and the entire imperial phalanx barked in reply. The front line lowered and braced their spears. Vahldan remained undaunted. Indeed, he was thrilled by the way they enflamed his rage. He held the futhark sword low, tucked his shield close, and bent to roll with Gadöf's gait, steering to the spot in the foe's line with the officers and the rector behind it. He was invincible. He would smash through. The leaders were his to strike down.

On the last stride to impact, Vahldan raised the blade and ducked behind the shield. He sensed movement all around him, but there was no impact. The front lines had opened precisely in time to avoid him. But rather than passing through, he was swallowed into their formation. Gadöf stomped to a halt. Vahldan came to his senses to find men waving bright banners before the gelding. They'd spooked his warhorse, and he was surrounded by spears, all pointed at him. Just as he absorbed the peril, the soldiers all started to jab. Gadöf reared and bucked, screaming in fear and agony. Vahldan managed to stay in the saddle, but the attackers were out of reach. All he could do was flail at their spears, knocking away a fraction of their jabs.

Within moments, the poor horse was staggering. A final spear thrust connected with Gadöf's front shoulder, sending him to his knees. And Vahldan started to fall.

He reflexively kicked free of the stirrups and lurched clear of the horse's falling body. He hit the ground hard, landing on his shield. He struggled to get his feet under him. Tiberian soldiers tightened their encirclement, spears bristling from every angle as he finally gained a fighting stance. He spun and swung, again and again, unable to hit anything but the occasional spear.

His hauberk and shield absorbed jab after jab as he spun. He lunged and heaved, knocking the spear tips away with shield and blade. He glimpsed a spear tip coming high and yanked his shield up to block. He instantly took a hit to his leather-covered hip that staggered him. He twisted and slashed again, shattering spear after spear. But there were too many.

Behind him the lines had swallowed Jhannas and Teavar as well.

Both his guardians were bellowing and swinging, same as him. The Tiberian battle lines had reformed to absorb the charge of his army. The imperial shield wall had flexed back and tightened. The Gottari charge faltered. Rekkrs flailed uselessly with swords, unable to reach soldiers wielding spears. Many had been turned away.

The imperial phalanx held, with Vahldan and his guardians trapped inside it.

The exhilaration Vahldan had felt vanished into the blur and white noise of the ugliness. He was a child again, raging uncontrollably at everything and nothing.

Grinning Tiberian faces surrounded him, mocking him. "We dance with the lion," one shouted in Hellainic. He staggered and roared, his swings whiffing. The jabbing was starting to knock him about. He could hardly tell where his skin had been pierced from where his armor had held. He was losing blood and growing winded.

"To King Vahldan!" Jhannas's voice rose over the clamor. "Rally to the king!" The giant burst through the encircling foe. Vahldan and his huge guardian were back-to-back. The foe eased out of reach and reclosed the circle. As soon as either he or Jhannas broke a spear or knocked one of them down, another took its place. A spear tip bit into the flesh behind Vahldan's knee and he collapsed to a kneeling position. Another struck the center of his chest, sending him sprawling. He couldn't see Jhannas anymore. He lay gasping for air, hiding behind his shield.

A spearman appeared over him. Vahldan realized the man had his foot on his blade and the tip of his spear at Vahldan's throat. "Hold," the soldier growled in Hellainic.

With a roar, Jhannas reappeared and swung, severing the head of his attacker. The encircling foe instantly fell on the loyal giant. Jhannas was knocked to his knees at Vahldan's side, still swinging his broadsword but unable to stop the torrent of what were now savage spear thrusts. Vahldan realized they'd been trying to take them alive. No longer. He lay watching as a spear caught his savior in the back of the neck, its tip emerging in a fount of blood from Jhannas's throat, showering Vahldan in warm gore.

Vahldan heaved, rolling to push off of Jhannas's still-gasping body with his shield. His sword came free, and he swung, wild. The soldier who'd killed his guardian had yet to yank his weapon free. Vahldan's wild slash hit his wrist, sending the man shrieking in flight.

Vahldan was still surrounded, still unable to get to his feet. His lungs burned and his limbs were leaden. Even the ugliness now failed him. He fell back and landed next to Jhannas. His foes came on again, closing the circle, their savage grins renewed. He and they knew it was done. They held their spears at the ready but did not strike. It was him they wanted alive.

This was not supposed to be happening. His father's advice had failed him. Perhaps it was penance for failing his father.

"I am the lion!" he roared. "I am the Bringer! The glory is mine!" Even as the words came, the futility of it all slammed into him. He'd failed.

Elan was still near the fore of the charging Amalus army, but she had fallen some distance behind Vahldan and the giants. Hrithvarra was already blowing. Fear filled Elan's chest. Not for the charge. In the realization that she was asking too much of her aging friend.

"On, my brave beauty," she said in the mare's ear. "Just a bit farther."

A gap opened in the Tibairyan shield wall, allowing Vahldan and the two guardians to ride through. Elan reined to follow. The instant she galloped even with the Tibairyan line, two spears shot out, one from either side. She was able to slash one spear, but the other sank into Hrithvarra's flank. The mare released a pained grunt and staggered. Elan fought to steady her and stay in the saddle. More spears jabbed, and her friend floundered. She was trapped in a nightmare that couldn't end well.

A beardless and chinless Tibairya appeared in front of her. Hrithvarra reared and neighed. The man thrust and Hrithvarra's neigh became a scream. It seemed like Elan should've felt it herself as she watched the spear pierce her dear one's flesh. Chinless sneered and pushed. Hrithvarra twisted but could neither escape nor reach her tormentor with her flailing hooves.

Elan's searing outrage burst into fury. She got her feet under her on the tilting saddle and leapt over the mare's head. The chinless man was alive just long enough for his glee to become panic as Elan brought Biter chopping down. She tumbled into him a heartbeat after her blade cut flesh, and they landed in a heap with Elan on top.

Elan yanked the sword free to knock away another spear thrust. Sensing the next, she spun, slamming her shoulder into an imperial shield coming hard her way. The impact sent her reeling. She would've fallen but for another spear punching her in the stomach. It kept her on her feet and her cuirass kept her from being skewered. She gasped for air and sought for the space to swing, only to stumble on something behind her. She fell onto the curve of her prone friend's body, her shoulder blades landing on Hrithvarra's mighty chest. Elan slid to her butt and lay gasping, struggling to right herself, expecting a killing blow.

But none came. She felt dazed. Sunlight streamed through the tousle of hair that fell over her face. The feet of the Tibairya moved away. She heard Teavar's deep roar coming from behind the mare's body. They'd left her for dead, turning to face the bellowing giant.

Hrithvarra was alive but badly hurt. The bellows of her dear friend's huge lungs still drew and blew air, but with an audible wheeze. It was over. Elan struggled to her hands and knees to survey the field. Both of the giants were surrounded. As was Vahldan.

Vahldan. Her subject. He was losing, flailing and shouting in frustration.

He was her duty. If this was their doom, they must meet it together.

"Vahldan," she cried, but the battle's roar swallowed her voice. She couldn't straighten and could hardly breathe. "I... I can't." Just then, Hrithvarra's front leg twitched, her hoof thumping Elan on the hip. It was enough. She pushed and twisted and managed to get her feet under her. Vahldan lay four spans away, prone, surrounded by spears that did not strike.

Elan stayed in a crouch and launched herself up, hitting the soldiers that encircled Vahldan. She swung, hitting one on the side of the head. She reversed and backswung, hitting another in the thigh. Both men fell. She was inside the ring of spearmen surrounding Vahldan. It was as if Vahldan had awoken. His eyes found hers, alert. His shield hand was in hers and she yanked him up. Suddenly, as if by the will of the gods, they were back-to-back, swinging, blocking, parrying the shocked Tibairya who revived their attack.

Using each other to stay upright, they heaved and grunted, somehow working in perfect concert, somehow managing to fend off thrust after wild thrust.

The rumble and crash of battle was split by the high peal of trumpets. These were no Gottari horns. In an instant, and with remarkable discipline and efficiency, the Tibairya were formed up and in swift retreat, shields facing back. The Gottari lines had reformed and had renewed their attack. The army was coming again, this time with much more cohesion.

"I told you! I am the lion!" Vahldan bellowed after the retreating foe. "I am the Bringer!"

Elan tried to turn and instantly realized how much he was depending on her support. Teavar appeared and hooked an arm around Vahldan, holding him up. Vahldan managed to point with his sword. "Onward," he called hoarsely. "Attack!"

"Time to let it go, my king," Teavar said, huffing for breath himself.

The Gottari riders arrived and formed a protective crescent

before them. Arrows began to fall from on high again. The Gottari captains called for shields. The Tibairyan phalanx steadily withdrew to the gate, their mounted leaders already gone.

"Jhannas," Vahldan said with despair in his voice. "Come, help me. Jhannas has fallen."

Elan ignored him. She sheathed Biter and ran the other way, tears blurring her vision.

She arrived and fell onto Hrithvarra, hugging her neck and burying her face in her mane. Her friend's head moved. Hrithvarra groaned. She was still alive. Elan crawled into position to hold and stroke her head. The mare's big brown eye found focus on her. "Oh, my dear heart. I am so sorry. I shouldn't have brought you." Hrithvarra snorted and bobbed her head. Her meaning was clear. Her fierce friend wouldn't have been left behind by choice.

Mighty Hrithvarra would not have wished to pass from this realm in a stinking stable.

Elan's tears soaked into her still glossy coat. Hrithvarra's eye stayed on her, but each breath had become a gurgling rasp. She was fading. "Thank you," Elan said. "For saving me. So many times. Thank you for all of the lessons you bestowed. Thank you for being my dearest and most loyal friend. I will never forget. I will love you forever."

It was enough. Her friend's breathing was ragged, but with effort she released a soft nickering sound and bobbed her great head. It was what Hrithvarra had hung on to hear. "How will I go on without you?" Elan whispered. Hrithvarra's eye focused on her, imploring. Their communion was stronger than ever. Her friend was reassuring her. She nodded. "I will," she vowed. "I remember my dream. I will do my duty."

Elan watched the light leave her dear one's eye then. Hrithvarra's head grew heavy. Too heavy to hold. Elan collapsed on her, sobbing.

Suddenly the ground shook. Voices called and hoofs thumped. "Catapults!" someone called. Elan looked up. Flames dotted the field among the regrouping Gottari army. She heard a whooshing sound.

A flaming missile appeared in the sky, arcing from the top of the city's walls. It crashed into the wooden stockade, igniting it. The structure became a wall of flame, a barrier across the entire gap. Another and another missile flew, sending Rekkrs scurrying. One crashed and burst so near that its bounding balls of fire passed within a span of Hrithvarra. Elan found she couldn't bring herself to rise. Maybe defeat meant that her dream was dead, after all. She would be alone now, without purpose. Perhaps burning with her only true friend would be fitting.

Hands gripped her shoulders from behind. "Come, Elan. Time to go." It was Arnegern.

"No. I won't leave her. I can't."

"You must." Arnegern grabbed her under her arms and physically hauled her to her feet. "Come now." He wrapped an arm around her and guided her into a limping retreat. "Your friend is too heavy to bear from here. But we will still honor her." He coaxed her into a trot. "That's it. Come now. Do as Hrithvarra would have of you. Be as valiant as she was. Know that you will see her again on the other side."

Missiles burst and fire surrounded them. Somehow Elan kept going. She tilted her head to the sky as she ran, and her tears flowed to her ringing ears.

"He's right. I will see you again, dear heart," she vowed.

CHAPTER 32
COMMON FOES

"The Sassanada Empire differed from the Tiberian Empire in many ways. Foremost among them was the disjointed nature of Sassanadi governance. Unlike the Tiberians, whose bureaucracy, senate, and militum were all beholden to the emperor in Medicia, the Sassanada were really a collection of principalities, governed by their separate lords, or dahs. Each dah swore to bow to the rule of the supreme emperor, or xah. Still, the governing framework was looser, less binding.

During the War of Two Empires, the Sassanadi lord whose neighboring lands surrounded Tiberian Trazonia, one Dah Arstra, was at the vortex of the conflict. Whether one considered the dah the one who incited war or the primary injured party in the strife that led to it depended upon one's perspective. Regardless, neither side could refute that Arstra's grievance with Tiberia was longstanding and deeply felt, or that it left an enduring bitterness after the armistice.

Arstra, being the only dah with proximity to Pontean waters, was solely responsible for the buildup of the Sassanadi naval fleet used throughout the war. As a concession to the xah's peace accords with Tiberia, Dah Arstra reluctantly agreed to sequester his warships. He kept *them—in drydock but well-maintained—at Anaissa, the city of his high seat on the banks of the River Haleez."—Brin Bright Eyes, Saga of Dania*

MALVIUS'S MIND WAS A VORTEX. Sabas sat on the bed pallet with an exaggerated groan. Malvius sought the avenues to his next step, but they all seemed blocked. Or worse, led to his downfall. Or his imprisonment or his death or.... The thug's daughter appraised him as keenly as he did her. The boy stood solemnly, waiting.

"So? Can you help us?" Brin asked, breaking the extended silence.

"Why me? I mean, you two seem capable. You escaped on your own, after all."

Brin frowned. "But they still have my family. And Ago's mother." She arched a brow. "Why you? Who else?"

Clever girl, putting it back on him. "I can't think of anyone. But I also can't think of how I might help, let alone why I might risk trying."

Brin looked like she'd swallowed a bitter dose, her eyes downcast. "Ligaia wants to kill them, you know." She raised her big eyes to his. "We heard her. The only thing keeping her from murdering my family is Isidros. He's afraid he might still have to face my father. For now."

Malvius scratched his stubbled chin. "That sounds about right." He had to admit, the girl was good. He actually almost felt for her. He couldn't deny that his sister had a powerful vindictive streak. He took a sip of the brandy Sabas had poured. Both children simply stood there, not fidgeting, not chattering or whining, not even asking if they could sit. They weren't much like any of the children he'd ever known. Certainly different than he'd been as a child. It made him think about what he'd lost. He'd never dreamed he would consider having a child himself, let alone mourn the loss of one that had never been given a chance.

"Will he?" It was the boy. Malvius stared, unsure what he meant.

"Will Isidros have to face the king?" Agoraki clarified. "Will Vahldan win the war and come back?"

"Well, if Isidros and his men are still here, there's a good possibility King Vahldan has at least taken Nicomedya, at the far end of the Pontean Straits."

Malvius looked to Sabas, who nodded. "That's the rumor, Cap."

"It's a good start." Even though it didn't win the Straits.

"But rumor also says," Sabas added, "that the Tiberians moved the Nicomedyan garrison to reinforce Megaria. Makes that a tough shell to shuck."

Malvius covertly made a face. He wanted to control the flow of information. Sabas looked suitably abashed. "Sabas is right," he admitted. "The war is likely far from over. It won't be easy."

All but impossible was probably a better description. If the rumors he had gathered in Akasas were true, that Zafan had betrayed the Gottari and that the eastern fleet had sailed from Trazonia for the Straits, the circumstances grew even more dire for the thug king. There were good reasons why Megaria hadn't been sacked in centuries. The city had few approaches, was surrounded by a virtually unbreachable double wall, and its powerful catapults sat in command of the mouth of the Straits. Every ship that passed was in range. Add to that the city's defenses now being manned by two full imperial garrisons—likely experienced veterans. The cities of the Straits were too vital to have green troops assigned to their garrisons.

The Illyrican hills surrounding Megaria had few roads, and fewer still were passable. Without seizing Megaria, and lacking naval support, the Gottari army had no good way back to Thrakius. Isidros had all but trapped the Gottari at the Tiberian end of the Straits.

All the rector needed to do was hunker down and wait. Even if it took till spring, eventually the Tiberian militum would be sent. Considering the strategic and economic value of the Straits, the response would be delivered with crushing force.

And if the imperials won now, Isidros and Ligaia would win. Which meant that Malvius would lose. This time he might lose everything. As Raven, the wise whore from Akasas, had put it, his wagon had gone rogue. He could bail out—flee Pontea forever—or he could try to guide his runaway cargo to the best possible crash. A crash that might even be flipped to his advantage.

He gestured with the cup to Sabas. "Another," he said. Sabas reached and poured.

He sipped, relishing the burn. He squeezed his eyes shut. Gods, the thought of bailing out galled him. He simply couldn't let them win—not Ligaia and Isidros, and not Vahldan and the Gottari. Not like this. Who could know how the Gottari might react to imperial retaliation? They might simply melt into the northern hills. Many or most might live to return to their homeland.

Which would mean it was only a matter of time before it began all over again.

No! It wasn't just that he couldn't flee or that he had to win. He had to ensure that the Gottari were never again allowed to inflict on another city such an outrageous reign of terror. Well, that and he'd really prefer to keep his fleet and return to a life of luxury. Not to mention avoid being locked up or hung for patricide.

He opened his eyes to his audience of three, all staring at him. The girl looked thoughtful, concerned but not rattled. "So?" she prompted again.

Malvius downed his cup in one slug. "So, at least one thing is clear. We need to see to it that your father wins his war." At least it would help him to put his plan back on course. "We need to see that he comes home. Soon." It was the only way to stay afloat, to keep sailing toward his destination.

"How do we do that?" Brin asked. Agoraki looked as eager as she did. Sabas raised his brows too, clearly curious.

"I'd say we need an ally," Malvius said. "And I can only think of one that fits the bill." One with enough power and with whom he shared common foes. "Which means..." He stood and held his hands out to Brin. She reluctantly put her hands in his. They were large for her age. And calloused. Interesting.

He held her arms out, appraising her. She was really going to be something, this girl. The beauty, size, and strength of her warrior parents were already apparent. She was muscular, rangy. More than that, she had a natural grace of carriage that could not be hidden or diminished.

Brin's cheeks grew pink. "Which means?"

"Which means I'm going to need your help to win the favor of these potential allies." Malvius glanced at the boy. "Have either of you ever been aboard a ship at sea during hiatus?"

Eyes wide, Agoraki simply shook his head. Brin actually smiled. "I've never been aboard a ship in any season."

"Can I count on you both to help me to help Brin's father win? And to save your families from my evil sister in the process?" They both nodded. Malvius bowed over Brin's hand and gave its back a formal peck. "Well then, my brave Princess Brin of Thrakius, you and your loyal manservant Master Agoraki are about to embark upon your first sea voyage. An emissary to an exotic foreign port."

Brin's mother hated sailing. Elan had said so all of the time. Now Brin understood it. Three days back on land in Anaissa, waiting to be allowed to see the leader of this crazy place, and sometimes Brin still felt the ground swaying beneath her. The three days sailing across the Pontean had been the wettest, coldest, sickest of her life. She'd vomited till she was heaving up nothing, which felt horrible.

She'd just begun to feel better, but the plan for the day was bringing it all back. Maybe it was just nerves, but it seemed to her that the wild patterns and colors of the tiled walls, floors, and even the ceilings of the palace brought Brin's wooziness back. She was not looking forward to being seen by the man they called the dah—which was the weirdest name for a leader that she'd ever heard. Malvius kept telling her how vital to their plan her audience would be, and he seemed so worried that it made her worried. Worried to the point of feeling like vomiting again.

But the time had come. Might as well get past it. Brin fought down the sick at the top of her throat and hurried after Malvius and their leggy Sassanadi guide as he led them through the palace. The place seemed endless, and the corridors were twisty-turny. She kept almost falling. The bedamned floors were stone that was as slippery as the slimy rocks by the pond in the keep, only these had no actual slime. They looked like wet glass, and the pointy slippers Malvius had bought in the market to replace her sandals made it feel like she was walking on ice.

The huge blue frock that Malvius had insisted she wear only made matters worse. The frilly thing would've fit Heliopa the cook. Brin kept stepping on the hem and catching herself. She felt like one of the jugglers in the fountain square, performing for tossed coins.

Two Sassanadi guards were right behind her. Their stares were scary, like they'd hate her if they could be bothered to care. Brin gave them what she hoped was her mother's hard look as she hitched the frock up and wedged it in her belt. She supposed it messed up her royal appearance, but it was better than tripping all of the time. Ago, playacting as her servant, kept putting his hand on her back. He was only trying to help, but it made her feel like a helpless fool. Still, she was glad he was there. She couldn't imagine facing this without him.

Their foreign guide and Malvius paused to wait at a guarded doorway. Brin assumed that the dah's throne room was on the other side of the big carved doors. Brin didn't see any signal for it, but the guards suddenly reached to open the doors and hold them wide. Brin was shocked. The doorway led outdoors. The guide took them into a courtyard full of plants. She couldn't see a way out, but it was shady and it smelled good. It reminded her of the terrace at home. And her mother. And her Uncle Urias, who always teased Elan about her plants. The gods only knew whether they were all right. Or even if either of them was still alive.

Which reminded her that this mission was about saving her family.

There was no dais or throne. An older man was there, looking really closely at a tall, leafy shrub. He was beardless and looked a bit like Hesiod, but with shinier clothes. Brin guessed he was the gardener. Then their guide spoke Hellainic for the first time. "Exalted One, may I present the Princess Brin, daughter of King Vahldan the Bold of Thrakius. As well as Captain Malvius, of her father's naval fleet."

Brin hated pretending she was a princess. Almost as much as she hated being the one that was supposed to do the talking. But Malvius was sure it was the only way this dah person would listen to them.

The gardener who was actually the dah didn't bother looking. After the boys had bowed and she had curtsied as instructed, Urias's training made Brin stand still and wait without fidgeting or speaking first. But it also made her note that the dah was holding a little curved knife. She started to wonder if he'd heard. Who could be this focused on pruning a plant?

The gardening dah finally turned and gave a fake smile. "Ah, and so it is." Brin had no idea what he meant. "It's even brighter than I had imagined." She followed his gaze. Was he talking about her hair? Malvius had insisted that she wear nothing over her head, in spite of the headdresses and scarves every other female in this crazy place wore.

The dah came so close she could smell his perfume. She found herself glancing at the knife in his hand. He lifted his other hand and paused. "May I?" She couldn't be sure, but it seemed like this powerful leader wanted to touch her hair.

Brin glanced at Malvius. He nodded with his eyes all buggy. "Of course... um, Exalted One." She almost forgot what she was supposed to call him.

The dah fingered her hair. "It's soft." He pushed his flat hand against her curls and released them. "And springy." He sounded like

Despoina did when she learned something about other people—like it was fascinating but they were still beneath her.

Malvius frowned and gestured for Brin to speak. "Um, thank you," she said.

The dah went to a garden chair and sat. "Has it always been thus?"

"My hair?" He nodded. "Yes. It's the only way I can remember. Curly."

"And so very red?" What a weird question.

"Yes, always red." Brin wondered how she was supposed to get around to what they wanted from him.

"I see." The dah's stare changed. He looked mad now. His silence became more and more uncomfortable. It made her mad, too. Her family's lives were on the line. Brin raised her chin and gave him her Elan look. Malvius got her attention, eyes begging. He'd told her to stay friendly, no matter what. Elan always told her not to stare, too. But that had never stopped Elan—particularly when she was mad. In Brin's family, not staring was one of those things that was said but not done. Which reminded her how much worse her mother could make things when she was mad. Urias wouldn't approve of surrendering to emotion. She quietly sighed and dropped her chin.

When Brin glanced up, the dah was smirking. "You remind me of them."

"I'm sorry?"

"Your parents. You are fierce, defiant."

"You know my parents?"

The dah flapped his hand. "We have never been formally introduced. And yet they made themselves known to me. In a fashion which I shall never forget. I am sure Captain Malvius will recall the incident to which I refer."

The dah shot Malvius a look but then went on without waiting for an answer. "It was near the beginning of the war at sea. My father was still the dah, and he bid me to build, launch, and command our new naval fleet. Our first victory restored our control of Haleez Bay, and I was determined to expand our advantage. During one of our earliest patrols afterward, along comes a trio of merchant vessels, blatantly sailing down the river through my realm, making for the open sea. I knew they could only be smugglers and that smuggled goods could only postpone the war's resolution.

"When the scofflaws saw our signal to halt, they fled. They were fast, but we had the wind that day. My own flagship was able to hook theirs. I ordered her pulled in and called for my skirmishers to make ready to board her. Those on the deck of our prize seemed to be compliantly awaiting our justice. We were surprised to see that among them was a woman. But we were even more surprised when we were near to drawing them alongside. In an instant, they drew swords and vaulted to our deck—the deck of a fully manned warship, mind you."

The dah's smirk changed back to mad. "We knew they were Northmen, but their like was nothing my crew had ever faced. Slashing, spinning, shrieking; in no time these few had killed a half-dozen, injured twice that, cast thrice that overboard, and cowed the rest. They swiftly sliced our sail lines, broke our helm, and then vaulted back, cutting the tow lines to free themselves for their escape. It was quite clear who led them—the woman I mentioned and the tall man at whose side she remained. These two were striking to behold, yet so deadly. I vowed to hunt them down, bring them to justice. Ever after we have heard tales of them. We soon found that most every crew in the Pontean knew of the Teuton guardsmen of the smuggler Malvius, led by Vahldan the Bold and his warrior consort, Elan."

Whenever anyone told Brin that her parents were the finest warriors, they always seemed to want her to feel... *proud*, she supposed. Instead, Brin always felt sort of hollow. Hearing firsthand how deadly they were felt worse than hollow. Now the hollow spot had a sad feeling in it. Had they really killed men who were only trying to stop them from smuggling?

She fought to keep her face blank. The dah lifted one eyebrow. "It is said that your mother keeps her hair so red by washing it in the blood of her victims. In seeing and touching yours, I find this to be unlikely. Though refuting the tale does little to dispel her lasting impression."

Malvius took a step forward. "As I recall—" The guards swiftly moved to block him.

"Recall it as you will, smuggler. Do you deny a single word of my recollection? Speak!"

Malvius bowed his head and backed up. "No, Exalted One."

"So tell me, daughter of the fierce. Why would I agree to aid a murderous Teuton chieftain—a man I once swore to bring to justice? A man who has already stolen a city, named himself a king, and now seems intent upon seizing control of an entire sea?"

"I beg you to consider the Tiberian eastern fleet—" Malvius began.

"Silence, smuggler! I asked your so-called princess."

Brin looked to Malvius. Now he looked even more worried. Worse, he looked helpless. It made her stomach flutter. Then she felt Ago's hand on her back. This time she was glad for it. She drew a breath and released it. She calmed her mind, as Urias would ask of her. Within heartbeats she knew what to say. "Common foes, Exalted One."

Dah Arstra squinted at her. "Explain yourself."

"My father always says that you don't need to be friends to be allies. He says common foes make for reliable allies, even if you're not sure of them. I'm guessing that my father would be as unsure of you as you seem of him. I'm also guessing his greatest foe is the same as yours. Who knows? Maybe aiding my father can even push the Tiberians out of Pontea. And if my tutor is correct, it was when the Tiberians tried to take over all of the trade from the east that the last war began. Seems like that war never actually solved what you were fighting about. Which means you're still foes. Just ones who aren't actually fighting at the moment. Maybe it works out for you that my father *is* fighting them. Maybe helping him fight them could be the next best thing."

Brin may not have been allowed to leave the palace much, but Mistress Despoina loved it when she got curious. Brin could while away a whole afternoon by having that woman answer questions. And war had been on her mind a lot lately. Ever since her uncle had told her about the Blade-Wielders and how he'd been in battles alongside them. She'd also spent a lot of time listening to her father. Especially during dinner. There was nothing else to do but listen and chew.

It seemed like she might have said something right. He looked like he was thinking, and not as mean anymore. "If I were to do as you propose," the dah began, "I would be breaking a truce between our empire and Tiberia. How would you suggest I explain such a move to my xah?"

"You could say that you didn't actually mean to break that old truce. Only that you were aiding a new ally in need—one that will help keep an old foe from sneaking back around. Bullies are like that —they can't help it, even if they've already gotten in trouble. You could tell your xah that it's smart because even though this new ally is no friend, he'll be the one who's pushing back against the bully, rather than you. My father is already taking all the risk, so the bully you both hate is already focused on him. Besides, by the time your xah makes you explain yourself, he will already see how well things are working out. You'll already be a hero."

Arstra tilted his head back. Brin thought he might be imaging it. "The gods know it is well to have ensured an old enemy is cast out. But how am I to be certain that I can trust the so-called ally I have allowed inside through the pursuit of making it so? Especially one whose deadly criminal nature I myself have beheld?"

"That's easy. Think about it. There's my father, and then there's your whole empire. Of course you are the strongest of the two." Brin searched her memory and smiled. "My father also says that treaties are solace for the meek and mere deferments to the bold." She'd gone to her uncle to help her work through that one. "Which means you can only trust a man to act in his own best interests, no matter what he says or which treaty he signs." She thought about what Urias had muttered about her father. "Especially an ambitious man."

She glanced at Malvius. He still looked worried, but she saw he was getting more hopeful. It made her realize how alike Malvius and her father were. "What you really have to do is make sure that the best interests of someone like that match up with yours. But you also better stay ready to remind them of their place."

The dah rubbed his face, but she saw he was hiding a smile with his hand. "Your studies have served you well, fierce daughter. You should commend your tutors—your father among them." Brin curtsied and bowed her head. The dah turned to the guide. "Summon Admiral Haareen and Marshall Behnan immediately."

"It shall be done." The guide bowed fancier than anyone she'd ever seen.

The dah clapped. "Bring food and wine." He let his smile shine. "For our new allies."

CHOOSING DESTINY

"One might suppose that Vahldan's attack on Efusium was the point from which there was no going back—that all-out war with the Tiberian Empire then became unavoidable. But throughout the centuries prior, imperial cities had often been sacked and looted by foreign chieftains. It was rare for Tiberia to commit large movements of imperial troops to such conflicts.

I would argue that the point of no return was reached through an awakening to the seriousness of the threat to the Straits—that eminent channel of Tiberian trade and wealth. Once the imperial gaze was locked upon the Amalus, my father and his followers found themselves in an unbridled gallop to destiny."—Brin Bright Eyes, *Saga of Dania*

VAHLDAN MARVELED at how Gullwing slid through the Straits in silence and without sails, how Malvius's well-practiced rowers worked in such smooth unity without a called cadence. Malvius's fleet had already passed once under the catapults of Megaria by night. Five ships had taken the risky run though the Straits in order to get to the

Amalus army in Nicomedya. Now the same Hellain sailors were risking their lives, and Malvius his ships, a second time. For Gottari victory.

If he'd ever doubted the full support of Malvius and his men, his doubt had been erased.

The last time he'd tried to move against Megaria, things had gone horribly wrong. He'd learned that boldness had to be sought without hubris. Brute force and ruthlessness were useless without guile. Leading a campaign of conquest required forethought and patience, too.

And allies. Vahldan really did need others in order to accomplish his goals. He alone would not set the Urrinan in motion. Not to mention that he could not rely on the ugliness to aid him in accomplishing... anything. Indeed, any willing submission to it was a betrayal, of himself and of those for whom he cared most. He'd been such a fool. They were humbling realizations. Even more so in that they came in the light of humbling defeat.

The gray glow of the coming dawn revealed the grand silhouette of Megaria. Necessity forced them to sail past the city and out into the Pontean Sea. The plan required them to make landfall on the far edge of Megaria's eastern landing beach.

He climbed to the ship's aftcastle and went to stand beside Malvius at the helm. "We're still sure the Tiberian triremes won't show up?" he asked.

"The Sassanada admiral vowed to lure them into a chase in the opposite direction. They should be more than a day's worth of sailing away by now." The tightness of Malvius's smile was apparent even in the predawn light. He didn't need to see it, though. The tension between them had been apparent since the day they'd landed in Bafrana.

Vahldan swallowed hard. "I know I haven't said it nearly enough, but... well, thank you. Without you and your men, we'd be lost. *I* would be lost."

Malvius released a little laugh. "I could say the same to you and your men."

"I also need to thank you for what you did for my family. All of our families. It seems like there's hope now. Hope that had felt lost. Hope we wouldn't have had without you."

"None of us would have any hope without that daughter of yours. She really is amazing."

"So you said." Vahldan would never have dreamed it. "And you say Brin was quoting me? To a Sassanadi lord?"

Malvius actually snorted. "She made you sound better than you would have yourself. She made all of us look damn good. None of this would be happening without her."

Vahldan forced a smile, but it quickly faded. He'd felt a lot of things since their defeat—since his close call with capture, torture, and death. He felt pain, first and foremost. He was still stiff, achy, and bandaged. He had more wounds than he could count. But he also felt no small amount of shame. Much of it born of realizing he hardly knew his own daughter.

Brin had always been different than the other Amalus children around the palace. He hated to admit it, even to himself, but her silence and lurking, her wide-eyed staring—he'd feared she was... well, somewhat simple. He realized that the blame was his alone. Talk about being a fool! A daughter that clever was obviously staring in silence precisely because he'd been such a blusterous fool. He felt himself flushing just thinking about it.

"If you're worried about her, don't." Malvius was watching him. "The girl is a force to be reckoned with. In fact, I'm more worried about you than I am about her."

This time Vahldan forced a laugh and nodded, feeling even more abashed and wishing he'd actually been caught worrying about his daughter rather than himself. Gods, if he was going to sire the first king of a hundred Tutona kingdoms in Urrinan, shouldn't he try to be a decent parent? It certainly wasn't coming naturally to him.

"Almost there," Malvius said. "Better get up front." The captain nodded to the fore.

Vahldan gingerly climbed down to the main deck. Moving slowly to keep his leg straight, he made his way through his waiting team, laying a hand on each shoulder as he passed. Yes, he was leaning on them for needed support, but he was also offering reassurance and gratitude. Each warrior seemed to sense his intent, and many nodded in reply.

Gullwing glided by the site of their first battle with the imperials. If it could be called a battle. It had been more like a rout, made all the more embarrassing by having it delivered by a force that had been a fraction of the size of his. He gazed out over the dark landscape. It had been over a month, but the loss still stung. He couldn't see anything—not the bodies on the field, the scorched earth—not even the scores of lost horses. The thought made him think of another penitence he still owed.

He swallowed hard and looked at Elan standing at the prow. She, too, was staring at the passing shore. He moved in close and leaned on the gunwale to take his weight off the leg. She glanced over and looked away. He could still read her as no one else could. She was staving off sorrow and regret—seeking to firm herself for what was coming. She'd been hurting for a long while now. And he'd ignored it. In order to focus on his own goals.

Vahldan had been trying to find a way to broach what was now the most hurtful topic. He had told himself doing so would only revive her pain. But in the silence between them now, he knew it couldn't wait. He'd been a coward for far too long. And if something else happened today, well, something had to be said. If there was only time for one thing, it had to be this.

He could think of no other way to put it, so he simply said, "I'm so sorry." Elan turned to him, unreadable. She was blocking him. He hadn't realized this was possible. "About Hrithvarra," he added, in case it wasn't clear. Indeed, her pain was revived. She nodded, her eyes pools of sorrow, the depths of which she clearly had no intention of sharing. "I know how much she meant to you, how much you two loved each other. I feel like... If I'd only—"

"Don't," she said, looking away. "Not now." She rubbed her sore arm. "I admit, I was more than sad. I was angry. And much of the blame I assigned to you."

He nodded. He deserved it. "Rightfully so."

Elan glanced at him again. "The anger is fading. But it only makes the sadness more profound. I've faced up to the fact that I was the one who had her loaded onto that ship. I rode her from Nicomedya. I guess I'd presumed my doom would come before hers." Elan met his gaze. "You owe much to her, you know."

"I don't doubt that. Almost as often as you saved me, she delivered you to do so."

Elan shook her head. "Not just that. I made her a promise, right before she passed. It's why I'm here."

Damn, that squeezed his heart. "She was already unforgettable. She has my eternal gratitude." Elan gave him a single nod and looked out at the shore. Still feeling anxious and awkward, he reached over his shoulder to give his hilt a test tug. "In her honor, this time we... *I* will be sure to do better."

She gave him a wry smile. "*We* will. Presuming you'll let me back in, that is."

"Let you in?"

"Yes. If I'm going to vow to carry on doing my duty and admit that my duty is to you..." She firmed herself, raised her chin. "If I'm going to come back to you, you need to give me the access I had before. Hear me?" She faced him, nose to nose. "See me?" Those eyes. Gods, they always said so much.

"I get it," he said. How had he taken it so far? How had he actually chosen the ugliness over this amazing friend? "I vow to do that, too."

"Good," she said. "If you let me anchor you, maybe we can get back to some sort of balance. You have to admit, there was magic in the way we used to fight together. It almost seemed divine."

Vahldan shook his head. "I doubt Thunar will be offering me his blessing anytime soon."

"He will," Elan said. "Eventually, I mean. After all, the gods are still fickle."

He laughed. "Seems that's more relevant than how they favor the bold, eh?"

She shrugged. "All we can do is keep seeking to prove ourselves worthy. A bit of boldness may yet be a part of that."

They fell silent as the city loomed. The ship slid past the mouth of the Straits and sailed out into the Pontean. Their chosen landing came into view. He tugged on the straps of his buckler. He hadn't trained with a smaller Skolani shield in years, let alone worn one into battle. But the memory of his trust in it was returning—same as the memory of his trust in his guardian. Elan had rightfully pointed out that the unencumbered use of both hands would be vital to this mission.

Elan wore the rope coil over her shoulder. The hook was of Sassanadi make. They could only hope it would grab and grip as well as their new allies claimed. Besides the hook, they were relying on Malvius's memory of the city—particularly the outer keep and the wall-walk. Their target was at the eastern end, which Malvius admitted he'd only seen once. They also had to rely on Tiberian protocol—that the changing of the watch would occur at dawn, and that there was a laxness about staying alert through the gray hour prior to it.

Vahldan looked back at his team. They looked grim but determined. He took a final pass through his chosen team made up of his closest supporters. "Remember, it's all about speed. Everyone knows their role, right?"

Teavar nodded. "We do, my king."

"We're ready," Belgar agreed.

They looked calm. Not in the overconfident way he'd been before the last battle. These warriors were rock solid. Loyal and unflappable even in the aftermath of the disaster he'd inflicted on them. He didn't deserve their loyalty, but he damn well appreciated it.

The thought made Vahldan's chest clinch. Were they truly ready? Was he ready? Would he lose himself again? Could he even find his way to Thunar's Blessing without losing himself? Could he do this without either? Was he leading those he loved to folly again? Vahldan knew this was his last chance. If he failed now, this war was a bust. No one would follow him to a second. Who could continue to believe he was the Bringer if he couldn't manage a single victory over the soldiers of the very empire he was supposed to bring to ruin?

With his dying breath, his father had implored Vahldan to lead their people forth. Angavar had said that glory was the way. The man had poured his all into ensuring that his firstborn son had the chance to lift his people to their rightful place in the world. If Vahldan failed today, he failed that legacy.

He limped back up to the prow. Elan watched him, her expression stern. "It's going to work," she said. Besides perfectly reading him, she'd opened herself to him. He forced a smile and nodded. "Accept it. You are the Bringer. I finally have."

It stunned him. "Really? Now?"

"Yes, now. I can now see that I'd lost my purpose. And once I lost Hrithvarra too, I realized that I was in danger of losing my soul. I have to believe this is all for something—that it's going to be worth something. Otherwise, I might as well lie down and die. I need to believe. In order to do that, I need you to be who you were born to be. It's no small thing I'm asking. But I'm depending on it. We're all depending on it."

"I understand," he said. "I will."

"Why?" she asked with a brow arched.

He didn't understand at first. Then he finally understood. "Because I believe, too." His oldest and dearest friend gave him a single nod. It was the right answer.

Gullwing swung around, arcing for the landing. They turned to face the landing site. "This feels right," he said. "You and I, leading the way like this."

He spotted a faint smile transforming her to an earlier version of herself. "It does."

"For the first time in a long time."

"Too long."

Gods, she was fierce. And as beautiful as ever. "Thank you," he said.

"Thank you for accepting my advice." She raised a brow. "And for giving your word."

He'd truly accepted that she was right. About all of it. If they succeeded in taking Megaria, any unnecessary killing would only set back their cause. Death and destruction would only breed hate, creating an endless cycle. He'd agreed to do everything possible to avoid harming the city and the civilian population. Plus, this time they would accept Tiberian surrenders. Prisoners would be treated humanely.

Gods, he'd been a monster in Efusium. And a fool for long before that. He'd been horrible to her for so long now. How could he have risked losing her? For so long, he had wondered if he already had. He still wasn't sure where they stood.

"We're still us, right?" he asked. Her head snapped back, her eyes locking onto his. Her entire demeanor had shifted. "I mean, you once said that there was no longer any you or me, only us. Are we still us?"

She squeezed her eyes shut. When she opened them, even in the dim light, he clearly saw her pain. She slowly shook her head, and for the first time, he truly felt that same pain. "You know we're not. You're the one who made it so."

Now it was his turn to shake his head. "I never meant to harm us."

Elan scowled, glanced beyond him at the others, and lowered her voice. "You fucked it up and you know it. It can never be pure again." He opened his mouth, but she held up a halting hand. "Just listen," she said. "I made a vow. Because of Hrithvarra, I promised myself that I would do my duty. I am still your guardian. And yes, I need to believe. I will share Urrinan's destiny with you. And destiny's doom. I can see that our original goals for our people are still worthy. But never again will we be us. Not as we were."

It stung all the more because he knew he deserved it. Anything he said could only cause further damage. They gazed into each other's eyes as the rowers ceased and they glided in. The bow scraped the sand. He knew he shouldn't, but he had to say it. "I'm sorry," he said softly.

Elan regained her fierce grin. "You don't deserve it, but I'll be at your shoulder. Try not to fuck that up, too. Now go."

Vahldan nodded, turned, and vaulted over the rail. It was much farther than he'd imagined. He splashed in shallow, frigid water. The impact jarred his whole aching body, and pain shot through his wounded leg with each step as he hobbled to shore. He heard the others throwing the rolled rope ladders over the side, but Elan was true to her word, running right behind him; she'd jumped too.

She was absolutely right—he didn't deserve a thing from her. But with her at his side, anything was possible. He could still turn this war around. And if he could do that, maybe other things could be repaired. It provided hope—hope that fueled him.

In the growing light, they ran for Megaria's outer wall even as the others came ashore. Elan quickly outpaced him. Vahldan gritted his teeth and struggled to keep up by utilizing a galloping limp. Even with his new humility, he would be the one to lead this assault, dammit. The gods may be fickle, but boldness would still be a part of his destiny.

BRIN IGNORED her aching side and hurried on, following Ago's torch through the dark corridor. The thumping boots of the Sassanadi soldiers echoed in the catacombs. The sound was so loud it made her feel like they were about to trample her. Before getting to the catacombs, they'd climbed a rocky hillside to get to a cave. Once inside, they'd crawled uphill for what felt like the length of the entire city, docks to palace. When they were finally able to stand, they were forced to wade through a frigid pool. Her borrowed boots were sodden and heavy, her hands raw, her arms scraped, her legs wobbly, and her tunic was sweaty and chafing.

Without her uncle's training, she would have begged to quit. Without Ago, none of this would've happened. With the support of her two dearest friends, anything was possible.

The frantic pace was necessary. They were racing against the discovery of the fleet of Sassanada warships anchored in a cove east of the city. A sentinel on the seawall that surrounded the city's harbor was sure to eventually spot them. The warning bell would be rung.

Surprising Isidros and his thugs was sure to save lives.

Urias was always in her thoughts. Brin couldn't fail him again. Gods, how long had it been since they'd taken Urias food and clean bandaging? After days of sailing, then days of waiting for an audience with the dah, the grouchy little man had finally agreed to provide aid. Which had only led to more days of waiting while the dah's ships were made ready and their strike force was assembled. It was hard to keep track of the days, but Brin feared it had been a month or more. And Urias had been in terrible shape the last time she'd seen him.

Besides her uncle, Brin worried about the others, too. There was Kemella, who was always so kind. And beautiful Mara and her sweet babe. And Sairsa and little Rohdric. And even though she had issues with her father's qeins, she couldn't help but worry over Ligaia's hatred of Amaga and her unborn babe.

Ago finally stopped. The strike force had arrived outside the crumbling door to the dungeon. Ago pulled Brin aside. The Sassanadi captain behind her called up the two soldiers who'd carried the ram. The burly pair had hauled it all this way just for this.

Ago held up a hand, pausing them. "Remember, the stairs to the kitchens are straight ahead. The guards' chamber is to the left at the bottom of the stairway. There's always at least one guard, but there may be more. Once you're past this door, anyone who's armed is a foe."

The captain nodded. "My men understand." His accent was thick, but his Hellainic was serviceable. "You also must remember your part. Stay close. As soon as the palace is secure, you are to guide the squad assigned to seize the east gate. Speed is of the essence."

Ago glanced at Brin. As much as she hated it, this was their agreement. It meant they would soon part ways. "I understand," he said, though she knew he hated leaving her, too.

"The key cabinet," Brin reminded them.

Both the captain and Ago nodded. "We'll make sure you get the keys," Ago said.

The two with the ram stepped up, swung it short of hitting two times, then raised it further and slammed it into the decrepit door. The first strike nearly shattered the wood, but the latch and the hinge bands remained intact. The second blow knocked it loose. It had been so loud Brin feared the entire palace must have heard.

The two with the ram tossed it aside, drew their blades, and led their comrades down the corridor of cells at a run. She and Ago followed, Brin's heart pounding all the way to her ears. Their passage set the prisoners to calling and exclaiming. She stopped at her uncle's cell door, but Ago went on. She called to him over all of the chaos and noise. "Uncle? Urias!"

No answer. The bars were too high for her to see in. Her panic surged. She pounded her fist on the thick wooden door. "Please! Answer me. Uncle Urias!"

Finally, two hands gripped the bars. His face appeared at the door. "Gods, Brin—is it really you? I feared I'd lost you." Tears filled his eyes. Which brought tears to hers.

"I'm here," she said, touching his hands. His hair was a tangled mess and his bushy gold beard crawled down his neck. His cheeks were hollow and his lips looked like cracked wax. "We're getting you out." She had to get those keys.

Calls and replies in Sassanadi echoed through the corridor. "What's happening?" Urias asked. "Who are they?"

"Allies," she said. "They're helping us take back the palace."

Ago came running back. Looped onto his forearm were dozens of keys, from elbow to wrist. "Here," he said breathlessly. He took her hand and slid the large key rings from his arm onto hers. "They're moving on. I've got to go."

Ago turned and started running. "Which one?" Brin called after him.

"Sorry, don't know," he called. Then he was gone.

The other prisoners began calling from their cells, most in Gottari. "What's happening?" and "You have the keys?" and "Get us out of here!"

Brin ignored them and started trying keys in Urias's cell door. Some wouldn't go in, but most simply wouldn't turn. "Where have you been, Brin?" Urias asked as she worked.

"It's a long story, Uncle. You won't believe it when I get the time to tell it." She dropped the bad keys at her feet. The pile grew.

"Those men, they're foreigners?"

"Sassanadi." Fewer than half of the keys remained.

"Sassanadi? Why are they helping? What do they want in return?" Urias had instantly homed in on one of her worries. Even if they pulled this off, what would her father say when he returned to find his palace held by another imperial army?

"As soon as we get the chance, I'll tell you everything. I promise." Finally, one of the keys slid straight in. It didn't turn easily, but it turned, emitting a clank as the bolt released. And with only three keys left.

She pushed while Urias pulled and the door swung with a screech. He stepped unsteadily out. Brin gasped. "Gods, you're so thin." His filthy tunic hung on his bony frame.

"Open ours next." A pair of Gottari graybeards crowded to gape from the opposite cell.

"There's no time," Urias said. "We've got to get to Amaga."

Brin knew he was right. "We'll be back for you all soon. I promise."

Urias started and almost fell. She looked down at his swollen, bare feet, full of sores. "They took my boots," he said. She pulled his arm over her shoulder, taking his weight, and helped him to hobble toward the light of the stairway. Confused, angry, and fearful calls echoed behind them.

As they reached the base of the stairs, the palace's warning bells rang. She stopped. It seemed mad to walk right into what was sure to be dangerous.

Urias sensed her fear. "Be brave. They need us." She nodded, knowing it was true.

He beckoned her onto the steps before him and held her shoulders as they ascended. The tolling bells were interspersed with shouts. They made it to the top and Brin peered through the door that had been left ajar. The corridor to the kitchens seemed empty. She led him out.

They walked alongside the larder, and Urias stopped her at a stack of laundered wiping cloths. "My feet," he said. Brin nodded and had him sit on the bench beside the worktable. She got him a ladle of water from the nearby barrel. Urias drank while she wrapped each foot in cloth. She couldn't figure out how to secure them. She tried tying the corners, but doubted they'd stay put. As she fussed with covering his swollen feet, she sensed something had changed. She stopped and cocked her head. "Listen," she said.

"To what," Urias whispered.

"The shouting. It's stopped. Maybe the fighting is over. Maybe Isidros's men have all been rounded up. Or maybe they surrendered."

As if in reply to Brin's dim but rising hope, a chorus of male voices erupted, echoing down the main stairs from the entry hall. This time the calls came in Hellainic. Battle cries.

"They didn't surrender," Urias said grimly.

Knowing that Skolani trained with ropes, both throwing and climbing them, Elan's insistence that she take the lead was hard to argue against. Vahldan still didn't like it. He hated putting her in harm's way. They arrived at the base of the wall without causing any alarm to be raised. Damn, the wall looked impossibly tall from down here. And yet, Elan's throw got the hook over the parapet on the first try, with barely an audible clank.

"You practiced that," he whispered.

Elan gave him a wink and tugged on the line to check it. An instant later, she was climbing. Bracing herself with her feet on the rough stone, she scurried up as fast as a squirrel climbs a tree. Even after all of these years, her prowess never ceased to amaze him. She waved from the top and he started climbing. Halfway up his hands were chafing, his arms burning, and his wounded hip and calf were both screaming. He heard a distant voice and stopped, scanning the wall top. His wounded leg suddenly gave way, but he caught himself. Gods, what if he fell and left her up there alone?

He hated that he'd received so many wounds and that the time spent in recovery since then had weakened him so. The worst part was that the wounds felt deserved. The pain in his knee radiated up his thigh, and the ugliness began to boil in his belly.

"No, dammit!" he said under his breath. He had to be out in front for this. If the attack failed to achieve surprise, it had to be his failure. The rest of his army could still flee. But he would not fail. He couldn't. Too much depended on it. He focused, firmed his grip, and resumed climbing, faster now.

Vahldan stayed focused on the effort, reaching, grabbing, pulling, stepping. Before he knew it Elan's hand appeared before him. She pulled him over the parapet and ran in a crouch for the nearest bulwark. He limped after her. Thus far Malvius had been right—the curvature at the eastern end obscured them from the view of the rest of the wall top. They both drew their blades and peered around the corner of the bulwark. The five catapults were set at intervals along the curved front of the wall, each with ample space to pivot and maneuver. They were placed to dominate a large swath of the Straits, just inside its mouth. Malvius said the Tiberians had built this section of the outer wall just for this. Taking out these catapults was vital to the success of their plan.

As expected, the catapults were manned—perhaps two dozen soldiers in all. A hanging lit lamp illuminated each launching station. A few of the soldiers stood talking to one another, but most sat huddled in their cloaks. Some even seemed to be dozing. It was exactly as they'd hoped.

Elan pointed to the stairs. The next step was to let in the others. They stole to the stairwell door and Vahldan led the way, shield hand on the wall, shuffling down the stone steps in total darkness. A dim light glowed ahead. He stopped short, throwing out an arm to halt Elan. They would've soon tripped over an unexpected obstacle: a lone soldier reclining in the archway that led to the gate, his back against the wall and his boots propped up on the far side. A wall-mounted torch sputtered above him. Their arrival caused him to stir, likely from slumber. The soldier groggily stretched his arms, tipped his head back, and yawned.

Vahldan reached to place the tip of his blade at the base of the soldier's throat. The man's eyes sprang wide. He started to stand and opened his mouth to call out. Vahldan's adrenaline surged and he thrust. The man gasped, eyes bulging. He was wide awake now but not for long.

"Sorry," Vahldan whispered to Elan as his victim gurgled and slumped.

"No need. It was necessary," Elan said, tiptoeing back up a few steps to make sure they remained unheard. "This time," she added as she returned.

They each grabbed an arm to drag the slack figure clear of the stairs and Elan hurried to the gate. She worked the latch and lifted the crossbar. Vahldan yanked on the iron handle. The gate hardly budged at first but then suddenly swung more easily. Teavar appeared on the other side, pushing his way in. Vahldan and Elan headed back up, leading half of their team to the attack. The others would attack the guards at the city's open inner gate as soon as they heard the attack on the wall begin. He pressed past the burning in his knee and the ache in his hip, staying ahead of his team. He reached the doorway at the top. The sky had grown alarmingly light.

They had to be fast and deadly. Dawn was too near for missteps.

Timing was everything. As soon as they set the first fire, an alarm would undoubtedly go up. The other team had to strike those manning the gatehouse immediately, before the gates were closed. At that point his team would be in full view of the sentinels patrolling the inner wall. The ships were to arrive soon after. Success depended on the overwhelming of the catapult squads. He scanned the horizon to the west and caught sight of the fleet's sails. Time was up.

The ugliness flared with his apprehension and pain. He turned to Elan. "See me?" she mouthed. He nodded and pushed it down. Together they ran for the first catapult. Three soldiers manned it— two standing and talking, one sitting with his chin to his chest, dozing. He and Elan set upon the crew, achieving surprise. Vahldan bypassed the dozing man and swung at the first standing man. Elan came right behind him, swinging for the other. Both crumpled to the ground with gory neck wounds, but Elan's victim managed to cry out. Teavar got to the dozing man, shoving a blade into his gaping mouth as he woke.

The call and commotion had alerted the other crews. Calls went up and within moments the warning bells rang. This was not going well. Vahldan beckoned his squad to charge. The Tiberians at the next two catapults fled. "Get the fires going!" Vahldan called. Several Rekkrs ran to do his bidding.

The imperials regrouped at the far end of the wall-walk, between the fourth and fifth catapult. Half had poleaxes, and those with shields were forming a shield wall for their counterattack. The rising flames behind the Gottari lit the scene eerily. The imperial formation moved warily but steadily. They swiftly blocked the fourth catapult. Clearly the foe had spotted the arriving fleet because amazingly, even while under attack, the Tiberian crews continued to load the two catapults still in their hands. Crewmen scrambled to place their burlap-covered missiles into the slings, already cocked and ready to be fired.

Damn, these bastards were disciplined.

Vahldan scanned the horizon. The Sassanadi warships were coming fast, four to each landing beach. Arnegern led the force on the ships landing from the Pontean side and Eldavar led those landing on the Straits side. The final two catapults both faced the Straits.

A crewman at the fifth catapult lowered a torch to the burlap of the loaded missile and it was instantly engulfed. A call went up and the weapon released, snapping in a thunderclap. The missile whooshed into the sky like a comet, arcing down to land on the west beach, exploding to send balls of flame bounding across the landing zone.

"No!" Vahldan bellowed. He started out ahead of the squad and his knee buckled.

"Vahldan!" It was Elan. He righted himself and looked. "See me?" she called.

The flame within him flared like the missile. But this time it burned away the ugliness and the pain, leaving a clarity and untapped power he hadn't felt in years. Thunar's Blessing. "I do," he replied. He made himself pause to assess the situation. The trio at the fourth catapult had to be stopped.

The missiles! Each station had a brick storage cubby behind it. He turned to Belgar. "Quick, the torch." His cousin handed it over and Vahldan sprinted for the fourth catapult. He veered just before the bristling Tiberian shield wall and threw the torch like a javelin.

Still flaring, his throw landed it in the storage cubby as he spun away and headed back.

Vahldan expected an explosion, but it never came. Instead, a fire flared and then roared. Within heartbeats, flames leapt from the cubby to the fourth catapult, causing its crew to scurry away. The fire spurred the imperial formation not to flee but to advance. They came on in perfect cohesion.

"Here they come!" He raised his blade and pointed.

Even as his crew formed up to meet the advancing foe, the fifth catapult was being cranked back for reloading. The fourth catapult crew ran to the aid of the fifth, hoisting a missile. Vahldan glanced at the sea as they moved into position to attack. In spite of the flames dotting the shore, half of the fleet slid toward the landing. The Straits-side division of his army would hit the beach in mere moments.

Teavar called, "Shields up! Archers on high!" Arrows began to clatter onto the stone around them, shot from the higher inner keep wall.

Vahldan heard the whoosh of ignition. The second missile, loaded in the fifth catapult, was lit and ready to be fired.

BRIN FRANTICALLY TRIED to secure the cloth to Urias's feet. The shouting coming down the stairwell from the palace's entry hall grew more intense. A skirmish was raging, just a floor above Brin and her uncle. There was no way of knowing which side was winning. They had to get moving, had to get to her family.

"This isn't working," Brin said, fighting the rising panic.

"Calm," Urias said softly. "What will?"

Brin stood and searched the prep tables of the kitchen. She finally came across the twine Heliopa used to tie hens for roasting. "Good girl," Urias said. She rushed back, dropped to her knees, and tied the first wiping cloths to her uncle's foot. Urias pointed to the prep table.

"The knife." Heliopa had left a carving knife on the board. The old cook must've fled in a hurry. Brin snatched it and cut the twine. Hands shaking, she tied a knot and then cut a length for the other foot. She fumbled with the cloth and twine, trying to wrap his foot while holding the knife. Urias reached down. "I'll hold it." She slapped the handle into his palm and finished tying up the second foot. Urias stood and slid the blade into his belt at the back of his hip.

"This way." Brin led him to the servants' stairwell.

They were able to go faster with Urias's feet wrapped. He was weak but determined. "Are they still being held in servants' quarters?"

"Last I heard," Brin said. They left the rest unsaid. Any change would be for the worse.

She led the way and he kept his hand on her shoulder, occasionally switching sides. Her uncle grunted and wheezed, but every time she slowed he urged her to hurry. As they passed into the residence levels, they heard angry voices echoing up. "They're still fighting around the high hall," he said.

Brin wasn't surprised. "That's where Isidros spends his days."

They continued up, flight after flight, listening and checking the corridors at each level. "Some of the family has got to be here," she said at the second to the top level where her own quarters were. "The servants' quarters here and above are the largest." Urias let go of her shoulders, drew the knife, and led the way toward her residence. They were halfway to the door when it opened. They stopped short.

From behind the door, they heard Ligaia before they saw her. "Quit your whining and keep moving, witch."

The first thing Brin saw was the round belly, then Amaga's terrified face. Amaga's mouth was gagged and her hands were bound behind her. When she saw them, Amaga melted into sobs against the gag. Her legs buckled. Ligaia pushed her from behind. "Get going!" The captor came clear of the door and spotted Brin and Urias. Ligaia froze.

Urias took a single step forward and Ligaia's hand flew up, pressing a knife to Amaga's throat. Hers was no kitchen knife. The awful woman wrapped her other arm across Amaga's chest, pulling her back and using her as a shield to get inside. "Go back to where you came from, savages!" Ligaia was back in the residence in mere moments.

"I can't do that," Urias said. "I won't leave without my kin." Her uncle warily but steadily continued toward the door Ligaia hadn't been able to close. Brin followed, steadying Urias from behind. They got to the doorway and peered in. Ligaia was pulling Amaga further into the residence.

"I'm warning you, Captain. I've wanted to kill this witch for some time. The only way she lives is if you back off. Best take your foreigners with you, or the thug's whole family dies."

Urias slowly moved through the entry hall. "It's too late, Ligaia. It's over now."

Brin stayed in the doorway. Faint pounding and muffled cries caught her ear, coming from the stairwell. Female voices calling for help, coming from upstairs. It had to be Kemella and the others. Kemella was the only one who could reason with Ligaia. Brin turned and dashed up the stairs.

Brin got to the king's residence and stopped. What if Isidros or his men were in there? The banging sounded again, then another muffled call. There was no doubt. "Kemella?" she called.

"Brin? Yes, we're here!"

She hurried to work the latch and rushed into the entry chamber. There was no one there. The whole residence was tidy and lavishly refurnished but empty of people. The doors to the terrace were open, but that was empty, too.

The pounding resumed, right beside her, causing her to jump. The servants' quarters!

"Hold on!" Brin called. The door was barred with a wooden plank laid across hastily added brackets. It was wedged tight. She hit the plank with the butt of her hand till it stung, and one end finally popped up, causing the other to drop out. The plank clattered to the floor. Brin flung the door open. Kemella immediately wrapped her in a hug. Mara and Sairsa rushed to join them, each holding a child. "Thank Freya, you're all right," Kemella said. "We thought—"

"I'm fine," Brin interjected. She drew back. "But there's no time."

"Amaga!" Kemella cried. "Ligaia took her."

"I know. She has a knife. They're downstairs."

"No! My baby!" Amaga's cry echoed in the space. Brin realized her voice was coming from the open terrace doors. She rushed to the terrace parapet with Kemella right behind. Below them, Ligaia still held Amaga with an arm around her neck.

Ligaia had the knife's tip at Amaga's swollen belly. "I've heard you all talking," Ligaia spat. "This whelp is to be the precious heir to your horrible prophecy."

"You don't want to do this." Urias was out of sight, his voice calm but full of command.

"I do, and I will!" Ligaia made a fake stabbing move and Amaga squealed.

"Ligaia!" Isidros appeared on a terrace two floors below Ligaia, looking up. Several of his men were gathered around him.

"Up here!" Ligaia called.

"Stay where you are! We're coming." The anax and his men all rushed back inside.

"We've got to do something," Kemella whispered. "Freya help us."

Brin knew Freya wouldn't help. As her mother always said, the gods are fickle.

"ALL TOGETHER, REKKRS!" Vahldan called to his men moving in formation. Someone cried out in pain. An arrow from the higher wall had found its mark. The wounded man crawled back and the others bunched to fill the gap, still moving forward. He and Elan were forced to get behind those with larger shields. Vahldan's anxiety grew. This was taking too long. "Come on, men. We have the numbers—heed the flanks!" He was about to call for a charge when he saw it.

The second missile streaked into the sky. They'd been too slow.

The bedamned Tiberian catapult crew was already cranking the weapon back again. They simply couldn't allow a third shot. "On, Gottari! Now!" Vahldan called. His squad roared in unison and surged. The lines met, shields crashed. Poleaxes jabbed through their shield wall as Gottari swords slashed. Wrathful screams mingled with shrieks of pain. To Vahldan's immediate left a Rekkr fell, writhing in pain, his face split open and bloody.

Still, Vahldan's fire burned clear. This was not the ugliness. A poleax whistled toward him. He easily dodged it and slid between two of his men, slashing at the poleax bearer and dropping him. Elan vaulted from Ermanaric's shoulder to strike an overhead blow. Vahldan mimicked the move, pushing from Belgar's shoulder, crashing down on an imperial helm beyond. The Tiberians were taking heavy losses, but their formation would not break. The catapult crew was about to load the third missile.

The heat of the fire he'd set grew intense, the flames roaring and spreading. Inspiration struck. "Push them to the fire!" Vahldan called. The Rekkr line surged right. The movement sent several of the Tiberians closest to the flames into flight. A moment later the rest of the imperial line disintegrated. The fighting gave way to every Tiberian for himself, with the last few isolated and outnumbered. With the separation, the imperial archers on the higher wall increased their firing pace. Arrows clattered all around them.

"Elan! Teavar!" Vahldan called. They both turned. "Catapult!" Teavar nodded and Elan started running, leading the way through the scattered combatants.

The imperials called for a retreat, fighting to regroup as they backed away toward the stairwell at the far end. The catapult crew had the third shot ready to go when Elan cut down the first of them.

The others fled, except the one holding the torch. The bastard stared defiantly at them, knowing he likely wouldn't escape as he lit the missile and yanked the cord. The contraption snapped and leapt, the missile streaking into the sky as Vahldan brought Bairtah-Urrin crashing down on the brash crewman.

"The wall is ours!" Teavar shouted.

Vahldan growled and ran to the parapet. One of the ships was already ablaze. The explosion from the third shot had men scurrying from the flames. The landing was in disarray. The portable catapult they'd brought from the Bafrana mission had been unloaded and moved clear, but it was ablaze on the shore. "Dammit!" Vahldan shouted.

Down below, the men from Arnegern's division assembled at the liberated main gate to the outer keep. They were stranded there without the catapult to take down the inner keep's gate.

Vahldan scanned the shoreline. Dark shapes bobbed in the current at the water's edge near the still-burning ship. They were burnt bodies.

He turned away, growling. His gaze fell on the last catapult, still intact, clear of the dwindling flames. He strode to the weapon, struggling to keep his own internal fire from roaring out of control. "Shields! We need shields. Cover us while we move this bedamned thing." Ermanaric and Teavar began hacking at the ropes that lashed it in place. Belgar ran to the front parapet and called down, "We need archers up here! And whoever has fired a catapult!"

The bells in the city gatehouse fell silent. Half of the Gottari created a shield barrier while the others scrambled to push the weapon around and into place. They got it turned as the Gottari archers began firing back up at the inner wall. The return shots were swiftly reduced to a trickle.

Vahldan stood behind the machine, sighting it toward the inner keep's massive wooden doors. It finally seemed to be on target. "Lash it down." Men scrambled to retie it to the nearest cleats. "Crank it back and bring a missile!" he called.

"You said no burning!" It was Elan, holding someone else's shield nearby.

All he could think about was the burning ship, the black bodies in the water. "Not the city. Just those doors." Several worked to cock the machine while two Rekkrs carried over a burlap-wrapped missile. Once it was ready, Belgar appeared with a torch. "Light it!" he called. Flames flared. "Fire!"

The projectile whooshed across the outer keep and burst against the tall inner city wall, just a span high and to the right. His men cheered. The bowshots from the inner wall halted. The Tiberians shouted to one another in alarm.

"Get her ready," Vahldan called. "We're too high. Back it up."

"Remember," Elan said. "Nothing else burns. No civilian deaths."

"You have my word," Vahldan promised, hoping he could keep it.

"Then look at me," she said. Elan narrowed her gaze. "See me?"

He knew his eyes said more than he could. "I do," he said. "I'm angry but I have this." Elan gave him a reluctant nod.

Vahldan turned back to his crew. The catapult was repositioned and loaded. Belgar held the torch over the missile. "Light it. Fire!" The second shot hit closer to the door, and the burning debris piled up in front of the doors, the flames licking the façade, darkening the wood. But there was no more room to move. The tethers barely reached the cleats. "We need axes! Cut those wheels from the front." Without delay, men with battleaxes got to work. "Bring another missile!"

The third shot skipped against the stony ground and bounded up to explode on impact. The entire gateway was a veil of flame and smoke. They couldn't make out the result.

Gottari lined the bulwark, watching, waiting. The flames died down, revealing the wreckage of what had been the arched wooden doors. His men cheered.

Ermanaric appeared at Vahldan's side. "Tell them to form up for an attack. We're going in." The big man nodded and hurried off.

Vahldan turned and almost ran into Elan. "Easy," she said. "The foe isn't going anywhere. Rushing in will gain us nothing." She was right—the Tiberians were trapped. He drew another breath and emitted a low growl. "Hear me?"

"I still do," he snapped. Elan stiffened. He drew a deeper breath and sighed. "And you're right." He tilted his head to her and went to the seaside parapet. "Biggest shields will take the lead!" he called. "Take it slow on the approach! No more casualties." Men gathered into formation below, and Vahldan started for the stairs.

High trumpets pealed from the city. They all turned to find a man holding some type of imperial banner over the inner wall parapet. The man called out in Hellainic. "Vahldan of the Gottari! Hear me! We seek parley."

Just as Vahldan turned to look for his scholar, Attasar appeared at his shoulder. Vahldan nodded and Attasar cupped his hands and called, "Speak then! King Vahldan listens."

"Rector Horius, of His Eminence's imperial government, wishes to surrender the city!" The man lowered the banner. "His banner is yours, under the condition that none of the city's citizens come to harm. And that all who wish it are allowed to leave in peace. Including His Eminence's officials, officers, and soldiery. Do you accept?"

Teavar laughed. "Seems the snakes want out of their den."

Just as he was about to speak, Elan stepped into his line of sight. "Remember our bargain." He looked past her, back at the bodies along the shore. She moved to put herself back in his field of vision. "See me?" He met her gaze, pushing down the looming ugliness. Her gaze hardened. "You gave your word. You seek to be an honorable king? This is where it starts."

Vahldan turned to Attasar. "Tell them we accept. Line this wall with archers and have them send their soldiers into the outer keep first. Be sure they're all disarmed. I want every one of them brought out with their hands on their heads. We find any soldiers left in the city, they die. Understood?"

Attasar nodded and turned to relay his bidding. Before the

scholar called a word, Vahldan was on his way down the stairs. His leg wound flared with every step, but he pressed on. He limped across the field at a near gallop, wending through his men, past the wounded and those tending them scattered across the landing zone.

Several called to him but he went on, pushing down the pain, fear, and anger, striding through the dark smoke straight to the smoldering wreckage at the landing site. Instinct drove him on toward the dark forms that had been pulled onto the shore from the cold, gray water.

They were laid out in a long row. Too many to count.

BRIN'S THOUGHTS WHIRLED. Isidros and his guards must've eluded the Sassanadi raiders. Urias had backed Ligaia out to the terrace parapet but there was nowhere left for her to go. Pressing her was not wise. Brin had no doubt—Ligaia would not hesitate to hurt Amaga. And Isidros and his men were coming. How could things have gone so wrong?

"You hear that, Captain?" Ligaia sneered. "This is over for you, not me."

Brin knew she couldn't hesitate. Not again. Her uncle's training came to her. Assess the situation. Visualize the best outcome. Consider the worst consequences. Act.

She acted. Brin went to the far right end of the parapet and vaulted over. Falling feet first, she plunged into the potted fir tree, crashing through the smaller branches at the top until her feet and legs caught firm branches, stopping her. Still two span from the terrace, she reached out and pushed off from the wall. Slowly at first, the entire tree toppled and fell. She rode the trunk straight to Ligaia and Amaga.

Ligaia looked up and screeched, throwing both hands up to protect her face, releasing Amaga in the process. Brin leaned and flung her arms wide, her body and the tree knocking both women down. She landed mostly on Ligaia, who pushed her off and scrambled to her feet.

Amaga was rolling under the branches like an overturned tortoise, squealing. Brin lunged to grab and hold Ligaia by the ankles, toppling her again. Urias rushed to Amaga and lifted her from under her arms. He managed to get her upright, but then Amaga clutched his neck and wrapped her legs around his hips like a child. Brin's weakened uncle staggered off toward the residence with his pregnant niece in his arms, far too slowly to be called flight.

Ligaia's growl became an unholy roar. She pushed herself to her hands and knees and kicked her feet with startling strength, shedding Brin's grip and knocking her back into the tangle of tree limbs. Ligaia went after them, knife in hand.

Urias made it through the terrace doorway and hit his knee on the chaise. He stumbled sideways, hefting Amaga to regain his grip. Ligaia was sure to catch them. The woman was in a rage. Brin had no doubt: She meant to kill.

Brin got her feet under her and pushed free of the limbs. She spotted the kitchen knife on the terrace. It must've fallen when Urias lifted Amaga.

Brin snatched up the knife and ran.

Ligaia stepped around the chaise, steadily advancing. Urias rushed to the entryway, clearly struggling to hold Amaga. Ligaia was almost on them, clutching her knife in her fist.

Brin sped up, visualizing the needed outcome. She had to save her uncle, her family. This had to end and only she could end it.

Urias reached the entry hall and Amaga's legs hit the wall, causing him to drop her. He bent to help her up, but Ligaia was there, snarling, knife raised to strike at Urias's back.

Brin leapt. One foot hit the chaise and she dove headfirst, gripping the kitchen knife over her shoulder. She brought the knife down as she fell, plunging the blade into Ligaia's shoulder. Ligaia shrieked and fell, her knife arm coming forward and driving into Urias. He collapsed and all three of them landed in a heap on Amaga. All four of them wriggled to break free of the pile.

Brin was first to her feet. She was certain that her uncle had been stabbed and that Ligaia meant to do worse. Instinct drove her. She grabbed a fistful of Ligaia's hair and a scream erupted from her lungs as she yanked the wretched woman away from her uncle and plunged the knife into the side of her neck. Ligaia was still gasping and mewling as Brin shoved her aside. Ligaia's hand clutched the wound. The blood came oozing through.

So much blood.

Brin turned from the terrible sight. She threw the knife aside and dropped to her knees next to Urias. "Uncle? Are you all right?"

"No!" Amaga wailed, curling on her side and holding her belly.

Brin ignored her and gently rolled Urias over. He blinked and looked up at her. He was alive! Brin helped him to a sitting position and steadied him as he caught his breath. He reached over his shoulder and brought his hand back bloody. "Oh no!" Brin cried.

"I don't think it's deep," he said. "Don't worry, I'll survive."

They both turned to Ligaia lying on her back, both hands on her neck. "Not so sure about her, though," Urias said.

Ligaia's face was turning purple. "Savages." The word came in a whoosh of breath, and then the awful woman fell to stillness, eyes bulging. Brin stared in horror, holding back a sob.

A voice called from outside, followed by a Sassanadi horn. "It's Ago," Brin said, relief surging through her. She ran to the parapet. Ago was coming from the palace gateway alongside an officer at the head of a column of the dah's soldiers.

"I barred the door," Urias said, shuffling up beside her. "We should be safe until they reach us."

"Is she...?" Brin couldn't even look.

"She's dead," he confirmed.

Brin hugged herself and trembled. She felt stricken, like her limbs weren't her own. "Let it go," he said. She didn't know if she could—if she ever would. Urias took her hands in his. "Breathe," he said and took a deep breath. She mimicked him and they sighed it out together. She felt weak, and tears blurred her vision. "It's over now," he said. He wrapped her in his arms and held her.

Brin laid her head against his chest, and his voice reverberated. "When I heard the Skolani battle cry, I wondered which Blade-Wielder could possibly have come to save us." Her uncle drew her back and gently lifted her chin. "Turns out it was my amazing niece."

"I'm not... I can't..." She couldn't catch her breath, couldn't find the words.

"You are and you did. You did what you had to do. To save others. That's what a Blade-Wielder does. Thank you, Brin. Thank you for saving us."

CHAPTER 34
CORROSIVE FIXATION

"*Considering myself an outsider in my own family has offered the occasional benefit. One was that I lacked the obligation to legacy that lay heavily upon the others, as it had for generations prior. I saw how my father's obligation to legacy overshadowed everything he did. I believe it even led to his fixation on Urrinan.*

As an outsider, I better perceived how that fixation made his glory-seeking corrosive rather than uplifting. Unfortunately, in later years, I was privy to its pernicious effects on the generation that followed. In hindsight, including upon me. For as I was finally accepted and found the embrace of family, so too did I surrender to the demands of legacy."—Brin Bright Eyes, *Saga of Dania*

VAHLDAN LIMPED ALONG THE SHORELINE, moving as fast as he could from the wreckage to the victims, hoping his instincts were wrong. Many of those who attended to the fallen stood as he approached, most bowing their heads, all looking mournful.

The cries and whimpers of the living victims were devastating. A cluster of Gottari soldiers stepped aside as he came to the end of the line. Herodes kneeled beside the last blackened body, speaking softly, a reassuring hand laid upon the arm of the sufferer.

Before he could truly see, Vahldan knew. "No, damn you." He spoke it as a curse to the gods. "It should be me." He'd promised their mother. She'd made him promise—told him that family came first. His family's health and prosperity had been the one thing that had kept his grief over Frisanna at bay. He'd failed her, betrayed her memory.

He dropped to his knees across from Herodes. "Vahldan's here," Herodes said. His cousin's sorrow-filled gaze rose. "He's been waiting for you."

Vahldan gulped for air to swallow a sob. "Bring a healer," he implored.

Herodes shook his head and rose. "More than one has already been here." He put a hand on Vahldan's shoulder and left them.

The skin on half of Eldavar's face was horribly burnt, like crackled ash. The eye on that side was either gone or swollen shut. His little brother's unburnt eye leaked in a steady stream. Eldavar was shivering and rocking, both his hands clutched to his stomach— his left over his right. Vahldan took his brother's left wrist and saw that his right hand was a mangled mess.

His brother's lone eye found focus on Vahldan. "I am sorry, my king." Eldavar's words came hissing through chattering teeth.

"No. I'm the one who's sorry. This is my fault."

"I told our mother... I said I would watch over the girls... that I would be your shieldmate. I failed." Hel's grace, how could Eldavar blame himself for Vahldan's failure?

"No, no. You did it all. So well, my brother. Áithei will be so proud."

"We won?"

"Yes, of course. The whole war. Those you led here—they finished it. The Straits are ours. Because of our effort, the Urrinan has begun."

"Vahldan, please. My son. Rohdric... He is to be a shieldmate to yours... To the first king of our nation made whole, born of the wolf and the lion... Promise me..."

The first king. Vahldan cringed at the rebuke. He'd proclaimed himself the Gottari king, but their nation was not whole. So many failures. "I promise. I will see to it. They both will know of your honor, your loyalty, your bravery. Rohdric will serve our family's legacy. They will do as Mother bid of us. They will watch over each other and their kin. Together our sons will make us whole. I promise you. I will see to it."

Eldavar's breathing grew even more labored, but he nodded. He believed. His little brother suddenly grimaced. "Gods, the pain... Please." His brother's eye sprang open, wide but unseeing. "Áithei... Mother, please. Make it stop... Please."

Vahldan knew what he had to do. His vision blurred as he leaned down and gently kissed his brother's unburnt cheek. He rose and drew Bairtah-Urrin. The instrument of his father's demise would perform the same terrible duty for Angavar's second son. He gently pulled aside his little brother's hands and raised his tattered hauberk. The stomach wound was grislier than he'd imagined. His brave brother was convulsing now, panting fast. There was no time for delay.

He laid the tip on his brother's abdomen, just below the sternum, and pushed. In and up, the motion, the sensation, so sadly familiar.

A strange glow suddenly lit the scene, so warm, like the first day of spring had come. Vahldan realized it was the dawn cresting the mountains. Eldavar's rapid panting slowed, and he drew and released a long, even breath. His body grew still. Gods, his devoted little brother's last breath leaving him—how could such a thing be a relief? Why would the gods punish them so?

Vahldan had to set aside his sorrow and anger and self-loathing. He knelt to pray. For if anyone deserved guidance to the next life, it was Eldavar, son of Angavar.

"Oh Hel, great goddess," he began, his voice shaking. "She who guards over the spirits of the dead, this man comes to you now. As he kneels before you, know that he loved and was loved in this life. He is my brother, and he was loved by none more than I." A sob wracked him. All of his muscles clenched. Vahldan pushed down the useless rage and drew a breath, firming himself. He would not let the ugliness dishonor this moment.

"My brother's honor, his loyalty, were matched only by his courage. Please, watch over him, Hel, as I shall watch over his progeny. Welcome him in glory and send him to our parents' embrace. Remind him that I shall never let him be forgotten. He shall live on in the songs of Urrinan. Forever."

ARNEGERN'S BACK ACHED. So did his knee, come to think of it. The chamber had grown stuffy. Gods, he'd almost rather be back on campaign than standing around in here. Almost. He discreetly stretched as the fifth minor anax was led from the great hall of the Megarian palace. This one had been less than satisfied, same as the others. The worst part was, Arnegern knew the day was far from done. He realized that no one could know how much more difficult it was to govern a realm than it was to seize it in war. At least not until they tried it.

"Woden's wrath, how many more are there?" Vahldan asked.

"At least you get to sit," Arnegern muttered. Vahldan shot him an arch look. "At least you get to sit, *my king*," he amended.

"Better," Vahldan said with a smile. The king's mood was slightly improved, at least.

All of the Hellain lordlings who'd come today had pledged themselves to Vahldan's reign. They all needed access to the Straits, of course. Of course they all had a list of additional requests as well—things they sought in return for their support. Several had made veiled allusions to the Sassanadi being the true power behind Vahldan's ascent. Every last one of them asked him to rein in the Bafranii pirates, who since the Tibairyan retreat had been running amok. The implication was clear—the empire would've taken steps to make sea trade safer by now. Hiatus was over, after all.

Arnegern knew how such talk annoyed Vahldan. No one wanted to punish the Bafranii more than he did. But his naval ally, the Sassanadi Dah Arstra, seemed only mildly interested in using his precious naval fleet to pursue such dangerous and costly missions. Of course all of his own merchant ships would be escorted by naval vessels. Still, there were only so many ships.

The attitude of the Sass irked him. The bastards were reaping the benefits of full domination over the trading out of Trazonia to the western markets—something that wouldn't exist without Gottari blood, sweat, and tears.

Vahldan was understandably frustrated. They all were. The Gottari had won the war. But they had paid dearly for their victory. And Arnegern knew that among the costs, none was higher for Vahldan than the loss of his brother. Surely Vahldan's ongoing grief over Eldavar was a big part of his ornery mood. But there was no time for mourning. Everyone expected victory to deliver reward. And even those who did not sacrifice were willing to line up and claim a piece of the prize. Seizing control of a realm was only a first step. Returning it to some semblance of a profitable routine came second, and it was a monumental task. It was left to Arnegern not only to keep Vahldan's spirits up but to see to it that his vindictive impulses were delayed or deflected until a more useful and enduring approach could be coaxed from him.

Arnegern had to admit, he found his new role exhausting.

"Never say that your standing all day was my idea," Vahldan scolded. "As far as I'm concerned, you should go and sit. But who am I to allow it?"

Exhausted or not, Arnegern understood the role. And standing at the king's shoulder was a vital part of it. Everyone knew that Attasar was cranking the gears of procedure. Just as everyone knew that Teavar was the king's actual bodyguard. Arnegern was here to supply a proper word, direct the proper course, and to gloss over the unhelpful things Vahldan was prone to uttering. The job made him better appreciate the Wulthus captain, Urias. "I was born to stand at your side. My king."

Vahldan gave him a wry glance. "That wasn't yesterday. The gods know neither of us is getting any younger."

It made Arnegern think of Eldavar. His younger cousin had always been so energetic. He had to put it out of his mind. Best not to think of what was lost. Not when so much had been won.

It had been a month since the Tibairyan retreat, and this was the fourth day of granting audiences. The petitioners had only grown more numerous, the sessions more tedious. For the first few sessions, scores of Rekkrs had cheerfully attended, puffing up their chests over their status as conquerors ushering in a new Pontean Empire. Today there were fewer than a dozen, talking among themselves or eating and drinking. Earlier Arnegern had even caught Belgar and Herodes casting rune sticks on the bench between them. He'd given them a glare, and they stopped, but now they were both dozing off.

Attasar finally came back in. "Who's next?" Vahldan called. "What's the delay?"

"My king, Captain Malvius has arrived from Thrakius. He insists that you'll wish to—"

"It's a boy!" Malvius burst through the doors with an Amalus guard rushing after him.

Vahldan stood. "What? It can't be. It's too soon."

"It's true." Malvius brushed past the scholar and strode up the aisle to the dais. "I heard it from my king's own sister's lips." Malvius bowed and rose wearing a grin. "You have a son!"

"The heir to Urrinan," Arnegern said softly. Vahldan spun to face him, and Arnegern knew he'd never forget the expression he wore— full of shock and elation, yes. But with an underlying terror he'd rarely seen from his dear old friend.

CHAPTER 35
HARD FATE

"I don't recall exactly when the realization dawned that I myself had been born of the wolf and the lion. I knew, of course, that my uncle was of the Wulthus and that my father was of the Amalus. But then one day, as I overheard my father reveling in the prophesy and of the coming of the high king—born of the wolf and lion—who would be his son, I saw it all in a new light.

I newly perceived that the ascension of this destined figure relied upon a great deal of choice—mainly on the part of my parents. Once I was born, my father continued going to great lengths to seek a son, and my mother ever sought to keep me sheltered, isolated from my kinfolk and my heritage. My new grasp inspired a belief—one that only grew within me thereafter: I belonged elsewhere and among others. I found the thought liberating. And healing.

I may not have been born into the Skolani tribe, but I was born with a Skolani heart. And it was Icannes who somehow first knew it. Long before we met."—Brin Bright Eyes, Saga of Dania

· · ·

THE COLUMN of the Gottari army entered Thrakius's west gate on a fine spring afternoon. Vahldan wasn't sure what he'd expected, but it wasn't this. The high street was empty but for a few Hellain matrons heading to market with baskets on their arms and glowering expressions on their faces. No horns or bells signaled their arrival. No cheers or even a call of greeting. Few bothered to watch as the vanguard passed. There was only the echoing clip-clop of the hooves of their horses.

The four Sassanadi guards at the gate to the palace stood at attention, their chins high. They were immaculately and identically dressed, with their spears held exactly the same.

The first sign of respect the Gottari encountered upon their arrival in Thrakius was from foreigners—those who'd come to liberate a city he'd left defenseless.

Vahldan reined to a halt in the palace's front courtyard. "Finally home," he said.

Teavar grunted. Elan frowned and said, "In a manner of speaking, I suppose."

Stableboys scurried to collect their mounts. Elan allowed hers to be led away, which only reminded him of her loss. She'd normally have gone off to attend to Hrithvarra.

The crowd that awaited them in the courtyard outside the palace doors was solemn. All of their attention was focused on the wagons behind the vanguard and their grim cargo. Sairsa was foremost among them, veiled and garbed as a grieving widow. His brother's qeins held her girl babe at her breast as she proceeded to the bed of the first wagon. His normally bold and cheerful nephew Rohdric stayed at his mother's skirts.

The corpses were wrapped for burial. They were to be taken on to Dania. The bodies could be identified by the swords laid upon their chests. The shroud spared Sairsa a vision that would haunt Vahldan for the rest of his days.

An audible sob escaped Eldavar's widow as she gripped her husband's boot. Little Rohdric crossed his hands over his heart and bowed—a salute to his father that he'd obviously been taught. A sad thing for a boy so young to have learned.

Vahldan sent Belgar to direct and dismiss the arriving army and stood waiting as the widows moved among the wagons. He wasn't quite sure what to say or do. He couldn't just leave them and go inside. If he said he was sorry, would it be viewed as some sort of confession? He already felt horrible enough.

An older veiled woman joined Sairsa. Recognition of her only came when she moved to Jhannas's corpse, which was laid out beside Eldavar. She, too, kept her children close, each of them performing a ritual salute to their fallen father.

Jhannas's widow came to stand before Vahldan on her way back to the palace steps. Vahldan realized he couldn't recall her name. She was a beautiful woman, but she was far from demure. She didn't bow but stared at him instead. "My condolences for your loss," he ventured. "Jhannas was not just brave but one of the finest men I ever fought beside. He gave his life defending his king."

Jhannas's widow raised her veil to reveal swollen eyes. "You did this," she said.

Vahldan wasn't sure what she meant. "I'm sorry?"

The woman's lip curled. "No, you're not," she said. Vahldan glanced at the others. Was he missing something? The woman made no sense. "You can't hide from me," she went on. "I see the ugly truth in you." The ugliness flared and she stared even more deeply into his eyes. "There it is," she said. It sounded like mockery. She squinted. "You embrace it. That makes you a murderer."

Teavar and Ermanaric lunged to grab her by the arms. "That's enough," Ermanaric said. The woman didn't struggle. Indeed, she looked smugly satisfied as they drew her back.

"Leave her be," Vahldan said. "She has a right to speak."

His guardians released her and the woman stood straight. "All of this is your fault," she said, her voice shaky, brimming with anger. "The worst part is, you won't rest until we're all dead. Or enslaved.

What will you have to show for it? What, exactly, will the Bringer bring?"

Again, he had no answer. Anything he said would make this worse.

The angry woman shook her head. "It's sad, really. He loved you." She gestured toward the army. "As so many do. My husband loved you, and you threw him to your enemies' spears. For what? To feed your insatiable appetite? You're even greedier than the last Lion Lord."

Vahldan allowed himself a slight grin. "Luckily, I didn't share his appetite for the qeins of others. At least Jhannas could always rely on that." Everyone knew of Desdrusan's lust for this woman, though folk pretended they couldn't guess how far it had gone.

The woman's gaze momentarily flared. He suspected she might strike him. Instead, she melted into tears and fled. Vahldan sighed.

"That went well," Elan quipped.

Vahldan scanned the courtyard. Grave faces surrounded him. "Gods, you'd think we lost," he said. The murmuring crowd and the arriving warriors resumed the doings of a journey's end, but even in the greetings and embraces gloominess prevailed. "Is there anyone who's happy to see us?" he asked.

"Oh, I think you'll find a few glad faces inside." Vahldan turned to find a smiling wolf. "Welcome home, my king," Urias said with a bow. "Your family awaits you in the entry hall."

The Wulthus emissary was gaunt and pale, confirming all that Vahldan had heard he'd been through. "Thank you, Captain. You have my gratitude. I understand you saved my wife and son."

Urias shook his head. "Not I, my king. In that I would've failed without the real hero."

The wolf stepped aside and gestured to a lanky young woman with deep red curls and large blue eyes. She stood as tall as Urias's shoulder. Recognition came swiftly, but the fact that it hadn't been instant was a shock. Vahldan grinned. "So, Brin Bright Eyes, is it?" Gods, the girl grew like a wild vine.

"Father," the girl said prosaically. She offered a stiff and hasty bow from the waist. As pugnacious as her mother. Typical Skolani.

Speaking of whom, as Brin rose, her gaze brushed past him and a smile finally blossomed on his daughter's lips. "Hello, Mother," she said. The girl took two swift steps and wrapped her arms around Elan. No one seemed more surprised than Elan, who took a beat to hug her back. "I'm glad to see you were right," Brin said, still clutching her. Their daughter drew back from the embrace with a sly smile. "Just between us," Brin added.

Elan laughed. "Yes, baby girl—just between us." Elan's sudden happiness reminded Vahldan of days he'd thought long past, never to return. Perhaps he hadn't been paying attention.

"Greetings, Sister." Urias gave Elan a quick but warm embrace. "Come inside, all of you. There are children to meet."

They entered the palace and moved past a group of bowing crones and graybeards. The sight of them made Vahldan wonder how the elderly had endured their confinement. These seemed hale. Mindful of the gloominess outside, he didn't dare ask how many lives were lost during the insurrection.

He saw Mara first, holding her young son in her arms. His sister's face lit up. When he went to her, Mara bowed as best she could with her cargo. "Greetings, my king. Welcome home."

"We'll have none of that," he said and drew her into an embrace. "You know my name."

"It's horrible about Eldavar," she whispered. "I'm glad you were with him."

"Horrible," Vahldan agreed. "I said the prayers and made him a vow." He released her and looked down on her son. "Ah, Rekkr Ragnavar, I presume. What a fine warrior you are becoming." The boy grinned and buried his face in his mother's frock. "Sorry to have left your husband in Megaria. Arnegern is one of the few I could trust to handle such a delicate position."

Mara's eyes lit up. "Perhaps I could go to him? Malvius said the courier ships are running again."

Vahldan feigned a smile. "Perhaps. It's still a bit unsettled there. We'll see." His sister's expression fell. "Where's Kemella?" he asked to change the subject.

"With your son, of course. She's like a second mother to him—a real natural. Come, they're upstairs."

"In the study?" he asked, limping up the stairway after her.

"Gods, no," Mara said emphatically. "Your qeins has very strict rules. I do understand it as he's still a bit weak. But Baby Thaedan has very rarely left the residence."

"Thaedan?" Mara gave him a look but kept going. "What do you mean, a bit weak?"

After several flights, a striking young woman appeared on the next landing. "Do you want me to take him?" The woman reached to take Mara's son.

They'd arrived on Mara's floor, Vahldan realized. "Yes, thank you, Harma."

The name helped him to finish sorting out who she was. Herodes's daughter. She had her hair tied back and wore no face paint. The voluptuous redhead settled the boy on her hip, then bowed her head. "Welcome home, my king," she said. Damn. Harma's sly smile said she was recalling their last encounter, same as him.

Mara continued and Vahldan followed, his knee burning and his hip aching. He'd forgotten how far up it was.

They finally arrived at his residence's door. Mara knocked— something he'd never have done. Amaga answered it. His qeins looked him up and down without the slightest hint of welcome. Was she even paler? He swore her eyes were even more haunted than usual. "Are you well?" Amaga asked. Gods, the irony.

"I am unharmed," Vahldan replied.

"I'm asking if you're ill," Amaga snapped.

He frowned. "I'm not. Are you?" The gods knew she looked it.

Amaga rolled her eyes. "I'll not have you bringing in illness." She stepped aside.

Finally, a warm smile. Kemella came to him holding a swaddled bundle. "Welcome home, my king." His little sister held the bundle out to him. "Meet your son."

Vahldan took the bundle. Gods, it was light as a tuft of wool. Kemella pulled the swaddling back, revealing a shock. This being looked more like a shriveled old man than a babe. "What's wrong with him?" he blurted.

"Nothing!" Amaga's outrage was almost comical.

"He's getting stronger every day," Mara said, rushing to Amaga's side.

"The Elli-Frodei says it's only that he arrived a bit early," Kemella said. "Your qeins went through quite a trauma. But Mara is right— Thaedan grows stronger every day."

Vahldan held the babe out, hoping Kemella would take him back. He couldn't bring himself to look again. "Thaedan sounds like a wolf's name," he said to Amaga.

"The name honors both my father and his. It befits he who is born of wolf and lion. The goddess approves." She lifted her chin, challenging him to argue.

The babe wiggled and made a snuffling sound. Was he crying? It sounded like a lamb coughing. "You've frightened him." Amaga snatched the babe and turned away. He'd have been grateful but for her protective posturing. "He needs his rest. I think you'd best leave."

"Leave? These are my chambers."

Kemella came and took his arm, leading him to the door. "We thought you could temporarily use my quarters, my king. Just until your son gains his full strength." Vahldan's baby sister pleaded with her eyes as she opened the door and led him into the corridor.

"And here I thought I was the king," Vahldan said as she released him.

"I'll keep working on her," Kemella whispered. "You'll be back in no time." His sister winked and then closed his own door on him, with his qeins, son, and sisters inside, leaving him alone.

Worse, he was alone with aching wounds, at the top of all those bedamned stairs. So much for the return of the victor. Seemed it really was lonely at the top of the climb.

After getting every crew started on the unloading process, Malvius walked toward his cabin on Gullwing. Dexicos was huffing under his burden behind him. He hoped to get the goods that were yet to be stamped off and into the warehouses before calling it a night. They were moored at the main quay in the harbor at Thrakius, so they likely didn't have long. He entered to find Sabas had left a lamp burning, bless him. "Let's tap that before the harbormaster gets here," he said. "It's top-notch stuff—all the way from the Tiberian mainland. I'll get the cups."

Dexicos sat the cask on the table with a grunt. "No rush, Cap. The dockworkers say this new Sass harbormaster doesn't bother himself after nightfall."

Malvius set two cups on the table. "See? Things are getting easier already."

Dex drove the tap, set the mallet aside, and filled both cups with bright red wine. "I suppose the Sass aren't so bad. Still, seems we only traded one tariff collector for another."

"Ah well. There will always be open palms, waiting for a coin. It'll still be true even after we take charge. Wait and see."

"Till then, there's the thug on the hill," Dex said, seeming to leave something unsaid.

"Yes," Malvius conceded. When Dex spoke, it was often with the voice of the crews. Malvius hated the thought of his longsuffering crews growing impatient, but he couldn't blame them. He supposed he should know the scope of it. "And?" he prompted.

Dex shrugged and sipped. "Just that he's bound to get us into more trouble, is all."

Malvius barked a laugh. "I'm counting on it."

"Suppose so," Dex conceded. "Makes it hard, facing surprise after surprise, never knowing what's next, let alone when we'll finally tie off in a friendly port."

"*This* is still our home, old friend." He threw a thumb to indicate the docks outside and the city of Thrakius beyond. "Know that the final surprise will be felt by the thug. And on that day, he and everyone else will know whose home this is, too."

A soft knock on the door preceded Sabas's head popping in. "Got a visitor, Cap."

"Are our Sassanadi friends up late, after all?" Malvius asked.

"Doesn't really look Sass to me," Sabas said, sounding amused.

"Who, then?"

The door swung wide, revealing a boy waiting behind Sabas. "Found our young friend lurking on the docks. Seems he has something he'd like to say."

"Agoraki! A charming surprise. Come in. Long way from the kitchens, aren't you?"

"I suppose." The boy could be as laconic as his Skolani friend. Speaking of whom. "How's the girl?"

"Brin's fine. A bit different now. But I suppose I am too."

Malvius sipped. It really was fine wine—too good to offer any to the boy. "How so?"

Ago fidgeted, his coal-smudged cap in his hands. "I suppose we both grew up some."

Malvius didn't doubt it. He wondered how he would've handled what they'd been through when he was their age. Likely not as well. They were both more like Ligaia had always been. Ironic that they were the ones who had brought her down. It reminded him that he ought to resent them for the death of his sister. It should be yet another reason to hate the Gottari. But knowing Ligaia as he did, it was difficult to blame them. Complicating the issue further was the fact that he'd been the one to send these two against her. He reminded himself that his treacherous sister had been planning to marry his rival. Together the perilous pair had conspired to have him tried for patricide in order to steal his entire operation, thereby seizing control of his city.

In fairness, he could now see that Ligaia had played a vital role in setting up his endgame. Without her, he might have settled for an incomplete vanquishing of the Gottari. Misguided as she was, he supposed his sister belonged on the list of those he would avenge.

Perhaps he'd grown up a bit, too. "I suppose you have," he said to Ago.

Sabas and Dex sat, but Malvius left the boy standing. And fidgeting. "That's sort of why I came, Cap," the boy finally said. "My maaman says that since I served your cause, and since I'm so close to being a man, that... well, I deserve more than hauling coal. And I can't see the Gottari having me do much else. So I thought, maybe..."

"You're asking for a job?" Ago stared at his dirty hands and nodded. "Well, you never did get seasick, did you?" Malvius winked at Dex. "But a sailor's life is far from an easy one."

Ago's cheeks flushed. "Before you decide, there's something else you ought to know."

Nice to see a little fire in the boy. A little. "Go on," he said.

"After the Gottari first came, I overheard my maaman and your sister talking. They didn't know I was there. Not while they spoke." The boy shifted from foot to foot, eyes downcast.

"And?"

"I heard them saying that Ligaia, well, that she's my real mother." Malvius sat up straighter. The boy went on. "And now she's dead, and I feel like it's my fault. It makes me feel weird. And I can see Brin senses it. I hate her being afraid that I blame her. And I hate that some days I do. It's not so great on the other days, when I blame myself, either. Anyway, I wanted you to know, before you decide whether to keep me around."

"I see," Malvius said. He really was beginning to. After all, the boy clearly wasn't Sassanadi like the supposed mother. And Ligaia would've wanted to keep him close.

"I wouldn't blame you if you hate me for it, too. Or sent me away."

"I don't hate you, son."

The boy kept his head down but glanced up. "You don't?"

"No. Bad things happen. There's a war on. Don't flog yourself, Ago."

"Since you aren't angry, can I ask..."

"Go on." Malvius's mind reeled.

"Since you're her brother, I wondered if you might know who my father is."

"How old are you, Ago?"

"Fourteen. Almost fifteen."

The boy looked up, his veiled hope briefly revealed. It all made so much sense. The square chin, the straight brown hair, the hard gray eyes. Gods afire, the boy was more than just his nephew, more than a rightful heir to the anaxship. He was half Tiberian.

Tiberian nobility, at that.

Malvius knew exactly who the father was. "I'm sorry, son. I have no guess who your father might be." True in that his conclusion was much better than a guess. "But I'm sure that you are family now." And he knew he had to keep his new nephew close. The boy could either ruin everything or become a useful tool. "I'm also sure that I'd be honored if you'd come and sail with me. Right here, on Gullwing. How does that sound?"

Ago blushed and hid a smile. "It's more than I dared hope. Thank you, Cap."

"Dex will find you a hammock and a spot for your things," Malvius said. "Won't you, Dex?" His first mate nodded, stood, slugged down his wine, and beckoned the boy.

Agoraki stopped at the door. "Cap?" Malvius raised a brow. "My father—he couldn't be Isidros, could he?"

Malvius hid a smile. "I may not have a guess at who your father is. But I'm perfectly certain Isidros is not him."

The boy sighed and nodded. "Good. He abandoned my birth

mother to save himself. That's not the sort of man I want to be." Malvius had to admit, Isidros had once again proved himself remarkably slippery. Damn near admirably so.

"Ago, you're already a better man than that," Malvius said, with no need to dissemble.

ELAN WANDERED DOWN THE SERVANTS' stairway. She felt purposeless. Both Kemella's quarters and Vahldan's residence had guards at the door. She'd already finished off the meager serving of wine Hesiod had brought up with the dinner she'd mostly skipped eating.

About halfway down to the larder, she ran into the Sassanadi serving woman—Apontia they called her. "Is there something you seek, my lady?"

Feeling embarrassed, Elan simply said, "Nothing."

The woman raised both brows. "Are you sure? Only the kitchens down that way, yes?" Apontia's laughing eyes seemed to find mirth at Elan's expense.

"I was going this way." Elan headed down the flanking corridor of the second floor. It was awkward and obviously untrue, but she just wanted to get away from the woman. She headed for the main stairway. Lamplight shone from the open doors to the high hall. Vahldan often kept a flagon in there. She headed to the doorway for a look.

Vahldan sat alone at the end of the long table, with no guards in sight. He hadn't seen her so she leaned in. Indeed, a flagon sat on the table before him. She went in. "Can't sleep?" She went to the side table, got herself a cup, and set it in front of him.

"No. You too?" He set aside a chunk of wood and his carving knife, grabbed the flagon, and poured for her. She saw the pile of shavings on the floor beside him. He was making a mess for someone else to clean, but seeing him carving again made her glad.

"Hardly a wink since Megaria," she confessed.

Vahldan barked a lone laugh. "Might be a bad habit, sleeping outside pavilions and prowling corridors. I imagine it's hard to sleep in a bed all night after doing it for so long."

"You knew?" Elan understood that he was aware that she watched over him as he slept while on campaign, but Nicomedya and Megaria had been different. Guards had been assigned outside his quarters, but she couldn't trust anyone else. Not in a foreign city. Those who'd been assigned to the duty grew accustomed to her hovering and double-checking.

"Of course I knew."

"Maybe it is a bad habit. Shall I try to break it?"

"I wish I could tell you not to, but that wouldn't be fair."

Elan took a long sip, watching him over the rim. "I'm not sure fairness is something you and I can aspire to. Not anymore."

"I suppose not." He picked up the knife and the wood and bent over his work again. "It's been a long time since I believed this life could be fair."

No point in dwelling on an obvious truth. "It's good to see you carving again," she said, changing the subject. She resisted the impulse to reach for her kestrel.

"Feels like the only way to strip it all away, you know?"

"I do." She leaned to look. "A lion?"

Vahldan's smile was lopsided and his cheeks pinked. "Yeah. I guess I was hoping it would reveal some sort of truth."

"Like what?"

He shrugged. "Like even the slightest hint that I'm on the right path."

Elan hated hearing such talk. After she'd surrendered so much to stay, to keep believing. "You better know you are. You promised me. And I'm not the only one counting on it."

He stopped carving and leaned back, staring at the map on the wall. "Attasar tells me there are over a hundred cities in the empire." He shook his head. "We struggled mightily to take three."

"All that matters is that they're the right three."

"But look what it cost us."

Her annoyance grew. "Did you expect this to be easy?"

Vahldan focused on his carving again. "No. But..." He paused. "Gods, I didn't think it would be this hard, either. We couldn't even manage it alone. We fight off one empire only to become beholden to another."

"Indebted, not beholden. They're two different things." Elan smiled at the thought. "Have you heard what our daughter said to the Sassanadi lord to convince him to help? She said that common foes made good allies. You know where she got that, right?"

"She's... something." He gave her a crooked smile. "Isn't she?"

"She is," Elan said. He sounded like he'd never imagined that Brin might be special.

"Too bad *she* wasn't the boy."

Elan bristled. He'd gone too far. She pushed back her chair to stand.

Vahldan sighed. "Gods, not again. Please don't go. What did I say this time?"

"You really don't know?"

"No. I mean, yes... I think. I remember what else you said the day you told me you were pregnant, if that's what you're getting at. I haven't brought it up since, have I?" She pressed her lips tight, shook her head to concede. "Still, you of all people ought to understand how difficult this legacy thing is for me."

Elan leaned back in her chair. "I do. You inherited a hard fate. It makes me angry that you're so damned determined to pass it along. Like some kind of twisted father-son tradition."

Vahldan tossed the knife and carving to clatter across the table. "So that's what this is all about? The prophecy? I only ever sought to raise us up. I recall a time when we both wanted that. It's not like I asked for the rest of it. You were the first to say I might as well take advantage and use it."

"Oh, you better know this is about more than the prophecy. You told me you'd try to accomplish our goals without *her*. Turns out that was just another broken promise."

He rolled his eyes. "Oh, come on, Elan. You know I tried. Thadmeir turned me away. It was Amaga who chased after me."

Elan snorted. "And that justifies bonding with her? Let alone impregnating her."

"Damn it, you know it's what they all expected of me. It was the only way I fit into their twisted version of our people's ascent. I wouldn't have been able to raise an army without playing along. Hel's judgement, half of the Amalus would've walked away before the first battle, let alone the unaligned herdsmen we recruited. You damn well know that playing along has always been part of the bargain. Just as it's always included supplying the first bedamned king of a hundred bedamned Tutona kingdoms. You heard her, same as I did. Same as they all did. Amaseila spoke of her grandson, of our shared progeny."

Elan laughed bitterly. "Of course! That's what *she* wanted. You blame everyone but yourself, as if you've had no choice in any of it. But you've made every damn choice. And you certainly didn't choose me. You never chose Brin. You never chose us."

Vahldan's eyes flashed. "Am I missing something, Elan? Didn't you insist that your daughter would never play any part in this? As I recall it, your dream said nothing of a child. Weren't you the one who wanted your daughter to take your precious place in the tribe that banished you? Seems to me that the vagueness of Brin's destiny is really more about you."

It stung because it was true. Why should it sting? She still wanted to protect Brin from being drawn into this bedamned mess. She should've left the first time. Actually, she should've known to keep her distance in the first place. She started to get up again.

"No, wait. I'm sorry." Vahldan leapt up and blocked her from rising. "Forgive me. Please. I just... Gods, I hate this. It's not how this was supposed to go."

"How what was supposed to go?"

"Any of it!" He started pacing. "Our relationship. My ascent. The war. All of it."

"All right, Bringer. How was it supposed to go, then?"

He gestured at the map. "We were supposed to *win*! The empire was supposed to crumble, and we've hardly had a clear victory. And I never imagined doing any of it without you at my side. I feel like all I've done is fail. I failed my father, my mother, our people. And worst of all, I've failed you. And our daughter. I even failed..." He plopped back in his chair and swallowed hard. "...those who loved me without asking anything in return."

Elan knew whose name he couldn't even speak. Gods, she'd known Eldavar since he was a little boy. He'd always been so buoyant, so cheery. Sure, he could be naïve. But it was because he had been so committed, so positive, so loyal. Eldavar had always believed. It had been so pure, it almost made her wish she could've kept believing like that, all the way through. It was hard to imagine him gone, to think of carrying on without him shining brightly beside them. Eldavar's absence would make it hard for her to stay true to her duty by believing again now.

She reached to pick up the carving. It was already finely detailed, poised to hunt. She wondered how long he'd been working on it. "Even lions lose some fights. We both know that sometimes lions die. That doesn't mean the pride has failed."

Vahldan grabbed his cup, took a drink, and stared into it. "I knew. I knew my brother was in that fire, and I stayed on that wall. Till I was sure I could claim victory. I didn't go to him."

"You couldn't have saved him. Even if you'd tried sooner, would it have made his sacrifice more honorable? You stayed until we all won. You did your duty and Eldavar did his. He died fighting for you because he believed in you. Just as your father did. Just as your people do. And look at us. Here we are. We control the Straits, and most of Pontea has declared allegiance."

He snorted. "For the moment."

"You just admitted that you never thought it would be easy."

Vahldan leaned back. "You want to know what I thought? I imagined that somehow I'd take it all down. I thought that if I embraced the role of the Bringer, it would be enough—that the gods would reward me for playing along. I thought calamity would ensue. And oh, how I wanted to wreck it all. Especially for the godsforsaken wolves and those bastards in the guild. That's as far ahead as I bothered to look. I started a war with this vast empire thinking I could change things in a homeland that the world doesn't even know exists." He finished the last of his cup and slammed it down. "And— like you said—here we are. All I'm supposed to do is wreck things. That, and have the son who's capable of doing the rest. All I've done is wreck things for those I love. And now I've got this scrawny wolf pup upstairs."

As much as she hated Amaga, the woman's babe was innocent. "Hey, that wolf pup is your son. Every child deserves a chance. Especially from their parents."

He held up his hands. "All right, all right. I'm trying to admit how wrong I've been."

Something about it all reminded her of Sael. "Maybe that's the lesson."

"What? That I've gotten everything wrong?"

"No. Well, maybe that needed to be a part of it. But Urrinan has always been about change. Change wrought from upheaval. And, yes, the empire is vast. And mighty. Our little war can't possibly bring it down."

He laughed. "Thanks for bolstering my confidence."

"But so what? What if we can still change it? Without bringing it down. Maybe even change it for the better. Who are we to know how change will be wrought or where it might lead?"

"What do you have in mind?"

She shrugged. "I'm not sure. I'm just saying that rather than focusing on destruction, we should think about what our people have to offer. At its best, the beauty of the Gottari system lies in having wolves and lions lead together. It's prosperity and power combined—the coin and the sword. And the alliance with the Skolani is about shared benefit. Everything good in Dania stems from balance. No one ever says that about the empire. All anyone in the empire talks about is the corruption, the unfairness. Grandmother used to say that Urrinan won't destroy the world so much as remake it. She often spoke of it as a rebirth. Maybe that's why the leader born of the wolf and the lion will be the first among the Tutona to ascend. Maybe that's the sort of leader that can even change an empire. Maybe we should consider the change as being one that comes from within the empire as well as from without. If the empire really is so vast, so strong, so entrenched, maybe internal upheaval is the only way such a thing could possibly begin. Maybe it's about rebuilding something better after it's been torn down."

Vahldan's gaze grew distant. "From within and from without."

"With a bridge from the old world to the new," she added, recalling what Sael had said of Brin. Perhaps their daughter should have a role in making a brighter future for their people.

He found focus on her. A slight smile grew in appraising her. "Attasar tells me that Tiberian leaders hold great respect for Tutona warriors. He said that they even recruit them to fight for the empire in special hosts. He claims that even the personal guardians of the emperor are mostly Tutona, so highly are we esteemed." He picked up the lion carving and narrowed his gaze. "You're right. Who are we to know how change will be wrought?"

She recognized him. Once again, carving had brought him back to his true self. Elan hated that she still had feelings for him. She knew love and hate were two sides of the same coin. Her stormy feelings toward him would make her duty difficult unto their doom. But she actually liked this version of Vahldan. She thought she'd best retreat before a darker version reappeared. "And who are we to know when sleep will finally come? I'd best get to bed before I miss my chance." She stood and stretched. "You coming up?"

Vahldan stood, his smile growing wistful. "Thank you," he said.

"For what?"

"For restoring my hope. You've always been the best of us. Still are. None of it would've been possible without you. And I can't imagine taking the next steps without you. Thank you for staying." He leaned in, looking like he wanted to hug, or worse. "I just wish—"

Elan refused to allow this to turn ugly. She laid a halting hand on his chest. "Save your wishes for your qeins."

He harrumphed. "Please. You know what she's like."

"Maybe. But I'm not the one who bonded with her." She couldn't stomach his carefully cultivated look of hurt, so she headed for the exit. "Sorry, but I'm not taking another step without sleep."

"Hang on. I'm coming, too." He grabbed his knife and carving. "I'm going to give this to little Rohdric." He gestured with the lion. "The boy's having a tough time. He could use the distraction."

Elan marveled. Just like that, he was back. How could someone so prone to doing the wrong thing also be so admirable? "That's a fine idea," she said.

VAHLDAN FOLLOWED Elan up the stairs in silence. Every step made his hip hurt more. Elan had grown stubbornly silent, but he knew he deserved it. He paused two floors below his. "This is Sairsa's floor, right?"

"They'll be long abed, I think," Elan said.

He held up the carving. "I'll leave it with the guard. I don't want to forget."

She nodded. Once again, he thought he saw the same longing in her that he felt. Before he could say another word, she spun and started upstairs. He supposed he deserved that, too.

Vahldan sighed and stepped into the corridor. There was indeed a guard at the far end, but nearer still was a woman coming toward him. She wore a nightfrock and stooped to hold the hands of a toddler walking before her. It wasn't Sairsa or Mara or Kemella. The red hair and full figure stopped him in his tracks. She hadn't seen him yet. He really should turn and go.

The boy pointed and Harma startled. Too late. "Oh, my king," she said softly. She bent to Rohdric. "See who it is? Say good evening to your uncle."

"Good evening, Uncle," Rohdric dutifully said. Such a handsome little man, though his eyes were puffy and red.

Harma smiled brightly. "We're having a bit of a rough night," she said and looked back to the boy. "But we're trying to let Mama get some sleep, aren't we?" He'd heard from both Sairsa and Mara what a blessing Harma had been in helping with their children.

Vahldan squatted to sit on his haunches, ignoring the complaints from his hip and knee. "Maybe this will help." He proffered the lion carving to the boy. The nephew that he promised his brother would become the shieldmate to his own son. "I made it for you."

The boy carefully accepted it, studying it in silent awe. Harma stooped behind Rohdric, looking over his shoulder. Her frock hung down, providing a view of that marvelous cleavage he'd been trying to avoid ogling. "Oh, how beautiful. Can you say thank you?" she prompted.

"Thank you, Uncle," the boy murmured by rote.

"It's a lion," he said. "You know about lions, don't you?"

"Oh yes," Harma answered for him. "He knows all about them and what they mean to our clan. Don't you, Rohdric?" The boy nodded. "Trust me, my king, this one's a lion through and through." Harma beamed.

The boy dropped to the floor to set the lion on its feet and moved it as though it were walking. He and Harma stood to face one another. Freya's grace, she was luminous.

He had to look away. He smiled down at the boy. "A lion through and through, eh?"

"All he wants are more stories of famous lions. I was just telling him how his mama's father was so brave. He knows that both sides of his family trace their lines to the Arrivals."

"Same as hers," Rohdric added without looking up from the lion. The boy evidently meant Harma's parents.

"Same as mine," she confirmed. "As you can see, we're both very proud of our clan."

"Just as his father was proud of his little lion." Vahldan looked past her at the guard, diligently avoiding eye contact. He lowered his voice. "Perhaps I should've been as wise as Eldavar." He couldn't get the sight of his scrawny wolf cub out of his head. Or how Elan thought change might occur—from without and from within.

Harma studied him, radiating concern. "Perhaps the..." She shook her head.

"Go on," he said.

"Forgive me, my king. It's not my place."

"Please." He offered a reassuring smile. "I'd like to hear."

"I was just going to say that perhaps your next son will take more after you." She bowed her head, blushing. "My king," she added and gave him a furtive glance. The woman was not only beautiful, she was the feminine exemplar of the Amalus.

"Gods willing," he said.

EPILOGUE: AGENT OF URRINAN

"Each of us is a product of our parents and is shaped by our siblings. And yet, this matter of family is beyond blood alone. This I know better than most.

I have loved and been loved by two mothers. The training, advice, and support I received from an uncle was as fulfilling as any father could hope to offer a daughter. I have known two women as sisters, though I share a birth mother with neither of them. I have been the confidant and guardian of each of my sisters during their separate assents to the highest heights. I have overseen the destined rise to power of one brother and fought a war against another—neither of whom knew me as a sister.

I have witnessed the impact upon us of the love and guidance of the family we hold dear. Just as I have observed—and suffered—the lack of those things. The bonds of our blood cannot be denied. And yet, I stand in awe of the mere concept of family. It is a force that should be neither overlooked nor underestimated."—Brin Bright Eyes, Saga of Dania

The two praetorians stayed in Vernius's courtyard to wait, watering their mounts and looking impatient. Vernius had hoped the pair would simply deliver the summons and leave. Apparently they would be escorting him to the emperor's villa at Tivolius, whether Vernius wanted their company or not.

He went inside to collect his gear. It was ironic, having just arrived home from the campaign in Iberica so recently that his gear was mostly still packed. Jupiter's mercy, he hated the thought of getting back on a horse again.

Caelia appeared at the sleeping chamber's doorway, wrapped in his bed linen. "Who is it? What do they want?"

Vernius couldn't face her. "They're praetorians—bodyguards from the royal retreat in Tivolius. They've come with a summons. From Emperor Mycanius himself."

"You can't leave again already. You promised me."

Vernius frowned. "Did I? Exactly what did I promise?"

Caelia flushed from her neck upward. "I thought this time you would go and speak to my father. You didn't refuse to. It's why I stayed."

Had she really hoped he would ask for her betrothal? He glanced at her. She seemed both angry and ashamed. Perhaps, in the moment, he'd encouraged her. But they'd both willingly hurried past any sort of commitment. More than once now—as she'd pointed out. Perhaps it was the spirits of their ancestors encouraging them both. Or maybe it was simple lust.

But seriously, he really should be considering a path to an heir. The gods knew Caelia was eligible. His need was only growing more pressing. His neighbors' sons were already working his family's estate, tending the vines in his absence. It was only a matter of time before they petitioned the provincial bureaucracy for a lien. He needed a new plan, now that she was gone… Spell of Venus, could Ligaia really be gone? He never had been able to imagine betrothing another.

Still, he felt he had to be sure. He needed time. He could afford to encourage Caelia just a bit longer. Especially with the unavoidable delay awaiting him outside.

"I'll draft your father a letter. We can discuss it all when I get back."

Caelia fled to the bedchamber. "A letter?" she shouted. "If you think that'll be enough for Papa, you are mistaken. I'll be thrashed for this."

"Even he will understand that I can't disobey a summons from our emperor."

"No. He warned me not to come. He said you'd do this. He'll throw me out this time."

Vernius assembled his gear as she dressed. "Well, if he throws you out, come back here and wait for me. Better still, simply stay. Let your father wait with Proserpine for all I care. There's nothing I can do until I get back."

Caelia was dressed but rumpled, her hair disheveled. "Stay here? What would I eat? I have no handmaiden here. You have only one slave, Vernius. A manservant. What if he thought to bed me against my will?"

Caelia had always been dramatic, but this was too much. "Tertius has loyally attended this house since it was my father's. He is no rapist. I'll leave enough coin for you to go to the market and purchase whatever you wish. Enough even for a handmaiden. *One* handmaiden."

She pouted. "How can you be so sure? After all, he is a barbarian. He may be unable to control his urges. You would have to have him executed."

Caelia had always disliked Tertius. It was true, his manservant was gruff. But her dislike was more due to her desire for Vernius to purchase a household staff selected by her—sparing no expense, of course. He wasn't about to send away a faithful aging man. He buckled his sword belt, hoisted his pack, and went to the door. "That would certainly flatter and suit you, my dear."

She ran out after him. "What do you mean to imply?"

"There is no hidden meaning." He kept on to the stables. "Stay, or not. My offer to write the letter and to buy a handmaiden stands. But if you're staying, speak up! Because I'm leaving."

Her tone became pleading. "Vernius, you can't do this. What am I to do?"

"I count three options. Stay with no letter, take the letter to your father, or just go. We are mere moments from reducing the number to one."

Tertius appeared at the stable door with his saddled horse. Together they outfitted his mount with his gear and saddlebags. Vernius mounted and turned to find Caelia hugging herself, her cheeks streaked with tears. He bent from the saddle to kiss her, but she turned away. No letter, then. He patted her on the head. "I shall return as soon as I can. Perhaps I'll see you?"

She shook her head. "No, you won't. Last time you were gone for four years. Four *years*! And I waited for you, Vernius. I won't do it again. I'm already getting too old for betrothal."

All he could think to say was, "Forgive me." She shook her head. Apparently she wouldn't. He had nothing left to offer. He'd have to find a new path to an heir. This one seemed highly unlikely to bear the needed result. "I hope you find happiness, my dear. I must go."

The praetorians waited at the gate. He heeled his mount, then reined in beside them to wave farewell. Caelia wouldn't look so he didn't bother. He felt a pang of regret. She truly was lovely. Not to mention a spirited lover. Ah well. Duty called.

One of the praetorians said, "The day grows late, Lord General."

Vernius forced his gaze from the woman he had nearly married, from his loyal manservant, and from a home he'd not even had time to grow accustomed to again. "Lead on," he said. "We mustn't keep His Eminence waiting. I'm certain his need of me is dire."

It always was. And it always cost him a chunk of his life and a little more of his soul.

~

Vernius hadn't actually visited the emperor's lake villa at Tivolius, but everyone had heard of its opulence. He was already impressed and he hadn't even been shown indoors. Instead, he was led through a series of elaborate courtyards, then out on a raised walkway overlooking a reflecting pool as long as the metronome and outfitted with a sequence of matching fountains. The walk was flanked by scaled-down replicas of famous temples of the civilized world. It was dizzying in its breadth, beauty, and seclusion.

Aside from all of that, it was quiet, serene. If Vernius were emperor, he'd never leave.

It was said that Mycanius relished the mountain air. Few Tiberians knew that His Eminence had an increasingly debilitating respiratory ailment. Though it became obvious to those who were privileged to spend any amount of time with the man privately.

Vernius had expected to be led into a grand court where the emperor would be seated in magnificence. Instead, he was led to an outdoor living area, draped in gauzy fabric and lit with the soft glow of dozens of hanging lamps. The spot was furnished with chaises and cushions arranged over plush carpets and surrounded by greenery. He couldn't see the harpist, but skilled strumming floated on the light breeze, in perfect harmony with the tinkle of the nearest fountain.

The emperor reclined on a chaise, a goblet in hand, clad in lustrous purple and gold silk. Two others were present. The younger of them was a scribe, sitting at a table, ready to take dictation. The graying second was Vernius's superior, Facerius, the master commander.

Vernius stepped into the lamplight and knelt, bowing his face to the carpet. "Vernius Stallicus of Nardium, at your service, Highness."

"Get up, Vernius. I know who you are." Mycanius's voice was wheezier than usual. "Sit and let us get to exactly *how* you may serve me."

Not a promising start. The man sounded as testy as ever. Vernius rose and bowed to his commander before sitting upright on a cushioned chaise that was intended for reclining.

"I've been bragging about your prowess in handling our Iberican problem," Facerius said. "The Numtian tribal alliance is in tatters. Each of them is separately scraping for a chance to be in our good graces again, thanks to the thorough thrashing you gave to their warlords."

"A task well done," Mycanius added absently. "You have the gratitude of your people."

A task? Well done? These were not the words for war. The man had no idea. He never had to see the bloody corpses, the burned-out villages, the shackled lines of wretched captives to be sold as slaves. Maintaining order on the frontier was no mere task. And doing what was necessary to accomplish it should never be referred to as well done. It was always horribly done.

Vernius formed his lips into a tight smile and bowed his head. "I am humbled by your praise, Highness."

A serving girl appeared, proffering a tray with a lone bejeweled cup. He accepted it and she disappeared again.

Mycanius made an impatient gesture. "Well, Facerius, get on with it."

His commander's expression hardened. It was going to be worse than he thought. "In your absence, problems have arisen in Pontea. Have you heard?"

"I heard of the fall of Thrakius and the placation of a barbarian there. That was before I left Cispadaena for Iberica."

Mycanius grunted, put a fist to his chest, and burped.

"There's more," Facerius said. "The situation has grown worse."

Mycanius waved his hand, conveying his apparent increasing impatience.

Facerius went on, speaking more rapidly. "The barbarian in question—a Teuton of the Gottari tribe—married into a rival clan and proclaimed himself a king. Vahldan the Bold, they call him, if you can believe. The man subsequently raised an army and sailed to

Bafrana with the Pontean rector's blessing, ostensibly to put down an insurgency. Secretly, the barbarian and the insurgent pirates had formed an alliance. After they executed one of our diplomats and the sadhu, the Bafranii guided their new allies on a swift march over the mountains to Efusium. The Gottari snuck in by night. They must have had an ally on the inside. Of course the usual horror followed. Every soldier of the garrison was either burned alive or slaughtered when they sought surrender."

"Jupiter's mercy," Vernius whispered. "Efusium has fallen?" It was one of the jewel cities of the empire.

"That's not yet the worst of it." Facerius glanced at the emperor, who nodded. "Before Efusium's fires were out, this King Vahldan marched on the Straits. Our garrison commander there got word of their approach, thank the gods. The garrison abandoned Nicomedya and retreated to combine forces with the garrison at Megaria. They held out through most of the winter, but... Well, this is the shocking part: The barbarians gained the alliance of the Sassanadi dah in Anaissa. With the support of the dah's naval fleet, they took Megaria as well."

"A Teutonic chieftain holds the Pontean Straits? With Sassanadi backing?" Vernius was beyond stunned.

"Obviously, such an outrage must not only be righted with swift and devastating force, but an example must also be made."

The emperor sat up and leaned in. "If it is my last task in this world, I will see to it that this Vahldan the Bold is summarily strangled before a cheering crowd." Mycanius delivered his words in an ominously soft, prosaic tone. "Every Gottari male is to be slain. The women and children who survive shall be taken as slaves. The survivors shall live their people's humiliation each waking hour. It's not that they shall merely be taught a lesson, it's that they shall cease to exist as a people. And every barbarian within a week's ride of an imperial border shall hear of it." Mycanius sat back, breathing hard through his nose.

Vernius and Facerius sat contemplating the ramifications of this absurdly harsh, thorough pronouncement. As appalled as Vernius was by what had happened, all he could think about was how easy it was to order such an ugly reprisal from a cushioned chaise in a tranquil courtyard.

The music had ceased. There was only the scratching of the scribe's quill until Facerius said, "This campaign must be a top priority, of course. His Eminence will lead the campaign as soon as an overwhelming force can be mustered and equipped. We want you, Vernius, to act as second-in-command, leading the mobile reserve via Efusium. You shall have the honor of taking Nicomedya, which we understand to be lightly manned by the barbarians. From there, six other legions will rally to march on Megaria, hold the Straits, and finally converge on Thrakius. You and the mobile reserve are to sail from Cispadaena. The campaign must be swift and decisive."

"I understand." What Vernius understood was that Mycanius would lead the campaign in name only and that he himself would get none of the credit but all of the blame. He and his men would initiate a war and remain on the front lines throughout it. They would also be the ones to take the most casualties and to end up with the most blood on their hands. As always. "I am honored, Highness. I shall spare no effort to ensure total success," he said, as always.

Mycanius's toothy smile didn't meet his serpentine eyes. "I'm counting on it. For if I do not have the barbarian king's head by the next hiatus, I shall take yours in its stead, Vernius Stallicus of Nardium."

"Of course, Highness." He stood and bowed.

The emperor waved a dismissive hand. "Now go. Out of my sight, all of you."

Still saddle-sore, Vernius hobbled to keep abreast of Facerius, leading the scribe across the pristine grounds. Without looking, Facerius said, "Oh. There's one more thing. A dispatch addressed to you has arrived from Pontea." His commander handed him a folded parchment. "Seems it was sent during the siege of Megaria, but it finally made it through."

Vernius broke the seal and instantly recognized the hand of the script. His heart leapt. His eye was drawn to the lone line of Ligaia's second paragraph. The rest became a blur.

"You have a son," it read.

The End

Bold Ascension is book two of The Sundered Nation Trilogy.
Book three, coming soon, is titled Destiny's Doom.

GRATITUDE

Well, here we are again, at the end of yet another lengthy epic fantasy novel. Which means you've proven, yet again, that you are a special sort of story connoisseur. I still recognize—perhaps all the more for my experience with book one—that you have a great deal of choice in how to spend the valuable time you set aside for the enjoyment of story. I believe that you're special in that you not only see the value in reading fiction, you've demonstrated by getting here that you enjoy vast, complex stories. You seek characters that evolve and suffer setbacks and gain nuance, often resulting in conflicting goals and motivations. You don't mind if you're occasionally left thinking and feeling and don't always need tidy resolutions. You've embraced the heightened perspective that can be gained through immersion in an alternative world.

My recognition that you're special does not diminish the wide array of choices that you have. I am a very small fish in an expansive sea of excellent fantasy stories. I mentioned in this same section at the end of book one how important word of mouth and reviews are to debut authors, and I've come to see how vital it remains to little-known authors with a sophomore release—particularly for an incomplete series. In regard to reviews of The Severing Son, while I recognize that the quantity of them (at the moment) is not particularly noteworthy, it can't be denied that the overriding quality has been exceptional. The depth and incisive nature of each, and the personal applicability of them, continues to blow my mind.

You guys rock! And have been so generous. You've been a big part of my ability to reach new readers, which allows me to grow and to keep striving.

I remain honored to have received a bit more of your valuable time. I'm incredibly grateful to each and every one of you—particularly those of you who've provided a rating, written a review, passed along a recommendation, or even offered a social media shout-out. If you enjoyed Bold Ascension, I humbly ask for your ongoing support. Please do continue to review the series and/or spread the word. I very much hope that I've earned your interest in book three, and I look forward to seeing you in this same segment after that final edition of the bittersweet pair of words: The End.

If all goes well, that moment will only be the beginning.

As it shall be.

Vaughn

ACKNOWLEDGMENTS

Second editions of a trilogy have a reputation for being tricky to write, and Bold Ascension was no exception. In spite of the fact that it is neither a beginning nor an ending, I have striven to give as complete an arc as possible to each of the primary characters and to convey a new beginning and a fitting ending point for this phase of the epic tale of Vahldan and Elan.

It's funny, but most every one of the mentors and beta-readers I listed in the acknowledgements of The Severing Son has had an effect on this book, though the majority of them has never actually read it. It's an unusual circumstance in that Bold Ascension sprang from an original version of TSS that encompassed the entire tale of this trilogy. Many of those already mentioned have read that earlier version. Their input was critical to making The Sundered Nation Trilogy into what it's become. My gratitude to each of them remains undiminished.

There are those who have read and offered feedback for this specific book, and each has been instrumental in making it better. Besides my wife, who is first to read everything, Donald Maass was next to read a draft of Bold Ascension. Thanks, Don, for reassuring me it's okay to take a shadowy path on the way to seeking enlightenment. Big thanks to Keaghan Cronin as well for being not just among the first to read the earliest version of TSS, but for being among the very few to read The Sundered Nation Trilogy in its final form straight through. You've made the trilogy smoother. In the developmental stage, Therese Walsh (the Story-Whisperer) provided sustaining guidance, saving me from several gaffes and plot holes. Another heartfelt thank you, T, from among the millions of those that I owe you. All three of you have provided me with confidence when it was tough to come by.

I also want to thank those who've supported me through the publication of The Severing Son. I stand in awe of the talent of cover artist John Anthony Di Giovanni. John, you've captured the look and provided the feel of this world so beautifully, which extends the perfect invitation to readers. Thanks for making the series more special. The fantasy book reviewing, fantasy BookTube, and fantasy self-pub communities have been incredibly helpful and supportive. Among them, I need to single out Philip Chase for taking a chance on an unknown book, and author, and being the first to review TSS. Philip, there wouldn't have been much of a launch without you. I've also been blown away by the support of my longtime writing community, mainly the Writer Unboxed crew, many of whom are not necessarily fans of the genre. So many of you have read and reviewed and offered such encouraging praise. Each of you has been instrumental to an amazing beginning to my career as an author, and I can't thank you enough.

My gratitude to Isabelle Wagner for her incredibly sharp eyes and kind support throughout the proofreading process. The eleventh hour input from Ben Kahn and Kim Bullock has been vital to making this book a better experience for readers. Thanks to both of you.

Lastly, and most importantly, I have to thank Maureen. Simply put, there would be no books without my wife. Maureen—I am a writer because of your support, a storyteller because of your inspiration, and an author because of your aid. You have my enduring gratitude and all of my love.

About the Author

Vaughn Roycroft has aspired to write epic fantasy since his sixth grade teacher gave him a boxed set of The Lord of the Rings. He has spent many years striving to be worthy of telling the tale of Vahldan and Elan. He lives with his soul mate in a cottage they designed and built themselves, near their favorite Great Lakes beach. When he's not writing, he can often be found walking the woods and beaches, trying to keep up with his energetic black lab.

X ⓘ